FRISCO

Also by Daniel Bacon
Walking San Francisco on the Barbary Coast Trail
Barbary Coast Trail Official Guide

FRISCO

DANIEL BACON

Quicksilver Press

Frisco is a work of historical fiction and, thus, a blend of fictional and historical characters and events. Historical characters are depicted by the generally known facts of their lives. However, they are used in a fictional manner. Names, characters, places, and incidents are either the product of the author's imagination or are used fictitiously.

Interior illustrations courtesy of International Publishers,
New York, NY

Quote page 233, Waterfront Worker, courtesy of the International Longshore and Warehouse Union, San Francisco, CA.

Governor Frank Merriam radio address, page 352. San Francisco Chronicle, July 2, 1934

Article excerpt (revised) page 352-353: San Francisco Chronicle, July 2, 1934

Maillard editorial, page 305: San Francisco Chronicle, May 21, 1934

Letter to the editor, page 306: San Francisco Chronicle, May 21, 1934

Mayor Angelo Rossi radio addresses: page 370-371, from San Francisco Chronicle, July 5, 1934; page 416, from San Francisco Chronicle, July 9, 1934

Song lyrics (revised) page 430, unknown Irish composer

Published by Quicksilver Press
San Rafael, California
www.quicksilverpress.net

Printed in the United States of America

*To the memory of my parents George and Betty,
whose love and guidance will always be an inspiration.*

The toughest guys on the old S.F. waterfront, neither rubes nor tourists, called it Frisco, and no effete journalist would have tried to correct them.

Herb Caen, *San Francisco Chronicle* columnist and author of *Don't Call it Frisco.*

PART ONE

PACIFIC ODYSSEY

CHAPTER 1

November 8, 1932

The first time Nick Benson heard his father mention the depression, it seemed like a distant threat, as relevant as a flu outbreak in China. Apparently that was the plan. Government officials called it a depression, he later learned, because they thought it sounded less alarming than a recession. A depression being a minor dip, a mere pothole in the road to prosperity.

More like a sinkhole, Nick thought as he opened the newspaper to the Help Wanted section, now just one page. He scanned the employment ads. Most were for high-level positions requiring years of experience or menial jobs requiring little more than a pulse, nothing for a recent college graduate. Half-way down the page a headline caught his eye. He put down his coffee and read the ad. As the words sank in, his grip on the paper tightened and the room around him disappeared. Opportunities to work for a daily newspaper were few and far between, so this was like finding a Renoir sketch at a rummage sale.

His first inclination was to thrust a celebratory fist in the air and cry, *"Eureka!"* Then, remembering where he was, at the breakfast table with his family, he held his glee in check. Carefully folding the Help Wanted section, he slipped it into his breast pocket and glanced at his father to see if he noticed. As he hoped, Charles was still studying the front page and its headlines announcing the latest calamitous events. UNEMPLOY-MENT CLIMBS TO 24% . . . STREETCAR CONDUCTORS THREATEN STRIKE . . . HITLER DEMANDS CHANCELLORSHIP OF GERMANY . . . FEDS DESTROY

SIXTY CASES OF BOOTLEG WHISKEY. The only headline offering a ray of hope read, NATION GOES TO POLLS TODAY.

His mother Lillian also hadn't noticed him pocket the Help Wanted section. She was saying to her father Rune and to Nick's younger sister Sarah that a storm was expected later that day, so she planned to vote and buy groceries before it arrived.

After breakfast Nick and Charles got up to leave, both wearing gray double-breasted suits. Nick would have preferred to dress more comfortably — he still wasn't used to a tie cinched around his neck — but his father insisted that any businessman, to be taken seriously, had to look the part, especially during hard times.

"Don't forget your umbrella," Lillian said to her husband with an air of amusement. Everyone around the table smiled at the long-standing joke. When they were first married Lillian bought an umbrella for Charles, a good one with a hooked wooden handle. He never used it, though, saying it looked like an old man's cane and he wasn't going around town with anything resembling a crutch.

"A little rain isn't going to hurt me," said Charles.

Nick and Sarah silently mouthed the words along with their father, having heard the same reply repeatedly since they were toddlers.

Ignoring their antics, Charles planted a kiss on his wife's cheek, gave a nod to his father-in-law, and cast one last affectionate glance at his daughter. Then he and Nick donned khaki trench coats and fedoras and left their flat on Mason Street.

It was a short walk to the polling station. On the way they passed signs posted in windows proclaiming a preference for one candidate or another. Choosing a candidate hadn't been difficult for the Bensons. Two years earlier President Hoover raised import tariffs to record levels. As a consequence, trade shrank to a fraction of what it had been, and now the Benson Cargo Warehouse stood half-empty, a shell of its former self. Franklin Roosevelt, on the other hand, had pledged to cut tariffs as part of a program called the New Deal, and that was enough to convince Charles, who never before had voted for a Democrat, that Roosevelt was the best man to get the country moving again.

Having fulfilled their civic duty, father and son walked down Russian Hill, through Chinatown, though the Financial District, to a brick warehouse near the waterfront. In past years as many as six employees would have been waiting for them. On this day there were two. Charles unlocked the steel roll-up door and the four of them entered the cavernous building.

Sunlight slanted down through high windows onto stacks of cargo, and the air smelled of canvas sacks, oak barrels, wooden crates, and cotton bales. While the two employees swept up and otherwise tried to look busy, Charles and Nick entered a one-room office. As was his habit, Charles turned on a hotplate to heat up a pot of coffee and sat down at his desk. He hooked a pair of spectacles over his ears and opened the company ledger, a large accounting book with lined pages and columns of numbers. He began combing through it, scrutinizing each page as if hidden somewhere in the strata of rows and columns was an elusive vein of gold.

At his own desk, Nick took out the Help Wanted section and reread the ad. It was an opportunity he'd been waiting for since graduating two years earlier. Now that it was here, every fiber of his being wanted to call the number at the bottom of the ad. Doing that, however, would ignite a row with his father, so he put the paper aside and went to work checking invoices.

At mid-morning an auctioneer came to see Charles about a shipment of used tractor engines stored in the back. The consignee, the man who owned the engines, had intended to rebuild them and sell them for half the cost of new ones. Since farmers were struggling it must've seemed like a good idea. But the consignee had gone bankrupt and owed Charles a substantial storage fee. Charles got up from his desk and went into the warehouse to greet the auctioneer. Nick observed him through the dust-covered window between the office and warehouse. His father had the erect posture of a ringmaster with the requisite broad shoulders and trim build. Like Nick, his hair was dark brown, his eyes light blue. He shook hands with the auctioneer and handed him a bill of lading. While the auctioneer examined it, Nick could guess what he was thinking. If the tractor engines were in good shape it would be easy to find buyers, but who would be interested in forty used ones in various states of disrepair.

With a wrinkled brow that read bad news, the auctioneer looked up. Nick couldn't hear what he was saying but noticed his father hunch over like a tent pole bending under considerable weight.

Keeping an eye on him, Nick picked up the phone and called the *San Francisco Chronicle*. He reached the assistant managing editor and asked if the job listed in the newspaper was still available. It was. Nervously tapping his foot, he introduced himself and asked if he could come in for an interview. The editor ignored his question and began an interrogation of his own. Did he know what a dateline was? An embargo? A chaser? Did he have clips? While Nick answered he watched his father slump down on a wooden crate and stare at the worthless bill of lading.

When the call ended, Nick was torn between the thrill of having arranged a job interview and a worry about his father, who seemed unusually gloomy. He fixed a cup of coffee just the way his father liked it — black, one sugar — and brought it to him.

"Everything alright?" he asked.

Charles grunted evasively, which served as both "thank you" for the coffee and "I don't want to discuss it" to the question, a terse answer for Charles who among any ten men was invariably the most polite and gracious.

Unable to think of anything else to say, Nick returned to his desk and kept an eye on the clock for the rest of the morning. When lunchtime rolled around, he left the warehouse without telling his father where he was going. Charles had always assumed Nick would take over the warehouse one day, even after Nick changed his major at the University of California, Berkeley, from business to journalism, a move that prompted Charles to lecture him: *Don't be a fool, son. This business is all I've got. It's your inheritance.* In the end Nick decided he would rather be considered a fool then abandon his dream. After he graduated he only agreed to work at the cargo warehouse because newspaper jobs were as rare as hard liquor at a Prohibition rally.

During the streetcar ride to the interview, Nick tried to think of questions he might be asked and the best answers, but it was hard to concentrate. The chance to work for a daily newspaper, to report on major events, to see his byline printed on the page, was everything he hoped for. And now it seemed within reach.

He stepped off the streetcar at the corner of Fifth and Mission in the shadow of the Chronicle Building, a three-story, Gothic Revival structure surmounted by a square clock tower. He took the elevator to the second floor. When the doors slid open he stepped into the newsroom and stopped in his tracks, startled by the frenzied scene. Copy boys were running between rows of desks, ringing phones cried for attention, reporters pounded on typewriters (*clickety-clack, clickety-clack*), editors barked orders (*Jones, crane down Harrison Street, bodies, get on it!*). As he stood there taking it all in, a smile crept over his lips and a tingling certainty gripped him: *this* was where he belonged.

Rufus Steele, the managing editor, offered him a seat opposite his desk and accepted a portfolio of articles Nick had written for the *Daily Cal*, the student newspaper at the University of California. Steele had a mop of grizzled hair. His tie was loosened, top shirt button undone. He leaned back in his chair and read the articles while Nick looked on.

A few minutes later he handed them back with an indifferent shrug. "You've mastered the basics but this stuff is stale. It's got no flair or imagination." He leaned forward. "Listen, we don't just hand out information. We gotta reach people here" — he pointed to his head — "and here" — he pointed to his heart — "and here" — he opened his coat and pointed to his wallet. "If we don't amaze 'em, scare 'em, or titillate 'em, we ain't doin' our job. You just haven't been around the block enough times to know what makes people wanna read the paper. Come back when you've gotta few more miles under your belt."

It was like a door slamming in his face, Nick thought as he left the building. He boarded a streetcar and during the ride back to the warehouse comforted himself with the knowledge that it had been a long shot. Two of San Francisco dailies, the *Post* and the *Bulletin*, had gone out of business, and the ones that remained, the *Chronicle, Examiner, Call-Bulletin*, and *San Francisco News*, could afford to be choosy. Still, he wasn't about to give up. In fact being in the newsroom had, if anything, stiffened his resolve. If Steele thought he needed more miles under his belt, then that was what he'd do. *But what does that mean exactly?* he wondered. *Travel around the world on a rusty freighter? Work for a small publication until my writing chops are worthy of big city newspaper?* He was still pondering the possibilities when he reached the warehouse and slipped back into the office.

Later that day Charles left the building without saying anything, leaving Nick to presume he'd run out to do an errand. When his father didn't return at the end of the day, Nick dismissed the warehousemen and locked the doors, figuring Charles had gone home after his errand.

It was a cold, wet evening. A light drizzle floated down and mixed with oil residue on the streets, creating iridescent swirls in the lamplight. As Nick walked home he noticed a crowd gathered in front of an office building on Montgomery Street and idly wondered what drew them there. Communists sometimes mounted soap boxes to attract listeners while they delivered angry rants about the evils of capitalism, but that mostly happened at the waterfront. And, anyway, he didn't see anyone on a soap box. He intended to keep going until he overheard someone say, "That's the third one this year. Good thing he didn't land on anyone."

An urgent siren wailed from somewhere in the distance, its cry echoing off the buildings along Montgomery Street.

A sudden curiosity took hold of Nick. He changed direction and headed toward the gathering, mostly office workers wearing trench coats and fedoras, some holding umbrellas. As he drew closer he heard a few gasps and a voice say, "What a bloody mess? Don't think I'll be able to eat tonight." When he reached the gathering more people came up behind him and soon he was encased in humanity. He couldn't see anything other than the back of hats, but he wasn't in a hurry and was just as curious as everyone else. To pass the time while waiting to see what was attracting everyone, he began writing an article in his head.

During the evening rush hour, a large crowd gathered on Montgomery Street to witness a sobering spectacle.

"Alright, step back. Step back now," said a blue-coated policeman who arrived with a partner, the two of them herding on-lookers back.

Those at the front of the pack, who'd already seen whatever it was, began pushing their way out, their movements opening gaps through which Nick caught quick glimpses.

They were transfixed by the sight of a red puddle spreading across the sidewalk. Blood and lots of it.

The policemen continued to herd the crowd back, creating an open area around the pool of blood. An ambulance pulled up next to the sidewalk, disgorging two attendants in white uniforms. As those leaving pushed their way out, Nick made his way forward until he caught sight of what drew everyone there.

In the middle of the red puddle lay a prone figure resting on his side as if he'd fallen asleep. Witnesses could be heard saying that he jumped out of a fourteenth-story window and nearly hit a pedestrian when he landed on the sidewalk. The jumper wore a gray suit and khaki trench coat, standard dress in these parts. Blood oozed from his left ear and one foot was cocked unnaturally sideways, apparently broken by the fall.

The two attendants lay a stretcher on the ground and transferred the body onto it. As they lifted the stretcher, it tilted slightly, rolling the jumper's head toward Nick, who gasped.

2

The phone rang after midnight, piercing the silence in the darkened flat and causing mattress springs to groan as sleepers rolled out of their beds. Nick was the first to emerge from his bedroom, drowsy-eyed, his dark brown hair mashed against the side of his head. He shambled down the hall, his progress followed by his mother Lillian and sister Sarah who peeked out from behind their bedroom doors as he reached the candlestick phone perched on a wall niche.

"Hello?" he said, thinking that if it was a wrong number he'd like to sling a few choice words at whoever it was.

"You've got to help me," the caller said. Nick recognized the voice. It had a singsong quality, each word a note in a pleasing melody. Clarisa called it her Gaelic lilt. Tonight it had an edge of desperation. "Seamus bit a policeman's ear. While drunk, no doubt. He's locked up here at the Hall of Justice, and if I don't get him out tonight he might go berserk again."

Nick raked a hand through his hair. This wasn't the first time her father ran afoul of the law while under the influence of Guinness and God-knows-what-else, but it was the first time she'd called for help.

"Jail might be the best place for him," he said. "We can pick him up in the morning when he's sober."

"I wish it were that simple." Her voice shifted from urgent to exasperated. "He's got a chip on his shoulder the size of Gibraltar. If I don't get him out soon, I'm afraid he'll do something rash."

"Alright, I'll borrow mother's car and be there right away."

While steering the Hudson Essex with one hand, Nick cranked open a window with the other, hoping the cool night air would erase his grogginess. It helped but didn't make up for months of restless nights laying in bed thinking about his father. He'd been paralyzed with shock when he saw the body, unable to move or say a word until the ambulance sped off and the crowd dispersed. He walked home in a daze, wondering what torturous path had led Charles to the fourteenth floor. Had he contemplated it for days? Weeks? Months? Or had it been an irrational, spur of the moment act? And what, Nick wondered, would it mean to his own life? To his future? Would he, too, be susceptible to committing such a desperate act? And what would his family do without an income or head of household? There didn't seem to be any answers, only an uneasy feeling that things would never be the same.

When he'd reached home, his mother was seated in the front parlor, her face wet with tears. His younger sister Sarah sat beside her with an arm around her. His grandfather Rune stood at the window puffing on a meerschaum pipe, staring out at the night sky. Police detective Jack Blum was there too, seated on the sofa. An old friend of the family, Blum usually greeted Nick with a broad smile and a firm handshake. On that night he didn't look like he relished being there. He stood up.

"Your father jumped —."

"Yeah, I know."

"I just got off the phone with his accountant." The detective paused, leaving Nick to wonder what he was talking about. "This morning he informed your father that his business is insolvent."

"Insolvent? What about the warehouse?"

"He borrowed money to keep the business going, a lot of money. Yesterday his creditors filed liens worth more than the property."

"But that's no reason to take his life," Lillian blurted out, her voice strained with shock. "He has a family that loves him. I don't understand. Why did he do it?"

Why, indeed, thought Nick. His father had been a pillar of strength and dependability. A man you could count on, everyone said. Of course things hadn't been easy. Nick could recall Charles complaining about high tariffs as the country slipped deeper into a grinding depression. Still, despite the financial difficulties, his father's suicide was a mystery, and in his confusion Nick tried to imagine why Charles would take his life when he had a family that depended on him.

As he pondered the possibilities, a crushing weight settled on his shoulders. He sat down beside his mother and wrapped an arm around her. She leaned her head on his shoulder, silent acknowledgement that he was head of the family now. Without a job, though, or prospects for employment, he had no idea how he would fill his father's shoes. And his dream of becoming a reporter. He'd reluctantly tucked it into a box labeled Deferred Dreams for Another Day.

Now, five months later, time hadn't produced the healing effect it was supposed to. The image of this father's body still haunted him, as did the questions it raised. The best that time seemed to offer was a kind of permanent malaise, a mental stalemate in which Nick saw the horrific image day after day, and night after night, until it no longer sent shock waves through him, yet wouldn't let him be. That was why he wanted to go as far away as possible. Perhaps distance would do what time couldn't.

He parked the Hudson in front of the Hall of Justice, a four-story granite building with dark stains running down the front. A cluster of cops sipping cups of coffee watched him get out of the car and push through the front door. He bounded up a set of worn marble stairs to the second floor and looked down a long corridor. Clarisa was standing at the far end, peering intently through a window grill, her lush auburn curls cascading down to her shoulders, her slender figure clad in a black overcoat with a belt cinched around her waist.

As Nick approached, she was talking through the grill. "Please let me take him home. He'll be a lot less trouble and I'll bring him back whenever you want."

A policeman behind the grill with enormous bags under his eyes regarded her with a sympathetic yet firm expression. "Listen, darlin', if he was just a drunk I'd have no problem cuttin' him loose, but your father bit an officer's ear and that's a felony. I can't let him go until he's had a hearing."

A door beside the window grill opened and another officer emerged, pear-shaped with a fleshy face. White gauze and tape covered his left ear.

Figuring this was Seamus' victim, Nick stepped in his path. "May I have a word?"

The officer ran his eyes up and down Nick's six-foot frame. "What is it? I gotta get back on duty."

Clarisa came over and slipped her hands around Nick's arm. "I'm so sorry my father injured you."

The policeman frowned and shook his head with obvious irritation. "He's a crazy one. Called us Black and Tans. Said he'd drive us back to the sea where we belonged."

Seamus' behavior isn't all that crazy if you know him, Nick thought. Before immigrating to America, Clarisa's father had been a member of the IRA, the Irish Republican Army, a citizen militia dedicated to ending British rule over Ireland. The British army wore black and tan uniforms, and those colors came to represent occupation and oppression. During the 1916 Dublin Easter Uprising, Seamus was captured and later let go with a warning to steer clear of the IRA, a useless admonition he promptly ignored. In retaliation, the Black and Tans harassed his wife and daughter until he couldn't take it anymore and packed them off to America. All these years later he still harbored a grudge against anyone in a position of authority, especially in uniform.

"You're right," said Nick, "Mr. McMahon can go overboard some-times. But if you knew him, Officer — what did you say your name was?"

"I didn't," replied the policeman who waved his hand to brush them aside. When that didn't work, he folded his arms across his chest. "It's O'Rourke."

As Nick suspected, the cop was a mick and likely to be sympathetic to a fellow Irishman. "Well, Officer O'Rourke, sometimes after a few pints Mr. McMahon doesn't know what he's doing. But he's not a criminal." He put his arm around Clarisa and together they gazed at the officer with beseeching eyes.

"Listen, you two," O'Rourke said, raising a hand to his bandaged ear, "if every drunk in Frisco took to assaultin' an officer, we'd have a pretty sorry lookin' force. If your father wants to drown his sorrows, he should stay at home where he'll do the least damage."

"That's right," said Clarisa, "he should be home. Especially now on the anniversary of the Easter Uprising. Every year at this time he feels guilty about leaving Dublin and the IRA."

O'Rourke studied the supplication on her face, then lowered his eyes to the marble floor and appeared to be tussling with his conscience.

Clarisa parted her lips to speak, but Nick, sensing a shift in the officer's attitude, squeezed her arm to remain quiet.

The policeman looked up with a somber expression. "I've a cousin who joined the IRA. They sent him on a mission to Kilkenny to rescue a priest who'd been arrested for collaboratin' with the cause. When he and his mates got there, the Black and Tan's were waitin' for 'em and cut 'em down with machine guns." He shook his head. "The poor boggers didn't stand a chance."

Clarisa rested a hand on his arm. "It was a terrible time. Some lost their lives. Others, like my father, lost their self-respect."

"Then it's probably best he's over here," O'Rourke said, patting her hand. He observed her imploring gaze for a few moments, then sighed. "Oh, all right. I won't press charges this time, but if he pulls any more shenanigans we'll have to throw the book at him."

Clarisa smiled broadly and kissed his cheek. "Believe me, he'll be a lot less trouble in my custody, and I won't let him out of the house until he's himself again."

"Joe," O'Rourke called to the officer behind the grill. "I've decided to let McMahon off with a warning this time."

The officer named Joe led them into a long room with steel-barred cells along one side. Some prisoners lay on bunks, others were sprawled on the floor. An odor of vomit permeated the air. Stopping at a cell, Joe rifled through his keys, located the correct one, and unlocked the cell door. He stepped aside and waved Clarisa and Nick in. A prisoner lay on the floor, a splotch of dried blood caked on his chin. He had a wiry build, grizzled hair, and large, sinewy hands spotted with ink stains.

Clarisa knelt down and gently squeezed his arm. "Seamus, wake-up. We've come to take you home."

He stirred and fell still again.

Nick bent down, draped Seamus' right arm over his shoulder, and lifted him to his feet. On the way up he caught the sharp smell of spirits and beer.

The movement woke Seamus with a start, his eyes disoriented and fearful. "Whaaa? Get yer hands off me ya bloody Black and Tans!" He struggled ineffectually, arms flailing like a rag doll. "I'll not submit to yer heathen torture!"

"Father, it's me," said Clarisa, cupping her palms on his cheeks and looking into his eyes. "We've come to take you home."

Seamus regarded her with a confused expression, as if trying to understand how she fit into his delusional nightmare. Then a look of horror came over him. "Oh, Jaysus," he cried, "they have me daughter too! I'll kill 'em! Tyrants! Murderers! God damn their souls!" Eyes wide and bulging, he lunged for the officer. Before he reached the cell door, Nick grabbed his coattail and right arm, wrenching it behind his back while Clarisa stepped in front of him.

"No, father, it's all right. They're going to let you out. Just like they did before, remember, when they opened the gaol and set all the internees free."

Chest heaving, Seamus directed a look of scorn at the jailer who stepped back, nervously fingering the baton at his side. "So they're letting us free again?" he said. "But what about poor Connolly, executed in a chair because he was too wounded to stand," a reference to the leader of the Easter Uprising. He shifted his gaze to Clarisa. At the sight of her face his angry scowl dissolved into wan smile. "You're all I've got in this world. I'd do anything for you."

"Come," she said, pulling him out of the cell, "before they change their minds."

He stumbled forward, only managing to stay on his feet with Nick's help. Somehow in his besotted brain Nick's presence didn't seem out of place in his nightmare. In fact just the opposite. "You're a good man to help me out of this dungeon," he said, "but then you're an American and Americans aren't afraid to stand up to tyranny."

By the time they rolled up to his print shop at 123 Haight Street, Seamus had fallen asleep in the backseat. Clarisa roused him and together she and Nick walked him up a flight of stairs into a long railroad flat above the shop. They guided him down a hall to his bedroom. There, Clarisa laid him down, removed his shoes, and drew a blanket over him.

Nick stood behind her, hands on her shoulders, and for a silent moment they watched Seamus inhale slow, labored breaths, mouth drooped open, chin still caked with blood.

Clarisa turned around and looked up at Nick with admiring eyes. "Thanks for your help," she whispered, laying her hands on his chest.

Nick searched her face, wondering if this was the right moment to break the news, to announce he was leaving. It was a delicate matter and only perfect timing and compelling persuasion would pave the way for her acceptance. Deciding it wasn't the right moment — or perhaps he just wanted to avoid a confrontation — he leaned forward and touched his lips to hers, her lavender perfume enveloping him, triggering a deep desire.

Her mouth parted, her body pressed against his.

They wrapped their arms around each other, lips joined, tongues touching, the heat of their bodies merging. Nick felt self-conscious being so intimate in front of her father, but Seamus continued to breathe slow, shallow breaths.

They continued to embrace until Clarisa stepped back with an inviting, come-hither smile. Taking his hand, she drew him out of the room, down the hall, and into her bedroom. She shut the door and came toward him. He was ready. More than ready. They both lived with their parents, so it was rare to find a time and place with enough privacy for love-making, and a rare treat when they did.

There was no reason to rush, yet it took no time at all to remove their clothes and fall into bed. Her breasts were firm, nipples swollen, face framed by a halo of curls. He ran a hand over her hips, down her legs, and back up to a triangular thatch the same auburn color as her hair. Despite the late hour, he was alert and energized. He stroked and kissed her, moving from her face to her neck to her breasts, then down across her tummy. His tongue flicked up and down, causing her to moan with pleasure, her hips moving rhythmically. This went on for some time until, as if driven by some force greater than himself, he lifted himself on top of her.

As their love-making progressed, Clarisa closed her eyes and bit her lower lip as if something was bothering her. She often did this when they made love, prompting Nick to ask her about it one day, concerned that she wasn't satisfied with his performance or, worse, that she didn't care for him as much as he thought. Neither was the case. She seemed genuinely surprised to learn of the habit and said she hadn't been aware of it and didn't know why she did it. Later, quite by accident, he discovered that if he stroked her hair while they made love she stopped biting her lip, as if that extra bit of affection calmed whatever subconscious worry their loving-making provoked.

Afterwards they lay in silence, he on his back, she with her head resting on his chest. It was getting late and he would have to leave soon, but for now he was enjoying the warm afterglow.

Clarisa idly stroked his chest. "So have you made up your mind?"

The question took him by surprise. He had to think for a moment about it until its meaning became clear. Once he understood he hesitated, unsure how to answer. He'd hoped to avoid this topic tonight, especially after they shared themselves so intimately, but her question had to be answered. Or did it? He gently caressed her hair, hoping to lull her to sleep. It was a manipulative move, but he felt justified — this wasn't the time or place to discuss it.

Her eyelids drooped shut. Her breathing become slower and deeper. She seemed to have fallen asleep when suddenly, as if awakened by a bad dream, her eyes flew open and focused on him, her expression suspicious as if she knew what he was doing.

"Are you going to answer my question?"

The accusation in her voice forced him to look beyond her to a jagged crack in the plaster wall. He could feel her eyes bore into him, demanding an answer, demanding more than he could give. He willed himself to meet her gaze. They were only inches apart, yet he sensed a deep chasm between them, echoing with unfulfilled dreams.

He lifted the corners of his mouth into an uneasy smile. "Yes, I have."

"And," she persisted.

"I've signed articles. I'll be working on a ship."

Her body stiffened. Her lower lip began to tremble.

He knew she dealt with conflict the way a railroad switch diverts a locomotive: in only one direction or the other. Once she reacted, there would be no changing her mind, no hopping from one track to another.

If he was going to influence her, he had to do it now. He took her hand.

"Mother's only working part time and we're hanging on by a thread. I applied for a position with all the dailies, but there aren't any job openings." He didn't mention an offer from an insurance company to work as a filing clerk. She wouldn't understand that he couldn't be confined within four walls, that if he was to deal with the demons his father left him, if he was to acquire the real world experience the *Chronicle* editor said he needed to become a reporter, he had to go away, far away.

"How can you leave now?" Her voice low and resentful. "Are you willing to jeopardize a lifetime together?"

He caressed her cheek with the back of his hand. "Of course not. But I'm not willing to abandon this opportunity either. Besides, it's not as if I'll be sailing for the rest of my life, just a year or two until the economy picks up."

She rolled onto her back and folded her arms across her chest. "And what am I suppose to do while you're gallivanting around the world? I've got dreams of my own, you know. I won't put my life on hold for you."

There had been times when he was certain of his decision. This wasn't one of them. "I — I guess I can't expect anything else."

So there it was, like a dead carcass stinking up the room, neither one wanting to look at it yet impossible to ignore. A faint light shown through the curtains, softly illuminating the frown on her face. He could see it was no use. She wasn't going to accept his leaving; that train had left the station. He fought a sudden and intense urge to wrap his arms around her, to draw her close and inhale her sweet fragrance. For a moment he wanted it more than anything, more than life itself. Looking at her now, though, it was clear that the body he'd been intimate with just minutes earlier was now out of bounds.

He got up and slipped on his clothes. Part of him had known it would turn out this way. That's why he'd wanted to wait for a better time. He took one last look at her, staring at the ceiling with moist eyes, biting her lower lip, her body trembling slightly.

He turned to leave, hesitated, waffled, then, summoning more self-discipline than he'd ever summoned before, walked out.

}

The Victorian houses along Haight Street gleamed fresh and bright after a season of winter rains. Clarisa admired their fanciful gingerbread moldings and round turrets from a bygone era when people had plenty of money to spend on their homes. *A far cry from today*, she thought as she walked toward the nearest streetcar stop. She passed under a tree sprouting tender green leaves from which morning dew evaporated, scenting the air with the earthy fragrance of spring. It was a time, she reflected, of renewal, a time as it said in Ecclesiastes "to be born...and a time to get." And that's just what she intended to do as she boarded a streetcar with a *Chronicle* folded under her arm. Get a job.

After Nick announced his intention to leave, she received another unexpected shock. She arrived home one afternoon from State Teacher's College, where she was a student, and found a notice tacked on the front door demanding back rent and threatening eviction. She assumed it was a mistake until her father confessed that their bank account was nearly depleted and that his printing business was limping along, generating little income. It was a crushing blow and led her to the inescapable conclusion that she would have to leave school and look for work.

This wasn't the first time her family faced serious adversity. Sixteen years earlier the McMahon's had immigrated to America and settled in a third-floor walk-up in Philadelphia near the Delaware River. Clarisa could still recall the wide avenues lined with big-leafed trees and the funny way Americans talked, stretching their vowels with a nasal twang and pronouncing 't's like 'd's, as in atom or ninety.

Her father, accustomed to Ireland's cool climate, had difficulty adjusting to Philadelphia's humid summers and soon began plotting their next move. He was about to purchase train tickets when Spanish influenza swept the country, sparking a panic among frightened citizens who covered their faces with bandanas to fend off the dreaded grippe. The epidemic was particularly virulent in crowded neighborhoods where multiple families occupied the same building. Clarisa's mother nursed a sick neighbor down the hall and was soon stricken herself. In the course of a single day, blue splotches appeared below her ears and spread across her face, a sign her congested lungs couldn't provide enough oxygen to her blood. By the end of the day her entire body was blue and in the middle of the night she passed away.

Eight years old at the time, Clarisa watched the progression in horror, unable to understand how God could let her mother deteriorate so quickly. And when it was over she not only felt a tremendous loss, she was convinced that nothing in life was certain, nothing dependable, and it left her with a deep, abiding desire to reclaim the sense of security so abruptly stripped from her.

After the funeral Seamus moved with his daughter to San Francisco, and with the help of the city's Irish expatriate community, he opened a printing business below their flat on Haight Street. In the boom years following The Great War, the print shop rolled out a steady stream of handbills, sporting programs, political pamphlets, posters, and advertisers, and the brass bell attached to the front door greeted customers with a cheerful jingle. To manage his growing business, Seamus hired three apprentices who ran the presses round the clock, and he provided free printing services to a group of expats who supported the Irish Republican Army.

He also made a comfortable life for his daughter. Several times a year he took her to The Emporium to purchase dresses, hats, shoes, makeup — anything she desired. And on Saturday nights they went to the Castro Theater to admire Greta Garbo slinking across the silver screen or to laugh at Charlie Chaplin's endearing pratfalls.

When the stock market crashed in 1929, the print shop began a long slow decline. Month after month the brass bell on the front door jingled with less frequency, and one-by-one Seamus had to let his apprentices go until only he was left to answer the bell. Fortunately, he didn't mind working the presses himself. Ink flowed in his veins and words nourished his soul.

Over time his customers pared down to a few local merchants and the Workers School next door run by leftists who recruited students from the swelling ranks of the unemployed. Seamus said they were sincere and steady customers — radicals, it turned out, admired the printed word as much as he. And when they discovered he fought in the Dublin Easter Uprising, he was revered as a battle-tested comrade. However, the school often lacked funds to pay its bill, so Seamus had had to accept IOUs or partial payment for his services.

Clarisa alighted from the streetcar at the corner of Market and Fremont streets and joined a throng of pedestrians moving to and fro, men in suits with square padded shoulders, women in long coats and cloche hats. She made her way to the Matson Building at 215 Market Street and paused at the front entrance to look up at the skyscraper. Its grand arched entrance was thirty-foot high, and there were rows of windows stepping up sixteen stories to an overhanging cornice. She had never worked in a building this large and just the size of it was intimidating. *How many people work here?* she wondered. *Must be hundreds.* Taking a deep breath, she pushed through a set of revolving doors into a lobby echoing with the shuffle of footsteps moving in and out.

On the ninth floor she entered Suite 981, offices of the Waterfront Employers Association. The reception room was handsomely furnished with leather chairs and framed photographs of ships docked at the waterfront. From behind a desk, a gray-haired receptionist peered over reading glasses and handed her a job application. Several other women were already seated in the reception area, apparently there to apply for the same job. Clarisa sat down beside them and filled out the application. When she finished, she opened the newspaper to the Help Wanted section and turned to the job listings designated for women. Why listings were divided into those for men and for women, she never understood, as if men couldn't nurse the sick and women couldn't count money in a bank. She scanned the page and found the listing that brought her here.

> *Seeking experienced secretary. Must have presentable appearance,*
> *know shorthand, and type 80 words per minute. Ideal applicant*
> *has experience organizing meetings and seeing to the needs of staff.*
> *Forty dollars per week. Contact Waterfront Employers Association at*
> *Douglas 3913.*

Seeing to the needs of staff, she assumed, meant serving coffee and running errands, so there was at least one required skill she could handle. In truth, her shorthand was rudimentary, and although she knew how to type, her proficiency at eighty words per minute was questionable. She glanced at the other applicants. Three of them looked a good ten years older than her, while another, dressed quite properly in white gloves and black hat with lace veil, had to be fifty. She sighed. This was shaping up to be just another opportunity to practice her interviewing skills. Not that she needed it. She'd already been to three interviews that week and none resulted in a job, although she had attracted an offer from a cigar-puffing cretin who owned a string of movie theaters. He interviewed her in a dingy back office and leered at her from behind a cloud of cigar smoke, then offered her a job with a pitiful salary. The wage could have been a million dollars for all she cared, she still wouldn't have worked for him.

The applicants were called in one at a time. When Clarisa's turn came, the receptionist pointed down a wood-paneled hallway.

"Mr. Farnsworth's office is the third door on the left. Just go right in."

Despite the instructions, she knocked on the door and waited.

"Hold on a sec," came a voice from inside, then louder, "Come on in."

Clutching her application, she opened the door and stepped into a spacious office bathed in light from a large picture window on the opposite wall. In front of the window, a young man, presumably Mr. Farnsworth, sat behind a massive mahogany desk, holding a phone to his ear. He wore a navy blue, double-breasted suit. His hair blond, oiled, and neatly combed back. His youthful features reminded her of Joe DiMaggio, the handsome shortstop for the San Francisco Seals, but his complexion was pale as if he spent little time outdoors. The picture window behind him framed a view of the waterfront and San Francisco Bay, now shimmering in shades of blue and green. He silently offered her a chair in front of his desk, then fished a silver case from his coat pocket and extracted a cigarette.

She sat down and glanced around. A mahogany bookcase covered one wall, stocked with books and framed photos. Most of the photos appeared to be family portraits — mother, father, siblings (no wife or children, she noticed). Curiously, there was a photo of a black man seated at a grand piano, and not just any black man. She immediately recognized Duke Ellington smiling at the camera, hands resting on the piano keys as if he was about to play "Take the 'A' Train." Her eyes lingered on the photo and the hand-written inscription at the bottom. She wanted to lean closer to see if it was a personal note but decided not to, figuring that such a move would be presumptuous. Still, whether or not the inscription was personal, it was curious to see a photo of a black man in the office of an executive.

She continued her survey and noted a side door, presumably leading to the secretary's office. There were also two comfortable club chairs facing Mr. Farnsworth's desk, including the one she occupied. Her gaze finally settled on her interviewer. He was still on the phone and studying a newsletter on his desk with the title *WATERFRONT WORKER* across the top. She glanced at the newsletter, a crudely mimeographed publication on legal-sized paper. What intrigued her more, though, was the blond DiMaggio who appeared to be only a few years older than herself.

"Yeah, I've got a copy right here," he said into the phone. "Pretty amateur stuff . . . I know. It's illiterate drivel, and the letters to the editor are probably fabricated . . . No, there aren't any names on it, but there is a Market Street address. Listen, it's just a few Reds trying to stir the pot.

I don't think the men will respond to this kind of rubbish. I'll contact Emile Stone at the Blue Book Union. One of his men may have heard something." He glanced at Clarisa and held up a finger to indicate he was almost through. "Okay, don't worry, I'll look into it."

He hung up the phone and rose to his feet, extended a hand. "How do you do, Miss —"

"McMahon." She shook his hand and placed the job application on his desk. "Clarisa McMahon."

"Pleasure to meet you, Miss McMahon." He sat down, his blond hair highlighted by sunlight pouring through the picture window behind him. "I'm Roger Farnsworth, executive assistant to Thomas Plant, chairman of the Waterfront Employers Association and general manager of the American-Hawaiian Steamship Line. Among other things, I act as a liaison between our office and the shipping and stevedore companies that comprise the bulk of our membership." He leaned back in his chair and lit the cigarette with a matching silver lighter. "So tell me about your experience?"

Clarisa had come prepared with several possible answers to this question. She could offer the unvarnished truth, although considering the competition that would probably get her nowhere, or give him a list of fictitious past employers. The application had only asked for her previous employment, which she listed as a part-time waitress at Coffee Dan's where she worked to earn money for school tuition. So at this point she could still invent a job history and hope he wouldn't check it.

Before her conscience intervened, she plunged ahead. "I worked for my father's printing company as a secretary for several years . . . until he no longer needed me."

"No longer needed you?"

"Yes, the — the economy — things slowed down." She met his stare for a guilty moment, then shifted her gaze to the view through the picture window behind him. A row of finger piers jutted out into the bay where several freighters were anchored, all facing in the same direction like a herd of grazing cows. Beyond the bay the East Bay hills, green from spring rains, rose up to a cloudless blue sky. The magnificent panorama gave her an idea: perhaps she could steer the interview away from her previous employment. "You have a terrific view. It must be nice to enjoy that every day."

Roger Farnsworth shrugged dismissively. "I'm usually too busy to turn around much less waste time looking out the window." His hazel eyes locked onto her. "There are thirty-three steamship companies in San Francisco and four stevedore suppliers, and every one of them has problems they expect us to solve. So, as you can see, we've got a lot to handle."

His intensity disarmed her. She hadn't expected someone so young to be so serious. Collecting herself, she said, "That's quite a responsibility, considering the port handles eleven million tons of cargo every year and accommodates seven-thousand ships at forty-one piers. And, if I'm not mistaken," she continued, reciting a list of statistics rehearsed the night before, "there are seventeen miles of berthing space with a cargo capacity of nearly two-million tons, capable of docking two-hundred-fifty vessels at a time." She took a breath. "It's San Francisco's largest industry, if you include ancillary operations."

The information had come from Nick. During picnics on Telegraph Hill overlooking the waterfront, he would often identify the class of a ship from its profile and the company it belonged to from the colors painted on its funnel.

Farnsworth's expression changed from studied to admiring. "For such a young lady, you know a lot about the port."

She glanced around at the furnishings. "For such a young man, you have a very handsome office." It was an impetuous response and one she immediately wanted to lasso and pull back into her mouth.

Farnsworth didn't appear to mind. He grinned and tapped his cigarette on a glass ashtray. "So, tell me about yourself."

For the next twenty minutes she described her family's journey to America (leaving out her father's association with the IRA), her volunteer work at St. Patrick's Mission, a soup kitchen south of Market Street, her father's printing business which still survived, though barely, and her love of novels, museums, strolls in Buena Vista Park—anything that might distract him from asking questions about her secretarial skills. He listened attentively until he glanced at his watch and seemed startled, muttering that he hadn't realized how long they'd been talking.

Abruptly rising to his feet, he thanked her for coming in and said they would let her know the results of the interview. As she passed through the reception room, the remaining applicants shot reproving glances at her, obviously irritated at how long her interview had lasted. Ignoring them, she left the building feeling satisfied. She might be one of the youngest applicants, but if her intuition was correct, she was among the finalists.

4

In the pre-dawn darkness Nick peered down Telegraph Hill into a dense fog, obscuring everything below but a row of mist-blurred street-lights. Beyond the lights, the bay was discernible only by the scent of saline air and the occasional moan of a foghorn. Feeling a chill Nick tugged a white cap down over his forehead and shoved his hands into the pockets of a navy pea coat. A duffel bag lay by his side stuffed with clothes, a personal kit, a padlock, a dog-eared copy of *The Ports of Asia*, several pints of bootleg whiskey his grandfather Rune suggested he bring, and a box of chocolates his mother added at the last minute. She wanted to see him off, but he rejected the idea. He wasn't a schoolboy going to his first day of class. His grandfather agreed: *This ain't a holiday cruise, and you won't have time to wave goodbye.*

The voyage was scheduled to last several months, but Nick felt as if he was leaving for good, or at least leaving something behind forever. He hesitated before walking down the hill, his eyes scanning the gray mist, searching for any sign of her, hoping she'd come to see him off. He'd called Clarisa after he announced his intention to work on a freighter, hoping to make amends, hoping she'd come to terms with his decision. She hadn't. After learning he still planned to leave, she ended the conversation and wouldn't accept his calls after that. In a last ditch effort, he left a message asking her to meet him on Telegraph Hill at the place where they'd spent hours together on a blanket, eating cheese and crackers, drinking wine and gazing out at the bay. *Didn't all those hours count for anything, the talking, the kissing, the laughing, the teasing, the cuddling?* Those enjoyable moments seemed so precious now, so golden and light. His heart ached at the thought of never having them again.

The rasp of footsteps on the road leading up the hill pulled him from his thoughts. Is she coming to say goodbye?

A figure slowly materialized out of the fog . . . tall, lean, aided by a malacca cane, huffing and puffing billows of warm breath. Nick recognized his grandfather by his old seaman's hat and his white mutton-chop sideburns running down to a walrus mustache.

Rune leaned on the cane to catch his breath. "I know you were expectin' someone else," he said with a Danish accent. "I heard you leave a message for her." He reached into his coat and pulled out a leather-bound notebook. "There's two kinda women, son. Those made fer sailors and those that aren't. Some don't mind their men gone most of the time, some even prefer it. But most don't. It's the hardest part of life at sea. You'd tink it was the odd hours or typhoons. Nope, it's the feelin' yer cut off from everyting ya love." He handed the notebook to Nick. "Here. You can pour yer heart out into it. I've seen men go crazy with homesickness. This'll help."

"Thanks, grandpa." Nick stuffed the notebook into his duffel bag and hoisted it over his shoulder. "If you see her, tell her I said goodbye."

Rune saluted two fingers against the bill of his hat. "You'll do just fine, son. Captain Harding and I go back to before the war. He's stiffer than a batten board but fair. Just remember all I taught ya."

As the sky paled in the east, Nick descended a wooden stairway to the Embarcadero and turned south along the waterfront. The dawning light revealed a row of ships resting beside finger piers, their prows pointed toward the city, waiting for the day to begin. On the inland side, at Colombo Produce Market, truck farmers in tented stalls were stacking pyramids of artichokes, asparagus, beets, and lettuce. The scene reminded him of his youth when the waterfront near his father's warehouse was a world of savory odors and fascinating sights. On many an afternoon he'd roamed the Embarcadero among the Belt Line trains and flatbed trucks, enjoying the aroma of coffee beans roasting at the Hills Brothers plant and ground cinnamon wafting out of the Schilling Spice Factory. Sometimes he'd sneak onto the docks and watch longshoremen discharge bales of tea from the Far East or sacks of cacao beans from the Ivory Coast, all the while trying to imagine the places it came from.

Recalling those days reminded him why he was embarking on this journey and reignited his anticipation at seeing far-off lands. He reached the Dollar Company cargo shed at Pier 42 and entered through an arched opening large enough to swallow freight trains. Just inside the shed he passed a line of longshoremen in striped hickory shirts and black Frisco pants, waiting at an office window to collect their pay tokens. From the look of their haggard faces and soiled clothing he reckoned it must have been an all-nighter.

He exited through a side door, stepped out onto the dock, and came to an abrupt stop before an imposing wall of steel, rising straight up out of the water. He traced the outlines of a vertical prow, a weather deck, and a three-story midship house standing bolt upright like a Crackerjack box. The homely ship bore no graceful curves, no rounded surfaces, yet she elicited his admiration nonetheless, for sheer size if nothing else. He studied her lines until he saw two words painted on the side of her bow: DIANA DOLLAR.

He climbed up the gangway behind two stewards toting stores on board. At the top, a sailor with a clipboard stood guard.

"Nick Benson, reporting for work," he said, keeping his voice steady to conceal his nervous excitement.

The guard studied the clipboard and made a check mark. "You're bunkin' in the number three cabin on the starboard side." He pointed to the midship house. "Stow your gear and report to the bosun."

"Where will I find him?"

"Oh, you can't miss Slag. And if you don't find him, he'll find you."

The cabin was small, cramped, and dimly lit by a single porthole. Two sailors lay sleeping in their clothes on the bottom bunks of two double-decker bunk beds. A locker cabinet against stood against one wall, and a small open area in the center of the room was large enough for two, maybe three sailors to stand without elbowing each other. Nick inspected the lockers and found one empty. He dumped the contents of his duffle bag on an upper bunk and stowed his gear item by item, carefully burying the whiskey bottles at the back of the locker.

You'll need to make friends and allies, Rune had advised. *A swig of grog offered on a bone-chilling night can make all the difference.*

Reaching for the last item, the box of chocolates, he patted an empty bunk. *Empty?* He looked around. Aside from himself the only living creatures were the two sleeping sailors. Or were they sleeping? He mulled over the situation. How much fuss was a box of chocolates worth? Not much, he concluded. Still, it irked him to be fleeced so quickly, and if the theft went unchallenged, he might be labeled a spineless doormat.

"You're welcome to take a few pieces," he said to no one in particular, "just don't take the whole box."

One of the sailors awakened, a stocky fellow with hair greased back in a pompadour. He stretched and yawned in the exaggerated manner of a Vaudevillian actor. "Whassamatter? You lose somefin'?"

"I put a box of chocolates here," said Nick, pointing to the empty bunk, "and now they're gone. Since no one else is here, I guess one of you has sticky fingers." He smiled to hide his irritation, although as soon as the words left his mouth he saw the incongruity of trying to seem friendly while making an accusation.

The stocky sailor rose up on his elbows and kicked the other seaman's bunk. "Hey, Remy, Sherlock Holmes here sez someone stole his box a choc-o-lates. Sez he left 'em on his bunk and now they're *allll* gone."

The other sailor, a thin swarthy fellow with a caterpillar mustache and yellow cigarette stains on his fingers, stirred, eyes fluttered open. "Huh, wha'd you say Moon?"

"You seen a box a choc-o-lates." Moon nodded toward Nick. "Our new mate here sez they disappeared. Whaddaya think? Maybe the cockroaches carried 'em away." He laughed and eyed Nick with a mocking grin. "Your dear mother gave 'em to you, right? As a going-a-way gift?" He flopped back down on the bunk and knitted his fingers behind his head as if he hadn't a care in the world.

Nick turned away. *Damn those stupid chocolates.* He'd endured razzing as a freshman in college, but everyone in his class had so it hadn't seemed personal. Now, not ten minutes onboard and already he felt humiliated. He tried to shrug it off, and would have, but the indignity got the better of him. As though possessed by a truculent toddler, he whirled around and glared at the stocky sailor. *"I want my box! And I want it now!"* he wanted to say in the worst way, but the words caught in his throat and the humiliation burned as if he'd swallowed a red hot pepper. Instead, he stood there paralyzed with self-doubt, keenly aware that he was out of his element — even the oily, salty smell of the cabin was alien to him — and that he was woefully ignorant of the rules of engagement among seamen.

"Come on," he said somewhere between pleading and demanding, "give it back."

He took a step toward Moon to give added gravity to the request. It didn't do any good. Moon lay there coolly ignoring him as if he wasn't there. Nick glared at him, his eyes drawn to Moon's nose, narrow at the bridge, then flattened and flared at the tip as if it had been used as a battering ram or, more likely, a punching bag. It gave Moon a fearsome, don't-fuck-with-me look, and the longer Nick stared at it, the more it seemed to be saying: *Come on, mate, one more fisticuff won't bother me.*

He was marveling at how a nose could convey such an unequivocal message when a trill of eighth notes rang out and a voice boomed from the passageway. "Turn to! All hands on deck!"

Moon jumped up from his bunk and bumped into Nick, who flinched back, half expecting a fist to come flying at him. Instead, Moon gave him a wink and a click of the tongue, then grabbed his flat-cap and strode out the door.

"Don't worry," Remy said, as he got up from his bunk and put on an identical cap. "Moon doesn't throw a punch unless he's defendin' himself or a mate, and he's a damn good sailor which is what counts around here. A lubber like you would do well to stay on his good side."

"How did you know I'm a—." Nick paused, embarrassed to be sized up so quickly.

"A lubber." Remy glanced at his flat-cap. "Your lunchbox Stetson is whiter than an albino's butt, your palms are softer than a hooker's muff, and"—he reached under Moon's pillow and pulled out the box of chocolates—"no man who's ever been to sea before would even think of leavin' a treat like this on his bunk and turn his back." He opened the box, popped a chocolate into his mouth, and handed it to Nick. "Here, Moon won't care. It was just a joke. Now let's turn to before Slag comes gunnin' for us."

"I'll be right along," Nick called out as Remy disappeared into the passageway. He tore off his flat-cap, threw it on the floor, and ground it under his heel. Then donning the smudged cap, he headed out to the weatherdeck.

The crew was scurrying about preparing the freighter for departure. Nick joined Remy at one of the five hatch openings that led to the ship's hold. They covered the hatch with thick boards, then spread a waterproof tarpaulin over the boards, securing the edges of the tarpaulin with wooden wedges pounded through slots in the coaming, a low perimeter wall around the hatch. As he worked, Nick could feel a cadenced hum from the ship's engine vibrating the deck under his feet.

Next they turned their attention to the kingpost, a tall mast-like column beside the hatch. Two steel poles, called booms, were attached to the base of the kingpost, both angled out like giant fishing rods. Following Remy's lead, Nick unhooked a pair of guy wires that held one of the booms in place. Then he reeled in the boom with a topping lift line until it was vertically snug against the kingpost.

Three sharp blasts from the ship's whistle sent a cloud of steam into the air, announcing the pilot's intention to depart. The *Diana Dollar* slowly warped away from the pier, guided by a tugboat nudging her stern south, while a second tug pointed her bow north.

Proceeding ahead amid a slew of other vessels — paddle-wheel ferries, tramp steamers, cargo lighters, and fishing boats — the freighter slowly sailed past the Ferry Building, rounded North Point, and headed toward the Golden Gate. As the ship drew close to the mile-wide channel, Nick noticed a wooden trestle extending out from the south shore toward the future site of the south bridge tower. Trucks and leather-helmeted construction workers were filing back and forth over the partially-completed trestle, hauling lumber and equipment out to the end.

On the opposite shore, at Lime Point, excavation was underway for the north bridge tower. A steam shovel stretched its articulated arm down into the foundation cavity and scooped out pulverized rock, then swiveled out over the water and deposited a cataract of ochre debris.

Picking up steam, the freighter sailed through the Golden Gate, passing Land's End where waves crashed against steep cliffs and white foamy surf boiled around rock islands. Nick stood on the quarterdeck, looking back at the city veiled in gray mist. He bade a silent goodbye to Clarisa whom he pictured under a warm blanket, thick auburn curls draped over her smooth pale cheeks. Her absence earlier hadn't been unexpected. Still, he felt a pang of sadness as the Golden Gate faded in the distance and a cold wind buffeted his cheeks.

5

Clarisa tugged the last sheet of paper out of her typewriter and exhaled a sigh of relief. Her first day at the Waterfront Employers Association had come to a close, leaving her with a satisfying sense of accomplishment. She had arrived that morning with a nervous flutter in her stomach. It was one thing to talk her way into a job and another to actually do it. She'd managed the former with a bit of homework and a glib tongue. For the latter, however, she knew she was far less prepared.

Mrs. Butterfield, the gray haired receptionist, had given her a tour of the office and introduced her to Mr. Plant, her boss's boss, a man of about sixty with grayish close-cropped hair. He greeted her with a brief exchange of pleasantries, wished her well, then summarily sat down and resumed his work, leaving Clarisa with the distinct feeling that he didn't have a moment to spare. And no wonder. He was both the executive director of the Waterfront Employers Association and the general manager of the American-Hawaiian Steamship Line.

Her own office was small, furnished with a desk, two file cabinets, and a stack of boxes containing assorted documents. Though it featured no outside window, natural light entered through opaque glass panels on two doors, one leading to Mr. Farnsworth's office, the other to the hallway. A framed photo hung on the wall opposite her desk, a picture of a steamship moored at the waterfront. Sailors on the deck of the ship were leaning on the railings, looking toward the camera. She found herself imagining Nick among them, his eyes trained on her. She knew otherwise, of course, but it was a disconcerting distraction until she examined the photo, satisfying herself that the ship didn't bear the name *Diana Dollar,* the vessel Nick said he was on.

Her sensitivity was perhaps a result of having avoided him after he announced he was leaving. It had stirred long-buried emotions, the same terrible emotions of loss and grief that devastated her when her mother died. Only this time the pain of separation triggered an all-consuming anger she couldn't control or dispel. On the day Nick left, still wrestling with her emotions, she forced herself to rise early and made her way to Telegraph Hill. She stood behind a large eucalyptus tree until Nick arrived at their usual picnic spot carrying a duffle bag. For several minutes she wavered back and forth, torn between her anger at him for leaving her at a time when her father was sinking into self-pity and the landlord was threatening eviction and her deep affection for him. She was just about to come out from behind the tree, although whether to berate him or hug him she wasn't sure, when his grandfather appeared out of the fog. Startled by the sudden intrusion, she shrank back and watched as Nick headed down the hill, descending from sight like a setting sun.

During her first day at work she had acquainted herself with the staples of her new job — typewriter, bond and carbon paper, dictation pads, manila folders, pens, ink, and an intercom connected to Mr. Farnsworth's office. She rummaged through the file drawers, mostly correspondence and reports, tested out the typewriter, a Royal that needed a new ribbon, and threw out an empty bottle of gin the last secretary had apparently hidden in the back of a file drawer and neglected to remove.

After lunch Mr. Farnsworth dictated several memos. She recorded them in shorthand then typed them, grateful no one was timing her speed.

Overall, she was pleased at how the day had gone and that everyone seemed satisfied with her performance.

"Miss McMahon," said Mr. Farnsworth over the intercom, "would you please come in and bring a notepad and pen?"

She checked her wristwatch — five-thirty, the time she was scheduled to leave. *Why can't it wait till morning?* she wondered. Then she remembered how lucky she was to have landed a job and that if she wanted to keep it she'd better be a willing employee. She reached over and pressed a lever on the intercom. "I'll be right in."

Mr. Farnsworth was sitting at his desk, his blond hair oiled and combed back in perfect parallel lines. "I know it's time for you to leave," he said, "but I have a couple of letters I want to send out tonight. I hope you don't mind."

His smooth pale features behind the massive hardwood desk still looked improbably young; however, the double-breasted suit he wore fit his trim physique perfectly and compensated for his youthful appearance.

She sat down, pen and pad at the ready. "Fire away."

Both letters were brief. The first was a note of condolence to the wife of a shipping executive who'd died unexpectedly of a heart attack. The second, addressed to a Federal bureaucrat, requested a meeting to discuss proposals for the maritime codes stipulated under the National Industrial Recovery Act. Neither letter seemed terribly urgent or required immediate mailing, so perhaps this was a test of her efficiency. When Mr. Farnsworth finished the dictation she rose to leave.

"How was your first day?" he asked. "Have we overwhelmed you?"

"Not at all. Everyone's been great." She waved the pad. "I'll have these back in a jiffy."

It took less than twenty minutes to type the two letters and file the carbon copies. She prepared envelopes and delivered the lot to Farnsworth who looked them over and signed them.

"Please sit down," he said, handing the letters back to her.

Clarisa glanced at her watch. It was now nearly thirty minutes beyond her quitting time. Her father would be expecting her home to make dinner and would want to hear how her first day at work went. "Is there something else?" she asked, hoping there wasn't.

"Please sit down," he repeated, his voice neutral, giving no hint as to what was on his mind.

After she complied, he knitted his fingers together and rested his hands on his desk as if he was about to make an important announcement. She sensed that something might be wrong and his sober expression seemed to confirm it. Was he going to accuse her of misrepresenting her secretarial skills? Fire her? *Please don't let it be that*, she thought. Without this job, she and her father would have little income, and it wouldn't be long before they were evicted.

"I'd like to ask you a question," he said, still not revealing his frame of mind. "How do you feel — in general, of course — about jazz?"

The question was so unexpected, so out of context, Clarisa stared at him for a few moments unable to think of a response. Apparently, though, thank God, he wasn't going to fire her. Then she recalled the photo of Duke Ellington on the bookshelf. She'd glanced at it earlier that day and noticed that the hand-written inscription was made out to "Roger" but that it was brief as if to a casual acquaintance rather than a close friend. Her boss, she figured, had either met Ellington or was an avid fan.

In any case, his question seemed odd in this setting and she wondered where it was leading. Perhaps it would be best to play dumb. "You mean jazz…the music?"

Farnsworth grinned as if he was aware his question was unusual in this context. "Yes, jazz music. Do you like it?"

Clarisa searched her memories under the heading of jazz. A few recollections came to mind — Paul Whiteman and his orchestra performing at Bal Taberne, dances at the Blanco Club, jazz combos playing in the basement of Coffee Dan's. Nearly every memory, though, included Nick accompanying her to concerts or twirling her on the dance floor. She mentally shunted him off to the side and focused on the music. She loved the syncopated rhythms and the interplay of horns and wind instruments, all weaving together to create an intricate, energetic sound. Still, she wasn't comfortable with Mr. Farnsworth's inquiry. It seemed unnecessary and an inappropriate intrusion into her personal life, especially on her first day at work. After all, she was an employee, not a friend.

She chose a neutral response. "I've been to a few jazz shows but I haven't been able to afford to go for some time."

"Did you like it? The music, I mean?"

Clarisa lowered her eyes and smoothed her skirt. Her boss was attractive, intelligent, well-dressed, his hazel eyes and blond hair a handsome combination. Under any other circumstances she would be flattered by his attention and open to a personal inquiry. At the moment, though, she needed a job more than a suitor, and it seemed foolhardy to venture down that path, even a few steps.

She looked up. "Why do you ask?"

"You mean why am I interested in whether you like jazz, or why do I like jazz?"

"Why you like jazz is certainly no business of mine."

He studied her for a moment, then laughed. "So by inference you're telling me that why *you* like jazz is no business of mine?"

She shifted her gaze to the window behind him. She didn't want to come across as stand-offish, and it would be no trouble playing along with his question and answer session. But her intuition cautioned otherwise and it seemed as good a time as any to draw a line between her work and personal life.

"You're very perceptive," she said, adding a smile to sooth any hard feelings.

As the rebuff sank in, Farnsworth's face dropped. "I'm being too familiar, aren't I? We barely know each other and here I am prying into your private life. It's just that I wanted you to know that, while I work hard and I'm dedicated to this organization, I'm human too. When I leave this office, I put work out of my mind and find enjoyment in music — specifically jazz, any kind of jazz from traditional New Orleans to Chicago swing to New York big band. I just thought that if you also had an interest in it, we could, well, have something to talk about occasionally besides work. After all, we'll be working together a lot, so I was hoping...or I thought that...well —."

Clarisa watched his poised demeanor disintegrate into that of a tongue-tied youth. It was endearing but perhaps now was the time to step in and save him from himself.

"I understand perfectly, Mr. Farnsworth. I expect, in time, we'll get to know each other a bit more. No sense in rushing it though. Don't you think?"

"Of course, of course," he agreed. "Thank God my mother wasn't here. She's a stickler for manners like you wouldn't believe. Once, when I was a boy, I forgot to thank my aunt for a birthday present. Mother nearly called out the regiment and put me put in leg irons. Another time, she trotted me out to meet her guests at a dinner party, and instead of saying 'pleased to meet you,' I accidentally said, 'Mees to pee you.' Mother turned bright red and smacked my bottom all the way to my room."

Try as she might, Clarisa couldn't stop herself from laughing. Her boss joined in and for a moment the sound of their mirth filled the room. When it subsided the tension was gone, leaving them both more relaxed.

"I hope I'm not being too forward again," said Farnsworth, "but I'd like to offer you a lift home. It's no trouble, and it would allow me to atone for my *faux pas*."

"Oh, that's not necessary," Clarisa replied, rising to leave. "I can catch a streetcar."

He nodded toward the window and the view of the waterfront, now bathed in a warm afternoon sunlight. "It's a beautiful evening and I have a convertible. Please allow me to do this for you, especially since I've kept you so late."

Clarisa hesitated, weighing the consequences of a yes or no answer. She had established a boundary of sorts, so perhaps it wouldn't hurt to be a bit flexible. Besides, a ride home in a convertible sounded lovely.

The Stutz Bearcat accelerated up Market Street, its crimson body and chrome trim shining in the afternoon light. On the passenger side, Clarisa looked out at shops and restaurants and empty storefronts with For Lease signs. Roger threaded the Stutz through traffic, weaving around green and white streetcars, canvas-topped trucks, and slow-moving sedans. Pedestrians gawked at them as they zoomed by, some waving as if the sight of an attractive young couple in a shiny sports car lifted their spirits. At Van Ness Avenue they stopped at a red light, the Stutz purring contentedly. A group of youngsters in flat-caps and knickers stepped off the curb and approached them, oohing and aahing at the sports car's sleek lines and wire wheels. Roger tooted the klaxon horn — *aaaooohgaa! aaaooohgaa!* — prompting the youngsters to yell, "Do it again! Do it again!" When the light turned green, he gunned the engine and popped the clutch, catapulting the car forward.

Near Octavia Street Clarisa pointed to the right, indicating the way to her flat. When Roger continued up Market, she raised her voice above the growl of the engine, "My home is that way."

Roger glanced at her. "I know. Don't worry. I just want to show you the best view in town. It'll only take a few minutes."

A stab of anger flushed Clarisa's cheeks and she was about to protest when, out of the corner of her eye, she glimpsed two young women standing at the curb, enviously tracking the sports car as it went by. The evening *was* so lovely, the ride so dreamlike. A breeze caressed her face and her auburn curls fluttered in the wind. At Castro Street Farnsworth downshifted and pressed the accelerator, spurring the Stutz up a steady incline toward Twin Peaks. Halfway up the hill, houses lining Market Street disappeared, replaced by wild grass and chaparral. At a turn in the road, the city below came into view, a broad expanse of peaked roofs and red chimneys, green parks and wide avenues, an urban diorama in perfect detail.

At the top of Twin Peaks, Farnsworth guided the Stutz into a flat gravel lot and parked facing the view. He hopped out of the car, dashed around to the passenger side, and opened the door with a gallant bow and a sweep of his arm. When Clarisa stepped out, he offered her a seat on the hood, then sat down beside her. They spent a quiet moment gazing at the city below and the bay beyond it, spread out to the left and right like the wings of a giant condor. On the opposite side of the bay, random points of gold light dotted the East Bay hills, reflections of the setting sun against window panes.

"Look," said Farnsworth, pointing at the dots of light, "the Golden Eyes of the East Bay." He fell silent for a moment, then in a more thoughtful voice added, "I like to think they're the eyes of some higher power, reminding us that we're a part of something bigger than ourselves."

Clarisa glanced at him curiously. "You sound like my priest."

He shrugged. "I'm not really religious, but if you don't believe in something beyond yourself, some greater good, then we're all just bugs on a log hunting for food and shelter."

It was an intriguing statement and Clarisa wanted to ask him what he did believe in, but as she well knew it was too soon for personal questions.

Behind them, the sun dipped below Twin Peaks, casting a shadow over the city. As the daylight dimmed, streetlamps along Market Street lit up, forming a path of light to the Ferry Building whose square clock tower rose up above the waterfront.

Roger drew in a deep breath and let it out. "Up here, the view and fresh air puts everything into perspective, helps me see that most of what goes on down there is just a mad scramble for, oh, I don't know, a bigger slice of the pie, I guess."

Clarisa wrapped her arms around her knees. "Now you sound like a philosopher. What next, a politician?"

Roger shook his head. "Oh, God no. I'm too different for that."

"Different? You seem pretty normal. Or is that an act?"

"In a way I guess it is, but no more than most people. Did you read about the bank officer who was arrested for embezzlement? A family man from Alameda, wife, kids, Rotary Club, Air Raid volunteer, the last person you'd suspect of grand larceny. He was living a secret life completely at odds with his public image, yet no one knew it, not even his wife."

"So what made him do it?"

"A mistress with a taste for expensive clothes and French champagne." He shrugged. "I think we all lead double lives to one degree or another."

Clarisa raised her eyebrows. "And you?"

"Me? I lead a life outside the office that would probably shock most people."

"You're not an embezzler?"

"No," he said, laughing, "nothing so sordid. I'm an insomniac. I stay up most nights till the wee hours."

That explains the pale complexion, she thought. "So what do you do at night?"

"I usually go to nightclubs and listen to jazz. If my family knew they'd disown me, but I love it. It's one of the few real things in this town. No pretense. No jive, as they say."

"So how do you reconcile your passion for nightlife with your work at the Waterfront Employers Association? The two seem worlds apart."

"They are." He looked out across the bay at the earth's shadow creeping up the East Bay hills, extinguishing the Golden Eyes. "But I enjoy both worlds, and I don't want to give up either one. Music feeds my soul, while work feeds, well, my wallet for one, but also my sense of purpose and commitment. It may sound strange, but I get satisfaction out of helping the port operate smoothly. Our members may be hard-nosed capitalists out for a pot of gold, but they provide jobs for thousands of workers and their ships carry products people need." He paused. "And some of the money generated by the port, if even just a small fraction, trickles down into the hands of jazz musicians, creating, I suppose, a kind of symmetry to my life."

Clarisa couldn't help but compare her boss to Nick who rarely mentioned commitment, certainly not to her or to anything other than his own selfish dreams. Okay, maybe he wasn't *entirely* selfish, maybe her opinion of him was clouded by residual pain and anger, but she still hadn't accepted his decision to abandon her.

"Anything serious?" Roger asked.

"Serious?"

"Whatever you're thinking about looks like it's weighing on you, and I can't imagine it's my interest in jazz and shipping schedules."

The streetlights below were turning on, crisscrossing the city in a grid pattern. Off in the distance a crescent moon rose above the East Bay hills.

Clarisa sighed . "A friend left town recently and I suppose I miss him."

"Is he gone for good?"

"I don't think so but it probably doesn't matter. I handled his leaving badly, so I expect he's written me off as a lost cause."

Farnsworth laced his fingers together palms out and stretched his arms. "When I'm feeling blue, I go to a place on Pacific Avenue called

Purcell's So Different Club. They have the hottest Negro band in town, and when things get going the musicians sweat buckets, couples crowd the dance floor, and the whole place shakes. Pretty soon my troubles melt away."

"I'll bet they didn't teach you that at boarding school."

"That's right," he said, hopping off the hood. "Some things you have to learn on your own." He held out his hand and helped her down. "Thanks for being a sport and letting me shanghai you. Now let me chauffeur you home."

On the way down the hill, a bracing wind on her face, Clarisa felt refreshed and cleansed. The stress of starting a new job had vanished and this jaunt to the top of Twin Peaks had been a perfect ending. Even if she had been tricked into it.

6

The ship's bell rang three times, inciting a shuffle of footsteps toward the mess room where a line formed at the galley window. A steward handed Nick a plate of stringy corned beef entwined with flaccid strips of boiled cabbage, accompanied by two biscuits and a dollop of butter so pale it had to be diluted with shortening. He joined Moon, Remy, and others at a long table and listened as they talked about Port-au-Prince, Valparaiso, Tangier, Cebu, Kobe, Mombasa—places he could only imagine. The conversation eventually made its way to Shanghai, the first foreign port of call on this voyage, and here the sailors recounted good-humored tales of high jinx and peccadilloes, producing loud laughter intensified by anticipation.

After dinner the mess room converted into a social hall with sailors playing pinochle and cribbage, reading books and magazines, and writing letters. Nick retrieved the leather-bound journal from his locker, slid onto a seat in a far corner, took out his pen, and opened the journal to the first page.

Journal – May 5th, 1933

My first day onboard and I'm a fish out of water. The ship creaks and groans like a haunted house, and I stumble along the passageways, my feet unaccustomed to a floor that rises and falls in irregular rhythms. During the morning watch, my bunkmate Remy and I chipped loose paint off the foc'sle, a raised deck at the bow. It was mindless work and gave us a chance to get to know one another, our conversation wandering in various directions. At one point Remy asked me how I got this job. Hoping to bolster my sea credentials, I told him my grandfather sailed with Captain Harding years ago. Then it occurred to me that he might think I got the job through nepotism, though whether that will hurt my standing with the crew, I don't know.

About an hour into the watch, I noticed a puff of mist shooting up from the sea. I set down my chipping hammer and scanned the waves, wondering what it was. Before long a second plume shot up, and this time I could see a shiny hump breaking the surface of the water.

Excited, I jumped up and pointed. "Look, a whale!"

Remy didn't seem interested; he's probably seen a thousand whales.

I continued to look for the elusive creature until a strange thing happened. Remy began pounding on the deck with his chipping hammer as if he was banging on a drum. His behavior seemed odd until, out of the corner of my eye, I noticed bosun Cyril Slag standing a few feet off, hands fisted on hips, arms akimbo, face screwed into a frown.

I've been told his nickname is The Lizard and it isn't hard to see why. The skin on his neck is dry and scaly and his tongue habitually flicks over chapped lips. He wore a Greek fisherman's hat with a worn leather bill that shaded his dark brown eyes.

"Enjoying yourself Benson?" he said, sarcastically. It was then I belatedly realized that Remy had been drumming on the deck to warn me that the bosun was near. "Should I ask the captain to fetch you a deck chair and a cup of hot cocoa?"

"No, sir," I replied, hoping if I showed proper deference he'd leave me alone.

"Then you won't mind cleaning the heads for the rest of the watch."

Which is what I did. And I must say, it wasn't the kind of work I anticipated when I graduated from college.

After lunch I set out to explore the ship.

My first stop was the galley where "Cook" prepares our food. He's a plump fellow who wears a white tee-shirt over a large round belly and talks with a cockney accent. The galley is the nerve center of the ship. Everyone goes there for coffee and to hear the latest scuttlebutt. In fact, Cook already knew I had "connections" with the captain and that I'd been put on head detail. He also has an amazing ability to carry on a conversation while simultaneously preparing twenty-five servings of Yorkshire pudding without missing a beat on either score. As he navigated his ample girth around the galley, he warned me that bosun Slag is "like a pot 'o boilin' noodles. Turn up the heat and he'll blow his lid." He called the first mate, Chief Primm, a cold turkey with frozen joints. "A squirt of hot oil up his arse, that's whot he needs." And when it came to Captain Harding, he shook his head wistfully. "A pit'aful case, he is, like a beau'ifol soufflé that's fallen into a mushy mess."

I thanked him for the coffee and headed down the passageway to continue my exploration. I was near an open door when I heard a voice that reminded me of my school days, that sounded like an instructor talking to students. As I passed the door, I looked in. A sailor, sitting on a stool in the center of the cabin, was talking to several others seated on bunks around him. The sailor who was talking had brown hair, oiled and combed back, and a dimpled chin. He wore a sleeveless shirt, a style worn by the men in the engine room, and had a tattoo on each arm, an anchor on the left, a rooster on the right. Curious, I paused to listen until he noticed me and stopped talking. This alerted the others, who turned toward me and stared with hard expressions as if I was an intruder.

Mumbling an apology, I continued down the passageway, wondering what would cause such a chilly reception. Lost in thought, I stepped out of the midship house and bumped into a tall, rail-thin officer in uniform. He wore a white Van Dyke beard and rimless spectacles. His complexion was pale and etched with wrinkles covering a preoccupied expression, as if he was continually weighing one option against another. He brushed past me, then wheeled back around and squinted.

"You the Benson boy?" he asked in a raspy voice. He coughed as if the effort to talk irritated his larynx.

"Yes, sir," I replied.

I recognized Captain Harding from grandfather's description.

The corners of his mouth lifted momentarily. "Rune was a damn good seaman. You'll do well to follow in his footsteps."

"Grandfather thinks highly of you too, sir." I couldn't think of anything else to say and remained silent while the captain stared at me as if he was examining a curiosity.

Finally he said, "Come round to my quarters for a chat, say at eighteen hundred hours tomorrow." With that he walked off, leaving me to ponder another odd encounter.

I made my way up to the quarterdeck, the raised deck at the stern, and leaned against the railing. A white foamy wake trailed the ship and slowly dissipated into the green undulating sea. I'd been there five minutes when the sailor who talked like an instructor, the one with a tattoo on each arm, came up beside me. Taking a pouch of tobacco out of his pocket and a pack of papers, he rolled a cigarette and pinched off tobacco strands from the ends. Then hunching over to block the wind, he struck a match and lit the cigarette. He took a puff and introduced himself — his name is Will Bailey — and I did likewise. He seemed friendly enough, so I asked him about the chilly reception earlier. He shrugged and said it was nothing, that they were just "jawing." I doubt this but let the matter drop.

Bailey isn't much older than me, perhaps three or four years, but he's had a much broader experience than I. He's crossed the country three times on freight trains, sailed around the world twice, and, if he's to be believed, made love to whores on four continents. Made me wonder who's had the better education, him or me. He was raised in Hell's Kitchen, an Irish neighborhood in New York City, and was brought up Catholic, although he doesn't practice it anymore. Now he believes in only one thing, he says: destiny.

I asked if he meant fate or astrology.

He shook his head and said we have all a common destiny, a destiny in which everyone takes part. I must have looked skeptical because he went on to explain that if he or I were injured, the company would let us go to sink or swim on our own. Mankind has a greater destiny, he said, a destiny in which we all share the fruits of our labor no matter how much each of us contributes. It sounded like pie in the sky to me. My father built a company, and without his effort it would never have gotten off the ground. I mentioned this and said that my father deserved all the benefits he accrued from his effort. Then — and I should have predicted this — he asked how the company was doing now. He must have sensed my reluctance to answer because he changed the subject and made one of the strangest statements I've ever heard. Things aren't always what they seem, he said. For instance, the Dollar Steamship Company bought this ship, the *Diana Dollar*, with *our* money, meaning his and mine.

Such a thing is ridiculous, of course, and although he seemed ready to explain, I'd had enough of his nonsense and took my leave.

Nick turned his journal to the next page and tore out a blank sheet. At the top he wrote *Dear Clarisa*. Then his pen hesitated, the hand guiding it unsure what nature the missive should take. In light of their last meeting an intimate love letter seemed inappropriate. On the other hand, a breezy note could be construed as trivializing their relationship. Not that he knew what *that* was. Some schism had occurred. Whether it was minor and temporary or significant and permanent, he wasn't sure. In the end he chose a friendly, confidential approach, hoping his descriptions of the ship and the quirky crew would amuse her. He concluded the letter, after more hesitation, with the simple closing *Love, Nick*, figuring that in this context the word *Love* could be taken in any number of ways, from friend-love to old pals-love to lovers-love, thus covering all the bases while allowing Clarisa to choose her own interpretation.

At eight bells he stowed the journal and made his way up to the wheel-house for the evening watch. Long strands of pink-orange clouds were visible through the wheelhouse windows, streaking across the sky in parallel lines as if a rake had been drawn across them. It was the beginning of a beautiful sunset, and his gaze lingered on the salmon clouds, radiant against a deep blue sky.

"Ready to take the helm?" Chief Primm asked, nodding toward the helmsman who grasped a spoked wooden wheel. Second in command, Primm wore a crisp khaki uniform and a military-style CPO hat with an anchor emblem above the visor.

Nick knew he was expected to take the helm without hesitation, and he would have, but the enormity of the task at hand and his complete lack of experience suddenly dawned on him, paralyzing him with uncertainty. The freighter measured some four-hundred feet long by fifty-five feet wide at the beam. Within those dimensions it carried twenty-five sailors and tons of valuable cargo. The thought of controlling such an enormous beast without a lick of training seemed foolhardy at best.

Primm gave him a questioning look. "Your first turn at the wheel?"

Nick nodded.

"Can you read a compass?"

"Yes, sir."

"Then you'll do just fine." He turned to the helmsman. "Prepare to turn over the wheel."

"Helmsman standing down," the sailor said, stepping back. "Course three-hundred fifteen degrees."

Nick remained rooted to the floor, hoping the chief would understand his reluctance to take control of the ship after being onboard less than twenty-four hours.

Unmoved by Nick's apprehension, Primm nodded toward the helm. "She may be a modern vessel, son, but she won't steer herself."

His words, spoken matter-of-factly as if steering the ship was as natural as breathing, gave Nick the nudge he needed. He wiped his palms on his pants, stepped up to the wheel, and grasped the wooden spokes, scarcely believing he was in control of a ten-thousand ton vessel.

Primm pointed to a round brass pedestal in front of the helm, hooded by a half-dome reflection shield that partially covered a compass held level by a gimbal ring. "Your job is to monitor the compass and see that the arrow remains at three-hundred-fifteen degrees. If there's a change in course, you'll be given new orders, but that's unlikely as we're miles from land."

He observed Nick for a few minutes, then, complaining that the third mate was tardy for the evening watch, left the wheelhouse to find the errant officer.

Expecting the helm to be loose and free-wheeling, Nick was surprised to find it as stiff as the steering wheel of a fully-loaded Cadillac. And despite Primm's admonition, the ship *did* seem to be steering itself, holding it on course simply a matter of keeping a firm grip. After several uneventful minutes, he relaxed and once again savored the evolving panorama through the wheelhouse windows. The sky was now darkening from azure to indigo, and points of light flickered on one-by-one. As a twilit calm settled over the ocean, Nick smiled. For the first time since boarding the *Diana Dollar*, he felt confident in his decision to go to sea. This is where he needed to be and what he needed to do to ease the memory of his father's suicide and to acquire the worldly experience the *Chronicle* editor thought he needed. As much as he loved Clarisa, she would have to wait until he explored the world and was sufficiently seasoned.

In the serene twilight he marveled at his good fortune and breathed a sigh of relief. It was the first time he'd felt this peaceful since his father died. He glanced at the compass, now obscured in shadow by the reflection shield. Reaching down, he groped for a light switch on the side of the binnacle, found it, and flipped it on. Directional degrees are numerically designated at four points on the compass: zero at due north, ninety at due east, one-hundred eighty at due south and two-hundred seventy at due west. It took a moment to calculate the ship's heading. When he did the result stiffened the hairs on his neck. During his inattentive reverie the ship had veered off course eight degrees.

He glanced around the empty wheelhouse, wondering why the chief hadn't already burst through the door to harangue him. Then it occurred to him that if he himself hadn't noticed the change in direction, the crew was even less likely to perceive it. Still, the third mate would arrive any minute, and it wouldn't improve his reputation to be found steering off course. He rotated the helm a full turn and watched as the compass needle stubbornly maintained its position. He waited a few moments, his fingers tapping the spokes, then cranked the wheel another full turn. After an interminable minute that seemed to last an hour, the needle slowly drifted back to the three-hundred-fifteen degree mark.

His relief lasted only a moment. The needle passed its intended station and continued around the compass, ignoring Nick's mounting frustration. He reversed the wheel one full turn and watched as the needle slowly came to a stop and remained stationary before it edged back toward its designated course. Just before it reached three-hundred-fifteen degrees, he reversed the wheel a half-turn to prevent the compass from overshooting its mark again. Alas, the wayward needle ignored his strategy and swept past three-fifteen to three-eighteen and then — *damn it!* — to three-twenty. Expecting the third mate to arrive any moment, he desperately jerked the wheel back another half-turn. The needle continued on to three-hundred-twenty-five before it slowed to a halt, then rested as though tired before languidly reversing direction.

For the next ten minutes the freighter zigzagged back and forth, trailing a curvy wake in its path. The abrupt turns eventually rocked the vessel so that the ship's bell began to ring as if the freighter was in turbulent seas.

A spate of hurried footsteps echoed in the passageway behind the wheelhouse, announcing the return of the chief who burst through the door followed by the third mate.

"What the hell are you doing?" he yelled. "You've got the ship swerving like a drunken sailor."

Before Nick could answer, the captain came through the door, his clothes askew as if he'd dressed in haste.

While the chief cursed him from one side and the rumpled captain glared at him from the other, Nick gripped the helm and stared straight ahead, embarrassed, ashamed, and wishing he was a million miles away. The chief suggested they put him on chipping duty for the rest of the voyage — he wasn't fit to be a sailor — and the speechless captain, lip trembling, nodded in agreement. Then Primm sent Nick out to the flying bridge above the wheelhouse to replace the lookout who took his place at the helm.

Later that night, laying on his bunk, sleepless and frustrated, Nick dissected the incident from start to finish. It occurred to him that the chief, by leaving the wheelhouse without an officer in charge, had likely violated maritime regulations. Primm also failed to inform the captain of his absence and had taken advantage of the old man's shaky state to squelch questions before incriminating facts were revealed. The more Nick thought about it, the angrier he got, and before he drifted off to sleep, he resolved to tell the captain the entire story. Place blame where it rightly belonged, exoneration and revenge in one fell swoop.

The next morning the crew averted their eyes when Nick entered the mess room. Word of the wheelhouse incident had obviously spread to the entire ship, leaving his reputation in tatters. He sat by himself at the end of the table, eating a bowl of oatmeal and wondering if he'd have to spend the entire voyage in isolation. For a brief, self-pitying moment he even considered leaving the ship at the first opportunity. Then rejected the notion. He'd never be able to face his grandfather, and he'd never become a reporter by quitting when things got tough.

After breakfast Slag assigned him to chipping duty for the entire forenoon watch. Since watches were usually divided between hard labor and less demanding chores, like manning the helm or standing lookout, his punishment was obvious to all. As he trudged to the bosun's storage locker to collect the necessary tools, the shame of it weighed on him. He started by chipping loose paint off the aft hatch coaming and found it helpful to imagine his hammer striking the chief's close-cropped head. In that way, by the end of the four-hour watch he'd hacked away yards of paint and much of his desire for revenge.

At eighteen-hundred hours, he climbed the companionway to the captain's cabin and knocked on the door. No answer. Had the captain forgotten his invitation? Had he decided to cancel it after the wheelhouse incident? Nick was about to leave when he heard feet shuffling and a throat-clearing cough.

"Come," said a low voice.

He opened the door. The odor of pipe tobacco and the musty smell of an unventilated room wafted out of the cabin. Captain Harding was seated at his desk, shirt disheveled, feet in slippers, gray hair uncombed. Various items lay on the desk: a logbook, a pair of spectacles, a briar pipe, an overflowing ashtray.

Nick hesitated. "Is this a bad time? I can come back later."

"No, no," replied the captain, beckoning him in. "Have a seat." He pointed toward a chair next to his desk. "I just woke up from a nap. Didn't sleep well last night. A sailor nearly ran us aground." He wiped his eyes with a handkerchief.

Nick sat down and searched the old man's face for a trace of sarcasm. Could Harding have forgotten that it was he, Nick, who was at the wheel? And as embarrassing as the incident was, the ship had never been in any real danger. "I want to apologize for what happened, sir. It was my first time at the helm."

The captain squinted at him, then fumbled for his spectacles and hooked them over his ears. Even with glasses he gave no sign of recognition. "It was *you*? What do you want?" His lower lip quivered.

The captain, Nick recalled, hadn't been wearing glasses in the wheelhouse. Without them his eyesight must be poor, very poor, as he'd been just a couple of feet away. "Sir, you asked me to come up for a visit. I'm Rune Olufson's grandson. We met on the weather deck yesterday afternoon. Remember?"

The old man looked down at his desk, his eyes darting from object to object as if he were looking for something. "Oh, yes. Of course I remember." He reached for his pipe and a brown leather tobacco pouch. He pinched a wad of tobacco, tamped it into the pipe bowl, and struck a match. As he sucked in the flame, he seemed to regain his composure. After a few puffs, he studied Nick with an appraising eye. "Your grandfather was a crack mate, one of the best seamen I've ever known, stalwart, trustworthy, never complained or whined like the simpering salts today." He paused. "So you want to follow in his footsteps?"

Nick considered an affirmative answer just to score points but decided against it. "This is my first voyage, sir. It'll probably be a while before I know if this is my calling."

"You look a bit old to be coming up through the hawse pipe," said the captain, meaning to start out as a common sailor and work up the ranks. The captain removed the pipe from his mouth. "Most of us who started sailing before the mast, like your grandfather and I, earned our sea legs as cabin boys. By the time we were twenty, we'd been sailing for five years when the word really meant something." He pointed his pipe at a painting mounted on the bulkhead above his desk, a windjammer in full sail, waves curling off its bow. "Rune and I were mates on the *Julia Ann*. We knew every rope, spar, and plank on that girl, and so did everyone else onboard. But she was more than deck board and sail cloth; she held us together like a yard sling and we treated her like fine bone china."

"Grandfather remembers those days fondly too, sir."

"Rune never made the jump from sail to steam. A lot of sailors didn't for one reason or another — or didn't want to. It's not the same, not by a long shot." He gazed at the painting. "I wish he'd been with me in the Navy. I sure could've used him."

"Why's that, sir?"

The captain fiddled with his pipe. "Let's just say he was one of the most trustworthy men I ever sailed with. If he'd been with me during the war, my life would be different, much different." His gaze fell to his desk, moisture welling in his eyes.

Embarrassed for the old man, Nick decided to steer the conversation in another direction. "Granddad hated steamships but never said why."

The captain puffed his briar pipe, swirls of smoke drifting about the cabin. "You can't imagine the difference between sail and steam. Shipping nowadays is highly specialized. For most of us in the deck department, the engines are a mystery and so is the wireless equipment. Then there's the schedule. Company agents book the cargo and set the route, crews are assigned by the labor hall, officers by the company. Everything is worked out months in advance by someone who's never set foot on a ship. Makes a master feel more like a streetcar conductor than a sea captain."

"So how did you make the switch to steam?"

The captain stroked his Van Dyke beard and gazed at the painting as if the answer lay in the brush strokes. "Before the war I was a skipper on the *Star of Alaska*, a three-masted square-rigger, working the king salmon run. Every year from spring through fall, we sailed up to the Kenai Peninsula and filled the holds with fish, then returned south along the Queen Charlotte Islands to San Francisco. It's the most beautiful run in the world. Snow covered mountains soar right out of the water and shimmering glaciers flow down to the ocean like jeweled rivers." He puffed his pipe. "The war changed everything. My ship was obsolete, but I was too young to retire. When a friend in the Navy Department said they were desperate for captains, I applied for a position and was accepted right away. They sent me to training school for six weeks, then assigned me to a supply ship." He shook his head. "Believe me, I knew I didn't belong on the bridge, and so did the officers under my command." He paused. "We were on patrol off the Outer Islands when my ship aground. My navigator assured me we were in safe waters, but, well, the captain is always responsible no matter what happens. Soon after, I was asked to resign."

Nick felt a wave of sympathy for the old man. He'd made the switch from sail to steam too late in his career and hadn't been able to adapt. Hence, he lacked authority in the minds of his officers and perhaps more importantly in himself. The incident in the wheelhouse was an example. He must have known that the chief and third mate were at least partially responsible but couldn't afford to confront them and was too traumatized to even try. On the last legs of a shaky career, he needed his officers more than they needed him, so out of self-preservation he sided with the chief.

The realization buoyed Nick, and it made him wonder if there was any point in bringing up the incident and putting the captain on the spot. Still, he didn't relish chipping duty for the rest of the voyage. "About last night, sir, I should have asked for more instruction before taking the wheel. I hope I'll be given another opportunity. I know I can do it."

The captain nodded. "I'm sure you can, son. It's not difficult once you get the hang of it, and I expect any grandson of Rune could master it in no time." He puffed his pipe thoughtfully. "Tell you what, I'll see that you get another chance after we leave coastal waters if you keep your eyes peeled and ears open and come by every couple of days for a chat."

Is he asking me to be a confidant, Nick wondered, *or a spy?* The former was no problem. The crew already knew he had "connections" with the bridge. And if he met with the captain every few days, no one would notice. The latter, however, was another matter. A spy? He could never do it. Not in a million years. Yet he sure as hell didn't want to spend the entire voyage chipping paint.

"Alright, sir, but I'm not a spy or a snitch."

"I know, son. I'm not asking you to be one. Crews usually clam up when a captain comes around, so skippers rely on their officers to feed them information. This lot, though, doesn't confide in me. You'd just be helping me keep an eye on things."

Nick recalled his grandfather saying that ship captains are the loneliest men on earth. They bear the heaviest burden of responsibility and are treated with deference by the crew but not amity, even by their officers. Harding probably wants companionship as much as information, and if that's the case, keeping the old man company seemed a fair price for another shot at the helm.

7

"Put a few men in the hospital and the rest will fall in line. That's the way to handle labor," said Stanley Dollar, chief executive of the Dollar Steamship Company. He was speaking to a group of shipping executives in the conference room of the Waterfront Employers Association.

At the far end of the table, pen poised over notepad, Clarisa was struggling to stay focused on the meeting. She'd been out later than usual the night before, much later, and now was suffering the consequence. A yawn rose to her mouth. She compressed her lips to suppress it, but the yawn persisted until it pried her lips apart. Quickly covering her mouth, she glanced around the table, hoping no one noticed. Her gaze settled on Thomas Plant, her boss's boss, who sat at the head of the table wearing a harried frown.

"It's not that simple anymore, Stanley," said Plant. "Roosevelt is about to sign the National Industrial Recovery Act, which authorizes the government to establish codes of competition for every industry, including codes regulating labor relations. His administration is willing to work with us on this, but we need to draw up guidelines and present them to a congressional committee."

"That communist!" Dollar exclaimed. "God forsook America the day FDR took office."

"What exactly does the legislation say?" asked Roger Lapham, the silver haired president of the American-Hawaiian Lines.

"My assistant can explain," said Plant, turning to Roger Farnsworth.

Clarisa readied her pen and turned her attention to her boss who, to her amazement, looked fresh and alert, his blond hair neatly combed back, eyes focused. Hardly the picture of someone who'd been out the night before tripping the light fantastic.

He rested his hands on a stack of papers. "I've studied a draft copy of the National Industrial Recovery Act, and there are several provisions that pertain to our members. The most pertinent being section 7(a)." He picked up the top sheet and read a summary. "The primary directives of 7(a) are, one, that employees shall have the right to organize and bargain collectively, two, that no employee shall be required to join or refrain from joining a labor organization, and, three, that employers shall comply with labor codes dictating the maximum number of hours per shift, minimum pay, and other conditions approved by the President."

The executives around the table wore solemn expressions.

"What about the open shop?" asked William Roth, President of the Matson Navigation Company. The open shop referred to any company whose employees were members of different unions or no union at all, as opposed to a closed shop, in which all employees belonged to a single union. "If it doesn't preserve the open shop, the unions will take the upper hand. Who can forget when Reds convinced the unions to demand a seat on our Board of Directors. Can you imagine what a nightmare that would have been?"

"I can answer that question," said John Francis Neylan, general counsel to William Randolph Hearst, the newspaper magnate, and Hearst's representative at the Industrial Association, a coalition of large corporations that consulted with employer groups. "The Recovery Act specifically allows you to hire whomever you want and negotiate with whichever union you want. Since you already have good relations with the Blue Book Union, there's no reason to believe anything will change. In other words, it preserves the open shop and specifically outlaws the closed shop."

"What about the labor codes?" asked Cyrus Grant, President of W. R. Grace Line. "I don't want the government telling me how much I can pay my men. Once you give the Feds an inch, they'll want a mile. The next thing you know, they'll have rules about every little thing until the men are telling *us* what to do. Hell, I'm not turning my business over to the goddamn Bolsheviks in Washington."

"And what about foreign competition?" said Dollar. "The Japanese won't have to abide by these rules. It'll put us at a disadvantage and send our customers to overseas shippers just when we're getting back on our feet."

An indignant murmur rippled through the room.

"Gentlemen, gentlemen," Plant said, holding up his hands, "let's not let our imaginations spin out of control. Right now we're working with East Coast shippers on a proposal that we'll submit to the President's committee. We've also scheduled meetings with key congressional allies to build support for suspending codes for the maritime industry altogether. In any case, we should be able to continue as we have. However, it's important to keep in mind that we can't appear unreasonable. The country's in bad shape and everyone's clamoring for a change. I've hired McCann-Erickson, the PR firm, to help us manage public opinion and we can always count on newspapers like the *Examiner*" — he nodded toward

Neylan — "to educate the public. We need to convince the citizenry that our interests are their interests…"

As Plant droned on, Clarisa stifled another yawn and glanced at Roger Farnsworth who sat ramrod straight, focused and attentive as if he'd had a full night's rest. How he looked so alert was a mystery to her now that she'd experienced his other world.

During the previous weeks her boss had extended numerous invitations to experience his "other life," the one outside of work. Although tempted and secretly flattered, she steadfastly declined the invitations and the possibility of an unwise romantic entanglement. As time wore on, though, she began to reconsider and ultimately rationalized a night out as a one-time occasion to become better acquainted with her boss, whom she'd come to admire for his intelligence and dedication.

A month after starting her job, her curiosity aroused by the mystery of his secret life, she succumbed to his appeals. They discreetly rendezvoused after work at a newsstand near the Matson Building and strolled up Montgomery Street to Il Trovatore Café, a swank Italian trattoria on the edge of North Beach. The restaurant bar was illuminated by a backlit stained-glass window depicting lush Tuscan vineyards, and a radio was playing a romantic ballad crooned by Bing Crosby: *When a bird, young and free, hangs about a certain tree, it's a natural thing to do…*

"We'll have two martinis," Farnsworth said to the bartender.

Clarisa glanced at him. "I thought only beer and wine are legal."

"That's right, but Congress passed legislation three months ago overturning the Volstead Act. Since then fives states have ratified it, so it's just a matter of time before Prohibition is repealed."

"Isn't hard liquor still illegal?"

The bartender placed two martinis on the bar. "The cops don't care, never really did. And the Feds aren't interested anymore." He smiled, exposing two gold teeth. "So drink up and enjoy."

Farnsworth raised his glass and trained his hazel eyes on Clarisa. "Here's to an eventful evening."

She held his gaze for a moment, then averted her eyes, hardly knowing how to react to the flirtatious toast. It had been ages since she'd been out on a first date, and she'd never dated someone for whom she worked. It was an unusual situation, and she hoped she'd made the right decision to accept his invitation. She sipped the clear liquid, fresh and cool like a menthol lozenge. Then she swallowed. As the alcohol flowed down her throat it burned, triggering a coughing fit.

Farnsworth signaled the bartender to bring a glass of water.

"Must be an acquired taste," she panted, setting the drink down and taking a sip of water.

"Would you prefer something else? A glass of wine?"

"That would be good, Mr. Farnsworth."

"Oh, please, call me Roger when we're out of the office."

The bartender poured a glass of Chianti from a crystal decanter and placed it in front of her. He pointed at her martini and glanced at Roger. "Wanna finish it?"

"Sure, no sense in letting good liquor go to waste." He downed his own drink in one gulp and reached for hers.

"Clearly, you have no trouble," said Clarisa, who in the intimate atmosphere of the restaurant was beginning to feel more like a friendly acquaintance than an employee. "Does alcohol help you slip into your other world? Isn't that what they say, that it suppresses inhibitions and unleashes one's true nature?"

Roger reached into his breast pocket and pulled out a silver case, opened it and extracted a cigarette. "I drink good liquor because I like things of superior quality, whether it's a soft cashmere sweater, a great jazz band, or a beautiful painting." He lit the cigarette and exhaled a stream of smoke. "In fact, I enjoy beauty and pleasure in all its forms. That's why I like you."

"Oh, brother," muttered Clarisa, thinking it was a tacky line but flattered nonetheless. "Well, if the appreciation of beauty and pleasure is what really matters to you, then that makes you a hedonist, doesn't it? Which is pretty superficial."

"Oh, but it's not," said Roger, smiling. "It stimulates all the senses and makes me feel more alive than anything." He tapped his cigarette on an ashtray. "Let me give you an example. Say you knew a Mack truck was going to run over you tomorrow and squash you to smithereens. What would you do? Now be honest. Wouldn't you want to experience life to its fullest? Taste all you could taste, touch all you could touch, dance with abandon, run on the beach, laugh and sing until sunrise? I would. The problem with most people is that they're afraid of what others might think, afraid of not meeting expectations, of not being accepted. And it's all because society keeps our true nature bottled up with a lot of hell-fire taboos and arbitrary social conventions."

Clarisa stared into her glass. "If your hypothesis were true, I probably would want to do all those things, especially with someone I love. And I'd also like to bid a last goodbye to my father and friends. But my chances of dying tomorrow are extremely low, so I can't live each day as if were the last." She glanced at him. "Don't you feel a commitment to your family?"

Roger threw his head back and let out a bitter chuckle. "My family has done nothing but worry about what others think of them. They sent me to the right schools, made sure I met the right people, taught me all the polite things to say. Did everything they could to push me along the road to success." He waggled the fore and middle fingers of each hand, encapsulating the word "success" with visual quote marks. "They trained me like a show dog, so that now I have a solid exterior of respectability, a shield that protects the real me, the side that rarely sees the light of day."

"Am I about to see that side tonight?"

"It's not too late to back out, but believe me you'll miss out on the time of your life."

Clarisa snorted in mock disbelief. "You're pretty cocksure of yourself, aren't you?"

Roger admitted he was and it wasn't hard to believe. His manners were impeccable, his blond hair perfectly cut, cheeks dimpled, face angular in all the right places. Over dinner and a bottle of excellent wine, he regaled her with stories of his travels in Europe where he drank heavily in Paris with a crowd of writers and musicians who accepted him as a fellow traveler on the road to self discovery. Paradoxically, the best American jazz he ever heard was played in the nightclubs of Montmartre. He saw Josephine Baker, the Negro chanteuse, who mesmerized the City of Light with her spangled outfits and deliciously lascivious act, and met Duke Ellington whom he revered as a living god. It was also there that he found a world far different from the one in which he'd been raised, a world where the inhabitants were judged not by their social rank or bank account but by their creative talents and *joie de vivre*.

As he recounted his travels, Clarisa drew a parallel between him and Nick. Both of them had been struck with wanderlust and veered onto a path less traveled. The difference being that Nick was still on his odyssey while Roger had returned and fashioned a dual life: Mr. Respectable by day, and by night, well, she was about to find out.

After dinner they walked around the corner to a place on Pacific Avenue called Purcell's So Different Club. A slender hostess the color of café au lait greeted them, her marcelled hair tapered to points around her face.

"Good evening, Mr. Farnsworth," she said with a winsome smile. "I see you brought fine comp'ny." She clamped her hands around his free arm and escorted them inside.

The club was long and narrow, crowded mostly with Negroes and Filipinos listening to a jazz band playing at the rear of the club. The air was smoky and redolent with a cloying blend of perfume and cologne mixed with an earthier aroma that reminded Clarisa of fresh-baked cornbread. On their way in, a handsome bartender, sporting a pencil thin mustache, smiled at them with teeth that shone like pearls against his bronze complexion.

"The usual, Mr. Farnsworth?" he asked.

"And a glass of red wine for my friend."

The hostess seated them at a table near the stage where they had a view of the musicians playing piano, drums, bull fiddle, saxophone, guitar, clarinet, and trumpet. A chorus of four Negro women fronted the band, wearing what amounted to glittered skivvies and diaphanous silk capes. They gyrated their hips to the music while belting out a Billy Austin tune:

Well a fellow is a crea-ture who always has been straaange.
Just when you think you're his, he's done gone and made a chaaange.
Is you is or is you ain't my ba-by?

The infectious rhythm vibrated Clarisa's chest and traveled down the length of her body to her toes, now tapping in time to the music. She'd never been to a colored nightclub before and in her ignorance had imagined a voodoo-like scene, with performers in feathered headdresses, chanting mysterious incantations and making primitive gestures for an excitable crowd. Looking at the well-dressed audience sipping cocktails, smoking cigarettes, and enjoying the music in the same manner as whites, she had to laugh at her misconceptions, and it made her realize how little she knew of this other world.

When the floor show was over, the music continued and couples took to the dance floor. Roger pulled her to her feet and guided her through a series of dance numbers — the Texas Tommy, Lindy Hop, East Coast Swing — until they were breathing deeply, cheeks glistening with perspiration.

They left the nightclub after one drink and strolled up the street to a string of other clubs — the Hippodrome, Spider Kelly's, the Jupiter, the Andromeda — stopping at each one long enough to have a drink and a spin on the dance floor.

At midnight Clarisa was still alert and energized, but the smoky air irritated her eyes and the loud music now felt smothering and claustrophobic. Roger suggested they go for a drive and get some fresh air, explaining that earlier that day, in anticipation of their date, he'd parked the Stutz nearby. She readily agreed.

They headed west toward the ocean, the top down, a cool refreshing breeze swirling past. Shadowy figures walked along the sidewalks, and lampposts cast pools of yellow light on the street. At Stanyan and McClaren Drive, Roger guided the Stutz into Golden Gate Park and suddenly the convertible, like a pent-up greyhound set free, sprang to life, hurtling down a dark, deserted road lined with eucalyptus trees. They sped past the Conservatory of Flowers and sprinted through a series of winding curves. Near Stow Lake the Stutz skidded around a turn, throwing Clarisa against the passenger door. She gripped the door handle and glanced at Roger with a look of alarm, though he was fully absorbed in the thrill of speeding through the deserted park. She was about to say something when a police siren blared out from behind them, lights flashing.

Roger glanced at the rearview mirror and smiled as if he expected the cops to pursue them, in fact welcomed it. He tightened his grip on the steering wheel and floored the gas pedal, spurring the car around another curve, its tires squealing as it shot past Spreckels Lake and barreled down a straight stretch alongside the buffalo paddock. Too terrified to say anything — or was it too *thrilled* — Clarisa kept one hand on the door handle and the other on the dashboard to keep from sliding side to side. They skidded around the final turn near the Dutch windmill and hurtled down the last hundred yards to the Great Highway. Roger blew through a stop sign and nearly hit a flat-bed truck as the Stutz made a sharp screeching slide onto the beachside boulevard, pointing south. He stomped on the gas pedal and accelerated the Stutz down the straight highway, the engine revving at the peak of its limit, the road beneath them a dark blur.

As the speed and excitement of the chase vanquished her fear, Clarisa felt a surge of exhilaration, her heart racing, curls fluttering in her face. She leaned her head back and gazed up at the night sky, the Milky Way flowing brightly across the heavens like a whitewater rapid.

The Stutz made another screeching turn onto Lake Merced Boulevard. When it swerved Clarisa glanced back at the patrol car, its lights flashing a mile behind.

They sped around the lake on a road flanked by tall Monterey pines. At the southern end, Roger jerked the car around a sharp hairpin turn and headed back toward Golden Gate Park. He veered onto Sunset Boulevard and gunned the engine, now roaring as it pitched the car forward.

When they reached the park, Roger reined in the Stutz and turned toward the ocean, slowing to the speed limit as if he were headed for a leisurely day at the beach. At the Great Highway he crossed over and steered into a gravel lot. They rolled to the far end, to a spot overlooking the water, where Roger killed the motor and turned off the lights.

They sat in silence and watched starlit breakers roll toward them, landing with percussive thuds on the beach, foam surf splaying up onto the shore and dissolving into the sand.

Clarisa raked a hand through her wind-tousled hair. "I take it this isn't the first time you provoked the police into a race around Lake Merced."

Roger reached his arms up toward the sky as though stretching them, then lowered one onto the seatback behind Clarisa. "They like to hide in the park like perverts, then put on a noisy show so that everyone obediently pulls over."

"Everyone but you?" said Clarisa, who noticed Roger's fake stretch leading to his arm on her seatback. To avoid the next dating cliché, the one where he attempted a clumsy kiss, she scooted toward the passenger door and angled to face him. "Was that supposed to impress me?"

"It is more fun with a passenger," he admitted, "but to be honest, it's not much of a contest. This angel" — he patted the dashboard — "could outrun those cop clunkers with three blown cylinders."

"Then why do it if the outcome is so predictable?"

"Didn't the speed and danger of being caught give you a thrill? Without a cop chasing us, it'd be like playing poker for matchsticks."

"I was more frightened than thrilled. You could have killed us on one of those turns."

Roger grinned. "You didn't look frightened. As a matter of fact, I'd say your expression was more of rapture than fear."

Clarisa clamped her lips to subdue a nervous smile. It *had* been thrilling — the wind, the roar of the engine, the wail of the siren, the blur of the road. Her body still tingled. "Okay, it was fun. But why risk a fatal crash for something as meaningless as a car chase? Isn't there anything more worthwhile you'd endanger your life for?"

Roger turned and stared at the combers rolling toward the beach.

Her question seemed to have hit a nerve, though she had no idea why. She rested a hand on his arm. "Look, I didn't mean to put you —."

The sound of tires on the gravel lot interrupted her. Their heads whirled around, and through a blinding floodlight Clarisa made out the black and white markings of a patrol car as it rolled up to their bumper, trapping them in place. She gripped Roger's arm. Ignoring her, he pulled out his silver cigarette case and lighter from his jacket pocket, and lit a cigarette. While Clarisa furtively glanced back, he calmly stared at the seascape, blowing smoke rings into the windshield.

Two officers with flashlights emerged from the patrol car and walked toward them, boots crunching on the gravel, vapor billowing from their nostrils. The officer on the driver's side ran his flashlight over the red sports car and then into their eyes.

"Thought you gave us the slip, huh?"

Roger exhaled a stream of smoke. "With all due respect, officer, we *did* give you the slip."

The cop bristled. "A big shot, huh? Suppose your mother stepped in front of your car and you mowed her down. You wouldn't be such a big shot then, would you?"

Roger sighed as if he found the question tedious. "I've been driving here at night for years, and I've never seen my mother, nor anybody else's mother walking around. And if my mother *were* foolish enough to frequent this area at night, she'd deserve any misfortune that might occur."

Frowning at the insolent response, the officer yanked the car door open. "Alright, get out. You too young lady. Put your hands on the hood."

As soon as Roger stepped out of the car, the cop grabbed his arms and pulled them behind his back. He shoved him over to the hood, pushed his head down, and frisked him. Meanwhile, the other officer politely opened the door for Clarisa and helped her out but didn't bother to search her.

"Lemme see your driver's license," demanded the first officer.

Roger stood up and removed his wallet from his coat pocket.

The cop snatched it out of his hand and thumbed through the contents until he found Roger's license. "Let's see…Roger Farnsworth…five-feet eleven…175 pounds…born April 18, 1906. Well, whaddaya know, Jake. This guy was born on earthquake day. No wonder he's got a screw loose. Hey, what's this?" He pulled a business card from the wallet and held it up to Roger's face. "What are you doin' with the chief's card? And don't tell me he's a personal friend, cause I've heard that story too many times before."

"Sorry to disappoint you, but I've had the pleasure of meeting Chief Quinn on several occasions. As a matter of fact, he was at our offices just the other day. My boss is a personal friend of his."

"Oh, yeah?" said the officer, his tone less hostile but still suspicious. "If you know the chief then tell me his wife's name?"

"I've only met Mrs. Quinn on a couple of occasions, and never informally or on a first name basis."

"Right" the officer said, the edge back in his voice. "If you don't know her name, you're lyin'. Anybody can print one of these cards to try and wiggle out of a jam. It don't mean nothin'." He grabbed Roger's arm and pulled him toward the patrol car. "Jake, we're takin' this joker in for reckless driving."

Roger wrenched his arm from the officer's grasp. "I didn't say I didn't know her name, only that I didn't know Mrs. Quinn on a first name basis. Her name is Julia and her children are Francis and Priscilla."

The officer glanced at his partner who shrugged as if to say, looks like his story's legit.

"Since no one was hurt," Roger said, "and no property was damaged, shall we let bygones be bygones?" He held out his hand. "If you'll return my wallet, I'll make it worth your while."

The policeman hesitated as if gaging Roger's offer. Apparently greed won out over ethical qualms. He handed the wallet to Roger, who removed a sawbuck and held it out. A faint smile appeared on the cop's face as he accepted the money and shoved it into his pocket. "Hey, any friend of the chief's is a friend of ours."

"And any friend of Alexander Hamilton," his partner added, "is a friend of ours, too."

The officers returned to their squad car and drove off. As their tail lights faded into the night, Clarisa wrapped her arms around her waist and shivered. Roger hurried around the Stutz and draped his jacket over her shoulders, then helped her into the car.

During the drive to her flat, Clarisa tried to keep her eyes open, but her lids sagged and her head leaned onto Roger's shoulder. The next morning she couldn't recall the ride home or the walk up into her flat, and if the alarm clock hadn't gone off she would have slept till noon.

Stifling another yawn, she redoubled her efforts to concentrate on the pep talk Thomas Plant was giving, although his platitudes were hardly worth recording.

"The way ahead will have its bumps and potholes, but things should be business as usual and well under control."

"What about this *Waterfront Worker*?" asked Stanley Dollar, waving a copy. "It's everywhere now, stirring things up with wild accusations, filling the men with communist propaganda. Who's behind it anyway?"

"We've been looking into that," Plant replied. He turned to Farnsworth. "What's the latest?"

Clarisa shifted her attention to Roger whose alert expression gave no hint of his activities the night before. *Could I fall in love with him,* she wondered? *He's smart, charming, handsome, has a good salary. His nighttime activities are odd, but most women would overlook that considering all else.* The fact was, though, she didn't know him well enough to risk a romantic entanglement and, above all, her priority was to keep her job

And, of course, there was Nick.

"The address on the masthead," said Farnsworth, "is a law office on Market Street connected with the Marine Workers Industrial Union, a communist-front organization. The paper says it's issued by a group of longshoremen. So far we haven't developed inside contacts or a list of names. This is a secretive group, so it may take awhile before we know more. We'll keep working on it."

"See that you do," Stanley Dollar shot back. "Those commies are everywhere. They've even opened up an office across from City Hall. I'm telling you it's a disease that infects the men, and if we don't stamp it out now, it'll spread like an epidemic."

8

With a continuous breeze on her portside and a canopy of gray clouds overhead, the *Diana Dollar* steamed up the coast in choppy seas dotted with whitecaps. Nick worked diligently at his assignments — chipping paint, scraping rust, washing decks, and polishing brass — until calluses formed on his hands and his fingers curled like the tines of a fork. During those times when he paused to gaze at the view or engage in conversation, bosun Slag invariably appeared, fists on hips, tongue flicking out over chapped lips, to order him back to work with a sharp reprimand. Nick wasn't sure why the bosun was riding him, perhaps to break him in. In any case, he accepted the tough treatment, hoping that Slag would eventually lay off.

The evening watch was his favorite time of day. On clear nights he stood on the flying bridge above the wheelhouse, watching the stars come out until the sky was dotted with more points of light than his city-bred eyes had ever seen. He found a stargazing guide in the messroom and used it to identify constellations: the Big Dipper chasing Little Dipper around Polaris, Cassiopeia bathing in the Milky Way while Perseus stood guard. And it never failed to remind him that his own problems didn't amount to an ant hill compared to the vastness of the universe.

At a remote point on the Washington coast, the ship turned towards land and entered a narrow channel leading to Grays Harbor, a large bay ringed by forested mountains, one behind the other as far as the eye could see. At the innermost end of the harbor, bluish smoke from a dozen lumber mills hovered over Aberdeen, a logging town whose dank piers were constructed of rough timbers and smelled of wood sap and creosote. The *Diana Dollar* berthed alongside several other freighters, prompting Nick to wonder why so many ships were docked at such an isolated port. Then when the area beyond the waterfront came into view, the reason was clear. Thousands of freshly felled logs, stacked in neat bundles, were sprawled over hundreds of acres.

To prepare the ship to receive cargo, the crew removed the hatch covers, lowered the booms from the kingposts, and greased the hoisting cables. This done, bearded stevedores in caulk boots clattered up the gangway to operate the winches. Within minutes they were hoisting logs up over the railings and into the holds, and for the rest of the day a great cacophony reverberated throughout the ship as logs, dangling on fall lines, descended into the hold and beat against the side of the hull.

During dinner the crew talked excitedly about going into town to a popular tavern. Since it was Nick's first port of call and his first chance to step on land as a sailor, he was eager to join them — that is until the bosun ordered him to stand gangway duty for the evening watch. As his shipmates tramped down the gangway, he waved them off with a rueful smile, unable to hide his disappointment at what seemed like senseless duty in such an isolated port.

Midway through the watch Sparks, the wireless operator, strolled by and stopped to chat. He had no duties while the ship lay in port, and when he understood the situation he offered to stand the last two hours for Nick who gratefully thanked him, promising to return the favor.

At the bottom of the gangway Nick remembered his letter to Clarisa. He bounded back up to his bunkroom, stuffed it into his coat pocket, and retraced his steps. A set of train tracks guided him across the Chehalis River to a street lined with Western storefronts and plank sidewalks. At a general store he shoved the letter into a postal slot, then headed toward a building with windows ablaze with light.

Honky-tonk music mixed with loud conversation spilled out of the building as he approached. He pushed through a pair of swinging doors into a cloud of tobacco smoke that made everything inside appear fuzzy and dream-like. Loggers and stevedores sat at a long bar and around a dozen tables, and from the odor of sweat and sawdust it was certain that most of them had only a passing acquaintance with soap and water. A female bartender, the only woman in the place, greeted him with a silent nod. Her dark unruly hair, pinned on top of her head, and her coal black eyes gave him the impression that, if need be, she could handle herself in any situation.

He ordered a beer and looked around the crudely built tavern. It was constructed of whole logs, mortised at the corners and mortared along the seams. A wooden Wurlitzer jukebox stood against the back wall, spinning well-worn records that popped and crackled as it played country-western tunes. A buck's head on the wall above the jukebox bore two magnificent eight-point antlers, its glass eyes gleaming dully in the smoke-filtered light.

"Hey, Nick!

Moon Mullins was motioning to him.

Moon, Remy, and three others were seated at a large round table made from the cross-section of a cedar log, its edge encrusted with bark. Beer mugs and shot glasses cluttered the tabletop.

"Ain't you on gangway duty?" Moon asked as Nick sat down.

"Sparks wasn't interested in coming into town, so he took over for me." He glanced at Remy who was hunched over the table, walking two wobbly fingers toward the center and muttering to himself. "What're you doing, Remy?"

The wobbly fingers paused. "Counting rings. I'm at four hundred twenty-eight and not even halfway finished. This thing could be a thousand years old." The two fingers resumed their journey.

Moon's face was shiny with sweat. "I'd rather watch paint dry."

Nick ran his palm over the concentric circles, admiring the huge slice of wood. "Cedars are one of most durable species on earth. Some live more than two-thousand years."

The wobbly fingers paused again. "Imagine that, born before Christ."

"Imagine that," Moon mimicked in a childlike voice, "born before Jesus fuckin' Christ." He stood up and steadied himself against the table.

"A'right mates, lissenup!" He turned to the next table. "Shaddup greasers." Will Bailey and the engine room crew looked over. "The deckmen hereby challenge the black hole gang to an arm wrestling match."

"What'er the stakes?" someone asked.

Moon grinned and wiped a sleeve across his forehead. "Losers have to carry the winners back to the ship piggyback."

A minor uproar ensued as the deckmen and engine room gang traded barbs and catcalls. Six men sat at each table, so it was decided they would pair off for a first round. The winners would then go on to a second round until two men, one from each department, were left for a final match. Will Bailey declined to take part and joined a table of loggers where, Nick noticed, he had no trouble introducing himself and joining their conversation.

Moon rolled up his shirtsleeve, revealing a muscular forearm tattooed with a bare-breasted mermaid lounging on an anchor. He sat down opposite his opponent and after a brief match pinned the fellow's arm to the table. To celebrate his victory he danced a lap around the table, smiling and waving his arms like a circus tent evangelist.

Remy followed and quickly lost, too inebriated to put up much of a battle.

Nick was up next against a young blond fellow named Jack whose bangs hung over his eyes. Days of chipping paint had toughened Nick's arms. Even so, the two were well-matched and remained deadlocked while the other sailors gave them encouragement.

"Come on, Jack!" someone from the engine room hollered. "You can beat Schoolboy!"

Nick hated the nickname, though he understood its origin. Aside from the officers, he was undoubtedly the only college educated sailor onboard, and although he'd been careful not to mention it, the crew had pegged him as a college graduate. Now, in the heat of battle, the repugnant nickname gave him the incentive he needed. He leaned forward, grunting and straining, putting everything he had into it.

Jack was straining as well, his face red and sweaty as he maintained resistance.

A burning ache ran down Nick's forearm to his elbow. He tried to ignore it, but as the seconds passed it became increasingly painful. Just when he thought he'd have to ease off, Jack grimaced and his arm leaned back slightly. Encouraged, Nick made one last effort, pushing with all his might. Jack's arm inched back again.

Finally it gave way — *whomp!* — Jack's knuckles slamming on the table.

The deck department erupted in cheers, and for a moment Nick's newcomer status was forgotten as they patted him on the back and celebrated the victory.

Every patron in the tavern was now gathered around the table, rooting for one side or the other. At the back of the crowd an impromptu bookmaker began taking bets.

The remaining first-round matches were split between the two teams, leaving three winners from the deck department and two from the engine room. It was decided among the deckmen that Moon and Nick would take on the remaining engine room opponents, with Moon to go first against a burly fellow named Haggis who wore denim overalls and a train engineer's cap perched on top of a bald head.

Moon sat down opposite his opponent, spit into his palms, and rubbed them together with a confident smile. He planted his elbow on the table and clasped Haggis' hand.

"Get set, go!" somebody yelled.

Moon aggressively leaned forward and seemed to put everything he had into it. By contrast, the burly Haggis remained calm, face relaxed, mind seemingly a blank slate. They were deadlocked for some time until Moon began trembling and grunting as he plied all his strength, the blood vessels on his forearm bulging, knuckles white, face red.

In desperation he exclaimed, "I can beat you, you big lummox."

The words fell on deaf ears. Haggis held steady, unperturbed, as if he was waiting for Moon to run out of steam. This went on for another minute until Haggis leaned forward and began pushing Moon's trembling arm back.

Moon gasped and groaned and strained, though it did no good. All at once his arm gave way and fell back on the table — *whomp!*

The engine room crew thrust their arms up in victory and howled in delight. At the back of the crowd, the bookmaker paid off winners and pocketed the rest.

Nick sat down to face his next opponent, the sailor who had beaten Remy earlier.

The engine room crew, sure of their ace-in-the-hole, offered to concede the match and go straight to a final round between Nick and Haggis. The deckmen agreed. When Nick sat down, the bookmaker judiciously examined the two opponents and announced the odds: 10 to 1 in favor of Haggis. Nick didn't disagree with the assessment and only hoped that the match against Moon had worn down Haggis enough to allow him a respectable showing. He grasped Haggis' hand and was surprised at how smooth and supple it was, perhaps from spreading lubricating oil on engine parts.

"Get set, go!" somebody yelled.

Nick applied pressure, holding back some in reserve; Haggis responded in kind. They both held steady and at first it appeared to be an even match. After a time Nick applied more pressure, and again Haggis matched his effort pound for pound. Nick knew that Haggis' superior size and strength would eventually prevail and that Haggis was waiting for him to tire. Hoping to hold on as long as possible, he bowed his head and closed his eyes, concentrating on keeping up a steady pressure.

All around them spectators yelped and cheered and craned their necks, some climbing on tables to form a balcony at the rear.

Tuning out the noisy clamor, Nick focused on the relentless pressure, growing stronger every second. A burning pain returned to his arm, and as it increased he wondered if he'd held out long enough to avoid humiliation. Thus absorbed, he failed to notice a figure elbow his way through the crowd, or to see a pair of hands grab his collar and yank him up out of his seat.

His attention suddenly diverted from the match, Nick's arm went limp and in an instant it toppled back onto the table under the crushing power of Haggis' strength. With one pair of hands lifting him up while another hand pinned down his arm, he felt his elbow wracked at an unnatural angle and about to pop out of its socket.

He cried out in pain.

Haggis quickly released his arm. The frenzied spectators froze.

Nick opened his eyes and found himself face to face with bosun Slag, still clutching his collar and staring at him with a frown that made him even more intimidating.

"What the hell are you doin' here, Benson?"

Between the dull ache in his arm and the shock of being pulled from the match so abruptly, it took a few moments for Nick to understand the question. "Sparks . . . Sparks took over gangway duty for me."

"No one leaves their post without my permission!"

Slag released Nick's collar and shot a glance at the rest of the crew who regarded him with a mixture of fear and recrimination. "That goes for all of you. Now get back to the ship."

His angry words broke the silence, and somewhere at the back of the crowd a bettor demanded his wager from the bookmaker, saying the match was annulled by the interruption. When the bookmaker declared Haggis the winner, claiming Nick's arm hit the table as he was yanked to his feet, the two men began arguing.

Meanwhile, the crew silently shuffled out of the tavern and trudged back to the ship, their silence broken only by the hoot of an owl hidden in the folds of the ink black forest.

9

The *Diana Dollar* sailed out of Grays Harbor and steered north into rolling seas that gently rocked her from side to side. Bosun Slag sent Nick forward to paint the number one kingpost, making no mention of Nick's absence from the ship the night before. For his part, Nick was grateful that the incident was buried. In retrospect he saw that the bosun had had good reason to be upset — he'd left his post without permission — and hoped Slag wouldn't hold it against him. With brush and paint can in hand, he climbed up the kingpost on horizontal pegs and reached the top twenty-five feet above the weather deck. He hung the can on the highest peg and paused a moment to enjoy the view. A sparkling ocean spread out in every direction, and off in the distance a thin green ribbon marked the coastline.

Clink! Clink! Clink! The paint can tapped against the kingpost as the post heaved up and down while swirling in circles in rhythm to the pitch and yaw of the ship. Gripping the post with one hand, Nick dipped the brush in the can with the other and began applying a coat of paint. It wasn't a difficult job. The hardest part was maintaining his grip on the oscillating post, especially when switching the brush from one hand to the other.

He was just getting the hang of it when a queasy sensation rolled through his stomach. The breakfast he'd eaten that morning — scrambled eggs, pork sausage, buttered toast, and coffee — felt like partially set concrete sloshing around inside him. He paused again to gaze at the horizon. In relation to the ship it appeared to be rising and falling, an optical illusion that brought on another wave of queasiness and triggered a flood of saliva. He wiped his brow, accidentally grazing his face with the brush and leaving a streak of paint across his cheek. His palms were now wet and slippery, compromising his grip. He hooked an arm around the post to better secure himself and tried not to think about plummeting to the deck below.

Determined to keep going, he dipped his brush in the can and began applying more paint, trying to ignore his stomach, trying to concentrate on his work. But it only made him more aware of the unsettled queasiness in his gut. Still, it was bearable.

Just when he thought he could manage, a wave of nausea rolled through him, followed by another wave and then another, like a relentless pounding surf. His head began to reel, and when he looked down at the deck below it was blurry and pulsating like the sea.

His stomach tightened and convulsed, sending a flood of bile up his esophagus, coating it with acid and leaving a nasty taste in the back of his throat. Dizzy and alarmed, he dumped the brush in the can and started down. He'd only stepped down two pegs when his stomach convulsed again, halting his descent. This time gray-brown slush surged up his throat and gushed out of his mouth, hitting his right arm as it cascaded to the deck below. He heaved several more times until his stomach was drained and then continued to dry retch, viscous spittle dangling from his lips.

"Hey," Moon called from below, "didn't anybody tell you to aim it over the side." When Nick didn't reply, he put a foot on the first peg.

"Leave him," said the bosun, who appeared out of nowhere as if he'd been watching all along.

"But he's liable to fall in that condition."

"Naahh, he won't let go."

For the next ten minutes, paralyzed by vertigo and a stomach-churning nausea, Nick held on for dear life, each minute an eternity. Slag finally allowed Moon to help him down. When they reached the bottom, Nick's legs buckled and he collapsed onto the deck like a jellyfish. Moon helped him to his bunk, assuring him that the nausea would only plague him for a day or two and, once past, would be gone for good unless the ship was caught in a typhoon. It was called Neptune's Hazing, he explained, a greeting from the sea god to every newcomer.

Arms wrapped around his torso, Nick lay on his bunk while waves of nausea rolled through him. In between the waves he came to the conclusion that the bosun had sent him up the kingpost knowing he would become seasick— a punishment for leaving his post the night before. And while it was comforting to know that Neptune would be done with him soon, he wasn't sure about Slag.

The *Diana Dollar* steamed through the strait of San Juan de Fuca into Puget Sound, and for the next six days she made brief stops at the ports of Seattle, Tacoma, and Everett to pick up lumber, rail tracks, and mail bound for the Far East. The bosun made Nick stand gangway duty each night, preventing him from going ashore, a fate Nick accepted without complaint, though he regretted not being able to explore the northwest ports.

On the nineteenth of May, six-thousand tons of cargo stowed in her hold, the *Diana Dollar* sailed out of Everett beginning the twenty-eight day journey across the Pacific Ocean. By midmorning the freighter had cleared Cape Flattery at the tip of the Olympic Peninsula and was sailing into open seas.

Nick wrote in his journal every day, finding it therapeutic as his grandfather had suggested. The topics varied depending on his mood. Sometimes he described his experiences as if he was writing a newspaper article, hoping the practice would hone his reporting skills. Other times he composed brief sketches of the ever changing seascape or his quirky shipmates. He also wrote letters to Clarisa and his family and asked Remy to mail them on their last evening in Everett. As fate would have it, a waterfront bar stood between the ship and the nearest mailbox. The next morning Remy sheepishly returned the letters, confessing that he and two mates had entered the bar before he deposited them and after numerous drinks had staggered back to the ship, the forgotten correspondence still tucked in his pocket. Nick took the undelivered letters and put them in his locker, figuring he wouldn't have another opportunity to mail them in time to reach San Francisco before he returned. What would Clarisa think, he wondered, when she received no correspondence beyond his first letter. Would she assume he'd put her out of his mind. That he considered their relationship over. He hoped not.

Journal – May 21st, 1933

The captain, bless him, was true to his word. Yesterday evening I reported to the wheelhouse for my second chance to man the helm, and this time I received proper instruction from Paul Conner, the third mate. For starters, I learned you don't steer a ship by compass alone. The forward kingpost indicates a change in direction much sooner. When the kingpost shifts in relation to the horizon, you adjust the wheel to bring it back in line, but only a spoke or two, not the wild half-turns of my first try.

Within an hour I felt comfortable at the helm and remarked that steering a ship was like driving a car down a straight highway, requiring constant vigilance and minor adjustments to stay on course. Conner agreed but said there's a major difference. Every day the ship must change course to maintain a straight line. It sounds contradictory, but the reason is simple. The shortest distance between any two points on the globe is the great circle route, an arc on the earth's surface whose center point is the center of the earth. To follow this arc, which on a flat chart looks like curve, the ship must periodically change compass directions.

Every day at noon Conner takes a reading with a sexton. Then with this information he calculates our position using navigation tables. If the sun is hidden behind clouds, however, the sexton is useless. In that case Conner has to resort to a time-honored, though not especially accurate method called dead reckoning. For this, he starts from the last known position, then factors the speed of the ship, the direction, and the effect of the current. One or two days of dead reckoning isn't bad if the weather is calm. Beyond that or in foul weather you can lose your bearings.

I asked him how he calculates the effect of the current.

You look at the ship's wake, he said. For every three degrees the wake veers from the ship's course, you can figure about one knot of current.

On this leg of the voyage we're sailing into the Kuro Current, also known as the Black Current because of the ocean's dark blue color. The Kuro Current flows up from the Philippines, so it's relatively warm. Off the coast of northern Japan it meets the Oya Current, a cold counter current eddying south from Kamchatka. That's the most dangerous part of our voyage, according to Conner. When the cold Oya Current meets the warmer Kuro, the moist sea air can congeal into a fog so thick you can't see the bow from the wheelhouse. Even at midday! And at night it's like being trapped in an underground cave. If you're in an area with rocks, shoals, uncharted islands, or other vessels, it's dangerous to continue, so you have to stop, drop the deep-sea anchor, and wait until the fog lifts. And that can take days.

The *Diana Dollar* pushed westward over endless miles of ocean, and as each day melted into the next, the crew fell into a comfortable, languorous rhythm. Their duties weren't onerous at sea, and with their bunk and meals provided, they had few worries. This relaxed pace was soothing to

Nick, and little by little the memory of his father's lifeless body receded, although never completely disappeared.

One mild evening, the winds calm, sky clear, the crew congregated on the weather deck to chat and spin a few yarns. Nick joined them and listened as sailors took turns recounting tales from what seemed like an endless supply of stories.

"We were off the coast of Madagascar," one sailor began, "when lightning struck the foremast. By God, the whole ship lit up like a roman candle, and the wireless operator was knocked to the floor and lost all his hair…" As soon as he finished, another man jumped in. "Why that ain't nothin' compared to the time we were in Cochin. It was so damn hot our rubber soles melted and Cook fried an omelet on the deck…" Some stories were as dramatic as pulp fiction. "We were off the Dardanelles when we ran smack dab into a Beaufort 10 storm. Howling winds drove the waves into huge peaks, and combers crashed on the deck like concussion bombs. A loose guy wire was whipping around, so two men went out to secure it. They almost reached it when a huge wave swept them off their feet and into the water. We tried to turn the ship to save them, but the waves were so tall the rudder wouldn't answer the helm. We floundered for hours until . . ."

Nick enjoyed the dramatic tales. When a good storyteller built up momentum and embellished his yarn with vivid details, you couldn't tell the difference between fact and fiction, and it really didn't matter.

During a break in the conversation, he left the weather deck and made his way up to the captain's cabin. Knocked on the door.

"Come," a voice commanded.

Captain Harding was seated at his desk, pipe in one hand, book in the other. He smiled as Nick entered. "I've been thinking about you." He held up the book, its cover threadbare and embossed with the title *Robinson Crusoe*. "Have you read this?"

Nick sat down. "No, sir."

"I first read it in my teens, and I've reread it a dozen times since. Funny thing is, it prepared me for this command better than any manual."

Nick was relieved to see the captain in good spirits. "I thought it was about a castaway marooned on a deserted island."

"It is, but mainly it's about surviving in an isolated situation with little help from anyone else. And that's a damn good description of commanding a ship." He set his pipe down, removed his spectacles, and rubbed his eyes. The back of his hands were dotted with age spots, and his face looked older and wearier than when he conducted his daily inspections. "Have you come for one of our chats?"

"Yes, sir."

"So, how do you like life at sea?"

Nick fidgeted with his shirtsleeve. He wanted to talk about Slag's harsh treatment but wasn't sure if he should mention it. After a moment's hesitation, he went ahead anyway. While the captain puffed on his pipe and listened, he described the humiliating punishment on the kingpost and how the bosun scolded him every time he paused and had put him on chipping and paint duty for the entire forenoon watch. He tried not to sound like a complainer, but he wanted to convince the captain that Slag had been picking on him unfairly, certainly more than any other sailor onboard. When he finished, he glanced at the old man.

Harding's face was tilted up toward the painting of the windjammer above his desk, eyes focused beyond it to what seemed like another place and time.

After a period of silence Nick coughed politely.

The captain removed the pipe from his mouth. "I was recalling my first days as an ordinary seaman. Every young man coming up the hawse pipe thinks the bosun has it in for him, that life onboard is unfair, that he gets the worst jobs, the lowest pay, and the roughest treatment." He looked at Nick with an expression that said: *Don't take it too hard, we all go through it.* "A sailors' first voyage is his most difficult, but if he works hard, obeys orders, and learn the ropes, it pays off in the end."

Nick had hoped to convince Harding that the bosun's tough treatment was more than just a strict boss breaking in a new hand, that it might be motivated by a resentment of Nick's connection with the captain or perhaps his education. Now that he looked back, though, he could see that the old man was probably right. Slag had been tough on him because of his inexperience and had been training him in the same way that he himself had been trained.

"We work in God's country," the captain continued, "though it's an unforgiving God. We can't afford to make mistakes — lives and millions of dollars of cargo and equipment are at stake. Discipline is critical to everything we do, from the captain on down. It's not like working at a five 'n' dime or pushing paper in an office. We face life threatening situations, so everyone has to do their part without hesitation. And that requires strict obedience. I expect the bosun is just trying to teach you a few lessons. Don't take it personally." He paused. "Anything else on your mind, son?"

Nick felt embarrassed to have complained about a few harsh words. The captain was right. He'd have to tough it out and make the best of it.

"No, sir. Everything's fine."

"Here," said the captain, holding out the book. "It's a good read. Come back and tell me what you think about it."

10

The red neon sign above Big Dipper Donuts buzzed and flickered, casting an intermittent glow on Clarisa as she walked by. A warm sweet fragrance wafted out of the shop from freshly baked donuts, pastries, and éclairs displayed in the window. She turned the corner into a narrow back street and continued to the middle of the block, to a breadline formed at the entrance to St. Patrick's Mission. Most men in line wore scuffed shoes, frayed coats, and battered fedoras, their faces unshaven. Yet in spite of their downtrodden appearance, they greeted Clarisa with warm smiles, and she returned their greeting with a smile of her own.

She began volunteering at St. Patrick's Mission two years earlier, and at the time, the breadline snaked in the direction she just came from. As the economy worsened and jobs became increasingly scarce, the line lengthened until it reached Big Dipper Donuts, a torturous situation for those forced to stand within sight of the freshly baked goods and smell the sweet aroma, and also for Clarisa, who saw their hungry faces reflected in the bakery window, staring forlornly into the shop. Eventually, she couldn't stand it any more and convinced Father Shannon to redirect the breadline in the opposite direction.

Inside the mission she donned a white apron and joined other volunteers toting large pots of stew and urns of coffee from the kitchen to a serving counter in the dining room. Another volunteer commented that the day's main course looked like what's-it stew. She peered into a pot at orange, green, and beige lumps, floating in a muddy broth laced with a stringy substance she guessed was chipped beef, and had to admit that the identity of the ingredients was open to question. Still, it would be the best meal of the day, perhaps the only meal, for many waiting outside.

At six o'clock the men shuffled in and lined up at the serving counter, each gratefully accepting a bowl of stew, two slices of bread, a pat of butter, and a cup of coffee. It was Clarisa's job to hand out the bread and butter, and along with it she gave each diner a gracious smile. Some of them were sturdy roustabouts who only worked part-time and were unable to make ends meet. Others were sailors stretching their dollars before shipping out again. Still others, by their soiled clothing and weathered faces, were clearly destitute, relying on the soup kitchen for survival. For these poor souls she offered her warmest smile and an extra slice of bread.

During the meal Father Michael Shannon, monsignor of St. Patrick's Church and director of the mission, made his way around the room. He chatted amiably with the men, largely blue-collar Catholics who preferred St. Patrick's Mission to other soup kitchens where they were required to listen to hellfire sermons as a price for their meal. It was evident that the diners appreciated his low key approach and easy manner, for even the most hardened among them managed a smile when he stopped to chat.

After finishing his rounds in the dining room, the silver-haired priest went to the kitchen, placed his hands on the shoulders of each volunteer, and thanked them with an informal blessing. It was a casual benediction that only a priest with Father Shannon's natural warmth could manage without seeming awkward, and every volunteer, whether Catholic or not, was visibly heartened by the gesture.

When it was Clarisa's turn, he grasped her hands between his palms. "We hardly see each other anymore outside the mission. I guess the teenager who once relied on my counsel no longer needs an old man's advice. I hope it's a sign that things are going well."

Clarisa managed a half-hearted smile. She would like to have said that everything was fine, that she was working at a new job with a good boss, and that she'd fended off an impending eviction. Instead, a subtle but distinct worry was gnawing at her. She'd only received one letter from Nick and that was weeks ago. Now she wondered if he'd forgotten her altogether. Men seemed to have the ability to move on much quicker than women, so perhaps he'd already met someone else. A girl in every port, wasn't that what they said about sailors.

Shannon seemed to sense her pensive mood. "Will you walk back to the church with me? It's on your way home."

She searched his face. "What's on your mind, Father?"

Smile lines curved around his lips. "Mainly, I'd like to catch up."

In the dim light of a lingering sunset, they ambled along Mission Street, their shadows swept around in half circles by the headlights of passing cars.

Father Shannon walked with a slight limp. "Tell me, darlin', how is Seamus?"

"Not good. A couple of months ago he drank himself into a blind rage and bit a policeman's ear. Nick and I managed to get him out of jail, and he's calmed down for now, but he's having a hard time. His printing business has nearly dried up, and he's humiliated that I'm the one earning a steady income."

Shannon nodded thoughtfully. "A lot of families are facing the same trouble. A third of the men in my parish are unemployed, maybe more. If things don't improve, I'm afraid the situation could get ugly." They walked a few more paces. "And how is Nick?"

"Gone. Shipped out on a freighter as a deck hand."

"At least he's working. That's better than many."

"I gave him a hard time about leaving, so I don't know if we'll be seeing each other again."

"Has he written?"

"Once."

"Well, I'm sure they keep those boys busy, and there aren't many opportunities to post mail. I wouldn't give up on him." He cast a sideways glance at her. "Is everything alright?"

Clarisa wasn't sure how to respond. Should she mention the rage that consumed her when Nick announced he was leaving? That it had ignited deep feelings of abandonment and anxiety. She was contemplating what to say when the words suddenly blurted out as if they had a life of their own. "I don't understand it. Nick and I were in love, about to settle down. Then after his father died things changed. Our life together didn't seem to matter to him anymore." Her eyes glistened. "I tried to hold on to him, tried to keep him from leaving, but it didn't do any good. He slipped farther and farther away until . . . until he was gone."

Father Shannon wrapped an arm around her. "There, there, darlin'."

Clarisa rested her head on his shoulder, and it reminded her of her teenage years when his supportive ear and sage advice helped her adjust to life with only one parent. He was a Godsend then, but that was years ago. She pulled herself upright and lifted her chin. "I warned him I wouldn't wait for him if he left."

"That's a tough stance to take with someone you love. Are you sure you want to close that chapter just yet?"

It was a question she'd pondered many times, and like the toss of a coin the answer came up randomly one way and then the other. Of one thing she was certain: she wanted the stability of someone she could rely on, someone with whom she could build a lasting relationship, a family. Her mother's unexpected death had been a terrible loss, and now that her father seemed to be slipping into his own private hell, she couldn't — she wouldn't — wait forever to build a life of her own.

"I'm not sure of anything," she murmured. "I'm just living one day at a time. At least I have a job."

"That's good." He nodded. "Who are you working for?"

"The Waterfront Employers Association."

Father Shannon stopped. "Really? Do you know anything about it? Its history?"

"Not really."

He continued on again and glanced down at his gimp leg. "I got this limp years ago when the Waterfront Employers Association crushed the Riggers and Stevedores Union. Strikers who stood up to them were beaten, arrested, and thrown in jail. One poor fellow's arm was pulled out of its socket. I was conducting a prayer rally at the waterfront when a gang of hired hooligans attacked us. Since then wages have gone down, hours are longer, safety precautions cut back."

They arrived at the steps of St. Patrick's Church, a tall brick building with arched windows and a square tower.

Clarisa stopped and faced Shannon. "I didn't think priests got involved in politics. Aren't you supposed to be more concerned with sinners than strikers?"

"You can't separate the two, my dear. If men can't find work or make a living wage, they're far more likely to give in to one temptation or another. The church believes that economic oppression is a sin against humanity and supports the right of workers to demand decent working conditions. Of course, there are conservative clerics who equate unions with communism, but" — he grinned — "I'm not one of them."

His words raised an issue that Clarisa would have preferred to ignore. She liked her job, even enjoyed it, and the Waterfront Employers Association certainly wasn't a nefarious organization. Self-interested, yes, but not evil per se. Now her priest, whom she regarded highly, was suggesting that it was a den of philistines. She'd heard its members refer to dockworkers in demeaning terms, and she was under no illusion that the goal of the organization was anything other than to help its members accrue as much profit as possible. So far, though, she'd been able to overlook the derogatory rhetoric and concentrate on her duties. Yet here and now, standing in the shadow of the church, she felt as if she was being asked to take sides, and it irritated her to be placed in such an untenable position.

"I suppose," she said curtly, "you think I'm working for the disciples of Mammon, but I'll tell you straight out, I won't quit my job. It's the one thing that's going well in my life, and it's the *only* thing keeping the landlord at bay. So, I won't do it. No matter what you say."

Her fit of pique seemed to amuse Father Shannon, who regarded her with a disarming smile. "My dear, it was the furthest thing from my mind. In fact, I would encourage you to keep your job. There's no telling what you'll learn, and, Lord knows, salvation and redemption come in many forms."

11

For twelve days the *Diana Dollar* steamed across a vast ocean that sparkled by day and glimmered softly at night. On the thirteenth day a row of dark specks appeared on the starboard horizon, the Aleutian Island chain, connecting North America and Asia. A slew of new species also appeared. Huge brown albatrosses circled the ship looking for food scraps discarded by the galley, and closer to the water squadrons of short-tailed shearwaters, flying in formation, skimmed over the waves and plucked fish from the sea.

A pod of blue-nosed dolphins romped in the ship's frothy wake, bounding to the surface like playful children and dipping back down, their upturned lips making them appear perpetually cheerful.

Nick was leaning on the quarterdeck rail, watching the dolphins, when a nearby voice said, "They look so damned happy, don't they?"

Nick looked up. "Oh, hi, Bailey. Just what I was thinking. They seem to have few worries compared to us."

Will Bailey pinched a hand-rolled cigarette from his shirt pocket and lit it. His sleeveless arms were streaked with lubricating oil, his fingernails caked with grime. He drew in a puff and looked out at the undulating waves. "Yeah, on the one hand, we're more capable. We produce our own food and vehicles to distribute it. We know how to construct huge bridges and build enormous ships." He pointed to an albatross circling overhead. "We've even invaded their territory. Yep, we're top dog on this planet." He nodded toward the dolphins. "On the other hand they work together for the benefit of all, don't they? You don't see one dolphin doing all the work to feed another, do you?"

Nick shrugged. "I'm no expert but I guess not. They have to work together, otherwise the pod wouldn't survive."

"That's right, all for one and one for all. That's where they got us beat six ways to Sunday. Somewhere along the line we decided it was okay for a few of us to hold all the cards, while the rest of us work our tails off. And those holding the cards get to keep the profits produced by the rest of us, as if we're slaves." He glanced at Nick as though to gauge his reaction. "Course, we're free to go home at night and fall asleep from exhaustion until it's time to go to work the next day, but is that really much different than slavery?"

"Sure it is. They have to pay us for our labor. And we can quit any time to work for someone else or start our own business."

"Can we? Right now twenty-five percent of American workers are unemployed. That's eleven million without jobs. And how can you start a business if the boss pays just enough to survive?"

"I hear they're going to start some sort of insurance for the unemployed. That'll help."

Bailey tapped the ash off his cigarette. "Maybe, but it's a temporary fix. After that we'll be right back where we started" — he held out his hands — "with nothin' but the dirt under our fingernails. No, my friend, we need a fundamental change in the way things work."

Nick recalled the outrageous statement Bailey made the first day they met, claiming that the Dollar Steamship Company bought the *Diana Dollar* with his and Bailey's money. It didn't make sense then — and it still didn't — but now he was beginning to see where the oiler was coming from.

"Are you a communist, Will?"

Bailey smiled a tight-lipped smile as though he'd heard the question before. "I won't lie to you, but before I answer, let me ask you somethin'. Would it matter if I was? Isn't truth, truth, no matter who's sayin' it?"

"It matters to men like Hoover. They think communists are born liars and want to overthrow the government."

"Whatta you think?"

Nick paused. "I don't know. I've never met a communist."

"Let me answer your question by tellin' you somethin' about myself. I grew up with five brothers and sisters, and my mother scrambled every day to feed us. Times were tough and the only thing that gave her solace was the church. So she made sure we learned our catechism and went to confession every week. I don't go to church anymore, but I still remember the story of Jesus. I remember thinkin', why don't he just shut up when the Pharisees call him a blasphemous liar? Why does he go on preachin' when he knows the authorities are after him, claimin' he's violatin' Roman law and creatin' civil unrest?" He glanced at Nick. "Ya know why?"

"Well . . . I expect it was because he believed so deeply in his gospel."

"That's right. His mission was greater than himself. He was after the big bonanza, the salvation of mankind. It didn't matter if people thought he was a whacked out preacher, he was going to continue till his last dyin' day." A dolphin leapt out of the wake and emitted a high-pitch squeal, then plunged back into the water. "All I'm saying is judge me by my words and deeds, not by labels."

"Alright," conceded Nick, "let's forget labels. Tell me what you're doing on this ship? I gotta a feeling it's more than oiling crank shafts."

Will nodded. "I do have more on my mind than grease monkey work, but it's not to overthrow the gov'ment. This is your first voyage so you haven't seen the changes in the shippin' industry. In the past few years wages have gone south. No overtime pay, of course, so most guys hardly make enough to support themselves. And if you're injured the company dumps you on the beach with a coupla bucks and replaces you like a fouled spark plug. Course, everyone is afraid to speak up, cause they don't have a union to stand up for 'em."

"What about the Sailor's Union of the Pacific? My granddad used to belong to it. Said it was run by a Norwegian."

Bailey nodded. "Old Andy Furuseth was a militant organizer when he started, but he's been in Washington D.C. so long, hobnobbing with politicians and shipowners, he's lost touch with the rank-and-file. I doubt he's got a thousand members."

"Is that what you were doing the other day when I interrupted your meeting? Organizing a union?"

"I'll let you in on a little secret. I'm the most disorganized guy I know. I'm really more a magnet that brings the men together till their own glue takes hold."

"Must be easy pickin's these days, what with the lousy economy."

Bailey shook his head. "It's never easy. Organizin' sailors is the hardest job there is. With a factory or a coal mine, you got the same guys goin' to the same place every day. You can take your time buildin' an organization. Sailors, on the other hand, are a movin' target, and they're easily replaced by college kids off on a slummer."

Nick shot a glance at him. "Is that what you think of me? A college kid on a slummer?"

"Whooa!" said Bailey, holding up his hands. "Remember, I'm the guy who hates labels. Over the years, though, I've developed a talent for judgin' a man's character — you have to in my line of work. You're not here on a slummer." He turned to go. "We'll be meetin' again in a few days. Why don't you join us?"

Bailey headed back to work, leaving Nick to ponder the invitation. He certainly hadn't planned on getting involved in a union and, after further consideration, decided it would be wiser to stay away from something he had no stake in. He was about to leave when one of the dolphins peeled off from the pod and swam away. One by one the others followed until they were all gone, leaving Nick to ponder another question. Had the lead dolphin made the decision for the rest? Or did they somehow come to a consensus, the leader merely the first to act on it?

That evening he took his journal to the messroom and began an entry. As he jotted down his thoughts, a cockroach wandered across the page, its antennae thrust forward, gesticulating back and forth sniffing for food. Nick didn't bother to brush it aside. What was the point? Another one would be along soon. The roaches had appeared shortly after the ship left the mainland, rambling freely about the vessel as if they knew there was little the crew could do to eradicate them at sea. When he asked about the sudden and puzzling infestation, his bunkmates shrugged indifferently as though inured to their presence. Even Cook was philosophical when an occasional cockroach dropped into a pot of stew simmering on the stove. *A bit 'o fresh protein never hurt a body, roight?*

On the sixteenth day out from Puget Sound, Nick rose from his afternoon nap and glanced out through the porthole at an ominous black curtain on the horizon. When he was a boy, his grandfather often regaled him with stories of storms at sea, of waves pounding the ship and gale force winds blowing so hard they could knock a man down. Now it looked like he was about to experience it firsthand, and it brought back the thrill he felt listening to his grandfather's tales.

Over the next couple of hours the squall closed to within five miles, and by the time the crew sat down to supper, a slashing rain pelted the ship and twelve-foot swells buffeted her hull, causing coffee to slosh around in cups and books on shelves to tip back and forth.

After the evening meal Nick donned an oil-skin jacket and trousers and stepped out onto the weather deck to take a closer look. He grasped the railing and gazed out at a whirling mist that blended ocean and sky so that one was indistinguishable from the other. A lumbering swell rolled toward the ship from the portside. As it drew near, a slicing wind blew spindrift off the top and hurled it against the hull with a whipping sound. When the swell hit the hull it broke over the bow with tympanic thunder, smothering the foc'sle with white frosting that drained through the scuppers and flowed back into the ferment. Driven by the wind, sheets of rain pounded against the midship house and vibrated guy wires that whistled and pinged against the kingposts in rapid arpeggios. The discordant sounds and chaotic rhythms were strangely beautiful and frighteningly powerful, and for the first time Nick understood the need for constant maintenance to protect the vessel, for even a modest storm flogged the ship with a corrosive force that no paint could withstand for long.

He stepped back from the railing and turned toward the midship house. As he pivoted, his shoes lost purchase on the deck and slid out from beneath him. He toppled like a fallen tree and landed on the deck, and from that moment forward time attenuated, each second unfolding with slow limpid clarity.

The deck felt like slime-covered rock, offering little friction as the ship tilted toward the portside. Nick slid toward the railing, his momentum carrying his feet under it. One foot passed over a metal ridge at the edge of the deck. He dug his other foot against the ridge, but it, too, bounced over as if the soles of his shoes were coated with oil. He continued to slide, his legs jutting out beyond the edge of the ship. He reached out for the railing with both hands. One hand missed but the other managed to grab it, saving himself from hurtling into the sea below. For a moment he lay there, heart racing, chest heaving, rain pelting his face.

When the ship rocked back toward the starboard side, he pushed himself away from the railing and slid toward the midship house until he was able to grasp a vertical standpipe. Using it as a hand-hold, he pulled himself to his feet, though his shoes now felt slippery as if he was standing on ice. He gripped the pipe tighter with one hand and leaned over to wipe the deck with the fingers of his other hand. He raised them to his nose and sniffed, detecting the faint odor of lubricating oil. As he suspected, someone had spilled oil and neglected to clean it up.

Holding onto the railing attached to the midship house, he took baby steps back to the doorway, slipped inside, and slumped to the floor. It took a minute for his breathing to calm, during which time it occurred to him that he could've been seriously injured — a broken leg or worse. And what would have happened to him then? Would the company take care of him? Pay his medical expenses? Rehabilitation? The questions reminded him of Will Bailey and their discussion a few days earlier. He hadn't planned on going to the union meeting, hadn't figured it was his business, but now he had a clearer understanding of what Bailey was talking about.

He went to his locker, removed a pint of whiskey, and took a swig. The liquor warmed his insides and calmed his rattled nerves. He took a second swig, recapped the bottle, and stuffed it into his back pocket, then headed off to Bailey's bunkroom.

When he arrived a meeting was in progress. As before, Bailey sat on a three-legged stool talking to sailors seated on bunks around him. When Nick entered the bunkroom, the sailors looked up and stared at him with blank expressions as if they weren't sure he was a friend or foe.

Nick removed the bottle from his pocket and held it out. "I don't know if this is allowed, but if it is I'd like to offer it."

The faces softened and the men snuck glances at Bailey to gauge his reaction. Following their glances, Nick extended the bottle toward the oiler.

"Normally, I don't allow liquor," said Bailey, "it clouds the brain. But it is a nasty night and it certainly won't hurt to take a nip." He took the bottle and gestured toward an empty spot on one of the bunks.

As Nick sat down, he recognized Haggis, the burly arm wrestler from Captain Grays, and Moon Mullins, who nodded and winked. When the bottle was emptied and dispatched out the porthole, all eyes turned to Bailey who, wearing his sleeveless shirt, was sitting hunched over, his tattooed forearms resting on his knees.

"As you know, those of us who keep the engines running, who steer the ships, who maintain the equipment, who risk our lives in all kinds of weather, who eat the worst food and live in the closest quarters, are paid the least. In fact, our slice of the pie is a drop in the bucket compared to the owners' share. And the irony is, it's our dough that paid for this ship."

There it is again, Nick thought, *the same preposterous claim.* He glanced at the others to see if they were equally skeptical. When no one spoke up, he decided he couldn't let the comment go unchallenged. "I find that hard to believe. How could the likes of us pay for this ship?"

"I'm glad you asked, because it *is* hard to believe. The *Diana Dollar* was constructed by the United States Shippin' Board for the war effort. All told, they built three-thousand vessels at a cost of over three-billion dollars. Paid for by *our* taxes. But the amazin' thing is, the first of these ships didn't slide down the ways until a month *after* the armistice was signed. So none of this gigantic fleet ever saw a single day in battle."

Moon held his hands out palms up. "Why in blazes did they build so many ships after the war ended?"

"In two words, money and politics. Companies supplyin' products to the ship buildin' project lobbied the government to continue the operation despite the end of the war. And representatives from districts benefitin' from the project joined in as well. It was a juggernaut the politicians couldn't and didn't want to stop. They justified the whole thing by claimin' that America had to rebuild its merchant marine fleet destroyed in the war, but what they didn't say was that they were buildin' ten times the number of vessels that had been destroyed."

A driving rain drummed against the ship as it rolled from side to side, creaking and groaning.

"After the ships were built, the Shippin' Board established a regular overseas service. They hired private companies to sail the ships and paid them a percentage of gross revenues. Now understand, you can take in millions in gross revenues and still lose money if your operation is inefficient. And that's exactly what happened. The private operators had no incentive to run a tight business, so they raked in huge profits while the entire operation drained money from the gov'ment like water out of a bullet-riddled bucket."

Heads around the cabin shook in disbelief.

"The politicians couldn't ignore the red ink, so they scrapped about a third of the fleet and sold the rest for less than ten percent of what it cost to build 'em."

"Is that when the Dollar Company bought this ship?" Nick asked.

"That's right. Every West Coast shipper bought vessels at rock bottom prices. But that's not the end of the story. Not by a long shot."

He removed a pouch of tobacco from his pocket and deftly rolled a cigarette while the men looked on. He seemed to know that he had them hooked and took his time lighting the cigarette, then blew out a stream of smoke and continued.

"Even with this tremendous windfall, American shippers still claimed they couldn't compete with foreign lines, so they convinced the gov'ment to give 'em contracts to deliver mail to foreign ports. It sounds reasonable until you know that the contracts are based not on the amount of mail delivered but on the number of miles the ships sail. So, no matter how much mail the ships carry, or how little, shippers are paid a set amount. And it ain't peanuts."

An elderly sailor, chewing a chaw of tobacco that bulged his cheek, asked, "Is that why our ship usually sails to the Orient fully loaded but returns half empty?"

"That's right. Dollar makes money whether or not his ships carry an ounce of cargo. He's collected over nineteen million dollars in mail contracts and borrowed another ten million from the government at extremely low interest rates to buy more ships." Bailey then began enunciating each word slowly and distinctly as if talking to a child. "Now here's the kicker. The gov'ment and shippers justified this subsidy by claimin' that the operatin' expenses of foreign lines are much lower. To compete, they said, shippers needed mail subsidies in order to pay good wages to American seamen."

A burst of laughter filled the cabin, punctuated by sniggers and exclamations of disbelief.

The old sailor exclaimed, "Dollar should try livin' on thirty-six bucks a month. Hell, that probably don't pay his cigar bill."

The men laughed again, an edge of bitterness creeping into their mirth.

"That's an interesting history lesson, Bailey," said another sailor, "but what's it got to do with us? Ain't no politicians gonna offer us contracts. An if'n we make a stink about it, Dollar'll just dump us on the beach."

"If we don't make a stink about it," another man chimed in, "he'll go on getting fat while we eat scraps off the floor."

There was general agreement to this statement, and for several minutes the men offered various opinions about the situation and what could be done to fix it. While the discussion progressed, Bailey sat back and smoked his cigarette, observing it with an air of detachment.

Being new to the shipping industry, Nick remained silent, reluctant to express an opinion. Bailey gave him a conspiratorial wink as if to say, *it's alright, you're one of us now*, but Nick didn't feel that way and remained silent until a sailor wearing a knit cap and wool sweater turned to him and said, "Hey, Schoolboy, whatta you make of it?"

Looking at the faces around him, Nick wondered if he could possibly say anything that would add to the conversation. These men were lifelong sailors, hardworking, dedicated to the trade, with few other options. He, on the other hand, bore no commitment to the seafaring life and had no particular stake in it. Maybe Bailey was right. Maybe he was taking a job from someone who really deserved it, who really needed it. He felt like an imposter and wanted to slip away. But the men were looking at him with genuine interest, and he felt obliged to make some attempt at answering the question.

"I'd say you need to do your homework. Find out what's worked in the past and what hasn't. You younger fellows should listen to the older ones. You can learn from their failures as well as their successes. And the older fellows should listen to the younger ones and draw strength from their energy and enthusiasm."

Bailey reached into a duffle bag, removed a stack of pamphlets, and passed them around. "Here's some information about the Marine Workers Industrial Union, the new union for seafarin' men. It's like old Ben Franklin said, 'if we don't hang together, we'll surely hang separately.'"

The storm departed and once again the sea sparkled under a radiant sun. Nick continued to labor diligently, refraining from idle conversation and completing his assignments as inconspicuously as possible to appease the bosun and maximize his shore leave in Shanghai. One morning Slag sent him forward to the fo'c'sle to organize the storage locker, a grimy chamber lined with cubby holes crammed with tools, equipment, paints, and grease pots. A square opening in the floor led to another storage locker below. Lacking a porthole, the lower locker was dark and gloomy, so most crewmen avoided it and, instead, dropped tools and equipment into the square opening or onto the floor beside it.

Nick spent the first couple of hours organizing the equipment in the upper locker, separating the items to go below and dropping them through the opening. When this was done, he climbed down a ladder into the dim lower chamber, illuminated only by light from the square opening above. He had to grope around like a blind man until his eyes adjusted to the gloom. Then without a break, he worked for the rest of the morning and lost track of time in the absence of sunlight. When the noon bell announced the change of watch, he was wrestling a chain into a bin, its clattering links drowning out all other sounds.

A few minutes later footsteps shuffled into the upper chamber.

"It's about time you cleaned this pigsty," said a voice. Nick recognized the precise, clipped diction of Chief Primm.

"I had Benson work on it this morning," replied another voice, this one looser, gravelly, with a steel edge. The bosun. "Got him trained like a hurdy-gurdy monkey. Works twice as hard as the others and keeps to himself."

"Is he still about?"

Footsteps approached the square opening.

Having heard them talk about him, Nick wasn't keen on being discovered. He looked for a place to hide. A paint splattered tarpaulin lay on the floor nearby. He dropped down, slipped under the tarpaulin, and froze, hoping his presence wouldn't be noticeable.

"I can't see nothin'," said Slag. "Hand me that torchlight."

Through a gap under the tarp, Nick watched a beam of light zigzag across the floor, holding his breath while it crossed over the tarpaulin and scoured the rest of the chamber.

"He ain't in there," said the bosun, shuffling to his feet.

"All right, let's go over it again," said Primm. "Once the captain is ready, we'll show him to the other officers. After that, we'll have to keep him quarantined in his cabin. When the effect wears off, there's no telling what he'll say."

"Aaah, he'll be a loose anchor by then. The crew already knows he's ready for the scrap yard. They won't believe a thing he says. You worry too much."

"That's my job," snapped the chief. "If I don't see to the details, we'll be in hot water up to our eyeballs. Anyway, the old man's nearly blind, and he's been holed up in his cabin for days. If he makes any mistakes, the rest of us will sink with him, and I don't intend to see my career torpedoed by a washed-up schooner pilot."

"What makes you think they'll promote *you*?"

"Why wouldn't they? They'll need a master to complete the voyage. And once I'm acting captain, it's a cinch they'll keep me on. You'll get what you want, too. A hundred pounds will be plenty to set you up. You can stow it in the captain's quarters once I move in."

"Good. It's my only chance to break out of this racket. I've worked my fingers to the bone, and what do I got to show for it? Nothin' but a pair of sea legs and a permanent sunburn. If I don't get out now, I'll die on one of these rust buckets."

Nick heard what sounded like a foot kicking something, a tool perhaps. It skittered across the floor, fell into the square opening, tripped down the ladder, and landed squarely on his hip. A sharp pain dug into his hip, causing him to groan.

"Did you hear that?" said Primm.

"What? The wrench hitting floor?"

"No. It sounds like someone's down there."

"I don't think so, but you're welcome to check."

Footsteps approached the square opening, and once again a beam of light zigzagged across the floor and up over the tarpaulin. Nick held his breath, hoping they'd think his groan was the wrench landing on the tarp with a dull thud instead of banging onto the floor.

"I guess you're right," the chief said. "Anyway, just remember, if we do this right you won't have to step onboard a ship again. Just make sure you do your part."

With that their footsteps shuffled back across the locker and through the door.

Nick stayed under the tarpaulin to make sure the conspirators were gone for good. While waiting, he reviewed the conversation. *Once the captain is ready . . . when the effect wears off . . . a hundred pounds will be enough to set you up.* The information was frustratingly vague, yet one thing was clear: the chief and the bosun were plotting to get rid of Captain Harding so Primm could take his place. And once Harding was gone, Primm would allow Slag to hide some sort of contraband in the captain's cabin that the bosun could sell when they returned home.

It reminded Nick of something his grandfather once said: *Chief mates are the most dissatisfied men aboard ship. They've dreamed their whole life of becoming captain, and now they're close . . . but not there yet.*

12

A disembodied voice summoned Clarisa over the intercom, startling her the way she imagined Moses must have been startled when God spoke to him from out of the blue. She gathered her notepad and pen and headed toward Mr. Farnsworth's office. She sometimes thought of her boss as a dedicated, hardworking executive, other times a charming, jazz-loving night owl. No matter how she thought of him, though, she always treated him with professional deference at the office, both to hide their budding friendship and to keep it from interfering with their work.

A man of about thirty was seated in front of Mr. Farnsworth's desk. His right arm cradled in a cotton sling.

"Mr. Gibbs," said Farnsworth , "this is my secretary, Miss McMahon." Gibbs stood up and reached over with his left hand to shake hers. His forehead was broad and bulbous and loomed over a small nose and mouth. "Mr. Gibbs is an investigator with the Pinkerton Agency. He'll be giving us a report. As you can see, he's unable to write it himself, so we'll need you to take notes." They all sat down. "Alright, Gibbs, let's get started."

"Well, sir, yesterday morning I went to the waterfront opposite the Ferry Building, you know, where the men gather for the shape-up."

"The shape-up?" Clarisa asked.

"Yes, ma'am. That's where they hire prospectors to work at the docks."

"Prospectors?"

"It's what they call dockworkers hired off the street for the day."

Farnsworth added, "About a third of the stevedores on any given day are prospectors. The rest work on regular gangs."

Clarisa's eyebrows lifted as she jotted a note.

"Do you have another question?"

She shook her head. "No. That's all."

"Were you dressed in work clothes, Gibbs?"

"Yes."

"Used ones?"

"No, sir. I don't have used work clothes. I bought an outfit at one of those cheap john shops on Front Street."

Farnsworth frowned. "Okay, go on."

"About six-hundred prospectors were there. I went around tryin' to pick up information, but didn't find out much till this guy showed up carryin' a bundle of newspapers like the one you showed me."

Gibbs pulled a copy out of his coat pocket and laid it on Farnsworth's desk. It looked to be about four pages, mimeographed on legal-sized paper and stapled at the corner. A crude hand-drawn masthead at the top of the front page depicted a freighter berthed at a pier with the title WATERFRONT WORKER imposed on the illustration. The text below was typed in columns divided by uneven hand-drawn lines.

"He was sellin' 'em for a penny a piece, sayin' it was the straight dope on how to improve workin' conditions. No more slave mart, bully bosses, speed-up. That sorta thing."

Clarisa looked up. "Sorry, but I want to make sure I write this down correctly. Slave mart?"

"It's a term the radicals use for the morning shape-up," said Roger.

Clarisa's brow lifted again as she recorded the information.

"The men snapped up the papers," Gibbs continued, "and when any-one said they couldn't afford a penny, the guy just gave it to 'em. I bought a copy and asked him if I could help distribute it. He looks me up and down and asks if I'm a longshoreman. 'You bet.' I sez. So he told me to stick around. Said he'd introduce me to the fellow he gets 'em from.

"At seven o'clock the hirin' boss came over from the Ferry Building. When he got close, the men ran out and crowded around him like a litter of squealin' puppies. It was quite a scene, and for awhile he just stood there while guys stuffed dollar bills and bottles of hooch in his pocket." He glanced at Clarisa. "Pretty nice racket, huh?"

Busy jotting notes, she didn't reply.

"Anyway, a coupla cops pushed the men back off the street and ordered 'em to shape-up. They formed a half-circle around the hirin' boss and waited while he picked out guys and sent 'em off to the docks. In all, he hired about two-hundred men. Of the ones left, some took off to scout other docks, while the rest said they'd stick around in case someone broke a leg or somethin' and a job opened up."

Clarisa's brow shot up again, prompting Roger to hold out a hand to halt the report.

"Is there something wrong, Miss McMahon?"

Clarisa looked up from her notes. "Why do you ask?"

"Your eyebrows are bouncing up and down like a Sunday morning congregation. It's really quite annoying. Do you think you could keep them in their place?"

This was the first time her boss had said anything to her that was remotely critical, and she wasn't sure how to react. She certainly wasn't in any position to challenge him but couldn't hide her disgust.

"I shall try," she replied, enunciating each word with stiff restraint, "although I don't see why my eyebrows should bother you. Unless, of course, you find Mr. Gibb's description of the shape-up as distasteful as I do."

Roger sighed. "Look, I wish we could hire all of them full-time. But the fact is, cargo through the port has declined by thirty percent, and half the prospectors are drifters and dust bowl refugees without a lick of experience. There just isn't enough work to go around, and our members aren't running charities."

Gibbs glanced back and forth between Roger and Clarisa, who stared at one another as though engaged in a silent test of wills.

Roger was the first to break off eye contact. "Alright, Gibbs, continue."

"I was waitin' for the newspaper guy when a stevedore wearing an eye patch jumped up on a box and read out loud an article in the *Waterfront Worker*. It was about a walkin' boss named Big Load Thompson, about how he yells at the men to speed things up and doesn't care if they get hurt. When the guy with the eye patch finished — they called him Pirate Larsen — he said it would be poetic justice if one of those big loads fell on Thompson. That really tickled the men.

"Then a fella wearin' a suit and tie showed up and called everyone together. Said he's startin' a local chapter of the International Longshoremen's Association. Accordin' to a new law, he said, they don't have to stay in the Blue Book Union no more. Now they're free to join any union they want."

"Did you get his name?"

Gibbs reached into his coat pocket and drew out a notepad. He leafed through it. "Here it is: Holman, Lee Holman."

"Go on."

"Holman saw a copy of the *Waterfront Worker* and said it was a no-good Commie rag. Said that no self-respectin', red-blooded stevedore would be caught dead readin' it. He told 'em if they join up with the Reds, they'll be takin' orders from Moscow, but if they want to join a bona-fide American union, they'd better sign up with the ILA and pay their fifty-cent dues."

"Excuse me," Clarisa said. "ILA?"

"International Longshoremen's Association," Roger explained. "It's headquartered in New York and affiliated with the American Federation of Labor. Go on, Gibbs."

"About an hour later, the newspaper guy returned and said he's gonna take me to see the guy who runs it. We went to an empty lot on Howard Street with tall weeds growin' in the back. I followed him in till I smelled a set-up. I stopped and told him to bring the guy out where I could see him. He said it was a big secret who this guy is and there's no way he could show his face in public. I shoulda listened to my instincts. When we got to the back of the lot, two guys jumped out from behind the weeds and started sockin' me pretty good. I managed to get away, and as I ran off they yelled that the next spy they caught wouldn't get off so easy" He held up his sprained arm. "I guess I was lucky to get outta there with this."

"Can you give us a description of them?" Roger asked.

"Oh, yeah. One guy was —."

"Good." Roger stood up. "Go out to the reception area and give it to Mrs. Butterfield. She'll forward it to Miss McMahon so she can include it in your report."

As soon as Gibbs left, Roger raised his hands in the air and flopped them down in a gesture of disgust. "What an idiot. He didn't fool them for a second." He went to the window behind his desk and looked down at the waterfront. "What we need is someone with calluses on his hands *and* a brain in his head, someone we can trust." He turned to Clarisa. "Your friend, the sailor, he graduated from Berkeley, right?" She nodded. "When's he due back?"

"Not for another six weeks, but he's never worked as a longshoreman."

"Doesn't matter. Lots of stevedores used to be sailors. As long as he doesn't try to pretend he's an experienced stevedore, they'll accept him. It'll take time, of course, but it's doable."

Clarisa shook her head. "I doubt he'd go along with it. Besides, he and I aren't exactly on speaking terms right now. You should probably recruit someone already working on the waterfront."

"Maybe you're right. I'll call Emile Stone at the Blue Book Union. One of his men might take this on." He sat down and rubbed his forehead. "I never thought I'd be recruiting spies. But Plant thinks the labor situation could get ugly, and if it does, we'll need information."

Clarisa recalled a similar warning from Father Shannon. "Do you think it will get ugly?"

"I don't know, possibly. In the last few months waterfront strikes have broken out in Baltimore, New Orleans, and Boston, not to mention a coal miners' strike in West Virginia and a steel lockout in Pittsburgh. Discontent is sweeping the country, and there's no reason to believe we're immune here on the Coast."

Clarisa straightened her posture, ready to leave. "Is there anything else before I type this up?"

Roger picked up his cigarette case, turned it over in his hands, and set it back down. "Look, I'm sorry about the eyebrow remark. I've been a bit jumpy lately. We've warned our members about the seriousness of the waterfront situation, but it hasn't sunk in yet."

Clarisa felt vindicated — and also sympathetic. Not many men would apologize so forthrightly to a subordinate, especially a woman. "Apology accepted. I meant no offense. I've heard things weren't so good at the waterfront, but like most people I didn't know the details."

Roger was visibly relieved. "Listen, I've got to go to a formal party at the Dollar mansion. I expect it'll be a tedious affair, and you know me, I'd rather be cutting a rug at Purcell's. If you were to come as my escort, however, it would certainly improve the situation."

Clarisa looked down at her skirt. She was receptive to another evening with her boss, but to be so open about it was cause for concern. If Mr. Plant saw them together, he might suspect that Roger was fraternizing with the help.

"Do you really think it's a good idea?" she said. "Once our friendship is out in the open, it'll be impossible to sweep back under the rug."

"Oh, God. You're not worried about appearances as if we're characters in a Jane Austen novel? This is the twentieth century."

"That may be, but office relationships between men and women, even if innocent, are not considered appropriate. If Mr. Plant were to discover that you and I were seeing each other socially, he'd probably fire one of us, and it wouldn't be you."

Once the words were out, she wondered if their relationship *was* so innocent. She sensed her boss wanted something more, something closer. But men were prone to infatuations that could evaporate in an instant, and she had no intention of becoming a fleeting fling for an executive off on a slummer. What bothered her more, though, was her own uncertainty. *Am I suppressing a budding affection in order to deny its existence? In order to protect my job and, just as important, my heart?*

While she mulled over the invitation and all the thorny issues it raised, Roger leaned back and took a cigarette from his case. He was about to light it when he stopped. "I've got it. I'll tell Plant that when I'm out of town on business, you'll have to deal with our members directly. It would be good for you to meet them informally, so they'll come to trust you the way I have."

Trust. The word reminded Clarisa of Father Shannon and the advice he gave her: *There's no telling what you'll learn, and, Lord knows, salvation and redemption come in many forms.* A spasm of guilt shot through her. She did her best to suppress it and hoped it wasn't noticeable. After all, she hadn't done anything to compromise the trust Roger placed in her. Far from it.

"Do you think Plant will believe it?" she asked.

"I don't see why not," said Roger, radiating a confidence that Clarisa, despite her cautious nature, found attractive and reassuring.

13

The *Diana Dollar* steamed south toward the East China Sea, the air warmer now and humid, the sea less deep blue, more plankton green. Nick continued to work diligently, chipping loose paint, applying primer and top coat, polishing brass, manning the helm, standing watch, and overall giving the bosun no cause to harangue him but keeping his eyes and ears open for any sign of betrayal.

After he overheard Primm and Slag discuss their mutinous plot, his first impulse was to report it to Captain Harding, who would surely want to know of a plan to depose him. Then, upon further consideration, he realized he would be putting the captain in a difficult position. An unsubstantiated accusation of mutiny, a serious charge which the two plotters would surely deny, would make the captain appear paranoid and Nick himself vindictive against a tough boss. Until he had something substantial to offer, some tangible proof, it would be unwise to reveal what he knew.

He discussed the situation with Moon, who offered to break into the chief's cabin to see if they could find the drug Primm was planning to use to incapacitate the captain, if that was his plan. Nick was sorely tempted but rejected the offer. Entering an officer's cabin without authorization was a serious offence. If they were caught, they would be fired and left high and dry in Shanghai.

He also mentioned the mutinous plot to Cook. If there was any scuttlebutt about it, Cook would catch wind of it first. Nick didn't ask him to spread the story but figured Cook would drop hints about it, and those hints would likely reach Slag and Primm, who might decide to call off their plan if they thought it was common knowledge.

A high-pitched whistle roused Nick from sleep one morning He hadn't heard this particular whistle before and wondered what it meant. He waited a couple of minutes. When nothing happened, he concluded that if the whistle indicated something important, someone would tell him. The gentle motion of the ship, rocking side to side like a bassinet, drew him back into a pleasant slumber. Not for long, though. The whistle blew again and then a few minutes later a third time. It seemed to be going off at regular intervals, and if its purpose was to keep him from sleeping it was doing a damn good job. He also noticed something else, or rather the absence of it. Aside from the whistle there was no other sound, no vibration from the ship's engine, no shuffling feet in the passageway, no chipping hammers beating on the deck, nothing but a strange dead silence.

He propped himself up on his elbows. The light in the cabin was dim, unusually so, and Moon and Remy were gone. He jumped down from his bunk, slipped on his clothes, and stepped out into the passageway. It was empty and quiet. *Where is everyone?* Perhaps in the messroom. He headed off in that direction, and on the way he passed a porthole and glanced out at . . . *Nothing?* No sea. No sky. No sun. Nothing but an impenetrable gray wall that matched the color of the ship. He stopped, rubbed his eyes, and looked out again. Still nothing. As he stared out at the gray world, he felt a pang of loneliness, and for a moment he imagined he was the only person onboard, hundreds of miles from land with no hope of seeing another living soul. *The Diana Dollar was found adrift at sea, abandoned save for the skeleton of one poor sailor left behind.*

A creeping fear gripped him. He was awake — there was no doubt about that — yet it felt like a nightmare. He stepped out of the midship house and peered into the gray matter. It was everywhere, all around him, as if he was embedded in the brain of some immense creature. Faint sounds accompanied the silence, the soft purl of waves lapping against the hull, a sinister creak from somewhere inside the ship. He looked toward the bow and could just make out the nearest kingpost, now a misty apparition. Beyond that the ship disappeared, swallowed by the gray matter.

Eeeeeeeeeeeeeee!

The high-pitched whistle pierced the silence again, and also dislodged a memory: *When the cold Oya Current meets the warmer Kuro, the moisture in the air congeals into a fog so dense you can't see the bow from the wheelhouse. You have to stop, drop the deep-sea anchor, and wait until the fog lifts.* Ahh. Now he understood. The whistle was a warning to other ships reckless enough to sail in this pea soup that they'd better steer clear.

He found the crew gathered in the messroom, speaking in low tones as if they too felt an oppressive loneliness in the smothering fog. Apparently he'd overslept, lulled by the gentle rock of the ship. He sat down beside Moon and Remy, who were playing pinochle. It wasn't their favorite game but gambling wasn't allowed and poker games only occurred in cabins when officers weren't snooping around. No one knew how long the fog would last — a few hours, a few days, on rare occasions a week or more. Beyond that, Nick couldn't get much out of his shipmates, though he understood why. The gray blanket had deprived them of light and blue sky and something to do other than sit around and wait for it to lift. Worst of all, it was holding them hostage just when Shanghai was just a few days away. Ever since they'd put to sea, the men had recounted colorful stories about the fabled city, its exotic fleshpots, lively watering holes, mysterious opium dens, colorful back streets and alleys. And it was dreams like these that kept them in high spirits and from feeling like rats trapped in a cage.

If the sailors were glum the first fog-bound day, they were in a worse mood the next, grumbling and muttering and moping about like grounded teenagers. Nick wrote in his journal to pass the time and checked in with Cook every few hours to see if he'd heard any news about the mutineers. So far, though, things were quiet. *Too quiet?* And he began to wonder if Primm and Slag had abandoned their plan or hatched some other plot.

On the evening of the second day, a loud wail erupted in the passageway, sounding like a coyote's howl combined with the cry of an injured child. Moments later a spate of footsteps pounded on the floor. Nick peeked out of his cabin to see what was going on just as a sailor ran by, his face contorted in fear as if he was being chased by a ghost. Not far behind, two sailors were running after him.

"What's wrong?" Nick yelled.

"He's gone berserk," said one of the sailors.

When they caught up with the crazed man, they tried to hold him down, but he fought them off, yelling and screaming as if they were torturing him. Nick and Moon ran out to lend assistance. After a short scuffle they were able to take hold of the wild man's limbs and carry him to the sickbay cabin. Paul Conner, the third mate, arrived and shoved a sedative into his mouth, then clamped it shut until he swallowed it. The sailor eventually calmed down and fell asleep as if the ordeal had drained him of all his energy.

It was an odd incident, and after much discussion it was generally agreed that the dense fog had unhinged the sailor and driven him to distraction until he cracked.

The following day the ordeal was repeated in a strangely identical way. First a screaming wail, then a wild-eyed sailor (this one the young blond from the engine department) running down the passageway, face contorted in fear. The chase, the capture, the sedative. The unstable fellow was put into sickbay with the first one, who after a long sleep was groggy but appeared to have recovered.

After the second incident, and with heavy fog still holding the ship hostage, the crew was on edge, and it wasn't long before they were glancing at each other suspiciously, looking for signs of madness. Who would be next? Who would go berserk?

Captain Harding was nowhere to be seen; he'd been holed up in his cabin since fog descended on the ship. Chief Primm, who in the absence of the captain had assumed his duties, kept both men confined to sickbay, saying that until the fog lifted he couldn't be sure they wouldn't have a relapse.

The entire crew was anxious now, waiting for the next man to crack. One sailor was so touchy that when another man accidently bumped into him, he accused him of doing it on purpose and shoved him hard. If others hadn't separated them, it would have come to blows.

The situation was feeling desperate, like a powder keg ready to blow, and it didn't help that Harding hadn't been seen for days.

On the third fog-bound day, Nick was afraid that something had happened to the captain, that Primm and Slag might have drugged him and were keeping him incapacitated so he couldn't communicate with the crew. It was time, he decided, to see if the old man was alright.

He knocked on the captain's door.

A pause. "Yes?"

"Benson, sir."

A weary sigh. "Come."

The cabin was stale and musty as if it hadn't been aired for days, the bed unmade, ashtray overflowing. Harding sat at his desk, staring at the painting of the *Julia Ann* mounted on the bulkhead in front of him. His face was covered with stubble, and the hand holding his briar pipe trembled slightly, his other hand absently stroking his Van Dyke beard.

Nick sat down in the chair beside his desk.

The captain's eyes remained fixed on the painting. "There is nothing more graceful or awe inspiring than a windjammer in full sail. It's like a great billowing cloud floating over the waves." He glanced at Nick. "I feel sorry for those of you who will never have a chance to see a three-master in full flight with top gallants set, a spanker over the quarterdeck, three jibs on the bowsprit, and skysails taut from the trades. You can't imagine how proud it makes the crew, from the captain down to the cabin boy." He set the pipe down and took off his glasses, wiped them with a kerchief, then put them on and gazed at the painting again. "Sure, life was tougher. You're at the mercy of the elements. One day you're stuck in the doldrums, the next day heeled over to the bulwarks. And sometimes we had to tack a thousand miles to make five hundred toward our destination. Every day was a challenge, everyday an adventure.

"But the sailors, oh my goodness." His face brightened and it seemed to Nick that remembrances of the past were passing before his eyes. "To watch them scramble up the rigging and leap from yardarm to yardarm, then slide down the stays like acrobats. It's truly a magnificent sight. They took such pride in their work, each man trying to outdo the other, each watch trying to out-sail the last." He paused, sighed, and turned to Nick. "What's on your mind, son?"

Nick was glad to see Harding in reasonably good shape and apparently in full control of his faculties. While listening to the captain, he decided it would be better to tell him everything before Primm and Slag made their move, before it was too late. And perhaps it would encourage the old man to come out of his cabin and show the crew who was in charge. He repeated the conversation he overhead in the foc'sle and explained why he hadn't reported it earlier, and why he decided to report it now even though he had no solid evidence.

"The men are in a terrible state, sir. They need your leadership."

The captain sighed again. "You're right, they do need leadership."

"So you'll be coming out, sir."

"I'm afraid not, son."

"What? Why not?"

Harding stroked his beard. "After we hit the fog bank, Primm came to me and claimed that things had gotten out of control. The men were spooked, he said. One man had gone berserk and a union organizer was exhorting the crew to take over the ship."

Nick gasped. "That's a lie."

"Then he said I was an incompetent master and tried to bully me into turning over my command. I was outraged, of course, and threatened to lock him up for mutiny, but he said all the officers felt the same way. None of them wanted to serve under me any longer. I was so upset I couldn't sleep or eat. The next night another sailor had some sort of psychotic breakdown. Afterwards, the chief threatened me again, saying the situation was intolerable."

The captain pinched a wad of tobacco from a leather pouch, tamped it into the pipe bowl, and struck a match, his hand trembling as he held the flame over the bowl. He drew in a breath, bending the flame down into the bowl, and puffed several times, igniting the tobacco into an orange coal. "It was such a strange state of affairs, what with the ship swamped in fog and the crew as jumpy as fleas on a dog's tail. I suspected that Primm had something to do with it, but to be honest, I wasn't sure he was wrong. I've known for a long time that my days on this ship were numbered. This might've been my last voyage anyway."

"So what happened?"

"I agreed to resign when we reach Shanghai. He made me do it in front of the other officers so I couldn't recant afterwards."

Nick was stunned — both at the news of the captain's resignation as well as the realization that by not reporting the conversation earlier he may have helped the mutineers. Primm and Slag must have discovered that their secret plot wasn't so secret and changed their strategy. And in the end it worked out better for them. With the captain leaving voluntarily, they avoided the possibility of an investigation. He rubbed the back of his neck. "Isn't there any way we can expose them?"

The captain shook his head. "I hate to disappoint you, son, but I'd rather not fight it. I'm too old and too tired to deal with a bulldog like Primm nipping at my heels. A master can't effectively command his ship without the support of his officers. Believe me, I know." He nodded toward the painting. "I'm really a windjammer captain masquerading as a steamer skipper. It's time I joined your grandfather reminiscing about the good ol' days."

Nick was deeply disappointed that he hadn't prevented Primm and Slag from deposing the captain, and he was certain that the two sailors who went berserk had been drugged as part of the plot. He also felt sorry for Harding, who had sailed all his life, risen to the rank of captain, and now was being tossed off his own ship like a worn out spark plug, just the way Bailey said.

14

"These are the times that try a father's soul," said Seamus McMahon, paraphrasing Thomas Paine, the great firebrand of the American Revolution.

Clarisa had just announced her intention to attend a soiree at the Dollar mansion, and now, as she set their dinner on the table, Seamus was lecturing her on the evils of parasitic capitalists, equivalent in his judgment to the British occupiers of Northern Ireland. She wasn't surprised by his reaction. Nor was she without a strategy to deflect it. When he finished, she calmly yet firmly explained that it was a work-related event, requiring her attendance. She had no choice but to attend.

Seamus wasn't convinced. For some time he'd dropped hints that he suspected her relationship with her boss had crossed the line from professional to personal. He'd never made a direct accusation, but every day, as if to remind her where her loyalty should lay, he asked if she'd received any word from Nick Benson.

"Any news, luv?" he said, scooping up a forkful of noodles.

"About what?" Clarisa replied, knowing full well his meaning.

"You know, the sailor who's working hard to bring a stake back to his one true love."

"I'm sure I don't know who you're talking about, because I haven't heard from any sailor and don't expect to."

"You will, luv." He patted her cheek affectionately. "Have patience. You will."

Clarisa wasn't as confident as her father. It had been weeks since Nick's first and only letter arrived. Since then she'd sorted through the mail each day with anticipation, but her expectations had diminished as each day proved as barren as the last.

When Saturday evening arrived, Roger Farnsworth appeared on her doorstep looking as handsome and debonair as a fashion ad in *Collier's Magazine*. Clad in a black tuxedo, matching cummerbund, and patent leather shoes, he cut an elegant figure, and as usual his golden mane was perfectly cut, oiled, and combed back in parallel lines. His hazel eyes widened when she opened the door, her slender figure wrapped in a blue satin strapless gown and matching shoulder wrap, her neck ringed with a string of pearls, hands covered in white kid gloves up to her elbows.

Unaccustomed to seeing each other in such stylish attire, both of them stared in silence until Roger found his voice. "You look sensational."

Clarisa smiled and spun around, the hem of her gown twirling and shimmering in the late afternoon light. She didn't have the money for such elegant gown but was fortunate to have a good friend who worked at a consignment shop on Fillmore Street who loaned her the ensemble. As she spun around, her auburn hair flew out behind her, then settled on her shoulders as she came to a stop.

Roger held out an arm. "Shall we make a night of it, my princess?"

She attached herself to his arm. "It does feel like a fairy tale. But I must warn you, I'm a complete fake. The gown, the shoes, the jewelry, everything's borrowed. I'm just a poor girl pretending to be a Vanderbilt."

Roger put a hand over hers. "Not to worry. Everyone else attending the soiree isn't more than two or three generations from scraping cow dung off their shoes. They may act like royalty, but, believe me, they're pretending too. Besides" — his eyes traveled up and down her form-fitting gown — "you'll be the belle of the ball."

They floated across the sidewalk toward the Stutz convertible shined to a gleaming finish. It was a magic moment, and everything around them seemed soft and fuzzy as if they were in a Hollywood movie.

A group of students from the Workers School next door stood nearby watching them. The students could have been extras in their movie, but these extras, frowning at the Stutz, seemed to be from a different sort of movie.

"Hey, rich boy," one of them called out, "where'd you get the jalopy? Your daddy buy it for you?" The others snickered.

Roger opened the car door for Clarisa, who, as she sat down, she gave him a smile of encouragement, hoping their magic moment wouldn't be spoiled. He shut the door, pivoted around, and faced the students. They all wore shapeless cotton trousers and open-collared shirts. A wry smile crept over Roger's face, showing his contempt. "Nietzsche says there are those who can't improve their lot, who become jealous and embittered and obsessed with taking away from others what they can't create for themselves. He called them tarantulas, and I expect he was talking about you."

The students stared blankly, apparently not expecting to hear the German philosopher Nietzsche quoted by a tuxedo-wearing rich boy.

A tall fellow with a thin aquiline nose stepped forward. "Easy for you to say. You've got yours while the rest of us struggle to pay rent."

A murmur of agreement rippled through the group. A pencil flew out of the group toward the Stutz, pinged off the front fender, and landed on the sidewalk.

Clarisa was certain no good would come from the exchange. "Let's go," she said.

Roger continued to stare defiantly at the students. Another pencil hit the car and landed at his feet. He shook his head in disgust. "You think everyone who has money is the enemy? Well, you're wrong. I'm not the enemy. You're your own worst enemy because you have no idea how to make something of yourselves. You'd rather hate me because of my success. And that makes you no better than fascists."

The thin nosed student took another step forward, fists clenched. "Whatta you know about fascists? Why I aughta teach you a lesson. Go back to Nob Hill, before I —." He stepped forward, the others close behind.

Clarisa jumped out of the car and slipped in front of Roger, her wrap trailing on the ground. She faced the students, her fists planted on her hips. "Stop it! Both of you. This is crazy." She glanced back at Roger. "Get in the car." While he sauntered around the Stutz and settled into the driver's seat, she held the students at bay with a stern gaze.

"Say, aren't you Seamus's daughter?" the thin nosed student asked. "You oughtn't to be consorting with the enemy."

"I'll consort with whomever I like," Clarisa retorted. "You should be ashamed of yourselves. You're acting like a mob."

When the car door shut, she gathered up her wrap, draped it over her shoulders, and climbed into the convertible. Roger revved the engine and rammed the stick shift into gear, grinding the transmission. As the Stutz took off, one of the students spat on the hood, while the others jeered and yelled insults.

"I'm sorry," said Clarisa. "I've never seen them act so foolishly."

Roger gripped the steering wheel and swerved the Stutz onto Market Street, tires squealing.

Clarisa glanced at him. "I hope you're not going to let them ruin the whole evening."

"They don't bother me. Their kind are boringly predictable."

Clarisa was puzzled. *Is he upset with me for taking control of the situation? If I hadn't, who knows what would have happened.* Men could be such nincompoops. And not for the first time she wondered why their egos were so enormous, yet so fragile.

The cool evening breeze whistled against the windshield and tousled her hair. Roger turned onto Van Ness Avenue and sped past City Hall, its magnificent dome shrouded in fog. Feeling a chill, Clarisa pulled the wrap down over her shoulders.

At Hyde Street Pier Roger parked behind a line of cars waiting to board the Sausalito ferry. A short time later the *Eureka* ferry approached the pier, its side-mounted paddle wheels churning in reverse, slowing the vessel as it glided into its slip. Once the vehicles from Marin County rolled off and sped away, the line of cars drove on. Roger and Clarisa got out of the Stutz and climbed up a companionway to the top deck. The ferry's paddle wheels began to turn, sloshing water and pushing the *Eureka* out of its slip and into the bay. They stood at the railing and looked out at the Golden Gate, now covered by a great billowing fog bank that hugged the water like a giant dust cloud. The front edge of the fog was splintered into wispy fingers that divided the sunlight into slanting rays, forming luminous pools of light on the water.

Looking into the fog bank, Clarisa imagined the ocean beyond it, stretching mile after mile after mile. Somewhere on that ocean a freighter was steaming away from her, taking Nick farther away. She pictured him on its fo'c'sle deck, squinting into the setting sun, looking forward to new destinations, new adventures. *Is he getting used to life at sea? Even liking it? Will he want to continue sailing after this voyage and give up what we had?* At the moment nothing seemed certain, and it gave her an uneasy feeling. Part of her still loved him, still craved his affection, but already her love seemed to have diminished, at least a bit. And given enough time it might reduce down to . . . well, who knows.

"Sorry about my boorish behavior," said Roger.

His words pulled her into the present. Her questions about Nick, though, remained. She glanced at Roger. He was about the same size as Nick, had a similar athletic build. Both were smart and attractive. Both were —. She stopped herself. It didn't seem right to hold them up side by side as if she was trying to decide which dress to wear. She brushed her thoughts aside. "Apology accepted."

"I'm just not used to being ordered about —." His voice trailed off.

"By a woman?"

"And a subordinate at that."

"Only at work."

"Right," he said, giving her a meaningful look that implied a world of possibilities, "and in no way do I want this evening to resemble work."

His suggestive comment prompted Clarisa to ponder the situation. Tonight would be their — what? — fourth evening out, and still she wasn't sure what their after-work relationship was. Or, for that matter, if she wanted a relationship at all. He'd been a perfect gentlemen and a delightful companion. Yet it was clear from his lingering glances and flattering compliments that he wanted more than an occasional date. Of course, it would be simple if he weren't her boss; she could be far less cautious.

"Look," said Roger, pointing to an enormous concrete monolith on the San Francisco side of the Golden Gate, towering several stories high and surrounded by scaffolding. "That's where they'll tether the suspension cables for the bridge, and, there"—he pointed to an identical structure on the opposite side of the Golden Gate—"is the other one."

Clarisa recalled the ground-breaking ceremony for the bridge earlier that year. She attended with Nick and his grandfather, thinking it would be a low-key affair, and was surprised to see two-hundred thousand others at Crissy Field, along with an army of vendors hawking pennants, programs, and commemorative pins.

The ceremony began when three sky-writing planes buzzed over the Golden Gate, leaving trails of smoke where the bridge would one day stand. Mayor Rossi stood on a temporary stage and read a telegram from ex-President Hoover, heralding the project as "a bridge between golden dreams and a new world of progress and prosperity." This inspired one heckler to yell, "What the hell does the guy who gave us Hoovervilles know about prosperity?" A reference to hobo encampments on the outskirts of towns, occupied by the unemployed and their families.

Curiously, Rune was put out by the whole affair. "Why would anyone want to cross the Golden Gate in a cramped steel contraption when they could stand on the deck of a ship and enjoy the view with the wind in their face?"

At the time Clarisa thought he was a grumpy curmudgeon, but now, with breezes caressing her cheeks and sunbeams streaming through the fog, she had to admit he had a point.

The ferry reached Sausalito and docked near the Northwest Pacific rail terminal. Roger drove onto the State Highway, a two-lane road leading north over a series of wooden trestles spanning brackish inlets and reed-covered marshes. Beyond the trestles, the road continued over rolling hills covered with golden grass and dotted with live oaks. The air grew steadily warmer and smelled of dried grass and sun-baked earth, a welcome change from San Francisco's chilly breezes. Clarisa took several deep breaths, and with each breath and with the late afternoon sun kissing her face, the cares of the city melted away, leaving her feeling as if she was suspended in a warm bath.

Ten miles north of Sausalito, in the town of San Rafael, Roger steered the Stutz up a long circular driveway flanked by an expansive lawn and flowering azaleas. At the top of the driveway they came to a stop in front of a Victorian mansion with a roofline of intersecting gables and a covered porch that curved around the side of the house. A handsome young valet, about eighteen years old, opened the passenger door and assisted Clarisa out of the car. As she alighted, he smiled at her in a way that made her feel wonderfully attractive in her pearls and blue satin gown, and it also calmed the apprehension she'd been feeling about facing a room full of "parasitic capitalists."

Roger slipped an arm around her waist and guided her up the front steps to the covered porch. The front door was open, allowing the sweet fragrance of gardenias to waft out from inside. They entered a spacious six-sided foyer paneled with redwood and burled ash. The buzz of lively conversation emanated from a room off to their right. Heading in that direction, they came to a great room, in which guests were sipping champagne and nibbling hors d'oeuvres served by maids in black dresses and white aprons.

A plump, gray-haired woman wearing an old-fashioned beaded dress broke away from a cluster of guests and approached them. She was short and rather frumpish, with a wide peasant nose and a warm welcoming smile. "It's been ages, Roger," she said, extending her arms and embracing him. "Welcome to Falkirk."

Roger gestured toward Clarisa. "Mrs. Dollar, may I present Miss McMahon."

"A pleasure to meet you, my dear."

Clarisa immediately felt at ease with her host, who appeared to be a pleasant, guileless woman, not the haughty blue-blood she feared. "Falkirk?" she asked.

"My late husband, Robert, was born in Falkirk, Scotland and, well, once a Scotsman always a Scotsman." Her face lit up. "My, you two make a handsome couple and we are a bit on the older side tonight, so it'll be nice to have a few young faces to liven things." She escorted them into the great room, paneled in redwood up to a lofty ceiling with box beams and crown moldings. Summoning a maid with a tray of champagne glasses, she handed them each a glass. "We're celebrating my granddaughter Diana's birthday. She's eighteen and quite a beautiful girl."

That would be Diana Dollar, Clarisa surmised, the namesake of the ship Nick was on.

Mrs. Dollar studied them with a curious expression. "Have you two known each other long?"

"A month or two," Roger replied.

"A budding romance?" she asked, arching an eyebrow.

Roger remained silent, leaving Clarisa to wonder if that was where they were headed. It seemed both possible and impossible, tempting and out of the question.

"Oh, don't answer that," Mrs. Dollar said. "Whatever you two are up to, I wish you the best." She looked beyond them. "Ah, the Grants are here. Do excuse me." She smiled and headed off toward the new arrivals.

Sipping their champagne, Roger and Clarisa observed the other guests, many of whom Clarisa recognized from meetings at the office or pictures in the society pages of the newspaper. Wives favored printed chiffons and crepes in summer shades of fuchsia and yellow. Their husbands were uniformly clad in black tuxedos, starched shirts, and black ties. Several men were standing near a punch bowl, huddled around a short gentleman with a fringe of gray hair, a Fuller brush mustache, and an impish grin.

"Isn't that —." she whispered to Roger.

"Governor Rolph. I'll introduce you later."

Above a large tiled fireplace hung the portrait of a gaunt, white-haired gentleman with a goatee beard and a schoolmaster's stern expression. Clarisa gestured toward it. "Robert Dollar?"

Roger nodded. "Founder of the Dollar Steamship Line, and the most driven shipper that ever lived. He started as a cabin boy in Scotland and worked his way to Canada where he learned the lumber business. He migrated to California, bought redwood land up north, and acquired a small packet boat to ship his lumber to market. From that humble beginning, he built the largest steamship line under U.S. flag. He died last year at the age of 93, and now his two sons, Stanley, whom you've met, and Harold, run the company."

A brash voice echoed in the foyer.

A hulking figure with a shiny bald head ambled into the great room, his wife trailing a step behind. He had a thick bull neck that bulged over his collar, and his upper lip was curled into a devil-may-care expression. By contrast his wife was small with frizzy red hair and wore a taffeta dress that rustled as she walked.

"Daddy Warbucks and Little Orphan Annie?" Clarisa whispered.

"Emile Stone, president of the Blue Book Union."

Mrs. Dollar had left the room to attend to some detail, so no one greeted the couple. Stone reached into his breast pocket, pulled out an enormous cigar, and patted his pockets for a match, seemingly without success. He looked around for someone with a match but faces turned away when his gaze came their way. Undaunted, he called out in a thick gravelly voice, "Anybody gotta light?" The room quieted as guests furtively glanced in his direction, though no one made a move. He caught Roger's eye and came over, his wife still a step behind, her face puffy under one eye.

"Gotta light, Farnsworth?"

Roger removed a lighter from his breast pocket, flipped it open, and sparked the flint.

Stone puffed the enormous cigar to life. "Ain't often a union man is invited to the Dollar mansion. Kinda old-fashioned for my taste. So what's the occasion?"

"Plant thought it would be a good idea to close ranks now that the International Longshoremen's Association is recruiting men."

A drop of perspiration trickled down Stone's cheek. "Well, tell Plant we got things under control."

"That's not what I hear."

"Listen, as long as the shippers and stevedore companies demand a Blue Book from the men, the ILA don't stand a chance."

"Then tell me this: how can we demand a Blue Book and claim we're for the open shop?"

Stone poked a blunt finger on Roger's chest. "That, my friend, is your problem, but if you don't you'll be in for a rough ride."

Clarisa looked beyond Stone at the other guests, all talking, drinking, eating, and enjoying themselves. In addition to the governor, she spotted the mayor of San Francisco, several shippers, and a host of investors and their wives. Her gaze traveled back to Stone, who was eyeing her as if he was about to say something, and, considering the whiskey on his breath, she wasn't eager to hear it. She glanced at Roger with her best get-me-out-of-here expression.

He took her elbow. "Excuse us."

Stone held out an arm, blocking their path. "Aren'tcha gonna introduce me to the young lady?"

"Later," said Roger, brushing past him, a move so blatantly rude Clarisa gave him a questioning glance. "He's an ass," Roger muttered.

"True, but isn't he right about the open shop? If enough men sign up with the ILA, the Blue Book Union could lose members."

Roger took her empty champagne glass, handed it to a maid, and replaced it with a fresh one. "That may be, but tonight let's make merry." He clinked her glass with his. "And let tomorrow take care of tomorrow."

They wandered over to a large picture window with a view of Mount Tamalpais rising above San Rafael, its darkened slopes backlit by a lingering sunset. Since the days of the Miwok Indians, the mountain's profile had been compared to a reclining woman, and in the waning twilight it seemed to evoke a mystery as old and immutable as time itself.

"The Sleeping Lady looks lovely tonight," said Roger.

"That she does," agreed another guest.

Clarisa glanced at him and instantly recognized Herbert Fleishhacker from photos in the newspapers. A succesful banker, Fleishhacker was also a well-known philanthropist, who made large donations to civic projects like Kezar Stadium and Fleishhacker Pool. He was also part owner of the Dollar Steamship Line.

"Oh, hello, Mr. Fleishhacker," said Roger.

"Good evening, Roger" Fleishhacker said, shaking hands. His head was covered with a comb over and his bulbous nose and enormous ears were too large for his face. But his features were offset by an impeccably tailored suit and silk tie held in place by a pearl tie pin. His wife stood beside him.

Roger placed a hand on the small of Clarisa's back. "May I present my secretary, Miss McMahon. Tom and I thought it would be good if she got to know our members."

Mrs. Fleishhacker raised an eyebrow. "Do you really expect us to believe that that's the reason this lovely young woman is your companion tonight?"

Roger bowed his head. "I would never presume to guess your beliefs."

Mrs. Fleishhacker laughed. "Spoken like a true diplomat." She turned to Clarisa. "So, are you one of the Philadelphia McMahons?"

Clarisa shook her head, hoping Mrs. Fleishhacker wouldn't pursue this line of questioning.

After an awkward silence, Roger intervened. "Actually, she's one of the Dublin McMahons. Her father owns a printing company in the city."

"Really," said Mrs. Fleishhacker, her eyes running up and down Clarisa's gown.

Embarrassed by the deception and feeling a bit like a stock animal at auction, Clarisa averted her gaze. It was just the kind of thing she had hoped to avoid, yet she knew it was a possibility and had made a promise to herself not to pretend to be anything other than what she was. Taking a breath, she met her examiner's eyes. "The truth is my father escaped Dublin after the Easter Uprising and runs a small print shop on Haight

Street, which happens to be failing at the moment."

"I see," said Mrs. Fleishhacker. "Well, don't feel awkward, dear. We Jews have had our share of escaping danger over the years. Many Jews and Irish from humble backgrounds have done well in San Francisco, so it shows good judgment that your father came here."

Emboldened by her kind words, Clarisa turned to Mr. Fleishhacker. "There's a rumor going around that you're the mysterious Mr. X who donated the funds to build St. Patrick's Mission. I'm a volunteer there and would love to know if it's true." She was referring to an anonymous philanthropist, dubbed "Mr. X" by newspaper reporters who suggested several possible donors, including Fleishhacker.

The tycoon's expression gave no hint one way or another. "If I were to admit that I was this Mr. X, which I don't, do you know how many organizations would come after me with requests for donations?"

"Quite a few, I imagine."

"Hundreds, which is probably why the donation was made anonymously. Once people think you're a soft touch they won't leave you alone."

"But you've made numerous contributions to the city. Why not be open about donating to the poor?"

"My dear," said Mrs. Fleishhacker, laying a hand on Clarisa's arm, "it's one thing to contribute to a new opera house or a sports arena — everyone applauds you — but when it comes to large donations for the poor, believe it or not, criticism often follows. Some say you're only trying to assuage a guilty conscience, others say you should do more, and others accuse you of attracting more dispossessed into the city at a time when we can ill afford to take care of our own." She patted Clarisa's arm. "But how wonderful of you to donate your time to the mission. Our city could use more good Samaritans like you."

Throughout the evening Roger introduced Clarisa to several more guests whom she recognized from the society pages, including a couple that struck her as oddly mismatched. William Roth, the tanned, handsome president of the Matson Navigation Company, could intelligently discuss subjects as diverse as French wines and pre-Columbian art. By contrast his wife, Lurline, daughter of the founder of the Matson Company, was a homely, long-faced matron with a single-minded interest in thoroughbred horses. For what seemed like an eternity, Mrs. Roth preached the advantages of raising Arabians over quarter-horses at her estate in Woodside called the Why Worry Ranch.

Why worry, indeed, thought Clarisa as she feigned interest, *when your father has left you millions.*

Mrs. Roth eventually changed the subject to the IRS, which had slapped her with a bill for $43,000 in back taxes. "They have some nerve claiming my ranch is a hobby. Why I've worked my fingers to the bone training for the Nationals."

Clarisa nodded politely, wondering how much one would have to earn in order to owe that much in taxes. Roger saved her from another tedious soliloquy when he took her arm and guided her to the cluster of men beside the punch bowl, now empty. As they approached, the men were laughing uproariously, and from the look of florid faces and playful grins there was no doubt where the brandy punch had gone. Governor Rolph was still at the center, wearing a carnation pinned to his lapel and black cowboy boots that boosted his five-foot five-inch frame.

"Governor," said Roger, shaking Rolph's hand, "I'd like to introduce you to my secretary, Miss McMahon."

"Charmed, I'm sure," Rolph said, taking her hand and kissing it. His eyes moistened as if her arrival had struck a nostalgic chord. "You remind me of Clara Bow, the motion picture actress, the one they called the It Girl. When I was mayor of San Francisco she used to take the train up from Los Angeles. I'd meet her at the station and escort her to the St. Francis Hotel for cocktails. Sweet girl, and one of my more pleasurable duties as mayor. Unfortunately no one of your charming presence comes to Sacramento. No reason to. It's really a farm town that's grown too big for its britches." He laughed with a kindly gleam in his eyes.

Clarisa felt an immediate liking for the governor. "I'm sure you've brightened it considerably."

Rolph's smile broadened. "I like to think so. If you come up to the capitol, I'll show you around, especially" — he winked playfully and nodded at Roger — "if you leave this young fellow back at the office."

Before ascending to the governor's mansion, Rolph had been a popular mayor, who spent as much time drinking and womanizing as he did performing his mayoral duties. In those days he was affectionately known as "Sunny Jim," an appropriate moniker for the man who helped San Francisco rise from the ashes after the 1906 earthquake and fire. Rolph also bridged the gap between the city's rank-and-file and its business leaders, sitting at the head of Labor Day parades as well as on corporate boards. And his goodwill served the city during contentious strikes when he kept them from escalating into violent conflicts. Being governor, Clarisa suspected, wasn't nearly as easy or fun. There were deep fatigue lines around his eyes and a web of broken veins across his nose and cheeks, although it wasn't unexpected considering the flood of dust bowl refugees pouring into the state.

"Have you two met my replacement at City Hall?" Rolph asked. "He's not as much fun as I am, but Mayor Rossi is still worth meeting." He drew them over to the man on his right who, by the look of him, could have been Rolph's younger brother. Mayor Rossi, like Rolph, had a carnation in his lapel, a hairbrush mustache, and a fringe of gray hair around his bare scalp. "Angelo, this is Roger Farnsworth of the Waterfront Employers Association and his secretary, Miss McMahon."

Rossi nodded politely to Clarisa and shook Roger's hand with a firm grip. "Your organization is doing a great job. We've had no problems at the port for over a decade, and it's our most important industry, has been since the Gold Rush."

"You talk like a native son," Roger said.

Rossi smiled with obvious pride. "My parents emigrated from Genoa and traveled through San Francisco on their way to the gold country, where they settled. When I was growing up, they always talked about how beautiful the city was. After my father passed away, my mother moved us to San Francisco, and, sure enough, it was just as beautiful as they said."

"Spoken like the city's number one booster," said Roger Lapham, the stout, silver-haired president of the Hawaiian-American Steamship Line. "Don't you ever turn it off?"

"I'll never turn it off," Rossi shot back. "And you know why? Because I believe it here" — he thumped his chest with his fist — "in my heart. San Francisco is the greatest city on earth."

"Well, one thing's for sure, for a flower vendor you've sure got ba —" he glanced at Clarisa — "backbone."

Roger shook Lapham's hand. "If anyone knows about backbone, sir, it's you. May I introduce my secretary, Miss McMahon?"

Clarisa grasped his hand. "You must be Mr. Plant's boss."

"Guilty as charged," Lapham replied, his ample cheeks flushed with punch.

"So what makes you so knowledgeable about backbone?"

Lapham looked down and swirled the drink in his hand. "It's not a claim I've ever made."

"He's being modest," said Roger. "He was caught behind enemy lines during the Great War and blinded by mustard gas. When his eyesight returned, he fought his way back through the German line to his division.

By then, he'd been gone two weeks and written off as a casualty."

"Reports of my death were exaggerated," said Lapham.

Everyone laughed, including Clarisa, who marveled at her good fortune to be in such a beautiful home with delightful company and a handsome escort.

At midnight Roger put his arm around her waist and nodded toward the front door. *Is it time to go?* During all the fun she'd lost track of the hour. They said their goodbyes and stepped out onto the front porch where the temperature was still deliciously warm. The valet approached, but Roger waved him off and guided Clarisa around the side of the house to a path that led up the hill. She walked beside him through a grove of oak trees whose gnarled limbs reached protectively overhead. The smell of dried grass filled the air, as did the chant of crickets, rhythmically rising and falling. They came to a field of waist-high grass bathed in moonlight. Roger led her to the middle of the field, and here they stopped to listen to the crickets and enjoy the warm night air.

"Look," he said, gesturing across the valley to Mount Tamalpais, now silhouetted by a starry sky.

Clarisa leaned her head on his shoulder and gazed at the stately peak: solid, timeless, immutable, its grandeur accentuated by a backdrop of luminous stars. She imagined what it would be like to be a mountain, to have waterfalls cascading down her shoulders, golden poppies and wild irises tangled in her hair, a coat of chaparral on her slopes, tender damp moss nestled in her cool canyons, and a halo of red-tailed hawks circling overhead.

A soft breeze rustled the oak leaves and swayed the grass.

Roger reached around and pulled her to him, his grip gentle yet sure. She'd half expected him to do such a thing. After all, it had been a romantic evening far beyond her expectations — the storybook mansion, the elegant guests, the convivial conversation. She closed her eyes and let the warmth of their bodies merge as the music of the crickets rose and fell in her ears. They held onto one another in the warm night air, swaying slightly, their breathing synchronized.

Clarisa was beginning to wonder what would happen next when Roger parted from her and spread his jacket on the dried grass. He took her hand and gently drew her down beside him, the grass crinkling as it conformed to their bodies. Laying on their backs within this hidden nest, this womb of golden grass, they gazed up at the stars and let their minds drift, their bodies relax, the hypnotic rhythm of the crickets swelling and receding, swelling and receding.

Clarisa was so relaxed that when Roger rolled over and pressed his lips to hers, she gave no thought to anything other than the pleasant sensation. They kissed for a long while until Roger nuzzled his face in her hair, his breath warm on her neck, his left hand tracing the curves of her body, caressing her arms, hips, legs. She closed her eyes and basked in the simultaneous sensation of relaxation and stimulation, her body tingling with pleasure yet every muscle at ease. A thought floated to the surface: *Have things gone too far?* Then another thought. *Should I stop it? Can I stop it? Do I want to stop to it?* She couldn't decide and watched as the thoughts drifted away like leaves floating on a slow moving river.

Along with the chant of the crickets, a rhythmic sensation pounded in her ears — *boom-boom, boom-boom, boom-boom.* She listened, wondering what it was until she recognized the beat of her heart, strong, steady, pulsing.

His lips found hers again, firmer and more insistent this time.

Their breaths quickened, wheezing in and out of their nostrils as their mouths locked in a passionate embrace. Within the womb of golden grass, time became measurable only by the beating of their hearts and the tempo of their breaths. The warm air swaddled their bodies so that when they removed their clothes, it seemed as if each article fell away like molting skin, revealing a new outer layer, soft and sensitive, warm and inviting. When they joined together, she stiffened and groaned with pleasure, fully engrossed in the sensation, fully resonating with the rhythm of their lovemaking. How long it lasted, a minute, an hour, she couldn't tell, but when it was over her heart still pounded, her chest heaved, and perspiration covered her cheeks.

As her breath calmed, she emerged from the trance of lovemaking and looked up at the sky. A blanket of stars filled her vision, each one radiating arrows of light, bright and luminous. She bit her lower lip and sank into her thoughts. It had all happened so fast and so dream-like, as if the evening was destined to end this way. *I couldn't have stopped it if I wanted to, could I?* She resisted any inclination to think about the consequences, or about the world beyond this moment. Yet an anxious feeling crept over her, and for a moment the stars seemed to dim as if some unseen cloud was passing overhead.

15

On the fourth morning of their captivity, the crew awoke to find the Kuro fog bank gone, the gray mist having evaporated as quickly and mysteriously as it arrived. Everyone returned to their usual duties, and in no time the rhythmic hum of the engine breathed life into the *Diana Dollar* and the men onboard. With the ship now sailing full-steam ahead and life returning to normal, Nick decided it was best to put the mutinous plot out of his mind and concentrate on his duties, at least for now. His attention was further diverted when the mountainous Japanese coastline appeared on the starboard horizon, the first sign their transpacific journey was nearly over.

Two days later the freighter cleared the southern tip of Japan and sailed into the East China Sea, a body of water known for hazards both natural and man-made. As a precaution Chief Primm posted double lookouts to keep an eye out for uncharted shoals, roaming pirates, and the Japanese military, known to stop and search merchant ships in violation of international law.

Primm had assumed the role of acting captain, and poor Harding made only occasional appearances. When Harding did emerge from his cabin, Primm treated him with patronizing deference as if to let everyone know that while the old man was still the captain in name, he was in charge now. Harding endured the pretense, but Nick saw flashes of humiliation in his eyes, and as time wore on he emerged less and less from his cabin.

On June 10th the *Diana Dollar* steamed into the mouth of the Yangtze River, a lumbering yellow estuary, miles wide and flowing toward the ocean with a gate so imperceptible it looked more like a stationary bay than a river. Nick was eager to catch his first glimpse of the Asian continent but was disappointed when he spied a flat, treeless plain with few distinguishing landmarks and little activity. The river traffic, it turned out, was much more interesting. A cavalcade of Chinese junks, Norwegian tramps, American oil tankers, British passenger liners, Japanese barges, Dutch coal colliers, and sea tugs navigated in and out of the Yangtze, trailing white foamy wakes and billows of black smoke.

The *Diana Dollar* dropped anchor off Taku Bar, a large sandbar at the mouth of the river. Early the next morning a cutter pulled alongside to drop off the bar pilot, who would guide them a short distance up the Yangtze to the Whangpu River and a half-day's sail up the Whangpu to Shanghai. Two sailors dropped a Jacob's ladder down to a corpulent American bar pilot, dressed in a white linen suit and a blue pilot's hat, who grasped the ladder and with surprising alacrity ascended up to the weather deck.

Nick was manning the helm when the bar pilot entered the wheelhouse.

"Where's the captain?" the pilot said to Chief Primm.

"The old man's feeling under the weather."

"Not yellow fever, I hope. We had two cases last month and both ships were quarantined."

"No, nothing like that." He motioned the pilot forward. "She's all yours."

The pilot stepped up to the wheelhouse windows and surveyed the broad yellow estuary. "Full ahead."

The chief repeated the order, and the third mate swung the arm of the marine telegraph upright to "Full Ahead."

"Fifteen degrees port, helmsman," commanded the bar pilot.

"Fifteen degrees port," Nick repeated, turning the wheel with an assuredness he'd lacked five weeks earlier.

The ship steamed past Ch'ung-ming Island and veered south into the Whangpu River, a quarter-mile wide tributary flanked on both sides by dirt levees. Beyond the levees, rice paddies extended into the distance as far as the eye could see, now brilliant green with spring shoots. Rice farmers wearing woven conical hats, stood thigh-deep in the muddy water, their arms thrust down into the rich alluvial mud.

Chief Primm offered the pilot a cigarette and lit it for him. "Anything new since the fireworks last year?"

The pilot shook his head. "Aside from the Japs acting more arrogant than ever, you'd never know anything happened. After the bombing, they pulled most of their troops out, and what was left of the Chinese Nineteenth Route Army retreated to Chowkow. The Jap Zeros left Chapei a mess, though. They flattened just about every building in the district. It took the Chinese months just to clean up the debris. Strange thing is, in the foreign settlements you wouldn't know that all hell had broken loose next door. British, American, and Chinese taipans are still throwing up buildings along Nanking Road like it was Fifth Avenue — tall ones, too, with fancy Art Deco exteriors, rooftop gardens, and indoor pools. They say it'll take more than the Jap military to stop Shanghai from growing."

An hour upriver scores of wooden sampans huddled along the banks like schools of fish feeding on the reeds along the shore. Crouching figures on the decks of the sampans were pounding the reeds into strips and weaving them into mats and baskets.

Farther upriver the rice paddies disappeared, replaced by factories and warehouses. The first of these was a huge shipyard resounding with the clang of industry and the buzz of workers crawling over ships propped up in drydock. Beyond the shipyard stood a succession of steel mills, cement plants, silk filatures, chemical works, and cotton mills, each spewing clouds of black smoke from tall, slender brick chimneys.

When they reached the outskirts of Shanghai, there were dozens of warships anchored in the middle of the river — destroyers, minesweepers, cutters — convoyed by nationality and bearing flags from the United States, Great Britain, France, Germany, and Japan.

"I'd forgotten how large the foreign fleet was," said Primm, "or has it grown?"

"They've all added ships since the bombing last year," the bar pilot replied. "Without gunboats the foreign taipans would have to kowtow to Chinese warlords or, worse, be run out of the country by communist insurgents." He raised his right hand. "Slow ahead."

As the freighter slowed to a crawl, two tugboats approached and maneuvered her up to the wharf at the Dollar Drydock and Shipyards. Once the ship was secured to the wharf, sailors lowered the gangway for customs officials who climbed aboard to check the ship's manifest. When this was done, Chinese longshoremen dressed in loose nankeen shirts and trousers clamored up the gangway under the sharp eye of an American walking boss. The longshoremen removed the tarpaulins from the cargo hatches, uncovered the hatch openings, and descended into the hold. Within minutes the *chuck-chuck-chuck* of steam-powered winches could be heard along the wharf as logs and rail tracks emerged from the freighter and dropped down to lighters moored on her starboard side.

At the end of the day, the crew showered and jostled for position around a tiny mirror to shave and comb their hair, all the while jabbering about their favorite watering holes and fleshpots. Nick put on his shore clothes, a loose short-sleeve cotton shirt, khaki trousers, a white flat cap, and was about to leave when he remembered Captain Harding.

He went to the captain's cabin and knocked. No one answered. He turned the handle and opened the door. The cabin was shipshape, the bed made-up, desk cleared of papers, nautical almanacs neatly stacked on the shelf, ashtray cleaned. The lingering odor of pipe tobacco hung in the air. He still wasn't certain the captain had decamped until he noticed a blank spot on the wall where the *Julia Ann* had skimmed over the ocean like a great billowing cloud. He paused to absorb the loss, to grasp some meaning from the old man's departure. For somehow it seemed greater than that, as though he was witnessing not only the end of a long career, but also the closing strains of a maritime tradition going back through the ages. And in that moment he could see a pair of skysails taut from the trades, slowly descending into the horizon like winged angels falling from sight beyond the curvature of the earth.

He caught up with Moon and Remy at a water taxi stand. The afternoon sun hung low in the sky, painting a gold patina on the placid river, its surface gently rippled by ships and sampans plying back and forth. A motorized launch with a striped awning picked them up and chugged upstream across the river. As it came to a turn in the Whangpu, they passed a tributary spilling into the river. Beyond that the industrial port abruptly ended, replaced by a sight so extraordinary, so monumental, so unexpected, Nick stared in awe.

"The Bund," Remy said. "You can't mistake it for anything in the world."

Indeed. A row of buildings, huge in scale and grandiose in design, extended along the river for nearly a mile. What made it even more extraordinary was that the buildings were all Western in design, as if each had been magically transported from some European capital and planted here intact. There were tiered towers and gleaming domes, soaring spires and copper cupolas, Doric columns and pyramidal roofs, forming a hodgepodge of architectural elements and styles. They did have one thing in common, however: the exhibition of ostentatious wealth. And although the effect was one of mismatched grandeur, it was grandeur nonetheless.

The water taxi deposited them in front of a rickshaw stand, and the moment they stepped onto the wharf a crowd of ragged, imploring rickshaw drivers huddled around them, tugging at their arms, attempting to draw them toward their rickshaws. In the roiling hubbub the more aggressive rickshaw men pushed and elbowed others aside, some of whom tumbled onto the pavement only to bounce back up and fight their way to the front again. Having grown up near San Francisco's Chinatown, Nick was comfortable around Asians, but these poor men — their clothes threadbare, breath sour, unwashed bodies emitting an odor of sweat and grime — were a disturbing sight.

They each chose a driver and hopped into their rickshaws.

"Follow me," yelled Moon, as his rickshaw pulled out into the stream of traffic flowing along The Bund.

For the next hour, among a swarm of cars, taxis, trucks, trolleys, bicycles, rickshaws, and wagons, they toured the streets of Shanghai, a city far more modern than Nick had imagined. There were wide thoroughfares lined with grand hotels and huge department stores, neon signs blinking on and off, and theater marquees announcing performances in English and Chinese. Pedestrians were also a surprise. Nick had expected to see robed mandarins wearing silk caps and long braided ponytails. Instead, the sidewalks were crowded with handsomely dressed Chinese, wearing the latest styles from New York, London, and Paris, as well as pitiful beggars covered in rags and mud. Without a doubt, Shanghai was a teeming metropolis, its streets echoing with the same honking horns, piercing whistles, screaming vendors, and clanging streetcars as San Francisco, only more so.

They traveled along Nanking Road through a district festooned with red banners hanging over the street, emblazoned with Chinese characters. This section of Shanghai, Nick knew from reading *The Ports of Asia*, was known as the International Settlement, one of two foreign-controlled zones within the Municipality of Greater Shanghai, a sprawling Chicago-sized city. Governed by a British and American Municipal Council, the International Settlement maintained its own police force and courts and was adjacent to the French Concession, the other foreign-controlled zone.

At the Shanghai Race Club, the rickshaws doubled back along alleys and side streets redolent with punk incense and colorful produce. The wares of small shops spilled out onto the sidewalks, and on some street corners, sidewalk vendors tossed meat, vegetables, and noodles into large steel woks that sizzled and hissed and scented the air with the tantalizing odors of garlic, ginger, and onions.

They disembarked from the rickshaws at Rue Chu Pao-san in the French Concession, a street whose sole trade appeared to be bars and nightclubs encrusted with neon lights advertising leggy chorus girls and Oriental floor shows.

"This is it," exclaimed Remy, sweeping his hand out across the scene like an impresario. "Blood Alley, the Barbary Coast of Shanghai."

They entered a nightclub called The Forbidden City and squeezed into a spot at the bar among merchant seamen, military personnel, and civilians. A pukka-walla fan above the bar slowly rotated a long horizontal pole with spoke-like arms attached to tulip-shaped fans. They ordered a round of beers and toasted their good fortune to have been given ten days in Shanghai while the ship was undergoing routine maintenance.

At the rear of the nightclub a bevy of attractive young women, white and Asian, were seated around a polished dance floor, all of them wearing low cut gowns with skirts slit up to their thighs, most smoking cigarettes with bored expressions.

"Taxi dancers," Remy explained to Nick. "A dime a dance."

Opposite the bar a score of round cocktail tables was strangely bereft of patrons. When Nick asked about it, Moon nodded toward the taxi dancers.

"As soon as you sit down, you'll be pestered by hens wantin' you to buy 'em a drink. Most guys have a few belts at the bar before they spend their dough on the ladies. But don't worry, things'll pick up when the music starts."

They finished the first round and ordered a second. When the drinks arrived, Moon raised his glass. "Here's to good times and willing women." They clinked glasses and quaffed their beers.

Nick noticed a lone Chinese gentleman sitting at one of the cocktail tables, wearing a dark pin-striped, double-breasted suit and a large gold ring fitted with diamonds. His eyes darted nervously around the room, though his face remained impassive. None of the taxi dancers approached him.

Nick nodded in his direction. "Who's the suit?"

Remy glanced over his shoulder. "He's a Green Gangster. The Green Gang controls the rackets on Blood Alley. Liquor, drugs, women, gambling. But don't worry. If you stay outta trouble and pay your tab, you got nothin' to worry about from him."

A band of Filipino musicians in black tuxedos mounted the bandstand and struck up a dance tune. This had the taxi dancers tapping their feet and patrons migrating to the tables. The three sailors finished their second round and joined the migration. As Moon predicted, the moment they sat down three heavily rouged women approached, two slender blondes and a voluptuous brunette.

One of the blondes, wearing a fluffy white boa over her shoulders and smiling with fuchsia lips, laid a hand on Moon's shoulder. "Allo, boys. You buy Katrina a bottle of vine?"

Moon clutched her arm and drew her to an empty chair. "Why not? Have a seat, ladies."

The three women gaily flounced down and settled into their seats with triumphant smiles. The second blonde removed a cigarette from her purse and leaned toward Nick, exposing milky cleavage. She held the cigarette to her lips, indicating a desire for a light. Nick patted his pockets to show he had no matches, then turned to watch the band. He would've preferred to have skipped the nightclub scene altogether and spend the evening touring the city. But it was a rare opportunity to bond with his bunkmates off the ship, and there would be more opportunities for exploration during their stay. Consequently, he wasn't keen on tangling with a taxi dancer whose sole objective was to lighten his wallet.

A Filipina chanteuse, wearing a gold-sequined off-the-shoulder gown, stepped onto the bandstand, snapping her fingers as she approached a microphone. She began belting out a tune:

It dooon't mean a thiiing, if it aaain't got that swiiing.
Doo-ah, doo-ah, doo-ah, doo-ah, doo-ah daaay.

"You no like Sonja?"

Nick turned to the blond taxi dancer. "Talking to me?"

Her flaxen hair was curled in the style of Jean Harlow, and her lower lip protruded into a coy pout. "You no like Sonja?" she repeated.

The question seemed silly. "Sonja, I don't know you well enough to dislike you."

Taking it as a compliment, she smiled and rubbed his arm. "You handsome man," she purred. "You buy Sonja a drink?"

A thick glaze of rouge covered her face, perhaps to hide her age, which as far as Nick could tell was anywhere from thirty to forty. Even so, it was evident she was a beautiful woman. Her lips were delicately curved, nose finely sculpted, cheeks full, eyes almond-shaped and imperceptibly hooded, a vestige perhaps of a marauding Mongolian ancestor. Still, the prospect of fending off a phony seductress attempting to squeeze dollars from his pocket while pretending rather badly to be attracted to him, no matter how beautiful she was, seemed a waste of money. He looked over at Moon and Remy, who apparently had no such qualms and were already pawing their partners.

The Filipina singer held out her arms and plunged into the bridge:

It makes no diff'rence if it's sweet or hot!
Just keep that rhythm, give-it-everything you got!

Sonja drew a strip of dance tickets out of the top of her gown. "I cannot sit if you no buy drink, but if you buy dance is cheaper, and we sit together afterward. Yes?"

Nick figured she wanted to dance in order to build up his thirst and encourage him to buy drinks later on. Despite the obvious ploy, he was inclined to go along. The music reminded him of dances back home when he and Clarisa learned to move in sync, the slightest motion on his part telegraphed to her so that their friends said they looked like they'd been dancing together for years. The memory brought a smile to his lips. "Alright, let's give it a whirl." He handed her four bits for five dance tickets.

Sonja proved to be an energetic dancer, twirling like a ballerina and moving with classical grace, her blond curls flopping up and down in time to the music. Yet she lacked a certain fluidity as if she knew the steps but hadn't mastered the nuances one learns when a dance is indigenous to one's own culture. Still, it was the most fun Nick had had since leaving home, and he used all the dance tickets in the first set.

They returned to table, cheeks flushed, beads of sweat glistening on their foreheads.

"Hey, you kids look great," said Moon, his arm wrapped around Katrina's shoulder. He poured two glasses of wine. "Here, have a drink on me."

Nick sipped the wine and listened to the music and conversation. The scene reminded him of a phrase he'd heard bandied about but only now was beginning to understand. After weeks at sea, sailors crave fun and affection and this presented them with a challenge known as the "sailor's dilemma." The chances of finding affection in respectable society were nil, so seamen often faced the choice between loneliness and carnal temptation. With their pockets flush with cash and their shore time limited, it was easy to understand why the latter often prevailed.

Sonja leaned toward him and brushed her lips against his ear. "You good dancer," she cooed. "You have girlfriend?"

Not knowing the answer, he shrugged.

"You break up before leaving America?"

Surprised at her accuracy, he gave her a searching look. She was either highly intuitive or had met dozens of men like him who were unsure of their relationships back home. He shrugged again. "Maybe."

She laid a hand on his arm with a knowing smile as if she'd heard his story before and didn't care if it was true or not.

"And you?" he asked.

She nodded towards the bar. "See beeg guy over there." A large Slavic-looking fellow stood at the bar, glancing their way, actually staring at them. He wore the simple clothes of a workingman, but something in his face — a long thin nose, neatly trimmed mustache, and intense eyes — gave him a regal, even haughty air. "His name Sergey. He vant me for vife, but he haf no money. We both come from Russia. Many White Russians in Shanghai. His family reech before Bolshevik revolution but lost all money and property. Now he work low pay joob, but say no good for aristocrat to clean toilet. I tell heem I must work too, but he hate what I do."

"Do you hate what you do?"

"Oh, no," she said, rubbing his arm affectionately. "I like. I like you. You like me?"

It was a silly question that didn't deserve an answer. "What did you do before coming to Shanghai?"

"I study Russian literature with private tutor. You like Pushkin? Tolstoy? Dostoevsky?" She laid a hand on his thigh and smiled flirtatiously.

Nick glanced down at her hand. *Should I remove it?* he wondered. The situation was, to say the least, artificial. Nevertheless, the sensation of a beautiful woman's touch on his thigh was not unpleasant. He let it stay.

"*Crime and Punishment,*" he said, "is a brilliant tale of desperation and deception, don't you think?"

"Oh, yes." She nodded enthusiastically, failing to catch the implication.

"So what do you think of the Bolsheviks?"

Her face scrunched into an angry scowl. "Everyone in Russia *hate* Bolsheviks. Lenin stole country from us. He keel many peeples, then make peeple slaves for government. We try to fight heem but lose." She stubbed out her cigarette as if trying to squash a painful memory.

"If everyone in Russia hates the Bolsheviks, how did they succeed?"

"Lenin lie to peeple. He say peeple run country better than Tzar. Then he make heemself dictator and murder Tzar."

"But weren't people fed up with the Tzar?"

Sonja shook her head. "Oh, no. Only Socialists and Bolsheviks hate Tzar. He friend to all Russian peeples."

"Really?" Nick said skeptically, figuring she was from a well-to-to family that benefited from the Tzar's feudal regime.

She shrugged. "Okay, is true. Not everybody love Tzar. But at least he not lie to peeple like Bolsheviks. I warn you, do not let Bolsheviks come to America. They sing *Internationale* about starving peeples, then steal everyting for themselves." As if a switch flipped in her head, her expression brightened into an exaggerated smile. "Forget past, handsome American."

Her hand squeezed his thigh and she leaned into him, rubbing her bosom against his arm. "Let us dance, drink. Night is young. No?"

A shadow covered her smile.

They both looked up at Sergey, who was standing behind them, frowning. He yanked Sonja's hand off Nick's thigh and barked something at her in Russian. Nick didn't understand the words but had no trouble discerning their meaning. She spat something back at him, also in Russian, and tried to wrench her arm out of his grasp. Keeping hold of her hand, he continued to berate her, and she responded just as vehemently.

Nick got up and faced them, wondering what to do. It seemed like a lover's quarrel more than anything. He was tempted to back away until a look of pain crossed Sonja's face as Sergey roughly pulled her to her feet. Everyone around them suspended their conversations and looked over.

"Let her go," Nick said in a firm, calm voice. "You're hurting her."

Sergey ignored him and tried to pull Sonja away. She resisted and yelled something that sounded like a plea to let go.

Nick grabbed his arm. "Listen, pal, she's just trying to do her job. Let's not make a big deal out of it."

Up to this point the Russian's anger had been directed at Sonja. Now his attention turned to Nick, his pupils shrinking into pinpoints of rage. He shouted something in Russian, prompting Sonja to yell, "*Neyt! Neyt!*"

Nick figured Sergey had told him to butt out or else but maintained his grip on the Russian's arm.

Sergey gave Nick a hard shove with his free hand, pushing him back against his chair. Nick stumbled backward, lost his balance and toppled over the chair, landing onto the floor. Having taken care of Nick, the Russian slapped Sonja with the back of his hand, whipping her head around and opening a cut at the corner of her mouth.

From across the table, Moon leaped out of his seat and headed toward the Russian, who, anticipating the blunt-nosed sailor, held out his free arm to ward off the attack. Before Moon reached him, a flash of gold streaked out of nowhere and landed on the Russian's cheek with a loud *smack!* The blow knocked him off his feet and onto the floor, where he lay unmoving, apparently unconscious.

"What the hell happened?" Nick asked as he got up off the floor.

"It was like poetry in motion," Remy said with a crooked alcoholic grin. "The Green Gangster came over like he's mindin' his own business, then cold-cocks the Russian. He's wearing this big gold ring that lands on his cheek, and from the sound of it I think he broke his cheekbone."

Nick scanned the gawkers surrounding their table. "Where'd he go?"

"I dunno. He walked off."

Blood trickled from Sonja's lip, dripping onto the front of her gown. Nick handed her a cocktail napkin. "You okay?"

She nodded. "But I need to go home."

Journal – June 18th, 1933

. . . I offered to escort Sonja to her apartment and was glad she accepted, as it gave me an excuse to leave the nightclub and see more of Shanghai. After saying our goodbyes, we walked several blocks through the French Concession and into a neighborhood of narrow meandering streets that appeared to have changed little in the last century. Buildings here were poorly maintained, many missing sections of plaster, exposing mud bricks and hand-hewn timbers. We passed an old weathered temple, and from its open windows came voices chanting incantations and loud cymbal crashes and the smell of sandalwood incense. Farther on I noticed a pungent odor like that of roasted pumpkin seeds, drifting from a dark alley. Sonja said it was opium and that hundreds of opium dens were scattered throughout Shanghai.

We arrived at a rundown apartment building of an indeterminate age. The stairs were chipped and broken, windows cracked or covered with cardboard, paint so weathered it was impossible to tell the original color. I had expected to deliver her to her door and leave, but she invited me in and I can't say I hesitated. Our conversation had been halting due to her rudimentary English and my non-existent Russian, yet it was clear that she was intelligent and well read. She lives with several others including her mother in a dingy, three-bedroom apartment (her father was killed during the revolution). Everyone was asleep when we entered, including two figures laying on a couch in the living room.

The place had a melancholy air. The furniture was worn and shabby, and the walls were bare except for a pair of religious icons with gold painted frames embedded with semi-precious stones. These, I imagine, were among the few possessions her family managed to hang onto from the days before the revolution.

She made a pot of tea and took me to her bedroom. Her mother was in bed and woke up when we entered. Seeing me, she got up and left. I protested, saying I didn't want to be an inconvenience, but Sonja said her mother could sleep in the next room.

We drank tea and talked for a long time. She lives in a colony of White

Russians, all refugees from the Soviet Union who fought against the Reds, lost, and escaped with little more than the clothes on their backs. She and her compatriots refuse to become Soviet citizens, and as a consequence they have no passports. Now she claims to be a citizen of the world, a nice concept but hardly practical. With no papers she can't immigrate to Europe or America, and if she were to leave the foreign-controlled sections of Shanghai and venture into China, she would become prey to white slavers who would force her to work in a brothel.

Before the revolution her family owned several tracts of farmland south of Moscow near the Oka River. I asked if she knew the peasants who worked her family's land. She said no, though she didn't strike me as an insensitive person, just someone from a world that accepted as providence a feudal system in which a fortunate few were entitled to the benefits afforded by the labor of many.

During our talk we discovered that both of us had lost our fathers under tragic circumstances. It was a poignant moment, and as if she were comforting an old friend, she reached out to hug me. I didn't want to take advantage of her sympathy, and I had no intention to, but somehow by mutual consent and, I think, desire, our lips touched and a friendly hug quickly evolved into a passionate embrace.

What happened next was less love-making than two people trying to forge a connection, trying to compensate for a loss that had changed our lives and scarred our souls. We took off our clothes and held each other, almost like brother and sister. Her body was as beautiful as her face, not an ounce of fat, I suppose from dancing every night. I have to admit that during the next hour, while our limbs were entwined, while our eyes locked onto each other, while our passion ignited, I fell in love. Fell in love with her sad smile that revealed a fear of what lay ahead but also a determination to survive. Fell in love with her milky skin, her gentle thrusts that met my own, her soft lips that made quiet groans until both of us stiffened with pleasure as we reached the inevitable climax.

Of course, I didn't feel the same deep love I have for Clarisa or my family. It was more like a love of all humanity focused onto one person, one vulnerable person sharing herself in the most intimate way.

Afterwards we lay on our backs and stared at the ceiling, silent within our thoughts, still strangers, still two fatherless children with a gaping hole inside.

Eventually I got out of bed, pulled on my clothes, and was about to say goodbye when I wondered if should offer her compensation. *Sailor's dilemma?* She wasn't a common prostitute and never hinted at payment, perhaps to maintain her dignity. Yet I had the feeling that I wasn't the first man she brought home, and it was obvious that she and her mother needed money. I bent down and kissed her goodbye. She smiled and thanked me for seeing her home. I smiled too, thanked her for the tea and conversation, and slipped a five-dollar bill under her pillow.

16

The Blessed Virgin Mary stood in a wall niche to the right of the altar, her marble face softly glowing from light through St. Patrick's stained-glass windows. Father Shannon was leading mass at the altar, but Clarisa was focused on the glowing face, wondering what the Blessed Virgin thought of her now that she'd had relations with someone to whom she wasn't married, or even committed to for that matter. She knew what she thought of herself, and her shame was multiplied by the fact that she'd succumbed so easily to the sweet but fleeting release.

Prior to the Night of the Golden Grass, as she euphemistically thought of it, the last thing she would have considered herself was a loose woman. Yet somehow when Roger led her up the hill, where the air was warm and sensuous, where stars blanketed the sky and crickets played a rhythmic chant, she was carried away by his gentle caresses and soft murmurings. Even now, thinking about it, a spark of pleasure glowed within her until she noticed the Blessed Virgin looking down at her with the sad eyes of a disappointed mother.

Her remorse had started as soon as the lovemaking was over, and it continued to gnaw at her until she became quiet and withdrawn. To relieve the guilt she punished herself with penitent labors, cleaning and dusting every corner of the flat, then scrubbing the kitchen floor so vigorously Seamus asked if she was planning to serve dinner on it.

On Monday morning she was equally reserved, refusing to make eye contact with Roger and speaking to him only when spoken to.

Her distant behavior seemed to confuse and bewilder him, prompting him to ask if he'd done something wrong or if he'd offended her in some way. "Please tell me," he begged. When she shrugged noncommittally, he demanded an answer. When she didn't respond, he lost his temper and threatened serious consequences if she refused to offer an explanation.

Knowing he didn't mean it, she remained silent and watched as he slumped down in his chair and heaved a sigh of resignation.

Defeated by her wall of silence, he apologized for his emotional outburst, saying that he only wanted to know what on earth would cause her to act in such a distant manner, especially after their magical evening at Falkirk.

She knew it wasn't fair to torture him so. She just couldn't find the words to express her conflicting emotions. During his apology she wanted to reach out and console him, wanted to let him know that she alone was responsible for her distant behavior. By then, though, the wall she'd built around herself was too formidable to breach, so she remained silent behind it, miserable, racked with guilt.

After the mass she approached Father Shannon and asked for a private meeting. He led her down a hallway into a cozy wood-paneled office furnished with an antique oak desk and matching credenza, both covered with disheveled stacks of books and paper. An orange calico cat lay curled up on one of the stacks, languidly licking its paws beside a large multi-paned window that looked out onto a courtyard

"Pardon the mess," Shannon said as he sat down behind his desk. "Sister Rose keeps threatening to discard anything with a date earlier than the Armistice, but so far I've managed to keep her at bay."

Clarisa brushed cat hair off a chair in front of his desk and sat down.

The priest studied her with a kindly yet curious expression. "I'd like to think you came by to warm an old friend's heart, but I fear that's not the case. Tell me," he inquired gently, "is something troubling you?"

Clarisa bit her lower lip. This wasn't going to be easy. She avoided his gaze as she recounted the Night of the Golden Grass in faltering words that came slowly at first, one drip at a time as if from a leaky faucet. As the story unfolded the drips came faster and faster until they formed a continuous stream. And it, too, sped up and swelled, becoming a raging torrent so powerful it seemed to rip every garment from her body until she sat before God and her confessor clothed only in her naked shame.

When she finished she fell silent, her eyes nervously darting around the room, still looking everywhere but at her priest. A ray of sunshine poured though the window onto the calico cat, now laying curled up in contented slumber, its chest slowly rising and falling in the warm afternoon light. The sight of the sleeping feline brought a smile to her face, and in that moment she felt the weight of guilt disappear, as if a dark cloud had dissipated into thin air.

As this feeling of liberation swept through her, she shifted her gaze to Father Shannon and gave him a shy, tentative smile.

The silver-haired priest returned her smile and nodded knowingly. "Confession is a powerful healer. Secrets weigh us down like stones tied to our ankles, and the more we try to ignore them, the greater the weight increases until we find ourselves drowning in shame. What you have done is not so much a sin against God as it is against yourself. If you care for this man, there's plenty of time to explore the mystery of love. Being intimate with him so quickly, however, will only corrupt the process. On the other hand, if your true affection lies with another, an intimate relationship with this man will undoubtedly be destructive."

He paused, and for the first time in a week Clarisa was able to hold the gaze of another without wanting to hide under a rock.

"God doesn't expect us to be perfect," he continued, "but he does expect us to be true to ourselves and to Him. You're confused, so it's good you're looking for guidance. And there's no better place to put your trust than in our Lord Jesus Christ." He leaned back in his chair and studied her for a moment, then said, "So tell me, how are things otherwise? Is your job going well?"

Relieved to be moving to another topic, Clarisa described the somber mood at the Waterfront Employers Association since the passage of the National Industrial Recovery Act. "They're concerned about renewed union activity. Rog —." She stopped herself. "Mr. Farnsworth suggested they raise longshoremen's wages back to eighty-five cents an hour to keep the men satisfied, but our members won't hear of it. As far as they're concerned, the longshoremen should be grateful to have any work at all."

Shannon shook his head. "It's a shame. The employers have little empathy for the men who work for them. What are their plans?"

"They've been discussing what to do if a new union forms and goes on strike. At the last board meeting a salesman showed them a riot gun that launches teargas grenades to control crowds. He offered to provide the guns for free if the employers agreed to purchase the grenades from his company."

The priest paled. "That sounds like the hand of the Industrial Association."

Clarisa nodded. "Their executive director, Paul Eliel, met with our board and suggested they create a strike fund, just in case."

"Are you familiar with the Industrial Association?"

Clarisa shook her head.

"It's a coalition of large corporations — Southern Pacific Railroad, Pacific Gas and Electric, Standard Oil, and the like — formed back in the '20s to break the unions. At the time, ninety-percent of San Francisco workers labored in closed shops in which employers hired only union members. Wages were reasonable and companies prospered, especially during the war years. After the war, when the economy slowed, employers slashed wages. Of course the unions resisted, so the Industrial Association amassed a huge war chest and picked off the weaker unions until only twenty-percent of workers labored in closed shops. Now wages are half of what they were."

"You think the Industrial Association will support the waterfront employers if it comes to a strike?"

He nodded. "The port is crucial to San Francisco. If it's disrupted, the entire city would be affected, and you can bet the Industrial Association won't stand for that."

The calico cat was peering out the window, its head jerking back and forth as it watched a leaf swirling in the wind. Clarisa watched the cat for a moment, then shifted her gaze back to Shannon. "Mr. Eliel says the Industrial Association just wants to maintain stability so that businesses can weather the depression. He claims that most union organizers are communists who want to disrupt the economy and drive it into the ground to promote a revolutionary agenda."

"Do you believe that?"

She hesitated. No one had ever asked her opinion before on that particular matter. In fact no one at the office seemed to care what she thought about anything. And why should they? She was just a secretary. "I — I don't know. He seems credible and doesn't strike me as a Philistine."

"No, he wouldn't, would he?"

17

Journal – June 28th, 1933

Sailor's delight (red sky at night), sailor's dilemma (loneliness vs. temptation), and now this: sailor's disease.

So what is this malady that afflicts men of the sea?

Let's start from the beginning. When the symptoms appeared.

My night with Sonja was incredible. After all, how often does one get to canoodle with a beautiful Russian aristocrat? The next day, though, I still had a yearning for female company. Of course I was tempted to see her again — who wouldn't be? — but it would have been for physical reasons and I wanted something more meaningful, something to satisfy my need for genuine affection as well as intimacy. Naturally my thoughts turned to Clarisa, again and again and again. One might say obsessively, and these obsessive thoughts had a disturbing effect.

I was visiting the Shanghai Museum of Art when I saw her.

She was standing in a display case, a Tang Dynasty figurine, tall and willowy, with a hint-of-a-smile and an alluring pose that perfectly captured Clarisa's essence. I must have stared at her for ten minutes, hoping she would step out of the case, life-sized and animated. Another time I was walking along the Whangpu River when her tongue ran down my cheek. Surprised, I looked around, but of course she wasn't there. Then I felt her again, a plump raindrop grazing my face.

I've also had yearnings to see mother, Sarah, even Rune. I try to picture what they're doing, how they're holding up, and then I feel guilty for having left them at such a difficult time.

This intense homesickness came to a head on our last night in Shanghai. Captain Primm (how I hate the sound of that) ordered the crew to stay aboard ship to ensure an early departure the next morning for Manila. I was in a dreadful mood and decided to break out one of my bottles of whisky. I opened my locker, and to my surprise I discovered they were all gone, every single bottle.

I had a pretty good idea where they went.

I confronted Moon and Remy, who, to their credit, admitted they broke into my locker after spending their shore-leave pay on Russian taxi dancers (Moon was a lock-picker in his youth), and drank my liquor down to the last drop. Of course I was furious and wanted to give them a thorough tongue lashing. But their remorseful hangdog expressions melted my anger, and other than this incident they've been swell mates.

Feeling defeated, I lay down on my bunk and sighed like a homesick puppy.

"You alright?" Moon asked. When I failed to answer, he took a close look at me and said, "Hmm. I think you've got a bad case."

"Bad case?" I said. "Of what?"

"Sailor's disease. It can hit rookies pretty hard. Sometimes a seaman can sink so low he won't leave his bunk or even threatens to jump overboard."

That was encouraging. "So what's the cure?"

"I know," said Remy. "Get drunk with a couple of mates and howl at the moon."

"Oh, now there's a great suggestion," I said sarcastically, since we had no liquor to administer his so-called cure.

We were contemplating this sad fact when Moon's face lit up.

Looking pleased with himself, he explained that the crew hadn't expected to be confined to ship that evening, so no one had stocked up on liquor for the next leg to Manila. We could take orders, he suggested, collect payment, including a delivery charge to cover a few bottles for ourselves and one to pay off the gangway guard, and sneak off the ship.

"It'll be as easy as selling moonshine in a dry county," he predicted.

And he was right.

An hour later, with a list of orders and a wad of cash, we snuck down the gangway and scurried upstream to a wooden dinghy tied to the wharf. Remy and I took the oars while Moon leaned back on the stern rail and smoked a stogie.

During our trip across the river, Moon hatched another idea. He'd heard me say I couldn't send a letter to Clarisa that would reach her before we returned home. He suggested I send her a telegram instead, offering to use some of our profits to pay for it. This touched me deeply. Eight weeks ago I was a stranger to these two knuckleheads, a stranger who didn't know a barnacle from a binnacle. Now they were my mates, filching mates maybe, but mates nonetheless.

We tied the dinghy to a wharf on the shores of Yangtzepoo, a gritty industrial area, and headed inland through a neighborhood of brick factories whose windows were ablaze with light from blast furnaces. At Paoshan Road we turned left into a shopping district and found a liquor store. Moon suggested we buy three bottles now, one for each of us, then go find a telegraph office and come back for the rest after sending the telegram. Remy and I readily agreed, and in short order the three of us, fortified with swigs of whiskey, were on our way to the telegraph office.

To get there we entered a lively neighborhood, echoing with the cries of children playing in the street under laundry hanging on lines spanning overhead. Farther on, the cheerful clamor died away, the laundry lines replaced with white paper lanterns strung above the sidewalk. The street here was the cleanest I'd seen in Shanghai, and also eerily quiet.

Several Japanese soldiers came swaggering toward us, taking up the entire sidewalk. We had to step out into the street to let them by, and after they passed, Remy whispered, "Little Tokyo."

In the next block we stepped aside again, this time for two beautiful geishas with jet-black hair bundled on their heads and mask-like faces painted snow white with thick black eyebrows. They wore wooden stilt shoes and took tiny steps, yet they carried themselves with amazing grace considering the precarious nature of their footwear. As they went by, we removed our hats and bowed gallantly like the three musketeers. They tittered at our theatrics, and it made me think that the world might better off if geishas ran the military and soldiers were the entertainers.

At Hongkew Road, a major thoroughfare, we stopped to watch the flow of traffic and pedestrians. Shanghai is an international crossroad, a diverse mixture of natives and sojourners, and here the full pageant is on display—foreign taipans riding in limousines driven by Chinese compradors, deformed beggars beseeching French attaches, pious Buddhist monks walking past equally pious Baptist missionaries, rouged streetwalkers eyeing prospective clients, Chinese vendors hawking hot tea, and British and American businessmen hurrying to the next meeting, all of them seemingly oblivious to the ominous gunboats floating on the Whangpu.

As the parade went by we swigged our liquor and discussed the contents of my telegram. Moon thought I should propose, and Remy came up with a rhyme: *Roses are red. Violets are blue. Marry me, sweetheart, and I'll sail home to you.* I shook my head. Clarisa certainly wouldn't be impressed with such an infantile effort. I made my own attempt at composing a message, but I could barely hear myself think above the street noise and a loud annoying buzz in my head. Gulping another mouthful of whiskey, I closed my eyes to concentrate, but the buzz seemed even louder with closed eyes. Then bright lines burst across the inside of my eyelids like an explosion of shooting stars.

There was no doubt about it. I was plastered.

Better walk it off.

I took a tentative step into the flow of pedestrians, leaning this way and that to keep my balance. When this proved successful, I took another step, holding out my hands as if walking on a tightrope. A few more unsteady steps convinced me that if I kept moving I could somehow straighten myself out. I continued to weave down the sidewalk until an elderly woman pushing a shopping cart came toward me. I tried to navigate around her but tripped on my own feet and bumped into the cart, toppling it over and launching her groceries across the sidewalk. I slurred a few words of apology, though my spastic tongue couldn't form sentences that either I or the old woman could understand. It must have been obvious that I was a drunken sailor because she cut me off with a torrent of unintelligible invectives and angry gestures.

To make amends I bent down to retrieve a strange brown fruit with mace-like spikes. Not a good idea. The buzz in my head rose to a deafening roar and a sudden eruption surged up from my gut. I tried to hold it down, but the effort disrupted my concentration and then my balance. In one simultaneous motion I fell to the ground and ejected a soupy mixture onto the sidewalk, then landed in the partially digested slurry. With my head resting on the sidewalk, I watched a troop of shoes march across my vision — silk flats, two-tone brogues, woven straw sandals — until it all went blank.

Sometime later, how much later I had no idea, I was roused by a patchwork of painful sensations. My tongue was dry and swollen, a sharp pain stabbed my right forearm, a grinding headache wracked my brain, and a rocking motion tortured my stomach.

"Sleeping Beauty awakens," said a voice.

With considerable effort I pushed myself upright. We were about halfway across the Whangpu River, glowing with the gentle luster of reflected moonlight. Moon and Remy were at the oars, rowing slowly toward the opposite shore.

"How long have I been out?" I wondered aloud.

"A couple of hours," said Moon.

"Two hours, eh?" I rubbed my shirtsleeve and winced as the pain in my forearm flared. *Did I fall on my arm?* Just then the sound of clinking glass drew my eyes to a wooden crate full of pint bottles. "How did you get me and the booze back to the boat?"

"We rented rickshaws," said Remy. "None of us were in any condition to walk, so it worked out fine."

I thought for a moment. "How come it took two hours to buy the booze and get back to the boat?"

"We had to take you somewhere to clean you up," said Moon.

I wiped the side my face with the back of my hand. No trace of vomit. My forearm still throbbed, but there was no blood and it didn't appear to be broken. "Where did you take me?"

"A little joint near where you passed out," said Moon.

"A whorehouse?" I asked, figuring that was why it took two hours.

"Nope," replied Remy. "We coulda gone whorin', but we didn't cuz we was thinkin' about your perdic'ment. You know, with your girl."

My girl? I was about to ask what he meant when the pain in my forearm flared again. Curious, I unbuttoned my cuff and rolled up the sleeve. A white gauze bandage covered my forearm.

"That's our present," said Moon. "Since you didn't send a telegram to your girl, we figured it was the next best way to show her you were thinkin' about her."

"Present? PRESENT!" I ripped off the bandage.

The pain was excruciating but I hardly noticed. For there, tattooed on my forearm, was a single solitary word: **CLARISA**. I stared at the permanent letters on my arm, not knowing whether to scream at the audacity of my bunkmates or cry at my own foolishness. Both responses, I decided, were a waste of energy and risked offending my mates. On the other hand, I don't expect the "present" will score any points with Clarisa.

Oh, well, if nothing else it's a memento of the voyage.

18

Hands clasped behind his back, head bowed down in thought, Father Shannon strode across town to Alamo Square, a hillside park in the Western Addition. A number of large Victorian houses surrounded the square, and opposite its northeast corner stood the largest house of all, a stately thirty-five room mansion occupied by Archbishop Edward J. Hanna. Three stories tall with a French Mansard roof, the mansion was often referred to as San Francisco's second City Hall, a perception not far from the truth.

Catholics composed a majority of the electorate in San Francisco. Consequently, mayoral candidates with any hope of success made a pilgrimage to the mansion to ask for the archbishop's blessing, and though he officially remained neutral, candidates judged to be out of step with church values made little headway among the city's Roman Catholic constituency.

Father Shannon knocked on the leaded glass door.

A wimpled nun opened it and scrutinized him with the guarded air of a gatekeeper.

Shannon removed his fedora. "Is His Grace in?"

"Is he expecting you?" she said, her voice indicating she already knew the answer.

"No, just a spontaneous house call. If he's busy, I can return another time."

"He's always busy," she said, emphasizing *always* as if everyone was aware of that fact except, apparently, the poor ignoramus in front of her, "but I'll let him know you're here."

She retreated into the mansion and returned several minutes later, gesturing to him to follow her, saying his Grace had a *few* moments. They climbed a wide circular stairway that wound inside an oval atrium bathed in light from a skylight centered over the stairs. At the top of the stairs she nodded toward an open door.

Shannon entered the archbishop's office and was struck by its simplicity. Unlike his own disheveled office, no piles of papers were to be seen anywhere, and the leather-bound books on the shelves lining the walls were neatly arranged in perfect rows. The archbishop sat at his desk talking on the phone, his massive hands laboriously scratching notes on a yellow legal pad, head bent over, revealing a bald pate ringed with dark hair flecked with gray. After he concluded the call, he jotted a few more notes.

"At my age, Michael," he said as he wrote, "memory is like a deep well. Every new fact falls in and is lost forever if I don't jot it down right away."

Shannon recalled the archbishop in his younger days when he was a figure of impressive size and robust stature. Now, at the age of seventy-three, he looked thinner and a bit frail, although he still had a strong chin and dark eyebrows. He glanced up.

"You look like a freshman divinity student, standing there with your hat in hand." He motioned to a leather wingback chair. "Have a seat." He finished his notes and flipped the page over. At the top of the next page he wrote Father Shannon's name in neat flowing script. "I was hoping this was a social call, but I can see by the furrow in your brow that you didn't come to enquire about my angina."

"Well, no, I mean yes, Your Grace, I did want to talk about a certain matter." It was then he noticed Hanna's chalky complexion and sagging cheeks. "But I hate to burden you if it's not a good time."

"Because of my heart condition?" The archbishop smiled. "Well, you needn't worry about that. The good Lord has provided me with the best physicians in the country, who tell me if I take it easy I'll put off meeting my Maker for years to come. And the good Lord also saw fit to ease my burden by ending Prohibition."

"Prohibition, Your Grace?"

"You can't imagine the hundreds of applications that came across my desk asking for a license to make sacramental wine. Even from non-Catholics. You'd have thought we guzzled the Eucharist by the barrel."

They both chuckled.

"I'm also getting relief," Hanna continued, "from the breakneck growth of the last decade. Ours was the fastest growing archdiocese in the country. I dedicated a new parish church every other month, and each one required mountains of paperwork. God may have commanded us to go forth and multiply, but Rome wants it documented in triplicate." He let out a sigh of resignation. "Recently, though, the financing hasn't been available to fund new building projects, so at long last I can concentrate on programs." He studied Father Shannon. "Speaking of programs, how is the mission?"

"Good and bad, Your Grace. We're doing a bang-up business. Every week the lines grow longer, and we're seeing more families join the hungry. If things keep going this way, we'll have to open up another location. Though Lord knows how we'll manage that."

"Is that why you came to see me?"

Shannon set his hat on the archbishop's desk and straightened his posture. "No, Your Grace. Plainly put, trouble is brewing on the waterfront. A new union is forming and there's a new anger and militancy I've not seen before. Longshoremen earn less than fifty dollars a week, *if* they can find a job, and many cannot. And it's dangerous, back-breaking work, made worse by inadequate safety precautions." He scooted to the edge of his chair. "The majority of dockworkers are Catholic, so we need to exert our influence and see that they don't resort to violence. At the same time, we should stand up for them. They'll face a formidable foe that can muster all the resources of corporate capital and government intervention."

Hanna nodded solemnly. "I understand, but it's vitally important we don't appear to take sides. We're just as represented in the boardrooms as we are in the halls of labor. If we are to maintain trust on both sides, we need to stay away from developments for now. I know you, Michael — you want to jump into the fray and direct things from the start. But trust me, now is not the time."

Father Shannon leaned forward. "Your Grace, as you know the

encyclical *Quadragesimo Anno* affirmed the right of workers to form unions and strive for decent working conditions. Shouldn't we be encouraging our men to do just that, perhaps under our auspices? Many of our people are desperate. I see their troubled faces every day, not from afar in an ivory tower, but up close so I can smell their humiliation and rage. If we don't act now, they could be trampled by corporate interests or seduced by communist organizers. In the coming months I predict we'll see a battle for the hearts and minds of workers." His hands unconsciously clenched into fists. "And it will be as much a contest between God and atheism as it is between capital and labor."

Father Shannon sat back, hoping he hadn't stated his case too vehemently or gone too far with the "ivory tower" comment.

Thankfully, the archbishop didn't appear offended.

"Michael, as long as I've known you, you've possessed a great compassion for the poor and working class. You are truly a hero to your parish in this time of economic hardship. And I share your concerns — deeply. But we are not in the business of organizing or directing labor unions. If we choose one union over another, we risk alienating men from the other side. If we take sides in a labor dispute, we risk losing our credibility as spiritual leaders. So I must forbid you from taking an active role other than to offer religious guidance and physical care."

"Your Grace," pleaded Shannon, his voice rising in frustration, "you've been actively involved in the Catholic Welfare Council for years, lobbying Congress and speaking out on social issues."

"That's right. But those are broad issues where we hope to influence public policy, which is quite different from taking sides in a labor dispute."

"With all due respect, the only difference I see is that your hands remain clean. The Communists and the Industrial Association aren't burdened with the same sanitary compulsion." Shannon stood up and snatched his hat off the desk. "If we stay off the playing field, I'm afraid the church will be in danger of a fate worse than perdition." He turned and walked toward the door.

"And what's that, Michael?"

Shannon pivoted around, his figure backlit by light from the atrium. "Irrelevancy, Your Grace. Irrelevancy."

19

Captain Harding wasn't the only sailor left behind when the *Diana Dollar* embarked for Manila. Nick learned from Cook that Primm had sacked Will Bailey for union organizing and that Bailey would have to make his own way back to the States. Primm also wasted no time in establishing his authority. He called the crew into the messroom and announced his intention to run a tight ship. Every man was expected to keep his shirttails tucked in and report to duty by the bell or face a deduction of wages, and no alcohol consumption or gambling would be tolerated, nor would the crew be allowed to hold meetings of any kind.

"A tight ship?" Cook remarked as he leaned on the galley counter while Nick poured a cup of coffee. "Primm don't know the meaning of it." He pointed to rodent pellets trailing across the galley floor and cockroaches climbing the bulkheads. "Those buggers could've been dealt with in Shanghai, but that would have meant jettisoning all the galley contents and replacing it with fresh stores after cleaning the entire vessel."

"So why didn't Primm do it?"

"Because the cost would have been deducted from the captain's bonus at the end of the voyage."

Two days later the *Diana Dollar* crossed the Tropic of Cancer and entered the Torrid Zone, an equatorial region where a merciless sun beat down on the ship and turned it into a broiling oven. The portholes were left open to draw in what little breeze the trade winds provided, but Nick found it nearly impossible to sleep, his armpits perpetually wet, his crotch itching from heat.

On the fifth day out they passed Corregidor, a rock island situated at the mouth of Manila Bay. An hour later the port of Manila came into view, its sprawling waterfront stretching along the shore. A British liner came steaming out of the port, water peeling off its bow. The *Diana Dollar* moved past it and continued on toward a row of finger piers jutting into the bay. As they drew closer, Nick could see ships of every shape and nationality — Greek tramps, Japanese traders, Norwegian flush deckers, American frigates — all of them bustling with Filipino longshoremen loading and discharging cargo. Beyond the waterfront, white-washed buildings with red tiled roofs and churches with square towers occupied a flat basin surrounded by verdant hills.

Its propellers turning in reverse, the *Diana Dollar* slowed to a crawl and nuzzled up to a pier piled high with what looked like dark brown dog turds. Stationed near the bow, Nick and Remy held a thick mooring line, ready to toss it to a dockworker waiting on the pier.

"What's that?" Nick asked, nodding toward the pile.

"Copra," said Remy, as they heaved the mooring line over the side of the bow, "It's coconut meat that's been pried out if its shell and dried in the sun until it shrivels into dark sticky pieces." At just that moment a foul oily odor assaulted them, as strong as skunk spray and nearly as obnoxious. "And you won't believe what it's used for."

"Fertilizer?"

"You'd think so, but no. It's used to make soaps, perfumes, and cooking oil."

As soon as the mooring lines were secured and the hatch covers removed, a gang of barefoot Filipinos pattered aboard and secured conveyer belts from the wharf up to the ship. The smelly brown copra was soon flowing up the conveyers and cascading down into the holds where gangs of small, muscular longshoremen armed with large scoop shovels spread the meat evenly throughout each hold.

A legion of large buzzing flies accompanied the copra, zigzagging above the coconut meat like an aerial patrol. Before long they were careening around the rest of the ship so maddeningly the crew retreated to the midship house and closed off all means of entry. Without ventilation the ship became unbearably hot, igniting a debate as to whether it was better to roast inside or open the portholes and concede defeat to the buzzing horde. The debate ended when a resourceful crewman found netting fabric and placed it over several open portholes, though it still provided little relief from the smothering heat.

For the rest of the day the conveyor belts rattled and hummed as inch-by-inch the longshoremen rose up on the stinking fruit, their feet and hands coated with a dark, sticky residue.

After dinner the crew donned their lightest weight clothing and tramped down the gangway, eager to abandon the sweltering ship. As the sun set behind the jungled hills surrounding Manila, Nick, Moon, Remy, and Haggis, the burly arm wrestling champion, strolled along the waterfront, glad to be away from the oily stench of copra and thankful that Manila, unlike noisy Shanghai, was a calm, relaxed city. Autos and streetcars rolled along the streets, but more common were two-wheeled passenger carriages, called *caramatas*, pulled by small brown ponies.

The city's architecture also had a relaxed feel. Influenced by centuries of Spanish colonial rule, smooth stuccoed buildings featured covered balconies and thick stone columns, and every few blocks stood a Catholic church with arched wood doors and a bell tower.

Near a crumbling fortress wall leftover from the Spanish era, Nick and his mates entered a thatched-roofed bar, its walls covered with woven grass mats, floor boards cut from hardwood logs. Ceiling fans slowly rotated above merchant marine and Navy sailors swigging cold beers and making conversation at a long mahogany bar. Opposite the bar, more sailors sat at tables, sipping drinks while they admired young Filipina waitresses in colorful sarongs tightly wrapped around their bodies as they carried trays of drinks or sat with customers.

The four sailors made their way to the bar and ordered a round of beers, ice cold and refreshing. Between swigs of beer, their conversation drifted from one topic to another, punctuated by easy laughter and good-natured teasing. Sailors were natural-born storytellers, Nick observed, and loved nothing more than to recount an unusual adventure, a difficult challenge, or an encounter with an eccentric character. He also noticed that the crew had bonded during the voyage, and this was especially evident when they congregated off the ship and swapped stories and jokes like old friends.

He mentioned this to Moon.

"It's a funny thing," said Moon, a rivulet of sweat rolling down his temple. "We're like blood brothers when we serve on the same ship, and we get to know each other better than our own kin. But as soon as the voyage ends, we drift apart like flotsam in a storm." He wiped his brow with the back of his hand. "That's why I've always joined one union or the other. It's the only way a sailor can keep a lasting bond with his mates. I'm no radical like Bailey, but I respect what he's doin'. When it comes right down to it, seamen don't got many allies on the beach, and we can use all the help we can get."

"What do you think'll happen to Bailey?"

"Oh, he'll be alright. They gave him his back pay, so he'll have a few bucks to keep him afloat till he signs on with another ship."

As the evening wore on, sailors paired up with waitresses and retreated arm-in-arm through a door at the back of the bar. It wasn't hard to guess what was going on and this puzzled Nick. The Philippines was primarily a Catholic country, so he didn't expect to see prostitution practiced so openly. It was only tolerated, he guessed, because it brought money into the economy. He thought no more about it until a high-pitched scream cut through the general din, quieting conversations as heads swiveled around looking for the source.

After a few uncertain moments, someone said, "Must be havin' a rip roarin' time back there."

Salacious laughter filled the bar, breaking the tension.

Nick didn't join in. One of the girls was being hurt or badly scared, and he could only imagine what would cause her to scream so. He wasn't prepared to do anything about it, and put it out of his mind until another frightened scream broke through the din. This time no one paid much attention, but Nick couldn't enjoy himself knowing someone was in trouble and might need help. He glanced at Moon and tilted his head toward the back door, indicating the direction it came from. Moon nodded, showing he understood Nick's concern. They set their beers down and shouldered their way through the crowd to the back door.

With Moon behind him, Nick opened the door and slipped into a dim-lit hall, a row of doors along one side presumably leading to private rooms. They headed along the hall, listening for anything unusual. A girlish giggle came out of one room, and from another they heard someone grunting "unh, unh, unh, unh."

When they reached the end of the hall, the sound of a sharp slap came from somewhere behind them, followed by a whimper. Turning around, they started back down the hall. The grunter was now speeding up and gaining volume — "UNH! UNH! UNH! UNHHHHHHHH!

A muffled scream came from a room up ahead. Hurrying forward, they were about halfway down the hall when they heard another slap followed by choking sobs and loud hyperventilating breaths. The stopped in front of the door where it came from. Nick wrapped his hand around the door handle and glanced at Moon. He nodded, indicating he was ready to go.

Nick turned the handle and pushed the door open.

A wiry figure, bare to the waist, his back to them, was on his knees between the legs of a Filipino girl who lay on her back, naked, arms tied together over her head. In the muted light of a kerosene lamp, Nick could see a sock stuffed in her mouth, her face swollen, tears streaming from her eyes. The kneeling figure held a pocket knife with the tip pressed against her throat. A trickle of blood ran down her neck.

"Whoever you are," the half-naked figure said "turn around and get the hell outta here." Then in a mock light-hearted tone, he added, "We're just having a little fun. Aren't we?" He punctuated the last word with a prod of the blade. The young woman let out another muffled scream, her face distorted in anguish.

The hairs on Nick's neck stood up. The man's voice was familiar. And so was the scaly skin around his neck.

It was such an unexpected turn of events, Nick hesitated, wondering what to do. Then he glanced at the girl's frightened expression and all his doubt vanished.

"I don't think she's having any fun at all," he said, keeping his voice calm, even.

Slag's head jerked around, his profile shadowed and menacing in the dim light. "I might have known." He jumped to his feet, the muscles in his shoulders taut, the knife blade in his hand dully reflected in the lamplight. "It's a good thing we're off the ship. If you two end up in the gutter, everyone'll figure it was a drunken bar fight over a two-bit whore."

Moon tugged on Nick's shirt. "Come on," he whispered "let's go. It ain't worth gettin' killed over. He'll toy with her for awhile and let her go."

The bosun was torturing the girl, alright, but as Moon suggested it was doubtful he'd do any permanent harm. *So why risk my own neck?* He would like to have said he was compelled to defend a helpless girl from a sick sadist. Or that he was appalled at the cruelty and malice in the bosun's eyes and had to do something. But that wasn't it. The events of the last few weeks still stuck in his craw. The constant harping, the harsh assignments, the forced departure of Harding and Bailey, all conspired to keep his feet planted. This wasn't about the girl — God bless her sorry soul — it was personal.

"Come on," Moon repeated, as he stepped back into the hall. "I'm going back to the bar."

Nick heard his footsteps retreat down the hall and the bar noise spike as Moon opened and shut the hall door.

"You'd better follow him, Schoolboy," said Slag, circling the knife.

Behind him the girl lay whimpering on the mattress, strands of wet hair clinging to her face, her legs now brought up to her chest in a fetal position. An odor of fear pervaded the room. At first Nick thought it came from her. Then he realized it was oozing from another source: himself.

The knife blade slashed through the air.

Nick flinched back, barely avoiding it.

"Come on, Schoolboy," Slag taunted, "now's your chance to get back at me."

Nick watched the tip of the blade circle around. Was he being foolish to think he could challenge an armed sadist without a weapon of his own? Not that he knew how to use a knife in combat. No, if he was going to survive, much less prevail, he'd have to disarm his opponent. But how?

The answer came sooner than expected, and it was the bosun's own words that triggered it. When Nick was a schoolboy, a real schoolboy, his mother urged him to use words instead of fists. And she'd been right. He avoided a number of scrapes by bluffing his opponent into thinking he was a good fighter or by offering an unexpected compliment to appeal to his opponent's vanity. Looking at the bosun's knife, he had a feeling that neither of those tactics would work. However, there was another one that might. It was risky because it wasn't meant to avoid a fight, but it might even the odds.

He shifted his focus from the blade to the boson's dark brown eyes. "You've got a knife, but without it you're a pathetic twerp. Just a sick sadist terrorizing a defenseless girl." The bosun's mouth twitched, the muscles across his chest tensing. "Of course, with a knife even a pathetic twerp like you can pretend he's —"

"I'll show you who's pathetic," said the bosun. He tossed the knife away, lowered his shoulder, and lunged at Nick, hitting him in the solar plexus. The blow knocked Nick back onto the floor. Slag cat-like sprung onto his chest and pinned down his arms with two sharp knees.

The blow to Nick's chest had knocked the wind out of him, and before he could recover Slag grabbed his head and pounded it against the floor until Nick's eyes glazed over and stars shot across his vision.

The young girl screamed or tried to, but what came out was a frightened croak. Yet it was enough to divert the bosun's attention.

He yelled over his shoulder, "Shaddup!"

During the diversion, Nick used his legs to lift his torso at an angle so that Slag tipped to one side and had to reach over to steady himself. For a split second the weight of his left knee lifted, allowing Nick to wrench his arm free. He threw a wild punch upward, not knowing where it would land. As it happened, it hit Slag at the base of this nose, jamming the cartilage and dislocating the septum, a lucky hit on one of the most sensitive parts of the body.

The bosun howled in pain, his tongue thrust out, uvula quivering like a stalactite in an earthquake.

Nick waited to see if the punch was enough to defeat Slag, or at least make him back off. While Nick waited, the bosun cleverly joined his hands together as though holding his nose, then drove them down like a sledgehammer. The blow struck Nick square on his chest, sending shock waves of pain down to his heart. The bosun raised his fists for another assault. Before a second blow could come crashing down, Nick reached up and jammed his thumb into Slag's Adam's apple. It was surprisingly soft, the trachea giving way like a ripe peach.

"IEEEEEEEEE!" the bosun gasped, clutching his neck and toppling over backward.

Nick wriggled out from underneath him and crawled over to the girl, who lay curled up sobbing. While Slag continued to writhe in pain, Nick untied her arms and handed her a sarong laying nearby. After she covered herself, he helped her to her feet, wrapped a protective arm around her, and led her out of the room, stepping over the bosun, who still lay on the floor gasping and grimacing.

They walked down the hall and stepped through the doorway into the bar. Patrons near the door noticed them and stopped talking, starting a rippling effect that spread through the room until everyone was silent, eyes focused on the girl's swollen face and bloodied neck. Nick guided her through the crowd toward the entrance. When they reached Moon, Remy, and Haggis, the three men stepped in front of them to form an advance guard that cleared a path through the sea of solemn faces.

"BENSON!" a chilling voice cried from behind them.

Nick looked over his shoulder.

Slag was standing in the rear doorway, chest smeared with blood dripping from his nose, a visible bruise on his throat. "I'll get you, you sonofabitch," he said with quiet determination, "if it's the last fuckin' thing I do."

20

The *Diana Dollar* pulled away from the copra dock, beginning the long voyage home. Nick stood at the stern rail, watching the waterfront recede, his thoughts drifting back to the night before — the bosun's cruelty, the anguished expression on the young woman's face, how he himself had come perilously close to losing his life. He was comforted by the knowledge that his shipmates, aware of the bosun's threat to retaliate, had promised to watch his back and come to his defense if necessary.

He noticed a group of Filipinos gathered at the end of the dock waving at the ship, bidding them goodbye. He thought it was the longshore crew until he saw children and adults huddled around a familiar face, the young woman from the night before, grinning from ear to ear. He returned the wave, guessing she must have brought her family to see him off. Strangely, her smile faded, arms flopped down. He was pondering this odd behavior when a voice spoke:

"She's just a whore, you know."

Bosun Slag stood against the rail a dozen feet away, looking like an alley cat, his nose swollen, Adam's apple stained with a dark purple bruise. "There's a thousand more like her who'll sell themselves for two-bits."

How can anyone be so evil? Nick wondered. *Did the isolation of working on a ship bring out the worst in him? Or had he been born without a conscience?* Not that it mattered. Either way, he was a sadistic sociopath, and Nick was not about to take his threat lightly.

Two days later the last of the Philippine islands faded into the aft horizon, leaving only rolling swells and wind-swept ocean between the ship and its home port. Even the seagulls screeched a last goodbye as they wheeled around and headed back toward shore, abandoning the sky to a penetrating sun that beat down on the ship and reddened the necks of sailors working on deck.

Nick was in the messroom one afternoon, writing in his journal, when Haggis sat down next to him and asked if, being a college graduate and all, Nick could help him with a problem. The burly sailor went on to say that a few days earlier he'd been working in the engine room when he saw two cockroaches racing to avoid the footsteps of the chief engineer. As he watched them scamper across the floor, he was reminded of a traveling flea circus he'd seen as a young boy, operated by a bearded showman who flung open a large portmanteau mounted on wooden legs to reveal a colorful arena with a troop of trained fleas. Under the "tiny top," as the showman called it, the Lilliputian performers raced teensy chariots around a circular track, inched across a tightrope of sewing thread, and were blasted out of a tiny cannon through a burning ring of fire.

The pleasant memory, coupled with the sight of two roaches running for cover, inspired Haggis in a way he'd never been inspired before. He went to the ship's carpenter, explained his idea, and together they spent the next two days building it. When it was done they admired their handiwork: a box six-feet in length, two-feet wide, open at the top, with four-inch high perimeter walls. Partitions inside the box divided the space lengthwise, creating six long runways. They also cut a slotted starting gate that neatly slid down across the partitions, creating small cubicles at one end of the box.

Ready for a trial run, Haggis captured a half-dozen cockroaches, not a difficult task in the roach-infested ship. He inserted a roach into each cubicle behind the starting gate. With the carpenter looking on, he lifted the slotted board out of the box and waved his arms, hoping the roaches would tear down the runway like spirited thoroughbreds. Instead, to his dismay, the shiny brown insects acted more like lost wanderers, circling aimlessly about and ultimately hunkering down as if they needed a rest.

When he finished his story, Haggis glanced at Nick and asked if he could figure out a way to make the roaches run down the track.

Not wanting to burden Haggis with the fact that a degree in journalism gave him scant knowledge of biology in general and no knowledge of roaches in particular, Nick assumed a thoughtful air and promised to get back to him in a day or two.

After Haggis left, he finished his journal entry and headed to his cabin to take a nap before his next watch. In the humid, sticky, brutally hot air, he tossed fitfully and sweated beads of perspiration that rolled off his body onto dampened sheets. Unable to sleep, he gave up trying and opened his eyes just as a cockroach ambled across his bed, its odor-sensitive antennae swishing madly about in the copra redolent air. A spot of sunlight from the porthole lay in the roach's path. Nick watched as the insect paused at the edge of the spotlight, then carefully detoured around it as if it was a bubbling tar pit. It had never occurred to Nick that roaches avoided bright light, and in that moment a flash of Newtonian insight inspired him to roll out of bed and go in search of his burly shipmate.

He found Haggis in the carpenter's shop, sitting on a stool, chin resting on fist, staring forlornly at the racetrack. Nick's heart went out to the big galoot. It was a silly thing to fret over, but, as he himself knew, in the confines of a freighter far from home, even minor anxieties could draw sturdy men into a black hole of depression.

"I've got an idea," said Nick.

Haggis looked up with a blank expression.

As Nick outlined his idea, Haggis' expression became hopeful, and once he understood the plan, he was smiling with anticipation.

First they drilled holes through the end-wall of the box near the starting gate. Then they inserted small light bulbs into each hole and wired them to a six-volt battery borrowed from the engine room. While Haggis went off to capture more roaches, Nick devised a switch that turned on the lights when the slotted starting gate was lifted out of the box. He further intensified the effect by lining the area around the lights with reflective swatches of aluminum foil.

When Haggis returned with the roaches, they placed them in the cubicles behind the starting gate. Ready for a test run, Nick lifted the gate out of the box. The light bulbs instantly flashed on, prompting the roaches to flee, their spindly legs moving rapidly back and forth. They sprinted about halfway down the track, but then slowed and came to a stop, apparently far enough from the lights to ease their discomfort.

Stymied again, the two sailors stared at the racetrack, wondering what, if anything, they could do motivate the roaches to run along the entire length of the track. This time it didn't take long before the light of inspiration turned on, or perhaps it would be more accurate to say turned off.

Nick instructed Haggis to place the roaches back in the starting cubicles. He then switched off the light in the carpenter's shop and pushed the door almost shut so that only a thin sliver of light shown around the edge.

In the darkened room Haggis lifted the starting gate. When the light bulbs turned on, they flooded the roach track with glaring intensity, and this time, as if fleeing for their lives, the startled roaches dashed forward, their legs jerking back and forth with amazing speed as they raced toward the other end of the box. Like spectators at a racetrack, Nick and Haggis whooped and cheered as the roaches reached the end of the track and crossed the finish line.

News of their success spread through the ship, and it wasn't long before curious visitors came to see the jury-rigged roach track. Nick and Haggis proudly showed off their invention and invited each visitor to capture a roach and compete in a tournament to be held the following Saturday night in the messroom.

The crew responded to the invitation with unmitigated enthusiasm, including the carpenter who provided colored paints with which to daub on each roachster's back for better identification. Scarcely noticed before, the ubiquitous roaches were now the object of passionate attention. "There's a fine specimen," one sailor would say to another as a particularly large cockroach scurried across the floor. Arms outstretched, the men would dive for the potential ringer as if it was a ten ounce gold nugget.

Crewmen soon discovered that the quickest roaches were also the most difficult to control. More than once a speed burner, fished out of its holding box and about to be placed behind the starting gate for a trial run, would wiggle out of its trainer's hand and dart under the nearest cabinet to freedom. Enough roachsters were lost this way that it was not unusual to see cockroaches wandering the ship with colorful stripes across their back. One ingenious sailor solved the problem by fashioning a leash with sewing thread, and it wasn't long before every roachster wore a leash, the thread color often complementing the paint daubs to present a dashing ensemble.

The day before the race, Nick received a summons from Captain Primm. Seated inside the captain's cabin, Nick listened while Primm reminded him that gambling wasn't allowed and that serious consequences would result if it occurred. Nick assured him that the race was just for fun and that each contestant had chipped into a pool to be awarded to the top three winners.

While they were talking Nick glanced around the cabin, recalling the promise he overhead Primm make to Slag. *A hundred pounds will be plenty to set you up. You can stow it in the captain's quarters once I move in.* It had to be narcotics, and he noted several places where the cache might be stowed. Customs agents usually didn't search a captain's quarters unless they had reason to, and Nick planned to give them one.

On Saturday night the crew gathered in the mess room and huddled around the roach track on a mess table. Each contestant clutched a jar or small box containing his roachster, its name written on the container. The race track was festively painted with red, white, and blue bunting, and on the outside the name BAILEY RACEWAY was printed in large block letters in honor of the departed sailor.

"Gen-tle-mennnn!" Nick called out in the dramatic style of a prizefight announcer. "We've collected forty-five dollars in prize money. Twenty will go to the winner, fifteen to the runner-up, and ten to show. By order of the captain, no outside betting is allowed. Contestants, prepare your racers and let the competition begin!"

The first six roachsters were carefully placed in their starting boxes. At a signal from Nick, Haggis switched off the lights, throwing the room into darkness save for the orange coals of burning cigarettes. For an expectant moment, all eyes were glued to the track, all lips silent.

"On your mark!" Nick announced. "Get set, go!"

He lifted the slotted board out of the box, turning on the light bulbs. This incited the roachsters to tear off down the track amid a clamoring uproar from the crew. Perhaps because of the hubbub, the cockroaches reacted with little consistency once they passed the halfway point. Some continued down the track, others shambled along in fits and starts. Contestants clapped and yelled in an attempt to spur on their roachsters to victory. One poor roach stopped just shy of the finish line and wouldn't move any farther. Another racer, apparently confused by the uproar and the haze of cigarette smoke, crawled against a sidewall and refused to continue. Most, though, continued to the finish line, and when a roach named Little Marlene was the first to cross it, her owner whooped in delight.

Between heats, Nick and Haggis tallied the results and organized the next heat. Occupied in this way they failed to notice spectators making wagers among themselves, surreptitiously exchanging dollar bills when the lights were off.

It was ten o'clock by the time the heats had eliminated all but the final six roachsters. Eager with anticipation, the crew pressed forward as the six were introduced. There was Mighty Mite, Little Marlene, Joe Hill, Frisco Filly, Scotch Boiler, and Spirit of St. Louis. As each roachster was introduced, its owner proudly held it up, then placed it in one of the starting cubicles.

"Gen-tle-mennnn!" Nick said, raising his hands to quiet the room. "This is the final race and will determine the top three prize winners!"

The crew craned forward to get a better view, while someone pounded a bare-handed drum roll on the table. When Haggis turned off the lights, the room fell quiet as everyone waited for the race to begin.

After a suspenseful pause, Nick jerked the starting board up, flashing on the light bulbs. All six finalists, reacting with inbred fear, spurted down the track toward the finish line. By now, though, they were accustomed to the bright lights, and all of them stopped well short of their goal.

Spectators, especially those who'd placed bets, yelled and howled and frantically waved their hands like marooned castaways. Under this tremendous din Mighty Mite came to life and lunged forward, causing sailors to cheer even louder. In desperation owners of the other racers snapped their fingers and clapped their hands, spurring the rest of the roachsters into action led by Frisco Filly and Joe Hill, both of whom quickly passed Mighty Mite and closed in on the finish line with Little Marlene, Scotch Boiler, and the Spirit of St. Louis trailing far behind.

A roar of excitement filled the messroom.

A moment later the roar was cut short when the overhead lights unexpectedly flicked on, flooding the messroom with illumination and bringing the race to a sudden halt. All eyes turned to Haggis, who grinned sheepishly, for his elbow had accidentally flipped on the light switch. He quickly turned off the lights. By now, though, the roachsters were far from the starting lights and seemed content to stay put. It had been a long evening madly dashing down the track. The racers looked wearily moribund, their bodies slumped to the floor of the track, their antennae drooped over like flaccid flower stems.

Out of the back of the pack, Scotch Boiler suddenly came to life and darted forward as if he were late to his own wedding. He crossed the finish line a full six inches ahead of his nearest opponent, inciting a clamor of joy and despair that motivated Frisco Filly to dart over the finish line in second place with Joe Hill a close third.

The unintentional interruption of the contest caused the losers to protest and the winners to argue with them. The entire throng was in such a state of uproarious commotion that no one noticed Primm and Slag slip into the room and station themselves near the door.

In the center of the agitated pack, Nick and Haggis discussed what to do. They could rerun the race, which would likely produce another winner and cause confusion, or they could declare the contest over.

Nick raised his arms to quiet the room. "Gentlemen, since each roachster was equally effected by the lights, we are ruling it a valid race with all prizes to be awarded to the winners."

A roar of cheers and groans greeted the announcement. At the back of the pack, losers reluctantly slipped dollars into the hands of winners.

21

"I warned you gambling is forbidden," said Captain Primm, fists on hips, eyes roving back and forth between Nick and Haggis. "I could have you dismissed without pay."

Cigarette butts and the remnants of squashed roaches littered the empty messroom, abandoned by the crew when the race ended and Primm's presence became known.

"But sir—" Haggis protested.

"There are no *buts*," Primm interrupted, "only *asses* who fail to obey orders."

Despite the stern admonition, Primm seemed perversely satisfied to have caught the two offenders red-handed, and so did Slag who stood behind him, one side of his mouth curved up in a perfidious smirk.

Nick was certain that Slag had convinced Primm to sneak into the messroom, knowing bets might be placed and knowing the captain would hold him responsible. "We told the men gambling was prohibited, so how can we be responsible if they made bets behind our backs?"

"You two staged this—this *contest*," Primm said, pointing to the roach track with the words BAILEY RACEWAY painted on the side, "and I warned you not to permit gambling. It was your job to make sure everyone obeyed the rules." He glanced over his shoulder at the bosun. "What do you think? Should we confine them to quarters for a few days and dock their pay?"

"Naah, I wouldn't be so hard," Slag replied in a mock solicitous tone. "After all, they were just tryin' to give the men some fun. A slap on the wrist should do."

"What do you suggest?"

"A few days cleanin' the holds ought to do it. Nothin' like good hard dreck to set a sailor straight."

"Okay, I'll leave it to your discretion. As for you men, I don't want to hear a peep out of you for the rest of the voyage. If the bosun reports any problems, you'll be confined to quarters until we reach Frisco."

It was obvious to everyone onboard that Nick's punishment was Slag's retaliation for the incident in Manila. The only question remaining was whether Slag's taste for revenge was satisfied, or did he have something more in mind. Since Nick had no way of knowing, he figured it would be safer to count on the latter, and that meant he would have to watch his step until the voyage was over.

The next morning Nick and Haggis climbed down into the number one hold to begin serving their sentence. The rancid oily odor of copra was noticeable throughout the ship, but here in the hold it was as thick and disgusting as an outhouse. Slag handed down two ladders, two wooden pallets, rags, scrub brushes, and buckets of soogey-moogey, a caustic cleaning compound composed of lye, soft soap, and water. He promised to let them out at the end of the watch if they finished cleaning half the hold. He then closed and locked the access door, cutting off all light except for two ceiling lamps that cast a dreary glow on the copra but left the far corners in brooding darkness.

Starting at one end of the hold, they stood the ladders upright on pallets and leaned them against horizontal I-beams supporting the weather deck above. While they were setting things up, a swarm of copra flies emerged from the shadows and buzzed around them like security guards harassing unwanted intruders. Nick couldn't imagine a worse place to work. The fetid smell of copra nearly made him gag and the soogey-moogey added its own noxious fumes to the stagnant air. He climbed a ladder, dipped his brush into the soogey-moogey, and began scrubbing the ceiling. Since most of the work required reaching overhead, it wasn't long before their faces and clothes were streaked with grime, their arms and shoulders aching.

As the morning wore on, the temperature in the hold grew increasingly hot. Slag had provided them with two canteens of water, but it was gone by midmorning, leaving their throats parched, heads faint from dehydration. Periodically they had to climb down the ladders and tuck their heads between their knees until they recovered enough to go back to work, motivated by the bosun's promise to let them out at the end of the watch if they finished cleaning half the hold.

At noon Slag opened the access door and descended into the hold, clutching a rag over his nose to ward off the smell. After a cursory look around he gave them permission to leave and ordered them to return for the evening watch to finish the other half.

Emerging from the hold light-headed and wobbly, Nick went straight to his bunk and lay down, rising only to refill his canteen or use the head. At dinner time Moon brought him a bowl of chili and crackers. He wolfed it down and was revived enough to return to the number one hold for the evening watch. By then the air had cooled, and with extra canteens of water he and Haggis finished cleaning the number one hold well before the four-hour watch was up. Exhausted, they rested on pallets and stared into the gloom until the bosun arrived at midnight to release them.

When Nick returned to his quarters, his bunkmates were still up and deep in conversation. The galley had run out of chili before the entire crew had eaten. This prompted hungry sailors to confront Cook who explained that the company had failed to provide adequate stores. He offered to heat up some sausages but warned that meal portions would have to be rationed for the rest of the voyage.

Too tired to join the conversation, Nick lay down and fell into a deep sleep, his face still streaked with grime. The next morning, tired and sore, he ate a meager breakfast of one egg, coffee, and a piece of toast. He and Haggis then reported to the number two hold where once again the bosun locked them in for the entire four hour watch.

For a second depressing morning they scrubbed the hold, their shoulders aching, their hands red and wrinkled from constant contact with the acidic soogey-moogey. The ship was now eight days from San Francisco, and the only thing that kept Nick going was his desire to complete the job before they reached home. More than anything he wanted to stand on deck when they sailed through the Golden Gate and watch the city and surrounding bay come into view.

He was dipping his scrub brush in soogey-moogey when he noticed a movement in the field of copra, or at least thought he did. He paused to look closer. He couldn't see anything unusual and reckoned that in the dim light his eyes had played a trick. That is until he saw the movement again. Only this time it had legs.

He climbed down the ladder and crept closer until he was able to distinguish the outlines of a spider about four inches in diameter, covered with dark-brown fuzz the same shade as the copra. He froze. It was the largest spider he'd ever seen, by far. And he knew what it was: a tarantula. His knowledge of the fearsome creature was limited, but he recalled that the sting of a tarantula, though quite painful, wasn't lethal. He looked around for others and didn't see any, but sensed that more were lurking in the copra and warned Haggis to be careful.

At the end of the watch, the bosun poked his head through the access door. This time he gave them permission to leave without bothering to check their work, then hurried off as if he had more important matters to attend to. Nick gave it little thought until he found Moon, Remy, and two others in his bunkroom talking about events earlier that morning. Several irate seamen had gone up to the captain's cabin to register a complaint about the lack of food. Sailors are willing to endure extreme physical hardship — rough seas, foul weather, boiling and frigid temperatures — as long as they receive three squares a day. On an empty stomach, however, even the most hardened seamen can become grumpy and argumentative, especially near the end of a long voyage. Primm tried to shoo them away, saying there was nothing he could do in the middle of the ocean. However, they wouldn't be dissuaded so easily, and one sailor complained that the officers were still dining on fresh meat and vegetables while the crew was eating half portions of insect-ridden chow.

Angered by the audacious protest, Primm ordered them off the bridge deck and threatened to lock them up if they disturbed him again.

That evening Nick trudged to the number two hold in low spirits. The thought of spending several more days locked in a dungeon with belligerent flies, lurking spiders, and the smothering stench of copra was almost more than he could bear. He sorely missed the joy of manning the helm and standing watch on the flying deck above the wheelhouse, surrounded by an expanse of sea and sky. Haggis, who was accustomed to working in the engine room, seemed less affected by the gloomy atmosphere, although he too grew silent as the evening wore on. At midnight they sat down on their pallets and waited for the bosun to let them out.

"So what're you gonna do when we reach Frisco?" Haggis asked.

Get off the ship as soon as possible, Nick was about to say but stopped himself. He didn't want Haggis to think he was eager to part with his shipmates. The truth was, he liked most of the men on the ship, and their stops in foreign ports had been an exciting education. But the voyage had been tougher than expected, and he wasn't sure he wanted to repeat it. Perhaps he needed time on dry land before deciding what to do next. In any case, his greatest desire was to see his family and reunite with Clarisa. He'd thought of her every day and often wondered what their first meeting would be like. Had her affection for him deepened in his absence? Made her realize how much she loved him? Would she greet him like a returning war hero? Wrap her arms around him and give him a warm welcoming kiss? He hoped so.

He glanced at Haggis. "After I get settled at home, I'd like to have a beer with you and my bunkmates."

Haggis nodded. "Yeah, a beer would be good. Maybe two or three."

Just then the bosun opened the access door and let them out.

They reported for duty the next morning and climbed down into the number three hold. Exhausted and sore, they took rest breaks with increasing frequency and often stopped to rub their aching arms. Consequently, it took two days to clean the number three hold and three days to finish number four.

At the end of each day, when the bosun freed them, they staggered out, arms limp, faces dirty and blank from exhaustion. It was meaner work, Haggis declared, than planting alfalfa in prairie hardpan.

With rationed portions from the galley providing fewer calories, Nick saw his body shrink down to hardened muscle and his cheeks hollow. Haggis went through an even greater transformation. When they started he resembled a corn fed Holstein and now had the gangly look of a Texas longhorn. Nick apologized for dragging him into a mess more intended to punish himself for a past grudge than their alleged gambling violation.

Haggis would hear none of it. He wrapped an arm around Nick's shoulder and explained that folks from his part of Kansas were pioneer families who lived by the dint of their labor. He himself had never known a man of letters before, and it was an honor to have a friend as smart and loyal as Nick. Besides, without Nick's help he wouldn't have been able to stage the roach race, one of the greatest moments of his life.

Weary, homesick, and truly moved by Haggis's affection, Nick turned his face away to keep from openly weeping in front of the burly sailor.

The freighter was nearing the California coast, and the closer they were to their homeport, the more Nick felt a desperate need to be on deck when the ship sailed into San Francisco Bay. He and Haggis received permission to work straight through until they completed the last hold. For fourteen straight hours they struggled to finish, their hands swollen and cracked, bodies sore and exhausted. At ten o'clock that evening they were only two-thirds done, yet Nick was determined to finish. Standing at the top of his ladder, he reached as far as he could to scrub a dark spot. If he hadn't been so tired, he would have climbed down and moved the ladder. Instead, he stretched out farther and farther and almost reached the spot when the ladder suddenly slid sideways and slipped off the I-beam. As it fell, he dropped the brush and tried to grab hold of the beam but missed and tumbled down, barely avoiding the ladder as he landed on the copra.

Dazed and shaken, though not seriously injured, he lay on his back looking up at a swarm of flies circling above him like vultures over carrion. Haggis climbed down and extended a hand to help him up. Nick looked up at his friend and saw that Haggis, too, was exhausted and could barely hold his head up.

"Let's call it a day," Nick said, motioning to him to sit down.

Haggis slumped onto the edge of a pallet. "Don't you want to finish tonight?"

"Yeah, but I know it doesn't mean as much to you. You'd be down in the engine room anyway. I can't make you work all night on my account."

Haggis shrugged. "Sometimes we used to cut and stack wheat three days straight to save the crop before rain come in. This ain't so bad."

Nick knitted his fingers behind his head. "So how did a farm boy like you end up on a ship?"

Haggis picked up a piece of copra and squeezed it between his fingers. "When I was eighteen a Navy recruiter came through town and talked about all the places we could go if we signed up. Made it sound like a holiday cruise. Daddy didn't want me to leave, said he needed help to take care of the farm. But I got three brothers and two sisters, and I reckoned they'd be alright with one less mouth to feed." He shook his head and grunted in a way that indicated the folly of his decision. "The Navy didn't turn out as glamorous as the recruiter said. I spent two years workin' on a sea tug, pushin' ships in and out of Norfolk harbor, wishin' I was on one of 'em."

"So how'd you get into the merchant marine?"

"After my tour of duty was up, I went back to the farm. When I got there everythin' had changed. Drought had sucked all the moisture outta the soil, and dust storms whipped it into black blizzards. Mama stuffed rags under the doors, but it didn't stop the dust from comin' in. She used to say her bread was four parts flour, two parts water, and one part Oklahoma." One side of his mouth turned up in a rueful smile. "I knew I couldn't stay. My brothers looked like sticks and half the neighbors had moved on. I told 'em I'd find work on a ship and send 'em money. Four months ago I got a letter sayin' they were headin' for California. Haven't heard from 'em since."

The spongy copra, smelly and fetid though it was, made a comfortable bed. Nick's eyelids drooped and his exhausted body pulled him down toward a peaceful slumber. Fighting off the sandman, he asked, "So how ya gonna find 'em?"

"Don't rightly know. They said they was gonna try their luck at a place called King City. Sounds kinda nice don't it...King City, City a Kings... Guess I'll look for 'em there."

Nick opened his eyes and stared into the gloom, his head groggy, his body stiff and sore. He must have been asleep, perhaps for hours. If that was the case San Francisco was sure to be close, maybe within sight. He closed his eyes and pictured himself standing on the weather deck as the ship approached the city . . . waves crashing on Ocean Beach . . . the roller coaster at Playland looping and swirling around itself . . . the Cliff House perched on an outcropping, a herd of sea lions lounging on the rocks below . . . the Golden Gate flanked by ochre cliffs and white foamy surf . . .

A loud clang came from somewhere above him. He propped himself up on his elbows and looked for Haggis. His burly friend lay sleeping nearby, hands tucked under his head. Nick yawned and stretched. He rose to his feet and looked around. Something was different, he sensed. What was it? Then he noticed his own ladder laying nearby but not Haggis's. "That's funny," he murmured as he stepped gingerly across the copra toward the middle of the hold. The other ladder was in a far corner leaning against the bulkhead. He moved toward it and looked up at the ceiling, head back, jaw slack. "Well, I'll be damned." The ceiling was clean, every bit of it.

Haggis had finished the job.

Something else was different too. Nick cocked his head and listened. Footsteps padding above. Hose lines dragging across the deck. A spray of water against the ship. The clink-clink-clink of someone tinkering with a ventilator. Aside from the workaday noises, there was no other sound, no rush of water against the hull, no rhythmic hum from the ship's engine, a vibration that had become as familiar to him as his heartbeat.

It was as if the freighter had died.

A wave of nostalgia suddenly swept over him, a sense of having lost something. *Nostalgia?* That was a surprise. After what he'd been through, he certainly didn't expect to feel anything resembling nostalgia. Still, these steel bones and this rigid skin had been his home for nearly four months, and soon it would all dissolve into the past — the ship, the crew, the odyssey. And these men to whom he'd come to consider his brothers, and perhaps more importantly who'd come to consider him their brother, would drift apart in the currents of time.

The access door opened. A shaft of sunlight poured into the hold.

The bosun stood in the doorway. "You finished?" Nick nodded. "Good. Longshoremen'll be onboard as soon as Customs gives us clearance. Get your gear together." He disappeared, leaving the door ajar.

Haggis stirred. He rubbed his eyes and sat up, his face puffy, streaked with gunk. "Sorry, you didn't get to see the ship sail into port. I shoulda woke you when I finished." He rose to his feet.

Nick put an arm over his shoulder. "You've got nothing to be sorry for, my friend."

They emerged from the hold into the bright light of a clear, sunny day. Nick shielded his eyes from the glare and inhaled breaths of fresh clean air. The *Diana Dollar* was berthed beside the copra dock in Islais Creek, a small inlet south of the Embarcadero. A tall steel crane stood on the dock beside the ship, a large flexible vacuum tube dangling from the crane, presumably to suck the copra out of the ship. Nick surveyed the surroundings — a grimy rail yard with rusty boxcars, several old brick warehouses and corrugated Quonset huts, gravel and oil spots.

It isn't the beautiful Golden Gate, he thought, *but at least it's home.*

Moon and Remy had already packed their gear and were playing pinochle when Nick entered the bunkroom. They kidded him about his filthy appearance and suggested he take a shower before showing himself around town. Too tired to respond to their teasing, he opened his locker and began removing his belongings.

Strange voices drifted in from the passageway. A minute later two men entered the cabin wearing uniforms with U.S. Customs patches on their shoulders. Moon and Remy opened their bags for inspection. While the Customs agents looked through their things, Nick transferred his belongings from his locker to his bunk. At the back of his locker, he grasped his duffle bag and felt a lump inside it about the size of a loaf of bread. He pulled out the bag, reached in, and touched a package wrapped in paper and tied with string. He smiled. Moon and Remy must have replaced his whisky without telling him. He removed the package from the duffle bag, and then notice it was too light to be a bottle of liquor.

What is it? he wondered.

"All right, son," one the inspectors said, "let's look at your gear."

22

Clarisa hailed a taxi in front of the Matson Building and instructed the driver to take her to the Hall of Justice. As the taxi sped north on Kearny Street, she gazed out the window at shops along the way. There was one for ladies hats, another for cigars, another for phonographs, one for sheet music, typewriters, baked goods, magazines. Yet they all had one thing in common. Prominently displayed in the window of each business was an identical poster emblazoned with a Blue Eagle. Symbol of the National Recovery Administration, the Blue Eagle was similar to the American eagle on the dollar bill, its wings outstretched, head turned to profile, a sheaf of lightning bolts clutched in the talons of one leg and a cog wheel in the other. Beneath it were the words, WE DO OUR PART. The posters were part of a government campaign to promote codes of fair competition, a policy designed to help lift the country out of a deep depression. *I wonder if it's working?* Clarisa thought. The situation hadn't improved as far as she could tell—the breadline in front of St. Patrick's Mission was growing every week—but perhaps in time it would.

As the taxi approached the Hall of Justice, Clarisa reflected on her mission. Nick's mother Lillian had called to let her know that Nick was back, then in the next breath announced he'd been arrested for smuggling narcotics, a charge Clarisa found baffling and wholly unbelievable. *Could he have changed that much? It didn't seem possible. Or did it?* Anyone might resort to reckless behavior if the rewards were great enough and if they thought they could get away with it. *But would Nick?* And it raised another question. How did she feel about him now that they'd been apart for months, now that she was seeing Roger. She'd looked forward to his return, yet now that he was here she wasn't sure how things would unfold. Still, there was one thing she was certain of: she wanted to help in whatever way she could.

The taxi dropped her off in front of the Hall of Justice, a four-story, granite building with dark stains down the front. She pushed through the front door, climbed the worn marble stairs to the second floor, and headed for the desk sergeant's window. The baggy-eyed sergeant behind the grill didn't recognize her until she reminded him of the night several months earlier when she came for her father.

"Oh, that's right," he recalled, "the ear biter. As far as I know, darlin', your father isn't a guest of the city at the moment."

"I'm not here for my father. I'm looking for the man who was with me that night."

A guard wearing a ring of jangling keys escorted her up to the next floor and into a visiting room divided down the middle by a long table, prisoners on one side, visitors on the other. She recognized Lillian Benson and her father Rune sitting opposite a man whose face was coated with grime, cheeks sunken and gaunt, clothes streaked with splotches of gunk as if he'd been pelted by drops of mud. As she approached he looked up, his light blue eyes shining amid a dirty, unshaven face. *Can this be Nick?* He looked like a half-starved vagrant, not the man who left four months earlier.

He must have sensed her shock, for he leaned toward his mother and whispered, "Why did you tell her I was here?"

"I — I thought you'd want to see her," she stammered.

"Like this? You want her to see me in here, like this?"

"I had no idea —. Why didn't they let you clean up?" Lillian lifted a canvas tote bag from the floor and pushed it across the table. "I brought some clean clothes and a few things to eat."

A guard came over and took the bag. "I'll have to inspect it."

Clarisa sat down beside Mrs. Benson and gave Nick a sympathetic smile, hoping to conceal her shock. "Please don't blame your mother. I would have been terribly disappointed if she hadn't called me."

"The boy's been set up by a couple of freebooters," said Rune, puffing furiously on his meerschaum pipe. "We'll make sure they get to the bottom of it."

"Has he got," Clarisa said to Lillian, then turned to Nick, "do you have an attorney?"

He glanced at her sullenly and looked away.

His reaction left her speechless. He'd never treated her with hostility before, in fact, just the opposite. He was the most loving man she knew, kind, considerate, rarely raised his voice. *What could have happened to him to make him so upset? And why does he look like a starving vagrant?* Then all at once the answer became clear. Not only was he suffering from the stress of being arrested and incarcerated and whatever else had happened before that, his pride was wounded as well.

As if to confirm her assessment, he heaved a deep, despairing sigh.

She wanted to reach out and console him, wanted to caress his cheek and tell him everything was going to be alright. But his state of mind was so raw and so wounded, she was afraid any sympathy might make him feel worse. And that was part of her shock. The most level-headed person she knew, who had never so much as sniffled in her presence before, even after his father died, was now reduced to a tangle of raw nerves.

Still, she had to do something. "When I get back to the office. I'll make inquiries about an attorney. My boss knows some of the best in San Francisco."

"That would be kind of you, dear," said Lillian, "but we don't have money for a lawyer."

"I'll see what I can do. Don't worry, Nick. We'll find a way out of this" — she didn't quite know how to put it — "this situation."

Nick nodded but still refused to look at her.

For the rest of the afternoon Clarisa floundered in a realm of uncertainty. She'd been aware that Nick's return would force her to face choices she wasn't prepared to make, but his arrest was a wrinkle that took her by surprise. Paradoxically, it also set her on a firm course. By the end of the day her Florence Nightingale side had taken over and defined the situation in clear, concise terms: help those in need, worry about the rest later.

She went into Roger's office and sat down, knitted her hands together on her lap, posture erect, eyes focused. After her confession to Father Shannon and its healing effect, she'd been able to resume a normal relationship with her boss, both at work and outside the office. They'd begun dating again, and although she was fond of him, she'd made it clear there would not be a repetition of the Night of the Golden Grass, at least for the foreseeable future.

She cleared her throat. When Roger looked up she described Nick's situation as if it were a work assignment with a set of challenges and a clear objective. She concluded by saying that it boiled down to one salient fact: Nick needed pro bono representation to exonerate him from false charges that carried a stiff prison sentence. She also pointed out that it was in the shipowner's best interest to catch the real perpetrators, even if it led to the captain, for a corrupt skipper could cause serious problems.

While Roger listened he chewed on the end of a pen, his eyes wandering across his desk, occasionally flitting up to her and back down again. When she finished, he fixed his gaze on her with a steady, penetrating stare. "So, do you love him?"

She met his gaze with her own, and as she did a warm tingle spread through her, a tingle she couldn't wholly interpret. *Am I still vulnerable to his animal magnetism? Or has a latent affection for Nick, dormant while he was away, come back to life?* Whatever the case, she couldn't think about that now. "Does it matter?"

"Maybe."

"You mean, if I don't love him you'll help, but if I do, you won't."

"Not necessarily. I just want to know."

"Why? Isn't it enough to help someone because he needs it, because it would be the right thing to do?"

Roger snorted. "Don't be disingenuous. This isn't just *someone* we're talking about. This is your former lover who in all likelihood still loves you. If I'm going to help *someone*, I want to know where things stand."

Where *did* things stand? The question forced her to examine her own feelings for the umpteenth time, and the answer was still the same. She loved Nick. The affection between them had been too deep to erase in a few months. But that didn't mean she wanted him. Why didn't men understand that a woman could love someone and not necessarily be *in* love with him? Why couldn't they see love for what it is: a process, not a point in time. Passion is the love child of daily nuances not the other way around. Even so, if that was all there was to it, she could offer a simple answer. Nick and I met, fell in love, separated, and now all that's left are the attenuated feelings that resonated within her, would always resonate within her.

But that wasn't the entire picture. Over the previous months a seedling had sprouted, an attraction to Roger that had been immediate and visceral. Yet her affection had grown in measured steps. She'd been careful not to let herself give in too quickly, resisting the urge to submit to male dominance and privilege. Here and now, though, she could see the seedling had taken root, although it was too early to tell where their mutual attraction would lead. So how could she explain the vagaries of love in a way that made sense to a male brain embedded with Cro-Magnon sensibilities? She smiled at the thought, thankful that Roger couldn't read her mind.

Taking her smile as reassurance, Roger leaned back in his chair. "Look, I don't want to play the heavy and push you into a corner."

Clarisa smiled again, this time purposely employing a negotiator's most cunning tool: silence.

Roger returned her smile, and for a moment they gazed at each other with mutual admiration.

Then, as if he'd made up his mind, Roger sat up and set his pen on the desk with deliberate purposefulness. "I'll give John Neylan a call. He'll know what to do."

"Is he good?"

"He's general counsel for the Hearst Corporation. They don't come any better."

23

John Francis Neylan bore the patrician features of a Roman senator, long face, straight nose, big ears, bushy brown eyebrows. He reached across the table and shook Nick's hand, then set his briefcase on the table, sat down beside Roger Farnsworth, and snapped his briefcase open. He removed a legal pad covered with notes and adjusted his wire-frame glasses.

While Neylan checked his notes, Nick studied the two men, grateful to have their help but curious as to why they were here and suspicious of their motive. Farnsworth was dressed in an expensive double-breasted suit, his blond hair perfectly oiled and combed. He glanced at Nick in a lingering way that gave Nick the distinct feeling he was being appraised, although for what reason he had no idea. The lawyer also wore a tailored suit and silk tie, and this aroused Nick's curiosity even more as to why these two well-heeled men were here. Farnsworth had informed him that he was Clarisa's boss, but unless he owed Clarisa a favor, it seemed unlikely that he would take an interest in Nick's situation *and* bring a high-priced lawyer to boot.

"I don't suppose you're here because you think I'm innocent?" he said, hoping to shed light on their motives.

"You have Miss McMahon to thank," said Farnsworth. "She convinced us we may have a couple of bad apples on the *Diana Dollar*, and no ship owner wants his vessel embroiled in legal proceedings. Customs hasn't impounded the ship, but they could, especially if more narcotics are found. That doesn't appear likely, though. They searched her and didn't find anything, then posted a twenty-four hour watch during discharge to make sure nothing was buried in the cargo. If there is more opium, it was either jettisoned overboard at sea or transferred to another vessel before the ship docked."

"I wouldn't be so sure about that," said Nick, feeling better after three days rest and regular meals. "There are hundreds of nooks and crannies on the *Diana Dollar*, many well hidden or difficult to reach. No one knows the ship better than bosun Slag. I doubt Customs agents found them all."

"At this point," said Neylan, looking up from his notes, "the narcotics they haven't found is the least of your worries. It's the narcotics they have found we're concerned with. I've interviewed Mr. Slag, Captain Primm, your bunkmates, and a few others, none of whom saw anyone in your locker but you."

"That doesn't mean it didn't happen. Our cabin was often empty and those lockers are easy to break into."

Neylan peered over his glasses. "And you would know about that, wouldn't you?"

Roger glanced quizzically at the lawyer.

"Another sailor," said Neylan, looking down at his notes, "a Mr. Mullins, broke into Nick's locker and stole several bottles of liquor during the voyage. Do you think he might have planted the opium?"

Nick shook his head. "He's no drug smuggler, and even if he was he wouldn't do that to me. No, it was Slag. I overheard Primm telling him he could hide a hundred pounds in the captain's cabin if he helped him get rid of Captain Harding."

Neylan checked his notes. "Mr. Mullins did say you were convinced Primm and Slag orchestrated Captain Harding's resignation, but there's nothing more than your word to support that assertion. As for Harding, after he resigned his post in Shanghai he reportedly boarded a French schooner bound for the Society Islands. It could be months before he shows up, if ever, so at this point we can't count on his testimony. In any case, Customs didn't find anything in Primm's cabin."

"Because Slag moved it and planted some of it in my locker."

"And you think he did that because you had a fight with him in Manila, is that right?"

Nick nodded.

"Again, there's nothing but your word to support that claim."

Nick shook his head in disbelief. Not only had those two mutinous bastards gotten rid of Harding, they'd framed him too.

"Do have any money for bail?" Neylan asked.

"How much is it?"

"The judge will probably set it at ten thousand, so you'll have to come up with a thousand for the bail bondsman."

Nick shook his head. He didn't have five hundred much less a thousand.

"Okay, then, you have two choices. You can plead not guilty and languish in jail, possibly for months, while I prepare a case and we wait for a court date. Or you can plead guilty and throw yourself at the mercy of the court."

"But —," Nick protested.

Neylan raised a hand. "Hear me out. Your story seems credible to me, but we don't have a shred of evidence to back it. And the facts point to your guilt. On the other hand, you're a college graduate with a clean record, so I may be able to convince the prosecutor to lower the charges to a misdemeanor customs violation. With the right judge you'll receive probation or at worst a year in county jail."

Nick could hardly believe his ears. *A year in jail? For a crime I didn't commit?* The whole situation was ludicrous, bizarre, like some nightmare out of an Edgar Allen Poe tale. There had to be another way out of this. "And what if I refuse to go along with this charade?"

"If we plead not guilty and you're convicted, you're a felon facing five to ten in San Quentin. Simple as that." He paused to let it sink in. "And I haven't met a single man who went to prison and came out the same. It's a huge risk."

Nick sat back and let out a sigh. For all his thoughts of being accepted into the Brotherhood of the Sea, a sailor among sailors, it now appeared he'd been a bumbling landlubber pulling on the tail of a shark whose jaws were now firmly clamped on his rear end.

Neylan stuffed his notepad back into his briefcase and picked up his hat. "The arraignment isn't till Monday, so you have a few days to think it over. If you have any questions, call my office." He placed a business card on the table and stood up. "You coming?" he asked Roger.

"No. I'll call you later. Thanks for your help."

"Don't mention it." Neylan headed toward the door, then turned back around, scratching his cheek thoughtfully. "There was a time when I would've taken this case to the State Supreme Court. But I've lost too many cases defending clients with the evidence stacked against them. I know it's a hard pill to swallow. You have to weigh the risk of going to prison against certain humiliation and inconvenience." He smiled ruefully. "Well, good day, gentlemen."

Nick shifted his focus to Farnsworth, wondering why he hadn't left with the lawyer. Roger was looking at him again in that lingering, appraising way, and it gave Nick an uneasy feeling that something was going on, something he was unaware of and probably unprepared for.

Roger leaned forward over the table and spoke in a low voice. "There is an alternative."

"Oh, yeah?"

"Things are changing at the port, and it's important that my organization, the Waterfront Employers Association, is well-informed about what's going on. To do that, we need inside information on a variety of groups and individuals."

Nick figured he knew what Farnsworth was driving at, but he had to be sure. "You're looking for a spy?"

Farnsworth shrugged. "Let's just say we need someone who can join a longshore gang, someone with calluses on his hands" — he nodded at Nick's hardened palms — "and a brain in his head."

Now the situation was clear. Farnsworth must have known that

Neylan would offer Nick two unpleasant choices and that he would be predisposed to accept a third offer. It was a cunning move, yet he wasn't in a position to discount it.

"So how are you going to keep me from going to court?"

Roger waved a hand dismissively as if to say it wouldn't be difficult. "When you have the right contacts, there are ways to resolve situations that don't involve normal channels."

"Okay, but I've never worked on the waterfront. They'd spot me as an outsider in a second."

"A lot of longshoremen are ex-sailors. I understand from Miss Mc-Mahon that you spent your teen years running around the waterfront, so you probably know more than you realize. Plus you're smart, so it shouldn't take long to learn the rest."

The mention of Clarisa reminded Nick that it was she who helped to arrange this meeting, and it made him wonder how much information about himself she'd revealed to Farnsworth. "Does she know about this?"

"No. We'll keep this arrangement to ourselves. You and I will be the only ones who know. Besides, it's safer that way."

"Safer?" Nick scoffed. "Let's not kid ourselves. You're asking me to spy on dockworkers, and they don't have a reputation for coddling their enemies. If I was discovered, I'd be mincemeat."

His own words surprised himself. *Am I even considering Farnsworth's offer? Didn't I tell Captain Harding I could never be a spy?* In all the time he worked on the *Diana Dollar,* he'd never gone out of his way to gather information, and he never snitched on anyone or got anyone in trouble. But this, this was the real McCoy. There would be no pretending he was an innocent bystander helping an aging, over-the-hill captain.

"Look," said Roger, "I'm not saying it'll be easy or risk free. But if you're reasonably careful, chances of serious trouble are nil. You aren't the first person we've hired to gather information. I'll admit a few of our operatives have sustained injuries, but none has ever taken a one-way trip to Cypress Lawn. And the rewards will be well worth the risk."

Nick pictured himself working on the waterfront, laboring in the hold of a ship. The job would be hard, but that didn't bother him. And it couldn't be nearly as hard as scrubbing off grime inside the *Diana Dollar* ... the *Diana Dollar* ... He mentally searched the freighter for places a hundred pounds of opium might be stowed. There were scores of nooks and crannies ideal for hiding a package, yet one fact was undeniable: he wouldn't find it "languishing in jail," as Neylan put it. Still, the thought of becoming a spy was troubling, and not just because of risk to life and limb.

"I don't know," he said. "I'm not sure I could stomach the job. I've never been a snitch."

"Look, what I'm asking you to do isn't illegal, isn't sabotage, and won't harm anyone. I'll need you to look into certain things. Otherwise, you'll just keep your eyes and ears open and let me know what's going on. You'll earn longshoreman's pay of seventy-five cents an hour, plus another thirty dollars a week from us. That's sixty bucks a week and a get-out-of-jail-free card."

Put that way, the offer was tempting, especially when one of the best lawyers in town said that pleading innocent might land him in the hoosegow and pleading guilty would brand him a criminal and still risk incarceration. Farnsworth's option was the only one guaranteed to release him from jail and give him an opportunity to prove his innocence. On the other hand, it obligated him to put on wolf's clothing and run with the pack. He rubbed the back of his neck. Every option had risks and pitfalls, and they all stank to high heaven. Nevertheless, he had to make a choice.

"Alright," he said, "on two conditions. First, the obligation will last for one year. Period. No extensions. After twelve months, I'm done."

"Okay," said Roger, smiling now that Nick had one foot onboard.

"Second, I want Primm and Slag transferred to another vessel and shipped out immediately."

"You mean before they have a chance to remove the opium you think is on the *Diana Dollar*?" Nick nodded. "Under normal circumstances I couldn't possibly promise that, but you're in luck there. The Dollar Company has decided to pull the *Diana Dollar* from the schedule. Freight prices for low-value raw materials have been depressed by foreign-owned tramp steamers. The bulk cargo she's been hauling hardly covers her overhead."

"I thought Dollar made its money on mail contracts."

"It does, but the larger and faster 501-class President ships are picking up the mail subsidy, so there's no reason to run the *Diana Dollar* any longer."

"What are they gonna do with her?"

"Put her up for sale. Although it's unlikely she'll sell anytime soon in the current economy,."

"Where do you think they'll store her?"

Roger pursed his lips into an expression that said, *don't mistake me for a fool.*

It wasn't the response Nick was hoping for, but he understood why Farnsworth withheld the information. After all, if he were to find the opium and prove his innocence, they'd lose a spy. In any case, he felt confident he could locate the freighter if he snooped around a bit. "What about Primm and Slag?"

"Your accusations haven't gone unnoticed. No one quite believes you enough to fire them, but Dollar doesn't intend to take chances either. Right now they're both on the *President Cleveland* steaming around the world. Primm was demoted back to first mate and Slag has remained bosun. Neither one complained, and considering the job market, they're lucky to be employed." Roger clasped his hands together. "So, do we have a deal?"

It seemed curious that Slag would willingly ship out again when he knew the whereabouts of a cache of narcotics valuable enough to retire on. Then again, if the cache was on the *Diana Dollar,* he probably wouldn't be able to lay his hands on it for some time and figured that when he returned from his around-the-world voyage, everyone would have forgotten about it, making it easier to retrieve.

"One more question, what happens if I screw up?"

Roger smiled, though his hazel eyes were less friendly. "If you let us down we can easily reinstate the charges and have you locked up without the benefit of Neylan's courtroom abilities or his influence over local judges."

As promised, the Federal prosecutor's office ordered Nick's release, the charges held in abeyance pending further investigation, meaning the case could be reopened at anytime. On his way out of the building, Nick was about to toss his grime-spattered clothes into a trash can, but changed his mind and stuffed them into his duffle bag. Perhaps a bit of soap and elbow grease would clean out the gunk and erase a few bad memories.

He stepped out of the building into the noise and bustle of city life. Trucks and cars of every description rumbled along Kearny Street, and pedestrians hurried to and fro, scarcely noticing him. He went to the curb and paused to take in the familiar sights. Marquard's newspaper stand displayed racks of newspapers from a dozen different countries. Whole roasted ducks with shiny brown skin hung upside down in the window of Royal Jade Restaurant. The Leman Hotel advertised rooms with hot and cold running water for fifty cents a night. All was outwardly familiar, all the same as he remembered.

Yet it also was different. As if underneath the surface the city was now more complex, more ominous, as if every street, every building, every room, held secrets. *Why didn't I notice it before? I can't be the only one with something to hide.* He looked across Kearny to Portsmouth Square, a grass covered park on the edge of Chinatown. Wizened Chinese seniors seated on park benches were reading newspapers or playing cards, and fresh-faced kiddies frolicked on the lawn under the watchful eye of their mothers. He smiled at the playful scene, at the blessed normality of it, and for the first time since he stepped off the *Diana Dollar,* he felt at home.

Home also reminded him of Clarisa. He'd anticipated seeing her for weeks, pictured them embracing, both of them shedding tears of happiness as they greeted each other with tender kisses and gazed into each other's eyes with deep, heartfelt affection. The reality, however, had been so unexpected, so humiliatingly different that something inside him had snapped, releasing a flood of anger and shame. By all rights, he should be grateful that she'd helped him get out of jail. Instead, he felt humiliated that it was she, the very person who pleaded with him not to go, who rescued him. And it was this humiliation that prompted him to make a vow to himself. He wasn't going to resume their relationship until he resolved his problems, until he was able to face her as a free man. He even rejected the notion of asking her to help him find the *Diana Dollar.* That was one mess he was going to fix on his own.

At a break in the traffic he trotted across Kearny and headed up Clay, passing places he'd passed a thousand times before — the colorful shops of Chinatown, a row of sturdy Edwardians with rounded bays and lace curtains, the brick cable car barn. He found himself glancing at passersby, half expecting them to return his gaze with cynical knowing eyes. Of course they didn't, and this gave him hope that if he was lucky, if he played his cards right, he'd survive the next year in one piece.

He reached his family's flat on Mason Street, and as he climbed the terrazzo steps to the front door, he recalled Farnsworth's parting words: *"Forget the Diana Dollar. It's a closed chapter. And even if you find what you're looking for, how will anyone know if it belongs to you . . . or someone else?"* The way Farnsworth said it, the way he stared at Nick, seemed to endow the warning with a subtext Nick couldn't decipher. He inserted the key into the front door lock, his odyssey finally over. As he entered the flat, he put on a smile and mentally shelved the cryptic warning.

There would be time enough to sort it all out.

PART TWO

A SERVANT OF TWO MASTERS

CHAPTER 24

Journal – August 17, 1933

My homecoming was understandably a low-key affair. I gave my wages to mother who prepared a delicious roast beef dinner, cooked to perfection with a rub of garlic, salt, pepper, thyme, and rosemary. It was our first roast beef since father died, and we all eagerly devoured it while Rune, Sarah, and mother peppered me with questions about the voyage.

Mustering as much enthusiasm as I could, I described the friends I'd made, the colorful sights and smells of Shanghai, the desolate beauty of the sea, the dazzling display of stars each night. At one point, as I looked around the table, a wave of contradictory emotions rolled through me; on the one hand, a profound joy at seeing my family after a long separation, on the other, a festering worry that the agreement I'd made to secure my freedom was an unholy bargain. It now appears that I've embarked on yet another journey into the unknown, and like the previous one, there seems to be no turning back.

Mother baked an apple tart for dessert. While we ate it I announced my intention to find work at the waterfront, half expecting mother to launch into a histrionic sermon about wasting my college education. To my surprise, she didn't object and furthermore admitted that with four mouths to feed and her hours working as a bookkeeper at Samuel's Jewelers cut to one day a week, a paycheck, no matter how menially obtained, would be welcomed.

The next morning I pulled on a pair of dungarees, buttoned up a blue work shirt, and tied a red bandana around my neck as instructed by Roger Farnsworth. Then, like my father before me, I gave my mother a kiss on the cheek, said goodbye to Rune and Sarah, and made my way to the waterfront, taking a route nearly identical to the one father and I took to get to the warehouse. It seemed strange to be following in his footsteps, but I tried not to think about it and was grateful not to be wearing a tie cinched around my neck.

At the Embarcadero, a wide boulevard running along the waterfront, I joined several hundred others hoping to find work at the docks. About half of them appeared to be seasoned stevedores, recognizable by their leather work boots, black Frisco trousers, and striped hickory shirts. Like varsity athletes, they grouped together to distinguish themselves from the backbenchers, a mixture of down-on-their-luck transients, unemployed workers from other occupations, and smooth-faced kids fresh out of high school.

Everyone was periodically glancing over at the Ferry Building on the other side of the Embarcadero where, I was told, the hiring boss would soon appear. A clock tower rising up from the center of the Ferry Building tolled the hour at seven o'clock. As the bell faded, the hiring boss stepped out of the building wearing a brown leather jacket and carrying a clipboard. When he reached our side of the cobblestone boulevard, the men surged out onto the road and formed a wide semi-circle, called the shape-up, in front of two police officers who herded us back off the street. Several men broke ranks and ran up to the hiring boss to stuff dollar bills in his pockets or hand him bottles of booze. Apparently that's the only way some men can be guaranteed a day's work.

After accepting the gifts and shooing the donors back into the shape-up, the hiring boss walked back and forth, pointing to the lucky ones who, breaking out of the group with broad smiles, accepted a work voucher and hurried off to their assigned piers. Most were sent to China Basin to tote stems of bananas off of a freighter or to the copra dock at Islais Creek where they would be given shovels to loosen the copra so it could be sucked out of the hold with a vacuum hose.

Without a hint of recognition or predetermination, the hiring boss beckoned to me and handed me a voucher for a job at the Swayne & Hoyt dock at Pier 21. I stuffed it in my pocket and trotted across the Embarcadero, relieved that the first step of Farnsworth's plan had proceeded without a hitch. I turned north and walked beside a row of pier sheds designed in the classical style with peaked roofs, pilasters resembling Roman columns, and arched entrances large enough to accommodate freight trains. I hadn't gone far when I heard footsteps running up behind me. A moment later a fellow I recognized from the shape-up caught up with me and matched my pace.

"You assigned to Sweat and Hurry too?" he asked.

"Sweat and Hurry?"

"You know, Swayne & Hoyt." He held out a hand. "M'name's Fargo, James Fargo, though some call me Fargone after I've had a few too many." He looked to be about fifty-years old with leathery skin and grizzled stubble on his chin. A brown and white mutt trotted alongside him, tongue lolling out.

I grasped his hand. "Nick Benson."

"I ain't seen you before, have I? There's an awful lotta new fellas showin' up these days. Bet you're from Missouri or Arkansas." When I didn't respond, he asked, "You humped cargo before?"

"No, but I've worked on a ship. How 'bout you?"

"Been workin' hand jive for more'n thirty years. Started out as a dockman at the Chelsea piers in New York, then worked 'fronts in Baltimore, New Orleans, Galveston, San Pedro, all over. Useta be a roustabout could tour the whole damn country that way. I'd work a few weeks humpin' cargo, then ride the rails to the next port, just as free and easy as you please. No more, though. Now I'm lucky to keep me 'n' Rusty here in baked beans." He reached down and scratched the mutt behind the ears. "So, how'd you get this shift? They don't usually pick newcomers to fill a star gang slot."

Not knowing what to say, I shrugged and kept walking.

"I'll bet you slipped the hirin' boss a pint, and he reco'nized your bandana there."

Unnerved by the partial accuracy of his observation, I reached up and touched the scarf.

Fargo seemed to pick up on my nervousness. "Don't worry. It don't matter. It's just that nobody on the 'front wears a red bandana around his neck. You stuck out like a hoochie-coochie dancer at a Methodist picnic."

Silently cursing Farnsworth, who obviously wasn't familiar with long-shoreman attire, I removed the scarf and stuffed it into my pocket.

We arrived at Pier 21 just as a Belt Line locomotive with huge steel wheels rolled into the shed. We followed the locomotive into the cavernous building, as big as two football fields laid end-to-end. Rail tracks ran down the center, and on either side of the tracks, stacks of cartons, boxes, barrels, and bales were waiting to be loaded onto a boxcar. Fargo led me into an office near the entrance, where we gave our vouchers to a clerk who wrote our names in a ledger.

"You boys got your Blue Books?" asked the clerk.

Fargo produced a worn blue booklet from his coat pocket and handed it to the clerk who thumbed through it.

"Looks like you haven't paid dues since April," said the clerk.

"I ain't had but four, five days a month since then. It's hard to come up with dues when you can't pay rent."

The clerk returned the Blue Book. "Better get paid up soon. Where's yours?" he said to me.

No one had instructed me to obtain a Blue Book, so I shrugged.

"This is his first day on the job," Fargo said. "I'll see he gets one."

"Make sure he does. The business agent's been comin' round regular lately. If he catches you without a book or not paid up, he'll toss you off the job." He gestured toward a large open door on the side of the shed. "Alright, go on."

The side door led to a dock running alongside the pier shed. About eighty longshoremen were waiting on the dock beside a freighter streaked with rust, its name, *Point Reyes,* painted on her bow. The air smelled of fuel oil and salt water, and above the dock seagulls circled around searching for food. Fargo led the way to the gang foreman, a stocky fellow who grinned as we approached.

"Where ya been, Fargo?" he asked.

Fargo smiled, revealing wide gaps between his teeth. "Been lookin' for the Big Rock Candy Mountain. You know, where the bluebirds sing by the lemonade springs." He winked. "But my feet got sore, I couldn't walk no more, so I thought I'd come back for a spell a what for."

The stocky foreman laughed. "Still the poetic dreamer, I see." He nodded towards me. "And who's this?"

"This here is Nick Benson. Nick, this is Henry Schmidt, one of the damndest finest men on the Frisco 'front."

"Know how to rig a ship, Benson?"

"Yep. I used to work on a Dollar ship."

"Good. Then you and Fargo can work the hold." He raised his voice. "Let's get movin', boys. We gotta get this load discharged before BLT puts our asses in a vise."

"BLT?" I said to Fargo as we headed up the gangway. "Isn't that a sandwich."

Fargo shook his head. "Round here it means one thing: Big Load Thomson, the walkin' boss."

Five hold gangs, each with eight men, assembled at their respective hatches on the weather deck. I took a hammer from our foreman, a fellow named Joad, and dislodged the wedged wood chucks that held the hatch cover tarpaulin in place. We rolled up the tarpaulin and set it aside, revealing a layer of hatch boards. Four of us removed the hatch boards, supported underneath by steel I-beams that spanned the hatch opening. The other four men in our gang untied two booms from the kingpost beside the hatch and lowered the booms to the proper angle with topping lift lines. This done, they swung one boom out over the dock and secured it with guy wires angled down to cleats on the ship's railing. The other boom they secured over the hatch in the same manner.

Two winch drums at the base of the kingpost controlled a single fall line. Starting at one of the winch drums, the fall line ran up the boom angled out over the hatch to a gin block at the end of the boom. The line then dropped down to a cargo hook dangling above us, then back up to the boom angled out over the dock and down to the other winch drum. The winchdriver tested the drums, raising and lowering each end of the fall line independently. In this way he was able to control the position of the hook, moving it back and forth from over the hatch to over the dock.

Satisfied the winches were in working order, the winchdriver lowered the hook to Fargo who looped it around the center of an I-beam and hooked it to the fall line. The winchdriver raised the hook, cinching the line around the I-beam until it rose up off the hatch coaming. Fargo and I grasped the I-beam and steadied it while the winchdriver swung it to the side of the hatch and gently lowered it onto the deck.

Once the I-beams were removed, we climbed down a ladder into the hold and stepped onto the cargo. Flooded with natural light, the hold was a far cry from *Diana Dollar's* dreary dungeon. Not only was it well-lit but the cargo was more interesting. There were wooden crates, cardboard boxes, oak barrels, cotton bales, large spools of paper, and canvas sacks, all secured and carefully packed.

With quiet efficiency we went to work, starting with a shipment of avocados from Mexico packed in wooden crates. One-by-one we carried the crates to the area under the hatch opening and stacked them on a square pallet called a sling board. When the sling board was fully loaded, Joad hooked a looped rope, called a sling, around each end of the pallet, then hung the rope onto the cargo hook.

"Let 'er go," he called up to winch driver, who looked down from the hatch opening.

As the hook rose, it pulled the sling taut around the load and lifted it off the floor. When the load was above my head, I carried another wooden crate to the center of the hold and set it on a second sling board. The rest of the crew had gone for more crates, all except Joad, who stood there frowning at me.

"What the hell are you doin' in the square?" he asked.

I gave him a sullen stare, wondering if all bosses on ships were hard asses or just the ones I worked for. Joad was about my height, a little over six feet, but lankier with strong hands bulging with thick veins. We stared at one another until I said, "What square?"

"You mean you don't know what the square is?" He grabbed my arm and roughly pulled me from the center of the hold.

In no mood to take guff from anyone, not after what I'd been through, I wrenched my arm from his grip and gave him a shove, pushing him back on his heels. He looked startled for a moment, then laughed.

"Brother, you gotta lot to learn about shakin' hands with the cargo. You was workin' in the middle of the square, right under the fall line, the most dangerous place in the hold. If the cargo had broke loose while you was under it, you'd be smashed potatoes. You never work in the square when cargo's on the hook."

It occurred to me that for a second time in the space of five months, I was learning a new trade, a difficult task in the best of circumstances, and this wasn't the best of circumstances. Nevertheless, I couldn't afford to get fired on my first day. "I know I don't have a lot of experience, but I've worked on ships as a sailor and learn quick."

"That may be, but this is a whole different ballgame. And I need experienced men if they expect me to discharge twenty tons an hour."

Fargo came over. "Give him a break, Joad. He's a good kid and strong. Look at his arms and hands. He ain't afraid a hard work."

Joad studied me for a moment as though assessing my potential. After some hesitation, he nodded. "Alright, brother. You're lucky we're dischargin'. If we was stowin', I'd eighty-six you pronto. Just keep an eye on everyone else and follow suit. And whatever you do, don't hold things up."

For the rest of the morning I stayed close to Fargo and copied his every move, lifting, toting, and stacking cargo until my back ached and beads of sweat covered my brow. At first the work seemed to require little more than brawn and stamina, but I soon learned that every step required thoughtful consideration as well as knowledge and skill. Cargo is stowed both like a grocery bag — heavier items on the bottom, delicate items above — and a travel trunk — space efficiency maximized. Thrown into the formula is the order in which the cargo is scheduled to be discharged, which depends on where it's going, and also the compatibility of different cargoes. For instance, oak barrels can't be stacked over sacks of flour, both for reasons of stability and to prevent liquid from a leaky barrel ruining the flour below it. The overall stowing plan is drawn up by the ship's first officer who gives it to the supercargo who in turn passes it on to the hold crew. But these charts are simple diagrams, leaving the stevedores to improvise as they go along.

Discharging cargo is easier than stowing, although it often requires removing other cargo around it, then repacking the remaining cargo. It wasn't long before I understood why Joad needed experienced men. Hold crews utilize a hundred different techniques to pack cargo, and with boxes and barrels stacked dozens of feet high around the square, it's vital that it be properly positioned and firmly secured.

At noon a shrill whistle signaled the lunch break. With Rusty at our heels, Fargo and I headed across the Embarcadero to the Eagle Cafe, a popular waterfront joint serving simple food and cold beer. I bought a ham sandwich and a bottle of soda pop for myself and lent Fargo fifteen cents for the same. Back at the dock we sat down against the pier shed and unwrapped our sandwiches. Fargo tore off a piece and held it out to Rusty, who gobbled it down and looked for more.

"So what's the Blue Book Union?" I asked.

"Shoot, it ain't a real union. They just collect dues and let the men fend for themselves."

"Don't they negotiate with the employers?"

"Not really. More like the bosses tell 'em what's what, and they pass it on to us." He tore off another piece and fed it to Rusty. "When I first started workin' the Frisco 'front, my crew was smoked everyday for a month straight, and they didn't do nothin'."

"Smoked?"

"They got a blackboard at most pier heads with each gang's number on it and the pier where the gang is workin' the next day. Sometimes, instead of a pier number, they write down 'smoke,' which means you gotta show up and standby. Usually you wait around till lunch, then relieve another crew for an hour. After that you wait around again until the regular crew gets off, and then you might take over so the company don't have to pay overtime. You end up hanging around for twelve hours and get paid for three maybe four."

"So what's that got to do with the Blue Book Union?"

"After a month of being smoked, I went to the Blue Book hall over on Clay Street. I s'plained the situation to a couple of officials and asked if they could do somefin'. A big fellow named Stone said I had no business tellin' 'em how to run their operation. He grabbed me by the collar and the seat of my pants and shoved me out the door. Ain't been back since."

"So how come you're not on a star gang now?"

Fargo swallowed a bite of sandwich and gave Rusty another piece. "I used to work on a gang with a walkin' boss who was a real sumbitch. Kept ridin' me, wouldn't leave me alone. It was 'Fargo this' and 'Fargo that'. So I began sneakin' a bottle into work to keep from goin' crazy. Got to the point where I was stumblin' over my own shoelaces. One day I dropped a box on his foot." He chuckled. "I swear on my mother's grave, it was the drink that made me clumsy, but he claimed I did it on purpose and tossed me off the job. Ain't been able to get regular work since."

For the rest of the day my gang worked at a steady pace, each man moving in concert with the other so that the hook stayed in motion and the winch drums made a constant ratcheting noise. Occasionally Big Load Thompson peered over the hatch coaming and exhorted us to keep things moving, though it hardly seemed necessary. We were fully engaged in our work, and at one point I noticed Joad looking my way with an approving glance.

At the end of the shift, the gang gathered on the dock around Henry Schmidt, who announced that we'd discharged one-hundred-ten tons that day, a respectable quantity. He also broke the good news that Fargo and I could expect to stay on until the ship was fully discharged and stowed again.

That night I counted a dozen aches and pains across my body, from scraped knuckles to sore arms to a bruised shoulder. Despite the discomfort I was filled with a definite sense of satisfaction. Much of the work on the *Diana Dollar* — polishing brass, chipping paint, scrubbing decks — had been menial and inconsequential, unlike the old days when sailors actually sailed the ship, its progress depending on each man's effort. Longshore work, I learned, is more like sailing a windjammer, requiring teamwork and close cooperation. Moreover, at the end of the day I could see the results of our labor; there was noticeably less cargo in the hold. I also thought about where the cargo was destined — food that would fill hungry bellies, cement going into the foundations of the two bridges under construction, coffee to be served in restaurants. Looked at one way, longshoremen contribute to the progress of everything and everyone everywhere, and it left me with a feeling that I'd accomplished something important, or at least useful.

25

Under a gray overcast sky, Nick joined his longshore gang on the dock beside the *Point Reyes*. His aches and pains from the day before were still noticeable, but none was serious and he looked forward to learning more about the longshore trade. At a few minutes before eight o'clock, Big Load Thompson emerged from the pier shed, a tuft of chest hair curling out over his open-collared shirt. He climbed halfway up the gangway and turned toward the men on the dock.

"Listen, boys," he bellowed, his voice echoing off the pier shed, "you only averaged a hundred-ten tons per gang yesterday. That ain't enough. This ship is scheduled to shove off at the end of next week. You should be dischargin' a hundred-sixty tons per gang, and the only way to do that —" he paused and peered down at them with an expression that said they'd better pay attention and heed his words if they knew what was good for them "— you gotta increase load size."

The men groaned.

Fargo muttered, "Leave it to BLT to speed things up."

"I want a minimum of forty cases per load of boxed goods. Thirty sacks per load of grain, sugar, and coffee. And eight units per load of barrels and drums."

More groans.

Henry Schmidt cried out, "It'll be tough to keep the hook in motion with those sized loads, and the fall lines on this ship are rope not wire. We'll be risking a break."

Thompson leaned over the railing, chest puffed out. "I know you boys can do it. Black gangs working on the *Point Arena* discharged one-hundred-fifty tons per gang yesterday. You don't want those niggers showin' you up, do you?" No reaction. "You wanna keep your jobs, don't you?"

Still no reaction. He leaned farther out. "Well, don't you!?!"

"*Yeah,*" came a half-hearted response.

"Alright then, get to work!"

Nick's gang began the shift carrying eighty-pound sacks of flour on their shoulders as they hustled back and forth between the cargo and the square. During the first fifteen minutes, every muscle and joint in Nick's body resisted the effort and cried out for relief from the heavy weight. But once his limbs warmed up, he fell into a pace noticeably faster than the day before. After the flour was discharged, the gang went to work on a shipment of hardware in cardboard boxes. They formed a line between the cargo and the square and tossed the boxes from one man to the next to maintain the stepped-up pace. To reach boxes stacked above their heads, they built stairs with wooden crates and passed the cargo down so no precious energy was wasted climbing up and down the steps.

An hour into this breakneck pace, Nick noticed Fargo bending over to catch his breath. He asked him if he needed help but the old roustabout urged him to keep up with the others.

Towards midmorning the hook dropped down before the next load was ready to hoist out of the hold. Instead of letting it hang, a cardinal sin as it slowed the entire operation, Joad wrapped the rope sling over the load, roved one loop through the other, attached it to the hook, and signaled the hatch tender to hoist it up.

When the cargo reached the hatch opening, Big Load Thompson was leaning over the coaming, his hands cupped around his mouth. "That's not a full load, boys! You're falling behind! You gotta pile it higher!

The men redoubled their efforts, trotting to and fro to the relentless beat of the ratcheting winch drums. They were discharging a shipment of canned goods when Fargo tripped on the uneven surface and fell to his knees. The box in his arms dropped to the floor and split open, sending cans of Boston baked beans rolling across the hold.

Nick and Joad rushed to his side and lifted him up.

"Sorry, boys," Fargo said, rubbing his forehead. "Didn't have supper last night or, come to think of it, breakfast this morning, and I'm feelin' kinda woozy."

Joad pointed to a far corner out-of-sight. "Take him over there where he can sit a spell."

For the rest of the morning the hold gang moved even faster to make up for one less hand, and as they worked they could hear Thompson's thundering cries exhorting them with threats one minute and praise the next. On the one hand he declared they were "slower than niggers in a tar patch" (a claim Nick found ironic considering the black gang's speed the day before), and on the other he bragged that they were the best damn stevedores in the country, and he'd personally tell management they deserved a raise. Most of all, though, he seemed to relish the sound of his voice echoing in the hold.

The noontime whistle signaled the lunch break, and like long distant runners crossing the finish line, the men stopped in their tracks and put down whatever they were carrying.

Nick helped Fargo out of the hold and bought him a sandwich and a bottle of milk. They ate their lunch on the quarterdeck overlooking the bay, Rusty sitting beside them.

"This is young man's work," said Fargo. "If I had any sense" — he pointed to his head — "or cents" — he rubbed the tips of his fingers with his thumb — "I'd be retired by now."

Nick pulled a stick of beef jerky out of his pocket, tore off a piece, and gave it to Rusty. The mutt gulped it down and looked for more. "They say Roosevelt's talking about payments for workin' people when they get old. Senior Security, I think they call it."

"Sure wish they had it now. I'm awful tired of bein' tired."

"Where do you and Rusty live?"

"We're staying at a warehouse on Rich Street. Kinda funny, ain't it. Broke on Rich Street."

Nick tore off another piece and gave it to the dog. "A warehouse?"

"The price is right, but all we get is a cot and a coupla blankets. I usually grab dinner at St. Patrick's Mission. Last night they ran outta chow by the time we reached the front of the line. It's good thing I'm workin' this week. I'm sure tired of what's-it stew. Can't wait to buy some hamburger."

The mention of St. Patrick's Mission reminded Nick of Clarisa. The humiliation he felt when she came to see him in jail had disappeared, yet he still couldn't summon the urge to contact her. For reasons he didn't fully understand, perhaps pride more than anything, he wanted to feel in control of his destiny before he reached out to her. And that would require finding the opium and exonerating himself. Still, he often thought of her and was about to ask Fargo if he knew an auburn-haired volunteer at the mission when Joad knelt down beside them and laid a hand on Fargo's shoulder.

"Feelin' better?" he asked.

"Much better. Just needed a bit o' vittles in m' belly."

"Good, cause we gotta hustle to keep on schedule." He turned to Nick. "You're doin' fine. Longshorin' may look simple but there's a lot to learn. Stick with Fargo, he'll teach you. Oh, and by the way, don't let BLT's big mouth bother you. He knows we're the best in the business, but that don't stop him from puttin' the heat on us."

For the next four days Nick followed Fargo like a duckling follows its mother, mimicking his every move. And the *Point Reyes*, with its varied cargo, was an excellent training ground. Fargo showed him how to roll a three-hundred pound barrel on its edge without dropping it, how to buffer dissimilar cargos to keep them from chaffing against each other, and the secret to man-handling huge bales of cotton. By the end of the week Nick had learned how to secure a twenty-foot high wall of oil drums to keep them from toppling in rough seas and was able to discern, from the pitch and rhythm of the winch drums, where the hook was located and whether it was lifting a load.

After the cargo was discharged, Henry Schmidt took Nick and Fargo aside and explained that he was transferring them to the dock. "You're a quick study," he said to Nick, "but stowing cargo is tricky business and requires more experience than you've got. And Fargo, working on the dock will be easier on you too."

Neither minded the change. Nick appreciated the chance to learn the dock side of things, while Fargo was happy to be reunited with his faithful mutt, who hadn't been allowed in the hold but could now lay beside the pier shed within sight of his master.

Transferring cargo from pier shed to ship was nearly as strenuous as discharging it out of the hold, in part because Schmidt had reassigned three dock men into the hold, leaving the dock gang short one man. The remaining dock men divided themselves into two groups, one in the shed loading cargo onto dollies and wheeling it out to the dock, while the other group, Nick, Fargo, and Henry Schmidt, stacked it onto sling boards and prepared it for hoisting.

By mid-afternoon the dock gang had settled into a steady rhythm. Four other gangs were on the dock as well, one opposite each hatch. The ship itself resembled a gigantic fishing boat, reeling in load after load of cargo that disappeared over the railing and into the holds. Toward the end of the day, the shed men rolled a dolly out onto the dock loaded with nail kegs, small barrels constructed of pine staves held together with wire bands. Nick, Fargo, and Henry Schmidt stacked them six-high onto a sling board. When the hook dropped down from the ship, Nick grasped it and guided it over to Fargo, who hooked it onto the sling rope.

"Hoist 'er up," Schmidt yelled to the winchdriver, who was standing at the ship's railing, looking down at the dock.

The fall line pulled taut and lifted the heavy load off the pier. When it reached a point higher than the ship's railing, it moved toward the ship, but before it reached the railing one of the winches made a hollow stuttering sound.

Nick was helping Fargo and Henry prepare the next load of kegs when he heard the unusual stutter. The three men stopped and looked up at the sling load dangling uncertainly overhead, its progress stopped.

Big Load Thompson spotted them from the weather deck and bellowed, "KEEP WORKIN' BOYS," then to the winchdriver, "Hurry it up! We ain't got all day!"

"Somethin's wrong with the offshore winch, boss," the winchdriver replied. "It's cuttin' in and out."

"We'll fix it after this shift. Right now, we gotta keep things movin'."

The winchdriver tried again to reel in the offshore line, and again the winch drum made a hollow stuttering sound. The hook only moved a foot or so before it stopped abruptly, causing the load to rock back and forth like a pendulum.

"Jesus," said Schmidt, squinting up at the swinging load, "one gust of wind and it'll tip over for sure." He cupped his hands around his mouth and yelled to the winchdriver, "For Christ's sake, steady her man!"

The winchdriver waited for the rocking motion to subside. When the load was nearly still, he attempted to reel in the offshore line again. The winch, still stuttering, pulled the sling load toward the ship. A moment later it let off again, accelerating the rocking motion.

Back and forth the sling load rocked until the kegs leaned perilously out over the side of the sling board. The dock men below, joined by the shed men who'd just wheeled another load of kegs onto the dock, stared transfixed at the giant pendulum swinging back and forth above them. Like a flower blossoming into separate petals, cracks opened between the stacks of nail kegs until the stacks began to separate into individual columns. When the load swung one way the columns on the opposite side separated; when it swung the other way, centrifugal force pushed the columns back into place.

Watching the swinging load, Nick was ready to run if it fell off the sling board.

Wisely, the winchdriver waited for the rocking motion to slow. When it was nearly still, he tried again, this time inching the kegs toward the ship.

"Whew," Schmidt said, exhaling, "that was a close one." Everyone else breathed normally again as well. "Alright, let's finish this load."

The men returned to their duties and began transferring kegs from the dolly to the sling board. They were almost finished when a deep booming voice yelled, "Outta the way! It's gonna fall!"

Nick looked up. The sling load had stopped moving toward the ship, restarting the pendulum motion and further separating the already loosened columns. First one keg tumbled off the top, then another and another until a dozen kegs cascaded down in a continuous stream. The stevedores below scattered helter-skelter, their arms and legs churning across the dock. There wasn't time for panicked cries, only grunts as they tried to dart away from the falling kegs. Nick pushed Fargo toward the shed, but Schmidt, who was in front of Fargo, tripped and fell and the three men toppled to the ground like dominos.

Nick landed on the dock face down and knitted his fingers over the back of his head. Out of the corner of his eye, he saw a keg hit the pier with a tremendous crash and split apart, sending an explosion of sixteen-penny nails out over the dock in a bomb blast pattern. Several more cases crashed onto the pier nearby, and one landed with a dull thud followed by a sharp groan.

When the noise abated, he raised his head and looked forward at Fargo whose spine was arched like a bow. A nail keg sat squarely on his back as if someone had placed it there intentionally.

The old longshoreman moaned briefly, then slumped down onto the dock.

A tall, muscular Negro, hair flecked with gray, limped over and carefully lifted the keg off Fargo's back. "Quick, somebody call an amb'lance!" It was the same voice that had called out a warning just before the kegs came tumbling down. A longshoreman tore off toward the office. Before he reached the shed, the Negro called after him, "And make sure they know which pier it is this time!"

Nick scrambled over to Fargo and rested an ear on his back. He could hear a heartbeat but the old man's breathing was shallow. Rusty trotted over and sniffed his master's face, then licked his cheek with a pink tongue. When Fargo didn't react, he sat down and whined softly.

Men from other crews gathered around to stare at the motionless stevedore.

"He'll not be workin' for awhile, if ever," Henry Schmidt remarked to no one in particular.

Big Load Thompson pushed his way through the men gathered around Fargo. "All right, boys, an ambulance is on its way. Nothin' you can do here. Floor off this mess and get back to work."

No one moved.

"One of ours is half-dead," Schmidt muttered, "and all you can think about is to keep the hook movin'."

The men continued to stare at Fargo, and as more longshoremen joined them they huddled together into a solid phalanx, eyes unblinking, faces registering shock, fear, anger.

"You heard me," Thompson barked, "nothin' more we can do for him till the ambulance comes. Time waits for no man." Still no one moved. "Come on Schmidt," he said in a more conciliatory tone, "get the boys back to work."

"Sure boss," Schmidt said in a mocking tone. "I'll get 'em workin'. But first I got somethin' to say to 'em." He looked at the men around him, his face solemn. "We gotta finish this ship but we don't have to take this kind of abuse. It's time we done somethin', time we stopped the accidents, the slave mart, the speed-up."

"Now see here," said Thompson, stepping in front of him, toe to toe, his bushy chest puffed out. "No more speeches. Clean up this mess and get the men back to work or you're off the dock for good."

No one moved, and for a moment all was quiet save for the *chug-chug-chug* of a tugboat somewhere out in the bay.

Schmidt and Thompson stared at each other. Schmidt wearing a grim smile, his fists clenched. "Sure boss, I'll get 'em back to work. Just as soon as —"

Nick and the Negro exchanged a split-second glance. Then simultaneously they slipped between Schmidt and Thomson, forcing them apart.

"You heard him," Nick said, "floor off this mess and bring in the next load."

Like a punctured tire the tension released, dissolving the phalanx. As the men drifted back to work, Thompson pivoted around and strode back into the shed.

Nick turned to Schmidt. "Trying to get yourself fired?"

As though under a spell, the gang foreman stared at the men sweeping up nails, carrying broken kegs into the shed. "No, just tryin' to wake 'em up."

A shadow brushed by their feet. They looked down at Rusty circling around them with a hapless grin, tail wagging nervously, ears raised at attention as though his senses were on high alert.

"I guess I'll take him to the pound," said Schmidt. "Don't think Fargo will be able to take care of him any time soon."

Nick crouched down on his haunches and extended a hand toward the brown and white mutt who came over, breath quick, tongue lolling out. Rusty glanced over at Fargo, whined, then turned back to Nick, who stroked his head and scratched his ears. "No, I'll take him. The pound might put him to sleep and that would hurt Fargo more than a keg of nails."

An ambulance arrived with two medics in white uniforms. They lifted Fargo onto a gurney and wheeled him off the dock. By then the nails were swept up, the broken winch repaired (its steam pipe had sprung a leak and was temporarily fixed with duck tape), the crews were back at work, and the ratcheting drone of the winches reverberated along the dock.

For the rest of the day the longshoremen wore masks of grim efficiency, barely concealing their anger. Schmidt circulated among them, quietly encouraging them to attend a union meeting at the Labor Temple on Thursday evening to "settle things once and for all."

At the end of the shift Nick whistled for Rusty, who came trotting over, still wearing a hapless grin. It was fortunate that Nick had spent the previous week dispensing treats to Rusty during lunch, because the mutt seemed to accept that he was now in Nick's custody and willingly followed him off the dock. Near the pier head they came across Henry Schmidt talking with the Negro who had yelled a warning before the nail kegs came down.

"I know you ain't a longshoreman," Schmidt was saying, "but it's important you know what's going on. We gotta stick together. If we go on strike you may have to choose sides, and it's in your best interests to know what we're about."

"Pardon me for interrupting," said Nick, facing the Negro. "I just want to thank you for helping Fargo."

The tall, solidly built fellow shook his head wistfully. "Ah jus' wish ah could'a done sump'um sooner."

"Nick, this here is Tanglefoot Fleming," said Schmidt. "He's no stranger to injuries, or strikes for that matter."

"Oh, yeah?"

Fleming looked to be about forty years-old, with a broad nose, full

lips, and clear brown eyes. There was a gentleness about him and a dif-
fident manner that seemed incongruent to his commanding stature.
He bowed his head, apparently embarrassed, or perhaps pained. Nick
couldn't tell which.

"Few years back," said Schmidt, "the company recruited him to
replace striking longshoremen."

Fleming looked up. "They never tol' us we was steppin' into the middle
of a fracas. By the time ah fig'erd it out, it was too dangerous to scoot."
His looked down again.

Nick figured Fleming was reluctant to resurrect painful memories,
and thought the matter would drop. but something drove Fleming to
continue.

"Durin' the day we moved cargo, and after our shift they ferried us to
a ship where we holed up till mawnin'. Ah worked three weeks straight,
then tried to slip off the ship to see m' folks. Before ah 'scaped the waterfront, strikers set on me and —." He shrugged as if to say it happened a
long time ago and wasn't worth recalling.

Schmidt filled in the details. Striking longshoremen caught Fleming
trying to sneak away. They pummeled him with sticks and baseball bats,
all the while screaming racial epithets. Afterwards his jaw was cracked,
four ribs broken, an ankle crushed. When the president of Swayne & Hoyt
learned of the beating, he gave Fleming a permanent job as a janitor and
paid his medical bills, an ironic gesture considering that the company
didn't provide medical coverage for its dockworkers.

Fleming seemed philosophic about it. "I reckon m' injury was the
Lord's punishment for steppin' into someone else's quarrel, but this job
was compensation for an innocent transgression."

"We can't let that kind of thing happen again," said Schmidt. "You
lost a good ankle and the men lost a good union. That's why we need you
this time."

Fleming looked down at his gimp leg. "Ah don't know . . . Ah gotta
family, a wahfe an' three keeds. Gotta stay outta trouble the bes' ah can."

26

Nick tapped his fingertips on the bar as he contemplated a nearly empty glass of Anchor Steam Beer, its effervescence long gone. He was considering whether to order a fresh one, but a beer in this fancy restaurant set you back thirty cents, three times the cost of a beer at the Eagle Cafe. He checked his wrist-watch. Seven-twenty. So much for punctuality. A mysterious "Mr. Smith" had called and left a message asking him to meet at six-thirty inside the stone turret that "Uncle Julius likes so much." To arrive on time, Nick had showered, shaved, slipped on a pair of slacks, pressed shirt, and sport coat, then rushed to the rendezvous without eating dinner. Now, after a long day shaking hands with the cargo and a fifty minute wait, his stomach was grumbling, his mood no better.

At least the setting was interesting.

Julius' Castle resembled a medieval fortress, its exterior clad in faux stone, its crenellated roofline featuring a round turret. And like a fortress it was perched on a hillside, the east face of Telegraph Hill, with a commanding view of the bay. The Castle wouldn't have been Nick's first choice for a meeting, yet he had to admit it was an impressive location and one in which he was unlikely to be spotted by anyone from the waterfront. Even so, he was irritated at his summoner's tardiness, as well as the cloak-and-dagger theatrics employed to arrange the rendezvous.

He was about to leave when a tuxedoed waiter tapped him on the shoulder. "Your table is ready, sir. If you'll follow me."

"My table?"

"Yes, sir. This way, sir."

He followed the waiter through the restaurant, romantically lit by crystal chandeliers that cast a soft glow on diners seated at tables with views of the bay. They entered a private alcove furnished with a table covered in white linen and two chairs upholstered in maroon velvet. A dozen oysters on the half-shell rested on the table, as did a chilled martini, its glass covered with beads of condensation. The waiter extended a hand toward an empty chair. On the opposite side of the table, Roger Farnsworth occupied the other chair, cigarette in one hand, martini in the other.

Still irritated at the long wait, Nick remained standing. "I thought we were just going to talk."

"Oh, no," said Roger, expelling a cloud of smoke. "Come, sit down, enjoy."

The waiter pulled the chair back. When Nick hesitated the waiter gave him a stiff smile, indicating that he couldn't stand there all night. Nick reluctantly sat down. The waiter then removed a folded cloth napkin from the table, snapped it open with a flick of his wrist, and delicately draped it across Nick's lap, as if to demonstrate how things are done in a classy restaurant.

"Here," Roger said, pushing the martini toward Nick, "bottoms up and down the hatch. Isn't that what you sailors say?"

Nick ignored the offer and looked out the window to calm his irritation. A side-wheel ferry, churning a frothy wake, paddled across the bay from the Ferry Building toward the Oakland Mole, a mile-long pier extending out from the East Bay. His gaze dropped down to the pier sheds bordering the Embarcadero. From this distance their classically inspired facades made them look like grand exhibition halls rather than gritty cargo terminals.

Sufficiently calmed, he turned to Roger. "Look, this isn't some game, and I can't have dinner with you. I'm here to give my report, that's all."

Roger's face dropped. "I know this is serious. I just wanted to make the best of it and figured we could take this opportunity to get to know one another." He sipped his martini. "Clarisa says you and I have a lot in common."

"Oh, really," Nick said dryly.

"Well, we're both Cal grads. I'm class of '29 and you're '30."

The waiter arrived with a basket of sliced sourdough baguette and a saucer of butter pats. A second waiter set water glasses and menus on the table.

"If you don't want dinner," said Roger, "at least help me finish off the oysters and bread." He gestured at the cocktail on the table. "And there's no sense in wasting a good martini."

A plump green olive stuffed with red pimento sat in the gin and vermouth. *Oh, what the hell,* Nick thought. It *had* been hours since his last meal and the oysters, soaking in a cold broth of their own juice, looked delicious. He reached for the martini.

"Good," said Roger. "Let's toast to—" He paused thoughtfully. "I know, let's toast to the Blue and Gold, the colors of our alma mater." They clinked glasses.

Nick sipped the cocktail, flavored with juniper and vermouth.

Roger smacked his lips. "It's so good to drink decent liquor after all these years. Christ, one frosh in my fraternity nearly went blind drinking the bathtub variety." He set the glass down, picked up a demi-fork, and stabbed one of the oysters. "Did you belong to a Greek?"

"No, I lived in a boardinghouse," Nick replied as he smeared a pat of butter on a slice of baguette.

"Major?"

"Business, at first. My dad wanted me to take over his cargo ware-house and thought I should have the education he never got. After a year I knew it wasn't for me, so I branched out into art history, drama, litera-ture, whatever seemed interesting. In the end I graduated with a B.A. in journalism."

"I'll bet that caused a few rows around the house."

"Oh, yeah." Nick stuffed the baguette into his mouth and reached for a lemon wedge.

Roger nodded knowingly. "I went through the same ordeal. My father's a surgeon and wanted me to take up the scalpel." He grasped a knife and held it up like a torch. "I was a dutiful son, so I took pre-med classes" — he dropped the knife on the table, causing the dishes to jump — "and hated it."

Nick squeezed the lemon over an oyster, picked up the shell, and poured the oyster into his mouth, savoring the salty flavor and slithery texture.

"In my junior year," Roger continued, "I switched to music, athletics, and history until father threatened to cut off my expenses." He shrugged. "In the end we compromised on business."

"How'd you like it?"

"It was practical, but if I'd had my way I would have concentrated on music." His face lit up. "Did you go to the dances at Harmon Gym?"

His hunger now dulled, Nick nodded enthusiastically. "Don Mulfurd's Big Band and The Athens Club Orchestra."

"That's it." Roger grinned. "Well, I was the guy standing in front of the bandstand, bopping my head up and down like a basketball. I collected dozens of records and knew all the tunes. I still love music more than anything, and Clarisa says I'm not a bad dancer." He tapped his cigarette on a glass ashtray, his eyes fixed on Nick like a lion tamer gauging the effect of a deliberate prod.

Blindsided by the provocative remark, Nick raised his glass and downed the martini in one long, slow gulp to hide his surprise and give himself time to digest the comment. If Roger was seeing Clarisa, then he must know that he, Nick, and Clarisa had been serious. In that case, this not-so-subtle declaration was Roger's way of warning him that he was staking a claim and also to discourage him from resuming a relationship with her. In other words, a challenge. The gin warmed Nick's insides, and it also gave him a bounce of Dutch courage.

"Speaking of Cal, I was in the Frosh-Soph Brawl the year I was a freshman and you were a sophomore. But it wasn't the usual Brawl that year, was it?"

The question elicited a stony silence from Roger.

The Frosh-Soph Brawl was an annual competition between male freshmen and sophomores who met on Hilgard Field for a series of contests — tug-of-war, relay races, piggy-back jousts, and the like. It was typically a raucous affair beginning with a wild, free-for-all wrestling match between the two classes. The older and bigger sophomores invariably won the wrestling competition and traditionally stripped a few freshmen down to their skivvies and tossed them into the grave, a long pit filled with muddy water that would later be used for the tug-of-war contest.

"We planned our strategy weeks in advance," Nick continued. "We lined up on the field opposite you sophomores with our biggest guys in the middle grouped into a charging wedge. Behind them, we placed our best throwers armed with clumps of mud and grass. When the contest began, we charged forward and broke through the sophomore line, all the while bombarding you with dirt clods." Caught up in the telling of the story, Nick leaned forward and grasped the edge of the table. "Our plan worked so well your class retreated like jackrabbits, and afterwards we went on to win most of the contests and took the competition. The first frosh class in U.C. history to win the Brawl. Afterwards the *Daily Cal* described it as a complete rout, and the only ones who ended up in the grave were sophomores who fell in during the tug-of-war contest. Goes to show what underdogs can do if they get themselves organized."

He leaned back and studied Roger with a triumphant grin.

The waiter arrived and asked for their orders.

Feeling satisfied with himself and ravenous, Nick picked up the menu. "I think I will have something." None of the entrees were under a dollar-fifty, but he supposed the view made the expense worthwhile to those who could afford it. "I assume the Employer's Association is paying for this?" Roger nodded. "Good, I'll have the golden filet steak with fresh peas, potatoes a la king, and spumoni ice cream for dessert."

Roger ordered the sweetbread sauté with grilled mushrooms, squash

Florentine, and a second round of martinis. He lit another cigarette, took a drag, and blew out a stream of smoke. "There's something else you might remember about the Frosh-Soph Brawl that year. After it was over the Sophomore Vigilante Committee caught several freshmen without their dink hats." Dink hats were blue skull caps with tiny yellow visors that male freshmen were ordered to wear on campus by the student body executive committee. Freshmen hated the silly-looking hats and avoided wearing them whenever possible. Consequently, an enforcing body called the Sophomore Vigilante Committee patrolled the campus armed with wooden pallets, ready to spank any freshmen caught without his dink. "I was one of the Vigilantes. We surrounded a few frosh without their dinks that day. Not only did we give them a good licking, we also invited their girlfriends to take a whack. One Sally, who must have been peeved at her boyfriend, took us up on it and really let him have it. Show's what can happen when a guy doesn't treat his girl with the attention she deserves."

The waiter arrived with two more martinis and set them on the table. Both men picked up their drinks and sipped them, glancing at each other like pugilists between rounds.

"As I recall," Nick said, charging out of his corner, "the Vigilante Committee was the most hated group on campus, strutting around like junior Mussolinis, trying to impress girls with their strong-arm tactics. We figured they carried big paddles to compensate for their tiny dicks."

Roger winced from behind a haze of cigarette smoke but came back with a shattering counterpunch. "That's because the girls fell all over us. Losers say infantile things when they're jealous."

Try as he might, Nick couldn't think of a comeback. And it was true. For reasons he never understood, campus coeds seemed captivated by belligerent bullies who wore lettered sweaters and expensive penny loafers. In any case, this conversation was no longer about college days, and he saw no reason to continue.

The two combatants fell into a wounded silence, nursing their drinks until the waiter arrived with their meals and set them on the table.

Roger picked up a fork and speared a sweetbread. "How are things at the docks?"

"A guy in my gang went to the hospital," Nick said as he cut off a piece of steak. "I almost went with him. You guys keep records of that kind of thing?"

"No, but we should. I hate to admit it but our members seem to care more about how accidents effect the schedule than the men."

The comment was surprisingly frank coming from an employee of the Waterfront Employers Association, and it prompted Nick to wonder if there was more to Farnsworth than he assumed. "I'm going to a union meeting tomorrow night. I'll let you know what happens."

"Good. I also need some specific information, and you're our best man for the job."

"You mean I'm not the only one on your payroll working on the waterfront."

"Not hardly, but with your background you're a perfect fit for this assignment." He pulled a newsletter out of his coat pocket and laid it on the table. "Have you seen this?" The title across the top read WATERFRONT WORKER. Below it was a headline: THE BLUE BOOK UNION MUST BE SMASHED! NOW IS THE TIME!

Nick leafed through the pages. "Nope."

"A radical group called the Marine Workers Industrial Union started publishing it six months ago. Now they claim" — he pointed to a tagline below the masthead — "that it's published by rank-and-file stevedores, but it doesn't say who. We're not sure if it's actually a longshoremen effort or Reds pretending to be longshoremen. Either way, we want to find out who's behind it."

"Hmmm…I doubt anyone would tell me unless I joined the staff."

"Well you do have a degree in journalism."

"Yeah, but if I join the staff, I'd have to stay on. It'd be too suspicious if I quit right away."

"Okay, see if you can gather names some other way. If not you'll have to do what it takes."

After dinner Nick climbed the Filbert Steps up Telegraph Hill. This part of Filbert Street, too steep for cars, had been cultivated into a lush garden of roses, jasmine, honeysuckle, and trumpet vines. He passed a young couple admiring the flowers, and it reminded him of evenings he and Clarisa had strolled here, soft moonlight illuminating the garden, the air redolent with the fragrance of honeysuckle. Roger's indirect admission that he and Clarisa were dating was troubling, and during dinner Nick had had to suppress pangs of jealousy. At the moment, however, another aspect of the night's meeting occupied his thoughts: the possibility of working as a reporter, even though it would be for a radical newsletter bent on stirring things up.

It also raised a question: *Am I ready for such an assignment? Have I been around the block enough times, as the Chronicle editor put it, to be a decent reporter?* He felt like a different person now, and there was no question that his odyssey had dealt him a series of eye-opening, ego-bruising blows. *But am I seasoned enough?*

He reached the crest of Telegraph Hill and paused there to admire the nearly completed tower on its peak, fluted and tapered to resemble a Greek column. An article in the newspaper had reported that Herbert Fleishhacker, banker and president of the Park Commission, had orchestrated the selection of the tower for this site. It was constructed of reinforced concrete, and the company that supplied the concrete was substantially owned by none other than Fleishhacker himself. Few seemed to think there was anything wrong with the arrangement, and it reminded Nick of the *Waterfront Worker* and its efforts to shake things up. *What happens,* he wondered, *to those who buck the system, who challenge the status quo, who question the sweetheart deals and jab their finger in the eyes of the great and powerful?*

It was an unanswerable question, but he had a sneaking suspicion that before it was all over he was going to find out.

27

They streamed into the Labor Temple in wool coats, denim jackets, opened collared shirts, knit sweaters, black trousers, blue jeans, leather work boots, flat-caps, and fedoras. Nick slipped in among them and made his way into a spacious auditorium, the air hazy from cigarette smoke hovering over rows of chairs facing a stage. He scanned the room looking for anyone he knew, and from the broad smiles and friendly banter, he could see that there were high expectations for the evening ahead. He spotted Henry Schmidt seated near the stage, talking to someone beside him. Taking a chair in the row behind Schmidt, he leaned forward to hear what Schmidt was saying.

"Holman got himself elected president before anyone could put up other candidates. It was a quick maneuver — I'll give him that — but he won't get away with it this time. We got guys posted in every section of the hall, ready to propose another vote. As soon as one of us is recognized, Bridges will second it. By parliamentary rules, Holman'll have to proceed with a discussion and a vote."

Schmidt's companion glanced over his shoulder at Nick listening in on their conversation. He leaned toward Schmidt and whispered just loud enough for Nick to hear, "I think we got a stool pigeon behind us."

Is it that obvious? Nick wondered.

Schmidt turned, frowning. When he saw Nick his expression relaxed. "He ain't a stoolie." He acknowledged Nick with a lift of his chin. "It's Brother Benson."

A gavel pounded on the lectern, quieting the room. A man in a loose, ill-fitting suit stood at the lectern. He introduced himself as Aiden Morrow, acting secretary of Local 38-79. Behind him were three other union officials in suits, sitting on chairs facing the members. Morrow called the meeting to order and read the minutes of the previous meeting. When the minutes were approved, he introduced Lee Holman, a well-built fellow with thick brown hair and eyes that shined with confidence. He greeted everyone and heaped praise on them for joining the International Longshoremen's Association.

"Now that our local has two-thousand members," he said with a magnanimous smile, "it's just a matter of time before we're recognized as the sole union representative of every dockworker on the Frisco front."

He went on to describe a proposal for the maritime labor codes under the National Recovery Act, especially their three key demands: a wage increase of fifteen cents an hour to a dollar per hour, a six-hour work day (down from eight hours), and overtime wages of one dollar-thirty cents per hour. He ended with a promise that he would urge Joe Ryan, national president of the ILA, to adopt the proposal and present it at the NRA code hearings in Washington D.C. in November.

The men clapped and cheered and tossed their hats in the air as if Holman had announced an actual pay raise.

This puzzled Nick. It was only a proposal and faced numerous hurdles before it could ever be enacted into law. He looked around at the faces nearby. Some were etched with age, others flush with youthful enthusiasm, still others haggard from years of hard labor and exposure to the elements. All of them, however, appeared hopeful and optimistic, and it was then that he understood their exuberance. For, in this case, hope was its own reward.

When the applause died down Holman introduced Bill Lewis, president of the ILA's newly-formed Pacific Coast District. Lewis praised the progress of the Pacific Coast District in banding together for the first time every longshore union on the West Coast. He also emphasized the importance of the code proposal in future negotiations with shippers and stevedore companies and suggested that the Pacific Coast District should send its own delegate to the code hearings in Washington D.C. "to make damn sure they hear us loud and clear."

The members cheered and whooped and again tossed their caps into the air.

Holman resumed his place at the lectern, his hands held up to calm the assembly. He was grinning from ear to ear, clearly enjoying the progress of the meeting like an entertainer who has won his audience and can do no wrong. At various places throughout the auditorium, arms shot into the air. While Holman looked them over, he reached into his breast pocket, pulled out a handkerchief, and wiped beads of sweat off his brow, a magnanimous smile still on his face.

"Point of order," a stevedore called out, rising to his feet. He wore a frayed wool jacket and baggy trousers, the corners of his mouth stained with tobacco juice.

Holman pointed the gavel at him. "Speak, brother."

"I been readin' the by-laws," the man drawled, "and it says plain and simple we got the right to elect officers."

Holman leaned toward the microphone. "We held an election last month, brother. Weren't you here?"

"I was here and what happened weren't no election; it was a ram job. No one 'ceptin' you and your gang got a chance to talk or was allowed to toss their hat in the ring. There's others who want a chance to say their piece. And besides, we should elect an executive board so's we don't wind up with another Blue Book Union on our hands run by labor-fakers for their own edification."

Holman laughed. "Edification? That's a mighty big word. You sure you know what it means?"

"Sure do," said the longshoreman. "So how about it?" He turned toward the membership. "I propose a motion that we hold an election for officers and an executive board, and that any bona fide member who wants to run can put his name up."

A few scattered men applauded, and after some hesitation about half the members politely joined in.

Another longshoreman stood up. "I second the motion," he said with a thick Australian accent. "Everybody here knows we gotta right to this election and—"

Holman pounded the gavel. "Si'down, Brother Bridges. You're out of order."

Bridges remained standing, and for a pregnant moment he and Holman stared at each other, neither willing to back down.

Ever since Nick had heard Schmidt's plan to force another election, he'd been mulling it over and wasn't surprised by Holman's resistance. The trick would be to convince Holman that it was in his own best interest to hold another election. While thinking it over Nick had formed a rationale that might appeal to the union leader, but he was hesitant to present it to such a large audience, especially as he'd only been working at the waterfront a short period. On the other hand, if it worked he might curry favor with key leaders and open a few doors.

Besides, he had nothing to lose.

He rose to his feet. "Mr. President, if you please, an open election would not only comply with the bylaws, it would also boost your credibility and force the employers to accept you as our legitimate representative."

It was a stretch to assume that shipowners would recognize Local 38-79 just because it held an election, but Holman had little to risk since the men appeared to be solidly behind him.

Holman squinted at Nick through swirls of cigarette smoke. "Who the hell're you?"

Nick swallowed against a dry throat. "Benson, sir. Been working at Pier 19 for Sweat and Hurry."

The comment provoked a few scattered chuckles.

As more hands shot up for recognition, Holman rubbed his chin. Bill Lewis joined him at the lectern, and the two conferred in whispers, during which time the members discussed the proposal amongst themselves until a steady buzz filled the hall.

After Lewis returned to his seat, Holman pounded the gavel. "The young man over there," he said, waving the gavel at Nick, "has a point. You men know this union wouldn't be anywhere without me and that I'd give my life for you. More than anything I want us to get organized and succeed. So, if you want an election," he bellowed, raising the gavel in the air, "By God, you'll have one!"

The men burst into cheers, and once again Holman grinned from ear to ear. "Now what we're gonna do is take names after the meeting for anyone who wants to run. I'll post them in the office, and next week you can come down to headquarters and cast your vote."

With that, the meeting was adjourned.

On their way out of the auditorium, Henry Schmidt and the Australian named Bridges thanked Nick for his timely intervention and invited him out for a beer. Nick gladly accepted the invitation — who knows what he might learn — and together they walked a few blocks to a beer hall on Valencia Street called The Albion. The place had a comfortable well-worn feel to it. The wood wainscoting and plaster walls had aged to a leathery hue from years of tobacco smoke, and the walls were decorated with faded pictures of German castles and lively beer gardens with waitresses in puffy off-the-shoulder blouses serving steins of beer.

They ordered a round of beers and settled into seats around an oak table near the back. A short time later the bartender delivered a tray of dimpled glass mugs overflowing with white froth. The three raised their mugs, clinked them together, and gulped down the amber lager, brewed on the premises, according to Schmidt, by German immigrants using a recipe from the old country.

Bridges reached into his coat pocket and pulled out a horse racing form and pencil. His hair was dark brown, combed back, his eyes pale gray.

"Harry loves the nags," Henry said to Nick with a good-natured wink, "some say more than his wife."

"Actually, I rarely bet on the horse," Bridges remarked as he studied the form and circled a name. "I prefer to place my money on the jockey." His nose was long and pointed, made prominent by a high forehead and receding chin. He looked up at Nick. "You go to the races?"

"Nope."

The Australian went back to scrutinizing the form. "It's my way to relax. I go to the track most Saturday mornings before post time and talk to the jockeys. There's three or four of 'em that really know how to push the bangtails. They give me the straight dope on which ones 'er hot and which ones 'er deadbeats. See, I like to know who I'm bettin' on." He lowered the form and sipped his beer. "Now take Holman, he talks a good game, right? So the men are fooled into thinkin' he's the best man to lead 'em. But all he's done is collect dues and talk about the codes. Well, I say fuck the codes. No worker ever got a square deal from a gov'ment code. And, besides, there's only one code that'll help us."

He returned to the racing form and circled another name.

Nick gave Schmidt an inquiring glance but Schmidt just shrugged.

"So, what's *that* code?" Nick asked.

Bridges looked up and directed a steady gaze at Nick, during which time Nick felt as if the Australian was peeling back the layers of his soul, gauging his character at the deepest level and weighing it against some standard of his own. It was the longest few seconds of his life, and he hoped that at least part of himself remained concealed.

"Brother," said Bridges, "it's a code a commitment to the workin' class. I'm from Australia where workin' people are proud of their class, and everyone who works belongs to a union. Here in America there's a great aversion to acknowledgin' the class struggle, to acknowledgin' the conflict between the interests of corporations and workin' people. But it's a fact. And," he said, poking his finger on the table to punctuate each word, "it's no more evident than now. There's over a hundred thousand workers on strike across America and most of 'em have been gassed, shot at, and clubbed for tryin' to get a square deal for their families." He shook his head. "But most Americans still blindly hang onto myths handed to us by the bosses."

These were radical words, to be sure, but Nick was intrigued. Not many dockworkers, hell, not many professors he'd known spoke with such passion and authority, and it made him want to learn more. "What do you mean, sir?"

Bridges frowned. "Now don't go callin' me sir. You're no doughboy and I'm nobody's commander."

"Sorry, I was just wondering what you meant by myths."

Bridges laid down the form. "Take Harratio Alger. Everyone has bought into that rags-to-riches crap. Emile Stone, head of the Blue Book Union, is a perfect example. Now there's a guy who'd sell his mother down the river for a bottle of scotch. And I ain't kiddin'. He used to be a winchdriver. As soon as he got fixed up as a union official, he started wearin' forty dollar suits and bought a fancy house in San Mateo. He couldn't wait to abandon his class and move up the ladder. Now he's nothin' but a labor faker, pretendin' he's on the side of workin' people. The labor movement's full of 'em. Look" — he leaned forward, fixing his gray eyes on Nick — "if we're gonna beat the shipowners at their own game, we'll need jockeys with a whole lot more commitment to the rank-and-file than the likes of Stone and Holman."

The sentiment was contrary to everything Nick had learned from his father, and he felt compelled to challenge it. "What's wrong with trying to get ahead, trying to build a better life for your family?" Strangely, in the presence of Bridges his words seemed hollow and selfish.

"Look, there's nothin' wrong with wanting a better life, but not at the expense of your mates."

Schmidt chuckled. "Harry fancies himself a workin' class hero, so he rarely mentions that he was brought up in the lap of luxury."

"The hell I was," Bridges retorted as he picked up the racing form and studied it again.

"Okay, maybe not luxury exactly, but your father was a landlord, so I guess that makes it the lap of the bourgeoisie."

"You forget my uncle belonged to the Labour Party," Bridges shot back from behind the paper, "and was as dedicated a union man as you'll ever find."

The bartender approached cradling a black oval case in his arms about the size of a sleeping lamb. There were scuff marks across the top and the corners were threadbare. He set it on the table.

"Harry," he said, with a German accent. "You play." He tilted his head toward an unlit jukebox in the corner. "Music box broken."

"Thank God for that," Bridges said, still perusing the form. "I get tired of those damn polkas. Can't you put any other records in it?"

"*Bitte*," the bartender said, touching the case, "you play *Valtzing Mathilde*? Ve need a little music to liven tings."

Bridges remained hidden behind the form, so the bartender opened the case and withdrew an old mandolin, its finish worn down from years of strumming. He held it out. "*Bitte, Valtzing Mathilde.* You play?"

Bridges looked over the top of the form, his lips pursed into an irritated frown. "Oh, all right," he sighed, folding the racing form and setting it down. He took the mandolin from the bartender, rested it on his lap, and began plucking the strings and adjusting the tuning pegs.

"Folks in America," he said as he tuned the mandolin, "even most Aussies, think Waltzing Matilda is a cute little tune full of quaint words like 'jumbuck' and 'billabong.' But it's really a song about class struggle. Even the title has a meaning, going all the way back to Germany. Right, Henry?"

"What?" said Schmidt, who'd been eyeing two women at the bar.

"Tell Nick what *auf der walz Mathilde* means."

"Oh, well, *auf der walz* is an old German expression meaning to travel around, sleeping where you can. And *Mathilde* is a name, of course, but it was also the term given to prostitutes who followed the Prussian army. Then it came to mean keeping warm at night, and finally it referred to a bedroll. German immigrants brought the expression to Australia where it got jackknifed into 'waltzing matilda' and came to mean traveling around like a hobo with a bedroll swagged around the chest."

Bridges nodded. "The song's about an itinerant swagman who skins and eats a sheep owned by a rich squatter."

"Rich squatter?" Nick asked.

"In Australia's early days, every landowner was a squatter because there weren't any laws regulating land distribution and ownership. The squatters grabbed every good tract they could lay their hands on and ran everyone else off. Then they paid piddling wages to have their sheep shorn. In the 1890s sheep shearers struck for higher wages, so the squatters threw 'em off their land. Some of the shearers retaliated by burnin' down a barn packed with hundreds of sheep. In response, squatters and troopers hunted down the shearers and murdered 'em. One German immigrant, rather than allowin' himself to be captured, shot himself next to a small pond called a billabong. At the end of the song the swagman, like the German immigrant, prefers death to capture. There are those, like myself, who believe it speaks to the allegiance the swagman had to his class. Conservatives, on the other hand, say it demonstrates law over anarchy. In the end, the two interpretations allowed the song to become an anthem for all Aussies."

He finished tuning the mandolin and strummed a few cords. Patrons in the beer hall looked over as he began singing.

Once a jolly swagman camped by a bill-a-bong
Under the shade of a coolabah tree.
And he sang as he watched and waited 'til his billy boiled
You'll come a-waltzing matilda with me.

At the chorus everyone joined in, their combined voices blending together to fill the beer hall.

Waltzing matilda, waltzing matilda
You'll come a waltzing matilda with me...

On the last verse Bridges slowed the song to a dirge-like tempo and everyone, including the bartender, hummed along.

Up jumped the swagman and sprang into that bill-a-bong
"You'll never take me alive!" said he.
And his ghost may be heard as you pass by that bill-a-bong
You'll come a-waltzing matilda with me...

Later that evening, on his way home, Nick rode a cable car up Russian Hill, feeling pleased with himself. His timely comment at the union meeting had brought him to the attention of the president, Lee Holman, a move that might prove useful. He'd scored points with Henry Schmidt and Harry Bridges, who apparently had plans of their own for Local 38-79. He'd received an invitation from Schmidt to attend weekly meetings at Albion Hall, a meeting room above The Albion, to discuss strategies that, according to Schmidt, would make Local 38-79 a union dedicated to the rank-and-file. And on top of all that, he was about to receive wages as both a longshoreman and an informant.

Not that he'd forgotten the risks. For the moment, though, they seemed manageable.

28

As the week drew to a close, longshore gangs stowed the last of the cargo onto the *Point Reyes* and watched as the ship blew its whistle and backed out into the bay. Tired and worn out, Nick plodded home and fell onto his bed for a nap so long and deep that when he woke up he wasn't sure if the faint light through the curtains meant it was dusk or dawn. Groggy, hair askew, he shuffled into the dining room and found a note laying on the table.

Dear Nick,

I left a plate of dinner in the oven. No dessert. Though I suppose we should be grateful to have anything at all. When do you get paid??? We're two months behind on our grocery bill and a month behind on the rent.

By the way, THAT DOG pooped on the kitchen floor again. Really, dear, you need to take him out every day. I've tried putting him in the backyard but he's already dug up Mrs. Barbarini's basil twice. If he does it again I'm afraid her husband will put out rat poison. Couldn't you take him to work as his owner did? He mopes around all day like your sister. I'm afraid I'm not much company for either of them.

Rune and I are off to a concert in Washington Square. We'll be back by ten.

Sarah ran off with her friends to an exhibit at the Art Institute. Lord knows when she'll be back. I've had a difficult time with her since your father passed on. Perhaps you can have a word. She won't listen to me, and I'm terribly afraid she'll end up with the wrong crowd.

I do wish we could talk face-to-face. You've been out a lot lately in the evenings. I hope you're alright. And who is this Mr. Smith that keeps calling? He sounds nice but says little.

Love, Mother

Oh, I almost forgot. Clarisa phoned while you were asleep. She sounded a bit formal. Are you two still friends?

A warm pressure settled on Nick's foot. He reached down and stroked Rusty and received a lick of appreciation. If only his relationship with Clarisa were that simple. He didn't know what to make of his mother's assessment of her formal tone. Perhaps she was annoyed that he hadn't called. He still rejected the notion of contacting her until all charges against him were dropped. It seemed terribly important that when they met again, it be on equal ground, no sympathy, no pity, no recriminations.

Rusty's soulful brown eyes gazed up at him. Nick stroked him again. "We'll go see Fargo tomorrow. I promise. In the meantime, let's go for a walk. Whattaya say?" The word "walk" hoisted Rusty onto his feet, ears perked, tail wagging.

After dinner Nick donned a jacket and cap and trooped down the front stairs with Rusty at his heels. He stepped outside into a twilit evening, the air cool and refreshing, a few scattered clouds drifting east. He headed up Russian Hill to the crest and paused to look down at rows of streetlights marching single-file toward the ocean, climbing over hills and down dips, converging at some distant vanishing point.

He continued on down the hill, thinking how fond he was of long walks, both for the exercise and the opportunity for contemplation. A few weeks after his father died, he'd walked all the way to Ocean Beach and was so absorbed in thinking about his father, he scarcely noticed how far he'd come. When at last he arrived at the long stretch of sand, he was able for the first time since his father passed to think of him without feeling intense sadness or resentful anger. *Life goes on*, he repeated to himself as he stood at the seawall watching waves surge onto the beach and then retreat, leaving patterns of tangled seaweed on the sand.

Inhaling fresh ocean air and feeling cool breezes against his face, he'd recalled precious moments with his father. The time Charles laughed till tears came to his eyes when six-year old Nick danced with abandon around the living room like a whirling dervish. The day they rode a steam train up Mount Tamalpais and broke through a layer of clouds as they arrived at the peak, an island in a sea of white mist. A glorious Seals game when Gus Sur slammed a game-winning homer while they jubilantly tossed popcorn in the air.

Despite these pleasant memories, the circumstances that brought his father's life to an untimely end still haunted him like the lingering pain of stinging nettle. If only he could have done something to relieve his father's burden. Like most men of his generation, Charles wasn't able to admit weakness or lean on his family for emotional support, preferring to conceal his problems and hide his anxieties. In the end, his inability to share his burden must have eroded his spirit and left him feeling hopeless and alone.

Striding down Russian Hill, Nick reached Hyde Street. He started across when he noticed a young woman nearby with auburn hair the same shade as Clarisa's. It wasn't Clarisa but he averted his eyes anyway. Since his release from jail, he'd made a conscious effort to avoid thinking about her and vowed not to do so until he felt ready to make contact. When thoughts about her did intrude, he concentrated on whatever was nearby to block them out. Using this strategy, he shifted his gaze to the cable car tracks at his feet and listened to the gentle whir of the cable moving in the middle slotted track. It worked, as it usually did, until another thought occurred to him, a thought so startling, so unnerving, he stopped in his tracks, prompting Rusty to look up inquisitively.

The thought, a revelation really, so perfectly exposed an elemental truth about himself, he murmured, "Oh, my God, of course."

In the middle of Hyde Street, oblivious to the honking cars and frowning drivers, he was astonished at how obvious it was and wondered why he hadn't thought of it before, why he'd been so blind. Under the bright light of insight, he now saw his father's well-worn path laid out before him, saw himself following it, avoiding any appearance of weakness or vulnerability to maintain his self-image of strength and self-reliance, the same self-image he'd inherited from his father.

Now he understood why he'd been avoiding Clarisa.

As the realization sank in and all its implications became clear, the mental barrier he'd erected to keep her at bay dissolved in a pool of understanding, replaced by a newfound sense of purpose. Determined to blaze a new trail, his own trail, he rushed forward on winged feet, Rusty at his heels.

Twenty minutes later he reached his destination and knocked on the door. After a short wait, the door cracked open and a bloodshot eye peered out at him.

"Whadda you want?" asked a gravely voice.

"It's me, Nick." The bloodshot eye stared at him without recognition. "Nick Benson."

The door swung open, revealing Seamus McMahon, arms extended, a syrupy grin on his face. "Nick, me boy. By God, you're a sight for sore eyes." Embracing Nick with a bear hug, Seamus held on to him as if cling-ing for dear life. Then he drew back and pulled him through the doorway. "Come on in." When Rusty followed, he thrust out a foot that glanced off the dog's snout. "Get outta here, ya goddamned beggar."

"No. No," said Nick. "He's with me."

"Oh, Jaysus, I didn't know you had a dog. A mutt by the look of him."

"He's not mine." Nick bent down and took hold of Rusty's collar. "I'm taking care of him for a friend."

"There's an awful lotta stray dogs roamin' the city these days, most of 'em hungry and vicious. I thought your mutt was tryin' to pull a fast one. Well, come on in, the two of yous."

They climbed the stairs and walked down a hall to the kitchen. Seamus offered Nick a seat at the dining table, upon which stood a half-empty pint of Old Kirk's Whiskey beside a tumbler and an open book.

"I was just readin' *The Iron Heel* by Jack London," Seamus said as he went to the cabinet and took out a glass. "A helluva a scribe. Not Joyce, mind you, but a real thinker." He set the glass on the table beside his own and poured them each a drink. "I told Clarisa you'd be back. And when she only received one letter, I told her to keep the faith." He handed a glass to Nick and grinned. "Jaysus, it's good to see you."

Nick took a sip to be sociable. It was decent liquor but the purpose of his visit wasn't to make merry. He set the tumbler down.

Seamus had no such inhibitions. He downed his whiskey in one quick gulp. "Go on, boy, drink up," he urged, wiping his mouth with his sleeve. "It's good for cool summer nights, just like dear ol' Dublin. Go on now."

Nick took another sip and for the next hour, while Seamus refilled their glasses (mostly his own), he recounted his voyage across the Pacific and all his adventures. When his story reached Manila and he described the brawl with bosun Slag, Seamus slammed his tumbler on the table and swore that if the bosun ever bothered him again, he'd be happy to take care of the twerp with his Enfield rifle. Nick assured him that Slag and Primm were on a voyage around the world. This seemed to mollify the Irishman, although he repeated his offer to defend Nick if the capitalist lackeys ever returned.

The sound of a key in the front door interrupted their conversation. They listened as footsteps padded up the stairs. When the footsteps reached the top, Seamus rose from his seat and shambled down the hall, holding his hands against the walls to steady himself.

"Darlin', light 'o my life," he slurred, "welcome home."

"You're drunk," a curt voice replied.

"That's because we're celebratin', luv."

"We? Who's here?"

"Come on, luv. The native son has returned."

Seamus entered the kitchen, pulling Clarisa along by her coat. "Ta daaa," he said, holding out his arms toward Nick like a ringmaster. "It's the courageous sailor who braved the ocean blue to bring back a stake to his one true love."

Clarisa's eyes widened, her lips parted in surprise.

Nick stood up and smiled sheepishly, wondering if it had been a mistake to show up unannounced. He studied her expression — the raised eyebrows, the startled green eyes, parted lips, dimpled —. His gaze returned to her mouth. It was strangely blurred and misshapen. He studied the unusual sight until he realized that it wasn't her mouth that was misshapen but rather her lipstick smeared beyond its usual boundaries. No crisp red edge, no perfect bow-shaped outline. Instead a messy smudged blur, like a child who's been sucking on a red popsicle. He instantly recognized the look. It was how she appeared after they kissed at her doorstep.

Apparently reading his mind, she self-consciously put her hand over her mouth and excused herself. While she was away Seamus made a feeble joke about women and their attachment to the john. When she returned, the smeared lipstick was replaced by a neatly applied coat. She was also more composed and gave Nick an inquiring glance.

"Feeling better now that you're out of jail?"

"Well...yes," he stammered, embarrassed by the memory of his rude behavior at their last meeting. "Look, I — I came to apologize. I'm sorry I acted so badly. You were only trying to help." He lowered his eyes and so did she.

Seamus glanced back and forth between them. "Oh, come on you two." He grasped each of them by the arm and attempted to pull them together. "Kiss and make up. It's not as though couples don't have rows once in a while. Go on."

Neither budged, though their heads lifted simultaneously, eyes met.

Despite the proximity and intensity of their mutual gaze, Nick felt a gulf between them as vast and wide as the night he announced he was leaving, maybe more so. Her face was still proud and beautiful, as he remembered, but her green eyes were now dull hard orbs.

"I tried to send you a letter from Seattle but —" He shrugged, not wanting to explain that his bunkmate was so drunk he forgot to mail the letter. "After that there wasn't another opportunity to post mail that would have gotten here before I returned."

Seamus walked unsteadily over to the cupboard and took out another tumbler. "There you go, luv. It was all just a mix-up." He set the glass on the table with the other two and poured what was left in the bottle. "Let's have a toast and let bygones be bygones."

Without removing her eyes from Nick, Clarisa said, "We need to talk—alone."

"Oh," Seamus said, setting the bottle on the table. "Right. You two must have a lot of catching up to do. We can toast another time. I'll just finish this off and go to bed."

"No," she exclaimed, snatching the tumbler from his hand. "You've had more than enough." She went to the kitchen sink and poured the whiskey down the drain, Seamus following her, arms outstretched.

"Jaysus, child!" he cried. "Have you no love for you poor old dad?"

She spun around and glared at him. "Off with you," she ordered, pointing her finger toward the hall. "And don't give me any cock and bull about love. I need you sober more than you need love."

Muttering to himself, Seamus slunk off into the hall while Clarisa washed the glasses and threw the empty whiskey bottle into the trash can.

"You really shouldn't encourage him," she said as they settled on the sofa in the parlor. "He's only getting worse now that he doesn't have much to do in the shop. Almost all his business these days comes from the Worker's School next door, and they don't pay half the time."

"Sorry. He was already in his cups when Rusty and I arrived."

"Rusty?"

"I'm taking care of a dog for a friend who's in the hospital."

At the sound of his name, Rusty came trotting in from the hall and rested his muzzle on Clarisa's lap.

"He's darling," she said, stroking his head. "What happened to his owner?"

"A load of nail kegs broke loose over the dock and one landed on his back. I was next to him when it happened. It could've been me."

She glanced at him curiously. "You're working at the docks?"

"Yep. No more sailing for me," he said as cheerfully as possible, although it sounded more exaggerated than he would have liked.

"Hmmm. So how did you get out of jail?"

Nick had anticipated this question. "The D.A.'s star witnesses shipped out, and with those two liars gone the case against me was too weak to prosecute. They've dropped the charges for now."

Clarisa nodded, her gaze still on Rusty. "How do you like working at the waterfront?"

"It's hard work, but jobs are scarce and we need the money."

She glanced at him, her expression cold and implacable. "So, why are you here?"

Nick fidgeted with his coat button. The visit had been spontaneous, perhaps too spontaneous, and he was beginning to feel as if he'd stumbled into a trap of his own making.

"Well...I wanted to apologize and..." His voice trailed off.

"You mean you don't *know*?"

"Well, no...I mean, yes...I mean I wanted to tell you that my sailoring days are over. In fact the D.A. has ordered me to stay in town for the time being, so I couldn't leave if I wanted to. And I was hoping we could —"

She gave him a sharp glance. "*Ohhh*, so now that you're trapped here you want to get back together. Is that what you're saying?"

"Well, not exactly...I mean, I wouldn't put it that way."

"Then how would you put it? Because that's how it sounds. And since when did you become so wishy-washy?"

Nick raised his eyes to the ceiling and shook his head. "I guess...I guess I'm not used to groveling."

"No, you never groveled before, but maybe you should have because right now I'm not ready to run back into your arms. I warned you that if you left I wouldn't wait for you. Everything's different now. I've got a father who needs looking after, and I'm the only breadwinner around here. I've also got job responsibilities and I certainly don't have time for dreamers. And how do I know that if the D.A. removes your travel restrictions you won't be off on another adventure?" She looked him straight in the eye. "I just don't know if I can trust you, and I won't give my heart to someone who thinks it's disposable."

Her words stunned him into silence. Everything she said was true. Up to this point his every move had been made without consideration for her. He'd only regarded her in terms of how she fit into his life, not how he fit into hers. And she was right. If things hadn't gone so badly on the *Diana Dollar*, he might have shipped out again. But that was an academic "if." The reality of sailoring hadn't lived up to his romantic expectations, not by a long shot, and at most he would have signed up for one, maybe two more voyages.

In any case it was a moot point. He wasn't going anywhere, travel restrictions or no.

"I understand how you feel," he said slowly, deliberately. "My actions *have* been selfish, although not with any intent to harm you. And I agree that everything is different. I also have family responsibilities as great as yours." He paused and met her gaze. "All I can say is that there wasn't a day on the *Diana Dollar* when I didn't think of you, when I didn't recall your face or imagine your smile, when I didn't yearn for your touch. There were times when the thought of you was all that kept me going, horrible, taxing days that would have ground me down if I hadn't been able to summon your image. I'm so sorry I caused you pain because, well, you eased mine."

A tear formed in the corner of her eye.

Nick removed a handkerchief from his pocket and handed to her. She dabbed her eyes and took a deep breath, then another. He wanted to stay longer, wanted to have the tender reunion he'd once dreamed of. But that wasn't going to happen, at least anytime soon. He stood up.

"I know I don't have a right to expect anything from you. I just wanted you to know how I feel. I also know that trust is earned by deeds, not words, so for now I'll say good night and be on my way."

29

After Nick and Rusty trudged down the stairs and let themselves out, Clarisa dropped her head onto her hands and dug her fingernails into her forehead as she rocked back and forth, unable to calm the mix of emotions roiling within her.

The next day she attended mass at St. Patrick's, hoping to find solace in the rituals of the church, in the prayers, the frankincense, the Eucharist. They'd been part of her life since she was born, and time and time again it was where she turned during periods of uncertainty. Yet after all these years, God was still an abstract concept to her, an incomprehensible being whose motives she never fully understood and perhaps wasn't meant to understand. The church, however, was real and concrete, stained glass windows depicting Irish saints, thick marble columns supporting vaulted ceilings that soared up toward heaven, a serene sanctuary in the heart of the city, a place of kindness and caring.

After mass she approached Father Shannon and asked for a few minutes of his time. He led her into his office and sat down behind his desk, his calico cat curled up on a stack of books, its tail wrapped snuggly around its chest. Dispensing with small talk, she dove right in and described her confusion. It had started when Nick had been hostile to her at the Hall of Justice. Not long after that, she'd surrendered to Roger's advances again, although this time — she made a point of saying — they hadn't been intimate. Now, after Nick's declaration of what? love? commitment? — she wasn't really sure — she felt obliged to make a choice. She never intended to be involved with two men and didn't know if she wanted to commit to either one. What she did know was that her indecision was undermining her spirit and sapping her strength.

Hands clasped on his lap, face solemn, Father Shannon listened to her describe her dilemma. When she finished, he assured her that she was an intelligent, capable woman with the strength and ability to hold both suitors at bay until she decided which, if either, she loved. There was no reason to rush into a commitment and every reason to take things one step at a time. As long as she was honest with both of them and made it clear she wasn't committed to either one, he didn't see why she couldn't take as much time as needed.

Presented in such clear, concise terms, his counsel once again soothed her troubled spirit as if he'd cut down a stand of tall weeds surrounding her so that now she could see the way forward. She was feeling relieved when a thought jogged her memory. She recalled something Roger once said and this led to more memories until, when fitted together, they formed a disturbing picture, like the last pieces of a jigsaw puzzle finally falling into place.

Her breath sucked in and her hand went to her mouth.

"What is it?" Father Shannon asked.

"I'm — I'm not sure I should tell you."

"That's fine, child, but remember, a spirit unburdened is a spirit at peace."

With the weight of realization bearing down on her, Clarisa wriggled in her seat, unsure what to do. *Should I tell him?* She glanced at the priest. *If I can't trust him who can I trust?* He nodded encouragingly, his kindly expression dissolving her resistance.

"I — I think Nick may be working for my boss."

"For your boss? Doing what?"

"Some time ago Roger asked me if Nick might be willing to gather information about union activities. At the time I didn't think it was possible, but now…his arrest…his sudden release…working at the docks."

Father Shannon nodded gravely. Then he gave her a comforting smile. "Don't let it trouble you, dear. He's a capable young man. I'm sure he can take care of himself."

After she departed, Father Shannon swiveled his chair toward the window overlooking the courtyard. The day outside was dreary. Gray rain clouds hung overhead and the first few raindrops imprinted dark spots on the courtyard. The news that Nick might be spying for the Waterfront Employers Association was disturbing. He'd only met the young man on a couple of occasions, yet he had a strong feeling that Nick was not the type to spy and had only taken on such a dangerous role because he had to, perhaps to get out of jail.

Just then the calico cat jumped up on his lap.

Brushing her away, he swiveled back around and picked up the phone.

30

Journal – September 21, 1933

My visit with Clarisa was a flop and no wonder. I left town against her wishes, returned as an accused smuggler, then treated her badly when she offered to help. Not exactly the behavior of an ardent lover. I'm also tortured by the knowledge that she and Roger Farnsworth are seeing each other, although there is a ray of hope. Something in her manner, perhaps her anger and tears, indicated that her heart is undecided, and it's in that indecision that I'm pinning my hopes. In the meantime I'll have to put my personal feelings aside (no easy feat) and concentrate on the tasks ahead.

My work for "Mr. Smith" is proceeding as planned. Henry Schmidt invited me to a victory party at The Albion to celebrate Local 38-79's election returns. Unlike the subdued atmosphere of my first visit, the beer hall was packed with jubilant dockworkers standing three-deep at the bar and seated around every table. Lee Holman and his running mates won the offices of president, vice-president, and secretary. Unbeknownst to them, however, two-thirds of the elected executive committee are members of a secret slate of candidates, all belonging to the group that meets in Albion Hall above The Albion.

Spirited voices and gruff laughter swirled around me as I made my way through the boisterous crowd. I spotted Harry Bridges at a table near the back, seated with several others who all seemed to be talking at once, though Bridges didn't appear to share their giddy excitement.

"Nick!" a voice called out. "Gimme a hand."

Henry Schmidt stood at the bar, surrounded by longshoremen pressed in around him. He reached over their heads and held out a pair of beer mugs. "Pass these over to our table." I took the mugs and handed them to another longshoreman, then passed several more until there was enough beer on the table to serve everyone twice over. Schmidt pushed his way out of the pack and led me to a couple of empty chairs near Bridges.

"It ain't easy fightin' your way through a crowd of muscle-bound stevedores," Schmidt said above the din. "Hell, if we can set up picket lines this tough, the shippers don't stand a chance."

Everyone laughed, followed by clinking mugs, followed by long, gulping swigs.

Dutch Dietrich, a stevedore with a trim mustache and a mischievous grin, said, "We aughta set up kegs at every pier. That would convert the Blue Bookers."

Laughter resounded again, although Bridges didn't join in.

I asked him if something was wrong.

"It's too soon," he said.

"Too soon to celebrate?"

He nodded. "As my ma use to say, 'don't count your sheep before they're shorn.' We gotta long way to go before any of this means anything. A jockey can't afford to pat himself on the back if he's ahead at the fourth furlong, because if he's behind at the tenth he'll beat himself up. These men have been down so long they're mistakin' a small triumph for a major achievement. They gotta understand that we have a long, rocky road ahead. There's gonna be ups and downs, and we need to be prepared for every step, or we'll fall flat on our faces."

"Oh, for Pete's sake, Harry," Schmidt chided, "lighten up. It's good for the men to enjoy their victory. The more they appreciate each other now, the stronger they'll be when the going gets tough."

"Tell ya what, Henry. You worry about morale and I'll worry about direction, and between the two of us we'll see if we can keep this fuckin' ship afloat. A what?"

They clinked glasses with gusto, froth and beer spilling on the table.

"Henry tells me you've done some writin'," Bridges said to me. "Know how to use a typewriter?"

I'd mentioned my journalism experience to Schmidt in hopes it would attract such an inquiry.

"Perhaps a better question," said Schmidt, "is do you know how to *fix* a typewriter? We've got an old Royal that goes on the fritz at least once a day."

"I'd be happy to take a look at it. I used to fix my dad's typewriter," I lied with a ready expression. The truth is, I can type sixty words a minute, but other than to change ribbons I've never looked inside a typewriter, much less repaired one.

"We need writers to help mobilize the men," Bridges said. "Interested?"

"Sure," I replied, pleased at how things were developing. With any luck, I'd give Mr. Smith the information he wanted, find the opium on the *Diana Dollar*, and exonerate myself before Christmas.

With a beer mug in hand, Henry Schmidt got up, went over to the bar, and climbed on top of it. "Brothers," he said in a loud voice, as he lifted the mug above his head. "I salute you! Tonight we celebrate the first step in building a militant fighting union." The men cheered and whistled. "And let it be the first of many victories to come." More applause. "From this day forward we are all of one mark, bound together by the justness of our cause, the strength of our will, and the bond of our experience. Again I say, we are all of one mark."

"*All of one mark!*" the men repeated, holding their mugs in the air. The room quieted as everyone pour liquid amber down their throats.

"What does 'all of one mark' mean?" I asked Bridges.

"It's an entire shipload of cargo going to one consignee, so it isn't divided or broken up because it's all bound for the same destination."

Schmidt continued, "I wanna bring someone up to say a few words. A guy who knows the straight dope and ain't afraid to say it." He beckoned to Bridges. "Come on up, Harry."

Bridges waved his hand to decline.

The men clapped and whistled and cheered until a pair of stevedores grabbed Bridges' arms and lifted him out of his chair. His feet barely touched the floor as he was hustled to the bar and hoisted up on a forest of outstretched arms like the raising of a flagpole. Placed on this high perch he looked uncomfortable and reserved and glanced shyly at the men below whose faces were flush from beer and beaming with victory. He stuffed his hands in his coat pockets and began speaking, quietly at first, his eyes lowered as if the sight of two hundred enthusiastic stevedores might distract him.

"There's been a lotta talk about the Blue Eagle and the NRA codes. It's a favorite theme of conservative union officials who want us to be patient and wait for the gov'ment to adopt codes for our industry. They keep tellin' us to stay calm and don't rock the boat. Just pay our dues and have faith in them like a bunch of fuckin' sheep. Meanwhile, the gov'ment holds NRA rallies and organizes parades all over the country to convince us that if everyone adopts the codes, everythin'll be honky dory." He lifted his eyes and swept his gaze over the gathering. "Do you believe that?"

"*NOOO!*" the men shouted.

"Damn right," he declared, leaning forward, jutting out his long pointed nose. "No workin' man ever got a fair deal from the gov'ment. Why? Because the gov'ment's controlled by capital, not labor. And the codes they're proposin' will take away our right to strike. Well, let me tell you somethin', a strike is labor's best weapon. We'd still be workin' sixteen hours a day fer starvation wages if we waited fer the bosses to volunteer concessions. Hell, they'd bottle up the sun and the air if they thought they could make us pay fer it."

Murmurs of laughter rippled through the room.

This seemed to boost Bridges' confidence. He began pacing up and down the bar, making eye contact as he spoke.

"You've heard capital's favorite phrase: a fairs day's work for a fair day's pay. They love to sing it like a well-worn jingle. But what they don't mention is that wages in the U.S. are down thirty-eight percent, while corporate dividends are up a hundred-sixty percent. So, *nowww* we know what the bosses mean when they say 'a fair day's work for a fair day's pay.'"

The men chuckled sardonically.

"Let me give you another phrase, one that makes much more sense fer workin' people: An injury to one is an injury to all! Let me here you say it."

"*An injury to one is an injury to all!*" the men chanted.

"What does it mean?" His eyes slowly roved around the room as if he was talking to each man individually. "It means that our only chance for a square deal is to stick together. Whether you're a wharf rat or a star gang stevedore, you can't afford to forget your mates. We gotta get organized, form dock committees, build trust among the rank-and-file so we can call job actions on the spot when the boss speeds things up or ignores hazardous conditions. We can't afford to wait for the codes. Why?" He stopped pacing and squared his shoulders toward the men. "Because our success depends not on the gov'ment, but on ourselves. "

He resumed stalking back and forth along the bar, continuing in this vein for another ten minutes, the words tumbling out like newsprint from a press. He talked about a democratic union run by and for the rank-and-file, about an end to payoffs at the shape-up, and an end to forty-sack pallets that break apart and rain down on men like cluster bombs.

At the end of each point, he punctuated it with the question: "Roight?" And when he did, the men showed their assent with knowing nods. As he described abuses they endured and put into words frustrations they felt, a light crept into the their eyes and a grin formed on their lips. And as he continued to posit the question — "Roight?" — they responded in unison — RIGHT! — their voices infused with hope and tempered by ire.

Like everyone else I was transfixed by his performance. It was pure theater. He roamed back and forth, making one point after another, weaving a story that reached deep into the audience, arousing emotions and stoking a fire long dimmed.

Someone in the crowd, overcome with emotion, began singing a song that sounded like the *Battle Hymn of the Republic* but with different words:

It is we who plowed the prairies, built the cities where they trade;
Other voices joined in.
Dug the mines and built the workshops, endless miles of railroad laid;
Now we stand outcast and starving midst the wonders we have made;
But the un-ion makes us stronnng.
Sol-idarity fore-ev-er.
Sol-idarity fore-ev-er.
Sol-idarity fore-ev-er...

As the second verse began, I studied the faces around me: some weathered and etched with lines, others smooth and unblemished. Yet all of them were staring at Bridges with fervent determination, and I had the feeling that I was witnessing the genesis of something historic, a kernel that might grow into something far larger than any of us could imagine. As I looked around I caught sight of a figure near the front of the beer hall who, it was obvious, wasn't a dockworker. His hair was silver and he wore a white cleric collar, his eyes following Bridges with an admiring gaze. He looked vaguely familiar, and I was sure I'd seen him somewhere before but couldn't recall when or where.

31

Another rusty Swayne & Hoyt freighter, its holds stuffed with cargo, nuzzled up to the dock at Pier 21. It took a week to discharge the cargo and another week to fill it up again. On the last day Nick's gang carried eighty pound sacks of fertilizer on their shoulders, their bodies bent over like hunchbacks. It was grueling, monotonous work, offering little diversion from the onerous weight bearing down on them. The men whistled and hummed during the morning hours to bolster their morale, but by mid-afternoon their faces were dogged and slack, the older ones plodding along stiff-legged as if their legs were tree trunks.

When the evening whistle blew, signaling the end of the shift, Big Load Thompson yelled down from the weather deck that the ship was scheduled to sail in a few hours so they had to keeping going until she was fully stowed. The men groaned and complained but soldiered on, knowing they had no choice if they wanted to keep their jobs.

As the hours passed and the aching muscles in his shoulders and legs became increasingly painful, a terrible anger welled up in Nick. And it wasn't just his own suffering that bothered him. He'd promised Fargo, who was confined to a hospital bed, that he would visit him after work. At eight o'clock they were still far from finishing the job, and an hour later when the sun went down, Klieg lights were set up so they could keep going.

It wasn't until after midnight that the ship was fully stowed. Stevedores, utterly spent, emerged from the hold, leaning on each other to stay upright as they stumbled down the gangway. The dock men waited for them, and together they trudged into the pier shed to collect their brass pay tokens. On their way out of the shed, they were met by Big Load Thompson who reminded them to be back in the morning to work the next shift.

Nick had never been this tired before. Yet he slept fitfully that night, his slumber interrupted by surreal dreams. In one dream a distorted head, with a large pointy nose and huge lips, spiraled up a cargo line, all the while repeating a nursery rhyme, *"Jack be nimble, Jack be slow, Jack don't know which way to go. Hide behind a candlestick. If he hollers catch him quick."* The distorted head hit the gin block at the end of the boom, dislodging it and sending it plummeting down onto a woman with swollen lips who squealed and cried as a flaxen-haired musician stood over her playing a mournful ballad on the saxophone.

The strange vision startled him to consciousness. Then, just as quickly, his exhausted body drew him back to sleep, a pattern that continued for the rest of the night, never allowing him to settle into a restful slumber.

The next morning his mother roused him out of bed and prepared a breakfast of toast, boiled eggs, and coffee. He ate it in a groggy stupor, barely able to keep his eyes open, then staggered back to bed and slept until noon.

Stiff and sore but refreshed, he got up, dressed, collected Rusty, and drove to San Francisco General Hospital. A nurse in the lobby wouldn't allow him to bring Rusty inside, so he tied him to a tree, promising to return with Fargo, if possible.

In a ward on the fourth floor, the old longshoreman lay on his back, pale and unshaven, his atrophied arms and legs as thin as drain pipes. The injury to his lower back had damaged his spinal cord, leaving him immobile from the waist down, although his tongue was fully functional.

"If Rusty can't come up here," he pleaded with the ward nurse, "why can't my friend take me to him?"

The nurse shook her head. "I'm afraid we can't take the risk. Any movement might do more injury to your spinal cord. The doctor says you're to stay put for at least another two weeks. There's still a chance the nerves could heal and return feeling to your legs. It's a slim one, but it's all we've got."

Fargo crossed his arms over his chest and muttered, "Damn nurses, more like prison guards."

Nick sat down beside Fargo's bed and attempted to cheer him up with news about the election and the celebration at The Albion and other waterfront developments. Yet nothing seemed to interest the old man.

Unable to draw Fargo out of his sour mood, Nick glanced out the sash window beside the bed. A row of Italianate Victorians across the street stood side-by-side, and beyond them, off in the distance, the twin spires of St. Ignatius church rose up above the city.

Intrigued, Nick stood up and went to the window and looked down at the hospital grounds below. There were gingko trees, privet hedges, a lawn with brick footpaths. Rusty was sitting attentively on his haunches beside a gingko tree, inspecting every passerby. It seemed a shame the brown and white mutt couldn't cheer up his ailing master. Nick glanced over at Fargo who appeared to be napping. *Perhaps there is something I can do for him.* He went around to the other side of the bed and leaned against the bed frame. It slid a couple of inches.

The movement stirred Fargo, who cracked open an eye. "What the hell are you doin'? Can't you let me suffer in peace?"

Nick held a finger to his lips. "Shusshh." He quietly pushed the foot of the bed around until it bumped against the wall under the window.

Fargo raised his head and peered out the sash. "You're goin' to an awful lotta trouble to improve my view, but it won't do no good." He collapsed back onto the pillow "As soon as the nurse returns, she'll make you move me back."

Nick smiled patiently. "Be quiet and look."

"I already did. Nothin' out there but a mean city."

Nick leaned down and slid his hands under Fargo's head and shoulders and lifted him up. The old man's body smelled of ripe mushrooms and autumn leaves.

"Take another look. Tell me what you see."

Fargo frowned. "You're playin' games with me, and I don't apprec —."

"Shut up and take a look."

Fargo turned his head toward the window and craned forward.

Nick lifted him higher. "Look down and tell me what you see."

"My eyesight ain't what it used to be. I can see some grass, a few trees." He stretched a bit more, the wizened skin on his neck pulling taut over tendons and muscle. "I see…oh my gosh…Rusty — RUSTY!" Just then the dog's head jerked around. "Look, he hears me — RUSTY!"

There was no way Rusty could hear Fargo's voice from down there, especially with the window closed. Perhaps a car honked or someone called out to a friend. In any case, it seemed to hearten the old man to think he still had a connection with his loyal companion, however tenuous.

The next morning Nick arrived at Pier 21, feeling refreshed after his day off. As he walked through the pier shed toward the dock, the clerk called out and beckoned to him to come into his office. During Nick's absence the previous day, the clerk explained, they filled his spot with another man, and because he was a casual hired at the shape-up, he would have to wait outside until another position opened up.

Is it that easy to lose my job? Nick thought. It seemed so abrupt, so heartless. He was about to ask the clerk to call Roger Farnsworth when it occurred to him the request would likely blow his cover. With no other recourse, he went out to the sidewalk and joined several other casuals gathered in front of the pier shed. He stuffed his fists into his pockets and watched as flatbed trucks and Belt Line trains rumbled by, pondering his separation from his job and his gang. Even in the few short weeks he'd worked there, he'd developed a close working relationship with Schmidt, Joad, and others. Now it felt as if he'd been exiled from his clan.

He waited by the shed for half an hour. When no one was hired from the sidewalk, he trotted across the Embarcadero to the Eagle Café and placed a call to Farnsworth, who seemed unconcerned and suggested Nick stay put while he made arrangements for another position. Thirty minutes later Nick called again and received instructions to report to the Matson docks at Pier 39. According to Farnsworth, the ILA was making inroads there and he wanted to keep tabs on it.

A group of casuals was waiting in front of Pier 39 when Nick arrived. He walked past them and knocked on the office door. A clerk opened it and frowned, apparently thinking Nick was looking for work. He began shooing him away until Nick gave his name. Then, as if Nick had uttered a magic password, the clerk dropped his frown and ushered him inside. He entered Nick's name in a logbook and sent him out with instructions to join the gang working opposite the number two hold of the *Malolo*, a Matson freighter.

Work gangs were discharging crates of pineapples off the *Malolo* and another Matson ship, the *Lurline*, docked in tandem behind the *Malolo*. Unlike Swayne & Hoyt's rusty freighters, the Matson ships were in pristine condition, every surface freshly painted glossy white and pastel blue. Opposite each ship, sling boards loaded with pineapples in wooden crates dropped down to stevedores who transferred the crates to hand-pulled jitneys and pushed the jitneys into the pier shed where the crates were loaded into boxcars.

Nick introduced himself to the gang foreman, a stout fellow of medium height who barely acknowledged his presence. Figuring he was expected to know what he was doing, Nick picked up a pineapple crate from the sling board and stacked it onto a jitney. The men in his gang worked with quiet efficiency, and it soon became obvious that he'd been inserted into an already full gang. With an extra hand they were able to transfer the crates from the sling boards to the shed long before the next load descended from the ship. During the wait, no one spoke to him, and it occurred to him that these seasoned stevedores knew an extra hand wasn't necessary and were distrustful of a stranger appearing suddenly in their midst.

Nick uttered a silent curse at Farnsworth who, it was apparent, had little understanding of how longshore gangs operated. This was the kind of careless move that could land him in the hospital or worse. If he was to be accepted his entry couldn't arouse suspicion, especially if his job was to gather information. Caught in an awkward situation, he did the only thing that made sense: he kept quiet and worked hard but made a point of not working harder than anyone else. He didn't want to appear desperate for approval and arouse even more suspicion.

Near the end of the day, two men wearing suits and fedoras walked onto the pier. Nick wouldn't have noticed them but for his close monitoring of the men in his gang who communicated with the subtlest of gestures. Just a slight nod and glimmer of acknowledgment between two of them directed his attention to the men in suits. They approached the gang opposite the *Malolo*'s number one hold. He couldn't hear what they were saying, but the number one gang stopped what they were doing and huddled around them. Minutes later he could hear voices arguing back and forth until the two suits emerged from the group, grim-faced and agitated, heading toward his gang.

"Looks like the Blue Book goons are paying us a call," said the gang foreman.

One of the Blue Book men had a slit mouth with no lips. The other was heavier and wore his fedora rakishly tilted to one side. When they reached Nick's gang, the slit-mouthed agent said, "Alright, boys, let's see your Blue Books."

One longshoreman pulled a Blue Book out of his back pocket and handed it to him. While the Blue Book agent checked the book, the winchdriver on the *Malolo* peered down from the railing to see what was holding things up.

The agent returned the book with an approving grunt, then looked around at the rest of the men. "You gotta be paid up to work these docks. You boys know that. Now why don't you play it smart?"

The gang foreman rested his fists on his hips. "We are paid up. We belong to the ILA."

The slit-mouthed agent frowned. "The ILA don't mean nothin' here. Our union has the contract for Matson. I know you boys all have Blue Books, so you'll have to pay up or get off the pier."

After a moment's hesitation, the gang foreman turned to his men. "You heard him. We knew it would come to this sooner or later. Do we pay tribute to these do-nothin' labor fakers or walk off the dock? Either way it's a risk. If we go, we may never work here again. If we don't, the ILA may never be worth a damn."

While the foreman talked to the men, Nick glanced at them and sensed in their posture and in their clenched jaws and in the way they hung together and folded their arms across their chests, a readiness to take a stand. For a moment he was tempted to say something to spur them on. It was an ideal opportunity to promote himself as a loyal ILA man while taking little personal risk. And it wouldn't take much to push them into action, a few catch-phrases about brotherhood and solidarity and such. He wavered back and forth, urging himself to act while the iron was hot, then pulling back appalled at such brazen manipulation. *And what's in it for me? I never promised Farnsworth anything other than to keep my eyes open and report the facts.* Something else, though, a feeling he couldn't define, tipped the balance and pushed him forward.

"I'm new on this crew," he heard himself say, "but I don't plan on giving a dime to any company union."

"Me neither," said another.

For the first time since Nick arrived, the foreman acknowledged his presence with a slender nod. "I happen to agree with this fella," he said. "There's over two-thousand of us signed up with the ILA now, and we won't be bullied any longer into staying with the Blue Book Union. I say we spread the word to the other gangs. It's the ILA or bust."

While the two agents looked on, the gang fanned out across the dock and up onto the ship, telling everyone that they either had to pay dues to the Blue Book Union or walk off the dock. Within minutes stevedores were streaming off the pier and gathering out front beside the Embarcadero. By someone's count over a hundred and twenty men had walked off, leaving enough for only two gangs to discharge both freighters. The men looked determined, but the act of insubordination had been so quick and spontaneous no one seemed to know what to do next. A look of uncertainty began to spread from man to man.

Someone finally said, "Let's make a bonfire outta these damn Blue Books!" He pointed toward an empty lot across the Embarcadero. "Come on."

The men swarmed across the boulevard and climbed over a wooden fence into the empty, rubble-strewn lot. A stevedore fashioned a small wooden cross and planted it in the ground. He then nailed a Blue Book to it and added a sprig of foliage. Meanwhile, another man collected several Blue Books and piled them in front of the cross and a third man used his cigarette lighter to set them ablaze.

One by one the longshoremen filed by the makeshift pyre, tossing their Blue Books onto the pile until the flames gathered strength and blackened the cross.

The diminutive bonfire engulfed the Blue Books and turned them to ash. When the flames died down, men sat down on the rubble and pensively wrapped their arms around their knees, their exuberant defiance disappearing with the bonfire, a look of uncertainty returning to the faces. Nick began to worry that he'd made a mistake, that he'd encouraged them to walk away from their livelihoods and into a rubble-strewn lot for his own selfish purpose. He was about to go off in search of a phone booth to call Harry Bridges for advice when the clerk from the Matson office climbed over the fence and walked up to the smoldering ashes and smoke darkened cross. He paused beside the makeshift pyre, considered it for a moment, then turned to the men.

"I need six crews to finish unloading the ships."

No one moved, their faces impassive.

"What about the Blue Books?" someone said.

"Never mind the books. We gotta finish the ships."

32

Word of the Matson walkout traveled swiftly along the waterfront. That evening Nick received a call from Harry Bridges who had heard of Nick's participation and wanted him to write an article about it for the *Waterfront Worker*. Nick was flattered and pleased to receive the invitation. His interest, however, was tempered by the worry that if Bridges had traced his presence to the Matson docks, he might be suspicious that Nick been able to find work so quickly after losing his job at Swayne & Hoyt. He tried to detect any inflection in Bridges' voice indicating suspicion, but the Aussie sounded matter-of-fact as he explained that the Albion Hall group had taken over the *Waterfront Worker* from the Marine Workers Industrial Union now that it had proven itself to be a credible force within Local 38-79.

Bridges' calm manner still wasn't enough to convince Nick to accept the assignment. It was one thing to keep his ears open and passively glean information, another thing to infiltrate a group like a secret agent. Grasping onto the first plausible excuse that came to mind, he declined, saying he was the primary breadwinner of his family and didn't want to risk being black-balled by the shipping companies if they discovered he was writing for a union paper. Bridges assured him that it was the strict policy of the *Waterfront Worker* to protect the anonymity of its writers. He also talked about the importance of exposing labor fakers, union officials who pretended to support the rank-and-file while taking orders from employers, and of presenting the men with a vision of an aggressive union dedicated to their welfare. The *Waterfront Worker* would be their most valuable tool to organize dockworkers and counter lies in the daily newspapers.

"If things blow up," said Bridges, "you'll see a big difference between what the daily newspapers print and what you see with your own eyes."

Nick was aware that newspapers ran sensationalized stories, but out and out misrepresentation? It violated everything he'd been taught about journalistic ethics. "I doubt newspapers would make up fairy tales and report it as news."

"There's more than one way to tell a lie, Nick. They don't have to make stuff up. They just report the facts they like and interview folks who think like them. If they quote someone who presents opinion as fact or even lies outright, that's not their fault. It's easy to slant a story one way or another while pretendin' to be objective."

"Why wouldn't they tell the truth?"

"Just look at who controls the dailies. Take Herbie Fleishhacker. He's part owner of the *Chronicle* and an investor in the Dollar Line. And shipping companies pay significant advertising revenues to the newspapers, so the dailies are not about to bite the hand that feeds them. Why do you think they're full of scandals and crime stories?"

Nick knew the answer but didn't see the connection. "Because that's what sells."

"Sure, but that's not the only reason. If the bosses keep our minds occupied with fear and suspicion, they divert our attention from the things they don't want us to think about—decent wages, safe workin' conditions, medical care, jobs for everyone."

Bridges' words had a reassuring effect and not just because of his guarantee of anonymity. Nick was also drawn to the Aussie's clarity of vision. More succinctly and convincingly than any professor Nick had studied under, Bridges delineated the facts, sorted them out, and drew insightful and seemingly incontrovertible conclusions.

Under Bridges' persuasive spell, Nick began a transformation that allowed him to continue his duplicitous role while placating his conscience — namely, to trick himself into thinking he could serve two masters. Logically, he knew it didn't make sense, but emotionally it was the only way he could take the next step. By the time he agreed to write the article, he'd already begun construction on a mental partition to divide his dual and conflicting roles into separate compartments as though they were wholly unrelated.

After the phone call, he sat down at his desk in his bedroom and typed up a two-hundred and fifty word account of the walkout. When it was done, he read through it and immediately saw that it was a passable but uninspired example of stale journalism, devoid of feeling or insight as if the writer were detached and indifferent to the outcome. Crumpling it up, he tossed it into the wastebasket and inserted another sheet of paper in the typewriter. Before starting, he tried to envision a different approach, and it was then that he recalled the words of Rufus Steele, the editor at the *Chronicle*: *"We're not just about information. We gotta reach people here"* — he'd pointed to his heart — *"and here"* — he'd pointed to his head — *"and here"* — he'd opened his coat and pointed to his wallet.

Two previous editions of the *Waterfront Worker* lay on Nick's desk. He read several articles to absorb the writing style, and found them to be homespun, vernacular, and amateurish, yet bound together with a thread of urgency and energy. He put them aside and rewrote the piece, and this time it was better, although it was still too dry and detached. He set the second draft down and closed his eyes, reimagining the scene moment-by-moment, detail-by-detail. *What's the essence of the story?* he asked himself. *And what will it mean to longshoremen toiling on the waterfront?*

He drew in a breath and began again.

"The Blue Book is on the way out. On Thursday, Sept. 14ᵗʰ, stevedores working on the Matson Dock, decided amongst themselves that the Blue Book had ruled them long enough..."

₤

"Please come in here," Roger Farnsworth said over the intercom.

Clarisa gathered her pen and notebook and headed for his office, wondering if her boss had summoned her for work-related reasons or something more personal. They'd been having trouble lately separating their work and social relationship, and on occasion, when alone in his office, they fell into a familiar, even intimate, exchange like that of a close couple. As she entered his office, she hoped that he wanted her for personal reasons but quickly surmised from his sober expression that he was in no mood to socialize.

"The executive board is holding an emergency meeting," he said, standing up. "I'll need you to take minutes."

"What's happened?"

On the way to the conference room, he explained, "Blue Book agents expelled workers off the Matson pier and ignited a walkout. Without advance notice the company had no choice but to take the men back. It made Matson appear desperate and the Blue Book Union look like a toothless tiger. Plant has been busy managing the Hawaiian-American Steamship Line, so he asked me to develop a strategy to deal with the situation. Today I'll present it to the executive board."

As they reached the conference room, Clarisa could see that Roger was pleased to have been given this responsibility and confident in his ability to handle it. And it made him even more appealing.

As usual Stanley Dollar sat at the head of the table. "If we don't nip this thing in the bud, all of us will have the ILA at our throats."

Silas Grant, president of the McCormick Steamship Company, sat to the right of Dollar, William Roth of Matson Navigation to his left. Thomas Plant was seated at the opposite end of the table.

"It's the goddamned communists," Grant blurted out. "They're taking over the whole country."

"Let's not over react," said Roth. "The Blue Book Union has been around for fourteen years, and we have a good relationship with them. The ILA won't get far if we don't recognize them as representing the men. What do you think, Tom? What do your sources say?"

"I'm afraid I agree with Stanley," said Plant. "We have a cancer in our midst. We've got to take action or else the disease will spread to every limb and fiber of the waterfront. The ILA has already gained a significant foothold at the Matson, Dollar, and Luckenbach piers. It's unfortunate the Blue Book Union acted so hastily, but I can assure you that *that* won't happen again. I've discussed it with their president Emile Stone. They'll be in complete cooperation with us in the future."

Grant wrung his hands. "That's all well and good, but what can we do to prevent this from growing into a full-blown catastrophe?" Grant was always the first to squawk like Chicken Little, but this time the others nodded in agreement.

"I share your concern," said Plant. "So we've developed a comprehensive plan. Would you describe it for us, Roger?"

Farnsworth cleared his throat. "To prevent future walk-outs, we recommend a three-pronged strategy. First, we need to shore up the Blue Book Union. To that end, a wage increase of ten cents an hour effective January 1st should be sufficient. It's a small price to pay to make the Blue Book look good and, at the same time, take the wind out of the ILA's sails. Second, we'll identify ILA leaders and eliminate them from the waterfront. And lastly, we'll send a representative to Washington D.C. to convince the President to approve our shipping code proposal that prohibits strikes and requires the men to submit to mediation and arbitration if there's a labor dispute."

There was no reaction from the executives, and in their silence Clarisa sensed a reluctance to take advice from anyone so young. It was just for this reason, however, that she hoped they would adopt his strategy. They needed someone like Roger, someone with fresh ideas and a fresh perspective to dislodge them from old ways of thinking.

Stanley Dollar was the first to respond. "I'm not sure a pay raise is in order at this time, but I support your other proposals. The ILA must be stopped, the men put in their place. I for one pledge to purge the leaders from the ranks of my stevedores as soon as possible."

34

Nick entered Albion Hall wondering why Harry Bridges had summoned him there. It wasn't a Thursday evening when the Albion Hall group held their weekly meetings, so if he had to guess a reason, it would be the firing of three dozen ILA men during the last two weeks. *Does Harry want to confront me about it?* he wondered, hoping that it wasn't the case. The truth was, under pressure from Farnsworth he'd given him the names of four active ILA men. He didn't think they'd lose their jobs, and later, when he discovered they had, he felt awful about it.

He took a seat beside Henry Schmidt and listened as Bridges and Schmidt discussed the recent firings. Pirate Larsen and Dutch Dietrich were there, too. Were they the enforcers who would mete out his punishment once Bridges was through with him?

Normally calm and measured, Bridges spoke with a bitter edge in his voice as he recounted his efforts to persuade Lee Holman, president of Local 38-79, to do something about the firings. Bridges had gone to the ILA office on Steuart Street and warned Holman that if Local 38-79 didn't protect its members, no ILA man was safe and even the existence of Local 38-79 would be in jeopardy.

Holman didn't agree. Until they had a contract with the shipowners, he said, it was too soon to rock the boat. Bridges didn't see it that way, of course, and pointed out that hundreds of men had joined Local 38-79 after the Matson walkout, a clear sign they were hungry for change.

"The real reason for Holman's foot-dragging," said Bridges, "is that two-thousand men are now paying dues to Local 38-79, and Holman doesn't want to spend it on anything so frivolous as defending their jobs. To get me out of his hair, he sent me to George Creel to see what he could do. It was a fool's errand, but I didn't see another option."

As Nick listened, he was relieved that Harry's anger was directed at Lee Holman and not himself, at least so far.

Taking three of the fired men with him, Bridges had gone to see Creel, regional administrator of the National Recovery Administration, and described the recent rash of firings for no apparent reason. Creel was sympathetic but explained that the waterfront industry wasn't yet covered by NRA codes of fair competition, and until that happened his hands were tied.

"Two days later," said Bridges, "the stakes grew a notch higher. The Matson Navigation Company fired four longshoremen for wearing ILA buttons on their lapels. Again I took a group of longshoremen into Creel's office, and told him that the firings violated, if not the letter, at least the spirit of the NRA. This time he agreed to appoint a special board to hear the complaint and said he knew just the right candidates — a rabbi, a business attorney, and a labor official." Bridges glanced at Nick. "It sounded like the setup of an old joke."

Nick smiled, hoping his nervousness didn't show.

The subsequent hearing lasted an hour. Afterwards the board deliberated for a brief period, then ruled that the NRA had no jurisdiction in the matter. "No surprise there," Bridges remarked. It also ruled that the Blue Book Union's contract with the employers was valid and enforceable by law; to obtain its benefits and protections, longshoremen would have to become members. To show their sympathy to the fired men, the board urged all waterfront employers to hire members of the Blue Book Union and the ILA without discrimination. The advisory ruling, however, failed to convince Matson to rehire the four men.

Bridges turned to Nick. "So what do you think?"

Nick hesitated. Was this a straightforward question or a subtle probe designed to make him nervous and reveal his role in all this? An awkward silence followed while Bridges and the other men observed him, waiting for an answer. Bridges in particular seemed to be studying him with disarming intensity.

"Well, a—" Nick stammered, grasping for something to say. *Should I admit what I've done and throw myself at their mercy?" They wouldn't dare kill me, would —*

"What I mean is," said Bridges, "can you write an article about it?"

Nick glanced back and forth between Schmidt and Bridges, searching for any indication that they knew he was an informant. He found none and it was such a relief all he could do was let out a deep breath.

"Harry," said Schmidt, " you should have told him when he got here you wanted him to write an article. He would've taken notes. Now look at him. He's probably wondering if he remembers everything."

"No," said Nick, feeling lucky to have dodged a bullet and grateful to be given another writing assignment, "I remember. I'll get started on it right away."

Bridges gave him a nod. "I knew I could count on you."

Nick suspected that Bridges wasn't going to let the firings pass without taking further action. And he was right. A few mornings later when he arrived for work at Pier 39, Bridges and several other men were distributing flyers to stevedores waiting for the gate to open. Bridges wore a flat-cap, old work clothes, and a cargo hook dangling from his belt loop as if he'd just gotten off work, an outfit worn more for theatrical effect, Nick guessed, than any practical reason.

A few minutes before the shift began, Bridges positioned himself in front of the gate and called the men together. "Look, fellas, four of our guys have been fired for wearing ILA buttons. I know most of you belong to the ILA, so let's have a program where they hire these four men back or none of us goes to work. Otherwise, we'll never buck the Blue Book Union off our backs. Whattaya say?"

A stevedore carrying a metal lunch pail said, "I gotta wife and two little ones at home. If I don't go to work I can't support 'em. And besides, if we walk out the company'll just replace us with bums from skid row."

"I understand your worries, brother. I gotta wife and kids too. But, look, until we have a decent union we'll never have job security, so it's for our families that I'm askin' you to walk off the job next Wednesday." He held a flyer above his head. "We've already anticipated the boss's tactics and printed up three-thousand leaflets askin' everyone to support us and stay off the Matson docks. We're gonna distribute 'em at relief centers and unemployment halls. If the bosses can't replace us, they'll have to meet our demands. Three weeks ago you took a courageous stand when you walked off the job. Now it's time to take the next step."

"Yeah," a stevedore called out, "but that was to protect our jobs, not the union. My family comes before any union."

There was a murmur of agreement among the men.

"Tell me this," Bridges shot back, "when was the last time you had a raise?" No answer. "When was the last time you worked steady for a month straight?" No answer. "When was the last time the boss enforced safety rules?"

Posing each question with a liturgical cadence, he poked his finger in the air for emphasis. "When was the last time they slowed the work down to a reasonable pace?"

"Never!" replied a stevedore.

"When was the last time they guaranteed you a job beyond the day you were workin'?"

"*Never!*" repeated the stevedore, joined by others.

"When was the last time they paid you sick or injury leave?"

"*Never!*" responded more voices.

"When was the last time they paid your doctor bills?

"*Never!*" the entire group replied.

"When was the last time they improved safety regulations?"

"*Never!*"

He thrust his fist into the air. "And when did the bosses ever give us anything we didn't have to fight for?"

"*NEVER!*" the men cried with one gusting breath, their voices echoing off the pier shed and sailing across the Embarcadero to pedestrians on the opposite side who looked over at the longshoreman, their fists raised in the air like a field of sunflower stalks reaching for the sky.

"It's an amazing gift you have," Nick said to Bridges afterwards. "If you went into politics you could run for mayor or even governor."

Harry looked over Nick's shoulder at knots of stevedores deep in discussion. "It ain't hocus-pocus. All I do is express the anger that's already in 'em and show 'em how to harness it in a way that'll benefit 'em in the long run."

Three days later Nick received a call from Roger Farnsworth, asking for a full report. This presented him with a dilemma. Despite his mental partition, he was beginning to have qualms about informing on men who only wanted to improve their lives. This motivated him more than ever to search for the *Diana Dollar*. Toward that goal, he'd gone to the Merchants Exchange Building on California Street where records were kept of all ships home-ported in San Francisco. He found the *Diana Dollar*'s records, but it ended after her last voyage. A clerk confirmed that once a ship was taken out of service no further records were kept of its whereabouts. "A retired ship can be stored anywhere," he said, "as long as it's kept out of shipping channels. The best way to find its present location is to ask the shipowner directly."

The one thing Nick couldn't do.

In his report to Farnsworth, Nick described the plan to walk off the Matson docks, but only in general terms, figuring it was already common knowledge among the rank-and-file. Roger then pressed him to divulge the names of stevedores working for the *Waterfront Worker*. On this point Nick was thankful that Bridges kept the names of the other writers confidential, allowing Nick to claim ignorance, as he'd only been asked to write articles and send them to an address on 19th Street. He did mention the name of the editor, Harry Bridges, and felt justified in doing so because Bridges seemed to spend his time working on union-related business and not as a stevedore. How he made ends meet, Nick had no idea; maybe his wife worked. Anyway, it wasn't his concern, although he hoped that revealing Bridges' identity wouldn't harm his ability to pay rent.

Forewarned of the walkout, Farnsworth called Emile Stone at the Blue Book Union and instructed him to send extra stevedores to the Matson dock. Stone promised to scour the entire city if necessary to come up with enough men, but the words rang hollow. The Blue Book Union had been losing members to the ILA and was having trouble supplying enough trained men on normal workdays. Finding additional ones wasn't going to be easy.

It was time, Farnsworth decided, to tap into another source of labor.

He called Fats Jackson, leader of the Negro Stevedore Association, and asked him to assemble every able-bodied man he could find at The Jupiter, a nightclub on Columbus Avenue. Fats' reputation for gambling and whoring was well-known, but he'd always been friendly with the shipping companies and supplied men whenever needed.

The next day Farnsworth descended a staircase into The Jupiter, a subterranean dive with red brick walls, a jet black ceiling, and the lingering odor of sweat and liquor. It had been a popular nightspot ever since Jelly Roll Morton opened it in 1916. When Roger found it, Morton was long gone, replaced by Red Cayou and his Louisiana Stompers who played a saucy, upbeat style of Dixieland jazz. Roger took an immediate liking to the place, as it was one of the few clubs in Frisco where whites and Negroes danced together, a cavernous netherworld of syncopated music, sensual gyrations, and easy laughter.

It took a moment for his eyes to adjust to the dimly lit room, and when the dark shapes sharpened into focus he was pleased to see about eighty Negroes seated around cocktail tables facing a bandstand.

Fats Jackson wore patent leather shoes, a double-breasted suit, and a Stetson fedora with a one-carat diamond pinned to the hatband. He lifted his sizable bulk onto the bandstand. "Ah called you here," he said, "b'cause we gotta great opportunity you won't wanna miss. Mr. Farnsworth here" — he gestured toward Roger with a cigar-sized finger — "is a man of integrity and a friend of the Negro dockworker, so ah'm sho you'll be interested in what he's got to say."

Roger climbed onto the stage and thanked Fat's for his help. Then turning to the men, he explained that a walkout was likely at the Matson docks and that if it happened he would need experienced stevedores. He described the risks of crossing a picket line, the threats of physical violence and angry name calling, but if they were willing to take the risk, there was the possibility of a long term contract when the labor dispute ended. He admitted that Negro longshoremen had been given short shrift in the past (only five of the one-hundred fifty gangs on the Frisco waterfront were black) but allowed that this had been the Blue Book Union's policy, not the policy of the shippers. "If you stand by us now," he concluded, "we'll stand by you later, and I'll personally make sure your piece of the pie is expanded."

"You'd better take this opportunity," advised Fats, "and work as hard as you can, build up a reputation, and maybe we can get a five-year contract when the strike is over. It's possible."

The room fell silent. The men traded glances.

A large, imposing fellow stood up, his hair flecked with gray.

"What you want, Tanglefoot?" Fats asked suspiciously.

Tanglefoot Fleming glanced around the room, nodding at acquaintances. "Ah know most of you don't have work most times," he began, his deep voice expanding to fill the cavernous room. "What's been bad for the whahte man has been ten times worse for the colored. Half our men are outta jobs and the other half hardly make enough scratch to pay bills. So I'm sure many of you are mightily tempted by Mr. Farnsworth's offer, just as Jesus was tempted by Satan during his fo'ty days and nights in the desert. But as Jesus said, man does not live by bread—"

"Tanglefoot," Fats broke in, pointing a finger at him, "this ain't no church and you ain't no preacher. So siddown and shut yo' mouth."

"Wait a minute," said Roger, who never before had been compared to Satan but took no offense. After years of rubbing elbows with Negroes, he had a deep respect, even affection for the black race and had no intention of leading anyone into temptation — as Fleming put it — without full disclosure and consideration. "Let him speak."

"Thank you, sah." Fleming turned to the others. "If you men cross that picket lahne, you'll be scabbing against yo' brotha workers, and they won't forgit that."

"Why should we give a *damn* about them?" said another man. "They won't 'llow us in their lily whahte union, and they don't let us work but fo' docks."

"You gotta point there, for sure, but ah believe a new day is dawnin'. And when it comes we'll be workin' side b' side, whahtes and coloreds, together. If we betray 'em now, they may never trus' us again. And when this walkout is over, with all due respec' to Mr. Farnsworth, things'll prob'ly go back to bidness as usual. But if we support our whahte brothas, ah have faith we'll all be stronger in the by and by."

He took one last look around and sat down.

The men huddled in groups, talking amongst themselves in low tones while Roger and Fats looked on. Presently one group stood up, nodded respectfully toward the bandstand, turned, and climbed the stairs out of the club. Another group rose soon after, then another and another, all climbing out of the club until only Roger and Fats remained.

Talk among the Matson stevedores had been optimistic, even enthusiastic. Talk and action, however, were two different things, and it remained to be seen whether the men would put their jobs on the line again. When Nick arrived at Pier 39 on the morning of the planned walkout, a dozen Albion Hall men were there, led by Harry Bridges who pulled Nick aside and asked him to write a report on the day's events for the *Waterfront Worker*. Nick was grateful for the invitation, as it meant Harry valued his previous articles. He was also pleased that he'd gained Harry's trust, and not just because he'd be privy to inside information. Bridges fascinated him, his strength of conviction, his ability to unite the men, his dedication to their welfare, and his flair for the theatrical. He'd never known anyone like him.

Stevedores began arriving and were greeted by Albion Hall men who urged them to stay off the docks. As it turned out, they needed little urging. Four-hundred stevedores joined the walkout, and by eight o'clock they were marching back and forth in front of the Matson gate, waving picket signs and chanting slogans, preventing Matson from unloading its ships.

Lee Holman drove by the walkout and denounced it as a wildcat strike. "If you men stay off the job," he declared from his car, "you do so without ILA sanction." His warning, however, was too little too late.

35

In the months since Clarisa began working at the Waterfront Employers Association, her shorthand skills had improved, her confidence in her abilities grown. Seated at the conference table, she easily jotted down the statements of George Creel, the local NRA administrator, who was saying to a group of shipping executives that the Matson strike wasn't an NRA issue and wouldn't be until government codes were established for the maritime industry. Thomas Plant had invited Creel to the meeting to see if he might intervene, perhaps even order the men back to work.

Now that seemed unlikely.

Edward Marsh, a Federal conciliator, was there as well. "Technically, you're correct, George" said Marsh, pushing his black-framed glasses up against the bridge of his nose. "However, the Federal government is concerned that this strike could escalate. The President believes trade is crucial to our economic recovery. The country's already mired in waterfront strikes in Baltimore, Philadelphia, and New Orleans, as well as steel, auto, and coal strikes in the Northeast and Midwest. So the last thing we need is another strike tying up our ports. The President wants the wheels of commerce running smoothly, but he also wants them on the right track." He looked around the table. "You fellows don't want to throw a monkey wrench into the works, do you?"

"Hold on," said William Roth. "We didn't start this strike. The men walked out on us. They don't even have approval from their own union. I've still got fifty men on my docks. With another two-hundred I can move all the goods I need to."

"It's doubtful you'll find additional experienced men," said Roger Farnsworth. "We've been trying to recruit them but without much success."

"Then I'll bring them up from San Pedro if I have to. I won't let a bunch of radicals dictate whom I can and can't hire."

Herbert Fleishhacker clasped his fingers together. "Under normal circumstances, Bill, I'd agree with you, but this problem isn't going to disappear if you manage to recruit additional stevedores. And it could easily spread to other docks if the men become riled enough. We've enjoyed labor peace for fourteen years. I don't know, maybe we've been lucky, but things are changing. If we want to maintain peace we're going to have to be even-handed. What do you suggest, Marsh?"

Marsh pushed his glasses up again. "We've had success with arbitration in West Virginia, Ohio, Michigan, and Tennessee. To make it work, we appointed respected citizens to arbitration boards and asked both sides to agree in advance to abide by the board's ruling. Usually neither side gets exactly what they want, but if they perceive the process as fair, they'll accept the outcome."

"We tried that two weeks ago," Roth exclaimed, "and look where it got us."

"That's because you fired four men for wearing ILA buttons," countered Creel. "What did you expect?"

Roth glared at the bureaucrat.

"Look," said Marsh, "before we dig in our heels, let's think this through rationally . . ."

While the Federal conciliator rehashed the situation, Clarisa glanced at Roger, wondering what on earth had come over him. Up until a couple of weeks ago, he'd taken her out every weekend and introduced her to his friends, whose affected mannerisms and upper class accents he mimicked behind their backs, much to her amusement. After dinner they usually went to the Curran Theater to see a play or to the Balconades Ballroom to twirl on the wood sprung dance floor. At the end of the evening, he drove her home in the Stutz and planted a long good night kiss on her lips, sorely testing her vow to remain chaste.

Then suddenly things changed. The dates ended and he hardly spoke a word to her that he didn't have to. She certainly had no right to complain, especially after she let him know that she wasn't committed to him or to anyone else for that matter. Still, she wondered if he was merely preoccupied with some problem or if his affection for her had faded.

As for Nick, she hadn't seen him since his surprise visit, and no wonder. He tried to apologize, and she hadn't accepted it graciously, a mistake she now regretted. His visit also raised another issue. She suspected that he was working for her boss in some sort of undercover capacity, and this added a whole new level of complication, bringing back all her confusion as to how she felt about both of them.

At the moment neither one seemed eager to see her, and perhaps that was for the best. Now that her two suitors had backed off, the three of them could take a break and let things develop naturally.

In the meantime she was busier than usual at St. Patrick's Mission. The lines were growing longer every week and included families now, with hungry infants and bawling babies. While the diners ate, Father Shannon circulated around the room, administering encouragement and comfort, his kind eyes and warm smile a ray of hope in a sea of dispirited faces. After dinner, she often walked to St. Patrick's church with him, as it was on her way home, and it was during one of these walks that he agreed it was an excellent time for her to let things take a natural course.

Looking at Roger now, though, she couldn't help but wonder what had prompted his change.

"The maritime code hearings," Marsh concluded, "will commence next week in Washington, and with any luck we'll have a set of guidelines in place by the end of the year. Meanwhile, let's take steps to prevent this situation from spiraling out of control. Is that agreeable?"

All eyes turned to Roth whose disgruntled expression revealed his inner turmoil. "I don't like it. A company ought to have the right to hire or fire whomever it sees fit — for whatever reason. After all, if it wasn't for us they wouldn't have jobs. So why should we give in, even an inch?"

"Try not to think of it in terms of right or wrong, Bill," said Thomas Plant. "At this point it's a tactical business decision. Do you want to risk a widespread waterfront strike? Keep in mind, the special board sided with us last time. If they do so again, the men will have to quit the ILA and come back to work on our terms, as members of the Blue Book Union."

The arbitration hearing took place three days later. Clarisa was in Roger's office when Plant called with news of the decision.

Roger put down the phone and shook his head. "I didn't want to say anything at the meeting, but I had a feeling this might happen. The arbitration board ruled that Matson violated Section 7(a) of the National Industrial Recovery Act and ordered the company to reinstate the four fired longshoremen. In addition, they said it could no longer discriminate against members of the International Longshoremen's Association."

"What does that mean," asked Clarisa, "as a practical matter?"

"It means the ILA is now in business."

When news of the decision reached the waterfront, Nick congratulated Harry Bridges, who, in keeping with his cautious nature, shrugged and said, "This doesn't mean the war is over. In fact it's just begun."

In that regard, representatives of the waterfront unions and shipping companies were in Washington D.C. testifying at the maritime code hearings. Bridges asked Nick to write an article on the D.C. proceedings for the November issue of the *Waterfront Worker*. Nick's primary source of information was Henry Melnikow, an official with the San Francisco Labor Council, who was acting as the representative of the ILA Pacific Coast District at the hearings. In this capacity he submitted the Pacific Coast District's three point proposal to: 1) establish union-run hiring halls in order to eliminate the notorious shape-up and provide a fair, rotational hiring system; 2) form joint union-employer grievance boards, and; 3) adopt a uniform safety code.

Over the phone from Washington D.C., Melnikow described a competing proposal offered by Joe Ryan, national president of the International Longshoremen's Association. Similar to the Pacific Coast District proposal, it envisioned a system of local arbitration boards, subject to the review of a national board. However, there was one notable exception.

Under Ryan's proposal, the national board's decisions were final and prohibited all strikes.

This seemed illogical to Nick. Why would the ILA president give up the right to strike? In his talks with Bridges he'd learned that a strike, even the threat of a strike, was labor's best weapon when negotiating with management. What made Ryan's proposal even more puzzling was that it was nearly identical to the proposal put forth by the American Steamship Operators Association and ignored the hiring hall issue altogether.

Nick began his article with a comparison of Ryan's proposal and the one by the Pacific Coast District. He also reported rumors that Ryan had secretly met with representatives of the Steamship Operator's Association and quoted Ryan as saying to the longshoremen: "Give the shipowners a break. They aren't making any money." Then he listed Herbert Fleishhacker's annual income of three and half million dollars and the Dollar Line's twenty-two million dollar profit from purchasing government ships at a deep discount.

The process of gathering information and writing the article was immensely satisfying. When Nick finished it, he submitted it to Bridges, who praised its thoroughness, then in the next breath said it lacked heart.

"These are tough times. The men have a right to be angry. You're not only speaking to them, you're speaking *for* them. So don't hold back."

Nick figured the facts spoke for themselves, and it wasn't in his nature or training to put his personal feelings into his copy, so it took several more attempts before he was able to arouse sufficient indignation.

He showed Bridges a newly written final paragraph:

"We are getting sick and tired of guys like Ryan and Herbie hogging the turkey while we and our families don't even get gravy. Every morning we have to shape-up and then plug the docks looking for work, while do-nothing union officials and shipowners rake in the dough. And the miserable pay checks we get are so small it makes a man mad enough to spit in the face of Max Baer!"

Bridges cracked a smile. "Now that's more like it."

36

The day after the *Waterfront Worker* hit the streets, Roger Farnsworth slammed a copy down on his desk so ferociously it shook the door between his and Clarisa's office. Curious as to why her boss was so upset, Clarisa rose from her chair, went to the door, and opened it a crack. Unsure if she should intrude, she paused and listened as Roger muttered, "Lies, lies, goddamned lies." Then she heard the ratcheting click of a telephone dial and his voice asking the operator for "Sutter five, five, three, zero."

In the silence that followed, she had to stifle an audible gasp. The phone number was as familiar to her as her own.

"Hello," he said, "this is Mr. Smith. I'd like to leave a message for Nick . . . I want him to meet me at the usual place tonight at six-thirty . . . Right, he'll know . . . Thanks. Goodbye."

Clarisa tip-toed back to her desk with a child-like guilt for having eavesdropped, as well as an intense curiosity to learn more. At the end of the day she bid Roger goodbye, left the office, and crossed Market Street to a delicatessen opposite the Matson Building. Pretending to read a newspaper, she stood by the window and alternately scanned the newsprint and the Matson Building across the street. When Roger emerged, she monitored his movements from behind the newspaper as he crossed Market Street in a crowd of pedestrians and disappeared onto Front Street. Feeling a bit like Sam Spade, she rushed out of the deli, caught up to within twenty yards of him, and followed him as he turned left onto Pine Street and then right onto Montgomery.

Seven blocks later the street rose sharply up Telegraph Hill into a residential neighborhood. Her crowd cover now gone, Clarisa dropped back to a discreet distance and watched as he reached a set of stairs at the end of the block where the hill rose too steeply for cars. He climbed the stairs and disappeared at the top. Afraid she might lose him, she hurried up the incline in her pumps, wishing she had more sensible shoes. At the top of the stairs she peered over a concrete balustrade and spotted him a block ahead, still walking north on Montgomery.

She cautiously followed him another three blocks to the end of the street and watched as he disappeared into Julius' Castle. Rushing forward, she drew to within twenty feet of the restaurant, slowed, and came to a stop. *Should I go inside or wait or just leave?* The phone call had confirmed her suspicions, so she wasn't sure why she followed him except that, aside from her father, the two men she cared about most, who never would have met if it hadn't been for her, were meeting inside. Perhaps that was what bothered her. Nick and Roger were mixed up in something that had little to do with her, something she had no control over and to which she now felt a rising resentment. It had been much easier when they were unconnected, like two incompatible friends one sees separately but never together. By keeping them separate she could control when, where, and how much they were part of her life. Being an only child, she had always been able to command as much or as little attention from her parents as she liked, and when her mother died her father devoted himself to her as if she were Michael Collins, hero of the Irish independence movement. Having so little control over the current situation stirred up feelings of insecurity, feelings she knew all too well.

She wandered over to a low stone wall overlooking the bay. The view extended out across the water several miles to Oakland and Berkeley, but she hardly noticed. Her thoughts drifted back to the night Nick announced he was leaving and how enraged it made her feel. It had taken weeks to get over it, and like a continuing echo the anger welled within her again. This time, though, it pulled her down into a dark, scary place, a place she rarely went, a place where she was terribly afraid of losing something precious. She was eight years-old again, sitting beside her mother laying comatose on a bed of sweat-soaked sheets, wheezing, her mucus-filled lungs struggling for breath. It was terribly painful to watch, but she couldn't look away until her mother exhaled a final breath, leaving her with the terrifying feeling that she'd been abandoned to a world of overwhelming grief.

A wave of sorrow swept over her, drowning her in emotion. She covered her face and slumped against the stone wall, tears rolling down her cheeks. At the same time another part of her observed herself from above like a detached witness, as if the pain was so deep, so strong, her psyche dared not surrender completely lest she fall permanently into an abyss of hopelessness.

The tears eventually subsided, her emotions settled, the present moment came back into focus. She reached into her purse and removed a handkerchief, dabbed her cheeks and blew her nose. Taking a deep breath, she looked out beyond the wall and for the first time noticed the expansive view. Twilight had descended on the bay, now flat and placid, rippled only by a paddle-wheel ferry gliding serenely across the harbor, its brightly lit windows reflecting on the water. The ferry sailed between two concrete islands, two of four such islands between Rincon Point and Yerba Buena Island that would become the foundations on which the Bay Bridge would someday rise.

She took several more breaths and felt her inner strength return, this time stronger than before, as if the tears had released a frightened child, allowing her to leave that dark, scary world and merge with her adult self. She turned toward the restaurant and looked up at its windows, each one framing a pair of diners whose faces glowed in candlelight.

It's time to go, she thought, *and time to let go.*

37

Roger swallowed the last of his martini and motioned to a passing waiter to bring another round for Nick and himself. A copy of the *Waterfront Worker* lay on the table. He frowned and pounded his fist on it, causing water in the glasses to ripple in concentric circles.

"It's a bold-faced lie to say that Dollar made twenty-two million dollars on the purchase of his steamships. He bought them from the government because the Shipping Board was losing money hand over fist and was desperate to unload them. It's not Dollar's fault the Shipping Board over-built its fleet and sold them at rock-bottom prices. Besides, those ships are only worth as much as the revenues they generate. Without Dollar and the other shipowners, they'd be little more than scrap metal, and thousands of men wouldn't have jobs. It's just this kind of fact-twisting that inflames longshoremen against the shipowners for no good reason."

Roger was referring to Nick's article, although he didn't know that Nick had written it, and it gave Nick a secret sense of satisfaction that his words were causing so much frustration in his undercover boss.

Nick finished his martini and gazed out the picture window. A dozen freighters lay anchored in the bay, all pointing south like migrating geese, pulled into that position by an ebb tide. He saw no reason to argue the point but a notion occurred to him.

"What about the mail subsidies? Weren't they justified in part to help shippers pay decent wages? Well-paid workers don't usually cause problems."

The waiter picked up their empty martini glasses and replaced them with fresh ones.

Roger took a sip and sighed plaintively. "I tried to talk our members into giving the men a raise, but they won't hear of it. The old coots are too damn stingy for their own good."

They both chuckled and exchanged a knowing glance, indicating a mutual understanding that men above a certain age were self-centered nincompoops, a condition to which they themselves, by virtue of their youth, were immune.

The newspaper caught Roger's eye again. He poked his finger at the headline. "There's a new defiance at the waterfront we haven't seen before, and this rag is inciting it. Every issue is filled with radical garbage that indoctrinates the men with crazy ideas." He gave Nick a challenging look. "I want names and I want them soon."

Nick averted his eyes. He didn't mind reporting general incidents or planned activities, but informing on individuals who could lose their jobs troubled him deeply, and he was beginning to wonder if he had the stomach for it. His best option was to remove himself from the situation, but that required finding the *Diana Dollar* and the opium somewhere onboard.

In that effort he'd met with Jack Blum, the police detective and family friend who'd delivered the news of his father's suicide. Blum worked the Chinatown beat and knew the narcotics trade as well as anyone. Over a meal at the Jade Palace on Jackson Street, Nick recounted the story of how Slag and Primm framed him and his efforts to locate the freighter. Blum agreed that Nick's best hope was to find the remaining cache of narcotics and turn it over to the police, who would examine it for finger-prints. If the prints matched Primm's or the bosun's, he was home free.

But how can I find the opium if I can't find the ship? He pushed the thought aside and glanced at Roger. "What about the maritime codes? Any chance they'll be approved by the end of the year?" If they were approved his spying services might not be needed.

"God, I hope so. When the congressional hearings are over they'll send a set of codes to the White House for Roosevelt to sign. As soon as the President approves them, we'll be able to settle disputes without disruptions, and this damn thing"—he jabbed a finger at the *Waterfront Worker*—"will be irrelevant."

Nick sipped his martini. As it went down, a warm, delicious tingle settled at the base of his skull. The food hadn't arrived but it didn't matter. The alcohol seemed to have dulled his appetite. Roger was sucking on a cigarette, elbow planted on the table, chin dejectedly resting in the hand holding the cigarette. Nick looked out the window and tried to think of another subject to fill the void. On the opposite side of the bay at the base of the East Bay hills, the Claremont Hotel, brightly illuminated, stood out against a stand of dark trees.

"One New Year's Eve," he said, shifting his gaze to Roger, "when I was a senior at Berkeley, a group of us went to the lounge at the Claremont Hotel. They didn't serve booze in those days, so we taped flasks to our legs. One guy even wore bandoleers under his coat" — he made a criss-cross gesture on his chest — "rigged with bottles of gin. We ordered tonics, and as we drank them we refilled our glasses with hooch. A few cute girls from Mills College sat down near us. We started flirting with them, got them laughing, then took them out onto the dance floor. Just before midnight we all formed a rumba line and snaked around the lounge, singing 'bamp-bamp, bamp-bamp, baaa, bamp!' It was great fun except for one thing: the band was playing a foxtrot." Roger listened with an amused grin. "Pretty soon some old fart in a tuxedo complained to the manager, and they came out on the dance floor to stop us." Nick finished his martini. "You know what we did?"

Roger shook his head.

"We wrapped the rumba line around them and continued dancing. Even the musicians got into it and started playing a Latin number. The manager couldn't believe it and the old fart went apoplectic. But there was nothing they could do. Everyone else in the place was joining us." He smiled wistfully. "God, I loved those days."

Roger tapped his cigarette on an ashtray. "I know what you mean. Growing older isn't what it's cracked up to be." With that, he launched into a story about a midnight panty raid that ended with coeds fleeing in their skivvies and three of his fraternity brothers tossed in jail. No one got in trouble though. The police said it was a college prank and released them the next morning.

Nick countered with another tale of collegiate high-jinx, and so it went through dinner and several more martinis, one story after another, back and forth, each trying to outdo the other, each reveling in the recounting of past exploits. Somehow they forgot about the tedious hours studying for exams, the interminable lectures, the exhausting all-night cram sessions. All they recalled was the best of their college years — the close-knit friends, the drunken nights, the young-and-immortal moments — until by the end of dinner Nick felt an intense longing for those Elysian days and could see in Roger's bleary-eyed expression the same nostalgia.

At a pause in the conversation their eyes met, they grinned impishly, and as if by some predetermined signal they simultaneously broke into song, shattering the quiet decorum of the restaurant and turning curious heads toward their table.

Oh, they had to carry Harry to the ferry,
And the ferry carried Harry to the shore;
And the reason that they had to carry Harry to the ferry
Was that Harry couldn't carry any more.

Beating their hands rhythmically on the table, they threw back their heads and sang with wild abandon, the tendons in their necks bulging out.

Californrrnia! Californrrnia!
The hills send back the cry,
We're out to do or die,
For Californrrnia, Californrrnia . . .

By the end of the chorus, every patron in the restaurant stared, astonished at their drunken performance. The owner, Julius Roz, came running over, waving his hands in the air and shouting, "Whatsamatta for you? Thissa nice restaurant, notta roadhouse. You shaddup or get outta my place."

Now the Souse fam-i-ly is the best fam-i-ly
That everrr came overrr from old Ger-man-y...

Roz motioned to his waiters who roughly grabbed the two singers, yanked them out of their seats, and pushed them through the dining room and down the stairs to the street. Arm-in-arm they stumbled out of the restaurant, holding each other upright, still bellowing at the top of their lungs. They piled into a taxi under the watchful eye of Roz who stood arms folded, scowling, flanked by his waiters. The taxi roared to life and lurched down Montgomery Street, the voices of its two passengers echoing among the apartment buildings perched on Telegraph Hill.

38

Marinating in a jar of formaldehyde: *that* was how his brain felt. His face fared no better, resting on a soggy pillow coated with puke and bile. Reliving his college days had its drawbacks, and it was disappointing to know that he was already too old to hop out of bed after a night on the town. Determined to resist the effects of aging, Nick pushed himself up off the pillow. He was nearly upright when a stabbing pain pierced his head, causing him to collapse back down onto the soggy pillow and stare vacantly at a strip of daylight on the wall, unable to form a coherent thought.

A knock on the door.

"There's a call for you," his mother said.

Did the phone ring? He hadn't heard it. "Who is it?" he croaked.

"I don't know. Shall I ask him to call back?"

He wanted to stay in bed until the ache in his head went away and his body was reasonably recovered, but that could take hours and he was no longer sleepy. "No, I'll take it. Tell him I'll be there in a minute."

He swung his legs over the edge of the bed, dropped his feet to the floor, and propped himself upright. The pain in his head flared, sharp and penetrating. He bent over and rub his temples. He was still wearing the same clothes from the night before, rumpled and stained and smelling like his pillow. Rising unsteadily to his feet, he stumbled into the hall and headed for the bathroom.

Lillian and Sarah watched him from the end of the hall with polar opposite expressions. His mother held a hand over her mouth, eyes wide with alarm. Sarah, on the other hand, smirked sardonically and shook her head as if to say, *You are one sorry looking soul.*

Nick ducked into the bathroom, splashed cold water on his face, and rinsed the vomit from his cheeks. "Good God," he muttered, as he examined himself in the mirror. Two bloodshot eyes in a puffy, pallid face stared back, bits of half-digested food entangled in his hair. Only a bath would clean him properly. He shuffled back into the hall and picked up the receiver.

"Hello."

"Nick Benson?" a muffled voice asked, sounding as if he was talking through a cloth to disguise his voice.

"Yeah. Who's this?"

"One who doesn't want to see you hurt."

The caller paused as if to give Nick time to absorb the comment. As the words sank in, Nick's heartbeat sped up, sending another sharp pain through his head. He rubbed his temples, unable in his groggy condition to form a response.

"I know what you're doing," the muffled voice continued, "and I don't want to see you hurt. But if you keep doing it, I'm afraid you will be. Understand?"

A wave of panic swept over Nick, his jumbled thoughts running the gamut from fuzzy to chaotic to terrified. Lillian and Sarah were still gaping at him from the end of the hall, although now they both looked concerned as if they could sense his anxiety. He turned away from them and asked in a low voice, "Who is this? What do you want?"

The phone clicked dead.

His heart still thumping, he replayed the warning in his head, trying to determine what the caller meant. His groggy brain made little headway and was further distracted when a surge of bile rose up his esophagus and scorched the back of his throat. He dropped the receiver and bent over, clutching his stomach as it convulsed again, ejecting a gush of vomit up his throat and out onto the hardwood floor.

Lee Holman had opposed the Matson walkout, yet he benefited from it more than anyone. Hundreds of new members packed the Labor Temple at the November ILA meeting, eager to support the nascent union and hungry for work. Nick hadn't planned on attending — after the anonymous phone call he avoided large groups of longshoremen — but when Harry Bridges asked him to cover it for the *Waterfront Worker*, he reluctantly accepted the assignment rather than risk suspicion.

As for the anonymous caller, Nick had no idea who he was. It was possible the caller had spotted him with Farnsworth purely by chance, in which case he might never discover his identity. Moreover, he wasn't certain if the call was a warning, a threat, or both. The first possibility was far less dangerous than the other two; even so he vowed never to meet Farnsworth in public again and to limit their contact as much as possible.

After the ILA meeting Nick joined Bridges and Schmidt at The Albion for their usual pint of beer. They were seated at a table at the back when Schmidt remarked bitterly, "Lee Holman is up to his old tricks."

Holman had nominated Curly Cutwright as Local 38-79's representative at an upcoming ILA Pacific Coast District Convention and called for a voice vote before anyone had a chance to offer another name.

Bridges nodded. "It was blatant, hard-knuckle parliamentarianism."

"Why Cutwright?" Nick asked.

"He's Holman's stooge and can be counted on to promote Joe Ryan's no-strike code proposal."

"I still don't understand why a union boss would want to give up the right to strike."

"Sounds crazy, doesn't it, until you know that guys like Joe Ryan get all sorts of benefits from the bosses if they keep the men in line. I happen to know that Ryan takes his family on European vacations, and there's no way he could do that with his salary from the union. By the way, I have another writing assignment for you. I want you to report on the ILA Pacific Coast Convention in Portland."

"You want me to go to Portland?"

"We don't have the dough for that, but you can talk to delegates on the phone."

Over the next several days Nick conducted phone interviews with longshoremen who were excited to be at a convention with delegates from every port on the West Coast. The excitement even rubbed off on Nick who considered his reports more than just information; they were also first-hand, first draft accounts of events that might lead to real change on the waterfront, and perhaps poured over by future historians.

Toward the end of the convention, he was surprised to learn that delegates had voted to endorse Joe Ryan's code proposal, even with its no-strike clause. However, they did add a proposal of their own: the establishment of union-run hiring halls and a ban on the shape-up. This was largely due, Nick learned, to the efforts of Harry Bridges, who'd contacted leading delegates and warned them that union members could always be discriminated against if there wasn't a fair rotational hiring system.

The delegates also directed Pacific Coast District Secretary John Bjorkland to contact the Waterfront Employers Association and schedule a meeting to discuss a contract covering every port on the West Coast. And to show they meant business, they passed a resolution that if the employers refused to meet by December 10th, the ILA Pacific Coast District would proceed with a strike vote.

Roger Farnsworth learned from Nick that he could expect a call from John Bjorkland, and when it came he relayed a message from Thomas Plant: as long as the waterfront employers were under contract with the Blue Book Union there was no point in negotiating with the ILA. Bjorkland then offered to submit the matter of longshoremen representation to a vote of all dockworkers. If it had been up to Roger, he would have accepted the offer. Longshoremen, he suspected, were fed-up with the Blue Book Union, and if that was the case, the ILA should be given a chance to prove itself. His hands were tied, though. Adhering to instructions from

Plant, he informed Bjorkland that the Waterfront Employers Association wasn't interested in an election, and if one were held the WEA was under no obligation to accept the results.

Three days later, on November 28th, the *San Francisco News* published an exposé on the Federal government's mail contracts with the shipping industry. The article revealed the government's agreement to pay shippers a set amount no matter how much or how little mail they delivered. The information was already known in certain circles, but this was the first widespread publication of the annual $30 million subsidy reaped by American steamship companies.

The burgeoning rise of the ILA, along with the negative publicity and a threat of labor unrest, set off alarm bells at the Waterfront Employers Association. Thomas Plant called an emergency meeting and turned it over to Roger, who detailed the latest events. The shipping executives were somber and immobile as he enumerated the ILA's latest demands and distributed copies of the *San Francisco News* article.

William Roth, still smarting from the arbitration board's ruling, looked glum and dispirited. By contrast, Stanley Dollar exuded defiant confidence.

"Frankly," Dollar said, "I don't give a damn if the public knows about the mail contracts. There's nothing illegal or unethical about them. Hell, without subsidies half the shipping routes would go out of business, and if that happened American shipping would go down the tubes. Then we'd be dependent on foreign shippers who might turn against us in the event of another war. People forget that America was caught with its pants down during the Great War. American shipping is more than just maritime commerce; it's essential to national security."

Paul Eliel, executive director of the Industrial Association, agreed. "I'd like to suggest you retain McCann-Erickson on a permanent basis. They're the best public relations firm in the country and can arrange favorable editorials as often as needed."

"That may help with the general public," said Roger, "but it won't cut mustard with the longshoremen." He looked around the table. "I'd like you to reconsider a ten cent pay raise to eighty-five cents per hour. We can announce it as part of a new contract with the Blue Book Union and that should draw members back into their ranks and reverse the ILA's progress. In the meantime, our representative in Washington is lobbying Federal officials to include a no-strike clause in the maritime codes."

After a half-hearted debate, the majority agreed that a pay raise was probably the least expensive and most effective way to head off the threat of a strike. Roger contacted Emile Stone at the Blue Book Union and offered to host a Christmas party at the Blue Book Union headquarters to treat the men to a holiday banquet and to announce the pay raise. Clarisa handled the details, ordering decorations and a buffet and flyers announcing the event that were posted at every pier along the waterfront.

It was a cold, wet December evening the night of the Christmas party. Clarisa and Roger arrived early at the Blue Book Union hall on Clay Street, Clarisa wearing a festive burgundy skirt and jacket with a matching burgundy beret, Roger in a Brooks Brothers suit and silk tie adorned with reindeer. They helped set up tables with red and green tablecloths and supervised the caterers who carried in steaming trays of baked ham, roast turkey, stuffing, sweet potatoes, peas, and four dozen pumpkin pies.

Emile Stone, the bald-headed president of the Blue Book Union, puffed on a cigar as he strode around the hall, directing his men where to hang the garland and string the lights.

By seven o'clock the decorations were in place and four chefs in white toque hats stood behind buffet tables ready to carve the meat. During the next hour only a handful of gang bosses arrived, and when Stone announced the pay raise at nine o'clock it was to less than forty men.

Afterwards Roger drove Clarisa home on wet streets, neither one saying a word until the Stutz reached her flat.

Clarisa rested a hand on his. "I'm sorry it didn't work out as well as you planned. I don't understand it. We posted notices at all the piers."

Roger shook his head. "Too little, too late. If we had made the announcement two months ago when I first suggested it, we might have saved the Blue Book. As it is . . ."

She glanced at him. "Maybe it isn't worth saving."

"Plant thinks it is and refuses to recognize the ILA. Until he does, there's nothing I can do but follow orders."

"If the majority of men want to be in the ILA, why won't he recognize it?"

"Because he's afraid of dealing with an independent union. If there's one thing I've learned at this job, it's that shippers prefer fear and intimidation over negotiation and compromise. It's a double-edged sword, though. They only respond to the same tactics, so they tend to react rather than act and that limits their options." He nodded at the Worker's School next to the print shop. "Sometimes I think radicals are better at strategic planning."

The Worker's School reminded Clarisa of her father and his endless rants about the sorry state of things and how the rich were getting richer while the poor slipped further into poverty. "Maybe that's because plans are all they have. When your only asset is dreams, dreams become your reason for living."

They lapsed into silence, the rain gently pattering on the convertible's canvas top. Though the evening had been disappointing, Clarisa felt calm and serene and content. After her revelation in front of Julius' Castle, she'd let go of her expectations regarding Roger and Nick, and that freed her from worry about what lay ahead. Besides, there were other things to think about. So many were suffering now, hungry depressed souls who made daily pilgrimages to St. Patrick's Mission with downcast eyes and gaunt faces. *Where do they all come from?* Her work at the mission had become more meaningful than anything else in her life, and as a bonus it kept her from obsessing about her own troubles and the troubles of her father whose business seemed to be shrinking every month, driving him to the bottle for solace. As long as she was able to help others, there was hope, and as long as there was hope, she could face whatever lay ahead.

Absorbed in her musings, she failed to notice Roger wrap an arm around her shoulder until he impetuously pulled her to him and pressed his lips against hers. Taken off-guard she stiffened, her peaceful serenity shattered. His lips slid across her cheek to her ear, and in a pleading voice, he implored her to spend the night with him, begged her for the intimacy and sweet release they once shared. At the same time his hand ran up and down her thigh and under her coat, searching, rapacious, as if he were a starving indigent groping for food.

How can someone with such impeccable manners transform so quickly into an aggressive predator? It was baffling. Scary.

"Please don't deny me," he pleaded, his hand now moving up over her hips, her waist, and finally onto her left breast, groping, squeezing, caressing, "I've tried to forget the night we were together. I stopped asking you out because I couldn't bear to be with you and not have all of you. I've buried myself in work, but it's no good. I need you. Please, more than you know."

He was panting now, his lips running down the side of her neck, his face burrowing into her hair. His pathetic plea reminded her of how different he'd been the Night of the Golden Grass, how their bodies melded together so beautifully in the warm summer evening. He'd been wonderful that evening, strong, self-confident, masterful. Now he was just the opposite: insecure, wanting her as much for assurance as for intimacy. It wasn't attractive. She pushed against him with one hand, the other fumbling for the door handle.

"Please don't," she said.

His roaming hand found its way under her skirt and reached up over her stockings, his fingers searching and probing the inside of her thighs.

Without thought or premeditation, she swung her right hand at him and slapped his cheek, leaving a red blush. The impact stopped him, giving her a chance to look down and locate the door handle. She tugged at it and released the door latch, then in one quick motion shoved her shoulder against the door and tumbled out of the car, landing on the rain-soaked sidewalk, her beret askew, skirt hiked up above her knees.

He leaned across the seat, arms outstretched, his face a road map of longing and regret. "Oh, God, I'm sorry. I didn't mean—." He pushed himself upright and opened the driver's side door.

"No!" she exclaimed as she lifted herself up onto her feet.

Her protest stopped him. He looked back at her.

Quieter and with barely contained fury, she said, "Don't...get...out. I'm fine." She righted her beret and smoothed her soaking wet skirt. Under his remorseful gaze, she reached into the car and retrieved her purse. "I'll see you tomorrow," she said without looking at him. She walked across the sidewalk to the front door of her flat. "I'm sorry," she heard him say in a meek voice as she unlocked the door and slipped inside.

39

Journal – December 16th, 1933

Nothing has changed. Harry Bridges continues to give me writing assignments, my work gang treats me, more or less, as an equal, and I haven't detected hostility from anyone at the waterfront, or anywhere else for that matter. Still, it's unnerving to know that someone somewhere knows what I'm doing.

At the December ILA meeting Lee Holman stepped to the podium in a sour mood, perhaps sensing his power slipping away. I took notes for an article while Holman lectured us on the need to stick together and abide by the will of the union (i.e. his will) until the shipping codes are approved. The men listened politely, though with little sign of enthusiasm. I think most of them read my article in the *Waterfront Worker* criticizing Holman for not supporting the Matson strike, and it seems to have changed their attitude. They know the arbitration ruling, prohibiting shippers from firing ILA members, would not have happened if the Matson men hadn't put their jobs on the line.

After Holman's lecture Curly Cutwright gave a report on the ILA Pacific Coast Convention in Portland. At the end of the report Henry Schmidt asked Cutwright if he'd voted to endorse Joe Ryan's no-strike code proposal, something the men now seem to understand is a bad idea, and if he supported a proposal for union-run hiring halls.

Cutwright wiped his brow and shuffled his notes.

"It's not a difficult question," Schmidt said dryly. "Or is it?" provoking a few scattered chuckles. "Don't you remember how you voted?" he persisted, an edge creeping into his voice. He nodded toward Holman. "Perhaps our president can answer the question."

Visibly relieved to step out of the spotlight, Cutwright moved aside while Holman stepped to the podium and said, "Brothers, I'm sorry to report that the stenographer hired to record the convention was inexperienced and much of the notes are illegible. But" — he raised a finger as a hail of groans greeted his announcement — "I can tell you that Brother Cutwright represented you well, and you can be damn proud of the job he did."

District Secretary John Bjorkland was next at the podium. He recounted his conversation with Roger Farnsworth and relayed Farnsworth's message that the Waterfront Employers Association was not interested in meeting with representatives from Local 38-79.

A low, ominous grumble rolled through the auditorium. In its wake Henry Schmidt got up and reminded the membership of the hardships they faced every day. He told them about Joe Robbie, a stevedore and father of six who was killed last week at the 14th Street Terminal in Oakland when a block pin broke and dropped a three-ton load on him. While Schmidt spoke, the men listened closely and nodded, a stiff resolve in their posture. It was in that resolve, in the desire for self-determination written on their faces, that I saw a strength that struck me as noble and courageous but also potentially dangerous.

At the end of Schmidt's speech, Pirate Larson got up and proposed a resolution calling for a strike vote if the Waterfront Employers Association refused to meet with our representatives by the next meeting.

Thunderous applause greeted the proposal.

Seated behind Bjorkland, Lee Holman was frowning, clearly uncomfortable with the direction the meeting had taken but reluctant to publicly oppose popular sentiment.

Schmidt seconded the motion and Bjorkland, who still controlled the podium, called for a voice vote.

It passed unanimously.

The hall quieted as the significance of the resolution sank in. Those who felt an urgent need to act only a minute earlier now seemed pensive, shifting in their seats as it dawned on them that a strike vote could shut down the waterfront and separate them from their jobs, and perhaps lead to violence and deprivation. In that moment of uncertainty, I could sense the self-doubt and fear seeping into their thoughts, eroding their confidence.

A solitary figure rose to his feet on the far side of the auditorium. His long nose, high forehead, and receding chin were recognizable, even from where I was seated.

"Men," Bridges said in a loud voice, "you took a big step just now and I'm proud of you. Together, you're the most powerful voice in this union. Hell, you're the most powerful voice on the whole damn waterfront. Up till now, though, your voice has been ignored by union officials who don't want to challenge employers, who are comfortable with fat salaries and a submissive membership. And there's no question your will was ignored in Portland and Washington D.C. So I wanna propose a convention for rank-and-file members, excludin' paid union officials, a convention that will bring our members together from all West Coast locals to discuss what course of action to take and to begin setting up the machinery to ensure a successful strike, if indeed that is the course we take. There's much work to be done, much planning and organization, and not a little risk. If we band together, though, if we're successful, the benefits will undoubtedly transform the waterfront." He raised his voice. "As Father Michael Shannon once said in similar circumstances, 'you are engaged in a struggle not merely for better wages and workin' conditions, but for the dearest property of man: your self-respect.'"

Lee Holman glared at Bridges with the enraged eyes of a schoolmaster furious at a recalcitrant pupil. The effect on the men, however, was entirely different. The uncertainty on their faces had disappeared, replaced by a renewed confidence.

I was writing all this down, encapsulating the flow of events, when my pen abruptly halted as if welded to the page. Bridges had quoted a priest. What was his name? Ah, yes. Father Shannon. I thought about it for a moment until it came to me. That's right. He's the priest at St. Patrick's, Clarisa's church.

40

Lillian Benson hummed a Christmas carol as she set her best china dishes on the green damask tablecloth. The aroma of coffee, cinnamon, and bacon pervaded the flat, mixing with the scent of noble fir from the tree in the front parlor. She paused to contemplate her bittersweet mood. This was the second Christmas since Charles died. She had tried to make the holiday seem normal, keeping up old traditions and rituals, but a profound emptiness still dwelt in her heart. Thank God the rest of her household was intact, at least most of the time. Some days, though, her family seemed to be losing gravitational force, its members acting more like rogue comets than orbiting planets.

Rune sat in the front parlor reading the *Chronicle*, puffing on an unlit pipe that Lillian forbade him from smoking as it would ruin the fragrances of Christmas. Brightly wrapped presents lay on the floor around the Christmas tree, including several for Fargo that Nick would deliver to the hospital later that day.

Lillian carried a platter of waffles and bacon into the dining room and placed it on the table. She knocked on Nick's bedroom door and then on Sarah's. This wasn't like past Christmases when her children rose before dawn and eagerly took down their stockings from the mantle to enjoy the toys and treats inside until she and Charles joined them. Nick emerged from his bedroom in pajamas and robe, but she had to knock on Sarah's door once more before her daughter appeared wearing a distant smirk, an expression she often wore now that she was friends with a group of students from the San Francisco Art Institute.

An article in the newspaper about marijuana use among young people had described behavior unnervingly similar to Sarah's, a distant attitude, a disregard for proper etiquette, casual dress, eating binges at odd hours, an attraction to Negro music. When Lillian confronted her about it, probably too harshly, Sarah promptly rebuffed her with an it's-none-of-your-business, I'll-do-what-I-want attitude. If only Charles were here, he'd corral her maverick tendencies and teach her to be a proper young lady, attractive to a man with prospects. She sighed. At least her daughter lived under her roof where she could monitor her erratic comings and goings.

Christmas breakfast was an annual ritual at the Benson household, a holiday feast of cinnamon-laced coffee, fresh squeezed orange juice, Belgian waffles with whipped cream, and thick Canadian bacon. All made possible this year, Lillian remarked cheerfully as she passed a pitcher of juice to Rune, because Nick was making a handsome salary as a longshoreman. It certainly wasn't the kind of work she envisioned for her college educated son, but it was paying the bills nicely. Nick ignored the compliment, his expression nearly as distant as Sarah's, and that worried her. He had always been the more upbeat of her two children, doing well in school and making friends easily, so his moody disposition of late was a mystery to which she had little insight.

After breakfast she and Sarah cleared the table while Nick and Rune tossed logs into the fireplace, the flames crackling and popping, scenting the air with the woody fragrance of oak and Douglas fir. The day outside was gray and damp, producing a glaze of condensation on the window panes. Nick turned on the radio and tuned it to a station playing Christmas carols and holiday songs. When the table was cleared, Lillian carried a tray of fresh coffee into the parlor and set it on the coffee table. Everyone was seated around the tree, including Rusty who lay curled up on the floor, his belly full of bacon scraps.

Rune sat in his favorite stuffed chair, stroking his walrus mustache, recalling Christmases in Denmark. "We didn't have much in those days — papa drank his wages — but mama always managed ta have someting special under the tree. A pair of used skates from the community chest, a carved reindeer, a wool hat and scarf she knitted." He puffed his smokeless pipe. "She served a homemade fruitcake made with stewed prunes and rendered pork fat. It was solid as a hockey puck but, gosh darn, it was delicious. You never tasted anyting like it."

"Uggg," grunted Sarah, her nose scrunched up in disgust, "I wouldn't want to. It sounds awful."

Rune harrumphed. "You young folks want everyting to come in a store bought box with a fancy bow."

"That's not true," said Sarah. "In fact I made all my gifts this year."

She reached under the tree and retrieved a stack of presents. All of them were thin, rectangular, and wrapped in plain white paper with red ribbon. "Merry Christmas, everyone," she said as she passed them out. "You go first, grandpa."

Rune untied the ribbon and tore away the wrapping. "Oh, my gosh," he said with a grin as he gazed at it. He turned it around and held it up for all to see: a framed watercolor of a three-masted barkentine with webbed rigging splaying down from the masts to the bulwarks and a graceful bowline curving up to a bowsprit. "It looks like my old ship, the *Rikstaat*! The ship that brought me here."

At the age of twenty-five, Rune was a sailor on a Danish barkentine when it reached the Golden Gate on a densely foggy day. The captain ordered her sails lowered as the ship moved toward shore, unaware that they were ten miles south of the harbor entrance opposite Devil's Slide, a treacherous rocky promontory. The *Rikstaat* ran aground and as she broke up under a pounding surf, Rune bravely jumped into the cold choppy swells and swam ashore. Ever since then he'd claimed, with a playful wink, that he was the only immigrant to have swum to America.

"I was hoping you'd say that," said Sarah.

Lillian was impressed. "I didn't know you knew how to paint, dear. It's quite lovely. Where did you learn?"

"At the Art Institute. Nick's been paying part of the tuition, and I've earned the rest by posing for drawing classes." She cast an affectionate smile at her brother. "Now it's your turn."

"Posing?" Lillian asked, her eyes narrowing. "You mean . . . without clothes?"

"Mother!" Sarah said. "Don't be such a prude."

Lillian studied her daughter, realizing perhaps for the first time that Sarah was no longer the innocent girl she once cradled in her arms. She also noticed the resemblance to herself at that age when young men had cast lingering glances at her dark eyes and swelling bosom. She made a mental note to remind her daughter that she couldn't be too careful if she wanted to marry a respectable man, then turned to Nick and watched him unwrap his present. Like Rune's, it was a framed picture.

As Nick examined it a series of fleeting emotions crossed his face.

"Don't keep us in suspense," said Lillian, wondering what would cause her son to have such a range of expressions.

Nick held it up for all to see. Another watercolor. A gray freighter with upright kingposts, a raised foc'sle on the bow, a quarterdeck at the stern, a midship house between them. On its side was the name DIANA DOLLAR.

"Do you like it?" asked Sarah.

"Sure . . . of course I do," said Nick.

A strange uneasiness in his voice drew a sharp glance from Lillian. Something was weighing on his heart, and it was time, she decided, to sit down with him and pry out whatever it was.

The phone rang.

"I'll get it," Nick said, rising abruptly.

"We'll wait for you," Lillian called after him as he went into the hall.

While he was gone, she complimented Sarah on her budding artistic talent, deciding it was best for the moment not to criticize her for posing in the nude and ignite a row on Christmas. Besides, it was comforting to know that her daughter was engaged in something constructive. Art may not help her find a good husband, but it was a worthy hobby to fill her time until she did. When she said as much, Sarah responded indignantly that there was no reason a woman couldn't be an artist in her own right. Lillian was about to reply when Nick returned and slumped down on his chair, his face ashen, eyes focused on the floor.

"What is it, dear?" Lillian asked. "Who called?" He didn't reply. "Nick"—her voice rising—"what's happened?"

Eyes still on the floor, he spoke in a low voice. "It was the hospital. They called to let me know Fargo died." Lillian gasped. "Apparently, he has no known kin and since I was the only one who visited him, they contacted me." His chest heaved. "I knew he hadn't been doing well. His weight was down to less than a hundred-twenty pounds. I figured once he got on his feet again, he'd gain it all back." A tear pooled in the corner of one eye. He wiped his cheek with the sleeve of his robe and drew in a deep, disconsolate breath.

"I'm so sorry," murmured Lillian. "And on . . . Christmas Day." She recalled the last time Nick was this upset, when he was in jail. He hadn't responded well. "Can I get you something, dear?"

His eyes wandered across the floor to the presents under the tree. He combed a hand through his hair, his foot nervously tapping up and down, his other hand opening and closing into a fist. He rose to his feet, crossed the room, and picked up the stack of presents for Fargo. He studied them for a moment, his fingers rubbing the wrapping. Then all at once he lifted them over his head and slammed them down onto the floor with a tremendous crash.

"It's all a lie," he said, "a goddamned lie." He looked around. "I'm a lie. Everything here is a lie." He grabbed a branch of the Christmas tree and yanked it until the tree toppled onto the floor, sending ornaments skidding across the room, glass balls shattering like broken eggshells.

Lillian looked on incredulously as he picked up several more presents and threw them onto the floor, then stormed out and slammed the door to his bedroom.

She surveyed the tangled mess of broken ornaments, scattered presents, and toppled tree. "Do you have any idea what he was talking about?" Sarah and Rune shook their heads. "Because I suspect that this outburst was more than just about poor Fargo's passing."

Sarah groaned and rolled her eyes, the way a son or daughter does when a parent says something stupendously obvious. Lillian ignored the reproach and sent her into the kitchen for a broom while she and Rune lifted the tree upright and rehung the ornaments.

A short while later Nick emerged from his bedroom dressed in dungarees, a wool pea coat, and white cap. Without a word, he snatched the key to the Hudson from a hook in the hall and trooped down the stairs, Rusty trailing behind.

41

It had taken several exploratory trips before his luck changed.

Nick was driving around one Saturday afternoon when he found the South End Yacht Club, a ramshackle marina with a motley collection of boats berthed at half-submerged, seaweed-fringed piers. A boatyard beside the marina was home to a fleet of vessels in various states of repair, most propped up on timber stilts amid scraps of lumber and wood shavings scattered on the ground. It was an unglamorous operation, yet one eminently suited to amateur sailors of modest means who enjoyed working on their humble vessels while brandishing a paint brush in one hand and a bottle of beer in the other. It didn't take Nick long to figure out that this pastime, rather than sailing or fishing, was the primary enterprise of the denizens of the weathered marina, who yakked and yammered as they repaired their boats.

The manager of the South End Yacht Club was a crusty fellow named

Lenny Dross, who lived in a one-room shack at one end of the boatyard. He was the happy lord of his tumbledown domain, collecting rents for the owner while keeping a protective eye on the place at night.

When Nick drove into the marina that Saturday afternoon, his heart leaped when he spotted a familiar sight floating a couple of hundred yards offshore. The *Diana Dollar* was tied up side-by-side with four other mothballed vessels, devoid of cargo and floating high in the water.

Relieved to have finally found her, he sat down with Lenny Dross for a spell of three beers and described his voyage across the Pacific, omitting the details of his arrest. At the end of his account, he expressed a desire to stand on the deck of his former ship again. Dross, a former sailor himself who understood the call of the sea and the love of a vessel, offered him the use of a rowboat and by the third beer agreed to lend him a grappling hook and rope ladder to board the freighter.

When Nick drove into the boatyard on Christmas Day, Lenny Dross looked happy to have company and offered him a bottle of Christmas ale. Nick declined, explaining that he wanted to board his old ship, but agreed to accept the offer when he returned.

"So what in tarnation brings you out today of all days?" Dross asked, as he collected a grappling hook and rope ladder from an old wooden shed.

Nick gazed out at the clump of ships mothballed in the bay. "I guess you could say my salvation."

The marina manager gave him a curious glance. "Well, I hope you find it."

After helping Rusty into the dinghy, Nick untied the mooring line, stepped aboard, and pushed off from the pier. He nodded goodbye to Dross, dipped the oars into the water, and propelled the rowboat forward. It was a crystal clear day, the sun reflecting off the bay in glimmering sparkles, the East Bay hills bright green and in sharp focus. He felt a comforting warmth spread through his chest as he pulled on the oars. The rowboat picked up speed and glided toward the ships, and for the first time that day his spirits lifted, his mission finally begun.

Up close the *Diana Dollar* towered over him, her draft from waterline to weather deck the equivalent of a three-story building. Nick tied the rope ladder to the grappling hook and neatly folded the ladder so it wouldn't tangle. Grasping the stem of the hook, he stood up and swung it back and forth, increasing the height of the arc with each swing. When its zenith reached his shoulder, he gave the hook one final heave and sent hurtling it up toward the ship's railing. As the rope ladder unfolded, its weight increasingly dragged on the hook so that well before it reached the railing, the hook glanced against the hull with a hollow clang and dropped back down into the bay — *kerplop!* — sending up a fountain of water.

Redoubling his effort, he attempted a second toss. This time, offset by the added weight of the water-soaked ladder, his toss was equally short. On the third unsuccessful attempt, his arm began to tire, and on the fourth and fifth attempts he fared no better. It was no use fighting gravity. Either he had to lighten the apparatus or figure out another way to scale the ship. He looked down the line of ships and noticed they were tied together in sequence of size. Being the largest, the *Diana Dollar* was at one end, while at the other end, a derelict coal collier with dark streaks down its sides, was only half its height. He rowed down to the coal collier and repeated the maneuver until the hook arced well above his shoulders. With one final thrust, he sent it up over the collier's rail where it landed on the deck with a ringing clank. A quick jerk on the rope ladder drew the hook in until it caught securely on the railing.

"Yahooo!" he cried, feeling the first exuberant joy of the day.

Rusty, joining his master, stood up and wagged his tail.

Nick tied the end of the rope ladder to the rowboat and climbed up to the collier's deck. Pulling the dinghy with the hook and ladder, he vaulted onto the next ship and in this way moved across the line of ships until, with a tingle of anticipation, he climbed onto the *Diana Dollar*.

The freighter had an air of forlorn grace. Its decks were splotched with seagull droppings and coated with a layer of dust randomly patterned by winter rains. Aside from this superficial indignity, she appeared to be shipshape, devoid of rust, the paint that Nick and shipmates applied still intact.

For the next hour he poked around the abandoned ship looking for hiding places the customs agents might have missed. He walked the passageways and peered into cabins, each place triggering a memory. In the messroom he could still hear the excited cheers during the cockroach race. On the flying bridge he looked up and pictured the glittering night sky over the Pacific. And in the bosun's dingy locker he recalled Primm and Slag plotting their coup d'état.

While looking around the bosun's locker, he spotted a partially concealed access panel in the bulkhead. Curious, he rummaged through the cubby holes until he found a hammer and screwdriver. He spent several minutes chipping paint off the screws that held the panel in place, then several more muscle-wrenching minutes unscrewing them. Once the screws were out, it was easy to pry the panel from the bulkhead, though all he found inside was a ball of tangled electrical wires.

He sat down and scratched his head, at a loss for what to do next. He was flummoxed until he noticed another access panel in the bulkhead, and then another and another and another. In all the months he'd lived on the *Diana Dollar*, he hadn't noticed these panels covering the ship's mechanical systems, perhaps because they were so ubiquitous, a dozen in the bosun's locker alone. And, as it turned out, each one was covered with multiple coats of paint and resistant to opening. It took three hours of chipping and removing screws until he was satisfied no cache of opium was hidden in the bosun's locker.

He went back to the midship house and by habit turned left toward the galley, half expecting Cook to be manning the stove. He checked the cabinets, the stove, and the food locker, scouring every nook and cranny with his flashlight. Aside from cockroach carcasses, it was barren of food, utensils, and insects. Even the roaches had moved on.

The winter sun was nearing the western horizon, the light outside dimming. Lillian would have a conniption if he didn't return in time for Christmas dinner. He stuffed the flashlight in his pocket and went out to the weather deck. Unless Lady Luck smiled on him, it might take a dozen or more inspections to thoroughly search the ship, and since he only had time on the weekends, the search could go on for weeks, even months. He untied the rope ladder from the grappling hook and tied it to the starboard railing near the adjoining ship where it couldn't be seen from shore. Holding the hook in one hand, he climbed down the ladder and stepped gingerly into the rowboat where he was greeted by Rusty who vigorously wagged his tail, his rear end wobbling back and forth.

He sat down on the cross bench and scratched the mutt behind the ears, glad to have a companion happy to see him. Grasping the oars, he slowly rowed back toward the marina as daylight dimmed into a long winter's night. Most San Franciscans would be turning on their Christmas lights by now and gathering for a holiday supper, grateful to have a roof over their heads and a meal to share with family and friends. It made him think about Fargo who'd died alone in the hospital with no one at his bedside, not even his faithful dog. It was hard to believe the old longshoreman was gone, and it saddened him to think of how lonely he must have felt during his final days.

42

Dozens of longshoremen attended a memorial service for James Fargo at Duggan's Funeral Parlor. Most hadn't known him personally but were there to pay respects to one of their own, senselessly injured on the job. Nick delivered the eulogy beside a simple pine coffin resting on a table draped in black cloth. He began with an account of the day Fargo was injured and how he himself had come perilously close to suffering the same fate. He also talked of Fargo's struggle to recover from his injury and his joy at seeing his beloved Rusty before he died. He wanted to say more, wanted to say that Fargo's life meant something, that his death meant something, that under different circumstances he might have been an inspiration to the family he never had. But the words caught in his throat, and he couldn't get them out.

Harry Bridges took his place beside the pine coffin, his face somber and determined. "The Chinese have a saying. Death can come from a single stroke or a thousand paper cuts. Well, I can tell you that Fargo didn't die from a single accident. His death was meted out in a thousand ways, over a thousand days. And during that time he was beaten down, treated like a pack animal, made to feel worthless, and only valued when the boss had use for him.

"A new year begins soon, and I'd like to dedicate the struggle ahead to James Fargo, Joe Robbie, and all the others who've been ground under by an abusive system. We owe it to them, as well as to our families, to continue our struggle with courage and determination. We owe it to them to make sure that their senseless deaths don't go unnoticed or unheeded. When the going gets rough — and it will — and when things look bleak" — he patted the coffin — "let's remember our fallen brothers and draw strength from their memory so that their deaths won't have been in vain."

Under a cloudless sky, the funeral cortege led by a black Hearse drove to Holy Cross Cemetery in Colma, a suburb south of San Francisco. Among a field of granite tombstones and marble mausoleums, a priest performed the final eulogy and Fargo's body was laid to rest. Nick brought Rusty to the burial and afterwards they strolled through the cemetery.

Led by an inquisitive nose, Rusty trotted to and fro, sniffing and exploring, his tail waving back and forth like a feathery flag. When Nick lagged behind him, Rusty stopped and looked back at his new master, standing before a granite headstone, gazing at the inscription carved in block letters: CHARLES BENSON – 1885-1932.

It had been months since Nick visited his father's grave. Charles had departed so abruptly, so unexpectedly, it had taken Nick a long time to accept his passing. And when he did finally accept it, his grief gave way to a simmering resentment. The suicide had left the Benson family to fend for itself at the worst possible time, and also at the exact moment when Nick was about to depart from the path his father had paved for him and strike out on his own. Even now, more than a year after Charles' passing, Nick still felt a lingering resentment, and it made him turn away.

Rusty trotted over to him and looked up expectantly as if to ask why they had paused at this spot. Nick stooped down on his haunches, wrapped an arm around his furry friend and gave him a hug. As he did, a wave of sadness engulfed him, both for the loss of his father as well as for Fargo.

When the sorrow passed, Nick stood up and took a deep breath. Released from his master's grasp, Rusty trotted over to Charles' gravestone and sniffed around the base, circling it a couple of times. Then to Nick's horror, Rusty stopped, lifted a leg, and let lose a stream of urine that dribbled down the side of the gravestone. Nick was about to reprimand him when a strange sensation distracted him, a roiling unsettled feeling in the pit of his stomach. He wondered what it was as it traveled up his chest, into his throat, and out of his mouth, first as an odd choking belch, then as a long, uncontrollable laugh, like that of a hysterical madman. He grabbed his sides and doubled over, still laughing uncontrollably.

He was puzzled by this odd outburst until in the midst of his laughter it came to him: a sudden realization that one of life's great lessons and one of its great ironies as well is that no matter what you want, no matter how hard you work for it, you have little control over anything but yourself. Everything else is up to God or the laws of physics or the randomness of the universe, take your pick, so there's no advantage in holding on to resentments or dwelling on them.

A nearby family of mourners shot disapproving glances at him. Ignoring them, he drew in a deep breath to calm himself, straightened upright, and headed down the path, Rusty at his side.

43

After Roger's clumsy attempt to seduce her, Clarisa thought it best to shift their relationship back to a purely professional footing. She declined his invitation to attend a New Year's Eve ball and instead went to St. Patrick's Mission to serve dinner to a long line of men, women, and children whose faces brightened when they received their meal. She went directly home afterwards and found a note from Seamus saying he'd gone out for a celebratory drink but would return in time to ring in the New Year. Doubtful he'd stay sober long enough to keep his promise, she crumpled the note and tossed it in the trash can.

For the rest of the evening she read a book and listened to a radio broadcast of the Cy Trobbe Orchestra playing popular dance numbers at the Warfield Theater to an enthusiastic crowd. When the midnight hour arrived and the revelers at the Warfield whooped and hollered and rattled their noisemakers, she thought of Roger and Nick and wondered where they might be. Roger, she imagined, was either at the ball or a jazz club on Pacific Avenue; Nick was perhaps dancing with someone else at the Bolero Ballroom as they had a year earlier.

She knew Nick was waiting for her to make the first move, and she'd been tempted on many occasions to pick up the phone and call him. But the relationship between Roger, Nick, and herself had become so complicated, and the potential consequences so serious, she held her impulses in check and vowed to remain neutral until — she wasn't entirely sure — perhaps until she had a better sense of what lay ahead.

At a few minutes after midnight, she put herself to bed and lay sleepless in the dark, thinking how strange it was that a woman who three men claimed to love could feel so alone.

On the first workday of 1934 she arrived at the office determined to behave as if everything between her and Roger was normal. Roger did the same, yet it still felt awkward, as if they were pretending there was no history of affection between them.

At midmorning a delegation from Local 38-79 met with Farnsworth in the conference room. The meeting was brief, and after the visitors left he called Clarisa into his office. She sat down ready to receive instructions, expecting Roger to give her an assignment or dictate a letter. Instead he toyed with his cigarette case as if something was on his mind.

He looked up. "I hope I don't lose my job."

That was the last thing she expected to hear. "Why? What happened?"

"Plant is on vacation in Palm Springs and instructed me to present the employer's position to the ILA delegation."

"Did you?"

"Yes . . . and no. As I expected they presented a list of demands, starting with recognition of the ILA as the representative of West Coast dockworkers. I told them we're quite satisfied with the Blue Book Union and not interested in a contract with another union. Of course, they claimed the Blue Book doesn't represent the rank-and-file any more."

"Is that true?"

"Possibly. So I challenged them to prove their claim or drop their demands. It's not what Plant would have done. He would have shown them the door."

"So what made you do it?"

Roger leaned forward. "We can't bury our head in the sand. If we don't recognize the situation for what it is, it's bound to get worse, much worse."

Clarisa agreed. Ignoring the ILA wouldn't make it go away. It also struck her as admirable that Roger had jeopardized his job for a reason that, to her, made sense. She wanted to give him an encouraging smile, wanted to say something supportive and complimentary, and if their relationship hadn't been so awkward she would have. As it was, she hesitated, and in that moment Roger handed her a stack of papers and sent her back to her office.

A week later, at the January meeting of Local 38-79, the delegation reported Farnsworth's challenge. Nick wasn't surprised. Nor was Harry Bridges who had always said the employers were going to fight them every step of the way. After the delegation gave its report, Lee Holman pleaded with the men to be patient. The maritime code hearings would end soon, and when the codes were approved the ILA would stand a better chance of being recognized as the sole representative of West Coast longshoremen.

A heated argument ensued. Some longshoremen sided with Holman and asked for patience; others openly derided him for attempting to keep the membership under his thumb. At a pause in the discussion Bridges got up and proposed, as he did in December, a motion to hold a rank-and-file convention, excluding paid union officials, to formulate a unified platform and to decide whether to proceed with a strike vote if their demands weren't met.

Holman countered with a telegram from Pacific Coast District President Bill Lewis that said the District wouldn't sanction such a convention as "all ILA conventions were rank-and-file."

"They're pretty rank all right," shouted Pirate Larsen, prompting laughter and catcalls that went on for some time.

In the face of this derision, Holman began to look like an escaped convict cornered by a pack of yelping hounds. Not about to surrender, he pounded his fist on the podium and snarled that radicals were trying to take over the union and lead them all to ruin. Members, he bellowed, should stay the course behind Joe Ryan and the union leadership.

The men reacted with little enthusiasm, and during that moment Nick could see the power slipping away from Holman and traveling to Bridges who, still standing, insisted the motion be given a vote.

Holman reluctantly let the vote proceed.

The membership overwhelmingly approved the motion, along with a proposal to send Bridges and Henry Schmidt on a barnstorming trip up and down the West Coast to drum up support for it.

When the meeting ended, Bridges asked Nick to take over his duties as managing editor of the *Waterfront Worker* while he was on the barnstorming trip. It was an unexpected honor and one which Nick was sorely tempted to accept. He was in awe of Bridges' powers of persuasion and his clarity of purpose, and the weekly meetings with Bridges and his followers in Albion Hall were the highlight of his week. As managing editor, though, he would have to work closely with the staff and learn their identities. He desperately wanted to preserve his ability to tell Farnsworth that he hadn't penetrated the paper's inner circle, hoping that as long as he provided general information, Farnsworth would be satisfied. Besides, it was only a matter of time before he found the narcotics hidden on the *Diana Dollar.*

Or so he hoped.

After tussling overnight with the request, Nick called Bridges to decline with the excuse that his grandfather was ill and needed special attention. He then gave assurances that he would still monitor the maritime code hearings in Washington and report on them for the *Waterfront Worker.*

In that regard, Nick learned that Joe Ryan had reiterated his preference for compulsory arbitration at the code hearings and made no mention of abolishing the shape-up or preserving the right to strike. Nick reported this to Bridges, and a few days later Bridges called from Tacoma, sounding pleased. West Coast longshoremen were unhappy with Ryan's position. Consequently, he and Schmidt were having no trouble obtaining commitments to attend a rank-and-file convention in San Francisco.

Journal – March 3rd, 1934

It's been a dramatic turning point for the ILA Pacific Coast District, and for me as well. I attended the Rank and File Convention to report on the proceedings for the *Waterfront Worker*, and even though I wasn't being paid, it was the first time I felt like a professional journalist.

Delegates from every port on the West Coast gathered in an auditorium in San Francisco and divided themselves into committees to tackle individual issues and report their recommendations back to the main body. I spent the day going from room to room, monitoring their progress and taking notes. Right away I noticed a palpable tension between conservative and progressive delegates. Conservatives advocated a go-slow approach, at least until the maritime codes were enacted, while progressives, eager to confront the employers, pushed for immediate action. This struggle, it soon became apparent, would become a theme of the convention.

During the afternoon session I sat in on the Resolutions Committee meeting chaired by Harry Bridges who challenged the men to think beyond the pork chop issues of wages and working conditions and take an active role in advocating social change. Under his guidance, the committee approved a number of such resolutions. One called for the release of the Scottsboro Boys, a group of young Negroes from Mississippi who have been charged, many think falsely, with raping two white women. Another demanded a national system of unemployment insurance. While another called for a boycott of all German goods to protest Hitler's ban on trade unions.

Conservative delegates objected to the irrelevancy and time-wasting nature of advocacy resolutions. Their complaints, however, didn't stop Bridges from introducing one more resolution, this one demanding the closure of all "fink halls" — hiring halls ostensibly run by unions but in reality controlled by employers — to be replaced by hiring halls run by the ILA. It was a brilliant move. Conservative delegates, relieved to vote on an issue directly related to longshore work, forgot about Joe Ryan's proposal, which made no mention of abolishing the shape-up.

The resolution passed without debate.

On the third day of the convention, the entire delegation was gathered in the main auditorium to hear Henry Melnikow deliver a report on the final version of the maritime industry codes, now on President Roosevelt's desk and ready for his signature. I interviewed Melnikow many times when he represented the ILA Pacific Coast District at the code hearings, and found him to be honest and straightforward.

He began by saying that the proposed maritime codes called for an arbitration board, as Joe Ryan and the shipping companies had requested, and made no mention of union-run hiring halls. This was disturbing enough. Then he dropped a bombshell that took everyone by surprise. Taking off his glasses, he leaned on the podium and said, "None of this matters because the maritime codes will never be enacted."

A hush descended on the delegation. Men who barely had been paying attention or had been conversing with others were now looking at Melnikow with stunned expressions.

"The reason for this," said Melnikow, "is that eighty-five percent of ships calling on U.S. ports are of foreign registry and will not be bound by the maritime codes. Roosevelt is unlikely to support codes that put the American shipping industry at a disadvantage."

In the moments that followed, conservative delegates sat in glum silence, while Bridges, who never believed the codes were going to make a difference, wore a knowing smile.

Some delegates expressed the hope that despite Melnikow's report a walkout could be avoided. To that end, a negotiating committee was formed to meet with the Waterfront Employers Association.

Bridges and the Resolutions Committee drew up a list of demands beginning with recognition of the ILA and a deadline of March 7th, by which time if favorable consideration were not given, the ILA Pacific Coast District would take a strike vote within ten days.

By this time I had pages and pages of notes to draw from, yet one overriding fact was clear: we are now one step closer to a waterfront strike involving every port on the West Coast.

44

Members of the ILA negotiating committee filed into the conference room at the Waterfront Employers Association. Thomas Plant and Roger Farnsworth greeted them and offered them seats on the opposite side of the table. At the far end of the table, notepad and pen at the ready, Clarisa McMahon watched the negotiators sit down. None of them were familiar to her until the last person entered the room and took a seat. And he was the last person she expected to see.

Nick Benson looked healthy and strong, his light blue eyes a stark contrast to his tanned face. She suppressed a natural instinct to acknowledge his presence, and he ignored her as well. *What's he doing here?* she wondered. *He's only been at the waterfront for five months. It doesn't make sense that he'd be a negotiator.* Roger hadn't acknowledged him either, but that didn't mean anything. Nick would have warned him that he'd be attending. Then she noticed he was carrying a notepad and pen. Perhaps he was there to take notes too. Whatever the reason, she would have to ignore him, although she couldn't stop herself from glancing at him from time to time.

Plant started off by introducing himself and his assistant, his manner polite and warm as if he was chatting among friends. Clarisa was surprised by this. Through the door to Roger's office she heard them talking loudly before the meeting. She hadn't caught every word, but she did hear Plant exclaim, "I don't give a damn if they do threaten to strike. We've got a war chest that will outlast every man jack of them!"

John Bjorkland introduced himself as the ILA Pacific Coast District Secretary and announced that all West Coast longshoremen were now organized within the ILA and prepared to bargain collectively.

Plant grinned at him like a Cheshire cat, all teeth and no warmth. "Our organization only represents the port of San Francisco. We can't possibly negotiate on behalf of employers at other ports."

Bjorkland, a large man with a bulbous nose and big ears, scratched his head. "I was given to understand that employers are organized up and down the coast like East Coast shippers."

Plant again insisted he couldn't speak for other ports.

Clarisa found this odd. A significant portion of her boss's time was spent conferring with shippers from other West Coast ports, who often junketed to San Francisco for meetings and to soak up the city's nightlife.

"As a practical matter," Bjorkland persisted, "it makes sense for representatives from all ports to sit down together, so's we can settle our differences all at once. Can't the Waterfront Employers Association arrange for other ports to participate in negotiations?"

Plant launched into a convoluted answer that was so long and confusing Clarisa couldn't follow it, and it seemed as if he was purposely erecting a barricade of meaningless words to fend off the request. He ended by asking the committee to lay out exactly what the ILA wanted.

"Full recognition and a coastwise contract," Bjorkland replied.

"That's a closed shop. Section 7(a) of the NRA doesn't permit a closed shop."

"Not in every case. Closed shop contracts are allowed under NRA rules when both sides agree. The United Mine Workers contract is exclusive, and so are the preferential agreements between the ILA and shipping companies on the East Coast."

Plant denied any knowledge of those arrangements and insisted that, anyway, it wouldn't work on the West Coast. When Bjorkland remarked that the Blue Book Union had enjoyed a closed shop agreement, Plant deftly turned the point around and argued that the ILA had objected to the closed shop agreement with the Blue Book Union, in fact walked off the Matson Docks because of it, but now was asking for one for itself. Before Bjorkland could respond, he said, "I have information that there were *sixteen* Communists among the delegates to the Rank and File Convention."

Roger had mentioned to Clarisa that a number of delegates were members of a radical group that met at a beer hall on Valencia Street and that the group had received advice from Sam Darcy, a known Communist and labor organizer. How he learned this information he didn't say, although she suspected Nick was the source. At any rate, Roger never said that members of the group were Communists themselves.

Everyone in the room was speechless, though their expressions were revealing. Bjorkland's brow was furrowed, as if the remark had taken him by surprise, Nick was shaking his head, and Roger was staring at Plant with a look of incredulity.

After a moment of stunned silence Nick spoke up. "I don't know where you got that information, but it isn't true."

Plant frowned at him, and for the next few seconds while the room remained silent, Clarisa wondered whether Plant knew that Nick was working for his assistant. And if he did know, he must be wondering why his spy was openly challenging him. *Will it prompt him to say something in anger that might expose Nick?*

Plant opened his mouth to speak. At the same time a look of fear came over Nick's face, as if he, too, was wondering if Plant was about to blurt out an incriminating remark.

"Who the hell are you, young man?"

Nick swallowed. "Nick Benson."

Plant's eyes widened, and it seemed to Clarisa that until this moment Plant knew Nick's name but not his face. She glanced at the other longshoremen to see if they picked up on Plant's reaction. They were looking at him, but as far as she could tell, they hadn't connected the dots. At least not yet.

Keeping his eyes on Nick, Plant said, "I'm warning you." Then he shifted his gaze to other the longshoremen. "I'm warning all of you. The ILA had better clean up its ranks or the employers will never negotiate with you."

Plant didn't stop there. He continued to hurl attacks and accusations, one after another like a politician on the warpath. Under this barrage of criticism, the longshoremen slumped in their seats like battle-weary boxers who know their effort is destined to fail. Clarisa couldn't help but feel sorry for them. Optimistic when they entered, they now appeared stymied by Plant's hostility and his take-no-prisoners attitude.

When the attacks ended, a longshoremen with large gnarled hands and a gravelly voice spoke up. He described the long hours and dangerous conditions the men endured, the injuries they sustained. Talking in simple terms that a child could understand, he described their desire for a safe and stable workplace and a living wage. Clarisa was moved by his heartfelt assertions and certain that this plain-spoken fellow, with hands of clay and tongue of wood, made more sense than all the others combined.

Unmoved, Plant remained adamant that he wouldn't negotiate with the ILA now or for the foreseeable future.

When the meeting ended, the longshoremen walked out in dejected silence. Nick was the last to leave, and on his way out he glanced at Clarisa, his expression blank and inscrutable. It was impossible to interpret, yet she felt certain he was deeply disappointed. And no wonder. Plant had treated them as if they were a pack of worthless rabble-rousers.

"So that was our man Benson, eh?" said Plant. "He did a good job of pretending he's one of them. I almost kicked him off the payroll. Anyway, I think we handled that well." He glanced at Roger. "Even so, I want you to contact our members and set up a meeting with the mayor. We'll need to prepare for a strike just in case."

Roger stared vacantly at the opposite wall, seemingly lost in thought. He shifted his gaze to Plant. "This was probably your last chance to avoid a walkout. And you humiliated them."

Plant stiffened. "If we don't stand up to them, it won't be long before they dictate what color socks we wear. Our job is to protect our members. Giving in to the ILA would be suicide."

"Has it occurred to you that you offered them no option but to strike, not even a bread crumb to take back to their members?"

"Let them eat cake," Clarisa muttered, as she collected her notes and rose to leave.

"What?" asked Plant.

Roger shot an irritated glance at her. "That will be all Miss McMahon." He turned back to Plant. "By the way, how did you determine there were *sixteen* Communists at the convention?"

"Oh, that. I had to give them some number to make my information sound credible."

45

Everywhere he looked, he saw gold. Gold satin drapes, gold-plated chandeliers, rococo chairs covered in gold leaf, Corinthian columns painted to look like gold travertine. Even the carpet had swirling gold arabesque designs. Constructed during the Roaring 20s when money was no object, the building was furnished in the opulent style of a Louis XV palace. Now, in these lean times, it was hard to believe that anyone would spend so lavishly on a movie theater. Nick pushed through a pair of upholstered swinging doors and stepped onto a balcony overlooking an immense screen bordered with life-sized gilded statues. The Fox Theater was a cavernous, monstrous place, so large you could get lost in it.

And, thus, ideal for a clandestine meeting.

Images on the screen illuminated the theater enough for him to find an unpopulated area. He sank down onto a velvet-covered seat and watched the opening credits scroll up the screen. He hadn't come to see the movie, but it was a relief to take a break from the outside world, if only for a little while. All week he'd been thinking about the meeting at the Waterfront Employers Association. It had taken every ounce of self-control he possessed to suppress the jealousy he felt when he saw Clarisa in the same room with Roger Farnsworth. He longed to hold her, to feel her close, and seeing them together had only intensified his longing. At the same time he was painfully aware that she was on Farnsworth's team and that they were seeing each other and perhaps were lovers. The thought made him nauseous.

He was also disturbed by Thomas Plant's hostile accusations. Farnsworth had promised the longshoremen that if they demonstrated a preference for Local 38-79 over the Blue Book Union, the employers would negotiate with them. That, it turned out, was a lie.

The sound of footfalls padded from somewhere behind him. A moment later Farnsworth emerged from the shadows and sat down beside him, ignoring him as if they were strangers.

In recent weeks their meetings had been a cat-and-mouse game, with Roger asking probing questions while Nick offered generalized accounts, revealing enough to satisfy his interrogator, though not enough to implicate individuals. On this day Roger remained strangely silent. He stared at the screen, absorbed in the movie as if that and not their meeting was why they were here. Nick wanted the interrogation to begin, wanted to get it over with, but he too became engrossed in the story on the screen. Entitled *Employees' Entrance*, it was about an attractive, though financially desperate, young woman played by Loretta Young, who slept with the boss to land a department store job. She later became romantically involved with another employee, and the two had to hide their relationship to protect their jobs.

Although the plot was mildly interesting, Nick began to feel nervous. It was risky to meet in person, even in a darkened theater, and seeing a movie wasn't worth the chance of being discovered.

It was time to get the ball rolling.

"How are things at the work?" he asked.

Roger didn't answer.

After a few minutes Nick asked another question, and it too was met with silence. He had no idea what was going on and was about to write off the meeting as a waste of time when Roger let out a lengthy, dispirited sigh that sounded like the death throes of a mortally wounded beast.

What would cause such distress? Can something have gone wrong between him and Clarisa? Even the remote possibility piqued his interest.

"Do you want to talk about it?" he asked gently.

Roger remained silent for a moment, then said, "There's going to be a strike, right?"

It wasn't the answer Nick was looking for, but at least his interrogator was talking. "We're going to vote on it next week."

"When the strike begins, the identity of the *Waterfront Worker* staff won't be a priority. Since you've managed to avoid completing that assignment for the last three months, I'm sure you won't mind. But don't think that lets you off the hook. In fact, we'll need your eyes and ears more than ever. And you'd better produce or, I assure you, Plant will lower the boom." Roger cast a sidelong glance at Nick with an expression that showed he meant business. "We'll want to know who the strike leaders are and what they're planning. If there's some sort of leadership committee, we want you on it and a full report of every meeting. You've been working on the waterfront long enough, it shouldn't be hard to finagle a good position. Understood?"

"Yeah, understood."

Nick wondered if he should tell Roger about the anonymous phone call. It was never far from his thoughts, especially when he walked alone at night or passed a group of husky longshoremen. And when someone at work or at a union meeting looked at him for more than a moment, he averted his eyes, then glanced back at them to see if they were still watching him.

On weekends he continued to search the *Diana Dollar*, scouring her from the depths of the engine room to the top of the midship house. His numerous visits even prompted Lenny Dross to ask if he was looking for a pirate's treasure. What else, Dross wondered aloud, would motivate him to spend so many hours aboard an empty freighter. Still, there were dozens of compartments left to investigate and Nick estimated it would take at least four more trips to complete the search. It also raised the question: what if he failed to find the opium? He couldn't foretell the future, but if that was the case, he might be better off if he quit working for Farnsworth and turned himself in to the authorities. With a strike on the horizon, the union would be on the lookout for spies, and if they found any . . . Well, it was best not to think about it.

"Oh, by the way," said Roger, "wasn't your ship the *Diana Dollar*?"

"Yeah. Why?" Nick asked, more eagerly than he meant to.

Roger gave him a curious glance. "You still believe narcotics are onboard?"

Nick felt his cheeks flush. *There damn well better be or I'm screwed.* Then it occurred to him that Roger wouldn't care, and he certainly didn't want to give his interrogator the satisfaction of knowing how desperate he felt. "So what about her?" he asked as casually as he could.

"Dollar has offered her services. If the men go on strike, we'll tow her to the Embarcadero to house replacement workers so they won't have to cross any nasty picket lines."

This changed everything. Nick had always assumed he'd be able to search the freighter as many times as needed and for as long as needed. Now it appeared that time was running out, and if he didn't find the narcotics soon, he might never find it.

46

As the days passed, Harry Bridges exerted an increasing influence over Local 38-79. He was a master strategist, Nick now realized, who made moves that appeared insignificant at the time but in retrospect were brilliantly calculated. The first of these was the formation of a Publicity Committee, a subcommittee of Local 38-79's executive board. Most of the committee members belonged to the Albion Hall group, and as their first order of business they elected Bridges chairman.

Wasting no time, the Australian made his next move. The ILA Pacific Coast District had just held an election to decide whether the District should hold a strike vote if the employers refused to negotiate. "I want you to draw up leaflets," he said to the committee, "announcing a special meeting to discuss the results of the election."

"Does the Publicity Committee have the authority to call a special meeting?" Nick asked. "I thought only the president could do that."

"Don't worry about Lee Holman. Once the leaflets are printed and distributed, he won't dare cancel the meeting."

Three days later, as Bridges predicted, two-thousand longshoremen packed the Labor Temple auditorium. Lee Holman stood behind the podium, frowning, obviously not pleased to be there. He called the meeting to order and introduced Pacific Coast District President Bill Lewis, who formally announced the election results. The resolution to hold a strike vote if the employers refused to negotiate had passed by a margin of six to one.

The reaction was swift. The men leap to their feet, cheering and clapping, giving themselves a standing ovation, and from that moment the meeting took on a life of its own. Though Holman still held the gavel, he was losing control of the membership like a head whose body is working independently. Bridges, on the other hand, appeared confident, and at his signal an Albion Hall lieutenant offered a resolution to create a fifty-member Strike Committee to organize and direct things in the event of a walkout.

Holman questioned the need for an additional committee when an Executive Committee already existed to direct the affairs of the local. He pounded the gavel and called the motion out of order but was interrupted by multiple voices, all demanding that Bridges be given a chance to speak. The voices were loud and boisterous, preventing Holman from continuing, and they went on until he laid down the gavel.

The room fell mute as Bridges rose to his feet. In his usual succinct manner he described the vital functions the Strike Committee would fulfill, organizing dock committees, negotiating with employers, communicating with other locals, and running the day-to-day operations of the strike. "If the strike is to be successful," he concluded, looking directly at Holman, "it needs an organizing body dedicated *without reservation* to its success." This last remark hung in the air, and in the silence that followed Bridges and Holman glared at each other like two prizefighters ready to duke it out. Everyone present, including Nick, was mesmerized by the tension, and for a pregnant moment time stood still as the two men engaged in a silent battle of wills.

For reasons he didn't fully understand, perhaps to curry favor with Bridges, Nick felt compelled to break the logjam. He rose to his feet and in a loud voice seconded the proposal. Henry Schmidt immediately sprang up behind him and called for a vote before Holman could table the motion.

The tension now severed, loud applause erupted, especially from Albion Hall men who jumped up and whooped and hollered and clapped their hands. Holman hesitated, his eyes roving nervously over the men, whose ovation continued unabated in a show of support. Nick could see that Holman wanted to resist, wanted to bring the meeting to an end, and when his arm lifted the gavel, it was slow and stiff as if some unseen force was moving it against his will. The gavel paused for a long moment . . . then came down onto the podium with a bang, quieting the auditorium. In a barely audible voice, he said, "All those in favor of a Strike Committee, say aye?"

"*Aye!*" an affirmative chorus exclaimed.

"All those opposed?"

The silence that followed was as decisive and powerful as an 8.0 earthquake. It swirled through the auditorium, drawing the men together, galvanizing them toward a common destiny they could only imagine.

After the meeting a throng of well-wishers followed Bridges out of the Labor Temple and crowded around him, asking questions and offering comments. Nick and Henry Schmidt waited nearby. When the crowd thinned and Bridges looked ready to break away, they tugged on his sleeve and motioned to him to join them for their usual Thursday night pint at The Albion.

At a back table Nick, Bridges, Schmidt, Pirate Larsen, and Dutch Dietrich swigged beers and savored their victory.

"Did you see Holman's face when the strike vote was announced?" Schmidt chortled. "God, I thought he'd spit fire and sling thunderbolts."

"He's history now," said Dietrich, grinning. "Tomorrow night we'll elect Harry chairman of the Strike Committee and after that Holman'll be irrelevant. I gotta hand it to you Harry, you really cooked his goose."

Bridges shrugged. "All I did was expose him for what he is: a labor faker who's hangin' on the coattails of Joe Ryan and standin' in the way of a democratic union. There's nothin' more rotten than a dictator who pretends to be a man of the people. Mark my words, Holman will be gone in less than two months. Even the conservatives are beginnin' to realize he's a liability." He turned to Nick. "Once again you stepped in at a crucial moment. You seem to have a flair for the dramatic. You sure you're not an actor?"

Startled by the partial accuracy of the question, Nick felt as if his innermost being had been exposed, as if Bridges could see inside him. He studied Bridges to see if his fears were well-founded, but the Aussie's expression gave no hint as to whether the question was an innocent comment or a subtle probe. The truth was, Nick had been an actor in collegiate theater, playing a minor role in Oscar Wilde's *The Importance of Being Earnest* and a lead role in Carlo Goldoni's *Servant of Two Masters*. He enjoyed performing and being part of a cast, enjoyed the laughter and applause. But rehearsals and performances left little time for other studies, so he gave it up after a couple of semesters. Now, as it turned out, the experience was useful in his current situation.

"I tried my hand at acting," he said with all the nonchalance he could muster, " but I bumbled around so much everyone said I looked more Buster Keaton than Clarke Gable."

Bridges chuckled. "Well, you certainly have impeccable timing. By the way, how'd you like to serve on the Strike Committee?"

"As representative of my dock?"

"Nope. I'll have a million details to take care of when the strike begins, and I'll need a smart assistant who I can trust to handle some of the errands and chores. Interested?"

Nick scratched an imaginary itch on his neck to give himself time to think. Being Bridges' assistant was exactly what Roger wanted him to do. It would allow him to attend important meetings and be privy to inside information. At the same time, though, a wary voice inside warned: *it's too good to be true*. On the other hand, if he refused it might put him in jeopardy with Bridges, who wouldn't understand his reluctance, and also with Plant, who would send him to jail if he wasn't in a position to supply information. Moreover, he needed more time to locate the hidden cache on the *Diana Dollar*.

Concealing his ambivalence, he smiled. "It would be an honor, sir."

Harry wagged his finger. "Now, look here, I've told you not to call me that. I'm nobody's sir. We're all in this together and everyone's gotta do his part. Are you're with me?"

"All the way."

The next evening Nick attended the Strike Committee's first meeting at Local 38-79's headquarters on Steuart Street, just a around the corner from the waterfront. The ILA office was minimally furnished with a few desks, some folding chairs, a couple of file drawers, a bulletin board, and the ILA's navy blue flag tacked on a wall. There weren't enough chairs for the entire Strike Committee, so men sat on desks or stood against the wall.

Henry Schmidt called the meeting to order and asked the committee to elect a chairman. Since the committee was Bridges' idea, he was the first to be nominated, and when no one else offered to run, he was elected without debate.

Wearing old work clothes, a white flat-cap, and a cargo hook dangling from his belt loop, Bridges stood up to address the men. He wasn't wearing his usual attire but was dressed, Nick suspected, more for dramatic effect than any practical reason. He began pacing back and forth, his hands slicing the air as he outlined a plan to prepare for a strike. His words came in rapid-fire sentences and his thick Australian accent made them nearly unintelligible, yet they were inspiring nonetheless. It was another fine performance, as much for style as content, and by the time he finished Nick was sure that everyone there was prepared to follow him to the gates of Hell if necessary.

Hurried footsteps clambered up the stairs leading to the ILA office.

The door burst open and Pacific Coast District President Bill Lewis rushed in waving a telegram, NRA administrator George Creel close behind him. The telegram, Lewis announced, was from President Roosevelt. Creel had wired him, warning of an imminent waterfront strike along the entire West Coast. The president had wired back, asking the Pacific Coast District to call off the strike while he appointed a mediation board to help settle the dispute. Under the circumstances, Lewis explained, he'd taken the liberty to cancel the strike and had secured an agreement from the Waterfront Employers Association to meet and discuss the issues.

Creel added his own warning: "If you men go on strike there's liable to be violence. Some of you are liable to be injured, and some of you are liable to be killed. I urge you to delay it."

The committee members looked to Bridges. His expression was blank, concealing any indication of his thoughts about this sudden development. When Lewis followed their gaze, Bridges nodded toward a back office. The two men left the room and conferred for several minutes. When they returned, Bridges announced his support for a delay of the walkout to allow the mediation board time to see if it could settle the issues. The Strike Committee, however, would continue its work to prepare for a walkout in the event mediation was unsuccessful.

After the meeting Nick asked Bridges what convinced him to go along with the delay. Harry ignored him, and only when Nick pressed further did he reveal the terms. An old fashioned horse swap was how he put it: his support for a mediation board for the ouster of Holman.

"It's politics," he said curtly, as if no other explanation was needed.

This was the first time Nick saw the cold, calculating side of Bridges, and it bothered him until he realized that, besides being a charismatic leader, Bridges was an expert tactician. He could orate passionately one minute and make decisions like a chess master the next, be a hard-nosed negotiator or an inspiring general. Nick resisted the temptation to put him on a pedestal. But the more he worked with Bridges the more he was eager to please him, and the more he felt honored when Harry complimented him, even in an offhand manner. Bridges was unlike anyone he'd ever met. Material things seemed to mean nothing to him, acquiring objects a distasteful addiction. His world was one of ideas and ideals, not locked away in an ivory tower but skillfully applied to real situations in the real world.

Three days later Roger Farnsworth and Thomas Plant attended the mediation board hearing in the California State Building on McAllister Street. Although Farnsworth hoped otherwise, he didn't expect much would be accomplished. Plant had said many times he didn't see why the employers needed to compromise on any of the issues and didn't see any point in discussing them. They were only there so they wouldn't appear to be uncooperative.

The hearing proceeded as Farnsworth expected, that is until ILA Pacific Coast District President Bill Lewis appeared before the board and took a more conciliatory stance than previous ILA delegations. He expressed flexibility on the hiring hall issue and a willingness to arbitrate all others.

This seemed to offer a ray of hope.

Farnsworth, Plant, and Lewis met later that day at the Waterfront Employers Association office to see if they could hash out an agreement. Lewis again expressed flexibility and this softened Plant as well. As a result, Plant agreed to recognize the ILA as the majority union while still retaining the option to negotiate with other longshore unions. He also accepted, in principle, a hiring hall system but made no commitment as to how it would operate. On one issue, however, he remained adamant. The Waterfront Employers Association would negotiate only for the port of San Francisco. Agreements with other ports would have to be made on a port-by-port basis.

Roger wrote up Plant's new positions and delivered them to the mediation board. On balance he thought it was major shift that might bring the two sides together.

The mediation board agreed.

On April 3rd the board presented a settlement incorporating Plant's positions. The longshoremen would hold elections to establish representation and then begin port-by-port negotiations on wages, hours, and conditions. A hiring hall would be established, although details on how it would be run would be negotiated. If negotiations deadlocked the two sides would appeal to a local mediation board, followed, if necessary, by arbitration before a Federal board. As such, a strike would be unnecessary.

One of the mediators, Judge Charles Reynolds, admitted it was just a start and suggested the two sides shake hands and make it a gentleman's agreement. "After all," he said, motioning Plant and Lewis together, "agreements must be founded on faith and good will."

Like two schoolboys involved in a playground scuffle, the men dutifully shook hands.

Later that day, in a back office at Local 38-79, Harry Bridges cussed like a sailor. Nick had never seen him so angry and didn't know how to respond. Bridges was going on at length about the Plant-Lewis settlement, which he said, "violated every fuckin' resolution approved at the Rank and File Convention." When he finally calmed down, he ordered Nick to compose an article condemning the "phony agreement."

Nick got to work on it right away, and three days later the *Waterfront Worker* hit the streets with a banner headline reading: SELLOUT.

At the April ILA meeting the mood was feisty and cantankerous, the men clearly unhappy with the settlement. For his part Nick was gratified to see that his words had had a palpable effect and that the men now understood the full ramifications of the Lewis-Plant settlement. After the minutes were read and approved, Bill Lewis stepped to the podium with a sheepish grin. In a lame attempt to lighten the mood, he waved the agreement over his head and exclaimed, "Well, here's the damned thing I sold you out for."

No one laughed.

Pirate Larsen stood up, his eye-patched face scornful. "Is the *damned thing* even signed?"

"No, it's a gentlemen's agreement."

An explosion of laughter and ridicule filled the hall, the men waving their caps up and down as if to bat down the agreement.

For the next fifteen minutes longshoremen fired heated questions at Lewis, whose answers were vague and evasive, leaving everyone in an uneasy mood. When Lewis retreated from the podium, he was replaced by Harry Bridges, who summarized the progress the union had made during the last several months. "First and foremost," he said, "we formulated a solid platform at the Rank and File Convention, a platform everyone agreed is not subject to arbitration." He then read a telegram from the Portland ILA local expressing dissatisfaction with the "Frisco settlement." He concluded, "If we don't stick to our guns now, we stand little chance of succeeding in arbitration."

Bridges left the podium, making way for Bill Lewis and Joe Johnson, acting president of Local 38-79 now that Holman was gone. They pleaded with the men to give the leadership more time to negotiate. "Once we walk out," Lewis warned, "there's no turning back."

The warning hung in the air like a storm cloud, subduing the men into silence.

Johnson proposed a motion to extend negotiations ten more days, and although a grumbling impatience pervaded the hall, the motion passed.

47

The negotiating sessions were long and tedious, often dwelling on minor work rules while leaving major issues unresolved. Clarisa was there taking notes, and it seemed to her that Thomas Plant took an unnecessarily hard line, perhaps angry that his settlement with Lewis had been rejected. Privately, she overheard him complaining to Roger that radicals had infiltrated the ILA, and he would be "goddamned if he'd give them an inch. Even if a strike costs us ten million dollars, it'll be worthwhile if it means ridding the waterfront of their kind." Union officials were equally stubborn, insisting they would accept no less than a six-hour day, a dollar an hour, a union-run hiring hall, and a coastwise contract.

To keep negotiations going, the two sides drank gallons of coffee and puffed cartons of cigarettes, breaking only for short periods at the beginning of each hour while Clarisa emptied ashtrays and refilled cups. As negotiations progressed, she noticed Roger sinking deeper within himself, slowly withdrawing from the proceedings. It worried her. Their personal contact had dropped off precipitously since the Christmas party, and she felt him retreating from her at work too. Some mornings he arrived at the office bleary-eyed, clothes disheveled, as if he'd been out all night. Plant also noticed the change and berated him for his appearance, so she contacted his dry cleaners and had them send several suits to the office, where she kept them for emergencies.

At the end of the ten-day extension period, Clarisa had a dozen legal pads filled with notes but no significant breakthroughs. Looking at them, she shook her head sadly. All that talk and the two sides were still no closer to settling the major issues than when negotiations began.

A rainstorm pounded the Labor Temple as longshoremen packed into the auditorium to hear the results of negotiations. One after another union negotiators offered excuses for the lack of progress and promised results if given additional time. While the speakers droned on, the men listened in silence, faces blank, no trace of the fire and enthusiasm at the previous meeting. As time passed they slumped lower and lower in their seats, their mood made all the worse by the dreary weather outside.

Nick glanced at Harry Bridges, wondering if he would jump into the breach. Sure enough, after the negotiators were finished the Aussie rose to his feet, producing a hush over the auditorium as all eyes focused on him, all ears attentive.

"The negotiations are convoluted rigmarole," he said, "a ploy by the employers to give themselves time to prepare for a strike. Our demands all boil down to a few clear-cut issues, and further negotiations will only strengthen the employer's hand and put us at a disadvantage."

Bridges continued in this vein until Bill Lewis unexpectedly jumped up and blurted out, "You and your comrades are dragging us into an ill-advised strike for no other purpose than to advance your radical agenda."

Unfazed by the interruption, Bridges replied, "I see you want to wave a Red paintbrush to make your point. Well, everyone knows that name calling is the last resort of a weak argument."

Chuckles flitted across the hall.

Lewis pointed a finger at him. "God damn you!"

Howls of protest erupted at the coarse insult, too much even for seasoned longshoremen.

When the clamor subsided, Bridges continued, "Lewis says I'm dragging an entire union behind me. Well, I have no illusions of such power." His eyes swept across the room. "The real power rests with you, the rank-and-file. It's your decision whether you want to stay mired in fruitless negotiations or take an unequivocal stand for your rights as workers, as husbands, as fathers, as men. You don't need me to tell you what you want." He pointed to the negotiators. "And you don't need them either.

You already know what you want. And now it's time to act on it. I believe in a democratic union. If you decide to hold off, so be it, but if you decide to move forward and make a stand, you'll be taking the first step toward meeting the foe head-on and transforming yourselves from wharf rats to lords of the dock."

A score of Albion Hall men jumped to their feet, applauding enthusiastically; the rest, following their lead, roared with approval.

Joe Johnson banged the gavel and proposed a motion aimed at satisfying both sides. "Negotiations will continue until May 7th, by which time if our demands are not met, we'll pull the pin."

Thunderous applause filled the auditorium.

Caught up in the excitement and fervor, Nick applauded as well, and it seemed to him that the men had taken a decisive step and crossed the Rubicon into a territory from which it would be difficult if not impossible to retreat.

48

The sun rose above the East Bay hills, painting a gold patina on the bay, its surface calm and smooth as honey. Nick loaded Rusty and his rucksack into a rowboat. He was fully prepared to spend the entire day and the next, if necessary, aboard the *Diana Dollar*, as this weekend might be his last opportunity to board her before she was moved to the waterfront to house replacement workers. He rowed to the opposite side of the freighter and squeezed the dinghy between the *Diana Dollar* and the adjacent ship. It took a moment for his eyes to adjust to the shady niche, and when they did he was surprised to see that the rope ladder was gone, presumably removed when someone came to inspect the ship. He pondered the situation and saw no other choice but to borrow another ladder.

A few minutes later he approached Lenny Dross's shack and knocked on the door. It took several more knocks before he heard stirring noises and footsteps shuffling across the floor.

"Whaddaya want?" a sleepy voice answered.

Nick apologized for disturbing him so early and asked to borrow a hook and rope ladder.

The door creaked open.

Lenny was dressed in a torn singlet and boxer shorts. "I was gonna tell you I saw a party board her last week. There's been activity every day since then. Looks like they're dressin' her up for somethin'." He eyed Nick curiously. "Still haven't found your pirate's treasure?"

"Nope."

"Well, I don't have another rope ladder, but I do have plenty of rope. You'll have to shinny up, but I expect a young fella like you can manage."

Lenny slipped on a pair of sandals and led Nick to an equipment shed. In short order he presented him with a grappling hook and a coil of rope. "Now, I'm only loanin' ya this 'cause I want the rope ladder back."

Nick thanked him and hurried off.

When he reached the freighter, he tied the dinghy to the anchor chain, then secured the rope to the grappling hook. The rope was lighter than the rope ladder, and on his first try he was able to toss the hook over the railing and onto the weather deck. He snagged the hook on the railing, picked up the rucksack, and was about to swing it over his shoulder when Rusty barked and wagged his tail against the side of the dinghy — *thump, thump, thump.*

"Whatsamatter, boy?" He bent over and stoked the dog's head. "Tired of being left alone."

Rusty barked again and whined.

"Whatta you expect me to do? Put you in my rucksack and carry you up?"

Rusty's tail sped up and he licked Nick's hand.

It really wasn't fair to leave him alone on weekdays while he worked and then leave him in the boat on weekends as well. "OK, boy, let's give it a try." He set the rucksack down, picked up the mutt, and carefully wedged his hind quarters into the sack until only his front legs and head poked out the top. Hoisting the rucksack onto his back, he grasp the rope and pulled himself up hand-over-hand while gripping the anchor chain between his legs. Even with the extra weight it wasn't difficult, and he was able to pull himself up to the top and scramble over the railing.

For the rest of the morning he searched the engine room a second time, a difficult task as it was crammed with a complex array of pipes, conduits, crank shafts, ventilation tubes, ladders, and steel catwalks. Behind all that there were dozens of access panels, some only a few inches square, others a foot or two wide. During his first search he had passed over the most inaccessible panels, figuring they were unlikely prospects as most hadn't been opened since the ship was constructed. Now he couldn't afford to leave even one unexamined. The work was difficult and time consuming, and more than once he skinned his knuckles trying to loosen a screw in a tight spot.

While Nick struggled with the access panels, Rusty sniffed around the four-story engine room in an aimless fashion. Finding nothing of interest, he curled up near his master and rested his muzzle on his paws, contented to lay there for the rest of the morning, napping and keeping on eye on Nick.

At just before noon he raised his head and growled.

Figuring that Rusty was unaccustomed to the ship's odd creaking noises, Nick ignored him. Then a moment later Rusty rose up on his haunches and let out a bark.

Nick froze and looked up toward the weather deck.

Muffled footfalls and voices echoed from above.

Nick threw his tools into the rucksack and bounded up the stairs to the engine room entrance, Rusty at his heels. He peered out into the passageway. No one there, but the voices and footsteps were drawing closer. He tiptoed toward the entrance to the midship house and looked out through a porthole. The grappling hook was still hanging on the railing. The coast looked clear and he was about to step out of the midship house, when it occurred to him that he hadn't figured out how he was going to retrieve the hook once he'd climbed down to the dinghy. He tried to think of possibilities. Nothing came to him and footsteps were fast approaching.

Then it hit him.

If he tossed the hook into the dinghy, while keeping the rope looped around the railing, he could use the doubled up rope to climb down. Once in the rowboat, he could pull the free end of the rope down through the railing. If all went well, the entire operation would only take a minute. He set the rucksack down, folded the flap back, and stuffed Rusty inside. Hoisting the rucksack up, he slipped it onto his back just as a door on the other side of the midship house opened, prompting Rusty to let out another bark.

He hurried out to the weather deck and pulled the free end of the rope up from the rowboat. The footsteps and voices behind him were growing louder. There was no time to judge whether he'd pulled up enough rope. He grasped the hook and tossed it toward the rowboat. It sailed down toward the dingy, closer and closer to its target. Then suddenly the rope went taut, suspending the hook in midair until it swung toward the ship and banged into it with a loud *clang!*

"Just a minute," a voice behind him said.

A hand gripped his right arm. At the same time he heard Rusty growl, followed by a loud snap.

"Oww, goddamn it!" the voice yelled.

The hand loosened its grip on his arm

Without hesitation Nick grabbed the railing and vaulted over.

The draft from weather deck to waterline was better than thirty feet. He hurtled down, hair standing on end in the updraft. When he hit the water he plunged into the bay, creating a swirl of bubbles around him as if he was swimming in a bottle of green soda pop. He paused to let the water clear and allow his natural buoyancy to stabilize his position.

A growing pressure in his ears was the first indication he was still descending, pulled down by the straps of his rucksack. He tugged at the straps to slip them off, but they resisted and seemed to be caught in his clothes. The water was darkening from dull green to slate gray and the pressure on his eardrums was now a sharp jab. He tried flapping his arms to pull himself up. No good. The stabbing pressure in his ears was getting worse. His shoulder brushed against something. Wildly reaching out, his forearm hit it. He wrapped a hand around what he now realized was the anchor chain. This halted his descent, though he was in near total darkness, his lungs craving air.

Frantically, he tore one strap off his shoulder, then switched hands and removed the other strap. As the pack drifted away, he grasped the chain with both hands and was about to pull himself up when a startling thought broke through his single-minded desire for air. *Rusty!* He reached down and grasped for the rucksack. Nothing, his fingers clutching cold water. Using the chain, he twisted his legs above his head and pulled himself down, the pain in his ears and the urge to inhale nearly unbearable. He kicked twice and reached down again. This time his hand brushed against something soft and floppy. He reached for it and grasped what he hoped was Rusty's ear. With his other hand he reached for the side of the rucksack. He found it and pulled with his first hand until Rusty slid out. Curling an arm around the dog's chest, he took hold of the chain with the other hand and turned himself upright.

Kicking with all his strength, he pulled himself up the chain with his free hand, the pressure in his lungs squeezing against his chest. As he struggled upward the water resisted his efforts, slowing his movements to what seemed like a sluggish crawl. He closed his eyes and continued to kick in the darkness, his leg muscles burning from exertion, his lungs craving oxygen.

He lifted his head toward the surface, and in his mind's eye an image appeared, a glowing, blurry head suspended above him, slowly sharping into focus. Two green eyes, a delicate nose, pink lips. The eyes were looking down at him, sparkling and playful, the corners of the mouth curled up in a pleasant smile, a cloud of auburn hair framed by a halo of light behind it. He followed the image like a homing beacon, and as he continued up the light behind the head glowed brighter and brighter until it washed out the features and all that remained was a round yellow glow.

All at once the light exploded. At the same time his head broke out of the water, a bright sun above him, shining in his eyes.

He sucked in air with ravenous heaves, unable to think of anything but replenishing his lungs with oxygen. When his breathing slowed he examined the dog cradled in his arms. Rusty's eyes were shut, head flopped to one side.

He couldn't tell if his dog was dead or alive.

He swam over to the rowboat, lifted Rusty up over the edge, and placed him on the cross bench. Too large for the narrow bench, Rusty rolled off and slid down to the bottom of the dinghy. Cursing his clumsiness, Nick swam to the stern and pulled himself up into the boat, dripping wet, his chest still heaving. He scrambled over to the prostrate dog, picked him up by his hind legs, and dangled him head down, water dribbling out of his nose and mouth. When Rusty's lungs seemed clear, Nick laid him on the stern bench, the tip of his pink tongue peeking out of his mouth. Mouth-to-mouth resuscitation might revive him, but his long snout looked ill-shaped for the technique.

Perhaps there's another way, he thought.

He pushed the dog's tongue back into his mouth and closed his jaw. Covering Rusty's nose with his own mouth, he blew hard. As he did, Rusty's chest expanded. He pulled away and watched the dog's chest contract, expelling air. He repeated the procedure several more times, and on the sixth try Rusty's eyelids fluttered, his chest heaved . . . on its own.

"That dog's got quite a bite," a voice called down from the ship.

Nick looked up. Three figures were peering down from the railing, the sun directly above them, obscuring their features in shadow and making them looked like two-dimensional cutouts.

"Is he okay?" one of them asked.

Rusty's chest expanded and contracted in a steady shallow rhythm.

"Yeah, I think so," Nick replied, thinking it odd that a few minutes earlier they were trying to capture him and now were inquiring about his dog's condition.

"Is that you, Benson?"

Nick looked up and squinted at the featureless shapes. The voice was familiar but he couldn't quite place it. He stood up and shielded his face with his hands. When his eyes adjusted, he was able to make out a burly figure with an engineer's hat perched on top of its head.

"Haggis?"

"That's right. What the heck are you doin' here?"

"I could ask you the same thing," he said, not eager to answer the question.

"We're checkin' the systems and puttin' 'em in order. I guess they're sendin' her out again."

"I don't think so."

"Oh, yeah? What's up?"

Nick hesitated. Only someone with a connection to the owner would know where she was headed. "I — I heard she has a cracked cylinder."

"Then why're we fixin' 'er up?"

"I dunno."

"So, what're you doin' here?"

Nick looked down at Rusty, now shivering, his wet fur clinging to his body. Nick bent down and stroked his coat to warm him.

"Oooh, I get it," said Haggis. "You're lookin' for somethin'."

There was no need to reply. The crew must have heard that he'd accused Slag and Primm of framing him with a portion of the opium they themselves were smuggling.

"Say, I heard you was in jail. They let you out, huh?"

"Yeah, but the only way I can clear myself is to find the rest of it."

"Well, you better work fast. They want us finished by the end of the day. That's why we're workin' on Saturday." He paused. "Oh, and there's somethin' else. The *President Cleveland* is returning next week."

Nick looked up. "What's that got to do with me?"

"Primm and Slag are on that ship."

Nick slumped down on the bench, wet, weary, and discouraged. He was still certain the opium was somewhere onboard the *Diana Dollar*, but with the ship about to be moved and the bosun returning, his chances of finding it were slipping away. He laid Rusty in the sun, left a bowl of water, and pulled himself back up onto the freighter. Haggis lent him a few tools, and for the rest of the afternoon he continued the search, though his heart wasn't in it. He'd spent dozens of hours going over every square foot of the ship, and now time had run out.

At the end of the day, resigned to defeat, he thanked Haggis and climbed down to the dinghy. Still on his side, Rusty looked up at him listlessly. Even his dog had run out of steam. He rowed back to shore, contemplating the situation. In retrospect, he could see that ever since he left San Francisco a year earlier, his life had been one long descent, propelled by a string of missteps that had stripped him of his girlfriend, his freedom, his integrity, and, last but not least, his self-respect. The phrase *rock-bottom* came to mind, and it was disturbing to know that there was no end in sight. If anything, storm clouds were massing on the horizon, harbingers of a conflict that seemed destined to hold him in its grasp.

PART THREE

FRISCO ILIAD

CHAPTER 49

The atmosphere inside the Labor Temple was thick with excitement. Two-thousand longshoremen were packed into the auditorium, talking excitedly and shifting in their seats like students on the first day of school. Nick sat with Harry Bridges, Henry Schmidt, and the rest of the Albion Hall group, all trading knowing glances. A decision was about to be rendered, and there was little doubt as to the outcome.

Pacific Coast District President Bill Lewis opened the meeting with a report on negotiations with the Waterfront Employers Association. "Despite weeks of effort," he said dejectedly, "no progress has been made on the major issues, nor do I see immediate prospects for a breakthrough."

Joe Johnson, now president of Local 38-79, replaced Bill Lewis at the podium. "In accordance with a decision by the membership at the previous meeting, we will now proceed with a strike vote." All those in favor of going out on strike, say aye?"

"*AYE*," two-thousand voices responded.

"All those opposed?"

Silence.

After the vote the auditorium remained strangely subdued, no cheering or applauding or patting a neighbor on the back, no whooping or hollering or hats tossed in the air. The men had been inching toward this moment for months, and now that it was here they met it with calm determination, ready to face whatever challenges lay ahead.

Nick himself wasn't feeling so self-assured. He'd accepted the inevitability of a strike and the need of longshoremen to stand up for themselves, to fight for a better life for their families. A strike, however, would make his own position infinitely more precarious. The *Diana Dollar* was now out of reach and Farnsworth was demanding information that would require greater risks. As a consequence, for the first time since agreeing to spy on the union, he was convinced that it had been a mistake. A mistake that couldn't be reversed. A mistake that now put him in serious danger.

Every ILA local on the West Coast voted to join the strike. As a result, fourteen-thousand stevedores were set to abandon the docks in Seattle, Tacoma, Grays Harbor, Astoria, Portland, San Francisco, Oakland, Stockton, San Pedro, and San Diego.

That night, laying in bed, Nick wondered how the conflict was going to play out. What was going to happen when strikers and police confronted each other, when hard stares turned into hard knocks. He'd never served in the military, never fought in a war, never engaged in combat, yet now he had an inkling of what a soldier must experience when the tide of history sweeps him toward some unknown, incalculable danger.

The sun peeked over the horizon on the morning of May 9th, casting a fiery reflection on the bay. Roger Farnsworth drove the length of the waterfront and was struck, as never before, by the grim nature of the situation. The Embarcadero, usually bustling with trains and trucks and vans and workers, now resembled a locked-down fortress, ready for battle. The rolling steels doors to the pier sheds were firmly shut, and many were protected with wooden barricades and coils of barbed wire. Police officers armed with riot sticks and pistols stood guard in front of the steel doors, and more officers patrolled the two-mile long Embarcadero on horseback and Harley Davidson motorcycles. Glancing up at a rooftop, he spotted a lookout with binoculars and a field telephone, ready to report movements to radio squad cars roaming the waterfront.

While the police appeared well-prepared for any eventuality, the Waterfront Employers Association still had much work to do. As soon as Roger arrived at the office, he met with Thomas Plant to discuss the recruitment and utilization of replacement workers. It would be a monumental task, requiring some nine-hundred men to work the docks.

Despite the challenges, Plant expressed confidence in their ability to keep cargo moving through the port. "I talked with Police Chief John Quinn," he said. "He's received a $50,000 donation from the Industrial Association to purchase riot gear, teargas grenades, and the guns to propel them. Our members might need workers, but the cops weren't going to let strikers interfere with the ones we do recruit."

To house the replacement workers, Roger made final arrangements to provide the *Diana Dollar*, now berthed at Pier 22, with steaks, beer, ice cream, candy, snacks, linens, games, projector, movies, stewards to run the ship like a first-class hotel, and a water launch to transport them to other piers.

He opened up a copy of the *Chronicle* to check a full-page ad he'd placed in the form of a letter to longshoremen. The employers had agreed, the letter said, to numerous improvements in work rules and had voluntarily raised wages the previous December to 85 cents an hour, an amount within five cents of its all-time high during the Great War. It also called the ILA's demand for a closed shop illegal. His first draft hadn't included this last point because a closed shop wasn't illegal if both sides agreed to it, but Plant had insisted that technically it was correct and ordered him to include it. The letter ended with a warning that employers were now free to hire anyone they wanted. To drive the point home, it included an offer:

LONGSHOREMEN WANTED
Experience Desirable But Not Necessary
Apply at 23 Main Street
85 cents an Hour Straight Time
$1.25 an Hour Overtime
STRIKE CONDITIONS PREVAIL

• • •

Four blocks away at ILA headquarters, Nick, Harry Bridges, and a dozen other Strike Committee members were listening to Pirate Larsen read the same letter.

"Listen to this," said Larsen. "It says the wage issue alone remains to be settled." He looked up. "Are those guys on the level? We've been tellin' 'em for months we want a closed shop, a coastwise contract, and a union-controlled hiring hall. Now they print this garbage." His mouth was contorted in anger, made all the more ominous by his eye-patch. "We aughta burn down their office and run 'em outta town."

Others grunted in approval.

"We'll do nothing of the kind," said Bridges. "If we resort to mob violence we'll be playin' right into their hands. We gotta keep our heads if we're gonna make good decisions. A coupla thousand longshoremen will arrive here soon, ready to confront strikebreakers and armed cops. It's a loaded gun waitin' to go off, and we gotta make sure we don't shoot ourselves in the foot. The first thing we need to do is organize the men into some kind of constructive action."

"How about holdin' a rally in the empty lot across the street?" Dutch Dietrich suggested.

Henry Schmidt shook his head. "We need to keep the men occupied for more than a couple of hours. Frisco's got an anti-picketing ordinance but that don't mean we have to stand by and twiddle our thumbs. We gotta keep our guys busy, give 'em somethin' to do. This business of coming down here and holding an open-air meeting, that won't do."

"We need twenty volunteers to start up a soup kitchen for strikers," said another stevedore. "There's a place down the street that's perfect."

"Good," said Bridges. "You organize that. Now what about the rest of the men?"

Schmidt looked out the window at the Embarcadero, devoid of trucks and jitneys that usually rumbled over the cobbled roadway. "Say, I got it. What about paradin' up and down the waterfront and takin' a soap box along? When we get to the end of the line, someone gets up on it and makes a speech."

Heads nodded.

"Alright, Henry," said Bridges, "you gather the men out front and get 'em organized for a march. And make sure you put our beefiest guys at the front. Larsen, you recruit flyin' squads to scout the waterfront and bring back any information on where strikebreakers are workin' and where police are gathered. And send a squad over to the scab hirin' hall at 23 Main Street. We need to make access to the piers as tough as possible. Understood?"

Pirate Larson wore a tight-lipped grin. "I know just the guys for the job."

"I also need someone to check out a rumor that they've berthed a ship at Pier 22 to house strikebreakers."

He turned to Nick who averted his eyes, hoping Bridges would choose someone else. He'd seen all of the *Diana Dollar* he ever wanted to see. When Bridges continued to stare at him, he knew the request wasn't a request.

"Okay," he said, "I'll check it out and be right back."

The city was quiet, the sidewalks mostly vacant, a moment of calm before commuters streamed out of the Ferry Building. Nick stepped onto the Embarcadero just as a posse of horse mounted officers passed by. The *clop-clop-clop* of their hoof beats seemed especially loud in the absence of locomotives whose hiss and clang usually dominated at this hour. He headed south toward Pier 22 and walked by a transient hotel where men in work clothes stood in the doorway, talking quietly, waiting to see what the day would bring.

He trotted across the Embarcadero and continued south, passing a squad of policemen stationed in front of Pier 18, drinking coffee out of thermos bottles. They nodded as he went by as if it was perfectly natural for them to be guarding the pier, and their friendly manner disarmed him. *Will the strike really lead to violence?* he wondered. It was hard to imagine with a clear sky overhead and a shimmering bay below.

Before he reached Pier 22 he could see something was going on there. The steel door was rolled up and coils of barbed wire flanked each side of the great arched entrance. A makeshift gate connected the barbed wire, behind which stood a half-dozen police officers. Another officer, carrying a clipboard, stood in front of the gate. Nick crouched behind a Model T and watched them. From where he was positioned he could see the *Diana Dollar*'s red and black smokestack, peeking up from behind the pier shed, emblazoned with Dollar's trademark $ sign. He was gazing at the smoke-stack when a black paddy wagon pulled up in front of the gate. The officer with the clipboard opened the back door of the paddy wagon, revealing a dozen pasty-faced men inside, most appearing to be unemployed clerks and college students. The officer checked their identification against a list on his clipboard. Then he signaled another officer who opened the gate and waved the vehicle into the pier shed.

Nick hurried back to ILA headquarters.

When he got there hundreds of strikers were gathered in front of the building, crowding the sidewalk and spilling out onto the street. Henry Schmidt stood on a wooden crate, directing them to form a line. He was flanked by two men holding flagpoles, one bearing the Stars and Stripes, the other the ILA's navy blue flag.

Nick climbed the stairs up to the ILA offices now bustling with activity. Phones ringing, voices calling back and forth, men tramping in and out. At the center of it all, Harry Bridges was conferring with lieutenants and issuing orders to men who rushed off to take care of some detail or other. After Nick reported his findings, Bridges asked him to standby until he had another assignment for him.

With nothing to do for the moment, Nick wandered over to a group of reporters huddled around Bill Lewis and Joe Johnson. They were listening to Lewis explain that despite the strike, negotiations with employers and the mediation board would continue until all issues were resolved. So far,

Nick noted, the press hadn't figured out who was really running the show.

At eight o'clock Bridges called him over. "It's time to move. I want you by my side."

"You're gonna join the march? I thought you'd stay here and —."

"I wouldn't miss it for the world," said Bridges, who for the first time since Nick had known him was in a state of excited anticipation. "The talking is done for now. It's time to show the bosses who's got the real power." In a rare gesture of affection, he put an arm around Nick's shoulder. "We may not have guns or teargas, pal, but we've got guts and passion, and that's a tough combination to beat."

Organized four abreast in a line stretching down Steuart Street, the strikers waited for the signal to proceed, some carrying hand-painted signs saying "Full Recognition for the ILA" and "No Scabs on the Waterfront." Nick and Harry joined the line about a half-block back from the front. A short while later the precession moved forward and turned right down Market Street to the Embarcadero.

In the same place where men usually gathered for the shape-up, longshoremen silently marched across the cobbled boulevard and turned left beside a row of green trolleys parked in front of the Ferry Building. As they crossed the path of commuters now streaming out of the building, some commuters slipped through the line, while others stood and watched the strikers file by. Police had warned the strikers to stay off the sidewalk, so Schmidt led them down the right-hand lane, and since there was little traffic at that hour it created no problems.

Nearly a thousand strong, the strikers marched along the Embarcadero for about a mile until they reached the northern end of the waterfront near Fisherman's Wharf. Stopping in front of the W.R. Grace Line offices, they gathered around Henry Schmidt, who mounted a soap box. Unaccustomed to speaking to a large crowd, he cleared his throat and stammered and stuttered. It was painful to watch, but he persisted until his passion ignited and his tongue caught fire. He denounced the shippers for their intransigence and condemned W. R. Grace Line for employing Negro stevedores as strikebreakers during past strikes, promising that the ILA would no longer tolerate discrimination and allow shippers to drive a wedge between workers of different races. Nick thought the men might not like this idea but they were jacked up and boisterous and cheered loudly, releasing a latent, pent-up energy. Anonymous eyes inside the Grace Line office peeked out from behind Venetian blinds as the men whooped and hollered and shook their fists in the air.

After the speech the strikers lined up behind the flag bearers and headed back down the Embarcadero. A squad of mounted police trailed behind them as they marched past the Ferry Building and continued alongside the great pier sheds. Near the Hills Brothers coffee plant, the aroma of roasted coffee beans scented the air, taking Nick back to his youth when he'd wandered along the waterfront enjoying the rich smell of coffee, the piquant fragrance of cinnamon and nutmeg from the Schilling plant, and the briny odor of Dungeness crab boiling in cauldrons at Fisherman's Wharf. *And never in my wildest dreams would I have imagined myself marching in a line of striking longshoremen, working as a covert spy, and desperate to find a cache of opium.*

Traffic was busier now, forcing vehicles to slow and merge left to maneuver around the strikers. A messenger from the front of the procession came running up to Bridges and reported that a squad of mounted police was stationed a few blocks farther on. The men at the front, he said, wanted to know what to do.

"Keep movin'," Bridges ordered. "We can't stop now. Oh, and tell 'em to move off the road before somebody gets hit by a truck."

Compressing and elongating like a slow-moving centipede, the line lurched forward onto the sidewalk and continued south toward China Basin. When it reached Pier 22, the pier where Nick saw a paddy wagon deliver strikebreakers, longshoremen spontaneously grouped around the barbed wire barricade, waving signs and yelling, "*Scabs off the waterfront!*" The officers behind the barricade, no longer smiling, gripped their billy clubs as they nervously watched the raucous strikers yell and shake their fists. Nick and Harry were standing at the back, keeping an eye on things, when Henry Schmidt pushed his way out of the pack, shaking his head.

"I couldn't stop 'em," he yelled above the clamor. "They know this is where strikebreakers are being kept, and, frankly, I don't blame 'em."

Nick glanced up the street and spotted a paddy wagon turning onto the Embarcadero, heading toward them. When it was a hundred yards off it slowed for a moment, then turned around and sped off before the strikers realized its purpose. He alerted Bridges and Schmidt, who watched it disappear around a bend.

Bridges smiled. "I don't see any harm in lettin' the men blow off a little steam as long as it doesn't get outta hand. And if we prevent scab herders from bringing in strikebreakers" — he shrugged — "all the better."

A clattering rumble joined the din of yelling strikers. Faint at first, it grew louder like the approach of rolling thunder. Nick looked over his shoulder. A half-block away, galloping horses and officers in blue uniforms were charging toward them, reins flapping wildly, billy clubs raised in the air, a forest of clattering hoofs pounding the cobblestones.

"Lookout," he yelled, "here they come!"

Heads swiveled toward the gathering noise.

Strikers closest to the charge shrank back from the horses, but those in the center, wedged in place, were unable to move. A few stevedores bravely stepped toward the attack, ready to take the brunt, yelling at the top of their lungs as if their voices could provide a measure of protection. Just before impact the horses slowed, not to a stop but enough to allow strikers to sidestep them and grab their reins, blunting the charge. One brawny fellow grasped a policeman's arm and yanked him from his saddle. On his way down the officer clubbed the striker on the head, opening a gash and spilling rivulets of blood down his face.

Although the initial impact drove the strikers back, they quickly recovered and surged forward, pulling four more officers off their steeds. Before the strikers could take advantage of their counter attack, another wave of mounted police and motorcycles rammed into them, knocking several men to the ground. They were immediately set upon by other officers who clubbed them with a viciousness that took Nick by surprise.

Reeling from the renewed attack, the men scattered away from the pier and retreated across the Embarcadero. In the confusion Nick and Harry lifted one fallen striker to his feet and helped him cross the boulevard before the police could put him in handcuffs. A dozen others weren't so lucky. From a safe distance, they watched a paddy wagon drive up and stop in front of Pier 22. Policemen opened the paddy wagon's rear door and roughly prodded handcuffed strikers into the vehicle.

Bridges observed the rout with a defiant expression. "The cops think that clubs are trumps, but it's gonna take a lot more than sticks to stop us now."

The paddy wagon sped off and a cordon of officers lined up in front of the pier entrance, shoulder-to-shoulder, forming a solid blue wall.

Bridges turned to leave and motioned Nick to join him.

Nick was about to when he noticed again the *Diana Dollar*'s red and black smokestack, peeking up from behind the pier shed. He was looking at it when a thought suddenly occurred to him, an insight that nearly bowled him over. *Why didn't I think of it before?* He had assumed the bosun wouldn't store the narcotics outside and risk damage from the elements. It wasn't until this moment that he belatedly realized that Slag could have wrapped the opium in oil cloth and secured it to a hook mounted on the inside of the smokestack.

"Don't take it too hard," Bridges said, apparently thinking Nick was lingering because he was discouraged by the attack on the strikers. "It's just one battle. We haven't lost the war."

"What?"

"I said let it go. We've got work to do."

Nick turned and followed Bridges, periodically glancing over his shoulder as they headed toward union headquarters.

Bridges was right. Not only did the defeat at Pier 22 fail to subdue the strikers, it incited them. Nick spent the rest of the day assisting Bridges at ILA headquarters where every few minutes a striker came in to report a new skirmish somewhere along the waterfront. One fellow said that Pirate Larsen's flying squads were doing an effective job hunting down suspected strikebreakers and scaring them off the waterfront. In one case they accosted a man in a car near Pier 32 and ordered him to move along. When he refused they dragged him from his vehicle, pummeled him with fists, and overturned his car.

In another incident, sixty strikers attempted to storm the cargo shed at Pier 17 just as a water launch was delivering strikebreakers. They were trying to break down the door when police arrived in the nick of time to disperse them. Another group of strikers stationed themselves at the hiring hall on Main Street, where they surrounded potential strikebreakers and roughed them up before herding them away.

A pattern eventually emerged. Longshoremen spontaneously gathered to disrupt port operations until officers converged on the scene, at which point the strikers melted away to regroup elsewhere.

50

Despite harassment from strikers and the threat of violence, five-hundred replacement workers were hired on the first day of the strike, nearly all having little or no longshore experience. They were transported to various piers either by armored car or water launch and organized into work groups, supervised by the few experienced longshoremen still willing to work.

Thomas Plant spent most of his time in meetings and negotiations, leaving Roger Farnsworth to manage the day-to-day operations, ably assisted by Clarisa, who put her personal sympathies aside to concentrate on the tasks required to keep port operations going. On the first day of the strike, the awkwardness between them disappeared under an avalanche of urgent responsibilities. They hadn't resumed their old familiarity, but Roger no longer sulked like a wounded puppy and Clarisa supported his efforts in whatever way she could.

The following day they visited the hiring hall on Main Street to assess the labor situation. The hiring boss reported a slowdown in applicants, apparently due to thousands of leaflets dropped from a biplane on working-class neighborhoods, asking residents to support the strike and refrain from working at the waterfront. Still, there were enough applicants to add an additional one-hundred-fifty men to the rolls, among them thirty-five football players from the University of California whose coach was virulently anti-union.

Roger, Clarisa, and the hiring boss were going over the coordination of strikebreakers when a shrill whistle from outside interrupted them. They went to the window and looked out at a group of mounted officers blocking a long line of strikers marching toward the hiring hall. One striker, a fellow with a long pointed nose and receding chin, stepped forward and talked to the officers. Clarisa couldn't make out what he was saying, but the two sides must have come to an agreement because they shook hands and the mounted officers retreated into the street, allowing the marchers to continue forward toward the hiring hall.

Three additional officers stood guard in front of the doorway, although this seemed to be meager protection should the situation get out of hand.

As the strikers filed past the hiring hall, they peered in curiously as if passing an animal cage at the zoo. Some shook their fists, others yelled epithets condemning "scabs" and the "scab herders" who hired them. Clarisa hadn't heard the term *scab* before but had no trouble discerning its meaning, especially as the strikers' faces were contorted into every possible frown imaginable.

It was a chilling experience. Yet her heart went out to them, these men dressed in simple working clothes, shoes scuffed to a dull finish, coats soiled and wrinkled, flat-caps shading weathered faces.

In the long line she noticed the man with the pointed nose, the one who convinced the officers to let the march proceed. He was nodding his head, listening to someone on the far side whom she couldn't see. He slowed down to look into the hiring hall, and in that a moment the man walking beside him came into view also looking in her direction. In an instant their eyes locked and a bolt of recognition flashed between them. Without thinking, her hands reached up to the glass window separating them, her mouth parted in surprise. The pointed-nosed man noticed her abrupt movement, as did others, and he followed her gaze to the man beside him, who looked equally surprised.

For a moment the scene before her resembled a Renaissance painting in which a group of figures is frozen in time, each wearing an expression that betrays his or her thoughts. The moment elongated then snapped shut, and in the next instant the marchers pushed forward, the scene dissolved. She stepped back and turned toward Roger, who was staring at her intently as if he too noticed the silent exchange.

51

Harry Bridges shoved Nick into a private office at union headquarters and confronted him about the hiring hall incident. Nick admitted knowing the woman inside — it was useless to deny — but insisted their relationship had ended a year earlier before she went to work for the Waterfront Employers Association. He suppressed an urge to come clean and admit his affection for her, a confession that would call his loyalty into question. Instead, he claimed his connection with the enemy camp was an inconsequential coincidence, and to further dispel suspicion, he offered to resign his post as Bridges' assistant if the Aussie thought he wasn't trustworthy.

Dutch Dietrich poked his head though the doorway with an urgent request. While Bridges considered the appeal, Nick mulled over a plan he'd been forming that might help the strike and himself. He hadn't intended to broach it quite yet, but under the circumstances it seemed an opportune time to promote his plan and also shore up his standing as a loyal lieutenant.

When Bridges returned from the interruption, Nick pitched his idea. "Employers are using a marine launch to transport scab workers from pier to pier to avoid interruption from strikers. I'm pretty sure I can borrow a few boats and organize a marine picket to harass the operation. It might not stop the delivery of strikebreakers, but it will add pressure and might encourage them to quit. I know a boatyard operator who probably can arrange the whole thing for the cost of fuel."

Bridges nodded approvingly. Just then another head poked through the door with another request. Harry stood up. "I'll think it over and let you know. Meanwhile, I want you to stay on as my assistant where I can keep an eye on you." He cuffed Nick's head affectionately. "Now the next thing I want you to do is organize a visit to Butchertown."

Roger Farnsworth also noticed the hiring hall incident but had no time to dwell on it. Events were unfolding so rapidly and responses required so quickly, he'd had to put his personal life on hold. And that was probably for the best. His crude behavior after the Christmas party was an embarrassment, and to protect himself from further rejection he'd kept Clarisa at arm's length. His affection for her, however, hadn't diminished and, if anything, had grown. Since the strike began she was the rock on which he relied, helping him organize a slew of meetings, planning sessions, press briefings, and communications. He found her especially endearing when she bristled at the intransigence of the negotiators, who, he admitted, were making little headway.

After the demonstration at the hiring hall, he met with Police Chief William Quinn, who advised him to move hiring operations to the Marine Service Bureau on Mission Street. This was several blocks farther from ILA headquarters than the hiring hall on Main Street and also farther from the Matson Building which could become a target if a riot broke out.

Roger was skeptical but agreed. With Clarisa's help he spent an entire day orchestrating the move.

In the end, as he suspected, it was an ineffective maneuver. The next day several hundred strikers staged a rowdy demonstration at Pier 14 where replacement workers were discharging cargo from the *President Cleveland*. The police quickly converged on the scene and beat back the strikers with billy clubs, then chased them away, arresting those who lingered or were too injured to flee. An hour later two hundred angry strikers armed with sticks, lengths of lumber, brickbats, and rocks descended on the Marine Service Bureau. When they spotted policemen standing guard, they hurled a volley of rocks and brickbats, shattering windows and forcing the officers to cower under the onslaught. The strikers, spurred on by their success, rushed forward and engaged officers in hand-to-hand combat until police reinforcements arrived to drive them away. When the melee was over, five policemen were injured, one enough to be hospitalized, and three strikers were treated at Harbor Emergency Hospital for cuts and bruises.

Roger met again with Chief Quinn who was furious.

"I'm forming riot squads armed with teargas guns," said Quinn. "We won't give quarter to rioters any longer."

Roger convinced him that Pier 22 was the safest place to conduct hiring activities, so for the second time in three days, he and Clarisa coordinated the move.

At eleven o'clock that evening he phoned Nick, and both agreed it was too dangerous to meet in person. Pirate Larson's flying squads had been roaming the waterfront, attacking strikebreakers, sometimes stomping on their legs until their bones cracked. If they were to capture a spy, who knows what they would do. Nick reported on talks between the ILA Strike Committee and Mike Casey, head of the San Francisco Teamsters Union. Casey had rejected a sympathy strike but his drivers supported the longshoremen. Consequently, he offered to halt all drayage to and from the waterfront on the pretext it would be too dangerous. An announcement was expected soon.

Nick also reported on meetings between Bridges and representatives of the Sailors' Union of the Pacific, known as SUP. The president of SUP, Andrew Furuseth, was in Washington D.C. and had openly rejected a sympathy walkout, reminding his men that SUP had never fully recovered from an unsuccessful strike in 1921. Local SUP officials, however, disagreed and, Nick warned, would likely announce a walkout in the next few days.

This was troubling news. The Waterfront Employers Association had hired nine-hundred replacement workers, and although most of them had never lifted anything heavier than a BVD strap, discharging cargo from the ships had proceeded nearly on schedule. Stowing was another matter. Safely stowing cargo in a ship's hold required years of experience, and only a few dozen trained men were available. Still, the strike hadn't closed the port by any means. Strikebreakers were discharging and stowing cargo around the clock. However, if sailors walked off the ships and teamsters refused to handle cargo, work at the waterfront could come to a standstill.

Roger thanked Nick for the information and set a date to talk again in a few days. He hung up the phone and lowered his head down on the desk, his mind cluttered with a jumble of worries, recriminations, and urgent things to do. If only he could take a break from this unholy mess. He raised his head off the desk an inch or so, then let it slump back down, his jumbled thoughts fading to black.

The odor of bloody offal and sour brewery wort assaulted them long before Nick and Harry reached Butchertown. Located two miles south of the Embarcadero, the neighborhood received its name from a cluster of slaughterhouses on Innis and Yosemite streets. Other enterprises were there as well — shipyards, breweries, power stations, manufactories and the like, most of them emitting some sort of noxious effluent. Rows of modest homes and boardinghouses also occupied the area, the dwellings of working-class families whose children played among piles of fluttering trash, broken crates, shards of rusting steel, and pools of black oil. Negroes made up a significant percentage of Butchertown residents, and it was for this reason that Nick had asked Tanglefoot Fleming to help him arrange a speaking tour of the area's black churches.

It was a warm Sunday morning when he drove Harry Bridges to St. James Baptist Church, a small single-steepled church not far from the slaughterhouses. They sat down in the back row behind families dressed in their Sunday best, men in dark wool suits, women wearing extravagantly plumaged hats in deep shades of purple and green. Well-scrubbed children sat beside them, boys in dark suits like their fathers, girls in petticoats and dresses.

Reverend Cornelius Brown, minister of the church, stood on a raised dais in front of the congregation. He was about forty years old and wore a minister's collar and black robes. A simple white cross hung on the wall behind him. To his left a young man sat behind a Hammond organ.

The organist began playing a slow mournful ballad, each chord quivering with tremolo. After a few bars the congregation joined in, their voices filling the diminutive one-room church.

I'm tirrred and so weary, but I muuust go along
Till the looord comes and caaalls me away. Oh yes.
Well the mooorning's so bright, and the laaamb is the light
And the niiight is as black as the day. Oh yes...

Nick had never heard gospel music in this its natural venue and was impressed at how beautifully the sopranos, altos, tenors, and deep basses melded together into a sublime yet somber harmony that seemed to give a deeper, truer meaning to the words. When the ballad ended, Reverend Brown announced the arrival of a special guest who had come to talk about the waterfront strike. He invited Harry Bridges to come up, and as Bridges made his way forward heads swiveled around, eyes following his progress, the children craning their necks to watch him, as if it was rare for a white man to speak at their church.

Dressed in a dark blue suit with an open-collared shirt, Bridges stepped up onto the dais and thanked the reverend for allowing him the opportunity to address the congregation. He turned toward the families and described the situation at the port and the shipper's efforts to recruit replacement workers to break the strike. He acknowledged the discrimination endured by Negro stevedores and blamed it on the ignorance and prejudice of white longshoremen, as well as opportunistic shipowners who had a long history of pitting one race against another to gain advantage.

"Amen," a voice affirmed from the pews.

"It's time," he said, "that blacks and whites unite for mutual benefit and to confront a mutual adversary."

More amens.

He was pleased that Negro stevedores had voted to join the strike, but many strikebreakers were from the black community. He acknowledged the devastating economic circumstances Negroes were suffering under. Yet tempting as scab jobs were, they were only a temporary fix to a festering wound, and those that took them would undermine all workers. "The shippers are merely exploiting blacks as they have in previous strikes and will cast them aside when the strike ends." He concluded with an unequivocal pledge. "Negro stevedores are now welcomed to join the ILA, and if the strike is successful they will participate in an unbiased job rotation system with their white brothers."

While Bridges spoke, Nick noticed Tanglefoot Fleming a few rows ahead. Fleming had been enthusiastic when Nick asked him to help arrange a tour of the neighborhood. Harry's personal appeal would mean a lot to the black community, he'd said. He went on to explain that politicians rarely spoke to Negroes, banks didn't loan to them, companies only hired them for menial jobs, property owners wouldn't sell to them, and many establishments discouraged their patronage. Blacks might be accustomed to this treatment, he admitted with a trace of anger, but they certainly didn't like it or accept it.

When Bridges finished, the congregation applauded with enthusiasm and let loose a hail of emphatic "hallelujahs" and "amens" that resounded in the church like a rousing gospel hymn, continuing for some time. In the midst of this vigorous outpouring, Nick felt a burst of pride, and also another profound emotion. An awestruck sense that history was being made right before his eyes, that this lowly Australian immigrant, this self-taught orator, this rank-and-file leader was making good, at last, on the guiding American principle that "all men are created equal."

That afternoon Nick and Harry joined four-thousand longshoremen and their supporters on a march up Market Street from the Ferry Building to the Civic Center plaza in front of City Hall. It was an inspiring event, and when Bill Lewis announced that the teamsters had voted to halt all deliveries to the docks, the marchers cheered triumphantly.

Two days later, as Nick had warned, the Sailors Union of the Pacific voted to walk off the ships, transforming the longshoremen strike into a full maritime job action. The next day, for the first time since the Gold Rush, no American ships sailed out of West Coast ports, and in San Francisco, where mountains of cargo stood in every pier shed, fifty coastal and forty-four deep-sea vessels lay immobilized, unable to move a single piece of freight.

Nick was now spending most of his time at Bridges side, taking care of whatever tasks Harry assigned to him. One of his duties was to clip newspapers articles and give them to Bridges to keep him up-to-date on events at other West Coast ports where violent skirmishes had been escalating into blood-letting battles. He was perusing the *Chronicle* one morning when he came across an article that said President Roosevelt was sending his best mediator, Assistant Secretary of Labor Edward McGrady, to help sort out the situation. The article hailed it as a major development and heaped praise on McGrady as if he was Alexander the Great come to cut the Gordian Knot tying up West Coast ports. Nick clipped it and showed it to Bridges who was unimpressed.

"Nick, the gov'ment ain't gonna do anythin' for us. The only way we'll win this thing is to stick together and stand our ground."

As the days passed, Bridges projected a growing confidence. With sailors and teamsters now onboard, the waterfront strike was having a noticeable effect, and not just at ports. Timber companies in the Northwest, unable to ship logs to Asia, had laid off nine-hundred employees. Washington fruit packers reported the loss of thousands of pounds of rotting produce. A Philadelphia company announced it was canceling a shipment of steel bound for the two bridges under construction in San

Francisco Bay. And other firms were scrambling to arrange rail transportation to avoid the waterfront altogether.

Negotiations between employers and longshoremen were still ongoing at the offices of the Waterfront Employers Association. Outside the Matson Building strikers marched back and forth, chanting slogans, waving signs, and forcing negotiators to squeeze through their midst. Clarisa dreaded the daily gauntlet when she arrived each morning, although not because she feared for her safety. She just didn't see any progress toward a resolution, and it was abundantly clear, as she took notes at the negotiations, that both sides were more intent on prevailing than addressing each other's concerns. The shippers, resentful at having to negotiate with longshoremen as equals, ridiculed them in private and treated them with thinly veiled contempt at the negotiating table. The longshoremen were equally obstinate, repeating the same demands over and over as if Moses himself had handed them down on a stone tablet.

When Assistant Secretary of Labor Edward McGrady came to the negotiating table, negotiators on both sides magically became considerate and open-minded, hanging on to McGrady's every word and speaking in ultra-polite terms. To Clarisa, though, it was obvious that they were only pretending to be receptive while stubbornly clinging to their entrenched positions.

McGrady asked each side to give full authority to their representatives to make agreements, a common practice in labor negotiations. Both the ILA and the WEA initially agreed. Then each side placed strict limits on their negotiators that left little wiggle room. Furthermore, at Harry Bridges insistence, Local 38-79 passed a resolution making any final agreement subject to ratification by the rank-and-file.

Clarisa didn't understand why the negotiators were so stubborn until one day, as she was leaving the building, an Associated Press reporter accosted her and asked for an interview. She declined, saying she wasn't authorized to speak to the press. Undeterred, however, he continued to walk beside her, trying to engage her in conversation. He told her that intense media coverage had spread news of the strike far beyond the West Coast and that it had become a cause célèbre among union sympathizers around the world, drawing donations from as far away as Europe. Under this windfall Local 38-79's coffers had grown, enabling the strike kitchen to serve breakfast and dinner as well as lunch. Shippers, he said, were even better off, hoarding a multi-million dollar war chest derived primarily from the Industrial Association, a consortium of corporations that viewed the strike as a threat to the entire business community.

No wonder neither side was inclined to compromise.

After several days of fruitless negotiations, McGrady declared that he had never been involved in a strike in which negotiators weren't authorized to make a final settlement on behalf of their organizations. "I've been able to crack other strikes," he said to the press, "but I can't crack this one. There's a communist element that just doesn't want to bring this thing to an end."

As far as Clarisa was concerned, McGrady was just another pig-headed male who hadn't got his way. In her view it all boiled down to a few simple facts that neither side seemed willing to acknowledge. One evening in Roger's office, unable to contain her opinions any longer, she put them into words.

"Why won't shippers recognize the ILA as the sole representative of all West Coast longshoremen? Wouldn't it be easier to settle disputes between two organizations rather than split the coast into a patchwork of different unions and shippers? And why not agree to a union-run hiring hall? If a longshoreman is incompetent, a union hiring hall wouldn't prevent the company from requesting a replacement. And why won't the union recognize the shippers' right to run their operations as efficiently as possible? It's unrealistic to hold on to nineteenth-century practices. After all, ports need to keep up with new methods and inventions, otherwise they won't remain competitive and everyone will be out of work."

Roger listened to her analysis without interruption until suddenly he burst out in laughter. He covered his mouth, but it was a futile gesture that made him look like a schoolboy stifling an embarrassing outburst.

Annoyed at his reaction, but not offended, Clarisa stopped and waited for him to regain his composure. After all, they were both exhausted.

Roger took a deep breath to calm himself. "I'm sorry. It's just that you're approaching this whole thing with logic and common sense."

"And what's wrong with that?"

"It's just not realistic."

"Oh?"

"Maybe it's hard for a woman to understand, so let me try to explain. Neither side trusts the other. Longshoremen don't trust shippers because they've been treated like slaves for years, and shippers don't trust longshoremen because they're afraid that radicals won't stop making demands until they control the company or drive it into bankruptcy . . ."

While he droned on, Clarisa nodded politely, resisting the urge to swat him with her notepad. Of course she knew the two sides didn't trust each other, but until they accepted their intertwined fate, they wouldn't achieve a lick of progress. She sighed. It was difficult having to listen politely while men spouted obvious explanations and simplistic platitudes. Just once she'd love to knock some sense into them. Someday she hoped to raise a daughter who could speak her mind with a voice equal to men. *It isn't going to happen in my generation, but maybe, just maybe, the next one will be different.*

She studied Roger. There were dark crescents under his eyes, making him look ten years older, and his blond hair, normally a picture of perfection, hung over his ears. Still, he was just as handsome as the day they met, and in her estimation he would make a good husband if only he could conquer his demons and let go of his resentment at being trapped by convention.

If only he could free himself from himself.

52

San Francisco Chronicle, May 21, 1934
Strike a Red Outbreak, Warns
Chamber of Commerce Chief
The San Francisco waterfront strike is out of hand. This is not a labor dispute but rather a conflict between American principles and un-American radicalism. The welfare of business and of the entire public is at stake in this crisis. The leaders of the longshoremen are not representative of American labor. They seek the complete paralysis of shipping and industry and are responsible for the violence and bloodshed. There is no hope for peace until the Communistic agitators are removed. As president of the Chamber of Commerce, it is my duty to warn every businessman in the community that the welfare of business and industry and the entire public is at stake in the outcome of this crisis. J.W. Mailliard

• • •

The Mailliard editorial caused an uproar at ILA headquarters. Union officials issued a vehement denial, claiming the strike was a labor dispute, nothing more, and Harry Bridges issued his own statement, accusing Mailliard of waving a Red herring to confuse the issue. He also directed Nick to write a rebuttal.

For the first time since Nick began writing for Bridges, his thoughts coalesced quickly and the words came forth without hesitation. When the rebuttal was complete, he delivered it to the *Chronicle*, figuring it would end up in a trash can. He hoped otherwise, and the next morning he opened the newspaper with a measure of anticipation. He turned to the editorial page and scanned it. Halfway down the page he found what he was looking for — just the way he wrote it.

> *Dear Editor: Regardless of political affiliation every long-shoreman agrees that the inhuman conditions prevailing on the waterfront prior to the strike can no longer be tolerated. As much as anyone in America, longshoremen want to promote a recovery from the current economic crises gripping our country. To attain this, our purchasing power must be increased, a notion endorsed by President Roosevelt . . ."*

Reading his words gave Nick a burst of pride and also a dash of hope. He'd put his dream of becoming a reporter aside when his father died. Now, seeing his composition in a major newspaper, the dream sprang to life like a desert bloom after a rain. Still, his hope was tempered with the knowledge that he wasn't a free man and would have to prove his innocence before the dream could ever be realized.

To further that goal, he nagged Bridges to authorize a marine picket for the purpose of harassing boats that shuttled strikebreakers to the docks. It was a sound strategy, he argued, keeping to himself the conviction that it was also his only chance to prove his innocence, for his plan entailed more than just harassing boats.

Bridges hadn't rejected Nick's idea, but he hadn't embraced it either. Then a week later he relented, although for reasons unrelated to Nick's lobbying. His change of heart occurred on the day a longshoreman burst into ILA headquarters, babbling excitedly as he approached Harry and Nick.

"Steady yourself, man," said Bridges. "What's happened?"

"The men spotted a Belt Line train coming out of Pier 18 carrying hot cargo." Hot cargo being the term for cargo handled by strike-breakers.

"I'm not surprised," said Bridges. "Now that teamsters won't move cargo off the piers, the shippers have turned to the Belt Line Railroad."

"Why the Belt Line?" asked Nick.

"It's owned by the State of California, and its employees are civil servants bound by a yellow-dog contract that forbids them from going on strike." He turned to the longshoreman. "So what happened?"

"The men got sore and pushed a truck in front of the locomotive, then poured oil on the tracks. The cops tried to move 'em away with clubs but that only made things worse. Some guys are fightin' back with baseball bats and two-by-fours."

Harry glanced at Nick with a worried expression. "Pier 18 is just around the corner. Let's go take a look."

The three men ran down the stairs to Steuart Street and circled around the block to the Embarcadero. Just then shots rang out.

A few blocks away hundreds of longshoremen were running from Pier 18, scattering in all directions like a flock of startled pigeons. A dozen police officers were standing in front of the pier shed, some shooting their service revolvers in the air as a warning.

The three men hurried toward Pier 18.

On the way there Nick saw strikers doubling back and reengaging officers while other strikers managed to slip by the police and enter the pier shed. A few moments later strikebreakers came running out the pier shed's side door and onto the dock, chased by strikers who followed them until the strikebreakers leapt into the bay to escape harm.

By the time the three men came close to the melee, police were on the attack, advancing with billy clubs, holding them aloft and driving them down on the heads of strikers.

Some strikers fought back. Nick saw several men surround an officer and pummel him with fists, bats, and picket signs until other officers ran up and chased them away. The violence on both sides was shocking, and it seemed to spread like a contagious disease, radiating out from Pier 18 and infecting everyone in its path. Some officers were running after strikers, and when they caught up with the slow ones, they clobbered them with clubs and put them in handcuffs. Other officers defended the pier shed from strikers who were making more attempts to get past them. Meanwhile, groups of strikers were roaming the Embarcadero looking for any opportunity to surround an officer and give him a taste of his own medicine. Nick saw one officer try to club a striker. Somehow the striker managed to grab the billy club, and the two became locked in a heated struggle.

The battle was even at first. The police had superior weapons but the strikers outnumbered them twenty to one. The balance of power shifted when an unmarked police car screeched to a halt fifty yards from the conflict. Officers jumped out clutching teargas guns and aimed the guns at longshoremen. *Pop! Pop! Pop!* A volley of gas grenades flew into the midst of the rioting men, spewing white vapor that spread over the Embarcadero like a bizarre summer fog.

It was the first time Nick had witnessed a full-scale riot, and he found it impossible to remain calm. His whole body was tense, vigilant, ready to fight or flee at any moment. An officer approached him, billy club raised in the air, face angry as if he had a personal grudge against Nick. As the officer drew closer, Nick froze. He had no experience to draw on to deal with a situation like this, no way to decide what to do. The officer was within ten feet when Nick recalled a piece of advice his father once gave him. He wasn't sure it would work, but it was worth a try. He raised his hands in the air to make himself appear larger, then yelled as loud as he could and waved his arms back and forth. The officer paused and seemed confused by the unexpected gesture, just the way Nick's father had said a black bear would react in the wild. Bridges and the other man also began yelling and waving their arms.

Confronted with three bellowing men, the officer backed away and went off in search of an easier target. A short while later Nick saw him sneak up behind a striker and deliver a crushing blow to the head. The striker staggered forward, blood dripping from his skull and streaming from his eyes like tears. The officer followed him and mercilessly hit him again. The dazed striker collapsed to the ground and lay motionless amid the chaotic scene around him. Other strikers saw the beating too. Through the surreal haze of teargas, Nick watched them surround the officer and tackle him, then viciously beat him with fists while the officer curled up on the ground to protect himself.

A few daring strikers, holding wet rags over their faces, picked up teargas grenades and heaved them back at the riot officers who in the excitement had forgotten to put on their gas masks. Unprepared, the officers had to retreat.

More police officers arrived on the scene, some on horseback, others on foot, all clutching billy clubs and wielding them with devastating force.

"We can't let this go on," Bridges said. "Our men are gonna get slaughtered." He waved his arms and yelled at nearby strikers to leave the area. Nick joined him and together they drew several men away from the conflict, although most were caught up in the heat of the moment or were too far away to hear their cries.

As the battle continued, strikers charged forward, hurled stones and brickbats, then scurried away from horse-mounted officers who chased them and slammed clubs onto those they caught. Other officers clamped handcuffs onto the injured and roughly shoved them into paddy wagons.

More officers continued to arrive, and with greater numbers they managed to push the strikers away from the waterfront. It took another hour before the police finally gained full control and cleared the waterfront, the ground littered with sticks, baseball bats, two-by-fours, and spent teargas canisters.

Nick and Harry returned to ILA headquarters where men were huddled around a radio listening to a special news report describing the waterfront battle. Chief Quinn came on and announced that he was invoking the city's anti-picketing ordinance. Strikers would no longer be allowed on the waterfront side of the Embarcadero and would have to remain on the inland side, a hundred-forty feet from the pier sheds.

It was then Bridges endorsed Nick's proposal to form a marine picket.

53

Having been an able-bodied seaman and knowing first-hand the hardships sailors and stevedores endured, Lenny Dross was only too happy to help. He located four boat owners who agreed to lend their humble vessels to the union, three fishing boats and a cabin cruiser.

Now all Nick needed was four crews to man them.

Striking sailors were stationed opposite the Admiral Line docks at Pier 16. Two hundred sailors were gathered there when Nick arrived, milling around or sitting on the curb with little to do but look across the Embarcadero at strikebreakers transferring bales of cotton from a Belt Line train to a ship berthed beside the pier. A few sailors held signs reading DON'T SCAB and FULL RECOGNITION FOR THE SEAMEN'S UNION. Whenever traffic rolled by, they raised the signs and waved their arms. If a driver honked they cheered and shook their fists. Then, as the

310 • DANIEL BACON

vehicle sped away, they became listless and idle again.

Nick was looking for someone in charge when he overheard a sailor say, "Why are scabs botherin' to load cargo when they don't got the crew to take it out the Golden Gate?"

His companion shrugged. "Aww, it's all for show to demoralize us. After they load the ship, they'll tow her out into the bay until the strike's over."

If it's a shipper's ploy, Nick thought, *it appears to be working.*

He approached a seaman with the bearing of a chief mate and asked if he could help find volunteers. Others overheard him, and in no time a throng of restless, jostling sailors crowded around him, begging him to choose them. He felt sorry for them, these young, energetic men with little to do but watch traffic roll by. He was trying to determine how to chose the right guys when a sight both unusual and familiar caught his eye. A striped train engineer's hat, perched on a large round head, floated above a sea of white caps like a ship on a storm-whipped ocean.

"Haggis!" he cried.

The burly wiper pushed his way forward and embraced Nick, delighted to see the big galoot. They were smiling at each other when a voice behind Haggis said, "Aren't you glad to see your old bunkmates, too?"

Haggis stepped aside to reveal Moon Mullins, his tattooed arms outstretched like a long lost lover. He looked the same as ever, a white cap jauntily raked to the back of his head, a greased pompadour, boxer's blunt nose. Beside him was Nick's other roommate, Remy Lacoe, wearing a wry grin and a droopy mustache.

"You're a sight for sore eyes," Moon said, as he clapped Nick's shoulders. "Where the hell ya been?"

"On the beach humping cargo," Nick replied, his spirits lifted by the appearance of old friends. Then he shrugged. "Well I was before we pulled the pin."

Moon chuckled. "Jeez, you even talk like a goddamned wharf rat. Well, we won't hold that against you. So you're lookin' for sailors to man picket boats?"

Nick nodded. "I need four crews."

"Well, look no further. We'll fix you right up."

Moon and Remy pushed the men back and ordered them to form a line. With impressive speed they interviewed every interested sailor and presented Nick with four crews, each with an experienced pilot, engineer, and two deckhands.

• • •

Early the next morning, the eastern horizon glowing orange and gold, the striking sailors met at the South End Yacht Club. Nick assigned each crew to a boat. His crew — Remy, Moon, Haggis, and himself — boarded the *Tuscan*, a thirty-foot Monterey fishing boat that had seen better days. Paint was peeling from her wheelhouse and the cracks between the deck boards needed oakum and caulking.

Haggis poked his head down into the engine compartment. "I wouldn't take her on an ocean cruise," he reported to Nick, "but her diesel engine looks okay, and she don't have much bilge water."

Once the crews were at their stations and the engines started, Nick gave the signal to proceed. As they pulled away from the marina, he waved to Lenny Dross who stood on the dock and wished them good luck. With the *Tuscan* in the lead, the four boats chugged out into the bay and steered north along the waterfront. At Islais Creek Channel Nick glanced in at the towering copra crane, standing in quiet repose, its limp, motionless suction hose a testament to the port's closure. Two miles farther on, they reached the Embarcadero, its finger piers jutting out into the bay, devoid of the usual sounds of commerce — no ratcheting winch drums, no gang bosses barking orders, no stevedores calling for the hook to rise — instead, an unnatural quiet that drew silent stares from the sailors as they glided past the abandoned piers.

Ratta-tat-tat! Ratta-tat-tat! Ratta-tat-tat!

The sharp report of what sounded like machine gun fire rent the air, startling the deckhands who ducked for cover behind the bulwarks. When the noise let up Nick peeked over the side of the boat in the direction of the racket. A hundred yards offshore, construction workers in leather helmets were riveting steel beams together to form the western tower of the Bay Bridge. They were standing on temporary catwalks wrapped around a gigantic, double-columned tower rising up on a concrete island. Nick relaxed. The unholy racket had been the sound of their rivet guns.

As they passed the partially constructed tower Nick wondered what changes the new bridges would bring. *Will they draw communities closer together or move them farther apart as residents flock to outlying areas?* The question reminded him of his father who thought that progress inevitably led to greater prosperity, citing his own parents who could barely scrape two cents together, while his family (at least before the crash) thrived under American ingenuity and resourcefulness. Rune, on the other hand, saw things differently. More and faster contraptions, he declared, didn't necessarily lead to greater contentment.

Nick had followed the debate over the years and generally sided with his father. Now he wasn't so sure.

The picket fleet rounded Rincon Point and glided past one pier after another. As they neared Pier 22 they could see the stiff rigid profile of the *Diana Dollar* berthed next to the pier. A second ship, a Matson liner named the *Wilhelmina,* was parked on the opposite side of the pier. Dozens of sleepy-faced strikebreakers stood on the quarterdecks of the two ships, stretching and yawning and smoking cigarettes. A steam schooner, the *Wapama,* was docked at the end of the pier. Smaller than the other two ships, its house was perched on its stern, leaving the weather deck clear for lumber or bulk cargo. Today it would be a water taxi to ferry replacement workers to other piers.

Like pesky flies preparing to harry a horse, the four picket boats took up positions around the schooner. Nick hoisted up a cone-shaped megaphone and pointed it toward the men on the larger ships.

"Listen, everyone!" he said, his amplified voice drawing curious onlookers to the stern rails. "We're all in the same boat. The real enemy is the shipowner who exploits us with low wages and dangerous working conditions. If you join us, we can ensure safe working conditions and higher wages for all. Not just a few."

The strikebreakers gazed down impassively. One man cupped his hands together and yelled, "I like my workin' conditions and pay just fine. They got everything on this floatin' hotel but dames. But we'll consider your offer if you let us borrow your girlfriends."

The comment drew smirks and nervous laughter from other strikebreakers.

Red-faced and steaming, Moon Mullins wrenched the megaphone out of Nick's hands and pointed it toward the ships. "Listen you fuckin' finks," he bellowed, "if you don't quit scabbin' were gonna break every goddamned bone in your goddamned body! Then we're gonna feed you to the goddamned sharks until the goddamned bay looks like goddamned tomato sauce! Do I make myself goddamned clear!?!"

The smirks disappeared and some strikebreakers looked nervous, undoubtedly aware of the injuries inflicted by Pirate Larsen's flying squads. One scab waved his hand dismissively as he and the rest headed down the gangways to the pier and then onto the *Wapama.*

When the strikebreakers were aboard the schooner, its whistle screeched, sending up a plume of steam, signaling its intention to shove off. The

Wapama slowly warped away from the dock and inched forward until a picket boat darted in its path, the other picket boats edging closer to hem it in, forcing it to slow down and come to a halt. The strikers waved picket signs and yelled slogans, hoping to further rattle the strikebreakers, who looked down at them from an outside passageway on the ship's house.

The *Wapama*'s captain stepped out of the wheelhouse and waved his arms to signal the picket boats to stand off. When his warning failed to have any effect, he stalked back in and blew the ship's whistle, long and menacingly. The schooner surged forward, easily nudging the picket boats aside like annoying gnats. As it broke through the picket line, strikers fished rocks and tomatoes from their pockets and began pelting the strikebreakers who raised their arms to shield themselves as they made a hasty retreat into the ship.

The *Wapama* steered south toward China Basin, surrounded by picket boats in hot pursuit. Soon after the procession was underway, a harbor patrol boat joined them and slipped between the steam schooner and the picket boats. The patrol captain, speaking over a loudspeaker, ordered the picket boats to stand fifty yards off the *Wapama*, and to enforce the order, his officers waved shotguns and revolvers in a threatening manner. As the procession continued south past Mission Creek Channel, the picket fleet played a daring cat and mouse game, alternately moving closer to the *Wapama* when the patrol boat was on the opposite side of the schooner, then falling away as it circled back around.

Near Pier 50 the *Wapama* slowed to a crawl and glided into a berth beside a dock laid with railroad tracks. This was the western terminus of the Santa Fe and Southern Pacific rail lines. Railroad workers were still on the job, so the railroad piers had remained active during the strike. Now that ships were no longer sailing, however, they weren't operating at full capacity. After half the strikebreakers disembarked, the schooner pulled away from the dock and continued on to other piers, dogged by the feisty picket fleet as it delivered the rest of its passengers.

Its morning run complete, the *Wapama* returned to Pier 22 and berthed beside the dock. Nick reckoned it wouldn't make another run until the end of the day. Nevertheless, he had the picket boats drop anchor nearby so they could monitor the schooner until it went out again.

A light breeze ruffled the bay, tips of waves sparkling in the sunshine. Moon and Remy settled down on the hatch and leaned back against the pilot house, languidly smoking cigarettes and chatting about their chase that morning. Unable to relax, Nick paced the deck pondering his next move until he, too, succumbed to the pleasant weather and sat down to catch up with his old mates.

After their voyage on the *Diana Dollar*, Moon and Remy had shipped out on the *President Cleveland* under Slag and Primm, who'd been demoted back to chief mate. Primm's demotion and Captain Harding's mid-voyage resignation were topics of speculation among the crew, but Primm seemed unfazed by the notoriety, that is until Remy overheard him arguing with Slag in the chief's cabin one evening. He couldn't make out the words, but the anger and recrimination in their voices was unmistakable. A few days later a rough storm in the East China Sea buffeted the vessel for hours. After it passed on, Primm missed his regular watch in the wheelhouse and a search of the ship failed to locate him. When his oil cloth suit was discovered missing, it was assumed he'd been swept overboard during the storm, a rare but not unheard of occurrence.

Nick still remembered nearly slipping off the deck of the *Diana Dollar* during a storm. It had been an accident caused by spilled oil, yet he couldn't help but wonder if Primm's untimely demise had also been an accident, or something more sinister. He looked up at the smokestack on the *Diana Dollar*. If his intuition was correct the opium was stored inside, dangling on a hook, or at least he hoped so. Slag had only been in town a week, so there was still a chance he hadn't removed it, though it was a sure bet he'd try at the first opportunity.

Tonight there would be a new moon, a perfect opportunity to execute the second part of his plan, the part he hadn't revealed to Bridges. The *Diana Dollar* wasn't accessible from the Embarcadero but a marine approach might be possible. It would require two boats, one to motor over from India Basin and a second to row quietly up to the pier. He could do that alone, but if something were to happen to him he needed an accomplice to return the motorboat to the marina.

Moon flicked a cigarette butt into the bay. "How the hell did you get out of the hoosegow, Nick?" A seagull swooped down to grasp the cigarette butt, mistaking it for food. At the last second it recognized its error, pulled up, and flew off.

"I'm on probation and free as long as I stay out of trouble."

"So if you're arrested for picketin' or riotin', they could throw the book at you?"

"Yep."

"Funny, I didn't peg you for a gung-ho union man. You must really believe in this strike to risk going to prison."

Nick squinted at sun sparkles glimmering on the bay. "I didn't at first. I'd only been working at the waterfront a few months when we went on strike. And, frankly, I'm not planning on working there for long. But things change." He paused. "These longshoremen, they have more at stake than I do. I may be facing a prison sentence, but they're facing a lifetime of working without job security and in dangerous conditions. The outcome of this strike will affect them and their families for generations, and if they end up losing their jobs, who knows what'll happen to them."

"So what are you plannin' on doin' when it's over?" Remy asked.

An image of Clarisa popped into his head and his desire to repair their relationship. He set it aside. "I can't think about that now." He looked over at the *Diana Dollar* resting against the pier. "Right now I need to get aboard that ship and you two are gonna help me."

54

Under a moonless night sky, the South End Yacht Club was dark and quiet save for the gentle murmur of water lapping against boats. Wearing black pants and a black turtleneck, Nick led Moon and Remy to the *Tuscan* floating beside a seaweed fringed pier. He'd told Lenny Dross he needed the vessel for union-related business, a necessary fib so Dross wouldn't be alarmed when he heard them boarding the boat in the middle of the night. While Nick and Moon untied the vessel, Remy cranked the key to the diesel engine until it sputtered and growled and settled into a steady click-clacking rhythm. At Nick's signal he edged the boat away from the slip and steered out of India Basin into the bay, a rowboat tied to the stern trailing behind.

Despite the absence of moonlight, the bay wasn't as dark as Nick had hoped. Ambient light from streetlamps and buildings, as well as from dozens of ships anchored in the bay, created a glow that gently illuminated the waterfront piers. Fortunately it wasn't unusual for a fishing boat to be headed out to sea in the middle of the night, so their mission was unlikely to arouse suspicion.

Nick and Moon stood at the stern while Remy guided the boat parallel to the shore, moving past pier after pier. Just beyond China Basin, Nick signaled Remy to cut the engine and douse the lights. As the fishing boat coasted to a stop, he pulled the rowboat in and with Moon's help swung it around beside the stern. Moon held the dinghy steady while Nick boarded. Then he untied the rowboat and stepped aboard himself.

Nick frowned. "Get back in the boat. This isn't your affair."

"Don't be silly," Moon said as he pushed against the fishing boat, propelling the rowboat toward shore. "You may need a hand." He sat down and swiveled the oars out over the water, then dipped them in and pulled.

As the dinghy lurched forward, Nick lost his balance and plopped down on the bench seat. "Alright, but you're to stay in the dinghy. And at the first sign of trouble I want you to go back to the boat with or without me."

"Whatever you say," said Moon, his patronizing tone implying otherwise.

Nick hadn't wanted to involve his old shipmates in his troubles, and he couldn't fathom why Moon would follow him into a dangerous situation. Perhaps their loyalty to him ran deeper than he realized, or maybe they were just attracted to a midnight adventure. In any case, it was heartening to know that someone was watching his back.

The *Wilhelmina* and the *Diana Dollar* floated alongside Pier 22, their decks empty and shadowed. Nick tied the dinghy to a piling at the end of the pier, then lifted a grappling hook and rope from the bottom of the rowboat. The top of the pier was only twelve feet above the water. With one easy toss he hurled the hook up onto the pier and tugged on the rope until the hook caught on a raised curb at the edge. Once it was secure he glanced at Moon indicating he was ready to go.

Gripping the rope, Nick pulled himself up hand-over-hand until he reached the top and scrambled onto the pier. He paused to look up at the *Diana Dollar*. All the portholes were black save one, the captain's porthole glowing brightly, the cabin occupied most likely by the ship's manager. He crouched down and scampered across the dock to the pier shed. Pressing himself against the shed wall, he melted into the shadows and paused to listen for any unusual sounds. Other than a faint rhythmic hum from the donkey boiler powering the ship's lights, everything was quiet.

He sidled along the wall until he was opposite the freighter's gangway. He couldn't see a guard at the top but that didn't mean there wasn't one. He crept over to the ship and started up the gangway, taking one cautious step at a time. Near the top he heard a curious intermittent buzz. He stopped, unsure what to do. It sounded like snoring but he couldn't be sure. Throwing caution to the wind, he inched up the last few steps until a sharp snort nearly sent him scurrying back down. When the buzz started again, he breathed a sigh of relief, as he could now see a figure at the top of the gangway, laying on his side, hands tucked under his head, apparently not expecting unauthorized visitors in the middle of the night.

He tip-toed toward the sleeping guard until he was inches away, then gingerly stepped over him. He turned right and continued alongside the midship house to the entrance. It was pitch black inside. This didn't bother him as he knew the ship's layout by heart. He entered and moved along the passageway to the companionway. Without hesitating, he climbed up to the boat deck and was about to continue up to the bridge deck when he remembered the light from the captain's cabin. If he proceeded up the companionway, the manager might hear him. He turned and went to the door leading to the aft outside passageway. He recalled that the lever door handle usually squeaked when turned. Slowly and carefully he pushed down on it. There was a grinding sound of bare metal rubbing against metal. To his relief it wasn't loud and the door quickly unlatched. He pushed it opened and stepped through the doorway onto the outside passageway.

A series of rungs on the outside wall led up to the flying bridge above the bridge deck. Swiftly and silently he climbed to the top and stepped onto the flying bridge, bordered on all sides by a railing. He'd spent countless hours standing watch on this deck, scanning the ever-changing ocean and a star-studded sky. Tonight the view was equally beautiful. Lights in the windows of skyscrapers gave the buildings shape and dimension, and together they formed a luminous cityscape.

He approached the red and black smokestack in the center of the flying bridge. It was round, ten feet in diameter, and sixteen feet high. U-shaped rungs attached to the aft side of the stack formed a ladder to the top. He grasped a rung, cold and damp from the moist night air, and took a deep breath. This was it. In a few moments he would know if his only chance at redemption, his Holy Grail, was waiting at the top. He pushed off the deck and began to climb up, one step at a time. Halfway to the top he was reaching for the next rung when his foot slipped off the moist ladder. The sudden added weight on his other foot cause it to slip off too, leaving him dangling with one hand on the ladder. He hung there for a moment, heart pounding, visions of falling to the deck and alerting everyone onboard running through his head. He reach up with his free hand and grasped the ladder, then lifted his right foot to search for a rung. It took a moment of fumbling before he found it and steadied himself.

Ready to began the ascent again, he started up and was nearly at the top when a voice behind him said, "I wouldn't do that if I were you."

He stopped and sighed. *Is this ever going to be easy?* He glanced over his shoulder. A portly figure wearing a trench coat and fedora stood near the aft access ladder, smiling like a friendly uncle, a double chin hanging down over his shirt collar. His expression was so affable that Nick didn't understand the meaning of his warning until he caught the glimmer of dull metal in his hand, a faint but unmistakable reflection off the barrel of a snubbed-nosed revolver.

"There's nothing up there," the portly man said, waving the revolver toward the top of the smokestack. "Your *friend*" — he pronounced it with a dose of sarcasm — "removed it two days ago. Paid me a pretty penny to let him do it. So you better climb down."

Nick squeezed the rungs, his knuckles white. He'd spent months searching the ship, and now, after all the worry, all the risks, all the evasion, all the lying, he wasn't about to stop. Gun or no gun. He steeled himself. "Go ahead. Shoot if you want to." He started up the ladder again. At the top he peered down into a bottomless well, so dark that lights from the city couldn't penetrate it. He took a flashlight from his jacket and scoured the inside until he found what he was looking for: a steel hook, slightly rusted, indicating that it had been installed within the last year.

"Satisfied?" the man below said.

Nick shoved the flashlight into his pocket and climbed down to the deck.

The fat man was still smiling — *he's actually fat,* Nick decided, *not just portly* — but now there was a menacing look in his eyes. "Your friend said you might show up. Said he'd pay me to take care of you if you did." His smile disappeared as he waved the gun toward the access ladder. "Let's go."

Nick moved to the ladder and looked down. Half a dozen men were standing on the boat deck below. He looked beyond them to the edge of the ship. His chances of vaulting over the railing with enough momentum to clear the vessel and land in the water didn't appear promising. And since the weather deck was thirty feet down, a miscalculation would be disastrous, possibly fatal.

The fat man poked the revolver in his ribs. "Move."

Nick climbed down the ladder into the waiting hands of the men below, who grabbed his arms and groped through his pockets, removing his flashlight, knife, and wallet.

When the fat man came down, one of them said, "Hey, Joel, we caught another prowler down below. Got him in the dining room."

Dining room? It's a cinch these guys aren't sailors.

"Alright," said Joel, waving the gun. "Let's go."

They escorted Nick to the mess hall where more strikebreakers were huddled around Moon, seated at a table holding a cup.

"I tell you I don't want no more coffee," said Moon, slamming the cup on the table, his words slurred, eyes bloodshot and unfocused. "Don't you scabbin' finks got no booze."

"Shaaddup," a strikebreaker said, cuffing him on the head, "and drink up."

"Say," said another, "ain't he the one who said he was gonna feed us to the sharks."

"Yeah, that's him," agreed another. "I say we give him a taste of his own medicine."

The others nodded and one of them grabbed Moon's arm.

"Not so fast," said Joel. He motioned to Nick to sit in a chair next to Moon. "Get this one some coffee." The way he said *coffee*, it was obvious it wasn't going to be a friendly cup of joe. When the cup appeared, he pressed the barrel of his gun against Nick's temple. "Drink up."

"Go onnn," Moon slurred. "It taste godawful but it won't hurt you." He downed the last of his cup. "Now which one of you finks wants to go first? I'll take yous on one at time or alls at once."

Nick sniffed the coffee and detected a chemical odor. A Mickey Finn. He looked up. "What if I refuse?"

Joel put on his friendly uncle smile again. "I turn you over to these morons" — he motioned toward the men hovering around them — "who'll beat you unconscious and dump you in the bay with a chain wrapped around your legs." The smile hardened. "So I suggest you drink up."

Nick stared at the muddy liquid and tried to think of a way to escape. He had no money to offer them or valuables to barter. He couldn't overpower them. And now that they knew he and Moon were marine pickets, they certainly weren't going let them off easy. His only hope was that if their intentions were lethal, it made no sense to drug them. He heaved a sigh of resignation. *Better get it over with quickly.*

He raised the cup to his lips and chugged the contents.

As the liquid went down, a bitter metallic taste coated his tongue. He swallowed to clear away the taste and was about to ask for water when an odd sensation tingled at the base of his spine, then surged up his torso and into his head. All at once his body felt heavy as if he was going up a speeding elevator, then light, then heavy again. At the same time his vision went blurry. He blinked several times, trying to keep his eyes focused.

Someone nearby said something.

He looked up. Disembodied faces floated in the air around him, distorted faces with large unblinking eyes and thick red lips. It was a curious phenomenon, but he was distracted by something else, another strange sensation. His arms resting on the table no longer felt like his own, as if they were no more a part of his body than the table they lay on. This out-of-body sensation didn't disturb him. In fact, he felt oddly unemotional about it, all feelings of fight and flight having vanished, replaced by a detached, zombie-like numbness.

A voice spoke and hands lifted him to his feet, guided him out of the mess room and along the passageway. He still wasn't alarmed. His legs seemed to be functioning properly, not because he willed them to but by reflexive habit alone. As long as an outside force herded him he was perfectly content to move in any direction whatsoever. The hands guided him to the gangway and then down to the dock. Crossing the dock, they entered the pier shed, Moon beside him, flanked by two men who were guiding him as well. Moon's face was blank, expressionless, as if he too was in a numb, disconnected state. Nick tried to smile at him, tried to reassure him that everything was going to be alright, but his facial muscles didn't seem to be working.

They went to a door at the front of the pier shed and paused while one of the strikebreakers opened it. Someone guided Nick through it, Moon close behind him. They stepped out of the shed and walked several paces to the edge of the Embarcadero.

On the opposite side of the boulevard, men were standing around flames leaping out of a fifty-gallon steel drum, an orange glow on their faces, their hands outstretched to warm themselves. Bridges had ordered round-the-clock pickets stationed at strategic points along the waterfront, so these men, Nick figured, must be strikers.

That's good, he thought. *The strikebreakers are going to turn us over to the strikers.*

The man clutching Moon's arm yelled, "Hey, you fuckin' assholes. We ain't afraid of you."

The men across the Embarcadero looked over with startled expressions.

That was rude, Nick thought. *Why are they being so insulting?* He wanted to tell them to calm down, but when he tried to talk his mouth felt like it was stuffed with cotton and all he could manage was a groan.

The strikebreaker next to him yelled, "Come on, dickheads. What're you waitin' for?"

That seemed to motivate the strikers. Two of them picked up sticks, and in one swarm they all headed toward them, fists clenched, faces grim. When the strikers were still a distance away but closing in, the two strikebreakers leaned Nick and Moon against each other and scooted off. Nick heard their footsteps head in the direction of the shed door behind him. Then the door slammed shut.

The strikers came toward him with quick strides, frowning, silent, menacing. Oddly, Nick didn't feel afraid. It was as if he was watching a movie and not in any danger. The flames leaping out of the steel drum backlit the strikers, their faces dark except for the whites of their eyes. The two strikers carrying sticks raised them above their heads as they drew closer. The first crashing blow hit Nick squarely on the head. He toppled over like a bowling pin and landed on his face. A moment later Moon fell on top of him. A flurry of sticks, fists, and boots mercilessly pounded them. Nick didn't feel any pain, but he could feel blood seeping out of his ear and down his cheek. He also heard a loud snap like a bone breaking.

Amid the sound of pounding fists and sticks, a police whistle rang out, followed by a clatter of hoof beats on cobblestones. The last thing Nick saw before everything went blank was a blur of dark figures scattering away into the night.

55

Judging from complaints out of the Chamber of Commerce, the business community was hurting, and this, more than anything, gave Harry Bridges reason to believe that the strike was going as well as could be expected. In his experience the only effective leverage unions had against employers was economic pain. Consequently, when the *San Francisco Chronicle* reported that ILA National President Joe Ryan was flying in from New York to broker a deal between striking longshoremen and employers, he viewed it with amusement. The article characterized Ryan as a cooperative union official willing to compromise to get his men back to work. If anyone could settle the West Coast strike, he could.

Bridges knew otherwise.

It was well-known within the rank-and-file that Ryan ran the ILA's East Coast District as a personal fiefdom, employing ex-cons to harass anyone who questioned his authority. Moreover, Bridges was aware of a crucial detail the press had overlooked. Under ILA by-laws, the Pacific Coast District was an autonomous body, not subject to Ryan's jurisdiction.

On the day Joe Ryan arrived from New York, three-thousand long-shoremen crammed into Eagles Hall to hear what he had to say. Bridges knew from sources that Pacific Coast District President Bill Lewis had already taken Ryan to a get-acquainted dinner with Mayor Rossi and a group of business leaders, and considering Ryan's reputation it didn't surprise Bridges that Ryan's first move was to meet with the opposition.

When the six-foot tall, barrel-chested Ryan walked into Eagles Hall, men from the Albion Hall group booed and hissed as he made his way to the stage. The majority of members, however, willing to give him the benefit of the doubt, clapped politely, and after he delivered an upbeat speech promising an early and equitable settlement to the strike, they were even more enthusiastic.

Bridges wasn't so impressed. The goals of the strike had been firmly established, and while Ryan could make sweeping statements about ending the walkout, it wouldn't be so easy to negotiate a settlement that was acceptable to the rank-and-file. What concerned Bridges more was the involvement of the Industrial Association, a consortium of large corporations with political clout and a multi-million dollar war chest. Another editorial by J.W. Mailliard, president of the S.F. Chamber of Commerce and a member of the Industrial Association, complained that the strike was costing the city's business community nearly a million dollars a day in lost contracts and unfulfilled orders. Mailliard predicted that if the strike wasn't settled soon, it would cause a citywide disaster equivalent to the 1906 earthquake and fire. It was time, the editorial concluded, for the Industrial Association to take a lead role in the conflict and open the port, by force if necessary, should negotiations fail to reach a settlement. This, Bridges knew, would escalate the violence, a situation he hoped to avoid.

A year earlier Mahatma Gandhi had used nonviolent protests against the British to obtain rights for India's native population. Emulating Gandhi's strategy, Bridges ordered sit-down demonstrations on the

Belt Line railroad tracks running along the waterfront. The Belt Line's engineers were bound by yellow-dog contracts that prohibited them from joining the strike, but they sympathized with the longshoremen and halted locomotives at the slightest interference.

Bridges also took another significant step. Striking sailors had been instrumental in shutting off commerce at West Coast ports. If the long-shoremen were to settle with employers and go back to work, it would leave their seafaring brothers high and dry. For that reason, at a meeting of the Strike Committee, he proposed an additional condition for settling the strike. Longshoremen would not return to work until grievances from the maritime unions were also resolved.

"We are all of one mark," he reminded the Strike Committee, "sailors and stevedores, masters and mates. United we're strong, divided we'll fall."

The Strike Committee approved his proposal and agreed to put it up for a vote at the next meeting of the full membership.

Meanwhile, Joe Ryan met with Thomas Plant at the Waterfront Employers Association. Bridges figured that Ryan's efforts were incon-sequential and chose to ignore his meddling—that is, until Ryan announced to the press, "The only vital point at issue is recognition of the ILA. We don't give a hoot for the closed shop as long as employers recog-nize the union and give preference to union members. It has worked on the East Coast for nineteen years and has kept Communists and radicals from infesting the piers."

Irked by Ryan's Red-baiting, Bridges introduced a resolution at Local 38-79's June meeting, reaffirming their demands for a union run hiring hall, closed shop, coastwise contract, and solidarity with other unions. "Settlement for mere recognition may mean a lot to officials who draw fat salaries," he declared, "but the workers are going to hold out for nothing less than a closed shop."

The resolution passed unanimously.

Despite his lack of authority, Joe Ryan continued to meet privately with Thomas Plant. Clarisa took notes at the meetings, and at first blush the nattily attired Ryan seemed to be a breath of fresh air as he listened to Plant's side of things and sympathized with the shippers' concerns. When Ryan signed a settlement agreement with Plant after only four meetings, however, Clarisa was skeptical and suspicious that the process had proceeded so quickly and come to a resolution so easily.

That night, after serving meals at St. Patrick's Mission, she walked up Mission Street with Father Shannon and discussed the situation. Her suspicions were aroused, she said, when Ryan readily accepted Plant's offer of an employer-run hiring hall with only a union monitor. He also agreed to an open shop that allowed employers to hire union or non-union stevedores as they pleased. And under the agreement the ILA would have to bargain with employers on a port-by-port basis and arbitrate disputes on wages and hours. As far as she could tell, all Ryan achieved was recognition of the ILA as representative of its own members.

The silver-haired priest shook his head. "The men will never accept such a contract, and it will only confuse the public when a prominent union official contradicts his members. The hiring hall issue is at the heart of the strike, and both sides are prepared for a fight to the finish."

Clarisa recalled a personal note she'd jotted down during negotiations, a passing idea that had crossed her mind, then vanished as she took notes. "What if the hiring hall was run by the union *and* the employers?"

"That's already been rejected by both sides, especially the union, which believes it would inevitably fall under employer domination and become a tool to discriminate against active union members."

"But what if the hiring hall dispatcher was a union member? Wouldn't that protect them?" The dispatcher was the person who actually sent men out to the docks, so his role was crucial.

"Hmm." The priest nodded. "It might."

The day after Ryan and Plant signed the agreement, Bridges ordered his Albion Hall followers to distribute leaflets warning strikers that Ryan's settlement was a gift to the employers and a death sentence for the union. That night members of Local 38-79 met at Eagles Hall to discuss the issue and take a vote. When Joe Ryan entered the auditorium he smiled broadly as if he expected, or at least hoped, to be congratulated. Instead, the membership greeted him with catcalls and hisses, a few even yelling "traitor" and "sellout."

The leaflets had worked, Bridges observed, at least so far.

Bill Lewis escorted Ryan to the stage and asked the members to give him an opportunity to state his case. Wearing a dark blue suit and silk tie, Ryan blasted his detractors, branding them dangerous radicals with a communist agenda and calling his settlement the best deal the longshoremen could realistically expect. The men listened stone-faced and unresponsive, clearly not swayed by his rhetoric. Ryan then changed tactics and started wheedling, bullying, and cajoling the members, though this too had little effect.

The defining moment came when Pirate Larsen jumped on stage next to Ryan and exclaimed, "You know, fellows, this guy is nothin' but a fink, and he's tryin' to make finks out of all of us! Let's throw him out!"

The men applauded, and when the hall quieted down Joe Johnson called for a vote on whether or not to accept the settlement.

"All in favor say 'aye'."

Silence.

"All oppose say 'no'."

In one thunderous declaration of independence, twenty-five hundred voices roared, "*NOOOOO!*"

56

It wasn't until the caller mentioned Nick that Clarisa recognized the quavering voice on the other end of the line. Lillian Benson's faltering words were difficult to understand, yet when their meaning became clear, Clarisa instantly recognized the heartache of a mother whose son was in the hospital, hanging on by a thread. She knew she couldn't fully appreciate the depth of Mrs. Benson's pain. However, the anxiety she herself felt was the most she'd felt since her own mother passed away.

It'd been a depressing morning already. On the way to work, she saw a headline announcing the death of Governor James Rolph. He had been unwell for weeks, so it wasn't a complete surprise. Still, the finality of his passing sparked memories of the charming man she'd met a year earlier at the Dollar mansion.

She put down the phone and went to Roger's office, planning to tell him that a family emergency required her immediate attention. It wasn't that she wanted to conceal her real purpose so much as she was still uncomfortable with the relationship between Roger and Nick. She understood the reasons that bound them together but now believed that their Faustian bargain had compromised both of them in ways that neither fully understood. She'd tried in vain to figure out a way to separate them, and now felt guilty for not having done more to prevent this tragedy. After all, though it was for the best of intentions, it was she who brought them together.

Roger was reading a report when she entered his office, one of many piled on his desk. His blond hair hung down over his ears, his clothes rumpled, perhaps slept in.

She retrieved a clean suit from the hall closet and laid it on his desk.

"Do I look that bad?" he asked with a limp smile.

"I'm afraid you do. Don't you ever go home?"

He shook his head. "While Plant's dreaming up more proposals, who do you think's running things? I've got two dozen ship owners calling me five times a day, back-to-back meetings, and dozens of reports to read." He waved a sheaf of papers. "The only way I can get anything done is to camp out here and burn the midnight oil."

"Isn't the Industrial Association taking over the strike from us?"

The Industrial Association had formed a drayage company called Atlas Trucking, according to reports, and was purchasing trucks, hiring drivers, and securing warehouse space. Once all the arrangements were made, the IA planned to reopen the port under the protection of the San Francisco Police Department.

"Oh, them," Roger scoffed. "All they do is flood the papers with propaganda and rattle their sabers like boys playing cowboys and Indians. They don't give a damn about negotiating with the union or coordinating the men we do have on the job." He sighed and tossed the report onto his desk. "So, what's on your mind?"

"I — I have an emergency to attend to. I need a couple of hours off."

Roger lit a cigarette and sat back, his eyes trained on her as if he suspected she was keeping something from him. After several awkward moments, during which she shifted her gaze to the window behind him, he blew out a stream of smoke. "Are you going tell me about it?"

"I'd prefer not to . . . if it's alright. I won't be long." *Why am I being so timid? I'm his employee, not his slave.*

"You sure you don't want to tell me?" Roger persisted. "Confession is good for the soul. Isn't that what Catholics believe?"

Her eyes narrowed. *How dare you pry into my private life. I'm a model employee. The least you can do is allow me a couple of hours off without giving me the third degree.* She was about to voice her thoughts when she noticed a weary look in his eyes and a slump in his posture. He'd been struggling with a difficult situation, perhaps more difficult than someone of his experience and abilities could handle. The realization dissolved her anger.

She sat down. "I might as well tell you because you're bound to find out sooner or later. Nick's in the hospital, in a coma. He was found several days ago laying on the Embarcadero with another man. Both of them were badly beaten and neither had any identification, so it took a while before his family discovered his whereabouts. His mother just called from General Hospital, and I promised to come right away."

Roger's face dropped. "Oh, Jesus." He took another drag on his cigarette. "How bad is it?"

"They're not sure yet."

He pushed away from his desk. "Well, let's get going."

Clarisa rose from her seat. "I don't think that's a good idea. Your presence might raise questions, especially if someone from the union shows up. He's in enough trouble already, don't you think?"

Neither of them had acknowledged Roger's relationship with Nick, and Clarisa knew that she was skirting the edge of, if not actually revealing her knowledge of it. All the same, it couldn't be helped.

He nodded, indicating he understood her reasoning, and gestured for her to leave.

When she arrived at the intensive care ward, Lillian, Rune, and Sarah were in the corridor outside Nick's room. Two other men wearing flat-caps and Frisco trousers stood nearby. She didn't recognize them but figured they were friends of Nick from the waterfront. She joined his family and hugged Lillian, whose eyes were moist, face drawn and haggard. Rune stood stiffly beside her, his lips firmly set around a pipe stem, legs planted a shoulder width apart as if he were on the deck of a windjammer navigating rough seas. Clarisa extended a hand to Rune, but he refused to shake it.

Removing the pipe from his mouth, he regarded her with a wary expression. "Seems like the only time we see you is when the boy is in trouble. How come you don't come round when tings are doin' well?"

"Papa!" Lillian said. "How can you be so rude?"

Clarisa couldn't come up with an answer to Rune's question, at least one that made sense. For it was true. There had been plenty of opportunities to contact Nick and resume some sort of relationship. Now that he was badly hurt, her reluctance seemed petty and vain, and she didn't have a reasonable defense. She rested a hand on Lillian's forearm. "He's right. I haven't been a good friend. How is Nick?"

Lillian opened her mouth to speak, but before any words came out, her eyes welled up and her face contorted in grief. Sarah came to her side and wrapped an arm around her shoulder. Clarisa barely recognized

Nick's sister. A pouty teenager the last time she saw her, Sarah was now an attractive, fully-grown young woman with a decidedly bohemian appearance. Her dark hair was cut in a severe bob, and she was dressed in a man's black wool blazer, calf-length skirt, and paint-spattered shoes. Her eyes were rimmed with black eyeliner and what looked like hand-made silver earrings dangled from her lobes.

"The doctors say he's stabilized," said Sarah, "but he still hasn't come to and they don't know when or even if he will. Apparently, he took quite a blow to the head."

"What about the other fellow? Wasn't he with another man?"

"Oh, he'll be shipshape in no time," a voice piped up behind her.

She turned. One of the two men she saw earlier had approached her from behind and was now standing inches away. He was about her height and had a swarthy face, droopy mustache, and crooked smile. He gazed at her with yellowish brown eyes that trailed languidly down her figure and back up to her face.

"You must be Clarisa and just as beautiful as he said you were."

She stepped back, flustered and annoyed by the audacious greeting. In any other context she would have shot him a withering glance, but at the moment there didn't seem any point in dwelling on crude manners.

"That's right, I'm Clarisa McMahon." She arched an eyebrow. "And you are?"

"Remedius Lacoe, but folks call me Remy."

She shook his hand with little enthusiasm. "Nice to meet you, Remy. You sailed with Nick on the *Diana Dollar*?"

"That's right. Me and Moon, the other fellow what got banged up, were his bunkmates. Moon used to be a Golden Gloves boxer and tough as nails. He's laid up downstairs with a broken arm and a coupla broken ribs. Nothin' he won't get over soon."

"Do you know how they came to be — ?" her voice trailed off.

"You mean how they got the crap beat out of 'em?"

Clarisa winced.

"Nick was looking for opium on the *Diana Dollar*. He was tryin' to find it to prove who really smuggled it, so him an' Moon snuck aboard."

"Then he was beaten by strikebreakers?"

Remy shook his head. "That's the strange thing. Word out on the street is that he and Moon came out of the pier shed with two others who yelled at strikers, then ran back inside. Nick and Moon were left to face strikers who were mad as hell and thought they were scabs." He shrugged. "A case of mistaken identity."

"So, how did he get on the *Diana Dollar*?" She detected a blush through Remy's swarthy complexion.

"Well, miss, I really shouldn't tell you this," he said, pulling her away from the others and lowering his voice, "but see'n as how you an' Nick are, you know." He waggled his eyebrows. "We borrowed a fishin' boat and sailed over to the waterfront. Then Nick and Moon rowed to Pier 22, and that's the last I seen of 'em until they landed in this berth."

"Consorting with the enemy?" said a voice.

They turned to see who it was.

Remy's companion had approached them unawares, a compact fellow with a high forehead, long pointed nose, and a receding chin. "Loose lips not only sink ships, Remy," he said, eyeing Clarisa with an enigmatic smile that was both friendly and guarded, "they can sink strikes as well. You must be Clarisa McMahon." He extended a hand. "My name is Bridges."

Surprised to meet the man who had caused so much consternation in her employers, Clarisa shook his hand. "I've heard a lot about you."

"I'll bet you have." He glanced at Remy. "Miss McMahon, here, works for the Waterfront Employers Association."

Remy's jaw dropped. "Well, I'll be a Hong Kong hooker. I'm tellin' you, Harry, I didn't know nothin' about her workin' for the shippers. Nick never mentioned it. He just said they were, you know —."

Harry nodded. "Yeah, I know. Listen, leave us alone for moment, will you?"

As Remy slinked away, Clarisa faced Bridges. "You should know that just because I work for the WEA doesn't mean I agree with everything they do. In fact, it doesn't mean I agree with anything they do. But I certainly wouldn't tell them anything I hear outside of work. I'm a secretary, not a spy."

Bridges flashed an amused grin. "Not like your boyfriend?"

Clarisa gasped. "You — you know about Nick?"

He nodded. "For quite some time."

"Then . . . why —?"

"Why didn't I kick him out of the union or have him taken care of in a back alley?" He smiled, though there was a cynical edge to it. "Two reasons. All's fair in love and war. Among other things, Miss McMahon, I'm a tactician with limited resources and I'll use whatever advantage I can get. An enemy spy can be quite useful, *if* you know he's a spy. I only allowed Nick to learn information I wanted him to learn. And I gave him other information that, shall we say, was manufactured and I knew he would pass on."

His gray eyes reflected no light, as though all information that entered them was consumed and stored for future use. They were the eyes, Clarisa imagined, of a military commander or a marauding warlord, tough, calculating, aware. She wanted to look away but couldn't. "I suppose I can't blame you. You're fighting with everything you've got. So, what's the second reason?"

"I know why Nick's been spying. Blackmail isn't a pretty thing, Miss McMahon, but then I wouldn't expect anything better from your side."

"I told you — it's not my side. I just work there."

Bridges locked his eyes onto hers. "Then perhaps you'd like to help the right side."

His animal magnetism drew her toward him, the magnetism any effective leader wields to bend Fate to his will. Struggling to keep her equilibrium, she stepped back and forced her gaze from his. "As I said, Mr. Bridges, I'm not a spy. I do sympathize with your cause, but I can't betray my employer." She met his gaze again. As if by magic his aura of power had vanished, revealing a man with cares and worries, passions and insecurities. Now she saw him for what he was, a resolute leader with a crystalline vision, a vision he was prepared to give his life for no matter what the consequences, his strength derived from an intractable belief in his cause and an absolute commitment to its success. She found it both admirable and intimidating.

"Why are you revealing all this now?" she asked.

"I thought I could protect Nick. And no one was more surprised than I to hear that he was beaten by strikers. At first I thought it was a lie until my men confirmed it. Then they asked how he got onto Pier 22 and why he and Mullins come out with scabs."

"What did you tell them?"

"Don't worry. I covered for him. He's a decent guy who got caught in a bind. I told the men he was on an undercover assignment for me."

"That still doesn't explain why you revealed to me that you know he's a spy."

"I want you to tell your boss that the jig is up. Nick's no good as a spy for either side now, so they should let him off the hook. Besides, if he really was a drug smuggler, why would he risk his life trying to disprove it?"

"They might claim he was just finishing the job."

Bridges shook his head. "Bastards . . . Well, I'll leave it to you." He tipped his hat. "G'day, Miss McMahon. When Nick wakes up, tell him I came by."

As he walked away a question occurred to Clarisa. "Mr. Bridges, tell me something?" He stopped and turned around. "How did you know Nick was working for the WEA?"

A thin smile crept over his face. "Sorry, Miss McMahon, I can't compromise my sources, especially to someone who works for the enemy." He turned and walked down the hall.

Clarisa watched him disappear into an elevator. *He fooled everyone — Nick, Roger, even his own men. No wonder he's a fierce opponent.* Yet she still wanted to know how he learned that Nick had been a spy. *Who is he protecting?*

Across the hall the Benson family was conferring with a nurse. Clarisa joined them and listened as the nurse explained that Nick's condition was unchanged and that they would be notified as soon as he showed any sign of regaining consciousness. After the nurse departed, Clarisa promised to return and asked Lillian to contact her immediately if there was any change in his condition, no matter how slight.

On the streetcar back to the office, she debated whether to tell Roger about her conversation with Bridges. She finally decided against it, at least for the time being. If Roger suspected that Bridges was sympathetic with Nick, he might be more inclined to send Nick back to jail rather than let him go. And if there were any feelings of jealousy mixed in... well, the outcome was even more certain.

57

While meeting with the Executive Committee at ILA headquarters, Harry Bridges received a disturbing report. A lone striker, walking near the Embarcadero at night, had been ambushed by five men in brown leather jackets and khaki pants. Three of the attackers grabbed him from behind while a fourth pistol-whipped him and called him a "dirty red" and "commie bastard." The fifth man, older than the others and wearing knee-high boots, looked on as the assailants beat the striker to the ground. On his way down, the striker spotted an American Legion pin on the lapel of an attacker. Coincidentally, he himself was a veteran, having served in the quartermaster corps during the Great War. He hadn't been injured during the war, and in the hospital after the attack, he joked that a gang of Legionnaires had caused him more damage than the entire German army.

To Bridges it wasn't a joking matter. There had been a number of Red-baiting editorials in the newspapers, claiming that the leaders of the strike were communists bent on destroying the government and the capitalist system. Bridges had serious doubts about the equity of capitalism and he had friends who were communists, but his goal wasn't revolution. Besides, the real purpose of Red-baiting editorials was to draw attention away from the issues of the strike and inflame the public. The attack on a striker showed that it was working, so he issued a warning to all strikers to stay in groups, especially after dark

Standing in a crowded streetcar, Roger Farnsworth and Thomas Plant held on to the safety bar as the streetcar lurched forward up Market Street. They were on their way to a meeting at City Hall hosted by Mayor Rossi, who up to this point hadn't been involved in the conflict.

"Why is the mayor jumping in now?" Farnsworth asked.

"Joe Ryan has been in the northwest working on an agreement with Dave Beck, the Seattle teamster boss. He and Beck are here now to present their proposal."

Ryan and Beck were natural allies, both of them conservative union officials who ran their respective organizations with an iron grip. Even so, Roger still didn't see why the mayor was now involved.

"Why didn't Ryan bring his proposal directly to us?"

"The Chamber of Commerce has been pressuring Rossi to step in. Mailliard thinks that if the mayor throws his weight behind an agreement, it might convince the rank-and-file in San Francisco to accept it. And if they accept it, the thinking is, the rest of the men on the coast will fall in line."

When Plant and Farnsworth entered the Mayor's spacious office, every major player was there, seated around a large conference table— Rossi, Ryan, Beck, Mailliard, Eliel, Johnson, Lewis, Casey, Dollar, Roth, Fleishhacker. Every major player but one, Farnsworth noted.

Harry Bridges was conspicuously absent.

The mayor greeted everyone and gave a short talk on the necessity of resolving the conflict before the city incurred further damage. Then he invited Joe Ryan to outline his proposal.

Ryan glanced around the table. "I've heard many of you say that Communists are leading the strike. That's true. But we can take control of this thing if you listen to reasonable persons like Bill Lewis and myself."

Ryan went on to detail a proposal similar to his earlier agreement. The major difference was that this one called for joint and equal control of hiring halls and prohibited sympathetic strikes to support other unions. It gave the longshoremen more than Ryan's previous proposal and pulled the employers incrementally toward the strikers' demands. Even so, troubling questions remained. Was it enough to capture the support of the rank-and-file? Roger was skeptical.

"Can you deliver the men?" he asked the ILA president point blank.

Ryan looked askance at him as though to say, *who the hell is this young upstart anyway?* He hooked his thumbs around his suspenders and swept his gaze around the table. "I give you my unqualified assurance that I can make an agreement on behalf of my membership that will be effective."

Mike Casey, head of the San Francisco teamsters union, and Dave Beck from Seattle, assured everyone that any agreement satisfactory with Ryan was enough for them to send their drivers back to the waterfront no matter what the strikers decided.

That night Farnsworth, Ryan, Plant, and Paul Eliel, executive director of the Industrial Association, met at Plant's house to hammer out the final details. The next morning, June 16th, the same group reconvened in Mayor Rossi's office to ratify the agreement. Prior to the meeting, Farnsworth had instructed McCann-Erickson to prepare a publicity campaign to promote the agreement. If Ryan couldn't convince the longshoremen to accept it, perhaps they could be stampeded back to work by an avalanche of press articles and editorials.

With smiling faces all around, Ryan and Plant signed the agreement on behalf of their respective organizations. Mayor Rossi, Mike Casey, and Dave Beck then added their signatures as approving witnesses.

After the signing Farnsworth and Plant boarded a streetcar headed down Market Street toward the Matson Building. When they got off at Main Street, Farnsworth was pleased to see a newsboy already hawking an early afternoon edition of the *Chronicle* with the headline: THE STRIKE HAS ENDED!

Harry Bridges was waiting in the lobby of the Chandler Hotel when Joe Ryan returned from the meeting at City Hall. Ryan glanced at him but kept walking toward the elevator as if he hadn't seen him. Bridges angled toward him and stepped in his path, forcing him to stop. He held up a copy of the *Chronicle*. "So, you think you can herd the men back to work like a bunch of fuckin' sheep?"

Though Ryan had a height and girth advantage, he appeared startled by the impertinent Bridges, as if no one had ever dared talk to him like that before. Half threatening, half pleading, he said, "Look, Bridges, I got no beef with you, but this strike has gone on long enough. The men wanna get back to work, and this agreement is the best they'll get."

Bridges inched closer and thrust his pointed nose into Ryan's face, forcing him to lean back. "How would you know what the men want? Did you ask them?"

Ryan grimaced.

Bridges waved the paper in his face. "You may think you've executed an agreement but this thing won't stick. You got no authority here and the sooner you know it the better." His eyes on Ryan, he slammed the paper on the floor, then walked over it as he stalked out of the hotel.

Three-thousand longshoremen were gathered in Eagles Hall to hear Joe Ryan justify his agreement and to vote on whether or not to accept it. Unfortunately for Ryan, he arrived thirty minutes late, and in his absence Bridges used the opportunity to characterize the agreement as a sell-out and a betrayal of everything the strike stood for. Others echoed Bridges' sentiments, some even calling for a general strike to shut down the entire city if their demands weren't met. By the time Ryan arrived, the rank-and-file had been whipped into a state of frenzy, and when he walked onto the stage, they erupted in a cacophonous din of jeers, boos, and catcalls.

Bridges smiled. Ryan, it turned out, had been an even weaker opponent than Lee Holman. In the space of three weeks, his blundering moves had turned a supportive ILA local into a hostile, agitated mob, and one that greeted his "agreement" with threats of bodily harm and a unanimous vote of rejection.

The outcome was everything Bridges had hoped for, yet he was angry that conservative union officials kept trying to sell the men short. It was time, he decided, to consolidate his power.

Following the rejection of the Ryan-Plant agreement, the men voted, as Bridges had proposed earlier, not to return to work until the demands of the longshore and all five maritime unions were met. Bridges then presented a proposal to form a Joint Marine Strike Committee to organize the striking unions under one banner. It would be composed of executive board members from each union and be authorized to conduct all future negotiations. He presented it as the next logical step toward building a united front and the best way to increase pressure on the employers. He also knew it would effectively strip union officials from the bargaining table and, if his plan worked, position himself as the undisputed leader of the strike.

The membership, demonstrating its increasing faith in Bridges, approved the proposal.

The Joint Marine Strike Committee met the following day, its first order of business to elect a chairman. Dutch Dietrich nominated Harry Bridges, a natural choice since the Committee had been Bridges' idea. Moreover, Bridges' reputation had grown during the previous weeks. He'd organized marches along the waterfront, supervised the creation of a strike kitchen to feed the men, recruited a group of pro-bono attorneys to represent arrested strikers, and spoken at every ILA meeting since the strike began. As a result, no one else put their hat in the ring.

His first act as chairman was to issue a press release listing the demands of the five striking maritime unions. The release also announced the unanimous vote rejecting the Ryan-Plant agreement, and it pointed out that the vote refuted assertions in some quarters that Local 38-79 was run by a small cadre of militant radicals.

Roger Farnsworth and Thomas Plant were meeting with Paul Eliel of the Industrial Association when news reached them that longshoremen had rejected the Ryan-Plant agreement.

"I was hoping for a miracle," Plant sighed, "but I must say, it's not unexpected. I still believe a radical element has taken over the union from elected officials, despite their denials."

"I wouldn't be so discouraged," said Eliel, who seemed buoyed by the news. "I'll wager it's a blessing in the long run."

"You don't consider it a setback?" asked Roger.

"Not at all. The primary concern of the Industrial Association is to preserve the open shop. You can't control the ILA by negotiating with them. Giving in to their demands will only encourage them to come back year-after-year asking for more. The only way to stop them is to marginalize the strike leaders and make the public see them as dangerous radicals. We knew they'd reject Ryan's proposal, and now they're talking about a general strike, which will surely antagonize the public."

Plant regarded Eliel with a grave expression. "You mean you encouraged me to negotiate in good faith, knowing it was a waste of time?"

"Come on, Tom. You didn't really think that blowhard Ryan was going to convince anyone of anything. In any case, it wasn't a waste of time. You played your part perfectly. We proved that the unions are unreasonable, so unreasonable they won't even listen to their own officials. When we open the port next week, the public will understand we had no choice."

Eliel's Machiavellian admission was stunning. It hadn't occurred to Roger that the Industrial Association aimed for nothing less than complete domination over the unions until it achieved total capitulation. Yet Eliel was probably right about one thing: a closed shop would likely leave militants in charge of waterfront labor. Even before the strike, longshoremen had refused to load ships flying the Nazi flag and were talking about refusing to load scrap iron onto Japanese freighters to protest the military buildup of that country. If they gained a closed shop, who knows what further demands they'd make. Some shippers even claimed that if the unions were victorious, they'd be taking orders from Moscow and America's ports would become a tool of communist expansion.

On the other hand, the rise of radicals on the waterfront, even Eliel tacitly admitted, was largely a result of callous treatment endured by longshoremen. ILA members were mostly regular joes who wanted nothing more than a steady job and a decent wage. They weren't saints, however, and if given a raw deal could be antagonized and provoked into desperate, even violent measures.

As Eliel continued to argue in favor of forcing the port open, Roger viewed him with newfound clarity. The IA executive director had proven himself to be a cunning tactician. To his way of thinking, the workers were little more than pack animals to be herded and molded into productive units, strikes merely the result of a few spirited broncos who needed taming. Somehow, though, this waterfront conflict had become more than a clash over wages and hiring halls. With violent strikes flaring up in Kentucky coal mines, Pennsylvania steel mills, Michigan auto plants, Southern textile factories, and California agricultural fields, the United States had become a country at war with itself. And it was as much a battle of words and ideologies as it was of picket lines and teargas grenades. In the middle of this conflict, men like Eliel and Bridges were playing for all the marbles, and it wouldn't end, Roger reckoned, until lives were crushed and one side or the other was victorious.

Eliel was now describing the IA's plan to open the port. "Five of our

Atlas trucks will pick up cargo from Pier 38, the McCormick Steamship Company dock, and drive it a few blocks to the Garcia & Maggini warehouse on King Street."

.Plant harrumphed, as if to say "big deal."

"It's a drop in the bucket," Eliel admitted, "more symbolic than strategic, and primarily aimed at convincing longshoremen that their strike is a futile effort. Once the operation is successful, however, the Industrial Association will expand the service to other piers until the men give up and return to the docks."

"What if your plan doesn't work?" asked Roger. "What if the men stay out and continue to harass our replacement workers?"

"The beauty of it is, we win either way. If they cave, we force them back into the Blue Book Union. If they resist, we crush them."

Roger didn't know whether he was impressed with Eliel's confidence or disgusted by his arrogance. "How can you be so sure you can crush them?"

Eliel held up a forefinger. "Number one, we'll have hundreds of police on hand. If the strikers try to stop us they'll be dealt with firmly and forcefully." He flipped up a second finger into a victory sign. "Number two, Governor Merriam has promised to call out the National Guard if necessary, and they won't tolerate lawlessness." A third finger flipped up. "And three, we have a fifty-million dollar war chest, so we can hold out longer than they can."

Plant looked queasy. "Maybe your members can holdout forever, but our shippers are hurting. The tugboat pilots just joined the strike. Now we can't even move our freighters to the docks much less send them out to sea."

"All the more reason to get moving," said Eliel with finality.

58

Roger returned to his office and summoned Clarisa on the intercom. The meeting with Paul Eliel had disturbed him, and also convinced him he needed time away from work to relax and unwind, if only for a short while. When Clarisa entered his office, he watched her cross the room, her slender figure, clear green eyes, cheeks with a tinge of rose. He hadn't looked at her that way—as a woman—for a long time, and it stirred a tumescent sensation that had been dormant for weeks.

He stood up. "I think it's high-time we took a break from work and give ourselves a reward."

"Oh, what do you have in mind?"

"A leisurely lunch at the most elegant restaurant in San Francisco should do."

The city seemed blessedly normal as they strolled up Market Street, a world away from the conflict embroiling the waterfront. Green and white streetcars rumbled along the boulevard, bells clanging, trucks double-parked to make deliveries, taxis nosing through traffic, their horns tooting, scattering pretty shop girls in polka dot dresses.

Roger tried to initiate conversation, but it had been months since they'd spent time together outside the office, so the exchange was hesitant and awkward. Moreover, Clarisa seemed anxious and preoccupied, although he couldn't tell if it was from overwork, Nick's condition, or some other problem.

At New Montgomery Street, they entered the Palace Hotel through a pair of leaded-glass doors and stepped into a lobby with a posh old-world atmosphere. The ceiling was coffered with box beams and crown moldings, the walls accented with torchiere lamps, floors covered in polished white marble. They walked through the lobby to an arched opening on the far side, crossed a central corridor, and came to the entrance of the Garden Court Restaurant. A maitre'd in a tuxedo greeted them and checked their reservation. He then collected two menus and led them into an enormous light-filled room, its entire ceiling an immense skylight made of thousands of pieces of glass. Massive crystal chandeliers hung suspended from the skylight, splintering the natural light into a dazzling display of countless sparkles that cast dots of dancing light on the room below.

"It's beautiful," said Clarisa as they walked past giant potted ferns whose fronds arched over tables covered with white linen.

"This used to be an open-air courtyard for horse-drawn carriages," Roger explained. "When automobiles came along, the skylight was added and the courtyard converted to a restaurant."

A genteel buzz of conversation filled the room from well-heeled patrons dining on French inspired cuisine. The maitre'd led them to a table and took Roger's order for a bottle of champagne. When it arrived Roger attempted to unearth the charm he'd kept buried for months. He was out of practice, and it took some effort to loosen his tongue, but his persistence paid off. By the time they finished the first flute of champagne, Clarisa's preoccupied expression had thawed and showed signs of relaxation.

While doing his best to amuse her, Roger contemplated his desire to win her affection. For months he'd suppressed his attraction to her to the point of convincing himself that the embers of passion had burned themselves out. It hadn't been difficult. Seeing her at work had satisfied his need for contact, perhaps in the way a husband and wife become accustomed to each other and give little thought to the state of their marriage. Then, on the day she hurried off to see Nick in the hospital, the reality of losing her hit him harder than expected. Quite suddenly his affection for her awakened, as if it had always been there waiting for the right moment to reignite.

During lunch they talked of small inconsequential things, purposefully avoiding any subject that might cause them to think about the strike or any other controversial subject. It was a pleasant break from their normal duties, and near the end of the meal, over a dessert of lemon meringue pie, Roger decided to dip his toe in the water.

"I'm glad we've been able to escape the pressures of work for a couple of hours. I'd forgotten how enjoyable it is to sit and talk with you."

Clarisa looked down at her dessert. "Yes, it's been a difficult time."

Encouraged, he plunged ahead. "I — I want to apologize."

She looked up. "For what?"

"I've been such a bore. Worse than that I've been an uncouth, sullen bore, starting in December when I lost my manners and since then —" He paused to reframe the thought. "I know I haven't been cordial lately. I was quite ashamed of my behavior, and I have a tendency to bury myself in work and late-night ventures when things aren't going well. So I'm afraid I haven't been a good boss . . . or friend."

Clarisa shrugged. "Even at your worst you aren't a terrible boss, and most of the time," she grinned, "you're quite tolerable." She picked up a fork and sliced off a piece of pie. "Perhaps now we can resume our friend" —

The conversational buzz around them hushed, causing Clarisa to break off her thought. Roger noticed heads turning toward the entrance, where a gentleman of about sixty, wearing a pink carnation pinned to the lapel of his suit, had entered the restaurant, followed by two others. Everyone had immediately recognized Mayor Rossi, and Roger watched as the mayor worked his way through the restaurant, pausing to shake hands, greet friends, and wave to acquaintances.

Rossi was passing their table when he noticed them and detoured over.

"Farnsworth, just the man I want to see." He shook Roger's hand, then turned to Clarisa and tapped a finger on his temple. "Miss McMahon, if I'm not mistaken."

"I'm impressed you remember me, Mr. Mayor." Clarisa held out a hand." It's been nearly a year since we met at Falkirk."

Rossi took her hand and clasped it between his. "Well, my dear, you created quite an impression. Why if Farnsworth and I hadn't been there, the late governor would surely have kidnapped you."

Roger admired the mayor's gracious manners. He wasn't as garrulous or flamboyant as Rolph, but he had a charm of his own.

Rossi let go of Clarisa's hand and turned to Roger. "You've heard the Industrial Association is planning to proceed on the 25th?" Roger nodded. "I think it's a mistake. I've been meeting with Bridges and his group from the Joint Marine Strike Committee. They're a tough bunch, too militant for my money, but they're still willing to negotiate. Granted, the two sides are far apart, but I think it's too soon to resort to force. You agree?"

Roger nodded again. "Once we go down that road there's no turning back, and it will undoubtedly get nasty."

The mayor lowered his voice to a near whisper. "Chief Quinn assures me he can handle the situation. He's stocking up on all sorts of riot equipment but between you and I, I'm not so sure. I've asked Eliel to hold off awhile longer. So far, though, he hasn't agreed."

"Can't you order him to wait?" Clarisa asked.

The mayor smiled wanly. "I wish it were that simple, my dear. The Industrial Association and the Chamber of Commerce have been complaining that the strike is costing them millions and hounding me to take action."

"Have you talked with the governor?" asked Roger.

"Yes, and he's just as anxious as Eliel to force the port open. But then he's not from San Francisco and doesn't have to live with the consequences." He shook his head sadly. "I wish Rolph was still in the statehouse."

"If the governor won't help," said Roger, "what about the next step up?"

"Roosevelt?"

"He's aware of the situation and the Industrial Association wouldn't dare defy him."

"You're probably right, but it's no good just calling for patience. He'll have to offer some way out of this mess."

"Congress just authorized the president to appoint mediation boards to help settle labor disputes, and assistant Secretary of Labor McGrady is already familiar with the issues. If Roosevelt appoints McGrady and two men from the Coast, one acceptable to employers and one acceptable to the union, the three of them might bring the two sides together."

"Good idea." Rossi turned to an aide standing behind him. "Look into it."

Roger felt a rush of pride at Rossi's acceptance of his suggestion. He stole a glance at Clarisa, then returned his attention to the mayor. "The trick will be to find the right men. The president will need recommendations. I'd suggest A.P. Gianinni and John O'Connell."

Rossi shook his head. "Gianinni won't get involved in anything controversial that might affect his banking business and O'Connell is too connected with unions. We need men in good standing with the community *and* with no direct connections to either side."

Clarisa muttered something under her breath.

"What, my dear?" the mayor asked.

Roger thought he heard her too, but when he looked over at her she was toying with her dessert and didn't appear to have heard the mayor's question.

"Say," the mayor said, rubbing his chin, "how about Archbishop Hanna? He's respected by the longshoremen, and I'll bet the employers won't have a problem with him either." Just then an aide tapped his shoulder. "Well, I see I'm late again." He shook hands. "It was a pleasure running into you. Remember, my door is always open."

After the mayor strode off, Roger turned to Clarisa. "Did you mutter Hanna's name just before the mayor mentioned it?"

She grinned. "I would never think of telling the mayor what to do. He's of a generation in which women are admired, not consulted."

"So you wanted him to think he thought of Hanna himself. Is that it?"

She shrugged. "As far as I'm concerned, the mayor suggested a brilliant candidate."

"Come onnn! Fess up."

"Sorry," she smiled coyly, "that's my story and I'm stickin' to it."

The ambient glow from the skylight melded light and shadow on her face, making it appear softly radiant. Roger felt a surge of affection, and the more he studied her face, the harder it was to restrain himself from blurting out an impetuous declaration. The lunch had gone well, better than expected, so there was no reason to rush things. He lit a cigarette and signed the bill, then suggested a leisurely walk back to the office.

Rising to their feet, they headed for the exit. As he followed her out, her perfume brushed against his face, its subtle notes of gardenia provoking another surge of desire.

59

Sounds from some unseeable source floated toward him. The metallic click of a door latch, the rasp of shoe leather, the rustle of cloth. The sounds seemed to be drawing closer until something — *a pair of hands?* — lifted his right leg and shoulder and rolled him onto his left side. He tried to open his eyes, tried with all his might, but couldn't do it and gave up. He then tried to move his right arm, and it too wouldn't respond as if his limb was a lifeless piece of driftwood.

This lack of control evoked a sobering question. *Am I dead and in some sort of purgatory?* He was mulling this over when a soft, wet sensation rubbed his back, his crotch, his buttocks. Although fuzzy on the details of purgatory, he was certain it didn't include a body washing service. *Then I must be alive!* It was an exhilarating thought until another sobering question occurred to him. *Am I paralyzed?* He tried to move a finger, tried several times. As far as he could tell it didn't budge, so he gave up and drifted back into a pool of pure gray nothingness.

Sometime later, how much later he couldn't tell, for time had no meaning in this gray netherworld, more sounds intruded into his consciousness. This time voices. He drew in a breath and filled his lungs with air, sweet satisfying air. Sweet not only because it penetrated the depths of his lungs, but also because he seemed to be in control of his respiration. Encouraged, he attempted to wiggle his fingers. It was difficult to tell, but he didn't think they moved. Next he tried his toes and they too seemed immobile as if his body was tightly wrapped in bandages like a mummy.

With nothing else to do he listened to the voices. There were two of them and they were vaguely familiar.

"I've been watching him for hours," said the first voice in a sad monotone. "There's been no real change. Poor dear. Sometimes his breathing slows and I start to panic, frightened he's leaving us. Other times it's stronger, as if he's about to wake up. It's a maddening roller coaster ride . . . . I just don't know what to do."

"You should go home and rest," said the second voice, this one pleasant and melodic. "I'll stay with him until visiting hours are over. If there's any change, I'll call you right away."

A deep, protracted sigh. "I suppose you're right. You'll call?"

"If there's any change at all."

A rustle of clothing, a gentle pressure on his chest, a soft pleasant sensation on his forehead. "Goodbye," said the monotone voice.

"Goodbye," the second voice replied.

Footsteps. A door opening and closing. Silence.

The silence went on for a long time, so long he began to wonder if he was alone. He wasn't sure until he felt a hand grasp his right arm and pull it out from under the covers. It gently caressed the top of his hand, a pleasing sensation that lulled him into a sea of tranquility where he had no need for plans or thoughts or ideas, where he was content just to lay there and enjoy the caresses. Presently the hand pushed up his sleeve and moved along his forearm, still gently caressing him. It made him feel safe and warm, and he was drifting off again when his peace was interrupted by the sound of a breath sucking in sharply. At the same time the caresses stopped and a single point of pressure rested on his forearm. He tried to understand what was happening, tried to conjure an image, but the gray oblivion was tugging at him again, pulling him down, drawing him away. As he sank deeper and deeper, the pressure remained on his forearm, on the same spot that once burned with a stabbing pain.

He didn't have time to contemplate what just happened, for an astonishing image appeared: a prone figure, face ashen, laying prostrate in a pool of blood. He was inexplicably drawn to it until he was close enough to see that whoever it was had dark hair, a sinewy build, and a face that was strangely familiar. He studied the face, wondering where he'd seen it before. Then a bolt of recognition hit him.

Can it be? Myself? It certainly looks like me.

He reached down to touch the lifeless body, and as he made contact it began to disintegrate and decay like an object under intense heat, until all that was left was a layer of fine dust. He was staring at his remains, puzzled by the strange vision, when a tiny seedling sprouted from the dust, a fragile stem with a single leaf in the shape of an eye. With amazing speed, the seedling grew larger and larger, adding offshoots and branches until it formed a bush with buds at the tip of each offshoot. Like a billowing cloud, the bush continued to grow and expand, its main stem swelling into a thick trunk that projected sturdy branches out over him, forming a dense green canopy. Astonished, he watched the buds blossom into white, tulip-like flowers that scented the air with the fragrance of vanilla and cardamom. The flowers began to drop their petals, first one and then another and another, until petals were drifting down all around him like falling snow. When all the petals had fallen, small red berries appeared where the flowers had been, crimson dots on a leafy background. The berries grew rapidly as well, ballooning into heavy fruits the size of pomegranates, weighing down the branches, bending them lower and lower until one came within his reach. Feeling a tremendous urge to touch it, he reached up to the red fruit and was about to grasp it when the leaves trembled and parted.

A large black snake thrust its head out, causing him to shrink back in fear. The snake's coal black eyes were trained on him as it slithered down from the tree, revealing a pattern of yellow diamonds on its back. When it was just two feet away, the creature opened its jaws, baring a mouth of sharp fangs and a forked red tongue. It let out a hiss that sounded like a punctured tire, its tongue undulating up and down. Before Nick could respond, it swooped down and coiled around him, binding him in its grasp. The coils began to inflate like a blood pressure gauge, tightening around him, squeezing him until he could barely breathe. Afraid he'd suffocate, he squirmed and wriggled and tried to push back against the pressure, but his efforts were feeble. The snake maintained its merciless grip.

He screamed, or tried to, and this too was futile. Nothing came out.

The snake's head drew closer, its slithery tongue flicking out, its coal-black eyes locked onto his. Though he desperately wanted to escape, wanted to end this nightmare, he was feeling weak and tired as if his life force was draining away. The creature's head was now inches from him, and to his amazement it began to change in incredible ways, expanding, becoming rounder, its black scales melding and lightening until its skin was as smooth as that of a mammal. Over the next minute the head morphed from serpent to simian to human until at last it had a new head, the head of someone he recognized . . . his father.

Unable to breathe and stunned by the fantastic vision, he stared helplessly at the creature holding him in its terrifying grasp. *Father, I'm dying!* his panicked mind screamed. *I'm dying!*

As if reading his mind, the protean head nodded.

60

Hands clammy, heart pounding, Father Shannon set the phone down, donned his hat and coat, and hurried out of the rectory as fast as his sixty-year-old legs could carry him. In his thirty-five years of service, he had never received a call from the archbishop. Not that he expected one. Archbishops presided over dozens of parishes. Priests usually called them, rarely the other way around. And when a call did come, it was invariably from an assistant, not the archbishop himself.

It wasn't just the call that put an urgency in his stride. He'd read the newspaper. The waterfront strike was at a stalemate, and the Assistant Secretary of Labor had flown in from Washington D. C. to try to calm things down before all hell broke loose. Archbishop Hanna had been called on before to mediate labor disputes. This led Shannon to believe that the personal summons he'd just received had something to do with the current situation.

When he arrived at the archbishop's mansion, the wimpled nun led him straight to Hanna's office. The archbishop sat facing the window behind his desk in a contemplative posture, hands steepled together, forefingers pressed against his lips. The city was shrouded in fog, buildings a block away colorless and wraith-like. From where Shannon stood the fog-filtered light formed a glowing nimbus around the archbishop's head fringed with salt-and-pepper hair. It reminded him of a darker-haired Hanna who had come to San Francisco some twenty years earlier, a rising star in the Catholic world at the time, famous for impressing the Pope with his rhetorical defense of St. Thomas Aquinas, for his compassionate care of poor Italian immigrants, and for his indefatigable energy.

Shannon's gaze wandered from Hanna to the wall beside his desk. It was covered with framed certificates, awards, academic degrees, and letters of commendation that evidenced a life of extraordinary accomplishments. One award was from, of all things, the National Archeological Society. *Good lord, are there any limits to the man's knowledge and insatiable drive? Is he not the embodiment of Nietzsche's Superman?* He leaned over to examine the award. As he did, the archbishop swiveled around and faced him.

Hanna's complexion was pale and translucent, like a wax statue in Madame Trousseau's museum, and his face was utterly devoid of vitality.

Shannon was shocked at the change in the archbishop's countenance since their last meeting. He straightened his posture and forced a smile to hide his thoughts. "I was just admiring your accolades, Your Grace."

Hanna removed a handkerchief from his breast pocket and spread it out on the desk, carefully smoothing the fabric. "Then it may surprise you, Michael, that of all the honors bestowed on me, this is the one I treasure most." The edges of the handkerchief were stitched with an intricate floral design, and in the center was a hummingbird embroidered with brightly colored thread.

"It's lovely, Your Grace."

"It was given to me years ago when I was a young priest in upstate New York. I was traveling on vacation, driving my beloved Stanley Steamer to Niagara Falls, when I came upon a family by the side of the road, looking miserable amid their travel-worn suitcases. Their old jalopy had broken down and they had no money. They'd been walking to the nearest town but it was too far, especially for the old nonna. I recognized the women's colorful head scarves as Italian, so I stopped my car and addressed them in their native tongue. From the look on their faces you would have thought I was the Holy Father himself." He chuckled. "Well, to make a long story short, I cancelled my vacation plans, drove them to Albany, and spent the week helping them find a place to live. I even wangled a job for the husband from one of our Catholic businessmen." He glanced down at the embroidered handkerchief. "Two months later, I received a dozen of these in the mail."

"A wonderful gift, Your Grace."

"I still have all twelve and carry one with me every day." The archbishop folded the handkerchief and put it back in his pocket. "Sit down." He gestured toward a leather wingback chair. "I'll come right to the point, Michael. I've been asked to serve as chairman of a mediation board to help settle the waterfront strike. It's a great responsibility, as you know."

"And a great honor, which you deserve."

The archbishop sighed wearily. "At my age, I don't need more honors. In any case, they want an answer right away, so I have an important decision to make. Before I do, I wanted to talk to you about alternatives."

"Alternatives?"

"Yes. I've decided to decline."

Shannon gripped the arms of his chair. "But Your Grace —"

The archbishop raised a hand. "Hear me out. I'm about to reveal confidential information, and you must promise to keep it here." He patted his chest.

"Of course," said Father Shannon, feeling honored to be held in close confidence.

"As you know, two years ago at my request the Holy Father appointed Bishop Mitty to be my Coadjutor. That was the first step toward passing on my responsibilities. What you don't know is that I've been diagnosed with arterial sclerosis. My heart is weak. I can hardly accomplish day-to-day tasks, and my doctor says any additional strain could be fatal." He paused to allow Shannon a moment to absorb the news.

During the pause Shannon felt a pang of sadness. He didn't often see the archbishop, but he'd always been comforted by the knowledge that a man of Hanna's caliber was leading the archdiocese.

Hanna continued, "I've been involved in these sorts of labor disputes before. They require long hours and diligent work. Believe me, I want to accept but it wouldn't be fair to all parties if the Lord were to cancel my plans in the middle of it."

It could have been a morbid joke, but the archbishop's expression was utterly serious.

"What is it that you want from me, Your Grace? I could never counsel you to endanger your health." Shannon leaned forward. "But you must know that you are uniquely qualified to take on this important task. I can think of no one else who commands as much respect and admiration from all parties. And I can think of no one else who will treat the men fairly, yet garner compliance from the employers."

"What makes you think I would favor the men?"

"Your Grace, you've spent a lifetime working to protect and nurture the poor and downtrodden. The men are merely trying to gain a measure of economic security and respect, but that means the employers will have to give up power and privilege they've exploited for years."

"What about the Communists? The newspapers seem to think that the union is controlled by them. If we give the Communists an advantage, they'll preach atheism and perhaps lead some of our men astray."

"That's exactly why it's imperative you take a lead role in the dispute. If the men think that Communists are the only ones willing to come to their aid, they'll naturally follow them. We must demonstrate the intrinsic value of Catholic compassion and justice. If you help them, they'll see our ability to improve their lives and that will renew their faith in the church."

The archbishop nodded, albeit reluctantly. "What about this man

Bridges? I've heard he's a silver-tongued radical. Who knows, maybe he's the devil. Either way, no one is more aware than I of the seductive power of poetic dogma and youthful exuberance." He pointed to a framed calligraphy hanging on the wall: *He, who inspires, moves mountains with a song.*

Father Shannon scooted forward to the edge of his chair. "Some time ago you forbade me from involving myself in union activities. Since then I've stood on the sidelines watching events unfold. I've heard Bridges. His power of elocution is remarkable because he understands the corruption and exploitation the men live under and isn't afraid to challenge it. He doesn't espouse communism per se, but he isn't religious either. If he can inspire the men to defy their elected leadership, he can surely lead them away from the church into secularism." Shannon's voice took on a pleading quality. "Let me help you take on this great responsibility. I've followed the situation from the beginning. I can handle much of the burden and help you sort through it."

The archbishop leaned back. "It will mean delaying my retirement for another six months."

"Your Grace, God has chosen a life of service for you. This one last burden will be the crowning achievement of an exemplary career. I beg of you to draw on your deep abiding faith and rise to the occasion."

Hanna inhaled a breath and let it out with an air of resignation. He lowered his eyes as if in prayer, and for the next several moments Shannon could practically hear the debate going on inside him, wishing he could say something to tip the balance. Silence, however, seemed most appropriate.

A determined expression slowly crept over the archbishop's face, an expression that reminded Shannon of a younger, vigorous Hanna.

"Alright," Hanna said, straightening his posture. "Enough of the inspirational pep talk. What I need is practical guidance. Tell me everything—facts, players, potential solutions."

61

Father Shannon wished he had done more to help the young man. When he learned from Clarisa that Nick was an informant for the employers, he'd called him anonymously to warn him not to continue on such a dangerous course. Unfortunately, it hadn't done much good. The poor fellow lay in a coma and no one knew when, or even if, he'd regain consciousness. Shannon prayed for him daily and planned to visit him when he had time. For now, though, he was busy assisting the archbishop.

On June 25th President Roosevelt appointed Archbishop Hanna chairman of the newly created National Longshoremen's Board. Hanna would serve with two other appointees, Oscar Kushing, a prominent San Francisco attorney, and Edward McGrady, Assistant Secretary of Labor — their mandate: to investigate the West Coast labor dispute and arbitrate if both sides agreed.

Father Shannon counseled the archbishop on the details of the strike, and a grateful Hanna asked him to serve as his assistant during the hearings. This couldn't have pleased Shannon more. For months he'd been watching the strike from the sidelines, wishing he could do something. Now, as Hanna's right-hand man, he had a chance to play a role and perhaps influence the outcome.

The National Longshoremen's Board began by asking the Industrial Association to defer plans to open the port. The IA reluctantly agreed but only for five days. Next, the board summoned representatives from the Joint Marine Strike Committee, the ILA Pacific Coast District Executive Committee, and the Waterfront Employers Association.

Over the next three days, as a high pressure weather system settled over San Francisco, pushing the fog back to the Pacific Ocean and raising temperatures, Archbishop Hanna and his colleagues listened to each group present their side. In Hanna's presence the usually stubborn longshoremen and arrogant employers were humble and contrite, as if they were standing in judgment before the Great Creator himself. When ILA officials appeared before the board, Hanna asked if they would accept a jointly-managed hiring hall with a neutral dispatcher. This had been Father Shannon's suggestion. Shannon knew that District President Bill Lewis would agree to it and would present it to the Pacific Coast District Executive Committee. Privately, however, he warned the archbishop that Harry Bridges wouldn't be so obliging. The strikers had been holding out for complete control of the hiring hall for months and wouldn't give up that demand easily. Still, he thought it was worth a try and offered to contact Bridges to see if he could convince the Aussie to accept a compromise.

The archbishop readily agreed.

Father Shannon had met Harry Bridges a number of times at

community meetings and social gatherings. Though he didn't agree with all of Bridges' ideas, he was of the opinion that Bridges was an honest union man with the longshoremen's best interests at heart. He'd even trusted Bridges enough to tell him about Nick's role as an informant after obtaining his assurance that Nick wouldn't be harmed. Later, when he heard that Nick had been beaten, he called Bridges for an explanation and learned that the poor fellow had been mistaken for a strikebreaker, an unfortunate and ironic twist of fate.

He called Bridges and described the hiring hall proposal. "Keep in mind, Harry, if the men are treated unfairly by the dispatcher, the union can appeal to an arbitration board or even go on strike again."

"It's an open-shop Trojan horse, Michael. The employers would flood the docks with non-union stevedores and that would undermine and eventually destroy the ILA. Besides, the rank-and-file will never agree to it."

Over Bridges objections, the Pacific Coast District Executive Committee approved the plan and submitted it to the National Longshoremen's Board. ILA President Joe Ryan also appeared before the board to voice his support.

Father Shannon disliked Ryan and his expensive suits and the way he talked like a Tammany Hall ward boss. In Shannon's opinion, there was nothing worse than a union official who feathered his nest at the expense of the rank-and-file.

At the end of his testimony Ryan, who was about to return to New York, took a parting shot at Bridges. "I'm convinced he's an agent provocateur on behalf of Communists and an obstructionist who doesn't want to settle the strike." He also rebuked Bridges for meddling in negotiations. "The Strike Committee isn't running the strike. It's controlled by the ILA Pacific Coast District. Bridges has assumed authority of running the whole thing when his Strike Committee is only responsible for organizing pickets and such."

Other ILA officials echoed Ryan, saying that Pacific Coast District President Bill Lewis was the elected and authorized spokesman for the men.

When Thomas Plant appeared before the board on behalf of the Waterfront Employers Association, he took immediate advantage of the ILA's infighting. "Who shall we deal with, Joseph Ryan or the District Executive Committee or Harry Bridges' Strike Committee? We've already made two agreements and both have been repudiated."

Not that it mattered. In the next breath, Plant rejected the District Executive Committee's proposal, saying it would lead to a closed shop, something the employers would never accept.

Meanwhile, the Industrial Association announced that if a settlement wasn't reached by Monday, July 2nd, it was prepared to proceed with its plan to open the port. Such a course, Father Shannon knew, would provoke a strong, possibly violent reaction, and he wasn't surprised to learn that several union delegates at the San Francisco Labor Council had proposed a general strike involving every union in the city if the Industrial Association attempted to move cargo with non-union labor. Though most delegates had rejected the notion of a general strike, they acknowledged that if corporations could crush the waterfront strike, every union was vulnerable.

By the weekend, two things were certain. First, the plan submitted by Bill Lewis and the District Executive Committee wasn't going to fly. Without the endorsement of either Plant or Bridges, the employers and the rank-and-file weren't going to budge. Second, temperatures around the Bay Area were rising. A heat wave was on the way.

Early Saturday morning Father Shannon took a leisurely walk down Mission Street to stretch his legs. It was a beautiful day. A warm summer sun had burned off the fog and morning dew was evaporating off the streets like a pot beginning to boil. He walked all the way to the water-front, and today it was unnaturally quiet, even for a Saturday morning. The great pier sheds were locked up tight, and solemn groups of picket-ers and policemen were stationed on opposite sides of the roadway, two entrenched camps separated by a no man's land of cobblestones and railroad tracks.

The aroma of hot coffee and sizzling bacon lured him into the Java House, a waterfront diner run by an ex-stevedore who manned the griddle while his wife took orders and served breakfasts. Unlike the quiet scene outside, the diner was crowded with a lively mix of police officers and strikers who mingled freely in what was considered neutral territory. Shannon was surprised to see so many out-of-work strikers until he spot-ted a sign offering half-price specials to all stevedores during the strike. Moreover, the fare here was undoubtedly better than the oatmeal served at the strike kitchen.

He sat down at the counter and ordered eggs, bacon, and coffee. Friendly banter among the customers and music from a radio gave the restaurant a cheerful air. Yet Shannon's mind was elsewhere, focused on the National Longshoremen's Board hearings the previous week and on what might bring the two sides together. There were only two days left before the Industrial Association would begin moving cargo, hardly enough time to sort it all out.

The music on the radio cut off, replaced by an announcer. *"We interrupt this program to bring you a special address from Governor Frank Merriam."*

The friendly banter quieted and all eyes turned to the radio.

"Ladies and gentlemen, as your governor it is my duty to inform you that California is facing a grave crises. Strikers, led by red agitators, are wreaking havoc all over the state. In the Central Valley they've prevented timely harvesting, costing millions in crop damage, and in seaports they're holding up thousands of tons of valuable shipments. Communists are responsible for considerable damage to property, but during this time of economic depression our state can ill-afford such wanton destruction..."

As the speech progressed, the strikers looked glum, as if their food had gone rancid, and the police officers appeared demoralized as well, as if they too had swallowed a bitter pill. Shannon observed the transformation with great disappointment. Merriam was placing blame rather than seeking solutions, and it was a remarkably stupid thing to do. He understood the governor's frustration. The economy was in shambles and labor disputes were only making things worse. Vilifying one side over the other as the sole cause of the problem, however, wasn't going to resolve anything.

When the speech ended and his breakfast arrived, Shannon picked up a newspaper laying on the counter. There were the usual articles about the strike, foreign trade, a kidnapping. Then an article caught his eye.

Raid on Communist Newspaper

On Friday evening five men wearing brown leather jackets and khaki trousers raided the headquarters of the Western Worker, a Communist Party publication at 37 Grove Street, a block from City Hall. According to eyewitnesses, the raiders shattered the front windows with baseball bats, entered the offices and proceeded to demolish furniture and equipment. Western Worker staff members, who had been working in the back room, rushed out to the front office. Confronted with superior numbers, the raiders dropped their implements of destruction, including a revolver, and fled across Civic Center plaza. The police arrived minutes later but took no action, speculating that the raid might have been an inside job as a play for sympathy.

Shannon set the newspaper down and stared at his breakfast, his appetite gone. It seemed that a war had broken out across America, a war pitting workers against employers, radicals against conservatives, unions against corporations. And unless men like himself are able to stop the rancor, things were going to get a whole lot worse before they got better.

62

A low morning sun in their eyes, hundreds of strikers crowded the sidewalks as they streamed east toward the waterfront. Negotiations under the auspices of the National Longshoremen's Board had proved fruitless, and now strikers were massing along the Embarcadero in anticipation of a move by the Industrial Association to open the port. Harry Bridges and Henry Schmidt watched the men walk along Folsom Street, some stopping at empty lots to pick up brickbats, cobblestones, railroad spikes, rocks, anything they could get their hands on. Though Bridges wasn't a violent person by nature, he knew they didn't stand a chance unless they stood up to the Industrial Association. Aside from the use of firearms, which he expressly prohibited, he encouraged the men to do whatever they could to disrupt the flow of cargo. It wasn't much of a plan, and he hoped violence wouldn't be necessary, yet deep down his intuition told him that before the day was through, blood would be spilled.

He and Schmidt joined the procession. When they arrived at the waterfront hundreds of strikers were already stationed opposite various pier sheds, watching for any sign of cargo movement. On the other side of the Embarcadero, squadrons of police stood guard in front of the great pier sheds that, for the moment, were locked up tight. According to a rumor the Industrial Association planned to begin operations at Pier 38, the McCormick docks, and it was there that the largest group of strikers was gathered. Unlike the classically designed pier sheds near the Ferry Building, the roof line of Pier 38 was rounded like the Alamo, and it wasn't lost on Bridges that the squadron of officers standing in front, like the men of the Alamo, were far outnumbered by those they faced. In this case, however, the Texans had far superior weapons than their opponents.

Bridges glanced up at Rincon Hill on the inland side of the Embarcadero, rising a hundred feet above the waterfront. Dozens of spectators were standing at the top, looking down at the scene below like fans at a ballgame. Directly below them, at the base of the hill, construction workers were building a huge concrete monolith nearly as high as Rincon Hill that would one day receive strands of cable from the Bay Bridge.

The two strike leaders spent the morning monitoring the scene until they received a report that the Industrial Association, at the behest of Mayor Rossi, had agreed to postpone any activities on the waterfront for twenty-four hours. It wasn't enough time to accomplish anything toward settling the strike but enough time, Bridges figured, for the IA to put its final pawns into place. When the postponement was announced, most strikers left the waterfront, thinking that nothing was going to happen that day. Bridges and Schmidt returned to ILA headquarters on Steuart Street where they, too, took the opportunity to make sure all their preparations were complete. They had organized a fleet of cars and scouts, who would keep an eye on the waterfront and report back to headquarters, recruited two doctors to treat injured strikers should violence break out, and sent out word to supporters and sympathizers that everyone was welcome to help the striking unions prevent the Industrial Association from moving cargo with non-union labor.

Towards the end of the day, Bridges and Schmidt decided to check on things at the waterfront. The afternoon sun was still high in the sky as they walked along the Embarcadero where the usual number of picketers and police were stationed opposite each other at various pier sheds. They were talking to a group of strikers opposite Pier 38 when five trucks rumbled onto the Embarcadero from a side street, escorted by several police cars. Bridges watched the trucks make a quick dash toward Pier 38, their solid rubber tires bouncing on the cobblestones, boxy sheet metal hoods clattering as they raced toward the pier shed's huge arched entrance. Just before the convoy reached the shed, its corrugated steel door rolled up and swallowed the trucks, and just as quickly it snapped shut. Mounted police then lined up in front of the door, flanked by officers on motorcycles and on foot, a move obviously pre-planned.

This confirmed Bridges' suspicion that the Industrial Association had only agreed to the delay so they could put their trucks into position. He sent men out along the waterfront to spread word about what just happened. In a matter of minutes breathless strikers came running from other piers, swelling the ranks opposite Pier 38 to several hundred agitated men. Bridges and Schmidt were standing at the front of the swelling crowd, and as more men arrived, the two strike leaders were pushed out onto the Embarcadero toward the line of horses, motorcycles, and blue-coated policemen protecting the pier shed.

"What's gonna happen?" Schmidt yelled above the din of agitated strikers.

"I don't know," said Bridges, feeling pressure against his back as the growing ranks continued to nudge them toward Pier 38.

Closer to the bluecoats now, Bridges could see the expressions on their faces revealing nervousness, determination, anger, or a combination of all three.

A striker yelled, "Come on, let's get those scab drivers!"

"Yeah," others shouted, "let's go!"

The crowd surged forward, pushing Bridges and Schmidt even closer to the line of horses and cops. As the gap between strikers and police narrowed, the men in blue tensed up and gripped their billy clubs. The horses, also sensing danger, lifted their heads and nervously jerked their reins. Bridges had figured that violence might erupt, probably would erupt at some point, but he hadn't expected to be thrust into it by an angry thong at his back. Moreover, until cargo emerged from the pier shed it was premature to resort to violence. He leaned backward against the pressure, trying to hold his ground, but his feet slid over the bumpy cobblestones as the men behind him continued to surge forward.

Just as the strikers seemed ready to charge, a police captain stepped forward with his hands in the air. "The men who drove those trucks are not on the pier," he yelled above the din. "They were taken off on a launch and the trucks are not being loaded. You can send two men in to satisfy yourselves that no cargo is being moved."

While the strikers hung back, Bridges and Schmidt followed the captain into the pier shed. The five canvas-topped trucks were parked in an aisle between two mountains of cargo. The trucks looked woefully inadequate for the job they were intended, but as Bridges well knew they could easily become a potent symbol of the IA's ability to force the port open.

Bridges assured the strikers that the trucks weren't being loaded and asked them to move back to the inland side of the Embarcadero. Dusk was coming on now. To prepare for an all-night vigil, the men lit fires in a half-dozen oil drums, the dancing flames casting a red orange glow onto the Alamo facade across the Embarcadero. Though it was a warm evening, the strikers were drawn to the flames and gathered around them, talking in low tones and glancing periodically toward the pier shed.

Hungry and tired, Bridges and Schmidt went to the ILA kitchen on Steuart Street to grab a meal. They sat down at a long communal table among longshoremen and sailors discussing the events at Pier 38 and what might happen the next day. The conversation was interrupted when a striker, standing beside a radio, called out, "Hey, listen. It's Chief Quinn." He turned up the volume.

"We're asking the public to stay away from the waterfront tomorrow unless you have business there. The Police Department will have its hands full preventing violence, and we do not want any innocent bystanders hurt."

Bridges smiled. "Quinn couldn't have broadcast a more attractive invitation."

Indeed, the following day thousands of strikers and sympathizers flowed toward the waterfront, and like the day before, many stopped along the way to arm themselves with whatever they could stuff in their pockets.

The waterfront was noticeably more tense than the previous day and more concentrated in one location. Hundreds of policemen were stationed in front of Pier 38 clutching billy clubs, teargas launchers, and shotguns. On the other side of the cobblestone divide, strikers crowded the sidewalks and spilled out onto the Embarcadero, blocking traffic along the roadway. Not that there was much. The usual flow of trucks, vans, and jitneys was entirely absent. Behind the strikers, spectators were once again gathered at the crest of Rincon Hill, watching, waiting, some looking through binoculars to survey the scene below.

Nothing much occurred during the morning hours. The ranks of strikers continued to grow until they backed up into nearby streets, police remained in formation, and the spectators on Rincon Hill waited patiently for the drama to unfold. At about eleven o'clock a line of policemen on foot, backed by horse-mounted officers, herded the strikers off the Embarcadero and placed wooden barricades in front of them to keep them off the roadway.

For two more hours the scene remained at a standstill.

Among a group of trusted Albion Hall men, Harry Bridges watched as horse-mounted officers position themselves in front of Pier 38. When they were in place, a line of blue-coated officers on foot took up position in front of them. It was now almost 1:30 p.m.

"I can't imagine the Industrial Association will hold off much longer," Bridges remarked to Henry Schmidt,

Schmidt frowned. "God, I'm hungry. I haven't eaten a thing since breakfast and that was a bowl of oatmeal."

Bridges glanced at him. "I don't know how you can be hungry at a time like this."

Schmidt patted his ample belly. "I'm always hungry, Harry."

A deafening roar erupted. The strikers around them stiffened as if jolted by an electric current and rose up on their toes to catch a better view.

"What's goin' on?" exclaimed Schmidt, craning his neck.

"The door's rollin' up," replied Bridges, peering over the crowd.

Eight police cars rolled out of the cargo shed at Pier 38 and turned left onto the Embarcadero, followed by the five canvas-topped trucks. A police captain, riding on the running board of the lead truck, held on with one hand while brandishing a revolver in the air with the other. As the trucks turned onto the Embarcadero, he bellowed for all to hear, "THE PORT IS NOW OPEN!" a taunting remark that seemed to dare the strikers to try to stop the procession.

If that was his intention, it worked. An angry clamor rose up from the strikers as they surged forward against the flimsy wooden barricades.

63

Clarisa left her flat, grim-faced and angry. Seamus had insulted her after he read a newspaper report that radicals had been arrested for distributing leaflets at the National Guard Armory, encouraging Guardsmen not to take up arms against strikers. Seamus was outraged that authorities had committed such a flagrant violation of the First Amendment, especially as he'd printed the leaflet free of charge for the Worker's School next door.

"This country doesn't live up to its principles," he complained over breakfast, "because men like your employers don't give a damn about the Constitution. Their brand of democracy is more akin to Hitler than

Washington."

Up until that point an unspoken agreement between them had kept them from discussing her job, a sore subject as Clarisa was the primary breadwinner, a situation that Seamus was loath to acknowledge. Now that her father had breached it, she felt free to reply, "You may not like my employers, but without the wages they pay me, we'd be out on the street."

"Oh, so now you're proud of whoring yourself for greedy capitalists."

During her streetcar ride to work, she calmed down enough to realize that her father's accusation was only partially aimed at her. When they first emigrated to America, Seamus held his adopted country in high regard, spending hours studying the Declaration of Independence and the Bill of Rights until he knew them by heart. "The first democracy in the world," he taught her proudly, "and the first colony to kick the British monarchy in the arse." But when the economy crashed and his business dried up, the old bitterness surfaced and he began to question America's brand of capitalism. "There's no cooperation here, just cut-throat competition. Big fish eat little fish until the only ones left are sharks."

He was also angered by the attack on the *Western Worker* offices and declared that they should have blown the raiders to "bloody 'ell." It even prompted him to retrieve his Enfield out of the closet, a bolt-action rifle he'd acquired during his days with the Irish Republican Army. At the kitchen table, he cleaned and oiled it, sharpened the bayonet to a fine edge, then stowed it downstairs in the print shop. "Just in case," he said.

Still, for all his frustrations he shouldn't have called me a—. She couldn't even bring herself to think the word.

When she arrived at the office, multiple phones were ringing, and Mrs. Butterfield, the gray-haired receptionist, looked harried and swamped with demands as she fielded the calls and took messages. On the way to her desk Clarisa caught a glimpse of Roger and Thomas Plant inside the conference room, surrounded by telephones all off the hook, apparently connected to callers vying for attention.

She kept busy for a couple of hours, typing letters and documents in her in-box. When it was empty, she peeked into the conference room, where Roger and Plant were still deep in phone conversations. Not wanting to disturb them, she returned to her desk and pulled a *Chronicle* out of her purse. At the top of the front page the headline read: PORT WILL OPEN TODAY.

At lunchtime, feeling cooped up and isolated in her windowless office, she decided to go out. On her way through the office, she passed the conference room and looked in. It was empty and Mrs. Butterfield confirmed that Mr. Farnsworth had left ten minutes earlier. This was puzzling to Clarisa, as he usually checked in with her before leaving the office.

There were no picketers in front of the building, reminding her that the strikers were massed at the waterfront. Curious to know what was going on, she bought a sandwich at a deli and headed south on Fremont Street toward Rincon Hill. Beyond Folsom Street the sidewalk sloped up, and a block later buildings gave way to a hillside covered with dried grass and littered with urban detritus.

Hundreds of curious onlookers stood at the top of the hill, all looking down at the waterfront with bored expressions, for at the moment nothing much was happening. She searched for Roger among the spectators, and being one of the only women there, men courteously tipped their hats and stepped out of her way until she found a spot with a clear view. From this vantage point she could see beyond the waterfront to the bay, where four partially-completed towers, evenly spaced in a straight line from San Francisco to Yerba Buena Island, rose up out of the water, each tower consisting of two tapered columns connected by diamond-shaped braces. Although it wasn't finished, she could see that when connected by a roadway, the bridge would be a marvel of modern engineering and design.

Her gaze dropped down to the waterfront. Two groups faced each other on opposite sides of the Embarcadero, each resembling a swarm of insects. The swarm closest to her was motley in color, a collection of white caps and dark fedoras stretching along the east side of the Embarcadero and into streets that fed into it. The swarm on the waterfront side, a dark-blue species, was organized in a rigid, orderly formation. Three lines of bluecoats formed the main body, backed by a line of horse-mounted officers. Additional officers on motorcycles flanked the main body, and more bluecoats with gold epaulets, presumably top brass, stood off to the side near command cars.

She ate her sandwich and monitored the scene below, although there wasn't much to see. The opposing swarms remained stationary, reminding her of a description of war as endless hours of boredom punctuated by moments of terror. She finished her lunch and was about to return to the office when someone exclaimed, "Something's happening at Pier 38."

The door to the pier shed was rising up and simultaneously an angry clamor erupted from the strikers, who pushed forward against a line of wooden barricades. Several police cars drove out of the pier shed, followed by five canvas-topped trucks, flanked and followed by a motorcycle escort. The caravan turned south, and as it rolled over the cobblestone roadway, strikers knocked over the barricades and advanced into the street until they met a line of bluecoats with billy clubs who halted their progress. Behind the frontline officers, another row of bluecoats bearing shotguns and teargas launchers stood at the ready.

"Looks like the cops have 'em well contained," one spectator remarked.

Indeed, at all points the blue line held the strikers at bay, allowing the caravan to proceed south two and a half blocks to a warehouse on King Street, making the trip in less than two minutes.

"All those cops just to go a coupla blocks," someone said. "The protection's gotta cost ten times the value of the cargo."

After the trucks were unloaded in the warehouse, Clarisa watched them travel back to Pier 38, presumably to pick up another load of cargo. Meanwhile, as water seeks the path of least resistance, the strikers flowed away from the Embarcadero, ranging along Brannan and Townsend to Second and Third streets, testing the police cordon at every intersection. One group of strikers approached an empty lot adjacent to the train station at Third and Townsend. A pile of red bricks lay inside the lot, attracting strikers who swarmed over it like ants on a piece of candy.

The blue-coated policemen saw the stockpile too. Several bluecoats broke ranks and sallied forward among the strikers, billy clubs flailing, trying to drive them from the potential missiles. Too late. Strikers began hurling brickbats at the officers, who cowered under the onslaught and hastily retreated, one retreating officer crumpling to the ground clutching his head. The bluecoats quickly organized themselves into a wedge formation and drove forward toward the strikers like a massive, multi-limbed beetle, its club-bearing arms mechanically rising and falling, cracking the skulls of those in its path who fell to the ground covering their blood-stained heads. The skirmish energized both sides, and like a colony of ants agitated by the stick of a doodling boy, the movements of the combatants sped up in random and chaotic patterns.

Clarisa noticed another group of strikers a few blocks away on Brannan Street, surrounding a flatbed truck with a load of canvas bags. It wasn't one of the Atlas trucks from Pier 38, but the men didn't seem to care. They yanked the bags off the truck, broke them open, and spread the contents onto the street.

Bang! Bang! Bang!

The sound of gunfire drew Clarisa's gaze back to the train station where police were firing revolvers into the air. The gunfire splintered the strikers into small nimble groups, each group alternately charging forward to hurl brickbats and spikes, then retreating while another group attacked from a different direction. Like watching a three-ring circus, Clarisa's eyes moved from one skirmish to the next. Back at the Embarcadero, strikers managed to breach the cordon protecting Pier 38 and surged forward to the line of horse-mounted officers, who whipped their steeds into the oncoming charge. She saw one officer pulled from his horse and set upon, and a horse struck on the head by a cobblestone.

Boom! Boom! Boom!

Clarisa flinched as explosive thuds rent the air. A cloud of gray teargas billowed up amongst the strikers, scattering them in disarray. Officers wearing green gas masks with ribbed breathing hoses that made them look like space invaders from Mars charged forward toward the strikers, who hurled missiles back at the alien-like creatures as they retreated off the Embarcadero.

A wailing siren again drew her attention to the train station. A police car drove up, stopped, and disgorged two officers, both wearing gold epaulets. She couldn't tell for sure, but one appeared to be Chief Quinn. A brick whizzed by him and smashed the windshield of his command car, shattering it into radiating shards. This seemed to enrage the bluecoats, who launched a dozen teargas canisters spewing toxic gas. The canisters landed amongst the strikers, who, as if playing a game of dodgeball, picked them up and tossed them back at the bluecoats.

The entire area from Pier 38 to the train station was now shrouded in teargas, forcing passengers who emerged from the train station to hold handkerchiefs over their faces as they hurried off into the city. The teargas also pushed strikers inland, followed by bluecoats in hot pursuit. Some strikers turned into South Park, a circular English-style commons with lawn and trees. Clarisa watched the strikers and police grapple inside the park, thinking how strange it was to see such naked animal aggression in what was normally a tranquil urban oasis.

As the afternoon wore on, the tide of battle alternately flared and dissipated. Police lines surged forward and ebbed back, as did the strikers, who spontaneously massed for attacks, then splintered apart at the crack of gunfire and the sting of teargas. Clarisa watched for an hour, deeply troubled by the blood and brutality, yet also mesmerized by it.

She returned to the office and for the rest of the afternoon found it nearly impossible to concentrate on her work, the scenes of battle fresh in her mind. At the end of the day, she left the Matson Building and walked past newspaper boys holding up the latest editions. *"Extra! Extra! Read all about the bloody massacre! The waterfront's a slaughterhouse!"* they cried. She bought a copy and read blow-by-blow accounts of the conflict, complete with statistics: twenty-four hospitalized, half police, half strikers, another fifty-five injured, fifty-two arrested. Eight trucks had been overturned by strikers, although none were part of the Atlas fleet. Four horses were injured; one had to be put down.

64

On the day of the waterfront battle, Roger Farnsworth received an unexpected phone call and it couldn't have come at a worse time. He and Plant were juggling multiple phone conversations in the conference room, alternating between authorities handling the conflict, mediators trying to avoid bloodshed, and supervisors managing replacement workers. When the unexpected call came, despite the chaotic situation, he slipped out of the office and hailed a taxi.

Two hours earlier, in a private room at San Francisco General Hospital, a faint vibrating glow appeared in the distance like the first dabble of sunrise to lighten the night sky. Still in his gray netherworld, Nick watched the glow brighten until a pinpoint of light poked through the mist like a shaft of sunlight breaking through the clouds. This too brightened and expanded until it became a radiant full moon, round and bright white. As bright as it was, it still seemed to be coming from far off as if from the end of a long tunnel, reminding him of descriptions of near death experiences.

Was my father right when he said I was dying?

He was contemplating this when the full moon flashed like an explosive charge, sending a sharp stabbing pain through his eyes and deep into his parietal lobe. He shielded his face to dim the blinding light, and in its place he saw the outlines of five metacarpal bones covered with a layer of pale skin and fine epidermal hairs. He stared, fascinated at the hand until it dawned on him that this vision, this five fingered paw, these wrinkled knuckles and unclipped nails, were not a dream.

His arm tired. His hand dropped.

Instantly the light bore down on him again, snapping his eyes shut under the intense glare. Slowly and curiously he cracked them open until his pupils adjusted to the light of an orbital fixture hanging from the ceiling. Without moving his head, his eyes circled the room in a clockwise motion. It was sparsely furnished with two chairs, a bedside table, and the bed he lay on. A tube attached to his left arm curled up to a drip bag hanging from a metal stand. He lay there, his mind blank, taking in colors and shapes and details. There were straight lines where walls met the ceiling, a bit of blue sky through a sash window, a painted door with a chrome knob. Footsteps on the other side of the door shuffled by, accompanied by voices, a squeaky gurney, someone laughing, another joining in. He was content for the moment to absorb whatever reached his senses.

To be. Not do. Just be.

The door opened and a nurse came in wearing a white uniform and stiff white hat. The rustle of her skirt and her footfalls sounded familiar as if he'd heard them before. When their eyes met, she smiled broadly as if seeing a long-lost friend for the first time. "You're awake," she said. "That's wonderful." She placed her fingers on his wrist. "Can you hear me?" Nick nodded. "You've been rolling over on your own the last few days, so we thought you might regain consciousness soon. Your mother will be happy. The poor woman kept a constant vigil until we convinced her you weren't going to come to your senses any sooner with her here." She picked up a chart hanging on the footboard and jotted a note. "I'm going to inform the doctor. How about some juice?"

She returned a few minutes later with a glass, lifted his head, and helped him take a sip. "The doctor's busy now, but he'll be here as soon as he can."

The cool liquid felt odd in his mouth as it seeped under his tongue and coated his gums, tingled his teeth. He held it in his mouth, absorbing the sensations and the tart sweet taste. When he tried to gulp his throat muscles didn't know what to do and resisted the effort, the liquid flowing down more from gravity than effort. He managed to take several sips, each one more naturally than the last, and this pulled him out of his hibernation. While the nurse replaced his drip bag, his grogginess faded and the mechanisms of his brain sputtered and sparked like a car engine starting up after a winter of disuse.

"Ho — how long?" he croaked.

"How long have you been in a coma?" She removed a thermometer from her apron pocket, shook it, and slipped it under his tongue. "Let's see." She checked the chart. "About fifteen days."

"Where am I?"

"San Francisco General Hospital. Now be quiet while I take your temperature."

Being quiet was the last thing he wanted to do. There were a dozen things he wanted to know. Like how he got here and what occurred in the time he'd been unconscious. When she left the room he closed his eyes and tried to remember what happened, though nothing came and it seemed as if his mind wasn't ready to concentrate. Strangely enough, when he gave up trying and let his thoughts drift, an image appeared, a towering gray object . . . a building . . . no, not a building, a ship, a freighter with a red and black smokestack. Slowly the image became more distinct and detailed like a developing photograph, and as soon as it was fully in focus, another image replaced it. Then another and another. A box of chocolates, a wooden helm, a reptilian face, a large head with a train engineers cap, a slashing storm, a burning tattoo, the stinking odor of copra. He watched passively as the images rolled by, one after another, until one jumped out at him, causing him to stiffen. He stopped the flow to examine it — a face, the face of his father suspended amid a leafy green background. He tried to understand its significance, to conjure some meaning, sensing that there was a lesson or parable attached to it. *What is it?* He held onto the image, not wanting to let it slip away like a dream not recalled after waking that fades and disappears forever.

"May I come in?"

The words jerked him from his thoughts.

A figure stood in the doorway, hat in hand, charcoal suit, blond hair. "I heard you were awake." His voice was calm and quiet, though a tense undercurrent lay beneath it. "How are you feeling?"

How am I feeling? He wasn't sure and it didn't seem important. He gazed at the young man and studied him without recognition until a name surfaced from somewhere in the depths.

"You took quite a blow to the head," said Roger. "Those strikers really let you have it."

"Strikers?"

"Don't you remember? Strikers attacked you. They thought you were a strikebreaker."

His memories were still a collection of jumbled shards that didn't fit into a cohesive picture. He needed more time to sort them out and piece them together, and he especially wanted to recapture the memory of his father before it faded away.

"They said you were on the *Diana Dollar* in the middle of the night and escorted you off for your own good."

Who said? When?

"I suppose you were looking for narcotics, but there wasn't any, was there?" Roger's lips pursed into a frown. "We had an agreement, Nick. When Plant found out you'd been on the ship, he was furious. He threatened to turn you in and would have if I hadn't spoken on your behalf."

None of this meant anything, and all he could do was try to fit the pieces together from a jumble of unconnected images.

"Don't you realize you could spend years in jail?"

The question jogged a few pieces into place, and from that point on he began the process of reassembling his life after the *Diana Dollar*, arranging the shards one-by-one, fitting them together into a crude mosaic. In spite of his progress many details remained unconnected, and it left him with an unsettled feeling, as if he'd lost his wallet and couldn't remember where he left it.

He looked to Roger for more answers. "Why are you here? What do you want?"

Roger smiled nervously, his forefinger tracing the edge of his hat brim. "Only one thing, and I'm prepared to trade for it." He paused. "Because you were injured, I can convince Plant that you're no longer any use to us, that we should let you off the hook. For good. No more threat of jail time hanging over your head." He lowered his eyes to the floor. "In return" — he shot a quick glance at Nick — "I want you to give her up." He sighed and seemed relieved to have laid out his proposition. "I love her. I want you to know that. And I know she has feelings for me, but —."

The broken sentence hung in limbo.

But what?

Roger studied the opposite wall, a look of pain in his eyes.

Ten seconds passed. Twenty seconds. A half-minute. Nick returned to his father's face amid the leafy green background. *Was there something he was trying to tell me?* In his mind's eye, the face was replaced by his father's lifeless body on a stretcher, an image that had haunted him every day for months. He hadn't thought of it since returning from the voyage, so perhaps distance *had* done what time couldn't: freed him from that horrible moment. He summoned Charles' face again in the leafy green tree, alive, eyes boring into him, telling him something, something important. *What was it?* A few more shards fell into place. The white blossoms, the prodigious red fruit, the snake with coal black eyes, the face of his father observing him as he died.

Or was it death?

"I can help you find another job," said Roger. "I've got contacts. Whatever you want to do, I'm sure I can help you get started."

The offer triggered a series of emotions — remorse, anger, guilt, fury, sadness — each one more intense than the last. All he could do was let them flow through him like passing squalls, and when the storm subsided his body was blank, not numb or dead but serene and quiet as if he'd been washed and hung out to dry in the sun. He wiggled his toes and with a rush of supreme joy watched the blanket at the foot of the bed move. He looked up at Roger.

"I don't want a different job. At least not now."

"No problem. We'll be employing hundreds of men on the docks."

"Not as a strikebreaker." The words flew out as if he'd vomited them.

"No matter. The strike will be over soon."

Roger recounted the events of the previous fortnight, and as the details unfolded Nick arranged more shards, fitting them together into distinct shapes and textures, melding them into a fully-realized picture.

When Roger finished, Nick said, "I want to go back with the men."

"The strikers? Don't be foolish. They're going to lose, and if Plant finds out you're collaborating with them, he'll send you to prison."

Nick wiggled his toes again. Delighted. "Doesn't matter."

"Doesn't matter? What about your family? How will they make ends meet if you're locked up?"

"We'll survive."

Roger gripped the brim of his hat. "And Clarisa?"

Nick looked up. "Don't you know?"

Now it was Roger's turn to be confused. "Know what?"

"We can't barter for her. It's for her to decide."

65

Joe Johnson, president of Local 38-79, received a request from Mayor Rossi asking for unfettered access to the Matson docks so the Belt Line Railroad could deliver a shipment of produce and polio serum destined for the Philippines. The Industrial Association had announced its intention to suspend trucking operations the following day in honor of the Fourth of July, but Belt Line engineers were willing to work on the holiday.

Harry Bridges advised Joe Johnson to put it up for a vote.

That night members of Local 38-79 crowded into at Eagles Hall to consider the request. Islands of white-bandaged heads dotted the sea of strikers, visceral symbols of the furious battle earlier that day. The first part of the meeting was taken up with longshoremen describing the day's events: choking teargas, ringing gunfire, crushing batons, gashed heads. By the time Rossi's request came to the floor, the men were in an angry, defiant mood and not inclined to cooperate with authorities. Bridges warned them that interfering with the state-run Belt Line Railroad would raise the ire of the governor. It didn't change their minds. The mention of Frank Merriam provoked an ugly roar of boos and hisses, and it was unanimously decided that a contingent of picketers would surround the trains to prevent the delivery.

When the meeting ended, stevedores poured out of the hall into a damp, foggy night, most of them turning up their collars and hurrying off to get a good night's sleep. A few lingered on the sidewalk and clustered around Harry Bridges, asking questions and offering opinions.

Henry Schmidt waited patiently until there was a break in the conversation. "Come on, Harry. We gotta go."

Bridges said his goodbyes and joined Schmidt and another stevedore who led them to an old Ford sedan. They piled in and drove out to Golden Gate Park, the road dark save for the occasional streetlamp, giant eucalyptus trees standing guard on both sides. A mile into the park, the driver stopped in front of the Conservatory of Flowers, a large Victorian greenhouse with a central dome flanked by two wings faintly glowing from lights within. The street was empty except for one other car, a battered Packard coupe with white sidewall tires. A hulking figure emerged from the coupe dressed in brown trousers and a pea coat.

The three longshoremen got out of the Ford to meet him. The driver introduced the stranger. "This here is Joe Miller. He used to be a Golden

Gloves champ. Him and I trained together at Zelinsky's gym."

Miller had a broad flat face as if his features had been imprinted by a coin stamp. Bridges shook his hand. "So what's up, Joe?"

"Well, Mr. Bridges," he said in a throaty voice, "I been instructed to make you an offer."

"Oh, yeah. By whom?"

Miller grinned sheepishly. "You don't need to know, but you can probably guess."

Bridges shrugged. "All right, let's have it."

"They'll pay you fifty-thousand dollars if you call off the strike."

Bridges brow shot up. "Fifty thousand?" A nice house in a good neighborhood could be bought for three-thousand dollars. Fifty-thousand was enough to buy a Pacific Heights mansion or retire to a tropical island. Bridges rubbed his chin as if considering the offer. "That's a lotta dough."

Miller's face lit up. "Yeah, I thought you'd be interested."

"Only one problem."

"What's that?"

"I can't call off the strike. Only the men can do that."

Miller's smile faded. "Oh, come on, everyone knows the men'll do what you say. One word from you and they'll be earnin' wages in no time. They believe in you Mr. Bridges."

Harry stuffed his hands in his pockets and rocked back on his heels. "And why do you suppose that is, Joe?"

"Well —" Miller looked up at the night sky as if the answer was written in the stars. A moment later his mouth opened and his head nodded up and down. "Ahhh, I getcha." His face dropped. "Well, listen, I ain't here to —"

"No, you listen to me," said Harry, poking a finger on Miller's chest. "Tell your boss he's welcomed to make a donation to the strike fund. We accept money from anyone without regard to religious or political affiliation. But he's barkin' up the wrong tree. I don't tell the men what to do. They tell me. So you go back and tell your boss."

66

The Benson family burst into Nick's room carrying bags bulging with assorted items. Nick was sitting up in bed, reading a newspaper with a headline announcing, PORT OPEN, RIOTS QUELLED. He looked up as they entered. When Lillian saw her son alive and awake, she gasped with delight, dropped her bags, and rushed to him, arms outstretched.

"Oh my goodness," she exclaimed, as she swept the newspaper aside and drew his face to her bosom. Then, pulling back, she brushed his bangs aside and kissed his forehead until he gently nudged her away. "You look so pale. How do you feel?"

"Like I overslept," he said with a faint smile.

In the time since he'd regained consciousness, the circulation in his limbs had improved, and, despite Lillian's concern, color was returning to his face. His nurses, encouraged by his progress, had hovered around him like mother hens, spoon feeding him oatmeal and other easily digestible food and plumping up his pillow. His doctor performed a battery of response and memory tests and was surprised and delighted by his rapid recovery and his ability to stand up and walk across the room.

Sarah joined Lillian beside the bed, smiling through tears that streaked black eyeliner down her cheeks. "It's good to see you."

Rune nodded in agreement. "The doctors weren't sure if you were going to make it, boy, but they don't know the strength of your Viking blood."

Reaching into a bag, Sarah pulled out a framed picture of Rusty and set it on a table beside the bed. "I wanted to bring him but they said he wasn't allowed, so I painted a picture of him."

Nick gazed at the three faces around him, faces he loved so much. "I feel much better now that you're here. I'm still weak, but the doctor says he only wants to keep me here a couple of more days for observation. Then I can come home."

"That's wonderful news," said Lillian. "And since you can't go outside for a Fourth of July picnic, we brought the picnic to you." She clapped her hands. "Alright, everybody. Let's get rolling."

Like a well-drilled marching band, the three visitors swung into action, emptying the bags and setting things up. Lillian spread a red, white, and blue striped tablecloth over the bed. Rune placed a radio on the window sill and turned it to an Independence Day program. Sarah placed a bouquet of red roses, white carnations, and blue irises on the bedside table. Then out came the feast, and in short order the family was seated around the bed munching on fried chicken, cornbread, and coleslaw, talking about the events of the previous two weeks. In the background, a medley of patriotic songs played on the radio, punctuated by commercial breaks with loud explosions and a Ben Franklin mimic, exhorting listeners to take advantage of Fourth of July sales.

"Oh, beauu-tiful for spaa-cious skies, for amber waves of grain..."

In between bites Lillian beamed like a sailor on shore leave. "This has always been my favorite holiday. No presents, no big fuss, nothing to do but spend time with your family."

"And watch fireworks obscured by fog," Sarah added, referring to the misty clouds that perennially covered San Francisco on summer nights.

Lillian frowned. "Now why does your generation always look at the negative side? Is it the depression that causes such a dark view?" She lifted the corners of her mouth into an exaggerated smile. "I grew up during the gay '90s, an innocent, hopeful time. No matter how difficult things were, we always tried to look at the sunny side of life."

"...and crowwn thy good with brootherhood from..."

"Even when the world was going to hell in a hand basket," Sarah muttered.

"Now what makes you say something so pessimistic, dear?"

Sarah rolled her eyes, and for the first time since his family arrived Nick noticed something different about his sister, an older more sophisticated look. Her hair was dyed jet black and cut into a severe bob, her eyes ringed with black eyeliner that intensified her brown irises and pale skin. *My God*, he thought, admiring her raven beauty, *she probably has to fend off every aspiring Picasso in town.*

"How's your painting?" he asked.

"Shssssh," said Lillian. "Isn't that the mayor?"

A voice with the oratorical solemnity of a politician spoke through the radio. *"On this Fourth of July, let us not forget in our self-pity due to the plight of national depression, the supreme difficulties that the founders of our country had to surmount so that this nation might become the land of the free — the asylum for the distressed of the world. Only our confidence in our beloved country will demonstrate the sincerity of our thankfulness..."*

"You see," Lillian said. "He wants us to see the bright side."

"...but today we face a battlefield, calling upon us for examples of

courage and fidelity fully equal to our founding fathers. Today we face a lurking danger — a hidden foe; one whose weapon is discontent, a weapon too easily wielded in a time of dark uncertainty like the present..."

Lillian nodded thoughtfully, her expression drooping a bit.

"The insidious poison which is seeping into the veins of our civil and religious life and imperiling the most sacred ideals of the home is communism. Like an infectious disease, it lurks in wait for those discouraged by failure on the ladder of success. This has been abundantly demonstrated by activities of some of the members in the strike, which has paralyzed the business of San Francisco's port for fifty-six days, ending only yesterday. It is our duty to use every effort to repel unlawful attacks against the life and property of those in no way responsible for the conditions we confront—"

"Turn it off."

All eyes turned to Nick.

"What's wrong, dear?" Lillian asked.

"Rossi should know better. He's using communism as a scapegoat for the failings of capitalism, and implying that longshoremen are gullible tools of a few radicals rather than resisters of good old American exploitation."

"Oh, dear," said Lillian, putting her fork down. "I was hoping you'd quit your waterfront job after all that's happened. Why, those hoodlums nearly killed you. How could you possibly want to associate yourself with them now?"

Nick glanced at her through solemn, inset eyes. "Because I deserved every bruise I got."

Lillian gasped. "How can you say that?" She reached out and stroked his cheek. "Poor dear. You must still be woozy."

He brushed her hand aside and let out a deep, disconsolate sigh. A sudden and tremendous desire welled within him to jettison all the secrets and lies he'd been concealing for months, to begin again with a clean slate. For that was what it amounted to. The terrible beating — a penance, if you will — had, in a perverse way, freed him to begin life anew. His father had been right in the dream. He *had* died, his old self disintegrated, allowing him to be reborn without the burden and obligation of unholy commitments. Slowly and falteringly, because he still felt intensely remorseful, he described his actions from the day he was arrested on the *Diana Dollar* to the beating he received on the Embarcadero. He talked about the men he'd betrayed and all the lies he'd told and lives he'd harmed. And when his story was over, he apologized for his behavior and asked for their forgiveness for bringing shame and dishonor to himself and his family.

Stunned by the unexpected confession, his family stared at their plates of half-eaten chicken and crumbled cornbread.

... And the rockets' red glare, the bombs bursting in air, gave proof ...

"Does this mean," Lillian began pensively, her lower lip trembling, "does this mean you've . . . you've become a radical? Because your father would roll over in his grave —" She broke off the sentence and wiped a tear from her cheek.

Rune gave her a handkerchief and Nick laid a reassuring hand on her arm.

She wiped her eyes. "I'm sorry. I still can't think of Charles without feeling a pain in my heart. He had his faults but he loved all of you. And he cherished his family more than anything."

"Yeah?" said Sarah. "Then why isn't he here?"

Lillian let out a gasp as if the question had tarnished the memory of her husband, as if her daughter was speaking ill of the dead. She glared at her, but Sarah defiantly returned her gaze, not willing to be cowed into submission. After a pregnant moment, Lillian sighed and shook her head. "I — I don't know. Believe me, I've wondered the same thing a thousand times."

...or the land of the freee, and the ho-me of the braaave.

"I know."

Everyone looked at Nick. He dropped back on his pillow, exhausted after his emotional confession. "Father saw himself as the quintessential American success story. He worked hard, played by the rules, and made good in the Promised Land. Consequently, he believed that anyone in America who tried hard enough could raise a family in comfort, and that those who didn't only had themselves to blame. Then when things went wrong, he thought he was a failure and couldn't see that it was the country that had failed him. In the end he felt worthless and alone."

"But he had us," Lillian said, "his family."

"Ironically, it was our judgment he feared most. He believed his primary purpose was to provide for us, to protect and care for us. When he went bankrupt, he thought that we would feel just as bad about him as he did about himself.

"He came to me while I was unconscious. I didn't understand why, and it wasn't until I woke up that the reason became clear. He was trying to tell me not to make the same mistake he made. He wanted to kill that part of me I'd inherited from him, the self-absorbed part that cared more about what others thought of him than doing the right thing." He reached over and squeezed Lillian's shoulder. "It's why I'm staying with the union for now. Those men out there aren't just fighting for decent jobs. They're fighting for something greater than themselves, for each other and their families, and it's giving them a sense of belonging, a bedrock of self-respect and dignity.

"I thought my salvation was in proving my innocence, but along the way I learned something. You can't trample on your honor and self-respect while trying to save yourself. You've got to stand up for what's right, no matter what the consequences. So you see, I've got to stay with those men, for their sake as well as my own."

67

A raucous drumbeat rumbled along the waterfront, traveling past the Java House, past the Hills Brothers Coffee plant, past the classically designed pier sheds, until it reached Local 38-79's headquarters on Steuart Street. Harry Bridges looked out the window. He couldn't see what was causing the commotion, but he had a good idea of what it was.

"Let's go see what's making the natives restless," he said to Henry Schmidt, pointing his thumb toward the waterfront.

They trooped down the stairs and went around the corner to the Embarcadero. On the opposite side of the boulevard, the Ferry Building stood quiet and empty, devoid of commuters on this holiday afternoon. Looking south in the direction of the drumbeat, they could see several hundred strikers gathered around a Belt Line freight train near the Matson docks at Pier 30. They headed in that direction, and as they drew near they could see men beating sticks on the side of the boxcars, chanting:

"NO-CARGO-GOES-BY-ON-THE-FOURTH-OF-JULY!
NO-CARGO-GOES-BY-ON-THE-FOURTH-OF-JULY!"

A train engineer peered down at the strikers, his face etched with worry. A dozen policemen stood nearby and watched, making no attempt to stop the strikers. With most of their brethren on holiday, they were no match for the hundreds of men surrounding the train. Having no hope of proceeding safely, the engineer shut off the diesel engine and signaled his crew to abandon the operation. The strikers fell quiet and parted as the rail workers descended from the train and crossed the Embarcadero toward the Belt Line roundhouse. After they were gone, the longshoremen erupted in cheers and drummed against the side of the train in rhythms that traveled all the way to the state capitol in Sacramento.

An hour later Bridges received a request from Governor Merriam, asking the ILA to allow the Matson Company an opportunity to move the perishable cargo to the Matson docks before it spoiled. Bridges put the request before the Joint Marine Strike Committee.

Without hesitation it was voted down.

Merriam submitted a second appeal for cooperation, accompanied by a threat to call out the National Guard if the strikers failed to comply.

The Strike Committee remained adamant.

That night, unable to sleep, Nick rolled from side-to-side, his thoughts alternating between descriptions of the battle he'd read in the paper, curiosity at how his friends had fared, and self-recriminations for not having been there. He tried to push the thoughts away but they kept coming back, again and again.

He sighed. *I couldn't wake up for two weeks and now I can't sleep.*

At two in the morning he gave up, rolled out of bed, and fumbled in the dark for the clothing his family had delivered in anticipation of his release. Though his legs felt wobbly, he was able to move reasonably well. His doctor said his recovery had been astonishingly swift. Most coma patients take weeks or even months to fully recover. Nick, he said, must have been in a light state of unconsciousness, and that would account for him being able to remember his dream.

Nick located the bag of clothes and slipped them on. He stepped out into the corridor and glanced down the darkened hall to the nurses' station illuminated by lamplight. Turning in the opposite direction, he quietly crept away and offered a mental thank you to the staff for the kind attention and skilled care he'd received. He emerged from the hospital and drew in a lungful of cool night air, grateful to be outside and on his feet. A yellow DeSoto taxi was parked in front. He would love to have taken a taxi, but having no money he headed north on foot along Potrero Avenue toward the waterfront.

It was good to be walking again, his leg muscles flexing and relaxing, his arms swinging in rhythm to his stride. A mile on at Townsend Street, his strength suddenly gave out near a dark empty lot, leaving him dizzy and weak at the knees. He staggered off the sidewalk into the lot, hoping to find a place to rest. A stack of railroad ties stood nearby. He headed toward them and on his way tripped on something that nearly knocked him off his feet. In the dim light of a distant streetlamp, he peered down at what tripped him, a six-foot long lump covered with cloth. Looking closer, he saw that the lump was actually a person stretched out on the ground, sleeping. When his eyes adjusted to the gloom, he saw a dozen other bodies huddled together under blankets around the dying embers of a makeshift campfire. He'd heard of hobo jungles. Like most folks, though, he thought they were on the outskirts of town and never imagined them in the heart of the city.

He slumped down on the railroad ties and bent over, dropping his head between his knees. *I'm in no hurry,* he told himself. *Just take it slow and easy.* When his head cleared and strength return to his limbs, he forced himself up and headed down Townsend toward the Southern Pacific train depot, the ground here still littered with stones and broken brickbats from the battle two days before. Two blocks beyond the depot he turned left onto First Street and walked to the base of Rincon Hill. Still feeling shaky, he decided to sit for a spell before tackling the climb.

It had been foolish to leave the hospital so soon and endanger his recovery, yet it didn't seem to matter. He'd already missed so much and couldn't stand the thought of missing whatever the morning might bring.

He rose to his feet and started up the hill, taking slow baby steps. Though it was just a modest two-block climb, his legs ached and sweat ran down his neck. He reached the top and walked onto a flat dirt plateau cleared of everything but a few piles of bricks to make way for an approach road for the bridge under construction. At the north edge of the plateau, a large clump of anise plants stood beside a factory wall facing the waterfront. He made his way there and crawled behind the anise to a space just large enough for him to curl up and catch a few hours sleep before daybreak. He closed his eyes and breathed in the smell of anise, a fragrance similar to licorice that took him back to his childhood, to Saturday matinees at the Alhambra Theater when he'd watched cowboys in ten-gallon hats gallop across the screen in a cloud of dust, kerchiefs flapping in the breeze.

68

Morning fog hung over the city, obscuring its loftiest peaks, including the newly completed tower atop Telegraph Hill. From the rooftop of the ILA building, the rear of which faced the Embarcadero, Harry Bridges and his lieutenants looked down at hundreds of blue-coated police officers deployed along the waterfront.

"Looks like they mean business," Henry Schmidt remarked. "They got new riot sticks, bigger and longer than the usual ones. Wonder who paid for em'?"

"I think we both know the answer," said Bridges, who'd heard from sources that the Industrial Association secretly donated funds to the police department for riot control equipment.

The police were concentrated at Pier 38 where Atlas trucks would resume round trips to the Garcia & Maggini warehouse on King Street, and at Piers 30 and 32 where the Belt Line railroad was expected to begin delivering and hauling away cargo. Radio squad cars were stationed at various points along the Embarcadero, and lookouts on rooftops scanned the waterfront with binoculars, reporting any developments on two-way radios.

A scout breathing hard came running up. "They're comin' from everywhere. Thousands of 'em."

"I can see that," Bridges said, looking down at strikers filling the sidewalks along the east side of the Embarcadero.

"And not all of 'em are strikers," the scout said. "I saw teamsters and streetcar drivers and warehousemen, even my old math teacher from Galileo High."

Bridges was pleased that workers from other unions were now supporting the strike. It was about time they understood that if the Industrial Association could destroy Local 38-79, it could destroy any union in San Francisco. However, even with the support of other unions he wasn't confident that the battle would be won today. He and his top lieutenants had marshaled their limited resources as best they could, but against a well-trained, well-armed police force, the odds of victory were slim. And he also knew that he couldn't afford to let the violence spin out of control, not against shotguns and teargas grenades.

"Henry, did you issue my order telling everyone to turn in their firearms so we can store them in the union safe?"

Schmidt nodded. "Yeah. No takers so far."

"I hope that means our guys who own firearms left them at home. This isn't an insurrection, and if it escalates into an armed conflict, we'll not only lose the battle, we'll lose public support."

Bridges could see bulges in the pockets of strikers who'd armed themselves with whatever weapons they could glean from empty lots and construction sites. He would've preferred a peaceful settlement, but without some sort of resistance, the Industrial Association would roll over them and destroy any chance of success.

At just before eight o'clock sunrays broke through the fog, casting a warm light on the Embarcadero and the thousands of strikers and sympathizers massed on the west side, concentrated like the police opposite Piers 30 and 32 and Pier 38. Above the waterfront, Rincon Hill again served as a lofty grandstand for hundreds of spectators, some laying their jackets on the dried grass to stake out positions, others sipping coffee in thermos bottles. Amongst them, vendors with trays strapped around their necks weaved through the crowd selling chocolate bars, chewing gum, cigarettes, and candy. The Fourth Estate was there as well. Film crews from Movietone News were positioned on two flatbed trucks, all set to film the action for cinema newsreels. Newspaper reporters also stood at the ready armed with pens, notepads and "PRESS" identification cards tucked in their hatbands. And photographers clutched bulky flash cameras ready to take pictures.

On each side of the cobblestone divide, police and strikers eyed one another with nervous anticipation, one side a well-equipped blue-coated phalanx, the other a ragtag collection of strikers and sympathizers armed with only found objects and an abiding rage.

Now the field was set. The players in position.

And so it came to pass that the conflict was as inevitable as a scheduled contest, and like a contest it began at the appointed time. The Ferry Building clock tower tolled eight o'clock. Simultaneously, as if the bell was a starting gun, a Belt Line locomotive rolled onto the Embarcadero, shunting two refrigerator cars toward the Matson docks. At the sight of the great mechanical beast, its bony arms cranking back and forth, its huge steel wheels grinding forward, a rumbling growl arose from the strikers and traveled across the cobblestone divide, echoing off the pier sheds and snapping the bluecoats to attention, their clubs cupped in their hands, their faces set in grim determination.

The strikers surged menacingly forward onto the Embarcadero and would have continued but a ranking officer stepped out from the blue line and yelled, "Move back!" This briefly stopped the strikers, as if they needed a moment to gird their courage, then a clamoring cry rose from their ranks, a visceral expression of their terrible anger. They charged across the roadway toward the blue phalanx, and from the opposite side hoof beats pounded on cobblestone as a line of mounted officers advanced to meet them. When the combatants collided, there was nothing tentative about their movements, nothing suggesting reason or subtlety, each side unleashing the full brunt of their anger, each side receiving blows that stained the street with blood.

Harry Bridges was taken aback at how quickly the embers of anger fanned into a raging, uncontrollable maelstrom. Within minutes, a wave of brutal aggression gripped the waterfront, each side attacking with unthinking fury, like two fighting cocks intent on inflicting the utmost damage with little regard to their own safety.

Two miles away at General Hospital, Clarisa entered the lobby with a bouquet of blue irises cradled in her arms. Lillian had phoned the day before and invited her to the Fourth of July picnic in Nick's room, but she declined with the excuse that his first waking hours should be spent with his family. Her real reason, however, was personal. She wanted her first minutes with him to be alone and without the distraction and observance of others. There was much to say, much she'd held back in her confusion and anger since his arrest and subsequent undercover role, and she didn't want the presence of others to inhibit their conversation.

While Nick was at sea, he had never been far from her thoughts, even when she was seeing Roger. After he returned and spurned her offer of help, she'd struggled with her feelings of abandonment and the confusion brought on by her attraction to Roger. As a consequence, she hadn't been able to reach out to Nick until she saw him unconscious in the hospital, his face calm and innocent as a newborn. Sitting at his bedside, stroking his arm, she noticed something peeking out from under the sleeve of his pajamas. Curious, she pushed up the sleeve and gasped. For there on his arm was her name imprinted in precisely rendered letters.

In one clean stroke, the tattoo cut her confusion away. All the objections propping up her rage, all the fears that held her back, all the doubts that plagued her, dissolved in a flood of insight that swept away the stilts of anger and left her feeling empty and drained. For days she tried to fill the void with long hours at the office, with volunteer work at the mission, with prayer, and with walks up to Buena Vista Park, where she looked out over rows of houses, past the green trees of the Presidio to the Golden Gate, and beyond that to the north tower of the Golden Gate Bridge now standing alone at the water's edge. Yet nothing worked, nothing filled the void, and she knew there was only one thing that could. She may have been a strong-willed woman fully capable of taking care of herself, but she still felt bound to Nick, bound to the love they once shared, perhaps now more than ever.

She took the elevator up to the recovery ward and entered his room, hoping her visit would be a pleasant surprise. He was laying on the bed, facing away from her. She snuck up behind him and planted a kiss on his cheek, but when his head turned, she pulled back, startled by the sight of a strange man with a large Roman nose.

He looked equally surprised, then held out his arms and crowed, "Come on sweetheart. How about another smacker?" He laughed, then grimaced. "Damn appendix kills me every time I crack up."

She scurried out of the room and found a nurse's aide chomping on a wad of gum. "Do you know where Nick Benson is?"

"You mean the cute one? He took a powder last night. You his girl?"

It was an impertinent question but she was too anxious to care. "Do you know where he went?"

The aide blew a bubble that burst with a loud snap. "No, but he left his things. I called Mrs. Benson and the poor lady just about had a heart attack. When she calmed down she said she was gonna ask the cops to find him, but I think they're all down at the waterfront. You heard any news? I got an uncle who's a motorcycle cop and a cousin who works on the docks. I sure hope they don't kill each other."

Clarisa rushed to a telephone booth in the lobby and called the office. Mrs. Butterfield answered, her voice quivering as she explained that the entire staff was in Mr. Plant's office looking down at the waterfront, where a riot had erupted. Clarisa was about to ask her to put Roger on the line when she heard muffled shots through the receiver.

"Oh, my god," said Mrs. Butterfield, "it sounds like a war out there."

"Listen," said Clarisa, her mind racing, "tell Mr. Farnsworth I won't be in this morning. Tell him . . . just tell him I'll be in this afternoon."

Before Mrs. Butterfield could ask why, she hung up the phone, hurried outside, and hailed a taxi, directing the driver to the Embarcadero.

He shook his head. "It's too dangerous, lady. They're shootin' people down there. We could get hit in the crossfire."

"Then take me to Third and Brannan. I'll walk from there."

69

From the roof of ILA headquarters, Harry Bridges watched black smoke billow up from burning vehicles, mixing with white teargas to form a gray haze over strikers and police battling each other. He hated to see the strike become a bloody conflict, and he felt sorry for the blue-coated foot soldiers who, after all, were only following orders. Yet all along he'd known that the employers weren't going to make significant concessions without a fight, so perhaps violence had been inevitable. Still, he couldn't stay on the sidelines any longer and watch his men get slaughtered by the mighty hardwood clubs.

With Henry Schmidt and Dutch Dietrich at his side, he rushed out of ILA headquarters and trotted down Steuart Street toward the waterfront. When they reached the intersection of Harrison and the Embarcadero, the situation was fluid, chaotic, and dangerous. A block farther south, in front of Piers 30 and 32, orange flames leaped out of two Belt Line freight cars, and sirens wailed as fire trucks careened along the Embarcadero toward the conflagration. The police were attempting to clear the street, now littered with brickbats and cobbles, but they were harried by groups of strikers leaking through their cordons and staging brief forays before separating into swirling eddies, chased by officers brandishing clubs. Some officers' uniforms were ripped and torn from flying missiles, and one bluecoat was being carried off on a stretcher.

A sharp bang followed by a dull thud drew their attention to a group of strikers near Pier 30. A teargas grenade had landed amongst the strikers, skidding and spinning as it spewed out a geyser of white haze. The strikers darted away from the teargas, leaving behind several injured men, who lay on the ground bleeding. Among them was a young boy, no more than fifteen, who lay unconscious in a pool of blood, his skull cracked, arm racked unnaturally behind his back. They watched an enraged striker, a piece of his scalp flapping where a club had torn it from the skull, pull a mountie off his horse. The striker was about to slug the mountie when another officer came up behind him and knocked him to the ground with a solid blow to the side of his head.

More sirens pierced the air from ambulances swerving through the battlefield toward the injured. The strikers, so enraged they considered any vehicle a target, hurled rocks and brickbats at the ambulances, whose side panels were scored and gouged.

Bang! Bang! Bang!

Officers fired their pistols over the heads of strikers, who scattered in disarray, running helter-skelter down the Embarcadero. Bridges, Schmidt, and Dietrich ducked behind an overturned delivery truck. As strikers ran by, Bridges waved his arms and called out, beckoning them to gather round. Before long some fifty men were huddled around him.

"We can't stay here against shotguns and revolvers," he shouted, pointing toward Rincon Hill. "Let's move to higher ground."

The impromptu brigade trotted onto Harrison Street and continued on as it rose up on an overpass above Beale Street. Schmidt stationed Dietrich and ten others on the overpass and gave them orders to erect a barrier across the road and arm themselves with rocks and bricks to drop on vehicles below, if need be. The rest of the group, some forty men in all, continued up Rincon Hill until they reached the top, now devoid of spectators, who had retreated when stray bullets whizzed by them and teargas wafted up from the waterfront.

Work had ceased on the Bay Bridge anchorage, the massive concrete monolith standing on the east side of the hill. Helmeted construction workers were gathered around their supervisor, vehemently pointing to nearby buildings whose windows had been shattered into jagged pieces by stray bullets.

Bridges looked down from the crest of the hill and watched as blue-coats methodically swept strikers off the Embarcadero and shoved the injured and captured into paddy wagons. Turning away from the water-front, he scanned the flat hilltop and spotted several stacks of bricks piled nearby, remnants of a factory that had been dismantled to make room for the Bay Bridge roadway.

"We'd better build some barricades!" he said, gesturing toward the bricks. He organized the men into two groups, one to pass bricks to the other, the second to build a wall at the edge of the hilltop overlooking the waterfront. With numerous hands at work, a four-foot-high, ten-foot-long wall was quickly erected and another begun nearby until it, too, was built and a third begun. When the brick fortification was complete, he gathered the men together, many of them bruised and battered and bleeding from cuts and gashes.

"We've taken a beating so far, but we ain't licked yet. Now here's what I want you to do."

Three hours after the battle began, the police were finally able to clear the Embarcadero of strikers and move inland, mopping up against scant resistance. When they reached the base of Rincon Hill, a strange eerie wail came down from the crest. They looked up to see twenty strikers charging down the hill, shrieking at the top of their lungs like a herd of howling banshees. Before the bluecoats could react, the strikers launched a volley of bricks and rocks, their missiles sailing through the air and crashing down around the officers. Several officers fell to the ground, while others ran from the surprise attack. The bulk of them, however, stood their ground and fired teargas grenades at the attackers, who let loose the last of their missiles and retreated back up the hill.

The teargas grenades landed in dry grass, igniting fires whose smoke mingled with the teargas to create a gray smokescreen. Into this thickening haze, bluecoats on foot and horseback charged up the hill after the attackers, firing their pistols at will and winging two strikers who hobbled up to the top and were helped into cars and whisked away. Amid smoke and teargas, the bluecoats continued up the hill, their progress hindered by the blinding, stinging haze.

Huddled behind the makeshift fortification, Bridges and his men held handkerchiefs and shirttails over their faces to ward off the teargas. Harry took a quick look over the wall, then shouted to the men around him, "Hold your fire till we see the whites of their eyes!"

Bluecoats on foot, backed by mounties, cautiously approached the brick fort, guns drawn with one hand, faces covered with the other. Bridges peeked over the wall again, then gave the signal. Like pop-up targets in a penny arcade, the strikers jumped up and threw brickbats down the hill, then ducked back down. The bricks knocked bluecoats off their feet and caused startled horses to rear up and whinny. When a second volley of brickbats came crashing down on them, the surprised bluecoats turned and fled back down the hill, firing their side arms wildly into the air as they retreated.

At the bottom of the hill, Ignatius McCarty, top salesman for the Lake Erie Chemical Company, could barely hide his glee. This was the opportunity he'd been waiting for. If he played his cards right, he could clinch a big sale and collect a tidy commission. While the police regrouped for another assault, he approached their commanding officer.

"Commander Cahill, I'll bet you'd like to flush out them commies before you make another charge."

Cahill, who was busy organizing his men, ignored him.

Undaunted, McCarty proceeded with his pitch. "Let me show you how you can shoot teargas grenades up over their fortification and make those fuckers cry like babies. No charge."

The commander still didn't respond.

Not about to let this opportunity slip by, McCarty passed out three new launchers of the latest design and kept one for himself. He showed the officers how to load grenades into the launchers, then aimed it toward the hill and fired. The grenade spiraled up and arced over the brick redoubt, landing in the flat lot behind the strikers. Acrid haze spewed out of the grenade in four directions, another company innovation, covering a wide area with burning teargas.

Bridges watched the teargas drift toward his men. In another few seconds, it would reach them and force a retreat. Covering his mouth and nose with a handkerchief, he ran into the spreading teargas, picked up the grenade, and heaved it like a football over the strikers and down the hill. The men cheered and whistled, but their joy was cut short when three more grenades spewing teargas landed nearby. This time, as each one hit the ground, a striker covering his face as best he could scurried over, picked it up, and tossed it back down the hill. The game went on for several minutes until the police changed tactics and aimed directly at the brick walls. Two grenades hit their mark and fell to the ground, flooding the air with gas that curled up over the walls, choking the men on the other side until their eyes bled stinging tears.

A striker near the end of the wall stepped out from behind its protection and ran toward the spewing grenades. As soon as he exposed himself, gunfire erupted from below and dropped him to the ground. When the gunfire ceased, Bridges peeked around the side of the wall and spotted the wounded striker about fifteen feet down the hill laying on his side, gripping his knee, blood seeping from under his hands.

Bridges had seen considerable violence that day, smashed heads and bruised bodies, but the sight of the helpless striker trying to stem the bleeding made him question his strategy of confrontation. He'd never intended to get his men embroiled in an all-out war and, in fact, wanted to avoid it. But the violence had affected him like everyone else, made him angry and frustrated and determined to fight back. He only wished that the men down the hill weren't cops, weren't workingmen like the strikers. He had an affinity for working people, had always had an affinity for working people. When he was a boy, his father, a real estate agent and property owner, sometimes asked him to collect rents from his tenants. It was a simple enough task, yet when a tenant was unemployed and couldn't pay the rent, Harry didn't have the heart to pressure him. "Just pay it when you're working again," he'd say, risking his father's anger.

He glanced down the hill. A score of bluecoats, wearing olive-green gas masks with small round windows, were lined up in formation to begin a second assault. He didn't want to fight the cops anymore. His heart wasn't in it, and ultimately it was a losing strategy. Yet he couldn't turn tail and run until he retrieved the injured striker who lay unprotected on the other side of the wall. The cops below hadn't begun to climb the hill, so he still had a chance if he moved quickly. He crawled out from behind the wall and slithered his way toward the wounded man. The bluecoats spotted him and fired their side arms as they charged up the hill. Under this volley of shots, he ducked down low in the grass, hoping their aim was hampered by the tiny gas mask windows and the smoke and teargas hovering over the hillside.

The rest of the strikers crouched behind the walls as bullets pinged off the brick fortification and zinged above them. During a short pause in the gunfire, another striker crept out from behind the wall, drawing fire as he took a flying leap toward one of the teargas grenades. In one quick motion, he scooped it up and heaved it down the hill. The grenade hit the ground just twenty feet below him, but gravity pulled it down the hillside, trailing a tail of billowing gas that joined with grass fire smoke to create a screen that obscured the bluecoats.

The daring striker then scrambled to the other grenade and with a backhanded toss, lofted it down the hill with the same effect. This done, he crawled over to the wounded man, and with Bridges' help the two of them pulled the bleeding striker up to safety behind the brick fortification.

"Kee-rist," Bridges said to the daring striker, who lay on his belly gasping for breath, "you tryin' to get yourself killed?"

The striker looked up, his face streaked with dirt and sweat. Bangs hung down over his eyes. "No, sir, just trying help."

"Now don't go callin' me sir—." Bridges stopped short and took a closer look at the prone figure. "Well, for the love of Pete." He elbowed Schmidt. "Look who's the goddamned hero."

Schmidt looked down, his forehead wrinkling in surprise. "Jesus, Nick, where'd you come from? I thought you were in the hospital."

Nick rolled over on his back. "I woke up just in time." He glanced at Bridges. "I was caught up in a terrible nightmare. Didn't know which end was up, but that's all over now."

Bridges nodded. "I was hopin' you'd come arou—"

"Here they come!" someone shouted.

Nick scrambled to his feet and hunched down behind Bridges, who peered over the wall at a line of bluecoats charging up the hill like a swarm of hungry locusts. They were coming so fast, his men wouldn't have time to retreat safely unless they pushed them back down the hill a second time.

"All right men," he said, raising a hand in the air, "on my signal. Let's give 'em what for."

He waited until they were twenty feet away, then dropped his hand.

A hail of bricks flew over the wall and rained down on the attackers. The strikers heard grunts and gasps and thuds and expletives, though they dared not look and expose themselves to gunfire.

Bridges reached down to grab another brick but his stockpile was depleted. "Damn," he muttered.

Then someone put a brick in his hand. "Here you go, Harrrry!"

Bridges turned. "Who the—?" His frown melted into grim smile at the sight of Nick who was grinning back at him. "Well, at least you ain't callin' me 'sir' no more."

A second hailstorm sent the bluecoats scrambling down the hill with dents and bits of red brick covering their backs. Commander Cahill, steaming at the ignominious retreat, stalked over to McCarty and demanded all the launchers and grenades in his possession.

"I want to cover the whole damn hill with gas," he fumed.

McCarty dutifully passed out a dozen new teargas launchers and a hundred grenades, then shoved a purchase order into the commander's hand. "Just sign here."

The crack of teargas launchers could be heard from blocks away as dozens of projectiles flew up over the brick walls and onto the top of Rincon Hill, creating a gigantic cloud that forced the evacuation of nearby factories and the retreat of Bay Bridge construction workers.

When the teargas ammo was spent, the commander sent his men up the hill a third time. Under cover of gas and smoke they reached the top and kicked down the brick walls, toppling them over into a pile of useless rubble. Beyond that, all they found was an empty lot, not a single striker anywhere and no evidence of their presence save for a few random drops of blood dotting the ground.

70

When Clarisa discovered that Nick had left the hospital, she instinctively knew where he'd gone. For the rest of the morning she skirted the riot zone searching for him, traipsing mile after mile in pumps ill-suited for the quest. Though she was tempted to move closer to the waterfront, she decided against it when she spied men running wildly along the Embarcadero amid clouds of swirling teargas and smoke. And ever present was the discordant sound of sirens wailing, guns blasting, voices hollering, engines revving, gears grinding, hoofs pounding.

Even blocks from the riot she encountered disturbing scenes. Two businessmen limped by on Harrison Street, complaining that policemen had chased them from the waterfront with billy clubs as if they were common laborers. On another occasion a dazed striker, the back of his head bleeding, face ashen, mumbled crazily to himself as he stumbled along the sidewalk. The sight was so shocking she didn't know what to do and was relieved when a car, driven by a striker, stopped and picked him up. And several times she saw ambulances race toward the conflict in pristine condition, only to emerge later pitted and scarred, driven by medics with pale, frightened faces.

As the noon hour approached, the last of the morning fog evaporated to reveal a clear blue sky. Noontime also signaled a temporary truce, and as if by mutual consent the combatants withdrew from the battlefield to nurse their wounds and fill their bellies.

When the din of conflict subsided, Clarisa cautiously made her way to the Embarcadero, now eerily calm and quiet. Policemen, who minutes before had been firing pistols and clubbing heads, were lounging in groups, eating sandwiches and soaking up sunrays as if they'd just finished a regular morning shift. The roadway was devoid of traffic save for ambulances picking up the injured, and strikers were absent too, having gone to the strike kitchen or to waterfront cafes. Though Clarisa was tired and hungry and her feet ached, she still had one more place to check before abandoning her quest.

"Ooohhh, my ear," moaned a young man sitting on the sidewalk in front of the Hills Brothers coffee plant. He clutched a large camera with one hand, while the other covered the side of his head.

Clarisa went over to him and bent down. "Do you need help?"

He looked up. One of his eyelids was bruised and distended, burying the eye. "I think my ear's been shot."

Clarisa stepped back, startled by the swollen face and the sight of blood trickling down his neck. For a fleeting moment she wanted to leave, wanted to run away from this field of bloody aggression. *Why do men have to be so angry at each other? So hurtful?* It made no sense.

Sense or no, she couldn't abandon the injured photographer.

"Let's take a look," she said, bending down again and gently removing his hand from his ear. Blood dripped from a half-moon shaped wound, as if a cookie cutter had neatly snipped off a piece of his earlobe. She took a clean handkerchief from her purse and pressed it against the wound. "Here, hold this while I help you up. Harbor Emergency Hospital is just a few blocks away."

"My camera," he said, clutching it tighter. "I gotta hang on to my camera."

"Okay, just take it easy." She grasped an arm and helped him to his feet, thankful he wasn't a large man.

"This has been the worst day of my life," he muttered, as he hobbled on a sprained ankle. "I've been beaten by strikers, clubbed by police, and shot in the ear. And you're the first person who's bothered to help." He paused and squeezed her hand. "I'm feeling woozy, so if I pass out make sure this camera gets to the *San Francisco News*. I've given my blood for these photos, and I want 'em published. Tell the editor they're from Rosenthal, Joe Rosenthal."[1]

"Sure thing, Joe."

"Thanks for your help."

"Don't worry. I was on my way to the hospital to look for a friend."

The photographer stepped off the curb onto Howard Street and winced

---

1 Years later Joe Rosenthal would take the most famous photograph of WWII during the battle of Iwo Jima. Afterwards he remarked that the San Francisco riots of 1934 were, for him, a much scarier experience.

as his foot hit the ground. "Well, I sure hope he's in better shape than me."

The scene at Harbor Emergency Hospital was much worse than Clarisa imagined. Injured strikers and policemen lay on rows of cots, blood oozing from gunshot wounds and cracked heads, their moans and cries of pain from broken limbs and blinding teargas a heart wrenching sound. A dozen doctors and nurses worked at the small hospital, all of them scurrying from patient to patient in aprons smeared with blood, working as fast as they could. Some were setting broken bones, others rinsing eyes blinded by gas. Still others were disinfecting wounds with iodine, stitching them together, and dressing them with gauze and tape.

Her arm around Mr. Rosenthal, Clarisa walked among the cots searching for someone to attend to his injuries. Groans and plaintive cries surrounded them, but what shocked her more was the sight of blood — blood on the patients, blood on the floor, even speckles of blood on the walls as if it had been haphazardly flicked there with a paintbrush.

She found a nurse to care for Mr. Rosenthal, then searched for Nick among the rows of cots. He was nowhere to be found, but during her search she could see that the staff was overwhelmed. And it wasn't long before her Florence Nightingale side took over, convincing her to suspend her quest and adopt another. When a nurse walked by, she offered to lend a hand and was given a bucket and string mop with instructions to keep the floors as clean as possible.

It was a frightful task. The grisly odor of fresh blood and the agonizing sight of twisted limbs and cracked heads confronted her at every turn. During her worst moments, when she felt like retching or running away, she resorted to a technique she sometimes used at the mission when encountering a malnourished individual. Instead of looking away or retreating, she imagined that she knew the injured striker or policeman, that he was a friend or acquaintance. Looking him straight in the eye, she forced herself to smile, then offered a kind word and a gentle squeeze of the hand. And in nearly every case, whether cop or striker, through grimaces of pain and agony, the patient responded to her kindness with a smile or return squeeze, as if to say, "It hurts like hell, miss, but I'll survive."

71

"I know I betrayed your trust. I — I don't know what to say."

Nick was sitting in a chair in a back office at ILA headquarters, head hanging down, eyes on the floor. Harry Bridges stood over him.

Bridges pursed his lips into a frown that conveyed disappointment more than anger. He opened his mouth as if to say something, then paused, one beat, two beats, three. His frown softened. "Look, you didn't betray me. You betrayed the men. Do you see that now? What we're doin' here, despite the rubbish printed in the papers, is as American as the Bill of Rights. We're organizin' men so they can stand up for themselves — black and white, Asian and Mexican, Catholic and Jew, men who've always takin' it in the shorts when they've gone up against the bosses."

And worst of all, Nick thought, *I've betrayed myself and those who trusted me.* The world had tested him and he'd failed miserably. As a measure of a man he felt two-feet small. He pressed his fingers on his temples to calm a dizzy light-headedness.

Bridges rested a hand on his shoulder. "Look, I know you're not cut out to be a longshoreman. But you're smart, see, and we need your talents. There are plenty of battles ahead and you can make a difference."

Nick looked up, thinking there was no way he could atone for his betrayal. "What can I do?"

"Have you forgotten?"

"Forgotten what?"

"You're my assistant, and I've still got more work than I can handle."

"You mean you want me to stay on? After what I've done?"

"Uh-huh." Bridges nodded. "This strike is far from over."

Henry Schmidt stood in the doorway. "It may not be over, but it's gonna run into a brick wall awful damn quick."

"Why? What's up?" said Bridges.

"The governor's called out the National Guard. They'll be here this afternoon, and they're aimin' to shut down the waterfront tighter than a drum."

"Shit. We can't fight machine guns and bayonets."

"True," said Schmidt, "but we sure as hell can shut down the rest of the city."

Harry shook his head. "I dunno. Support for a general strike is weak.

We've only received commitments from, what, four or five unions so far."

Schmidt rubbed his stomach. "I don't know about you boys, but I could eat a horse. How 'bout we talk it over at The Bulkhead?"

"I'll second that," said Nick, still feeling light-headed. "I could use some food."

The three men went next door to The Bulkhead Cafe, a popular seaman's bar and restaurant in the Audiffred Building. It was a rustic place decorated with maritime bric-a-brac: signal flags, marlinespikes, life preservers, glass buoys, webbed nets. They settled into a booth beside a window with a view of Mission and Steuart streets. Strikers were milling on the four corners of the intersection, digesting lunch and looking out for police who, for the moment, were conspicuously absent. Only the muffled explosions of teargas grenades somewhere off in the distance belied the relative calm.

"Sounds like the bluecoats are starting up again," said Bridges.

Schmidt flashed a grim smile. "Yeah, and after the shellacking we gave 'em on Rincon Hill, they'll be out for blood."

A waitress took their order for sandwiches and coffee.

Buoyed by their success on Rincon Hill, Schmidt lobbied Bridges to order one more stand before the National Guard arrived. They were discussing possible tactics when strikers outside began drifting inland from the Embarcadero as though herded by some unseen force.

"Uh-oh," said Bridges, "somethin's up. Nick, go out and check on it. We may not have time to eat after all."

Nick hurried out of the restaurant and into a crowd of strikers standing on the corner. He threaded his way to the curb and stepped out into the intersection until he had a clear view down Mission Street to the Embarcadero. A line of mounties and bluecoats were standing in formation. At the moment, though, they didn't seem to be going anywhere. He walked farther out into the intersection and looked south down Steuart Street. A cloud of teargas hovered over the street several blocks away.

The area around ILA headquarters had been a safe zone during the strike, a place where longshoremen and sailors could gather without fear of police harassment. A multitude of strikers, perhaps two-thousand in all, were congregated on all four corners of the intersection, some spilling out into the street, others into a gas station catty corner from The Bulkhead.

Nick stepped back onto the curb and was about to return to the restaurant when a black sedan drove into the intersection and stopped near the gas station. Two men seated inside were dressed in suits and fedoras. Plain-clothed cops, Nick figured. One of them climbed out of the passenger side, gripping a shotgun and frowning. He swiveled his head back and forth as if he expected trouble.

The strikers booed and jeered. Someone yelled, "Let's tip it over."

The cop turned toward the strikers grouped in front of the gas station. "Any of you sons of bitches want trouble," he said, "bring it on."

A cobble flew out of the crowd and landed near him. He dodged it and fired the shotgun over the heads of the strikers who scattered into the gas station. More cobbles and brickbats flew toward him from multiple directions. He crouched down as though deer hunting and glanced this way and that, trying to determine where the missiles came from. Strikers in the gas station, sensing his fear and confusion, moved back toward the intersection and lobbed more bricks at him. The cop dodged back and forth to avoid them, then fired another shot into the air. His ammo spent, he ran around to the driver's side of the car, the side facing the corner where Nick stood in a crowd of agitated strikers yelling epithets. The car window rolled down and the gunman received more shells from the driver. He inserted them into the shotgun and turned to face the strikers. Another brick flew at him from somewhere near Nick and hit his right leg, tearing his pants.

"Alright, you asked for it!" yelled the gunman. He aimed the shotgun toward the group Nick was in and fired.

A thunderous blast erupted.

Wild pandemonium ensued as panicked strikers pushed and shoved each other, trying to flee from the shooter. Seconds later another explosion roared and in the confusion Nick lost his balance, cognizant as he went down of a sharp ringing in his ears.

Bridges and Schmidt heard the shots and rushed out of the restaurant just as the plain-clothed cop jumped back into the sedan which sped off. Bridges looked through the crowd and spotted two men lying on the sidewalk, blood seeping from shotgun wounds. He headed toward them but was blocked by hundreds of others moving in the same direction. Worried that Nick might be one of the wounded men, he shouldered his way through the tightly packed throng, though it was tough going and his progress was interrupted by a squad of policemen who arrived and began pushing everyone back. When he finally managed to break through the crowd, he faced a husky bluecoat gripping a billy club.

"Get back," the cop ordered, jabbing Bridges in the chest, "or you'll get what they got. Get back, all of you."

As he backed up, Bridges heard someone say that an ambulance had been called and was on the way. He was attempting to get a better view of the fallen men when he noticed a line of horse-mounted officers moving inland on Mission Street from the Embarcadero, pushing strikers toward ILA headquarters. He glanced south down Steuart Street now clouded with teargas, sealing that avenue. It seemed that the bluecoats were trying to herd the strikers into a confined area, and his suspicions were confirmed when more strikers flowed into the intersection on Mission Street from the west. He stopped one of them.

"What's going on?"

"The cops are pushing us this way."

Hemmed in on three sides, the strikers began moving toward whatever escape routes they could find. Bridges pushed his way out of the crowd and found Henry Schmidt, motioning to Henry to follow him. They ducked into ILA headquarters and bounded up the stairs to the second floor. Bridges peered out the window and watched as strikers dispersed, some taking refuge in the Seaboard Hotel, a sailor's flophouse a few doors away, others heading north on Steuart Street, which hadn't been sealed off yet, and some, like himself, retreating into ILA headquarters.

Although more cops were converging on the intersection, almost all the strikers reacted quickly enough to slip away. A police squadron equipped with teargas grenade launchers arrived and stationed themselves in front of ILA headquarters. Bridges figured they were preparing to raid the headquarters and was about to order his men to erect a barricade at the front entrance when suddenly, without warning, the police aimed their launchers at the ILA building and the nearby Seaboard Hotel and fired off grenades. Two grenades smashed through ILA windows and landed inside. His men quickly tossed them back out, forcing the cops to retreat to the opposite side of the street. From there, officers pulled out their revolvers and fired at the buildings as if using them for target practice.

The men inside dove behind desks and chairs as bullets hit the outside wall and smashed through into the office.

"You were right," Bridges said to Schmidt, as they crouched behind an overturned desk, "the cops *are* out for blood." He wished he could call a truce and end the cycle of anger and violence. Unfortunately, it had taken on a life of its own and probably wouldn't end until it played itself out. When the shooting outside stopped and the cops moved on, he and Schmidt went up to the roof to monitor events along the waterfront. The sound of gunfire seemed to be everywhere now, and the acrid smell of teargas once again fouled the air.

The strikers were out-gunned and less organized than the police, yet they were agile and resourceful, moving the battle here and there and back again. In the confusion, police fired randomly into crowds, their bullets shattering office windows and hitting scores of innocent bystanders and strikers alike. More than once, Bridges and his lieutenants dove down as bullets hit the ILA building or flew past them.

72

The two strikers shot in front of The Bulkhead were the first to arrive at Harbor Emergency Hospital after the lunch break, causing an uproar as doctors barked orders and applied bandages to stem the bleeding. Their arrival also marked the onset of a new wave of patients. Those with the most serious injuries, including the two wounded men, were transferred to General Hospital. The rest were treated and released to make room for others.

Having proved her worth, Clarisa was given a battlefield promotion and put in charge of distributing bandages, iodine, sutures, surgical instruments, and blankets. And when the need arose, she applied towels to wounds until they could be dressed, wrapped bandages when a nurse had to rush off to another patient, swabbed iodine on minor cuts and scrapes, and dispensed aspirin. She was tending to a longshoreman when he regurgitated a squalid mixture of blood, teeth, and vomit, some of it splattering on her shoes. It happened so suddenly, she froze and stared at the gray-green mixture, dotted with pieces of teeth like a muddy soup with bits of white corn. She'd never experienced anything this repulsive before, and it seemed as if she'd entered an alien world in which order and civility were replaced with suffering and carnage. The rancid smell of vomit nearly overwhelmed her, causing her own gut to convulse. Fearing that if she looked at it another second she wouldn't be able to stop herself from throwing up, she rushed off to get a mop and bucket. When she returned, the longshoreman was swearing at a police officer who was badgering him with questions. She politely suggested to the officer that this wasn't a good time for an interrogation and herded him away.

Another man, mistaking her for a nurse, removed a jacket draped over his arm, revealing a hand cocked unnaturally at right angles to his forearm as if he were weirdly double-jointed.

"It's funny," he said, holding up the broken wrist with his good hand like a bizarre trophy. "It don't hurt much."

"It will when the shock wears off," she said, as she led him to a doctor.

During a lull in her duties, she glanced at a clock on the wall and was surprised that it was already half past three. The last several hours had flown by, and all she could remember was a blur of battered faces, guttural moans, vomit, and more blood than she'd ever seen in one day. It was probably best, she decided, that she'd been so busy. If she'd had more time to contemplate all the trauma, she might not have been able to keep herself from breaking down or leaving.

A nurse handed her gauze and bandages and asked her to wrap a policeman's hand. She was quite proficient at this now that she'd had hours of practice and was almost done when a familiar voice spoke up behind her.

"So there you are."

She finished taping off the gauze, wiped her hands on her apron, and turned around.

Roger Farnsworth looked relieved to have found her — that is until his gaze dropped down to the blood on her apron, and instantly his expression changed to shock as if it was the last thing he expected to see.

"Yes, here I am," she said, brushing a curl from her face with the back of her hand.

"I've been looking for you all afternoon. Mrs. Butterfield said you promised to be in this afternoon. When you didn't show, I got worried." He nodded toward the street. "It's a nightmare out there. I had to dodge rioters and bullets. Are you okay?"

"Yes. Tired but fine."

She glanced past him at strikers and police laying on cots waiting to be treated, some talking to neighbors, others staring off into space, contemplating the violence and anger they'd encountered that day. She noticed a striker at the far end the room, laying perfectly still, apparently unconscious. It was hard to tell at this distance, and her view was partially blocked by nurses and doctors walking between them, but he looked familiar. For a moment she wondered if her mind was playing tricks. Was she glomming onto an illusion out of desperate hope? Was this an unconscious effort to divert her thoughts from all the agony she'd seen that day?

Illusion or no, she swept past Roger and flew across the room.

"Oh, my God," she murmured as she reached him.

His eyes were closed, his face devoid of color. She lifted his head to her chest and held him close until a nurse passed by.

"What's wrong with him?" she asked.

The nurse shrugged. "He's been lying there for some time. His vital signs are okay, so with all this" — she swept her hand around — "we're letting him rest." She reached into her apron and removed a bottle. "Here, try smelling salts."

Clarisa opened the bottle and waved it under his nose. His fingers twitched, his head moved side-to-side, eyelids fluttered open, revealing a pair of light blue eyes. A sudden burst of relief washed over Clarisa. Those eyes, those beautiful blue eyes surrounded by dark lashes, were like twin beams of light on a dark night, guiding her home. She drank them in and held them in her gaze, not wanting to look away, not wanting to return to the horror that surrounded them.

His lips were dry, she noticed. She glanced over her shoulder at Roger. "Would you get a glass of water?"

"Is he alright?"

"I don't know. Please bring a glass of water."

"Okay. Okay," he muttered and wandered off.

Nick's eyes focused on the ceiling, on the nurses and doctors walking by, and then on the face hovering above him. He studied it without expression, as if for the first time.

"How do you feel?" asked Clarisa.

He inhaled a deep breath and let it out. "Hungry. Haven't eaten since yesterday. I must have passed out from hunger. We were just about to have lunch when —" He paused. "The last thing I remember was a shotgun blast. What happened?"

"Two men were hit. We just got word. They died. Were you there?"

Roger returned with a glass of water and handed it to Clarisa. She held it up to Nick's lips. He lifted his head and took a sip, then settled back down.

"Bridges asked me to see what was going on. When I reached the corner, someone fired at us. That's all I remember."

"Thank God you weren't hit." She cupped a hand on his cheek.

He put his hand over hers. "Do you know who was killed?"

"No, I've been here all afternoon. Did you hear anything, Roger?"

He didn't reply.

When she turned he was gone.

Newspaper accounts confirmed the death of two strikers. Both had been working in the strike kitchen down the street and were on their way to ILA headquarters to have their timecards punched, never suspecting that gunfire was about to cut them down. Thirty-eight others were wounded by gunfire, including several bystanders. Dozens, perhaps hundreds, were injured.

Harry Bridges led a delegation to City Hall to protest the police department's brutal handling of the riot. By then, though, it was a moot point. The cadenced tread of National Guard troops could be heard along the Embarcadero, effectively ending the war between the strikers and police. Guardsmen of the 40th California Division and 250th Coast Artillery, wearing wide-brimmed helmets, olive uniforms, and leather jackboots, set up sandbagged positions and fifty-caliber machine guns along the waterfront from China Basin to Fisherman's Wharf.

Despite the violence and chaos, the Industrial Association's trucks had been able to transfer cargo from Pier 38 to the Maggini & Garcia warehouse without difficulty. The amount was insignificant, but it proved that with police and military protection the port could be opened, however so slightly.

The following day Bridges addressed the San Francisco Labor Council, a coalition of the city's labor unions. "Now that the National Guard is firmly in control of the waterfront, the great arched doors of the Embarcadero have been flung open to swallow and spit out Belt Line trains and Atlas trucks without hindrance. Against military intervention no union is safe, no strike effective, no workingman protected. Only a general strike, involving all unions, will stop the Industrial Association from destroying the longshore and maritime unions and stop it from crushing every other union in Frisco."

Mostly men in their fifties and sixties, the Labor Council listened to his appeal and promised to set up a fact-finding committee to explore the practicality of staging a general strike. Bridges could see in their eyes and the way they whispered among themselves that these older, conservative union officials didn't support a general strike and would try to slow things down to avert it. He also knew that they considered him a radical upstart who had acquired too much power too quickly. Yet he also saw in their expressions a grudging realization that his assessment of the situation was correct, that the survival of every union in San Francisco was at stake, and that to head off disaster, it might be time to circle the wagons.

PART FOUR

LORDS OF THE PORT

CHAPTER 73

Not since the Gold Rush, when a semaphore on its peak alerted residents that a newly arrived ship had sailed into the bay, had Telegraph Hill attracted so much attention. The newly completed tower at its summit, standing 210 feet tall, was indeed a sight to behold. Slender and elegant, it resembled a gigantic fluted column capped by a lookout station said to offer a spectacular view of the city and bay, although so far the public hadn't been allowed inside to see it.

Nick and Clarisa strolled up the hill, Nick carrying a wicker picnic basket, Clarisa a blanket to sit on. It was a beautiful day, the sun bright but not overpowering, a perfect afternoon to relax and recover from the July 5th battle, now called Bloody Thursday. This was only the second time Nick and Clarisa had been alone together in over a year, and although there was much to talk about, much catching up to do, they were satisfied just to hold hands and enjoy each other's company as they walked to the top of the hill.

When they reached their old picnic spot overlooking the bay, they spread the blanket on a patch of golden grass and unpacked the picnic basket — a bottle of Chianti, a loaf of sourdough French bread, a wedge of Fontina cheese, and a brace of ripe golden peaches. While Nick pulled the cork from the wine bottle and poured two glasses, Clarisa sliced the bread and cheese and arranged them on a plate. She set the plate beside Nick.

"Do you know where I was the morning you left on your voyage?"

Nick handed her a glass of Chianti and thought back to that morning. It was then he realized that they were at the same spot where he waited for her, hoping she would see him off. "In bed?"

She pointed to a nearby eucalyptus tree with a guilty smile. "No, there, behind that tree."

"What? Why didn't you say goodbye?"

She looked down at her glass. "I was too angry and confused. I hated you for leaving but loved you nevertheless." She laid a hand on his arm. "I almost came out. Then your grandfather showed up and I . . . I don't know. I should have said goodbye anyway."

They sipped the wine and gazed down at the waterfront, now more a military occupation zone than a port. National Guardsmen were stationed in front of the pier sheds, some standing at attention with rifles on their shoulders, others crouched inside sandbag machine gun nests, ready to repel any attack. Military jeeps rolled up and down the boulevard, as did trucks towing artillery cannons, more for show, Nick reckoned, than any practical purpose. Beyond the waterfront, the bay was dotted with dozens of ships still waiting to be unloaded.

For the next hour, while they enjoyed the simple repast, Nick described his journey across the Pacific — to Grays Harbor, Seattle, Tacoma, Shanghai, Manila, and back. Details of the voyage had already begun to lose clarity under the weight of recent events, and some details, like the night he spent with the Russian taxi dancer, he left out altogether. He also described his work for the *Waterfront Worker* and the satisfaction it gave him to serve a cause he supported while honing his writing skills. He was afraid Clarisa might feel some resentment, for it was his desire to become a reporter that, at least partially, was responsible for their long separation. To his relief, she listened attentively and he detected no such ill-feelings.

When he finished, he asked her to recount her own experiences during their separation. She seemed hesitant at first, picking and choosing her words carefully. He figured that this was because she didn't want to discuss her relationship with Roger, and since he, too, had censored himself, he listened without interruption and didn't question her or ask for more details.

During a break in the conversation, he thought back to previous picnics at this location when, just like today, they sat on a blanket and shared a meal. He glanced at the bottle of wine and plate of food. Their picnic today was the same as before, yet somehow it felt different. *What is it? What's different?* Then it came to him. It was him. He was different; he wasn't the same person. In past years he liked to show off his knowledge of ships in the bay, identifying them by their shape and color, or he would daydream about them as vehicles to exotic, far-off lands. Now he saw them in a different light. Now they were tools of commerce, owned by capital and operated by labor. Now he was able to picture the men who worked on them, what they looked like, how they talked, what they did. He swirled the red wine in his glass. Even the Chianti tasted different, as if the grape picker, the crusher, the vintner, the bottler, the truck driver, the stevedore, the sailor, the shelf stocker, all who labored to create and deliver the ruby liquid had each infused their essence into its bouquet.

They lingered in the sunshine, savoring each other's company until the wine bottle was nearly empty. Nick was about to suggest they depart when he noticed moisture welling in Clarisa's eyes and a tear roll down her cheek. He reached up to catch it with his finger, and when he touched it his own eyes moistened. As if drawn together by an invisible force, they reached out to each other and embraced, crying openly, their tears an expression of joy at reuniting, as well as a release of tension from the nightmare of Bloody Thursday.

When they drew apart, Clarisa wiped her face with a napkin and inhaled deeply as if it was her first breath in a long time. "Oh, before I forget," she said as she opened her purse and rummaged through it, "I have something for you." She removed a carbon copy of a letter and handed it to Nick. "No one must know how you obtained it."

He read the letter, startled by its contents. "You got this from work?"

She nodded and told him how she obtained it.

On the day after Bloody Thursday, she and Roger worked nonstop preparing for the National Longshoremen's Board hearings and assisting waterfront employers, who were now gearing up to normal levels of commerce. Toward the end of the day, he handed her a letter he'd written at the request of Thomas Plant and asked her to type it. It seemed odd that he would ask *her* to type it, as Plant's letters, even those Roger wrote, were typically typed by his own secretary. She figured Plant's secretary was too busy to type it, that is until she sat down at her desk and read it.

Addressed to members of the Waterfront Employers Association at the port of San Pedro, the letter chastised them for spending WEA funds for private guards, then bragged that in San Francisco the cost of deploying police and National Guard had been borne solely by the government. Clarisa immediately understood the consequences should the letter became public. Not only would it embarrass Plant, it might tip public opinion against the shippers whose massive government subsidies had already been exposed. She wondered if Roger had given her the letter knowing she might pass it on. It seemed possible, even likely. But why would he?

74

Mourners were lined up outside ILA headquarters, waiting to pay last respects to Howard Sperry and Nick Bordoise, the two men killed on Bloody Thursday, whose bodies lay in state inside. Nick could have walked right in, but it seemed disrespectful so he joined the line and followed it into the building and up the stairs. While in line he had a chance to observe the other mourners, and from the variety of manner and dress, simple working clothes to tailored suits and dresses, he could see that they were from a broad cross-section of society, a testament to the profound effect the deaths had had beyond the waterfront.

Desks and chairs had been moved aside to make room for two open coffins that lay on a table draped with black cloth. A dozen floral wreaths, mounted on easels, scented the air as visitors filed by the coffins, some bending their knees and genuflecting, others raising their fists in a sign of militant solidarity, most just gazing solemnly at the fallen men.

After Nick paid his respects, he searched for Bridges and found him in a back office, meeting with several of his lieutenants.

The Aussie was in an unusually upbeat mood considering the somber scene in the next room. "I want everyone to come in early tomorrow," he said. "We're going to stage a funeral the likes of which this town has never seen. And, believe it or not, I convinced Chief Quinn to let us march up Market Street without police interference."

"You're kidding," someone said, the sharp report of gunfire and tear-gas grenades still fresh in everyone's mind.

"Absolutely not. I reckon Quinn feels guilty — as he should — for the way his stooges went berserk, so he's agreed to leave us alone. We're going to organize our own security to keep traffic off the street, but we aren't allowed to distribute flyers or carry placards, which is just as well. I don't want this to become a rally, or worse a riot. This'll be our chance to show the city who has self-control and who doesn't." He was referring to news-paper reports that portrayed the strikers as blood-thirsty rioters attacking police without provocation.

When the meeting ended and everyone else had gone, Nick pulled out the letter he obtained from Clarisa. "Here," he said, handing it to Bridges, "take a look at this."

Bridges read it and whistled. "This is dynamite. Where did you get it?" Nick shrugged, preferring to keep that to himself. Bridges smiled. "That's alright. I can guess. So you're back with your girl?"

Nick grinned, hardly believing it himself.

The next day at the stroke of noon, a brass marching band commenced the doleful strains of Chopin's funeral dirge, signaling the start of the procession. Behind the band the funeral cortege extended down Steuart Street for nearly a mile. Harry Bridges invited Nick to march with the strike leaders near the front of the line, but he declined, preferring to join his old shipmates. It was a bittersweet reunion, as many of them hadn't seen each other since landing on the beach eleven months earlier. Moon carried his broken arm in a sling but otherwise looked fit. Remy and Haggis were there, bruised from waterfront battles but not seriously hurt. Cook, his considerable girth hanging over his trousers, was there with the carpenter. And Sparks joined them to show his support even though wireless operators weren't unionized.

In stark contrast to the chaos four days earlier, the strikers marched in orderly formation six-abreast up Market Street, taking up the entire width of the boulevard. An honor guard of veterans followed the brass band, proudly carrying the Stars and Stripes and the ILA's navy-blue flag. Behind them, two flatbed trucks draped in black funereal cloth bore the coffins of Bordoise and Sperry, whose coffin was covered with an American flag, as he was a veteran. Two more flatbed trucks followed, each bedecked with floral wreaths, and behind them a pair of black limousines carried relatives of the two fallen men.

The strike leaders—Bill Lewis, Joe Johnson, Harry Bridges, Henry Schmidt, and the entire Joint Marine Strike Committee—walked in formation behind the limousines. They were followed by the great mass of longshoremen wearing black Frisco jeans and striped hickory shirts, their white caps tucked under their arms in deference to the occasion. Then came the sailors, marine engineers, masters, mates, pilots, oilers, water tenders, cooks, scalers, machinists, and welders, their footsteps treading up Market Street—*tramp, tramp, tramp*—before crowds of curious onlookers.

· · ·

From the Matson Building on Market Street, the staff of the Waterfront Employers Association gazed down at the procession, its orderly rows occupying the boulevard in either direction as far as the eye could see. Roger stood beside Clarisa, aware that Nick was somewhere below. He'd been wrestling with the fact that Clarisa had chosen Nick over him, a choice made clear at Harbor Emergency Hospital. And although it hadn't been a complete surprise, the finality of her decision had hit him like a punch in the gut. He was also aware that Clarisa knew Nick was somewhere below — an awkward situation — so they watched in silence, mesmerized by the solemn spectacle.

Thomas Plant, standing behind them, wasn't so impressed. "Helluva nerve they've got stopping traffic on the city's busiest street, especially after the disturbance they caused."

"They did lose *two* men," said Roger.

"I know. But they don't have to make a big show of it. This is just propaganda, if you ask me. I don't trust Bridges. He's up to something. Have you talked with our man — what's his name, Benson? — to find out what their next move is? They certainly won't be able to set foot on the Embarcadero again."

Out of the corner of his eye Roger caught Clarisa stealing a glance at him. "I'm afraid he won't cooperate."

"What!?!" Plant exclaimed. "Why not?"

"He's had a change of heart. Says he can't spy on the union any longer."

"He knows the consequences?"

"Yes and still refuses."

"Fine. Call Quinn and have him arrested. You've got another man in the union hall?"

"Yes," he replied, glancing at Clarisa.

Her expression was unchanged but the natural blush in her cheeks was deeper than usual.

"Well, then, see what you can find out."

"Excuse me," said Clarisa, as she whirled around and bumped into Plant. He stepped aside and let her by, his eyes following her down the hall until she disappeared.

"You think it'll work?" he asked Roger.

"I don't know. Let's give it a few days."

The funeral march proceeded up Market Street, attracting tens of thousands of spectators who witnessed labor's solidarity. No longer would newspapers be able to claim that the strike was led by a small cadre of violent radicals with negligible support from mainstream labor. Behind the strikers came block after block of marchers from other unions — teamsters, electricians, carpenters, bakers, streetcar operators, taxi drivers, hod carriers, musicians, waiters, printers, janitors, teachers, librarians. For the first time in history, San Francisco's workers were united in their disgust with intractable employers bent on destroying unions, and united in their desire for safe and stable jobs that paid a living wage. They waved no banners and chanted no slogans, but the unity that bound them together was self-evident in their discipline and decorum.

When the procession reached Duggan's Funeral Parlor on 17th Street, the low-slung building quickly filled to capacity. Nick and his former shipmates arrived too late to squeeze in, so they walked around the corner to The Albion, where they ordered mugs of lager and traded battle stories as they proudly displayed their cuts and bruises.

When that topic was exhausted Nick asked if anyone had run across the bosun.

Sparks nodded. "I saw him come out of a bar in Chinatown a few days ago. The lizard looked as ornery as ever, so I gave him a wide berth."

"If he's already sold the opium," Moon said, looking around the table, "he wouldn't be hangin' around a Chinatown bar. Hell, if I came into a few grand I'd have a dame on each arm and a chauffeur drivin' us to one a them hoity-toity joints where the waiters clean your ashtray every time you flick an ash."

Haggis sighed. "I'd buy me a farm and raise the biggest damn hogs in the county." His eyes brightened. "Then I'd build a house with electric lights in every room and a stove so big, mama could bake a dozen pies at a time."

"I'd buy a cottage near Bodega Bay," said the carpenter. "Then I'd build a fishing boat and spend my days hauling in salmon the size of cocker spaniels."

"Oy'd open a roadhouse there," chimed in Cook, "roight on the wharf, and serve yer catch." He pounded a sumptuous fist on the table, spilling froth. "It'd sure as hell beat servin' slop to sailors who grouse about moiy chow from mornin' 'til noight."

Of that they all agreed and toasted Cook and his future establishment.

Nick paid only partial attention after that, his thoughts instead centered on the bosun. He didn't know where Slag was or what he was doing, but he was reasonably sure of one thing: as Moon suggested, it was likely the bosun still possessed the contraband. After all, he was a sailor not a drug dealer, and there weren't many buyers who could afford a hundred pounds of opium.

The funeral march provoked an extraordinary reaction. Thousands witnessed it and thousands more read about it in the newspapers. As Nick traveled about the city, he noticed a shift in attitude among the public. On streetcars and in markets, along sidewalks and at restaurants, everyone was talking about the miles-long procession, and more significantly, they talked about the strikers with an air of sympathy and respect, as though for the first time they saw them not as radical agitators but as upstanding citizens who deserved a decent job.

This same reverence extended to the National Longshoremen's Board as it began a new round of hearings to determine the viability of arbitration. The day after the funeral Nick accompanied Harry Bridges to the Federal Building, where the strike leader had been asked to testify. The courtroom was packed with reporters, longshoremen, and other interested parties, including Father Shannon, Thomas Plant, Roger Farnsworth, and Clarisa McMahon. Archbishop Hanna and his fellow board members, Oscar Kushing and Edward McGrady, listened as Bridges described the humiliating shape-up and the disabling injuries and deaths common on West Coast waterfronts. Speaking extemporaneously and without notes, the strike leader held the room spellbound for more than an hour while he reviewed the events leading up to Bloody Thursday. He then denounced the reign of terror loosed on the strikers by city officials at the behest of the Industrial Association. Unlike previous hearings, the board listened to him without interruption, and for the first time many in the audience experienced the extraordinary oratory that had inspired and bound the strikers together for sixty-two days.

At the end of his testimony, Bridges produced the Plant letter he'd obtained from Nick and read it out loud. Addressed to the San Pedro employers, it bragged that unlike San Pedro, where the employers had paid for private guards, the city government in San Francisco had born the cost of combating the strikers. When he finished there was utter silence.

Plant shot an angry glance at Roger, who shrugged and turned up his palms, as if to say he had no idea how Bridges acquired the letter. Clarisa, who was seated on his other side, stared straight ahead, a mantle of sweat on her upper lip. Roger was glad she'd passed on the letter as he suspected she would. For some time, in his estimation, the employers had been obstinate fools who seemed to care little about their workers and more about holding on to power and control.

Archbishop Hanna rubbed his forehead, clearly stunned by the tone and content of the letter. Kushing and McGrady appeared equally disturbed. Bridges then presented another letter, this one from the Industrial Association urging its members to send financial contributions to aid in its effort to gain control of the waterfront.

"Contributors were asked to sign pledge cards and were given three to five years to pay," he said, his voice dripping with sarcasm. "In other words, strikebreaking on the installment plan."

Laughter broke out and continued until the bailiff called for quiet.

Archbishop Hanna asked Bridges, "Would the longshoremen consider binding arbitration by this board on all issues? I can assure you, you'll receive a fair hearing."

Harry clasped his hands together and leaned forward. "I've been asked that question many times before, Your Grace, and my answer is the same as it's always been. First of all, we've already agreed to arbitrate all issues except the hiring hall and a coastwise contract. Without control of the hiring hall, the ILA would be at the mercy of employers and eventually destroyed through discrimination and blacklisting, leaving the right of longshoremen to organize a farce. Moreover, this is not just a longshoremen's strike but a maritime strike. For the longshoremen to return to work without a settlement of the other unions would be an absolute betrayal. So any arbitration would have to include all striking unions." He sat back in his chair and splayed his hands on the table. "To be honest, though, I don't think the men are in any mood for it. After what happened on Bloody Thursday and now the occupation of the waterfront by the National Guard, there's a strong sentiment for a general strike."

"I urge you to reject such a drastic measure," said Hanna, "It could tear the city apart and derail progress toward a resolution."

"Your Grace, we intend to stay off the job until we have reasonable assurances — not mere pledges — that the strikers will have adequate job protections. For that reason a general strike is pending and all organized labor is watching this board and the outcome of its deliberations."

Thomas Plant was the next to testify. He presented a strident defense of the employers, pointing out that two previous agreements between the waterfront employers and the ILA had been rejected by the rank-and-file under the domination of militant radicals. He also reminded the board that the employers had previously agreed to a jointly operated hiring hall and to only hire registered men. Nevertheless, he concluded, the Waterfront Employers Association would be willing to submit all issues, except the hiring hall, to arbitration.

"What about the maritime unions?" McGrady asked.

"That's a different kettle of fish. My organization represents companies that hire dockworkers to stow and discharge cargo. There isn't a corresponding employers group for marine workers, so it's our opinion that they'll have to negotiate company by company."

Hanna appeared skeptical. "Aren't several of your members also owners of the largest shipping companies on the West Coast?"

"That's correct, Your Grace, but our members only constitute a fraction of the shipping companies that call on the Port of San Francisco. Other shipping companies have said they won't arbitrate, and we can't control them."

"Of course he would say that," Bridges said to Nick as they drove to a teamster meeting that afternoon. "The employers know very well that the ILA wouldn't have been able to shut down the port without the support of the maritime unions and that the maritime unions would never have gone out on strike if it hadn't been for the longshoremen. So they're trying to split us up. Divide and conquer. It's the oldest trick in the book."

Hundreds of longshoremen were gathered on the sidewalk in front of Dreamland Auditorium, corner of Post and Steiner, waiting to hear if the teamsters inside would join a general strike. It was a momentous decision as the teamsters union was the most powerful union in San Francisco, its support critical. Every few minutes someone would come out and report on what was happening inside. The latest news was that members of the San Francisco Labor Council were urging the teamsters not to make a hasty decision. Moreover, Teamster president Mike Casey had warned his drivers that if they left their jobs they would be violating union rules and risk losing benefits. Apparently neither argument was working. A noisy, rebellious clamor tumbled out of the building, and voices could be heard chanting, *"Brid-ges! Brid-ges! We want Brid-ges!"*

This was accompanied by the stomping of boots in time to the chant. *"Brid-ges! Brid-ges! We want Brid-ges!"*

Six teamsters came out of the auditorium searching for Harry Bridges. When they found him, they surrounded him and hustled him inside, Nick managing to slip in behind them. As soon as the rank-and-file recognized the Aussie they cheered and applauded as he climbed onto the stage and stepped up to the podium. Employing an oratorical device that Nick had seen him use before, Bridges spoke in a low, barely audible whisper. To hear him, the boisterous teamsters quieted down and craned forward, their attention riveted to the podium as, word-by-word, sentence-by-sentence, Bridges increased the volume and intensity of his speech. He detailed events leading up to the current deadlock, reminding the teamsters that the Industrial Association had employed non-union drivers to open the port. Unity, he urged, was the only way to combat this assault on union labor and defend their common interests.

When his speech ended, in stark contrast to previous speakers, a roar of approval shook the auditorium.

Mike Casey stepped to the podium and called for a standing vote on whether to join a general strike. For several seconds all that could be heard was the sound of men rising to their feet, and when the auditorium quieted, every teamster was standing, showing a unanimous desire to leave their jobs at midnight.

A general strike was one step closer.

75

Seamus McMahon was gobsmacked. An article in the Saturday morning *Chronicle* reported that teamsters had set up blockades at every major entry point into San Francisco—Bayshore Highway, El Camino Real, Skyline Boulevard, the East Bay ferry terminals—and that they were turning back incoming trucks except those carrying bread, milk, beer, laundry, and a few other exempted items. *Jaysus, what else do people need? There are times in Ireland when families would give their eye-teeth for a loaf of bread, a quart of milk, and a pint of Guinness.* If this was a "Stupendous Crises," as the headline declared, he'd like to send the editors to County Cork where they'd really learn the meaning of hardship.

As for the blockaded items, he reckoned the city could manage without them, and it would do the public good to acquire a few survival skills. Take gas, a luxury item as far as he was concerned, requiring ownership of a car, and hardly anyone he knew could afford one except for Clarisa's wanker boss who drove a fancy convertible, all shiny and spit-polished. And meat. *Hell, when I was a lad, we were lucky if ma put corned beef on the table once a week.* But beer. Now there was a real staple. Even the bloody Black and Tans know better than to stand between a man and his daily dose of suds.

He was sitting behind the counter in his print shop, waiting for someone, anyone, to come in and place an order. Saturdays used to be his busiest day, the bell over the front door jingling cheerfully whenever a customer entered. *Now where are they?* He didn't care so much about the lack of income as he did the lack of activity. It drove him crazy to be idle.

To keep himself busy, he'd polished and tuned his printing press until it shined like that wanker's sports car. Then he cleaned and oiled his Enfield rifle, breaking the weapon down into its component parts — barrel, bolt, trigger, magazine, butt, bayonet — laying them on the counter and cleaning each one with solvent and a bristle brush. Then he lubricated the parts with Yasker's Gun Oil and reassembled the lot. All in ten minutes flat.

A student from the Worker's School next door came by while he was cleaning the rifle and gawked at it as if it were Lenin's Tomb. Soon thereafter more students came in and asked to see it, some even wanted to touch it, but he drew the line there. They may have been able to recite *Ten Days that Shook the World* chapter and verse, but the closest they ever came to handling a firearm was the penny arcade at Playland. And he wasn't about to let them put their rabbity paws on it.

The San Francisco Labor Council met on morning Saturday to decide whether to support a general strike. Nick drove Harry Bridges to the meeting, and on the way Bridges explained the situation. "Twenty-eight unions have voted to join so far, but only if the San Francisco Labor Council agrees to back it. Our mission is to convince them that if they don't go along, they'll suffer the consequences."

"Consequences? Like what?"

"The Industrial Association has neutralized the waterfront strike. If they get away with it, it will set a precedent, and there's no doubt they'll try to neutralize every strike."

"Sounds like the Labor Council should be eager to support a general strike?"

"You'd think so, but most of 'em are conservative officials who like their cushy jobs and don't want to challenge the status quo."

Nick suspected that there was more to it than Bridges was willing to admit. He'd heard that some in the labor movement, influenced by

Red-baiting in the newspapers, were convinced that Bridges was a communist. And, worse, they felt threatened by his influence over the rank-and-file. Nick had never asked Bridges if he was a communist. If he was he hadn't mention it, and he certainly didn't have time for it. His work for the union kept him busy seven days a week, so busy he hardly had time for his own family. Or so he said.

Delegates from one-hundred fifteen unions were assembled in the Labor Temple auditorium, smoking cigarettes and chatting amiably or looking around with a wary eye. Bridges was one of the first to speak. He made a passionate appeal for a general strike, saying it would show the public that all San Francisco unions supported the waterfront strike and were opposed to interference from police and military. "It's Labor's Last Stand," he said to cheers from younger rank-and-file members.

John O'Connell, longtime official with the Labor Council, saw things differently. "General strikes have never been successful, and one now, particularly in this period of economic distress, will surely alienate a public deprived of transportation and food."

Bridges shot back: "If we take police brutality and military occupation lying down, the bosses will never let us win another strike. We might as well pack up and go home."

The debate went back and forth, sometimes degenerating into a shouting match as tempers flared and faces turned red. It eventually became clear that most delegates were angry at the police for their brutal treatment of strikers and at the Industrial Association for using non-union truck drivers, and that anger seemed to trump all other arguments. When the shouting subsided, there was little doubt as to how the majority felt. Every union that hadn't already voted to walk out, sixty-three in all, let their voices be heard. And all spoke as one.

The general strike was on.

76

Lillian Benson had never seen anything like it. *Has everyone lost their mind?* She'd been traipsing from one market to another, and all of them were packed with crazed shoppers as if it was the day before Thanksgiving and everyone was expecting a horde of hungry relatives.

The press had reported the Labor Council's decision to proceed with a general strike on Monday morning and warned of possible shortages. Consequently, shops were enjoying a booming business as residents rushed to stock up on items before the strike began. Lillian noticed other changes as well. Streetcars and taxis had suddenly vanished, presumably when drivers walked out in advance of the other striking unions. And the usual swarm of pedestrians and vehicles along downtown streets was now a slow trickle, giving the city an empty, abandoned atmosphere.

Giving up her search for an uncrowded market, she entered Perini's, a family-run grocery store on Columbus Avenue. Like everywhere else, customers were cleaning out the shelves, even of odds-and-ends like shoe polish. And there was a line snaking up and down the aisles to the checkout counter, which had a sign announcing a five-pound limit on flour and sugar.

After enduring the line in Perini's, she went to Iacopi Meats on Grant Avenue and was disappointed to find the front door locked and a sign in the window announcing it had run out of meat. In desperation she walked down Grant and ventured into Chinatown where shoppers crowded the markets, although this was normal. Chinatown was the densest neighborhood in San Francisco, and every Saturday Chinese residents flocked to the stores to buy produce, spices, tea, and rice for the coming week. She found a seafood market on Stockton Street with fresh fish laid out on a bed of ice. Unlike the markets she was used to, this one only stocked whole fish, no fillets or steaks, however, the prices were reasonable. She pointed to a sea bass. As the owner wrapped it in newspaper, she asked for directions to a poultry shop.

He shook his head. "No speak English."

She thought for a moment, then flapped her arms and squawked like a barnyard hen.

Smiling at her antics, he pointed across the street.

The poultry shop was narrow and deep, its walls lined from floor to ceiling with caged birds all clucking and cooing at once. The smell of feathers and bird excrement nearly drove Lillian out, but she braced herself, marched up to the counter and asked for a roasting chicken. The clerk removed a plump hen from one of the cages and presented it for her approval. She nodded and watched as he chopped off its head right in front of her, tore out the gizzards, and plucked its feathers as if the whole operation was as normal as brushing his teeth. Taken aback by the sight of blood and guts, she fumbled in her handbag until she found her coin purse to pay for the freshly slaughtered fowl.

That evening she proudly served baked sea bass, scalloped potatoes, and steamed broccoli flavored with salt, pepper, and butter. While Nick, Sarah, and Rune devoured the home-cooked meal she recounted her shopping adventures and the odd state of things, remarking that even during the Great War food staples hadn't been this scarce.

Afterwards they all gathered in the front parlor for what had become a rare event: a quiet evening at home together. While the radio played in the background, Lillian stitched a needlepoint design, periodically glancing at her father and her two grown children, happy to have them all gathered in one place. Rune was settled in a stuffed mohair chair, puffing contentedly on his meerschaum pipe, his head buried in a newspaper. Nick was on the sofa reading a book, while Sarah sat beside him, staring out the window with a bored expression, as if spending an evening with her family was a burden she was enduring rather than enjoying.

The familiar opening strains of the Amos 'n' Andy Show came on the radio. Lillian had always enjoyed the humorous misadventures of Kingfish, owner of the Fresh Air Taxi Company, and his cohorts, and during these difficult times a bit of laughter was a welcome relief. She reached over to the radio and turned up the volume.

KINGFISH: *"Ow wah! Ow wah! Little Queenie. What's dat regusting aroma? Sho seems like de Fresh Air Taxi Company ain't so fresh no mo'. Needs a good rubdown with some sweet lemon oil or sumfin."*

MADAM QUEEN: *"Looky here, Kingfish, I's wearing my new ody colonee, Lady of de Kasbah. Ain't it odiferous, darlin'?"*

KINGFISH: *"Humph."* (in a stage whisper) *"Brotha Crawford, I'm thinkin' it smell mo' like da Lady of de Rump Roast."*

BROTHER CRAWFORD: *"Yess suh, chief, check and double-check."*

Lillian chuckled. "Those colored folk sure are a hoot. Don't you think?" When no one answered, she rested the needlepoint on her lap. "Well, don't everyone answer at once."

Nick looked up from his book. "Mother, those aren't Negroes. They're white actors pretending to be Negroes."

"Really?" she said, resuming her needlepoint. "They sure sound colored."

"Actually, Negroes don't talk like that. Harry Bridges says it makes fun of them in a demeaning way and shouldn't be allowed on the air."

Lillian frowned. "Harry this, Harry that. If he's so smart, why's he gotten us into this mess? It's bad enough he's shut down the city and cleaned out the stores; now he wants to control the airwaves? Where will it end?"

Nick sighed. "Drastic situations demand drastic actions. Things will return to normal as soon as the shippers come to their —"

"Ladies and Gentlemen, we interrupt this program to bring you an emergency address by the Mayor of San Francisco, the Honorable Angelo J. Rossi."

Lillian stopped mid-stitch and stared pensively at the radio.

"My fellow citizens: In saying to you that all of us tonight face a situation of great seriousness and difficulty, I wish to also remind you that San Francisco before now has come triumphantly through great disasters. However, the current state of emergency is like none other we've face before, and tonight I ask all our citizens to pull together in this uncertain hour and stand up for the liberties and freedoms guaranteed by the constitution.

"On Monday morning, the city's labor unions have called for a general strike, which will effect the welfare of every man, woman, and child. In concert with many of our citizens, including respected members of organized labor, I have used all my efforts as Mayor to avert this calamity. It is my opinion that the labor movement is not threatened and has not been threatened during the past months. Unfortunately, through intimidation and hooliganism by a small group that has seized control of the International Longshoremen's Association, the strike has been ripped from the control of responsible labor leaders by alien radicals who oppose peace.

"Let me say to them, as well as to all our citizens, we are going to enforce order and protect and safeguard life and property with every method and procedure at our disposal. I am determined that those in this city who willfully seek to prolong strife for the purpose of overthrowing this government or the government of the United States will face all of the forces at my command and all other forces that may be required to prevent their carrying out their plans."

Lillian dropped her needlepoint. "State of emergency? What does he mean? What does he intend to do?"

"Amazing," Nick said, holding up his book. "Jack London predicted it in 1905 when he wrote *The Iron Heel.*"

"Predicted what?" Lillian asked.

"He warned of an attack on capitalist governments by the German aristocracy — the Great War —, followed by industrial overproduction — the Roaring Twenties —, followed by economic collapse — the Great Depression. He predicted that small farmers would lose their land to large banks, and that that would strengthen the corporations and turn farmers into migrant tenants. He also foresaw the popularity of socialism during economic collapse, giving rise to fascist states like Germany to combat working-class rebellion."

Rune lowered his newspaper and peered over the top, and Sarah, forgetting her boredom for a moment, regarded her brother with mild interest.

"But what does that have to do with the general strike?" Lillian asked.

"London predicted the rise of what he called the Black Hundreds — vigilante groups and hired guns like the Pinkertons — to combat strikes and militant progressives. He also described the creation of a national police force — the FBI — to combat subversive groups. And he predicted the creation of an elite class of workers who would form a buffer between the upper class and the majority of workers who labor in poverty."

Lillian shook her head in dismay. "Maybe I'm just plain dumb, but I still don't see what that has to do with the mayor's speech."

Nick laid the book down on his lap. "It all boils down to this. Rossi is comfortable with old line conservative labor leaders who head unions whose workers are paid just enough to keep them satisfied but who actually have little influence over their own unions. Along comes a guy like Harry Bridges who inspires a group of exploited workers to demand not just fair wages and safe conditions but also rank-and-file control of their union to promote their interests and protect their ability to stay organized. This not only changes the balance of power on the waterfront, it also threatens all other employers who control their labor force through conservative union leaders. The *I Ching* says —"

"The what?" interrupted Lillian.

"The *I Ching*, an ancient book of Chinese philosophy. I picked up a copy in Shanghai. It says, 'When power is threatened, violence will follow.' In other words, a general strike constitutes a direct challenge by labor to the politicians and the corporations who get them elected, and their first instinct is self-preservation. So Rossi is basically saying that he's going to pull out all the stops and take dictatorial reign of the city. We're gonna see more police, more National Guard, and perhaps the military on the streets of San Francisco. He's also encouraging civilians to join in and fight this so-called attack on government."

Lillian stared at him perplexed, not sure whether to be proud of a son who understood complex issues or alarmed at his radical notions. "I — I wish your father was here. I don't think he would approve of this kind of talk."

"Mother, don't make the same mistake as Rossi. Just because I'm in favor of union-controlled hiring halls doesn't mean I want to invite Stalin over for dinner."

"Well, thank goodness for that," she replied earnestly, "because we barely have enough food as it is."

Sarah rolled her eyes and groaned as she rose up from the sofa and headed toward the door.

"And where are you going, young lady?" Lillian demanded.

"Out, with friends." She vanished into the hall.

"Come back here. You heard the mayor. It's not safe outside. The city's in turmoil. I want to know where you're going."

Sarah reappeared in the doorway, wearing a hip-length black wool jacket, a pair of loose wool trousers, and a felt beret.

Lillian regarded her with disapproval. "You're not going out in that outfit, are you? My mother would never have allowed it."

Sarah adjusted her beret. "A few of us are going up to Telegraph Hill to see the murals in Coit Tower, and these," she looked down at her pants, "are much warmer than a skirt."

"But the *Chronicle* said the tower isn't open to the public yet, something about inspiring more civil disruption."

The city's Art Commission had hired twenty-six artists to paint fresco murals on Coit Tower's lobby walls, the theme: Californians At Work. Inspired by Mexican muralist Diego Rivera, the artists painted the frescos in rich earth-tones, portraying workers engaged in various occupations — picking and crating oranges, gathering calla lilies, butchering meat, pouring molten steel. But the newspapers had focused on a few controversial scenes.

One of these scene depicted figures reading leftist newspapers in a public library. Another was an iconic profile of the Golden Gate Bridge with the words *In God We Trust* imposed on the right side of the bridge, the pledge imprinted on U.S. currency, a symbol of American capitalism. On the left side was a hammer and sickle, the emblem of Soviet communism. In between these, over the center of the bridge, was the NRA Blue Eagle, symbolizing Roosevelt's New Deal. Though the rendering was designed to show the relationship between three economic systems — communism, capitalism, and something in between — the Art Commission felt it was "in opposition to the generally accepted tradition of native Americanism" (not to be confused with the traditions of Native

Americans). And this, of course, enraged the artists.

But what set off the greatest controversy was a doctored photograph taken by an intrepid *Examiner* reporter. He managed to sneak into the tower and had taken photos of the hammer and sickle and of the library scene located on another wall. Back at the newsroom, he cropped and pasted the two photos together with the caption, "Here is the painting in Coit Tower that has caused a bitter dispute between the artists and the Art Commission." With newspapers beating the drums of controversy and the waterfront in an upheaval, the Art Commission decided to delay the opening of the tower. This blatant censorship piqued the curiosity of adventuresome students who dodged evening patrols to peer through the tower windows with flashlights to view the offending frescos.

"It's art, mother," said Sarah. "I hardly think the murals are going to turn me into a raving revolutionary. Besides, do you want the government telling us what we can and can't look at? As an artist," she said, tossing a scarf around her neck, "I'm outraged."

With that she flounced out.

Lillian exhaled a sigh of resignation.

Rune, on the other hand, chuckled. "Forbidden fruit, my dear, it's always the sweetest."

77

Clarisa left the flat earlier than usual on Monday morning dressed in a forest green pleated skirt and matching jacket, her feet clad in a pair of rubber-soled Red Wings. Under normal circumstances she wouldn't be caught dead wearing hiking shoes to work, but with streetcar service discontinued, the two-mile trek to work was far too long in pumps, now tucked in her tote bag. The day was pleasantly brisk, and Haight Street, normally bustling with cars and trucks, was unusually quiet. Not that it was empty. Bread and milk trucks rolled by, as did the occasional automobile crammed with passengers sharing a ride to work. Still, the absence of motor vehicles gave the city a peaceful air, as if half the residents had decamped for a holiday weekend.

She turned onto Market Street and headed down a gentle slope toward the office buildings downtown, her arms swinging in a comfortable rhythm. There was little traffic on the wide boulevard and no clanging, screeching streetcars. Buoyed by the pleasant exercise, she quickened her stride, her heartbeat accelerating, her lungs pumping air. *Why haven't I walked to work before?* she wondered. *This is certainly more enjoyable than squeezing onto an overcrowded streetcar.*

Along the way she was joined by other pedestrians, salesmen with briefcases, secretaries wearing cloche hats, executives in double-breasted suits, stock-room boys sporting bow ties. The procession continued to grow until the sidewalk was congested, forcing walkers to step into the curbside lane, which forced the occasional motor vehicle to the center of the boulevard. *Brrrinng! Brrrinng!* Bicycle bells rang out as cyclists rolled past, the chime of their bells merging with the tread of shoe leather. Then something unexpected. Students on roller skates sailed by, their hair floating in the breeze, faces flushed and grinning.

Far from being nervous about the general strike, morning commuters seemed to be enjoying their trek to work. People who normally kept to themselves remarked to each other how lovely it was to be outside and not cooped up in a vehicle. This sparked friendly conversations that reminded Clarisa of stories she'd heard about friendships formed in the days after the 1906 earthquake and fire, when residents were diverted from their usual routine.

At the corner of Market and Van Ness Avenue, a boy wearing knickers and a flat cap and holding copies of the *Chronicle* called out to the passing throng: "Extra! Extra! Read all about the general strike! And how the Brits crushed one in 1926!"

Clarisa bought a copy and scanned an article describing how authorities in London had foiled a general strike by encouraging citizens, backed by the military, to attack strikers who were locked up by the hundreds. Another paperboy ran up and thrust an *Examiner* under her nose. She waved him off but not before she noticed the same headline on the front page: Aroused Citizens Defeated British General Walkout. The similarity of the two articles was obviously more than coincidence. Newspapers appeared to be making a concerted effort to rally citizens into taking the law into their own hands, a strategy that destroyed any pretense of impartiality.

Most shops along Market Street were closed and many had posted signs in their windows saying: "Closed till the boys win," or "Closed for the duration of the general strike." At Compton's Restaurant, one of nineteen restaurants authorized by the Labor Council to remain open, a line snaked out the front door and down the block. Some in line looked irritated at having to wait outside for breakfast, sorely tempting Clarisa to stop and ask them if they'd like to stand in line for meals every day and to remind them of the importance of helping the needy.

When she arrived at work, the office was bristling with energy. The general strike had reduced the rest of the city to a crawl, but waterfront commerce, under National Guard protection, was ramping up to normal levels. She went directly to her office and sorted through a stack of letters and memos in her in-box. She usually checked in with Roger at the beginning of the day, but after Bloody Thursday he'd been distant and only communicated with her when necessary. Besides, ever since she learned that Plant had ordered Nick's arrest, she knew her days at the Waterfront Employers Association were numbered. As soon as she found other employment — Lord knows when that would happen — she planned to give notice.

As for Nick, she warned him about the arrest order and begged him to leave town or at least remove himself from the strike. Once it was over, she reasoned, Plant might be persuaded to rescind the warrant and let the matter drop. Despite her warnings, Nick refused to consider the suggestion, saying he'd rather spend ten years in jail than run away like an outlaw for a crime he hadn't committed.

She talked with Father Shannon about Nick's refusal to heed her warning, hoping he would side with her and advise Nick to leave. Instead, he praised Nick's decision and said courage was not truly realized until tested by adversity. Did not Jesus rebel against the Pharisees and their temples of mammon at great personal peril? And did not he himself suffer personal injury — his gimp leg — while standing up to employer-hired hooligans. He was delighted that she and Nick had reconciled and advised her to support Nick's decision as a way to reinforce their reconciliation.

Outwardly, she accepted Shannon's counsel, but inside, her anger at Nick resurfaced. *If he hadn't abandoned me and gone off on a long voyage, none of this would have happened. We would be happily married by now, perhaps with a child. And then I'd have had what I've always wanted: a stable, loving family.* Her thoughts continued in this vein until a sudden insight altered her perspective. If Nick had plodded down a tried-and-true path, he might have become just another self-absorbed husband expecting her to be subservient and cater to his every whim. Instead, he'd undergone a remarkable change from restless wayfarer to committed journalist to loyal paramour. So perhaps in the end everything had worked out for the best.

She finished typing the contents of her in-box and carried a stack of correspondence into Roger's office for his signature. He was on the phone and motioned to her to sit down.

"Yes, we're aware of it," he said into the phone, "but it shouldn't effect our operation. As far as we've been appraised, the a . . . the engagements will occur well away from the waterfront, so it's of no concern to us."

Clarisa wondered what he was referring to. A possible confrontation?

"In any case," Roger continued, "we have our hands full . . . Right, port operations are gearing up and we've got a lot of catching up to do . . . Alright, keep me posted and I'll do the same."

He hung up the phone and reached for a cigarette, then lit it, his hands trembling. This didn't surprise Clarisa. They'd been under great stress for some time, and it would take more time to digest recent events and adjust to the final outcome, whatever that might be. She held her pen and pad ready, assuming he wanted to dictate a letter or a list of instructions. He tapped his cigarette on an ashtray and stared at his desk. She could practically hear the wheels turning in his head, mulling over something, but she had no idea what it was.

"I—I want to apologize," he said without looking up, his voice soft, contrite. "Once again, I've failed you as an employer and a friend." His hazel eyes lifted to hers, then settled back on the desk. "You've made your choice and," he shrugged, "I wouldn't be honest if I didn't admit I'm disappointed . . . no, more than disappointed." He sucked on his cigarette and exhaled a stream of smoke, then shrugged again as if engaged in an internal debate. "I wasn't going to say this, but now I think I will." He looked up at her. There was a freshness in his appearance that had been missing for some time. His blond hair was neatly cut and combed, his pale features once again crisp and youthful. Yet his eyes seemed to possess an infinite sadness. "I love you," he said quietly. "God knows I tried not to but I couldn't keep myself from . . . from loving you." He let out a breath as if relieved to have made the confession. "Anyhow, once this mess is over, I'm planning to take off . . . maybe to Brazil. They say the samba parties go on all night, so it sounds like the perfect place to forget all this." He swept a hand out over the desk, indicating everything before him, including, she assumed, herself.

In the silence that followed, Clarisa looked beyond him at the picture window framing a flock of clouds drifting over the bay, dark in the center, silver around the edges. Life is peculiar, she reflected. There was a time when she would have been his if he had declared his love for her so simply, so forthrightly.

But he hadn't, and that was that.

"*Sorry,*" they both said simultaneously.

"Go ahead," said Clarisa. "Finish what you were saying."

Roger sighed. "Our lives will drift apart soon, and before they do I want you to know that I'll always think fondly of you. Our friendship has meant the world to me and I'll take it wherever I go."

Clarisa gave him a sympathetic smile. They *had* spent many enjoyable hours together, both at work and outside the office, and many of those hours had been filled with laughter and engaging conversation.

"I've enjoyed your company as well."

She wondered if this was the right moment to ask him for help. Could he, would he, release Nick from the smuggling charge? Release him from their unholy arrangement? She was about to speak when he rose abruptly from his chair and turned toward the window.

"Of course, we're not out of the woods yet." He nodded toward the western tower of the Bay Bridge. "Work has stopped on both bridges. Union tradesmen walked out this morning, preventing four-thousand bridge workers from doing their jobs. Together, those two structures make up the largest public works project in the country, and now they're dead in the water, quite literally." He shook his head. "Something's got to give."

78

Nick had dreamt of this moment for months. During the voyage across the Pacific, he'd imagined it in every detail, in every way, and now that it was here he was savoring every moment. They were in a small hotel on Cosmo Place off Taylor Street, a cozy old inn with floral wallpaper and wood floors that creaked. He had surprised her after work, waiting outside the Matson Building until she emerged and then following her up Market Street to the cable car turnaround. In front of Woolworths he tapped her on the shoulder and gestured for her to come with him. When she parted her lips to speak, he shook his head and took her hand, silently leading her to the hotel, her warm hand in his. At the front desk, an old friend from college who managed the place smiled knowingly as he handed Nick the room key. No charge.

The room was sparsely furnished and not much bigger than the bed, but that was all they needed. The moment the door closed behind them, they sloughed off their clothes and pressed their bodies together in a passionate embrace. Dispensing with foreplay, they fell onto the bed and went at it like two eager teenagers in the backseat of a car. Slow sensuality would come later; now was the time to unleash a smoldering desire repressed for too long.

During this intense moment Nick felt a supreme joy as if his whole life had led to this, as if all the trials and tribulations he'd faced in the last eighteen months had been put in his path so that this moment, this exquisite moment, would be that much more meaningful. And the release was incredible, his pent-up desire exploding into a kaleidoscope of wondrous sensations and emotions.

They lay in each other's arms for a brief intermission before starting up again, this time with slow deliberate movements, both of them savoring the warmth and affection of each other's touch. When he was fully erect she gently pushed him onto his back and climbed astride him, keeping herself upright and lowering herself gradually until she took him deep inside. Their movements were calm now, the rhythm of their love making slow and sensual as she rocked back and forth, back and forth.

"It's so quiet outside," she whispered afterward, their legs intertwined, her head resting on his shoulder, her auburn curls draped on this chest "I wish the city were always this quiet."

Nick stroked her back. "It's too bad it won't stay this way for long."

"Why?"

"Members of the Labor Council say that the general strike is causing panic and that everyone is blaming the unions."

Clarisa frowned. "I haven't seen any panic. Just the opposite. The city has never been more peaceful."

Nick hadn't seen any panic either. He'd heard that a number of wealthy residents had escaped to their country homes and would stay away until the general strike ended. He'd also read a report in the *Chronicle* that an army of Communists was massing somewhere in Northern California, but there was no evidence to confirm such a claim. If there was any panic, it was being whipped up by forces opposed to the general strike, who seemed to be doing everything they could to end it.

"The Labor Council is considering a proposal that will allow more restaurants to open, more produce and meat trucks into the city, and allow streetcar drivers to return to work."

"What does Bridges say?"

"He warned the council that loosening restrictions would demoralize the strikers and give the wrong impression to the public, that the only way to protect unions from military intervention and police brutality is to keep up the pressure until the waterfront employers agree to a reasonable settlement."

"The council disagreed?"

"Yeah. I think they're going to approve the proposal."

"Why? Don't they want the general strike to succeed?"

"No, not really. They only went along with it because the rank-and-file would have torn them to shreds if they hadn't. Now they want to derail it."

79

Clarisa was taking dictation in Roger's office when his phone rang.

He picked it up. "Hello." He listened for a moment, then put his hand over the phone and whispered, "It's a reporter."

Clarisa couldn't hear exactly what the reporter was saying, but she was able to catch the gist. Vigilantes were roaming the city, attacking the homes and offices of known communists and radicals. There had been bloodshed during the raids and property damage, though to what extend she couldn't tell. The reporter wanted a comment from Roger.

"I don't know anything more than what you've mentioned," Roger said, "but as far as I'm concerned unlawful violence, even against leftist organizations, is to be condemned. This isn't the Wild West anymore."

Apparently that wasn't the answer the reporter wanted. Clarisa could hear him badger Roger for a quote to illustrate the waterfront employers' appreciation of patriots combating radical elements. The two parried back and forth until the reporter exclaimed, "Hey, I ain't got all day. I'm on deadline." The phone clicked dead.

Roger set it back in its cradle. "Now, where were we?"

Clarisa didn't respond. She was staring off into space, her mind racing from one thought to the next. If vigilantes were raiding leftist organizations, they might raid the Workers' School next to her father's print shop.

That alone wouldn't be a problem, but Seamus had posted handbills in his shop window that he'd printed for the school. If the vigilantes saw the handbills, they might think the print shop was part of the school, and if they confronted her father, who knows what he would do.

She jumped to her feet. "I'm sorry. I have to make a phone call." She hurried into her office and picked up the phone. "Mrs. Butterfield, please connect me to Ashbury 5482." She heard the phone ring on the other end, once ... twice ... three times ...

"Hello," said Seamus.

She hastily explained the situation and pleaded with him to take the handbills down from the windows, lock up the shop, and leave.

"Don't worry, luv. The folks next door heard about the raids and warned me." His voice was sluggish and slurry; then it hardened with resolve. "They said they're gonna pack up and leave, but I'll not run away this time. Those bastards forced us out of our own country, but they sure as hell won't drive us out of Frisco. This is America! Land of the god-damned free! I'll *kill* the bastards!"

"Please, father, leave now. You can return in a few hours."

Her words didn't convince him. All conflicts in his besotted brain seemed to have melded together into a single raging anger: Brits, vigilante — vigilante, Brits. *I'll kill the bastards!*

She set the phone down and picked it up again. "Connect me with the longshoremen headquarters ... That's right, you heard me. Do it, *now*."

A gruff voice answered. "ILA."

"I need to talk with Nick Benson right away. Tell him it's Clarisa McMahon."

She heard voices murmuring, feet shuffling, phones ringing.

"Clarisa? Is that you?"

She gripped the phone. "Thank God you're there."

"Why? What's the matter?"

"Have you heard about the vigilante raids?"

"Yeah, but we're staying away. It's not our fight. Why?"

"I'm afraid they'll mistake father's shop as part of the Workers' School. I tried to convince him to lock up and leave, but he won't listen to me."

"Hmmm. Okay, I'll gather some help and drive up there. Traffic's light. It should only take fifteen minutes."

"Please, hurry," she pleaded. "I don't know what he'll do if the vigilantes get there first."

She hung up the phone and then wished she'd asked him to pick her up on his way to the print shop. She wasn't sure she needed to be there now that he was going, but a feeling of dread came over her and she knew she couldn't wait to see what, if anything, might happen. She grabbed her purse, flung open her office door, and charged out into the hall in such a preoccupied state she didn't notice Roger until she bumped into him.

"Whoa," he said, gripping her shoulders. "What's the emergency?"

She wriggled her shoulders, trying to free herself. "Please let me go. I don't have time to explain. I've got to leave now."

He held firm. "Does this have something to do with the vigilante raids?"

"Yes, if you must know, my father may be in danger." She wriggled again. "Now let me go."

Roger tightened his grip. "Wait a second. If you'll tell me what the problem is, I may be able to help."

Clarisa stared at him questioningly. "What? How?"

"Never mind. If time is important, tell me what you know and I'll see what I can do."

A minute later he picked up the phone, Clarisa by his side. "Mrs. Butterfield, get me the Industrial Association . . . Hello, this is Roger Farnsworth at the Waterfront Employers Association, please connect me with Paul Eliel. It's urgent . . . Hello, Paul. I need someone to contact the vigilantes right away. Is that possible? . . . Why? To prevent a catastrophe. Now can you contact them or not? . . . No? Alright, forget it."

During the call Clarisa had time to think back to a phone conversation she overheard Roger having the day before, to something she heard him say, something about being *appraised of engagements well away from the waterfront*. When he hung up, she glared at him. "You knew about this, didn't you?"

"Yes, but I had no idea it would involve your father."

"Never mind. Did you drive your car today?"

"No."

"Then I don't have a moment to lose." She headed for the door.

"Wait," he called out as he reached for his hat, "I'm coming with you."

Nick tried to recruit volunteers at the union hall, but was unsuccessful. Everyone was either too busy with strike matters or reluctant to interfere with a pogrom against radicals. *"I'd lay my life on the line for Bridges and the union — you know that — but I ain't stickin' my neck out for no Reds."* Though he explained the distinction between the Workers' School and Seamus' print shop, it didn't seem to matter and he didn't have time to argue. He flew down the stairs to the street and headed toward the Hudson, grateful he'd driven to work that day. He was almost there when an idea struck him that sent him off toward the Seaboard Hotel a few doors away.

The lobby was packed with sailors lounging on beat-up couches, some reading newspapers, others writing letters, playing cards, or swapping stories. Now that the National Guard occupied the waterfront, picketers weren't allowed on the Embarcadero, leaving most to bide their time elsewhere until the strike ended. Bridges had confided to Nick that the situation was worrisome. An idle striker soon loses backbone, he said, and falls prey to conservative union officials in cahoots with employers. He'd organized work programs to support the general strike, and that kept some of the original strikers busy (they'd now been out for seventy days), but many were losing confidence, a deadly sign for the waterfront strike.

Nick scanned the lobby until he spotted what he was looking for. He rushed to the back of the lobby, to where Moon and Remy were playing poker with three others, while Haggis looked on. He briefly explained the situation and asked them to join him.

"Well, boys," Moon said, as he laid down three jacks, "I guess that ends the game." He swept the pot into his flat-cap.

"What a minute," whined another player, "you gotta give us a chance to win some back."

"Sorry, mate," said Remy as he, Moon, and Haggis rose to their feet, "duty calls."

The four men trotted over to the Hudson and slipped inside. Nick turned the key to start the twelve-cylinder engine. It growled and grumbled and turned over a few times until it finally caught on and purred to life. He wheeled the car into the street, drove two blocks to Market Street, and turned left. The wide boulevard was nearly empty. With a clear path ahead, he floored the gas pedal, accelerating the sedan forward until the engine roared and the car barreled up the boulevard.

80

The crash of shattering glass unnerved Seamus. An ill wind had broken through the front window next door, and once inside scooped up desks, chairs, file cabinets, typewriters, and phones, tossing them around like an intemperate toddler flings his toys. With each bang and crash, pictures hanging on the walls of the print shop vibrated and rocked out of kilter, as though an earthquake had shook the building. Seamus sat behind the counter, one hand resting on his Enfield, the other holding a half-empty pint of whiskey. He raised the bottle to his lips, took a swig, then set it down on the counter and watched the surface of the whiskey ripple from the thudding sounds next door.

Carefully and deliberately he opened a box of ammunition and removed a half-dozen bullets. He pulled back the bolt of his rifle — *click, slide* — inserted the bullets into the chamber and pushed the bolt back in place — *slide, click.* It was a satisfying sound. Solid. Hard. Metallic. Only Clarisa's sweet Gaelic lilt gave him more aural satisfaction.

She had asked him to close the shop and run away, leaving the fate of his business, his livelihood, his *home* in the hands of marauders. He clenched his teeth, his jaw muscles pulsing. He'd run away before and look where that got him. Wifeless and countryless. He wasn't going down that road again. His eyes swept over the shop. *This is hers too, damn it. Doesn't she see that?* For eighteen years, they'd built a place in the world, a home, a business, in a country that belonged to them as much as it did to anyone. *That's right. For the first time since coming here, I can finally say I'm an American. And Americans don't run and hide, not from anyone, especially self-appointed arbiters of right and wrong.*

A tear rolled down his cheek as he realized for the first time that this hilly windswept city, perched on the edge of a continent so far from his place of birth, was now his home, his true home. *I've reached the Promised Land. I've finally let go of*—. A loud bang shook the building, opening a jagged crack in the wall adjacent to the Worker's School. Above the crack, a framed photo of Michael Collins, hero of the Dublin Easter Uprising, dropped two inches and hung askew.

His eyes fixed on the front door, Seamus swigged another mouthful of whiskey. As it flowed down his throat, he recalled a song from his youth about the dark days in Dublin when the supporters of British rule harassed anyone who advocated an independent Ireland. He began to sing it in a low voice, altering the words to fit the times:

Through the windy streets of Frisco, in the dark of early morn,
vigilantes came maraudin', wreckin' little homes wit' scorn.
Heedless of the cryin' children, draggin' fathers from their beds, beatin'
sons while hapless mothers, watched the blood flow from their heads.
Not for them a judge or jury or indeed a crime at all,
bein' diff'rent means they're guilty, so we're guilty one and all.

When the discordant sounds next door tapered off, Seamus loosened his grip on the Enfield, thankful the ill wind had died down. Calm voices now drifted in from outside. He spotted a gray-haired man in khaki pants and white shirt checking his watch and studying a clipboard. Several others similarly dressed, although younger, were gathered around him, their shirts clinging to their spines where swaths of perspiration bled through. They leaned forward toward the gray-haired leader like athletes in a huddle. Seamus couldn't hear what they were saying, but the voice of the leader was deep and commanding, like voices of the British officers who led the Black and Tans. As best as he could guess, they were planning their next raid and receiving instructions. Good, that would mean they'd leave soon and he could go next door to survey the —. Out of the corner of his eye, a blur dropped down from the wall, the framed photo of Michael Collins, landing with a shattering crash, sending splinters of glass across the floor.

The vigilantes must have heard it too. They looked toward the print shop, squinting in the noonday sun. Two of them separated from the huddle, walked over, and peered in, covering their eyes from the glare. Seamus tightened his grip on the Enfield. The two men looked in for a few seconds, apparently unable to see him sitting in the back of the darkened shop. They were about to leave when one of them noticed the handbills taped to the front window. FREE BILL MOONEY. FREE THE SCOTTSBORO BOYS. UNEMPLOYMENT AND SOCIAL SECURITY INSURANCE FOR ALL. RENT DISPENSATION FOR THE POOR AND UNEMPLOYED. He pointed to the handbills and called to the others. "Hey, look at this." The rest of the posse crowded around and pressed their hands and faces against the shop window like children viewing puppies at a pet store, voices excited and agitated as though they'd made a great discovery.

The group parted as their leader approached the window.

One of the vigilantes banged his fist against the glass and said, "Long's we're here, might as well mop up this place."

Seamus swung the rifle toward the front door and rested it on the counter. He was seated well inside the shop, shrouded in shadow, hidden from the squinty eyes of the vigilantes, who stood in full sunlight. They hadn't spotted him, he reckoned . . . at least not yet.

81

His palm jammed on the horn, Nick raced the Hudson up Market Street, swerving around what few vehicles there were on the road. Moon was on the passenger side, Remy and Haggis in the back. The city was a blur as they streaked past shops and restaurants, past the Palace Hotel, past the flat-iron Phelan Building. At the intersection of Powell and Market a stooped figure stepped into the crosswalk, a little old lady in a dark overcoat pulling a wire basket on wheels. Nick slammed on the brakes, locking the tires in a sliding, screeching skid until the Hudson came to a jolting stop just inches from the old woman, who apparently was hard of hearing and tottered forward, the four men anxiously following her progress.

When she was safely out of the way, Nick floored the gas pedal and popped the clutch, the sedan lurching forward, jerking the passengers' heads back, accelerating faster and faster until the engine roared and pedestrians and buildings were once again a continuous blur.

A police officer directing traffic at Van Ness Avenue looked up as the Hudson bore down on him, horn blaring like a runaway freight train. At the last second he jumped out of the way, blowing his whistle ineffectually as the car hurtled past.

Seconds later, a siren wailed.

Remy looked over his shoulder through the rear window. "Two motor mounties aft," he said. "Either speed up or slow down."

Nick considered pressing the gas pedal and making the cops chase him to Seamus' print shop. And he would have but it occurred to him that they might ignore any trouble at the shop while they arrested him for reckless driving and evading a police officer. Making a snap decision, he lifted his foot off the gas pedal. The lumbering sedan decelerated, allowing one Harley-Davidson to pull ahead while the other edged up to the driver's side and herded the Hudson over to the curb.

The motorcycle officers lowered their kickstands, dismounted, and approached the vehicle, one on each side. Nick rolled down his window as one of the officers drew close, a husky fellow with a red mustache on a generously freckled face. He bent over and peered in at the four men, all wearing dungarees, blue work shirts, and white flat-caps.

Nick gripped the car door. "Officer, this is an emergency, a matter of life or death. Please let us go. In fact, join us."

"Oh, yeah? What kind of emergency?"

"There may be an attack on a print shop on Haight Street."

The cop unsnapped his chin strap and pushed his hat back. "Now why would anybody attack a print shop?"

"It's next to the Worker's School. We're afraid vigilantes might raid the print shop by mistake."

"Next to one of those radical joints?"

Nick nodded. "But we've got to hurry."

"Hmmm." The officer glanced inside the car again at the three sailors, then at Nick. "Lemme see your driver's license."

Nick pulled his wallet out of his pocket, removed his license, and handed it through the car window.

"Benson, eh?" The officer removed a folded sheet from his jacket pocket, carefully opened it, and ran his finger down the page, stopping halfway. Without changing his expression, he refolded the paper, stuffed it back in his pocket, then drew his gun from its holster and aimed the barrel at Nick. "All right, out of the car, all of you, and put your hands up."

"What?" said Nick. "I don't understand. There's an emergency and no time to waste."

The other officer looked just as surprised as Nick. "What's up?"

The red-haired cop swung the car door open and motioned Nick to come out. "Cover me," he said to his partner as he inserted his gun back in its holster. When Nick emerged, he spun him around, wrenched his arms behind his back, and clamped handcuffs over his wrists. "There's a warrant out for this one." He grabbed Nick's arm and turned him back around. "You're under arrest."

82

Seamus watched the gray-haired leader of the vigilantes shade his eyes from the noontime sun as he peered into the print shop. He looked to be about Seamus' age, bigger though, more muscular, and he carried himself with the erect bearing of a military officer. *Probably served in the Great War and is acting out his fantasies to lead his men into battle again.* Seamus knew the type. A super patriot who hated foreigners, commies, niggers, and Jews.

The vigilante leader looked up at the address over the front door, then scanned the paper on his clipboard. "Sorry, boys, this one isn't on our dance card."

The raiders looked disappointed and one said, "Sir, look at the Red handbills in the window. They're the same ones we found next door."

"This must be their print shop," added another. "If we don't take it out now, they'll be up and running in no time, and all our work next door will be for nothing."

Others made assenting noises. And a couple of raiders banged their fists impatiently against the print shop window.

"Don't be so eager," Seamus muttered.

The leader checked his watch. *Probably has a schedule to keep.* He looked at the print shop as if he didn't want to disappoint his men but sensed that something inside might be waiting for him. "You boys stay here. I'll go in and reconnoiter." He opened the front door.

The bell above the door jingled as he stepped across the threshold. He paused to allow his eyes to adjust, then surveyed the room, his gaze roving from file drawers to printing press to the counter. Then suddenly his eyes stopped at a fixed point and widened.

Seamus looked down to see what caught his attention. A sliver of light, tapering down to a fine point, reflected off a metal shaft — the bayonet on his Enfield.

The vigilante froze for what must have been a moment of indecision.

Then, as if transported back to the battlefield, he threw himself headlong onto the floor and landed with a loud thud. Seamus fired a warning round into the air, hoping to scare him off. It hit the ceiling, pulverizing plaster that rained down on the vigilante who, in one quick motion, rolled to one side and pulled a gun from his holster.

A blast of white light burst from the barrel.

Seamus felt nothing. The shot went wide, he assumed, but another was bound to come soon. He lowered the rifle and squeezed the trigger. The vigilante's pant leg flicked as if caught by a sudden burst of wind. In the next moment the vigilante dug a foot into the floor and launched himself forward like an arrow shot from a bow. Seamus was astonished at how quickly he closed the distance between them. *Is he crazy? Who would charge into a waiting Enfield?*

As the vigilante came close, Seamus lunged forward across the counter, his arms outstretched as he thrust the bayonet into the man's eye, the blade penetrating easily. Seamus gave it another push until it reached the back of his skull. The vigilante convulsed and wriggled like a fish on a hook, mouth agape, blood dripping down his face. He twitched like this for half a minute, the convulsions coming less and less frequently until he finally went still.

Seamus glanced through the front window. The raiders had retreated behind a car, their heads poking out. He looked back down at their leader and again wondered what kind of man would charge a waiting Enfield. Only someone, he imagined, who had already defied long odds on the battlefield. He was about to withdraw the bayonet when something peeked up above the counter. He couldn't tell what it was and looked closer until he recognized the dull shine of metal, though not just any piece of metal. It was the tip of a gun barrel pointing straight up.

In the next moment the barrel tilted toward him.

83

Nick paced back and forth in his cell, frustrated and angry. He'd only been four blocks from Haight Street when the motorcycle cops pulled him over. *Four blocks!* He'd tried to convince the paddy wagon driver to swing by the print shop on the way to the Hall of Justice, to no avail. Later, as soon as they booked him, he asked to use a phone to check on Seamus and was told it would be hours before his turn came. He didn't doubt it. Hundreds of others had been incarcerated and more were arriving every few minutes. He learned from another prisoner that after each vigilante raid, police had swooped in and arrested everyone for vagrancy or disturbing the peace. Clearly the whole operation had been planned and approved by the authorities, perhaps even the mayor. He pounded his fist against the wall. If only he had known that the police were in on it, he would have told the motorcycle cop that his wife was giving birth or concocted some other emergency.

Moon, Remy, and Haggis had been locked in a holding cell with prisoners from the vigilante raids. But for reasons no one explained, Nick was taken to the floor above and placed in his own cell. Tired of pacing, he threw himself down on a lumpy mattress that smelled of hair oil and body odor. He rolled onto his stomach and closed his eyes. The adrenaline in his veins from the race up Market Street had dissipated, and he was beginning to feel tired and listless.

The sound of keys jangling on a ring entered the cell block, accompanied by footsteps padding down the aisle beside the cells. A cell door clicked open and clanged shut, jarringly loud, so it was either his cell door, Nick figured, or one of his neighbors'.

"Since the two of yous have been arrested for the same crime," a voice said, "you might as well board together."

Nick rolled over onto his back and looked up, wondering what the guard meant by 'arrested for the same crime.' His new cellmate stood just inside the door, fists on hips, feet a shoulder-width apart as if he were standing on the deck of a ship, lips pursed into a frown, eyes dark and implacable as he stared down at Nick.

Nick stared back at him, disbelieving, speechless. This was the last person he expected to see.

Cyril Slag looked unchanged since their last meeting, swarthy, scabrous around the neck, a pointed tongue that swiped the edges of his perpetually chapped lips. The two men continued to eye each other, during which time Nick tried to figure out how the bosun, of all people, was incarcerated with him in the same cell. And from the frozen expression on the bosun's face, his nemesis was no less surprised.

"So, they nabbed you, too, eh?" Slag finally said. "That's funny. They don't usually arrest two men for the same crime unless they think the two of 'em are in on it together. Is that what you told 'em?"

Nick swung his legs around and planted his feet on the floor, still trying to understand how they ended up in the same cell. "Why would I do that? I didn't know where you were, and I've been too busy with the strike to care. Besides, once you took the opium off the ship, I figured it was gone for good."

"You're lyin'," the bosun said, taking a step toward Nick. "Somebody set me up. I've been workin' on a deal for a month and everything was tits up until the last minute. Then when I made the delivery this morning, BOOM!" He smacked his fist into the palm of his other hand. "The cops busted me, and my buyer vanished like it was all set up." He glowered at Nick. "Now why in the world would a drug dealer turn me in unless the cops were already onto me?"

The bosun's angry scowl reminded Nick of the night they fought in Manila, the hatred in his eyes, his blooded nose, bruised Adam's apple, his vow to take vengeance. The fear Nick felt that night came creeping back as of it had happened yesterday. He'd been lucky then, but would he be so lucky again.

He stood up and faced Slag, hoping his fear wasn't noticeable. "That's obvious. I told them about you and Primm when they arrested me on the *Diana Dollar.*"

"They didn't believe you, though, did they? And that was months ago."

"Maybe they were just waiting for you to return."

One side of Slag's mouth lifted into a wry grin. "Well, the joke's on them. This morning was a dry run."

Nick backed away to the rear of the cell. "You had a phony bag?"

The bosun's grin transformed into a confident sneer. "That's right. They didn't get squat. And as long as they don't have the goods, they got nothin' on me." He moved toward Nick, his sneer now menacing. "There's only one way they might pin somethin' on me now."

Nick wanted to move farther away but his back was against the wall. "Oh, yeah? What's that?"

Slag took another step forward. "If the buyer testifies against me."

Nick thought for a moment. "But what's the chance of a jury believing a Chinese drug dealer over the word of a white man?"

"Not much. Unless —" Slag broke off, maintaining a menacing stare.

Nick figured he knew what Slag was suggesting, but he wanted to be sure. "Unless?"

Slag stepped forward again until his swarthy, sun-beaten face was inches away, his breath stinking of cigarettes. "Unless you testify against me." He continued to stare at Nick, who felt frozen in place as if cornered by a rabid dog. "Now you wouldn't do that would you?"

Nick felt a sudden urge to run away or to call the guard, but the former was impossible and the latter would only confirm Slag's suspicions that he was collaborating with the cops. Being careful to avoid the bosun, he squeezed past him and moved to the front of the cell. "They wouldn't take my word. All the hard evidence is against me, not you. And, besides, they probably think we were in on it together. Anyway, why would I do that?"

Slag closed in on him again until his chapped lips were nearly touching Nick's ear. "Because of what I done to you."

Nick shuddered. It was true. He had every reason to hate the bosun — his tyrannical treatment of him on the *Diana Dollar*, his collaboration with Primm to oust Captain Harding, his sadistic treatment of the girl in Manila, his punishment of him and Haggis in the ship's hold, and finally the planting of opium in Nick's locker, a coup de grace that triggered a string of consequences far beyond what Slag could have imagined.

Yet strangely enough, Nick didn't feel bitter. It was as if both of them had been caught up in a drama much larger than themselves, each playing a predestined role only obliquely related to the other. Still, he needed to prove his innocence, and this extraordinary coincidence, the two of them incarcerated together, presented a unique opportunity. Somehow he had to use it to his advantage.

He squeezed past the bosun and stepped to the back of the cell. "That's all in the past. I've moved on."

"You want to clear yourself, though, right?"

"Sure. Without the opium, though, I haven't gotta chance." He tried another tack. "What about Primm? Can't we pin the narcotics you planted in my locker on him? He can't possibly care now."

The bosun let out a chilling laugh. "You're right, there, Benson. Dead men tell no tales. Primm shoulda stayed outta the storm."

The way Slag said it — with too much glee for Nick's liking — made it sound like he took some twisted satisfaction from it. *Could it be that the bosun had a hand in Primm's death? Remy had heard them argue before Primm disappeared.* Nick didn't really care how Primm died — the chief had been a mutinous bastard — but he was curious. "I wouldn't think a seaman with his experience would fall overboard accidentally."

Slag came toward him until he was inches away, his dark brown eyes boring into him. "Who said it was an accident."

Nick pressed his back against a cold concrete wall, hard and implacable like the bosun who now had all but admitted he was a murderer.

A slow grin crept over Slag's lips. He backed away, lay down on the bed, and tucked his hands under his head. "Who knows, maybe we could make a deal."

A deal with you? Nick wanted to say with as much incredulity as possible. *Go to hell!* Any deal with Slag would surely be fraught with danger and double-crosses. On the other hand, if he wanted to take advantage of this opportunity, if he wanted to find the narcotics, he'd have to play ball, even if he didn't know the rules. "What've you got in mind?"

"You help me sell the goods and I'll testify that Primm planted the opium in your locker because you tried to stop him from taking over the ship. Just like you said. That way we both get what we want."

"But they'll want to know why you didn't reveal that at the time I was arrested."

Slag shrugged. "I'll just tell 'em Primm threatened to sack me if I even considered ratting on him. I had to keep my job, didn't I?"

Nick was intrigued. Not that he trusted Slag, but he was beginning to see that, one way or another, this might somehow help him, perhaps even lead to his exoneration. There was one thing, however, that still didn't make sense. "You don't need my help to sell the opium, so what's in it for you?"

"You'll be my accomplice. That way you'll never be able to testify against me without incriminating yourself. You'll also be my cover. If anything goes wrong, it'll be your neck, not mine."

Slag went on to explain how the deal would go down. Nick would take the buyer's henchman to the hidden cache. The henchman would call his boss to confirm it. The boss would pay Slag and hand him the phone. Then Slag would give Nick the go-ahead to release the goods. He warned Nick that if he tipped-off the cops, he would swear they were in on it together, and since Nick had already been caught red-handed trying to smuggle contraband, no jury would believe he was innocent.

At first blush it seemed to be a fool-proof plan, certainly from Slag's point of view, and as Slag mentioned, Nick didn't have any other viable options. "Okay," he said. Then he couldn't stop himself from asking, "so where'd you stash the narcotics?"

"Sheesh," Slag replied in a way that said, *Don't take me for a fool.* "You'll find out when the time comes." He chuckled to himself. "Let's just say I planted it right under the cop's noses, but they won't find it, not in a million years."

Having searched the *Diana Dollar* for months, Nick didn't doubt him for a moment. "So what happens next?"

"After they release me and you make bail, I'll sign a notarized statement sayin' Primm framed you. Then you can watch me store it in a safety deposit box. When the deal is done, I'll give you the key to the box."

"How do I know you'll keep your word after I've done your dirty work?"

The bosun shrugged. "I'll have my dough. Besides, if I screw you, you can tip-off the cops. And, anyway, what other choice do you have? It's either cooperate with me or cool your heels in prison for a looong time." He chuckled again, clearly proud himself for forcing Nick to become an accomplice *and* a criminal.

84

Alternating between a fast walk and a trot, Clarisa and Roger hurried up Haight Street, breathing heavily after the two-mile trek up Market Street. In the block ahead, three police cars and an ambulance were parked in the middle of the street in front of Seamus's print shop. A cluster of solemn-faced men stood outside the shop, looking in as if they expected someone to emerge at any moment. As she drew closer, Clarisa uttered a quick prayer — *Dear God, let him be alright* — and broke into a run. Just before she reached the Worker's School, a uniformed policeman stepped in her path, arms outstretched, blocking her way.

"This area is closed," he said, then nodded to his left. "You can continue on the other side of the street."

"That's my father's shop!" said Clarisa, chest heaving.

The officer looked a little less certain. "Your related to the a —" Clarisa dashed to his right but he side-stepped in her way. "Wait a minute. You can't go in there just now."

She glared at him. "How dare you prevent me from seeing my father?"

"If something's happened," said Roger, "she has a right to know. You better let us by."

The policeman glanced at Roger wearing a tailored suit and polished wingtip shoes, his blond hair perfectly cut. "Okay. Lemme talk to the captain." He held out his hand. "But stay here."

Clarisa glanced over his shoulder at two attendants in white uniforms coming out of the print shop, carrying a stretcher covered with a white sheet. "Oh, no!" she cried.

The officer turned to look.

In that moment Clarisa darted past him and ran toward the attendants now stepping onto the street and about to lift the stretcher into the rear of the ambulance. In her haste she tripped off the curb and stumbled into one of the attendants, hitting him so hard he lost his grip on the stretcher, one side falling like a trap door, dumping a body onto the pavement.

Clarisa looked down in disbelief. Seamus lay on his back, eyes unfocused, mouth agape, a dark hole in the back of his throat. An excruciating pain shot through her, sucking all the breath out of her as if she'd been punched in the gut. She collapsed down beside her father. "Oh, God, nooooo!" she cried, lifting his head to her breast, her body trembling in spasmodic shudders, her face taut in anguish. This was the second time a parent had been torn away from her, and it brought back all the pain and agony from the first time, all the intense feelings of helpless, hopeless loss.

An officer approached but Roger waved him off. He crouched down on his haunches and gently placed a hand on her shoulder while she sobbed, rocking back and fort, the police and ambulance attendants looking on with uncomfortable expressions.

When her sobs subsided, she laid her father's head down and stroked his face, her hands, covered with blood, drawing a red streak across his cheek. His face was calm and serene, no trace of anger or bitterness. She hadn't seen him this peaceful in a long time and wondered if in his last moments he'd been able to do what he'd always wanted: stand his ground in the face of tyranny and erase the guilt and bitterness of having abandoned his native country all those years ago.

She hoped so.

Roger helped her to her feet. As she stood upright, her head spun and her legs felt rubbery, barely able to keep her erect. She turned and leaned against him, pressing her palms against his chest to steady herself. She took several deep breaths and then stepped back, eyes unfocused, barely able to see beyond the pain and agony.

Then something caught her attention.

"Oh, my God," she murmured.

Roger followed her gaze down to his chest, to two bloody palm prints painted on his suit coat, each finger and thumb perfectly imprinted as if by a stamp.

The palm prints, bright red on his gray suit, were, it seemed to Clarisa, a sign of guilt, a scarlet letter identifying the culprit responsible for this tragedy. In an instant her sorrow transformed into an intense, all-consuming rage. "You!" she said with icy disdain. "You knew about this… AND…DID…NOTHING!" She threw herself at him and pummeled his chest with her fists, as if it was he who had planned the raids, he who pulled the trigger, he who killed her father.

Roger didn't stop her. He took every blow, every accusation, every venomous epithet, as if he too felt responsible, and it continued until her anger was spent and she collapsed in his arms, weeping uncontrollably.

Behind him, the attendants lifted Seamus' body onto the stretcher and raised it up to the ambulance door. Putting their weight against it, they slid the stretcher into the ambulance beside another body, slammed the doors shut, climbed into the front, and drove off toward the morgue.

85

A jailer unlocked the cell door and motioned to Slag. "Come on, get your things. You're being released."

Slag got up from the bunk and headed toward the door. As he reached it, he looked back at Nick with a smug smile. "See you 'round."

The words left Nick with a queasy feeling, brought on by the realization that he was now in cahoots with a sick sadist who'd killed an accomplice when it suited him. He sat down on the bed and rested his head in his hands. He knew he'd taken a risk when he refused to remain an informant for Farnsworth, but he'd hoped that Plant would let the matter drop since he'd supplied them with information for ten months, just two months shy of the agreed upon period. And on top of all that, his arrest couldn't have happened at a worse moment. Had Seamus tangled with the vigilantes? Had Clarisa arrived in time? He knew the court would assign his case to a public defender and perhaps let him out on bail. But how long would that take?

The jailer returned a few minutes later and unlocked the cell door. "Let's go," he said.

Nick followed him up to the next floor and then to a door with a small window. The jailor unlocked it and waved him into what appeared to be an interview room, small, furnished with only a table and two chairs. This was where, he figured, he would confer with a public defender. While he waited, he went over Slag's scheme to sell the opium. The operation seemed fairly simple, and if everything went according to plan he would obtain the evidence he needed to prove his innocence. Could he rely on Slag to keep his word, though? *Not likely. And where does that leave me?*

When he was in the hospital he'd been certain of his ability to face any challenge, overcome any obstacle. Now the prospect of incarceration for a crime he hadn't committed, separating him from everyone he loved, scared the hell out of him.

The door opened and a man entered.

Nick stared at him, speechless, surprised for a second time that afternoon to see someone he least expected.

Jack Blum wore an enigmatic expression as he took a seat on the other side of the table. Nick hadn't seen the police detective since their dinner in Chinatown eight months earlier when he solicited Blum's advice about the smuggling charge.

"I expect you're wondering why you're here," said Blum.

There were many things Nick was uncertain of, but the reason for his incarceration wasn't one of them. "Because Thomas Plant told the D.A. to arrest me for smuggling narcotics."

Blum shook his head. "Nope. It was me. I had you picked up."

"You?" Now he was really puzzled. *Isn't Blum on my side?* His father had always said he was one of the few incorruptible cops on the force. "But why?"

"After you told me about Slag, I made a note to keep track of him when he returned. A week ago one of my contacts in Chinatown told me that a swarthy fellow with crusty skin had been trying to find a buyer for a sizeable amount of opium. I figured it was him, so I spread the word that anyone who helped me catch him would earn a big favor. When he arranged a sale with Quan Chen, I knew all about it."

"But then he tricked you."

Blum pursed his lips and nodded. "Pissed me off. So I arrested him anyway. Right away, though, I knew he wasn't going to incriminate himself. That's when I thought of you. I had you brought in and locked up with him, figuring he might talk to you. I didn't tell you because I didn't know if you were a good enough actor to pull it off if you knew what I was doing."

Good enough actor? Haven't I been acting for the last ten months? "So the smuggling charges haven't been reinstated?"

"That's right. You're free to go. But before you do, tell me what you and Slag talked about."

Nick hesitated. On the one hand, he could confess everything and hope that Blum would gather enough evidence to convict Slag and exonerate himself. Of course, Slag would claim that Nick had been his original accomplice, and a zealous prosecutor, pressured by Plant, could use Slag's testimony to convict him, even if Blum testified that he'd cooperated with the investigation. On the other hand, he could tell Blum that Slag hadn't revealed anything, and if Slag's plan worked, he would have an affidavit proving his innocence once and for all.

While Nick weighed his options, the detective watched him closely, undoubtedly aware of his ambivalence. "Look," said Blum, "I don't know what that scumbag told you, but I can see you're reluctant to talk. So I'll tell you what. I'm gonna release you and give you time to think it over. When you're ready to talk, gimme a call."

Nick smiled appreciatively. Part of him wanted to say more, wanted to make a clean breast of it, but as Blum intuited, he needed time to think it over.

The sun was setting behind Nob Hill when he emerged from the Hall of Justice, casting shadows across Kearny Street. He stood at the curb watching cars and trucks zoom by, relieved to be free again. At a break in the traffic, he sprinted across Kearny and walked through Portsmouth Square, a gently sloping park landscaped with lawn, bushes, and paved pathways. Now that he'd had another taste of incarceration, he was determined not to let it happen again. Yet he was keenly aware that Plant could have him arrested at any time or that Slag might double-cross him. And in either case he'd be locked up in a cell for who knows how long.

When he reached home he called Clarisa, hoping to learn that Seamus was safe and sound, that everyone was fine. No one answered and it gave him an uneasy feeling. He tried to ignore his apprehension and thought of reasons why no one had picked up the phone. Seamus might have gone out for a pint of Guinness, and Clarisa was probably at the grocery store shopping for dinner. Still, he couldn't shake the feeling that something was wrong and he couldn't wait any longer to find out. He borrowed the Hudson, drove to Haight Street, and parked. On the way to Clarisa's flat, he passed the Worker's School and glanced inside. The place was a mess, file drawers upended, books and papers strewn on the floor, a wooden desk broken into splinters, signs and pictures ripped from the walls.

A deep foreboding took hold of him as he surveyed the destruction. Those responsible for this tangled mess were clearly driven by reckless hatred, and where reckless hatred prevailed, terrible things happened. He hastened to the building next door and pressed the doorbell. Thirty seconds went by. A minute. He rang the bell again and knocked on the door. *Maybe they've they gone out and everything is alright.* He was about to go looking for them when he heard footfalls on the stairway, slow and irregular as if whoever it was was having trouble descending the stairs. The door opened and in the dim evening light Clarisa appeared, her eyes bloodshot and rimmed with red, complexion pale, hair in a tangled mess. That might not have been so bad, might have been how she looked after a late night out or a bout of flu, except that her mouth drooped down in an expression of utter hopelessness, and her posture was slumped and listless as if she was about to collapse.

Nick helped her back upstairs and into the front parlor, neither one saying a word. He sat her down on the sofa and put his arms around her, her head resting on his shoulder. They remained there for the rest of the evening, Clarisa sometimes crying, sometimes silent, never saying a word. Nick offered to make her a something to eat but she declined, so at nine o'clock he put her to bed and slept on the sofa.

The next morning, while she slept in, he made breakfast and picked up a newspaper on the front stoop. An article on the front page described the vigilante raids and included photos of demolished offices with mocking captions. PARALYSIS OF THE JOINTS! A SMASHING RAID ON RED NESTS. It detailed the results of the raids: thirty-five homes, offices, and meeting places invaded and trashed, and over four-hundred arrests. It was hard to imagine the authorities tolerating, much less abetting, such wanton violence, and it led Nick to the conclusion that if the goal of the United States was to create a perfect union, it still had a ways to go.

After breakfast he checked on Clarisa who was still sleeping soundly, her face buried in a pillow, her breathing soft and slow. He thought back to the days after his own father committed suicide, to the intense loss he felt, as if a limb had been severed from his body. It took a long time to heal from that, so sleep was probably the best medicine for now.

86

Roger Farnsworth looked down at Market Street from the ninth floor of the Matson Building. More cars were rolling along the boulevard than the day before and more streetcars too, protected by armed guards. It was the third day of the general strike, and already it seemed to be falling apart. He'd heard a report that the Labor Council had authorized all union restaurants and butcher shops to open and had lifted the embargo on gasoline and oil. He also learned that building contractors for the two bridges had called their employees back to work and that truck convoys, protected by highway patrol escorts, were once again entering the city.

San Francisco was coming back to life, although it still wasn't its old self yet.

After lunch he met with Thomas Plant to map out a strategy.

"I want to hold a press conference," said Plant, "to announce that the Port of San Francisco is now open for business. I think it will deflate the general strike and perhaps end the waterfront strike as well."

Roger shook his head. "The general strike may end soon but the longshoremen have too much at stake to give up now. I just got word that the Labor Council recommended all issues be submitted to arbitration. I'm inclined to agree. We can't let stubborn pride prolong the situation." His words became louder and more strident. "It's costing more than anyone can afford — us, the stevedores, the public." Overcome with emotion he pounded his fist on the table. "Damn it, it's time we end this thing once and for all."

Plant's brow furrowed into a startled frown, as if he couldn't believe his assistant had spoken to him with such vehemence. Roger didn't care. Seamus' death had changed everything. He could still see the lifeless body dripping with blood, the anguish on Clarisa's face. It had given him a new perspective on what was important and what wasn't. Unless the waterfront strike was settled, more people would die, more businesses would go bankrupt, more workers would lose their jobs, more families would struggle, and more children would go hungry. Winning now seemed less important than ending the conflict. Of course, he couldn't say that to Plant, but he could prod him into accepting arbitration.

Plant wasn't ready to concede. "I don't think we should give in while we have the upper hand. It's only a matter of time before the men come crawling back on our terms."

"And how long with that take? A week, a month, six months? In the meantime, our inexperienced replacement workers are having trouble loading and discharging ships, and their sloppy stowing has caused mounting losses. On top of that the accident rate has soared through the roof. If we open the port to normal traffic, they won't be able to handle it." He paused. "Besides, the National Industrial Recovery Act gives the men the right to organize. Sooner or later we're going to have to come to terms with them."

Plant frowned again. "I don't trust Harry Bridges. He's a Communist, and I have no doubt his ultimate goal is to take over the country and nationalize every business. It happened in Russia; who's to say it can't happen here. Frankly, I'm glad the vigilantes wiped out those radical groups. It's time someone put a stop to them."

At the mention of vigilantes, Roger recalled the demolished office next to the print shop and Clarisa's fists pounding on his chest, tears running down her cheeks. It wasn't fair to blame him for Seamus' death, but he understood why she had. She needed someone to blame, someone to hold accountable, and if blaming him helped her deal with her sorrow, he was willing to accept it, fair or no. Plant's comment also gave him an idea. To change his boss's way of thinking, he would have to fight fire with fire. *The only thing we have to fear is fear itself,* Roosevelt had said, but fear could also be an effective weapon against fear.

"The strike is bleeding our members dry," he said, leaning forward toward his boss. "The Industrial Association may have a huge war chest at its disposal, but without mail subsidies and freight charges our shipping companies are hurting. And if the public turns against them, the politicians might be tempted to eliminate the mail subsidies altogether. We also have to consider sabotage. Angry sailors and longshoremen can easily disable ships and damage cargo if they think they're getting a raw deal."

Roger continued in this vein for several minutes, detailing one dire scenario after another—ships run aground, cargo pilfered, waterfront wars. It took some time before the barrage of catastrophes got through to Plant, but it finally did.

He threw up his arms in disgust. "Alright, alright. Call Hanna and tell him we'll submit to arbitration, but do it now before I change my mind."

On Thursday morning the San Francisco Labor Council voted to kill the general strike it never wanted in the first place. Within hours San Francisco sprang to life. Restaurants threw open their doors, sending savory aromas out into the street. Icemen replenished ice boxes with blocks of ice. Butcher shops hung fresh meats in their windows. Movie theaters lit up their marquees. Bars turned on their colorful neon lights. Taxis and trucks flooded the streets. Shoppers swamped the sidewalks. Cable cars trundled along tracks with bells ringing, conductors calling out stops. It was as if the city's pulse had slowed to near death, then phoenix-like sprang to life.

Roger fervently believed that arbitration was the only viable solution to end the waterfront strike, yet there was one final hurdle to surmount. Shipowners hadn't agreed to collective bargaining with the maritime unions, and longshoremen had vowed not to betray their seafaring brothers. To overcome this obstacle, he convinced John Francis Neylan, attorney for William Randolph Hearst (and the same attorney who counseled Nick after his arrest), to host a meeting of shipowners at his estate in Atherton. Neylan was universally respected. If anyone could convince the shipowners to accept arbitration with the sailors, he could.

Roger hastily organized the event and seated the shipping executives at picnic tables under a large oak tree outside Neylan's home. Stanley Dollar was there, as was William Roth, Cyrus Grant, Roger Lapham, Herbert Fleishhacker and a dozen others. Neylan welcomed the executives, then encouraged them to vent their frustration. After all, it had been a trying time for everyone. It was also a brilliant strategy. Once the shippers had blown off steam and calmed down, he read them the riot act.

"For years you've treated the legitimate grievances of labor with atrocious neglect, and now it's come back to bite you." He continued on for some time and concluded his speech with a threat. "I'm going to announce your acceptance of arbitration to the press, and I dare you to deny it."

Unaccustomed to such a dressing down, the shippers grumbled and groused, complaining that never before had they been forced to accept government intervention in their labor relations. Yet in spite of their misgivings, they eventually came around and approved a statement agreeing to arbitration with the seafaring unions if the longshoremen also agreed to arbitration.

Roger arranged a press conference to announce the shipowners' decision, and it was his proudest moment. He'd done everything he could to end the stalemate. Now it was up to the longshoremen.

The following night Local 38-79 held a special meeting to consider a proposal that would authorize the ILA Pacific Coast District to hold an election to decide whether to submit all issues to arbitration. Harry Bridges was still fiercely opposed to letting arbitrators decide the hiring hall issue, and Nick sympathized with his position. After all, the longshoremen had declared for months they wouldn't relinquish the hiring hall issue to the uncertainty of an arbitration board. Yet he, too, was deeply disturbed by Seamus' death and had come to the conclusion that it was time for both sides to end the conflict.

The debate was long and bitter. Joe Johnson urged the men to approve the proposal, while Bridges opposed it, using every rhetorical weapon in his arsenal to convince the men it was a bad idea. In truth, though, the newspapers and Red-baiters had been wrong. Bridges was no mesmerizing Svengali, nor arm-twisting Stalin. His real power was to inspire and motivate the men to believe in themselves and the dreams they cherished and the ambitions they harbored. His true gift was his vision and voice, a voice that added passion to their aspirations and a road map to achieve them. In the end, however, the men had a will of their own. On Sunday afternoon every longshore union on the West Coast voted and the result was a landslide. Weary of the strike and ready to return to work, West Coast longshoremen accepted arbitration by a ratio of 6 to 1.

87

In contrast to the general strike, the waterfront strike ended as abruptly and decisively as it began. On the morning of Tuesday, July 31st, thousands of longshoremen and sailors streamed to the waterfront to breathe new life into the port. Nick roamed along the Embarcadero observing the renewed activity — freighters nuzzling their bows into berths, sailors lowering gangways, longshoremen uncovering hatches and securing booms with guy wires. Soon the ratcheting whine of cargo winches and the gruff cries of longshoremen echoed between ship and pier shed as bundles of steel bound for the bridges dropped down to outstretched hands, as cases of canned fruit from the Santa Clara Valley arched over railings and disappeared into holds, as men toted six-foot long stems of bananas to trucks that would distribute them throughout northern California. All along the Embarcadero, vehicles of every description, from hand-pulled jitneys to towering lumber carriers to canvas-topped trucks, transported cargo to and fro so that once again the waterfront resumed its role as the lifeblood of the city.

Instead of going back to work at the docks, Nick continued as Harry Bridges' assistant and as a reporter for the *Waterfront Worker*, now the official newsletter of Local 38-79. It was an exciting time. The longshoremen went about their work with an unprecedented confidence in their step and a lively bravado in their manner. And although the final out-come of the struggle was still in doubt, what was not in doubt was the power of the union to galvanize the men into a cohesive force dedicated to the well-being of its members.

On the surface it appeared as if nothing had changed. Belt Line trains shunted boxcars in and out of pier sheds; trucks rattled over the cobbled roadway; stevedores pushed, carried, and stacked cargo; goods flowed in and out of the port; and waterfront bartenders poured countless glasses of froth-topped beer.

But something *had* changed.

Walking bosses who belittled and cursed their crews, who issued threats to speed up the work, who set up phony competitions, who ignored unsafe conditions and undermanned crews, were met with sul-len stares and intentional slowdowns. In short order the men let their supervisors know that they were no longer wharf rats to be abused, no longer serfs to be ordered about like slaves. The old methods no longer applied, the walking bosses found, and a new civility entered into their engagements.

Nick wrote about the change, about how the men had formed dock committees to resolve issues and how they were working with the walk-ing bosses to keep the cargo moving in a safe and responsible manner. And when that failed, how they called quickie walkouts to back up their assertions. And no longer was "Safety First" a meaningless slogan posted on the side of a pier shed. As never before, management listened to sug-gestions. Not that things were perfect, far from it, but there was a world of difference between the way it was and the way it was now.

During that first week Nick was so caught up in the flurry of renewed activity and with checking in on Clarisa, who was bearing up with the help of Father Shannon, he nearly forgot about Slag and Blum and that entire mess. When it did cross his mind, he swept it aside and focused on whatever article he was writing or errand he was running, hoping that somehow it would disappear of its own accord. Inevitably, though, a call came from the bosun, who wanted to see him and go over the details again, including the location of the hidden narcotics. Slag suggested they rendezvous at Fort Point, the decommissioned Civil War-era fort on the south shore of the Golden Gate. It was a strange, out-of-the-way place to meet, but the cops, he said, had been tailing him and he wanted to make sure he could shake them before they met.

At nine o'clock on a chilly Friday evening, Nick parked the Hudson at the edge of the bay and sniffed the damp sea air. Waves pounded against a concrete sea wall, throwing spray up onto a guard rail made of huge chain links covered in rust. He got out of the car, stuffed his hands into his pea coat, and walked toward the fort, a forbidding brick building, three stories tall with small, narrow windows that made it look as much like a prison as a fortress. A flat area in front of the fort now served as a marshalling yard for the bridge building project. In the waning twilight, Nick could see trucks, trailers, temporary sheds, and assorted piles of building materials. The original plan for the bridge required Fort Point to be razed to make room for the approach roadway. As the oldest Federal fortification on the West Coast, it was deemed historically significant, so engineers designed two huge concrete pylons, one on each side of the fort, that would support the bridge approach and spare the historic structure below.

Nick looked out across the Golden Gate to the opposite shore, to the north bridge tower standing fully erect and glowing in the final minutes of twilight. The bridge was still a long way from completion and for now the north tower stood alone, tall and elegant, two tapered columns connected by horizontal struts that formed window-like openings through which one could see the surrounding hills and sky. A rare marriage of nature and architecture, each one enhancing the splendor of the other.

Wearing a Greek fisherman's cap and a wool coat, Slag was waiting for him next to the fort, smoking a cigarette. As Nick approached, the bosun tossed the cigarette down and ground it into the dirt with his heel. A foghorn bleated somewhere off in the distance, announcing the approach of a fog bank that would smother the Golden Gate before the night was over.

"Come on," said Slag, motioning toward the back of the building. "I know a place where there's no chance of being overheard."

Nick figured they were already in a private spot but didn't want to argue. He followed the boson around the fort on a shoreline road that continued out over the water on a wooden trestle. The trestle extended a thousand feet out to a large oval cofferdam, enclosing the site where the south tower would one day stand. Unlike the north tower, whose concrete foundation rested on the tip of Lime Point, the south tower site was situated inside the Golden Gate, a mile-wide channel that could be described as a mercurial river whose flows changed direction twice a day with the tides. Once the cofferdam had been constructed, the water inside was pumped out, leaving a dry well in which to build the south tower pier.

As they walked along the trestle, Nick could hear water riffling against the support columns, indicating tidal movement. To their right the sky was clear, the lights of the city reflecting in dancing flashes on the bay. To their left a gray mist crept toward them through the Golden Gate, pushed east by the prevailing westerlies.

When they reached the end of the trestle, Nick pulled up the collar of his pea coat against a cool breeze. On the opposite side of the Golden Gate, the steep auburn cliffs of the Marin Headlands rose almost vertically out of the water. Then to his right was Angel Island, lush and wooded, dark and mysterious, then farther to his right Alcatraz Island capped by prison walls, then the East Bay hills dotted with lights, and lastly San Francisco, its skyscrapers and steep hills reaching up to the twilit sky. It was an absorbing panorama, how Nick imagined it would have looked from the deck of the *Diana Dollar* when she sailed into port, if only he'd been on deck.

No point in dwelling on lost opportunities, he thought as he turned to the bosun. The two of them had uttered nary a word, and now that they'd reached their final destination he wanted to get the meeting over with and head home.

Slag seemed less inclined to proceed with urgency. He sauntered over to the edge of the trestle and faced the fog whose wispy tentacles now reached them. Nick followed him and looked down at the turbid water. Tails of rippling wavelets extended out from the trestle's support columns, indicating an ebb tide flowing toward the Pacific Ocean. He glanced at the bosun, who was nervously fingering something in his coat pocket.

"Do you believe in fate?" said Slag.

It seemed an odd question. "Why do you ask?"

"You and I" — he cast a sidelong glance at Nick — "we've had our dust-ups, and we've made each other's lives — how should I say — complicated."

"Yeah," Nick agreed, "but once we pull this off we'll be rid of each other for good."

The bosun wiped his tongue over chapped lips. "That's what I figured. But now I'm not so sure. Seems like we're destined to battle till one of us wins."

The hairs on Nick's neck bristled.

"You see," Slag continued, "once I worked things out, I realized somethin'. The only way the cops were onto me was if you went to 'em while I was away." He gave Nick a reproachful look. "And once you get my sworn statement, I figure you'll probably go back to 'em and squeal like a pig."

Nick tried to think of something to say in his defense, something plausible, but nothing came to him. Slag was right. He *had* gone to Blum and asked for help. *But why mention it now?* He noticed the bosun's right hand again, fingering something in his pocket, and all at once the answer became clear. He glanced around. There was no place to hide and only one long trestle back to shore. He ran through his options. He could deny the bosun's accusation and try to bluff his way out, he could plead for his life, or he could attack the bosun and hope for the best.

None seemed feasible.

Then another option came to him. He'd seen Harry Bridges grapple with a number of thorny situations, and the one consistency he could recall was that Bridges faced problems head on with absolute honesty, as if the outcome to himself was inconsequential.

It was worth a try.

"You're right," he said, fixing his eyes on the bosun. "I did go to the cops, but that was months ago. And I was planning to turn you in, but only to clear myself, not to take revenge. I really don't care what you do."

Slag regarded Nick with a surprised expression, as if he hadn't expected Nick to be so candid. "I gotta hand it to you, Benson, you've changed. When you first boarded the *Diana Dollar*, you were a fuckin' pansy. I did my best to toughen you, but I didn't think it did any good — till now."

A smile crossed Nick's lips, though he did his best to suppress it. A compliment coming from someone as despicable as the bosun was surely tainted. Still, it was the first time Slag had praised him and he couldn't help but feel a tiny bit of gratification. "Look, why don't we call it a draw. After we get rid of the opium, you leave me alone and I'll do the same for you."

The bosun removed his right hand from his pocket and produced, as Nick suspected, a small revolver. He stepped away and pointed the gun at Nick, the tips of the bullets visible in the rotating cylinder. "I can't do that. You know too much. Besides I have a score to settle. Remember Manila?" He waved the gun toward the edge of the trestle. "Move."

Nick didn't budge. Confronted with his own demise, he was certain of one thing: he wasn't going to go gently into the night. He weighed his options again. He could attack the bosun and hope that the first shot either missed or didn't hit a vital organ, or he could move to the edge of the trestle and quickly jump in before the bosun pulled the trigger, then swim underwater as far as a single breath could take him. If the bosun missed him on the way down, he'd have a good chance of escaping. Small revolvers were notoriously inaccurate beyond a short range, and he'd always been a good swimmer.

He stepped toward the edge of the trestle and was about to jump when a voice called out, "Drop it!"

Both men whirled around and peered into a gust of fog rolling over the trestle, obscuring whoever it was. A moment later the fog thinned to reveal a figure fifteen yards off, wearing a fedora that hid his face in shadow. He was holding a gun in both hands, looking down the barrel at the bosun. In the dim light Nick was just able to make out the familiar features of Jack Blum. *He must have figured out that Slag and I struck a deal. When Slag shook his tail, he must have followed me instead. Thank God he did.*

"Drop it, now!" Blum repeated.

In the blink of an eye Slag slipped behind Nick and jabbed the revolver against his temple. "Lower your gun and back off or he takes a bullet."

Blum hesitated, and in that interval Nick felt the pulse in his temple pounding against the cold, metal gun barrel. "All right, all right," Blum agreed, lowering his weapon while he backed away.

Another gust of fog rolled over the trestle and engulfed Blum. Before he completely disappeared Slag leveled his revolver at him and pulled the trigger. As the gun went off Nick leaned back, hoping to jostle the boson's arm enough to throw off his aim. He continued to lean back and pushed his feet against the trestle, forcing Slag to take a step back to keep his balance. In doing so, the bosun's foot slipped off the edge of the trestle and into thin air.

Immediately the dynamics of their dance reversed.

Falling backwards, the bosun wrapped his arms around Nick, who tried to keep from falling with him. Gravity, however, would not be denied. The two men toppled backwards off the trestle and landed in the water with a muffled splash.

Nick felt a snap in his ears as cold water saturated his clothes and swirled around his head, jolting his heart. He kicked toward the surface, the bosun still behind him, his arms wrapped around Nick's torso.

When their heads emerged, Slag sputtered, "You fucker, I'm gonna kill you for that." He jabbed the revolver at Nick's temple.

"Wait!" said Nick. "Can you swim back to shore?"

The bosun looked up at the trestle, now fifteen feet away and blurred by mist as the current carried them away toward open ocean. He glanced from side-to-side. Only the tips of undulating waves were visible out to about thirty feet, at which point water and fog blended together into a seamless gray curtain. A look of panic seized his scabrous face. He tightened his grip on Nick with one arm, the other still holding the gun to Nick's head.

"I'm a good swimmer," said Nick, treading water as best he could. "If we work together we can make it to shore."

With the trestle fading into the mist and waves splashing against him, Slag now seemed less determined to kill and more determined to survive. He foolishly stuffed the revolver into his coat pocket and wrapped both arms around Nick as if he was holding onto a life preserver.

Nick kicked his legs to keep his head above water, but with the bosun clinging to him it wasn't easy. "You gotta let go so we can swim to shore. I'll help you."

His plea didn't loosen the bosun's grip. With no other option he began crawling toward shore one stroke at a time, his legs scissoring, shoes kicking the water. Even under the best of circumstances towing another person is cumbersome. Fully clothed in a strong current, it's doubly difficult. Breathing heavily, Nick soon realized he wasn't going to swim a hundred feet much less a thousand. In desperation he grasped Slag's arms and tried to pry them off. Weighed down by their clothes, the two sank below the surface, the bosun holding on with a vice-like grip as if his life depended on it, and for a moment Nick wondered if he was trying to drown them both. As they sank lower and lower, Slag finally loosened his grip and pushed down on Nick as he made for the surface.

Unencumbered, Nick kicked diagonally upward, hoping to distance himself from the bosun before he reached the surface. When his head broke out of the water, he sucked in air several times, then looked around for Slag who was ten feet away, clawing madly at the water, his arms swinging up and over like a windmill, creating more splash than movement. Nick stripped off his pea coat and tore off his shoes, then circled in place to get his bearings. In all the jostling he'd lost his orientation and neither the undulating water nor the impenetrable fog gave him a clue as to where the shore lay.

88

The low, guttural moan of a foghorn rumbled through the mist, coming from everywhere and nowhere at once. Treading water in the cold current of the Golden Gate, Nick cocked his head this way and that, trying to triangulate the source. When a second moan reached him, his ears picked up subtle clues pointing to its general direction. There were two foghorns in the Golden Gate, one on the north side at Point Bonita, the other perched on Mile Rock just off Land's End near the south shore. He had no chance of reaching Point Bonita before the current swept him out to sea. If he swam toward Mile Rock on the ebb tide, however, he might reach it as long as the current didn't drive him past it.

He'd only heard the one foghorn so he headed toward it, hoping for the best. To conserve energy he swam in slow, measured strokes, relying on the tide to do most of the work. In this way he developed a steady rhythm, though he had no way to measure his progress or tell if he was even headed in the right direction.

He'd been a good swimmer in college, but his swimming muscles hadn't had a good workout in years. His arms soon began to tire and the cold water didn't help; his whole body was shaking as if he had palsy. Neither of these discomforts, however, was as taxing as the fear whispering in his ear. *You'll never make to it shore . . . The water's too cold . . . The tide's too strong . . . Your body's too weak.* To suppress these thoughts, he counted the strokes — *seventeen, eighteen, nineteen* — pausing every twenty to rest and look around at the tips of waves extending out into the gloom.

Another foghorn blast rumbled through the mist, this one higher-pitched than the first, ending with a low grunt. Each foghorn had a distinct call so that sailors could identify them. For this reason he was able to distinguish the second foghorn from the first, but he wasn't experienced enough to know on which side of the Golden Gate it was located. This latest blast seemed to be coming from somewhere off to his right. If that was the case, it meant that it originated at Point Bonita and confirmed his course toward Mile Rock.

Or so he thought.

As it turned out his calculations were wrong. Steep cliffs flanking the Golden Gate reflected echoes and counter-echoes; even a seasoned sailor could be fooled in a dense fog. Without reliable reference points, he'd been swimming into the current, so instead of moving swiftly toward Mile Rock, as he'd hoped, he had been swimming away from it. Yet he was still drifting slowly toward it on the outgoing tide.

A low growl carried across the water. He stopped to listen. *A boat?* Blum would have called the Coast Guard, and surely they would be searching for him by now. Like the foghorn, the growl seemed to be coming from everywhere and nowhere at once. Swiveling around, he yelled for help, calling in every direction, frustrated that he couldn't see anything or know where they were.

The growl, ignoring his desperate cries, slowly faded into the distance, leaving him winded and discouraged. He'd been in the water for about thirty minutes, his strength now seeping out of him. Strangely, he didn't feel as cold as before, though this, he knew, was a dangerous sign of hypothermia.

He started swimming again, his strokes slow and feeble, arms leaden, legs nearly useless. The effort wasn't just difficult, it also seemed pointless. He had no idea where he was, where he was headed, or his chances of reaching land. Still, something inside him, an unbroken desire to keep going, to survive, kept him going.

His arms eventually lost strength and wouldn't respond, so, turning over onto his back, he let himself drift with the current, his thoughts rambling as he bobbed up and down on the ebb tide, water lapping against his face. The whispering fear was now gone, as if his body and mind were prepared to let nature take its course. He floated like this for several minutes, eyes closed, calm and resigned. *Is this my fate?* he wondered. *Will all my efforts to put my life back together, to reunite with Clarisa, dissolve in an unforgiving tide?* He'd learned so much in the last year and a half, grown from a naïve dreamer to world traveler to experienced journalist. It seemed a waste to see it end now. *At least Clarisa and I had one last intimate moment together. Clarisa.* He pictured her, green eyes gazing at him, a halo of auburn curls. *What will happen to you? To lose both your father and me will be devastating, perhaps beyond repair. Whose shoulder will you cry on this time? Roger's? He and I competed for your affection and I prevailed, but he isn't evil. And if he loves you perhaps —.* His train of thought was interrupted by something pushing against his legs, moving them sideways to his left. At the same time his head and shoulders seemed to be moving to the right. *Am I . . . spinning?*

He raised his head to see what was happening. There wasn't anything unusual that might tell him why he was moving counter clockwise, no driftwood, nor sea creatures, only water, cold undulating water. He was about to close his eyes again when he noticed a jagged white line of foam floating on the water. And something else. The water on one side of the foam was darker than the other side. He recalled seeing this phenomenon before while standing on a bluff overlooking the Golden Gate, a white line dividing two shades of blue-green water. He later learned that during an ebb tide, the outflow from the bay squeezes through the narrow Golden Gate. When the tide reverses, a foam border forms between the waning ebb tide still flowing down the middle of the channel and a rising flood tide sneaking up its flanks like insurgents counteracting a larger force. A riptide. The water from the bay and from the ocean are different shades, though which shade was which he couldn't recall.

The two opposing tides spun Nick around and flung him into the current again. Only now he was moving in the opposite direction away from Mile Rock. Not that he was aware of it or that it mattered. He was too exhausted to care. He closed his eyes and drifted in a semi-conscious state, thinking that if he had to die, the Golden Gate was as good a place as any.

His senses were shutting down now. He couldn't feel anything and couldn't see much when he opened his eyes. His ears were useless as well; all he could hear was water sloshing in his ears and against face. He floated like this for some time, his awareness of the outside world disappearing, his mind no longer thinking, his body flotsam bobbing on the waves.

For a brief moment the water receded from his ears, and during that moment a faint sound, a low rumble, intruded into his consciousness. He ignored it but the rumble grew louder like the drumbeat of an advancing army. Eventually it was accompanied by a loud percussive thud, followed by another. His eyes flew open. *Are those waves pounding on the shore?* Even the remote possibility pulled him out of his stupor.

He rolled over and clawed toward the low rumble, one agonizing stroke at a time. The water seemed rougher now, lifting him up and dropping him down like the peaks and valleys of a gentle roller coaster. He also had the sensation of being hurled forward, then held in place, then hurled forward again. *Just keep breathing*, he thought as he struggled to keep his mouth free of water. *Just. Keep. Breathing.*

The up and down motion became increasingly pronounced, the highs higher, the lows lower. This went on for a several minutes until a great surge lifted him up, up, up, higher than ever before, until it reach a peak and paused. For a brief moment time seemed to stand still, as if Poseidon himself was contemplating his fate. *Will he keep me? Steal me from everything I've known — family, friends, lover? Or toss me back like a fish too small to keep?* In the next moment the sea hurled him forward and collapsed into a bubbling, churning soup that smothered his head and swirled around his face, shot up his nose and into his ears, buffeted his cheeks and hair, and drove him forward like a piece of lifeless driftwood.

Engulfed in this swirling foam, he closed his eyes and held his breath, each succeeding second elongating more than the last. One one-thousand, two . one . thousand, three . . one . . thousand, four . . . one . . . thousand . . .

His head hit something. Whatever it was was both hard and soft and scraped and scratched his face, tore at his clothes, and filled his gaping mouth with watery grit. He coughed uncontrollably, trying to expel the slurry, and each time he tried to inhale more slurry filled his mouth, triggering another coughing fit. This struggle to breathe would have continued but the water was less aggressive now, replaced by a cold sea breeze running over his back.

When his lungs finally cleared, he was drifting in and out of consciousness, only vaguely aware of his surroundings. Yet he did had enough wits to know that if he stayed here, stayed on this lonely beach he would die of exposure. Summoning his last ounce of strength, he dragged himself forward like a feeble sea lion, waves lapping over him and draining away. He managed to move a few feet until his strength gave out and his arms went limp. Maybe if he slept a while he could try again when his strength returned. He closed his eyes, thinking how comfortable the sand felt beneath him, how perfectly it conformed to his body. As he let go of consciousness and slid into oblivion, the last thing he heard was the sound of breathing . . . no, sniffing.

89

It took two days in the hospital to recover from hypothermia and exhaustion, during which time Nick was grateful to have been discovered by a golden retriever named Gracie and grateful to be alive. Clarisa spent hours at his bedside tending to him, a diversion that pulled her out of her doldrums and gave her something to focus on besides her grief. To pass the time she read to him, and he especially enjoyed *The Seafarer*, an Old English poem about the hardships of life at sea, the cruel weather, the unpredictable ocean, the isolation, and her Gaelic lilt was a perfect companion to the ancient words. *There I heard nothing but the roaring of the sea, the ice-cold wave, at times the swan's cry . . . Yet longing always came upon me to fare forth on the water . . .*

She'd been hesitant to read the poem to him and said it was understandable if he didn't want to be reminded of his traumatic experience. But Nick encouraged her. His near-drowning and his time on the *Diana Dollar* had given him a deeper understanding of the ancient poem and of the life his grandfather and Captain Harding had clung to until it disappeared in the onslaught of progress. The verses also reminded him of Slag, who had endured a lifetime of corrosive sea spray and inclement weather that wore away any veneer of compassion he might have had until all that was left was a hard reptilian core.

Not long after he left the hospital, he learned that Slag's body had washed up on Ocean Beach, his shoes still on, his pistol still tucked in his coat pocket. It was a relief to know that the bosun no longer posed a threat, but he was still keenly aware that Plant could still have him arrested at any moment. It was a cloud hanging over him and would remain there until he located the narcotics, although that seemed unlikely, for as Slag said, "Dead men tell no tales."

Eager to return to work, Nick resumed his position as Harry Bridges assistant and helped him prepare for the arbitration hearings. They worked long hours together, compiling information from various sources: government statistics, longshoremen interviews, newspaper accounts. Many of those hours were spent at Bridges' flat in Bernal Heights, working late into the night at the kitchen table, preparing a presentation and typing it. Nick knew that Harry would set the pages aside at the hearing and speak extemporaneously. Still, the process of organizing the information would provide Bridges with a foundation on which to articulate the rank-and-file position.

Those long evenings at the kitchen table were the most intimate moments Nick would spend with Bridges. His wife Agnes served them bottles of beer and his nine year-old daughter hovered nearby, doing her homework and glancing at Nick with the adoring eyes of a girl smitten by a handsome older man. With the strike now over and the urgency of conflict lifted from his shoulders, Harry was more relaxed and talkative, occasionally engaging in conversation that wandered in unexpected yet revealing directions. One evening Nick typed a couple of letters and asked for stamps to mail them. This prompted Harry, his hand wrapped around a bottle of beer, to reminisce about his mother, an Irish-Catholic who immigrated to Australia and married a Protestant real estate broker but never forgot her roots.

"When I was a boy," he recalled, "she sent me to the post office with the warning, 'don't buy the shilling stamps, 'arry, only the penny ones,' even though it meant covering the entire envelope with stamps to make postage. When I asked her why, she huffed, 'shilling stamps have a picture of George V, and I'll not have a son of mine lick the backside of an English king.'" He chuckled. "So, you see, Nick. It's in my blood to question authority. I can't help myself." His face turned solemn. "When I grew older, my father had me collect rents from his tenants. I hated it, especially when times were tough and they had to choose between paying rent and feeding their kids. That's why I ran off to sea. It's a beautiful thing, the sea — free, open, adventurous, connected to every port in the world. But as you know it can be a fickle friend. I was shipwrecked twice before I sailed through the Golden Gate, and I've been here ever since. So this is my home now and longshore people are my people, and I'll not lick the backside of anyone to see they get a square deal."

A tear welled in the corner of his eye, which he quickly brushed away.

Nick also felt more relaxed now that his duplicitous role was behind him. He described to Bridges the details of his Faustian bargain and his worry that he might be arrested again, especially as he'd stayed with the union. If only he could find the opium, he could put the whole matter behind him once and for all. But the only clue he had was Slag's own words that he'd hid the narcotics right under the cops' noses.

"Were those his exact words?" asked Harry.

Nick thought back to his conversation with Slag in the jail cell and went over it, word for word, trying to tease out any clues. It seemed like a lost cause until he remembered a detail that, at the time, seemed unimportant.

Two days later at the Hall of Justice, Nick walked into detective Jack Blum's office carrying two spade shovels on his shoulder.

"How are you at digging up evidence?" he asked Blum.

The detective glanced at the shovels with a bemused expression. "Well, I'm not afraid to get my hands dirty, if that's what you mean."

Nick nodded toward the door. "Let's go. I think you'll be interested in this."

On the way out of the building Nick recounted his conversation with Bridges and his recollection that Slag had said he'd *planted* the opium right under the cops' noses. Knowing the bosun's penchant for hiding his cache in a place so obvious no one would think of looking there, Nick had done some poking around. He looked up the portly manager of the *Diana Dollar*, who was surprised to hear from him, and learned that Slag had retrieved the cache late one night and carted it off in a hand-pulled jitney in the direction of Chinatown. Between the Hall of Justice and Chinatown there was only one place, Nick reasoned, where Slag could have "planted" his cache. A triangulation of facts pointed to it, and this time there weren't any echoes to throw him off course.

With shovels in hand, they walked across Kearny Street into Portsmouth Square, a sloped park located on the edge of Chinatown. Landscaped with lawn, bushes, trees, and paved pathways, it was a pleasant place for Chinese children to frolic and for seniors to play cards and read the newspaper. On the far side of the square, a clump of quince bushes formed a circular wall around a small open area about four feet in diameter. Children were using it to play tag, squeezing in and out of the encircled area and squealing with delight as they fled from the one who was "it."

When the kids moved on, Nick separated two quince bushes and led Blum inside. The ground was bare dirt, trampled by kids playing games. Nick had scoured the neighborhood and decided that this was the only spot near the Hall of Justice where Slag could have come in the middle of the night and buried the opium without being seen.

Or so he hoped.

They took off their jackets, rolled up their sleeves, and stabbed their shovels into the loamy soil, tightly packed but easily penetrated. They dug down, shovelful by shovelful, and tossed the soil onto a pile beside the hole. Two-feet down Nick hit something. It wasn't rock hard, but it wasn't soil either. He dug out the dirt around it, uncovering a green canvas duffle bag cinched at one end with a rope. He was tempted to shout, "*Eureka!*" but kept his emotions in check, afraid to celebrate too soon and jinx the discovery.

With Blum's help, Nick knelt down and dragged the bag out of the hole, brushed off loose soil, and took a deep breath. Could this really be the end of his search? The end of a long, arduous quest to exonerate himself. Ironically, the ordeal had forced him to learn more about the world, more about himself, more about love and honor than all his years at college. If the bag contained what he hoped, it would be the equivalent of a diploma, conferring a masters degree in life skills that no university could match.

He untied the rope and loosened it, then reached in and pulled out a large package wrapped in oil cloth and bound with jute rope.

Blum tipped his fedora back. "Well, I'll be damned."

90

On October 12th, 1934 the National Longshoremen's Board presented its decision to a packed audience of union members, waterfront employers, and press reporters from around the country. Nick attended with Harry Bridges and the entire Joint Marine Strike Committee, and the other side was represented by Roger Farnsworth, Thomas Plant, and Paul Eliel, executive director of the Industrial Association.

While they waited for the presentation to begin, Nick and Roger exchanged glances and nodded, silent acknowledgement that they were no longer adversaries — everything was settled, or about to be — and it gave Nick reason to think that under different circumstances, in a different time and place, the two of them could have been friends.

Archbishop Hanna and his fellow board members, Oscar Kushing and Edward McGrady, sat at a table facing the assembly. Nick had seen Hanna at previous hearings, and it seemed to him that the bags under Hanna's eyes were fuller, his posture more stooped, his hair thinner. Still, he was clear-eyed and focused and seemed relieved to have completed this important task.

The archbishop called the meeting to order and without further ado read the board's decision. It was dozens of pages but could summed up in these simple words: an award to the workingmen of the waterfront. Longshoremen had asked for a collective bargaining agreement covering the entire West Coast and received it. They asked for a six-hour day and received a six-hour day. They asked for a dollar an hour and were given ninety-five cents an hour and a dollar-twenty an hour for overtime, so that in an eight-hour day, wages would average one dollar and one cent per hour.

When the outcome was clear, Plant and Eliel got up and stalked out, and from the frowns on their faces it was obvious that even though the longshoremen had won the battle, the war was far from over. By contrast, Bridges and the Joint Marine Strike Committee congratulated each other with undisguised glee, and Nick, too, felt tremendous joy. All the angst, all the pain, all the violence, all the uncertainty, suddenly seemed to be a reasonable and necessary price for this momentous victory. And from the broad smiles on their faces, it was certain that every workingman there wanted to run wildly down the Embarcadero shouting, *We won! We won! We won!*

On the all-important matter of the hiring hall, Archbishop Hanna and his colleagues had grappled with it for weeks. They'd listened to hours of testimony and read hundreds of pages of documents and still couldn't envision a solution acceptable to both sides. Even Father Shannon began to think that a viable compromise was as unlikely as a blizzard in San Francisco.

During this period of deliberation, Hanna invited Shannon to his residence to discuss the issue over a glass of wine. He led him into his study and poured two glasses of port, then gestured to a pair of wingback chairs in front of a fireplace blazing with a crackling fire.

With firelight flickering on his face, Hanna outlined his quandary. "Employers will never accept a closed shop and longshoremen will never accept employer control of the hiring hall. The longshoremen also believe that joint or even government control of the hall will leave the door open for employers to discriminate against active union members."

Shannon shifted his gaze from the crackling flames to the archbishop. "Your Grace, I believe in the sanctity of the common man. Our Lord didn't choose a merchant, a warrior, a politician, or even a priest to speak for him. He chose a carpenter from a humble family. His Son worked with callused hands and simple tools to create things that helped others. In essence, His Son's life was one of service from manger to cross. This was no mere happenstance or random act. The Lord knew what he was doing when he chose Jesus to represent him, and there is a message in that choice that we all must bear witness to and heed.

"The church must stand with the common man, Your Grace. The Industrial Revolution has produced great wealth but also great disparity. Even Abraham Lincoln warned of the insidious power of corporations who would distort and foil democracy for their own ends.

Therefore, it is our duty to support the common man in his quest for dignity, not only within our holy walls but also in his everyday life so that he may learn to treat his fellow citizens with the same respect he himself receives."

The archbishop rolled his glass between his palms, its ruby red wine luminous in the firelight. "You always give a great sermon, Michael. Many learn the precepts of the church, but few articulate it as well as you. However," he sighed, "I must offer a solution that will stand in the real world and end the rancor, not prolong it."

Shannon studied the flames rising up into the chimney. They had reached this point many times before and gone no further, as if a brick wall stood in their path. This time his thoughts circled back to a conversation he'd had with Clarisa while walking from the mission to St. Patrick's. *She made a suggestion, hadn't she? What was it?*

He suddenly sat up with a triumphant grin. "What if you give each side what they want?"

Hanna regarded him skeptically. "How?"

"Award control of the hiring hall to both sides and allow registered longshoremen access without regard to union or non-union status."

"That would certainly satisfy the employers."

"Then designate the dispatcher a union man. He'll send the men to work on a rotational basis regardless of race and —"

"union activities."

"Exactly." Shannon nodded.

The archbishop straightened his posture. "And since nearly every registered longshoreman is already a union member, it will strengthen their hand and allow them to bargain with employers as equals, not as underlings."

Shannon nodded again.

The two men settled back in their chairs and gazed at the fire, its flames dying down to glowing embers. The room was quiet save for the occasional spark and crackle, and it smelled of burnt oak and leather-bound books, furniture polish and India ink. Shannon took another sip of port and savored its sweet earthy blend of fruit, soil, and sunshine, and once again he marveled at the self-evident truth that the simple things in life are what satisfy the senses and sooth the soul.

91

She wore a white satin gown with matching kid gloves, her hair pinned on top of her head, her left hand resting on the arm of Father Shannon. They walked down the aisle of St. Patrick's Church between scores of friends admiring her proud Celtic beauty and elegant gown. Borrowed from a friend who worked at a consignment shop, the gown was a single piece of flowing white satin that hung by two straps from her shoulders and draped cleanly down to a pool of fabric at her feet. She moved gracefully toward the altar, her face bathed in gentle light from the stained-glass windows, revealing for all to see the love and happiness in her eyes.

Nick was waiting for her at the altar in a black double-breasted suit inherited from his father. He had proposed to her the day he and Jack Blum found the narcotics, the day he was free from his unholy bargain, free to choose his destiny. It had given him such an exalted feeling of joy and liberation, he rushed to Clarisa's flat to tell her the news and ask for her hand in marriage.

She was sorting through her father's belongings when he arrived, trying to figure out what was worth saving and what to throw out. As she went about the task, her face was somber, eyes moist with emotion. He immediately recognized that it wasn't an appropriate moment to propose and offered to help her instead. They boxed up Seamus' papers — articles he'd written, a nearly-completed memoir, and various notes — all of which Clarisa planned to give to a local organization that supported Irish independence. Then she offered her father's considerable collection of books to Nick, a gift he gladly accepted.

When the sorting was done, Nick suggested they get some fresh air and enjoy the last of the sunny weather before the rainy season arrived. With Rusty leading the way, his tail swishing side to side, they strolled up to the top of Buena Vista Park and stopped to look out over the city, a broad expanse of rooftops and chimneys, church steeples and tall trees, green parks and wide avenues. While they enjoyed the view, Nick thought again of proposing and again concluded that it wasn't the right moment, that she needed more time to wear down the sharp edges of grief.

He turned toward her and stroked her cheek, wishing he could say something to erase the pain and ease the heartache. She sighed and faced him, wearing a wan smile that spoke of hope and desire and bittersweet sorrow. Their eyes met in a wordless exchange, and during that moment he saw their future spread out before them — an endless chain of birthday parties and holiday gatherings, of toddlers and teenagers, of laughter and sorrow, of new beginnings and old endings. It nearly brought tears to his eyes, and all at once he knew with certainty, with absolute certainty, that she was ready, that they were both ready.

When they reached the altar Father Shannon passed Clarisa over to Nick. Then, switching from surrogate father to spiritual Father, he stepped in front of them and faced the gathering of family and friends occupying the pews to the back of the church. Lillian sat in the front row with Sarah and Rune, holding a handkerchief to dab her eyes, already red and weepy. Harry Bridges sat behind her with his wife and children, and behind him there was Henry Schmidt, Pirate Larsen, Dutch Dietrich and all the other Albion Hall men. Joad, the hold foreman at the Swayne and Hoyt docks, was there with his family. And Moon, Remy, and Haggis were seated together, looking unusually dapper in sport coats and pressed trousers.

Father Shannon smiled at Nick and Clarisa for a pregnant moment; then he looked past them at the gathering. "We are here to bring this man and this woman together in holy matrimony. And while this is a new beginning, it is an ending as well, the end of a long journey taken along divergent paths that from this day forward will merge into one . . ."

PART FIVE

THE MEMORIAL

CHAPTER 92

April 14, 1990 – Mill Valley

It was emphysema that finally got him. I was saddened to hear the news but not surprised. Harry was eighty-eight and a heavy smoker most of his life. He only lasted this long, I'm sure, because of his stubborn resistance to abandoning a good cause.

The memorial service is today, and since I don't drive much anymore my granddaughter Tess is taking me.

She arrives at my home in Mill Valley dressed in jeans ripped at the knees, an orange tee-shirt, and a faded denim jacket that looks like it came from a thrift store. I ignore her sartorial shortcomings — after all, she's barely out of college — and offer her a cup of coffee. She smiles and declines, saying it's not allowed on her colon cleansing diet. Whatever that is.

We settle into her Mazda convertible, a red two-seater with the top down, and instantly I'm twenty-five again, eager for a joyride. It's funny how in our advanced years a part of us still thinks of ourselves as young, and sitting in a shiny red sports car is a perfect way to enhance the illusion. We head south on Highway 101, the bayside town of Sausalito below us, with its picturesque houseboats and sleek yachts, relaxed tourists and waterfront restaurants. The highway climbs up a long steady grade and then dips down and plunges into the Waldo Tunnel. I've made this trip countless times before, and still I get a tingle when a view of the Golden Gate Bridge appears at the end of the tunnel, its twin towers tall and erect, its cabled wings unfurled over the harbor entrance.

On the other side of the tunnel, the bay appears off to our left, its sparkling water extending all the way to San Francisco and its herd of skyscrapers pointing up to a clear blue sky. The freeway then winds down through the rugged Marin Headlands to the Golden Gate Bridge, and as we drive onto the span I glance at Tess wondering what she thinks of our excursion to pay final respects to the man who pulled me through my darkest hour. I tried to explain it to her once, hoping to interest her in a pivotal period of my life, but her face went blank and her lovely green eyes wandered away.

I don't blame her. It was a long time ago.

Though she may not share my interest in history, Tess is a wonderful girl, endowed with lush auburn curls like her grandmother. Unlike her grandmother, however, she wears an assortment of colorful tattoos, gold earrings, and studs in places no one of my generation would have thought possible. I once called it her tribal uniform, for all her friends have similar adornments, but she just laughed and pulled up my sleeve and pointed to the name tattooed on my forearm.

"See, grandpa," she said, with an amused grin, "you have one too, and I bet you wore an earring when you sailed to China."

I denied the earring but there's no denying the name on my arm.

Looking at it got me thinking about that time, and without really knowing why, perhaps a desire to keep the memories alive, I was drawn to my desk, to my old loyal Royal, and began to type it all down one moment at time. Once I got going I relived it all over again, the words flowing out in great gusts of story, memoir, and chronicle, all melding together like the savory flavors in a simmering cioppino.

When the manuscript was finished I wanted to show it to Tess, wanted her to know what happened all those years ago, but I knew she wasn't ready, at least not yet.

Someday I'll let her read it. Perhaps then she'll understand.

While we cross the bridge, I notice Tess glancing out at the mile-wide Golden Gate, silver-blue in the morning light. Then her eyes scale the red-orange bridge towers, and I wonder if it's possible for her to visualize the Golden Gate without the bridge. After all, the two have been wedded in movies and advertisements for more than half a century, so that now, like Antony and Cleopatra, it's nearly impossible to think of one without the other. Even I have trouble picturing the Golden Gate before cables swagged across it, and I was twenty-four — the same age as Tess is now — when bridge construction began.

We park near the International Longshore & Warehouse Union Hall, a remnant of the working port that vanished from the Embarcadero years ago. For decades it served as a hiring hall just the way Harry envisioned, rotational and non-discriminatory, a place to wait for a shift out of the elements, a home-away-from-home for the men, and later the women, of the docks.

The memorial service won't start for awhile, so we take a stroll along the waterfront. These days the Embarcadero is a construction zone, crawling with workers digging up the last of the Belt Line railroad tracks to make room for a light-rail line that will shuttle tourists between Market Street and Fisherman's Wharf. We detour around the construction, cross the Embarcadero, and wander onto Pier 39, a cargo pier long ago and now a succession of souvenir shops, seafood restaurants, and tourists licking ice cream cones.

Being here reminds me of the day when several hundred of us walked off the Matson dock and burned our Blue Books in an empty lot across the street. I mention this to Tess and she nods politely, though with little enthusiasm, as if I just described a Civil War skirmish.

We reach the end of the pier and look out at the sparkling bay and surrounding hills, still green from spring rains. The air is so clear that the derelict penitentiary buildings on Alcatraz Island, decommissioned thirty years ago, seem close enough to touch. To our left a gigantic container ship sails under the Golden Gate Bridge, its seven-story house sitting aft at the stern, its weather deck stacked six-high with identical blue containers. Not a single sailor is visible on her decks, making her look like a ghost ship or a remote controlled vessel. We watch her glide past us and continue on under the Bay Bridge toward the Port of Oakland, which decades ago sucked the life-blood out of the Embarcadero.

Some are under the erroneous impression that shipping was driven out of San Francisco by the unions. That's not the case. All West Coast ports are organized under the International Longshore and Warehouse Union, the union Harry Bridges and his followers founded in 1937 to split away from the old ILA.

In truth, it was geography that crippled the Port of San Francisco. Containerized shipping requires hundreds of acres of backspace to store cargo containers that are moved on and off ships with enormous cranes resembling mechanical Star Wars creatures. The finger piers of the Embarcadero, while state-of-the-art in the 1930s, were woefully obsolete by the 1960s. Meanwhile, the areas adjacent to the San Francisco waterfront were filled in with office buildings and condominiums, leaving inadequate room for container storage. On top of that Oakland is a day closer to points north and east than San Francisco, which sits at the tip of a forty-mile long peninsula.

But what a peninsula it is, with its undulating hills sensuous and inviting, its pastel houses marching block after block toward the sea, its towers of glass and granite rising up like a shining citadel. Many of my generation bemoan the loss of Frisco, the city of boxy streetcars and rusty freighters, waterfront taverns and ramshackle marinas. It's still there, though, or at least vestiges. And in spite of its ever-changing skyline, the city has done a fair job of retaining the old flavor. You just need to know where to look.

We walk back through Pier 39, past a juggler balancing a bowling ball on the nape of his neck and a video game parlor where kids in baggy jeans are crowded around machines that beep, squeal, and zing. When we reach the ILWU Hall, a six-sided pyramidal building, people are streaming in, longshoremen in white flat-caps, politicians and shipping executives in tailored suits, union officials in open-collared shirts, academics, radicals, reporters.

An animated buzz fills the cavernous building as people greet each other and look for a seat. A jazz combo led by the great jazz bassist Vernon Alley is jamming to *One O'clock Jump*, the music echoing in the canted dome ceiling. I look around for familiar faces, but most are decades younger than I. Many in attendance are African-American, reflecting the current make-up of the ILWU. Harry would approve of that. One evening at The Albion he told me that if he could choose only two men to work on the docks one would be black. When I asked him if that was to prevent shipowners from pitting white against black, he nodded. "You're damn right. But that's not the only reason." He gave me a meaningful look. "It's also the right thing to do. We need them because they're our brothers, see."

Someone overheard him and asked if he'd let his daughter marry one.

Harry looked askance at the fellow and replied, "Only if she loved him."

There aren't many in the audience who look old enough to have been around in '34. Henry Schmidt is gone, as is Pirate Larsen and Bill Lewis. And of those on the other side, none is alive either, not Plant, nor Neylan, nor Rossi, nor Lapham. Harry outlasted nearly all of us.

The music stops, the lights dim, and a documentary of Harry's life plays on a screen over the stage. It shows him as a vigorous, sharp-faced man in his thirties; the way I'll always remember him, dressed in work clothes and a flat cap. Then as president of the union, wearing a double-breasted suit, speaking at rallies and negotiating with shippers, then in a loose Hawaiian shirt, organizing dockworkers in Hawaii, then on trial for being a Communist, an ordeal he went through three times before the Supreme Court declared him innocent and granted him American citizenship. Then with Noriko, his third and final wife, whom he married in Nevada in 1949 despite an anti-miscegenation law in that state barring interracial marriage, then as a Port commissioner, sitting on the same commission with shipping men he'd fought against, who finally gave him the respect he deserved, and finally as a retired legend lecturing Bill Moyers about labor rights and his belief in worker control of the means of production.

The documentary ends and the lights flick on, illuminating a panel of speakers on stage, politicians, family members, friends. One by one they step up to the podium and deliver eulogies laced with heartfelt stories describing the swath Harry cut across San Francisco and the world at large, as well as their own lives. For San Franciscans love nothing better than an outspoken character, quick with a quip and ready to take on the establishment.

One plain-spoken fellow, a stocky, retired longshoremen, says that he and his wife live a decent life because Harry fought for a pension program. And while he talks I see something in his manner that reminds me of Fargo, who died penniless and alone.

I glance at Tess and see that she's listening to the stories, and I'm glad that she's not bored.

The eulogies go on for more than two hours, and no one leaves as the tales are amusing and inspiring. We all share a feeling of what Harry Bridges represented, of his spirit which we all want to cling to, which despite his death we all want to see survive. It occurs to me that we're like drunken homesick sailors who can't get enough hooch, because each sip momentarily relieves the pain of loss and gives us hope about ourselves, our families, and the future of mankind. We linger on and savor each word because there's a bittersweet sense that when it's all over, we have to let go and move on, and we don't want to let go. Each story elicits waves of applause, each anecdote gales of laughter — laughter intensified by sorrow.

When the speaking is done, the combo plays *Just a Closer Walk with Thee*, and we all stand and hold hands and sway and sing, just like at Civil Rights rallies in the Sixties. I look over at Tess and see tears rolling down her face. Beneath the tears, though, she's smiling. I'm happy because now I see that she has an inkling of what Harry and I and thousands of others went through to change the waterfront. Hell, to change the world. I squeeze her hand, her smile broadens, and I'm glad I brought her because now I think she's ready to read my manuscript. Now she'll understand.

We file out of the hall into a sunny afternoon that draws us back into the present and dries our moistened eyes. Tess takes the wheel, and during the drive home she has a slew of questions about Harry and me and what happened when I knew him.

I'm pleased that she's interested and assure her that when we return to Mill Valley I'll give her all the answers.

We return to Marin over the Golden Gate Bridge, and during the ride I look up at the thick suspension cables swagged between the towers and remember when bridge workers hung them. With rolling cable spinners that moved back and forth, they strung pencil-thin wires between the two towers until they had strung enough individual wires to make huge cables that would hold up the bridge roadway.

And once again I can see that Harry was right, that like strands of wire, if you bind enough individuals together you can accomplish anything.

As we drive off the bridge and head up through the Marin Headlands, more memories percolate to the surface. I think about Roger Farnsworth, who quit his job not long after the strike and sailed to Rio de Janeiro as he'd planned. He stayed for six months and returned wearing sandals and shaggy blond hair. His parents urged him to return to work, and although he said he would, he never did. The last I heard he took up the saxophone, moved to New York, and became a jazz musician.

A year after the strike, Cook landed a job at a seafood restaurant in Bodega Bay where he stayed until the owner retired and sold him the business, eventually becoming famous for his barbecued oysters and abalone steak. Moon and Remy continued to work on ships until WWII when I lost track of them, though I expect they ended up back East where they came from. Haggis moved to Redding, California, got married, bought a few acres, and raised hogs, chickens, and a brood of kidlets.

As for my family, Rune died in his sleep in the late 1930s, and till the end of his days he recounted his adventures at sea and his love of sailing. Mother tended a victory garden during WWII and continued to work as a bookkeeper until her retirement, then moved in with my family until she passed in 1955. Sarah and I are still close. She put her artistry to good use, first becoming a stage set painter for a theater company, then the first female professional set designer in the Bay Area. She married an actor who treats her like gold, and the two of them live a happy bohemian life in

Bernal Heights, not far from where Harry used to live.

After the strike I stayed with the union for a couple of years, writing for the *Waterfront Worker* until I received a call from Paul Smith, a young wunderkind who'd just become managing editor at the *Chronicle*. We had a long chat about the troubles of '34, during which he admitted being personally embarrassed by the *Chronicle*'s prejudicial reporting. He was the financial editor at the time, and the only journalist to conduct an in-depth interview with Harry Bridges, who'd been suspicious and tight-lipped until Smith asked him if he thought there was a class war going on in America. "Kee-rist," Harry replied, "you mean there's someone at the *Chronicle* who knows about the class war?" Smith's boss refused to print the interview, but now that Smith was in charge, he wanted to introduce new blood into the staff. He'd just hired a young columnist from Sacramento about my age, a wise-cracking bonhomie named Herb Caen, and he reckoned that with my experience at the port, I'd be ideal for covering the waterfront beat.

When I informed Harry that I was going to work for the *Chronicle*, he half-jokingly called me a capitalist stooge. I was hurt by this, as I still looked up to him and craved his approval, but Henry Schmidt took me aside and said that he knew for a fact that Harry was sad to see me go, though he was too proud to admit it.

I didn't see Harry much after that — we were both buried in our own lives. When we did run into each other, he liked to kid me about being a tool of the capitalist class, although he acknowledged that my reporting was accurate and even-handed.

Tess and I arrive home late in the day, the redwoods in the backyard casting long shadows across the garden, now starting to bloom with azaleas, rhododendrons, irises, and cosmos. Wearing a light-blue smock and a straw sun hat, Clarisa is kneeling on the ground, attacking a purple thistle that had the temerity of crashing her garden party. Like me, her hair is silver and her face is laced with wrinkles both fine and deep. I bring out glasses of lemonade, and we stand back, sip our drinks, and admire the floral profusion of colors and shapes. She asks how the memorial went, and I describe the service and Tess's reaction. She smiles and hugs me and says she's glad I went. Then her face darkens. It's still hard for her to think about that time, and she says she would rather remember the times before and after.

Feeling a great surge of affection, I wrap my arms around her and draw her close and, try as I might, I can't recall why I ever wanted to leave her.

SCENE LOCATIONS

Many scenes in *Frisco* are set in places that existed in 1934 and still exist today, so that interested readers might explore vestiges of old Frisco. The Embarcadero, in particular, is a wonderful place to visit. Many of the original cargo sheds still stand, and there are interpretive panels and pylons along the two-mile boulevard with historical photos and information. All locations below are in San Francisco unless otherwise noted.

Archbishop's Mansion (now a bed and breakfast inn) – 1000 Fulton Street

Audiffred Building (Bulkhead Café now Boulevard Restaurant) – 1 Mission St.

Chronicle Building – 901 Mission Street

Claremont Hotel – 41 Tunnel Road, Berkeley, CA

Coit Tower – top of Telegraph Hill

Copra Crane – Islais Creek Channel

Eagle Cafe – Pier 39, The Embarcadero (moved from the west side of the Embarcadero to Pier 39 in 1978)

Eureka Ferry Boat – Hyde Street Pier, Hyde and Jefferson

Falkirk Mansion (now Falkirk Cultural Center) – 1408 Mission Avenue, San Rafael, CA

Filbert Steps - Filbert St. between Telegraph Hill Blvd. and Sansome St.

Fort Point - Golden Gate National Recreation Area, south shore of the Golden Gate, end of Marine Drive

Garcia & Maggini Warehouse (a plaque on the outside of the building commemorates its role in 1934) – 136 King Street

International Longshore and Warehouse Union (where the Harry Bridges memorial took place) – 400 North Point

Julius' Castle (closed as of this writing but still worth a visit) – 1541 Montgomery Street

Labor Temple (now Redstone Building, a mural in the lobby depicts a scene from the 1934 strike) – 2926 16th Street

Matson Building (listed on the National Register of Historic Places) – 215 Market Street

Palace Hotel/Garden Court Restaurant – 2 New Montgomery Street

Pier 38 – The Embarcadero between Brannan St. and Townsend St.

Red's Java House – Pier 30 The Embarcadero at Bryant Street

San Francisco City Hall – 1 Dr. Carlton B. Goodlett Place

St. Patrick's Church – 756 Mission Street

ACKNOWLEDGEMENTS

A novel such as this, taking years to research and write, could never have seen the light of day without considerable advice and encouragement. I owe a debt of gratitude to my editor, Robyn Russell, and to my writing group: Joanne Miller, Ginny Horton, Ann Hyman, and Greg Bowman. I received insightful feedback from Dennis Sides, my brother David Bacon, and my dear friend Christine Hahn. The Encouragement Award goes to my good friend Richard Everett and his wife Nancy. The Putting Up With A Very Long Project Award goes to my wife Patty. I received expert help from former longshoreman Herb Mills, from ILWU librarian Eugene Vrana, who allowed me to cull through the original meeting notes of Local 38-79 and copies of the Waterfront Worker, from the staff at the History Center at the San Francisco Main Library, and from Thomas Fleming who helped me understand the African-American perspective. Honorable mentions go to Janelle Baumsteiger, Marianne Betterly-Kohn, Madelon Van Leir, Frank Coppola, Mary Jane Gessner, Jesse Hamlin, Leslie Harlib, Kevin Mullin, Carl Nolte, and Richard Johns. My graphic designer, David Ice, did a terrific job, as always. And a special thanks to Maggie McDonald.

Lastly, I'd like to tip my hat to Harry Bridges, whose courageous determination was inspiring and motivating. There are few people who have had such a direct, sustaining, and positive impact on so many others, and who asked for so little in return. He was one.

BIBLIOGRAPHY

Abbot, Willis J. *Story of Our Merchant Marine.* New York, N.Y.: Dodd, Mead and Company, 1919

Atherton, Gertrude. *My San Francisco.* New York, N.Y.: The Bobbs-Merrill Company, 1946

Bailey, Bill. *The Kid from Hoboken: An Autobiography.* San Francisco, CA: Circus Lithograph Prepress, 1993

Barry, John M. *The Great Influenza.* New York, N.Y.: Penguin Group, 2004

Boardman, Gwen R. *Carrying Cargo.* Camden, N.J.: Thomas Nelson & Sons, 1968

Dong, Stella. *Shanghai: The Rise and Fall of a Decadent City.* New York, NY: Harper Collins, 2000

Flamm, Jerry. *Goodlife in Hard Times.* San Francisco, CA: Chronicle Books, 1978

Flamm, Jerry. *Hometown San Francisco.* San Francisco, CA: Scottwall Associates, 1994

Ford, A. G. *Handling and Stowage of Cargo.* Scranton, Penn.: International Textbook Company, 1941

Gilliam, Harold. *San Francisco Bay.* Garden City, N. Y.: Double Day, 1957

Halliburton, Richard. *Royal Road to Romance.* Garden City, New York, Garden City Publishing Company, 1925

Hartog, Jan de. *A Sailor's Life.* New York, N.Y.: Harper & Brothers Publishers, 1955

Heuvelmans, Martin. *Cargo Deadweight Distribution.* New York, N.Y.: Cornell Maritime Press

Larrowe, Charles. *Harry Bridges: The Rise and Fall of Radical Labor in the United States.* New York, N.Y.: Lawrence Hill and Co.

Leeming, Joseph. *Ships and Cargoes.* Garden City, N.Y.: Doubleday, Durran, & Company, Inc., 1932

Nelson, Bruce. *Workers on the Waterfront.* Chicago, IL: University of Illinois Press, 1990

Padfield, Peter. *The Merchant Navy as a Career*. London, England: B.T. Batsford Ltd., 1962

Potter, Elizabeth. *The San Francisco Skyline*. New York, N.Y.: Dodd, Mead & Company, 1939

Quin, Mike. *The Big Strike*. New York, N.Y.: International Publishers, 1949

Radius, Walter. *United States Shipping in Transpacific Trade: 1922–1938*. Stanford University, California: Sanford University Press, 1944

San Francisco Chronicle. Chronicle Publishing Company, San Francisco, CA., May 8 to July 28, 1934.

Starr, Kevin. *Endangered Dreams: The Great Depression in California*. New York, N.Y.: Oxford University Press, 1997

Selvin, David F. *A Terrible Anger*. Detroit, MI; Wayne State University Press, 1996

Waterfront Worker: February 1933 – October 1934

Wellman, David. *The Union Makes Us Strong*. New York, N.Y.: Cambridge University Press, 1995

Woon, Basil. *San Francisco and The Golden Empire*. New York, N.Y.: Harrison Smith & Robert Haas, 1935

Work Projects Administration writers. *San Francisco: The Bay and Its Cities*. New York, N.Y.: Hastings House, 1940

Daniel Bacon is the creator of the Barbary Coast Trail, San Francisco's historical walking trail (www.barbarycoasttrail.org). He is the author of *Walking San Francisco on the Barbary Coast Trail* and co-hosted KQED's program *Sin, Fire, and Gold*. He lives in the San Francisco Bay Area with his wife Patty, son Brendan, and dog Foxy.

Made in the USA
San Bernardino, CA
27 October 2016